Praise for **JOE**

"Brown compels our admiration, Joe himself makes us care." —*Newsweek*

"Goes for the jugular . . . Painfully honest . . . A focused, driven story."
—*Chicago Sun-Times*

"The novel, written in a luminescent prose tempered by wit, moves gracefully forward by tracking the independent movements of its three artfully conceived and skillfully balanced principals. As their lives mesh, the novel's momentum, and its rewards, build. A fourth major role may be said to belong to the terrain itself, a Mississippi so vividly sketched you can all but mount it on your wall." —*The New York Times Book Review*

"Masterful . . . There isn't a bad sentence anywhere in this book. *Joe* is tougher than a night in a Georgia jailhouse." —*The Kansas City Star*

"A tragic, compelling new novel." —The Associated Press

"Gifted with brilliant descriptive ability, a perfect ear for dialogue, and an unflinching eye, Brown creates a world of stunted lives and thwarted hopes as relentless as anything in Dreiser or Dos Passos . . . A stark, often funny novel with a core as dark as a delta midnight." —*Entertainment Weekly*

"Brown has quietly established himself as among the finest of the new generation of Southern writers. His latest work is absolutely riveting in its rawness. Brown has unleashed all his skills in this story." —*The Denver Post*

"Larry Brown is one of the more distinctive prose artists of our time. . . . His prose is starkly poetic, his characterizations, occasionally darkly comic, are always uncompromising and convincing." —*The Houston Post*

"*Joe* appalls, repels, but ultimately fascinates . . . Larry Brown is a writer whose language and imagination redeem the very worst life has to offer; a novelist of unusual power." —William Kennedy, author of *Ironweed*

"This raw and gritty novel ranks with the best hard-knocks down-and-out work of Jim Thompson and Harry Crews. It's lean, mean, and original."
—*Kirkus Reviews*

JOE

Also by Larry Brown

Facing the Music, stories

Dirty Work, a novel

Big Bad Love, stories

On Fire, essays

Father and Son, a novel

Fay, a novel

Billy Ray's Farm, essays

A Miracle of Catfish, a novel

JOE

A novel by

LARRY BROWN

Algonquin Books of Chapel Hill   2003

Published by
Algonquin Books of Chapel Hill
Post Office Box 2225
Chapel Hill, North Carolina 27515-2225
a division of
Workman Publishing
225 Varick Street
New York, New York 10014

First paperback edition, Warner Books, October 1992. First Algonquin
paperback, October 2003. Originally published in hardcover by
Algonquin Books of Chapel Hill in 1991.
Printed in the United States of America.
Design by Molly Renda.

Library of Congress Cataloging-in-Publication Data
Brown, Larry
    Joe : a novel / by Larry Brown. — 1st ed.
      p. cm.
    ISBN 978-0-945575-61-0 (HC)
    I. Title.
PS3552.R6927J64   1991
813.54—dc20   91-12026 CIP

ISBN 978-1-56512-413-4 (PB)

10 9 8 7 6 5 4 3 2

for my big bad bro,
Paul Hipp

JOE

The road lay long and black ahead of them and the heat was coming now through the thin soles of their shoes. There were young beans pushing up from the dry brown fields, tiny rows of green sprigs that stretched away in the distance. They trudged on beneath the burning sun, but anyone watching could have seen that they were almost beaten. They passed over a bridge spanning a creek that held no water as their feet sounded weak drumbeats, erratic and small in the silence that surrounded them. No cars passed these potential hitchhikers. The few rotting houses perched on the hillsides of snarled vegetation were broken-backed and listing, discarded dwellings where dwelled only field mice and owls. It was as if no one lived in this land or ever would again, but they could see a red tractor toiling in a field far off, silently, a small dust cloud following.

The two girls and the woman had weakened in the heat. Sweat beaded the black down on their upper lips. They each carried paper sacks containing their possessions, all except the old man, who was known as Wade, and who carried nothing but the ragged red bandanna that he mopped against his neck and head to staunch the flow of sweat that had turned his light blue shirt a darker hue. Half of his right shoe sole was off, and it flopped and folded beneath his foot so that he managed a sliding, shuffling movement with that leg, picking it up high in a queer manner before the sole flopped again.

The boy's name was Gary. He was small but he carried the most. His arms were laden with shapeless clothes, rusted cooking utensils, mildewed quilts and blankets. He had to look over the top of them as he walked, just to be able to see where he was going.

The old man faltered momentarily, did a drunken two-step, and collapsed slowly on the melted tar with a small grunt, easing down so as not to hurt himself. He lay with one forearm shielding his face from the eye of the sun. His family went on without him. He watched them growing smaller in the distance, advancing through the mirrored heat waves that shimmied in the road, unfocused wavering shapes with long legs and little heads.

"Hold up," he called. Silence answered. "Boy," he said. No head turned to hear him. If his cries fell on their ears they seemed not to care. Their heads were bent with purpose and their steps grew softer as they went on down the road.

He cursed them all viciously for a few moments and then he pushed himself up off the road and went after them, his shoe sole keeping a weird time. He hurried enough to catch up with them and they marched on through the stifling afternoon without speaking, as if they all knew where they were heading, as if there was no need for conversation. The road before them wound up into dark green hills. Maybe some hope of deep shade and cool water beckoned. They passed through a crossroads with fields and woods and cattle and a swamp, and they eyed the countryside with expressions bleak and harried. The sun had started its slow burning run down the sky.

The old man could see beer cans lying in the ditches, where a thin green scum nourished the tan sagegrass that grew there. He was very thirsty, but there was no prospect of any kind of drink within sight. He who rarely drank water was almost ready to cry out for some now.

He had his head down, plodding along like a mule in harness, and he walked very slowly into the back of his wife where she had stopped in the middle of the road.

"Why, yonder's some beer," she said, pointing.

He started to raise some curse against her without even looking, but then he looked. She was still pointing.

"Where?" he said. His eyes moved wildly in his head.

"Right yonder."

He looked where she was pointing and saw three or four bright red-and-white cans nestled among the grasses like Easter eggs. He stepped carefully down into the ditch, watchful for snakes. He stepped closer and stopped.

"Why, good God," he said. He bent and picked up a full can of Budweiser that was slathered with mud and slightly dented, unopened and still drinkable. A little joyous smile briefly creased his face. He put the beer in a pocket of his overalls and turned slowly in the weeds. He picked up two more, both full, and stood there for a while, searching for more, but three were all this wonderful ditch would yield. He climbed back out and put one of the beers in another pocket.

"Somebody done throwed this beer away," he said, looking at it. His family watched him.

"I guess you going to drink it," the woman said.

"Finders keepers. They ain't a fuckin thing wrong with it."

"How come em to throw it away then?"

"I don't know."

"Well," she said. "Just don't you give him none of it."

"I ain't about to give him none of it."

The woman turned and started walking away. The boy waited. He stood mute and patient with his armload of things. His father opened the can and foam exploded from it. It ran down over the sides and over his hand and he sucked at the thick white suds with a delicate slobbering noise and trembling pursed lips. He tilted the can and poured the hot beer down his throat, leaning his head back with his eyes closed and one rough red hand hanging loose by his side. A lump of gristle in his neck pumped up and down until he trailed the can away from his mouth with his face still turned up, one drop of beer falling away from the can before it was flung, spinning, backward into the ditch. He started walking again.

The boy shifted his gear higher and stepped off after him.

"What's beer taste like?" he said, as the old man wiped his mouth.

"Beer."

"I know that. But what's it *taste* like?"

"I don't know. Shit. It just tastes like beer. Don't ask so many fuckin questions. I need to hire somebody full time just to answer your questions."

The woman and the girls had gone ahead by two hundred feet. The old man and the boy had not gone more than a hundred feet before he opened the second beer. He drank it more slowly, walking, making four or five drinks of it. By the time they got to the foot of the first hill he had drunk all three.

It was that part of evening when the sun has gone but daylight still remains. The whippoorwills called to each other and moved about, and the choirs of frogs had assembled in the ditches to sing their melancholy songs. Bats scurried overhead, swift and gone in the gathering dusk. The boy didn't know where he and his family were, other than one name: Mississippi.

In the cooling evening light they turned off onto a gravel road, their reasons unspoken or merely obscure. Wilder country here, also unpeopled, with snagged wire and rotten posts encompassing regions of Johnsongrass and bitterweed, the grim woods holding secrets on each side. They walked up the road, the dust falling over their footprints. A coyote lifted one thin broken scream down in the bottom; somewhere beyond the stands of cane they could see a faint green at the end of the plowed ground. They turned in on a field road at the base of a soapstone hill and followed it, stepping around washed-out places in the ground, past pine trees standing like lonely sentinels, where doves flew out singing on gray-feathered wings, and by patches of bracken where unseen things scurried off noisily through the brush.

"You know where you at?" said the woman.

The old man didn't even look at her. "Do you?"

"I'm just followin you."

"Well, shut up then."

She did. They went over the last hill and here the whole bottom was open before them, the weak light that remained stretching far down across an immense expanse of land that had been plowed but not yet planted. They could see all the way to the river, where the trees stood black and solid.

"It's a river bottom," said the boy.

"Well shit," said the old man.

"Can't cross no river," the woman said.

"I know it."

"Not in the dark."

The old man glanced at her in the falling light and she looked away. He looked around.

"Well hell," he said. "It's bout dark. Y'all see if you can find us some wood and we'll build us a fire."

The boy and the two girls put everything they had on the ground. The girls found some dead pine tops next to an old fence and they pulled them whole into the road and began breaking them into pieces small enough to burn.

"See if you can find us a pine knot," he told the boy. The boy left and they could hear him breaking through the brush up the hill. When he came back he was dragging a gray hunk of wood with one hand and carrying in the other arm some dead branches. He threw all this down and started off for more. The old man squatted in the dust of the road and began to roll a cigarette, his attention focused finely, aware of nothing but the little task at hand. The woman was still standing with her arms clutched about her, hearing something out there in the dark that maybe spoke to no ear but her own.

The boy came back with another load and said, "Let me see your knife."

The old man fished out a broken-bladed Case and the boy fell to shaving thin orange peelings of wood away from the pine knot. He drew the blade down, breaking the chips off close to the base. When he had a good handful whittled, he arranged them in some unseen formation of his own devising in the powdered gray dust.

"Let me see some of them little sticks," he told his little sister. She passed across a bundle of brittle tinder and he set this around and above the pine chips. He drew a box of matches from his pocket and struck one. In the little fire that flared, his face loomed out of the dark, curiously intense and dirty, his hands needlessly cupping the small flame. He touched it to one of the chips and a tiny yellow blade curled up, a tendril of black smoke above it like a thick waving hair.

"That stuff's rich as six foot up a bull's ass," the old man said. The little scrap of wood began sizzling and the resin boiled out in black bubbles, the flames eating their way up. The boy picked up another one from the pile and held it over the fire, got it caught, and added it to the fire. One of the sticks popped and burst into flame.

"Give me some of them a little bigger," he said. She handed them. They smiled at each other, he and little sister. Now they began to be drawn out of the coming dark, the five of them hunched around the fire with their arms on their knees. He fed the sticks one by one into the fire, and soon it was crackling and growing and red embers were breaking off and falling into the little bed of coals already forming.

He kept feeding it, jostling and poking it. He got down on his knees and lowered his face sideways to the fire and began to blow on it. Like a bellows he gave it air and it responded. The fire rushed over the sticks, burned higher in the night.

"Y'all go on and put some of them big ones on it," he said, getting up. "I'll go up here and get some more."

The girls hauled limbs and piled them on the fire. Soon there were red sparks launching up into the smoke. The stars came out and enveloped them in their makeshift camp. They sat under a black skyscape beside woods alive with noise. The bullfrogs on the creeks that fed the river were hoarse and they spoke from the clay banks up into the darkness with a sound the ear loves.

The woman was digging among her sparse duffel, pawing aside unusable items at the top of the sack. She pulled out a blackened iron skillet and a pint can of green beans. She set these down and looked some more.

"Where's them sardines?" she said.

"They in here, Mama," the oldest girl said. The youngest one said nothing.

"Well, give em here, honey."

The boy came crashing down through the bushes and laid another armload of wood by the fire and went away again. They could hear him casting about like an enormous hound. The woman had the knife up and she was stabbing at the can of beans with it. She managed to open it and with careful fingers she pried the jagged edge up and turned the can over, shaking the beans into the skillet. She set it close to the coals and started in on the sardines. After she got the can open she rummaged around in her sack and pulled out a package of paper plates partially wrapped in cellophane and set them down, took out five. There were five of the little fish in the can. She put one in each plate.

The old man immediately reached over with grimed fingers and picked up a sardine daintily and bit it once and bit it twice and it was gone.

"That was his," she said.

"He ort to been down here," he said, chewing, wiping.

The boy had moved far back in the brush. They listened to him while the beans warmed.

"How much longer?"

The woman stared into the fire with a face sullen and orange.

"It'll be ready when it gets ready."

She looked off suddenly into the dark as if she'd heard something out there, her face grained like leather, trying to smile.

"Calvin?" she called. "Calvin. Is that you?"

"Hush," he said, looking with her. "Shut that shit up."

She fixed him with a look of grim desperation, a face she wore at night.

"I think it's Calvin," she said. "Done found us."

She lurched up onto her knees and looked wildly about, as if searching for a weapon to fend off the night, and she called out to the screaming dark: "Honey, come on in here it's almost ready Mama's got biscuits fixed."

She gathered her breath to say more, but he got up and went to her and shook her by the shoulders, bending over her with the ragged legs of his overalls flopping before the fire and the girls silent and not watching this at all. The little one got up on one knee and put another stick on the fire.

"Now, just hush," the old man said. "Hush."

She turned to the oldest girl.

"You water's not broke, is it?"

"I ain't pregnant, Mama." Her head was bowed, dark hair falling down around her face. "I done told you."

"Lord God, child, if you water's broke it ain't nothin nobody can do about it. I knowed this nigger woman one time her water broke and they wasn't nobody around for a mile to help her. I tried helpin her and she wouldn't have me."

"I'm fixin to slap you," he said.

"She wasn't about to have me. I's standing out yonder by the pumphouse and they come in there three or four and tied her down and she had the biggest blackest thing stickin out butt first . . ."

He hit her. Laid her out with one lick. She didn't even groan. She fell over on her back in the dirt and lay with her arms outspread like a witness for Christ stricken with the power of the Blood.

The girls looked at her and then they looked at the beans. They were almost ready. The old man was crouched beside their mother, his hands moving and working.

The boy was running back down through the brush and the woods, the wire singing one high shrieking note when he hit it. He stumbled panting and on all fours to the fire and noted his mother lying stretched out on her back and his father bent over her in an attitude of supplication and saw his two sisters watching the fire with hungry looks and yelled out, over the noise of the bullfrogs and the maddening crickets screaming and the murmur of the water running low in the creek: "They's a *house* up here!"

oe rose early from a sleep filled with nightmares of shooting guns and swinging pool cues launched up in his face and stealthy blacks with knives who lurked around corners with their eyes walled white in the darkness or slipped up behind him on cat feet to take his life for money. At four-thirty he made some instant coffee and drank about half a cup. He put a load of clothes in to wash, moving through the brightly lit rooms while all around him outside the community slept. He turned on the television to see if there was anything on, but there wasn't anything but snow.

The dog was standing in the yard with his head up when he pushed open the door.

"Here, dog," he said. "Hey, dog."

He bent with the two opened cans of dog food in his hands and spooned the meat onto a concrete block at the foot of the steps. He moved out of the way when the dog moved in and stepped back up into the open door to watch him eat. Just a few grunting noises, the jerking of his scarred head up and down.

The coffee was cold in the cup when he sat back down at the

table. He pitched it into the sink and made another, then sat sipping it slowly with his arm laid out to rest on the cheap metal table, a Winston smoking between his fingers. It was five o'clock by then. He had some numbers written down on a piece of notebook paper that had been folded and rained on, and he spread it out before him on the table, smoothing it, silently rehearsing the numbers with his lips. The phone was on the table in front of him. He lifted the receiver and dialed.

"You goin to work this mornin?" he said. He listened. "What about Junior? He get drunk last night?" He listened, grinned, then coughed into the phone. "All right," he said. "I'll be up there in thirty minutes. Y'all be ready, hear?"

He hung up on a babbling voice. He listened to the clothes chugging in the machine and he listened to the silence he lived in now, which was broken most times only by the dog whining at the back step. He got up and went to the icebox and brought the fifth of whiskey that was in there back to the table. He held it in his hand for a minute, studying it, reading the label, where it was made, how long it was aged. Then he opened it and took a good drink. There was a canned Coke on the table, half empty, flat and hot. He made sure nobody had thumped any cigarette ashes in it before he took a drink. Coke, then whiskey, Coke and then whiskey. He wiped his mouth and capped the bottle and lit another cigarette.

He turned off the lights at five-fifteen and went down the steps and across the wet grass of the tiny yard and no one saw him leave. The stars had gone in but dawn had not yet paled the sky. The dog whined and nuzzled around his legs as if he'd go, too, but Joe pushed him away gently with his foot and told him to move, then got in the truck.

"Stay here," he said. The dog went back under the house. The whiskey went under the seat. He cranked the truck with the door still open, found the wiper switch and watched the blades slap against the dew on the windshield. The truck was old and rusty and it had a wrecked camper hull bolted over the bed, where the poison guns and jugs lay in wreaths of dust and where the scraps of baby pines left from the past winter had dried into kindling. Spare tires and flat ones, empty beer cans and whiskey bottles. He sat revving it until it would idle and then he shut the door and turned on the lights and backed out of the driveway. It coughed up the road, missing and lurching, the one red eye in the back slowly fading toward the dawn.

There were five of them standing beside the road with their hands in their pockets and the orange tips of their cigarettes winking in their lips. He pulled up beside them and stopped and they climbed into the back, the truck shaking and jarring as they sat. He stopped twice more before he got to town, taking on one rider at each halt. It was getting daylight when he drove into the city limits. He eased under the red light at the top of the hill and turned onto the project road with the back end sagging. The blue lights of the police cars that were gathered in the parking lot washed the gray brick walls in sporadic sapphire, while the strobes flashed and illuminated the junked autos and spilled trash and overflowing Dumpsters. He pulled up short and stopped and sat watching. There were three patrol cars and he could see at least five cops. He stuck his head out the window and said: "Hey, Shorty."

One of them climbed down from the back and walked up beside the cab to stand next to him. A thin youth in a red T-shirt.

"What's goin on, Shorty? Where's Junior at?"

The boy shook his head. "Somebody fucked up."

"Well, go see if you can find him right quick. I don't need to be around these damn cops. They'll think I did it."

"I'll go get him," the boy said, and he moved off toward the nearest building.

"Hurry up, now," he said after him, and the boy broke into a jog. Fifteen or twenty black people were standing in a group on the sidewalk, watching. Most of them were wearing undershorts or nightgowns. One cop was keeping the crowd herded back.

As he sat looking at them, the police led a man in a pair of white jeans to one of the cars. His hands were cuffed behind his naked back. They opened a rear door and one of them put his hand on top of the man's head in an oddly gentle act and kept him from bumping his head as he got in. Some of the workhands in the back end of the truck started out but Joe called for them to stay put, that they didn't have time. He lit a cigarette and saw a red glow moving through the pines behind them. He swiveled his head to see an ambulance coming slowly with the siren off. Somebody dead, no urgency, had to be. Then he saw the foot. Just one, turned with the toes up, sticking out past the left side of a patrol car. A black foot with a pale bottom unmoving on the asphalt. If he hadn't been in such a hurry he would have gotten out to take a better look. But the ambulance had pulled up now and the attendants were unloading a stretcher from the back. They wheeled it around, two men in white jackets. They bent over the body and then the foot was gone.

"We ready now," the boy said beside him. There was another boy with him.

"That you, Junior?"

White teeth gleamed in the dying night. "It's me. You let me have a cigarette, Joe?"

He pulled a pack off the dash and shook one out for him.

"Hell. I thought that might be you laid out yonder, Junior. What's done happened?"

He lit the cigarette for him and Junior stood there a moment. He smoked and yawned and scratched the side of his jaw with the fingers that held his smoke.

"Aw, Noony been drunk and talkin his old shit again. Bobby's boy shot him, Mama said."

"Just get up front with me, Junior. Let's go, Shorty. We got to haul ass."

He put it up in reverse and waited for Junior to come around. Junior got in and then he couldn't get the door to stay shut.

"Slam it hard," Joe said. "They all in back there?"

"I reckon. Shoot. I was still in the bed."

He backed the truck around quickly and pulled it down into low. He took off, but the gears crashed when he tried to shove it up into second. He pushed in the clutch hard and tried again. It finally caught, but the valves rattled as it struggled up the hill.

"I got to buy me a new truck," he said. The black boy beside him giggled like a girl. "Where's your hat, Junior?"

"Run off and left it. Shorty say you's fixin to leave me if I didn't come on."

"Hell, we late. Be daylight before we ever get out there. I guess ever one of y'all needs to stop at the store."

"I got to get somethin to eat," he said. "What you take for this old truck if you buy you a new one?"

"This truck ain't old. It's just got some minor stuff wrong with it."

They stopped under the red light and waited for it to turn green. Another cruiser came up the hill and turned in with its blue lights flashing. He pulled the shift down into low and took off again, clashed the gears and dropped it into third. The truck sputtered, lurched violently and died. He cranked on it and the lights dimmed until he pushed them off.

"Ragged son of a bitch," he said. It cranked finally and he wound the hell out of it in low, up to almost twenty-five before he dropped it into high gear. It rattled a loud complaint but it went on.

"Linkage messed up," said Junior.

"Let's see if we can fix it at dinner."

"All right."

They turned at the intersection and took the road that led out of town. The stores were just opening.

"Say you was still in the bed, Junior?"

"Yessir. I got off with Dooley and them last night. Don't even know what time we got in. It was late."

"I guess y'all was drinking some whiskey."

"Shoot. Whiskey and beer both. I won me a little money and then got drunk and lost it."

Joe looked out at the coming morning. It was coming fast.

"Shit," he said. "We got to hurry. Y'all can't stay with it in this heat. Gonna be ninety somethin today."

"You done got the ice?"

He started to touch the brake and then he shook his head, mashing the gas harder instead.

"Why, hell naw. We ain't got time to go back for it now. There's probably still some left in the cooler. Freddy may have some. We'll get some out there if he does."

"Let me get one more of them cigarettes off you."

"Up there on the dash, son. I'm gonna have to start takin cigarettes and beer out of you boys' pay. I went out to the truck other evening after we quit and it was one beer in the cooler. Y'all drink it up fast as I can buy it."

"Them old cold beers good when you get off," said Junior.

"Well I guess so when it's free."

They rode in silence for a few miles, the dark trees whipping past on both sides and the lights beginning to come on in the houses along the road. Once in a while they had to straddle a smashed possum.

"And say that was Noony that got shot? Was he the one that used to work for me? Little short guy?"

"Naw. That's his brother. Duwight. Noony the one been in all that trouble with the law. I think he spent about three years in the pen."

"He did? When was he down there?"

"I don't know. He been out I guess three or four years."

"I just wondered was he the one I used to know one time. What did he get put in the pen for?"

"I think he cut somebody. He just got to where he stayed in jail all the time. He's on probation right now."

"He is?"

"He was. Motherfucker dead now."

Joe got the last cigarette and crumpled the pack and threw it out the window. He leaned over the steering wheel with both arms as the old truck rushed along. He could hear faint cries coming from the back and he grinned.

"Goin too fast for them boys," he said. "How come that boy to shoot him? What? Did he come over there fuckin with him?"

"I imagine. Aw, I know he did. He always think he have to be fuckin with somebody. I knocked him in the head with a speaker one day."

"You did?"

"I sure did. He come over at Mama's one day, said I owed him some money. I told him he better get his ass out I didn't owe him shit. Told him he want some money get out and work for it. What I have to do."

"Then you knocked him in the head."

"Knocked a durn hole in his head. Mama said he got shot about three o'clock. Been out there till the garbagemen found him."

"You don't know what time y'all got in?"

"Naw. It was late."

"He wasn't out there when y'all got in?"

"I don't reckon. He mighta been."

Joe cracked the vent wider and flicked the ashes off his smoke.

"Well, I'll tell you," he said. "Folks lookin for trouble can find more than they want."

Junior nodded and crossed his legs.

"You right," he said. "You exactly right about that."

They unloaded from the back end at Dogtown like a pack of hounds themselves and went into the store talking and laughing and opening the doors on the coolers, reaching for milk and Cokes and orange juice. Joe watched them milling around inside while he pumped gas into the truck. Cars were coming along the road with their lights on, carrying people headed to work in the factories who had to be on the job by seven. He had done that and he was glad he wasn't doing it now. He shut off the pump and hung up the nozzle and looked at his watch as he went in.

"Y'all hurry up, now," he said. They were getting Moon Pies and crackers and sardines and cans of Vienna sausage.

At the counter Freddy looked up at him with a sick smile as the men lined up in front of him with their lunches. Freddy charged their food and drinks and smokes to them each day and was paid off on Friday when Joe brought them by. He kept their tickets in little pads beneath the counter.

"Hey, Joe," he said. He stopped writing, sighed deeply and put down his pen. "You want some coffee?"

"I can get it." He found a Styrofoam cup and poured it full, then dumped in a whole lot of sugar and stirred it well.

"Let's see now," Freddy said. He was examining Shorty carefully. "You're Hilliard, right?"

"Shorty," Shorty said, and pointed to another man. "He Hilliard."

Freddy shook his head and looked at Shorty's groceries.

"Y'all gonna have to start wearin name tags. I can't keep you straight from one day to the next."

"Y'all gonna have to hurry up," Joe said. "It's almost six-thirty. Where you got Jimmy at today?"

"All right," Freddy said. "That's got you. Who's next? You want a sack for that?"

"Yessir. Please."

He pulled out a small bag and started putting the items inside.

"Gone fishin," he said. "I'm fixin to fire that boy."

"He told me you'd done fired him three times."

"I'm gonna fire him for good if he don't start helpin me out some."

"Where did they go? Sardis?"

"Naw. I don't know. Off on some goddamn river somewhere. Him and Icky. They'll probably come in drunk today and won't have no money or no fish either, more than likely."

"You gonna see if he got any ice?" said Junior.

Joe set his coffee on the counter. "Yeah. Freddy, you got any ice?"

"I don't know. He didn't run yesterday but you can look in the freezer and see. There may be some left."

"Go see if he's got any, Junior." He looked at his watch again. "Y'all gonna have to get the lead out, now. It's almost daylight right now."

"They two bags back here," Junior called out.

"Well, go put it in the cooler, then. Put some more water in there, too."

He picked up his coffee and stood sipping it until the last hand had gone out the door with his little sack. Then he set it on the counter again and waited for the storekeeper to open the till. Freddy didn't look happy when he looked up from his money, and spoke to Joe.

"You couldn't wait a little while on this, could you?"

"What's the matter? You ain't got it?"

"Aw, I got it. I got it right here. My gas man's due today, though. If I can't buy gas I might as well not even keep the door open."

"When you gonna learn not to bet money you can't afford to lose, Freddy?"

"I never thought Duran would beat him."

"So you said."

"Would you let me give you half this week and half next week? She's gonna notice this as it is."

He thought about it for a moment, about winners and losers and high rollers and those who aspired to be. Finally he said: "All right. Give it here."

Freddy reached in quickly and took out three hundred dollars and handed it over, shaking his head with relief.

"I sure appreciate it, Joe. Business ain't been good lately."

"Looks pretty good to me," said Joe.

They were trying to finish up a tract of a hundred and seventeen acres close to Toccopola that they'd been on for eight days. He'd started with a crew of eleven, but he'd fired two and one had quit the second day. He stopped the truck on a bulldozed road deep in the woods, a slash of red dirt high in the green hills of timber. He sat on the tailgate with the file in his hand, while Shorty and Dooley held the blades across his leg for sharpening, a small pocket of bright filings growing in a crease in his jeans. When he had five ready, he told Junior to get the men started. Shorty had climbed into the back and wrestled the thirty-gallon drum of poison over on its side and he and Dooley were filling the plastic milk jugs with the thick brown fluid.

Joe raised his head and looked far down the tract to the dying trees they'd injected three days before. It was as if a blight had grown across the emerald tops of the forest and was trying to catch up to where they stood.

"Y'all won't need no water yet," he said. "Go on down there to where we quit yesterday and start in before it gets too hot."

"It ain't gonna rain, is it?" one said hopefully.

Joe looked up to a sky gray and overcast, with rumblings of thunder in the distance.

"It ain't gonna rain," he said. "Not till dinner anyway."

He finished with the last blade and tried to hurry the hands as much as he could while they in turn tried to prolong the beginning of their labor by filling their guns and priming the tubes.

"All right, let's hit it," he said. "Y'all done fucked around long enough. We got to finish by tomorrow if it takes all day."

The man who carried their water and poison took up a jug of each and followed behind them and they all went off down into the hollow to find their marks and begin. Joe got in the cab and pulled the whiskey out from under the seat and opened a hot Coke and sat there. He lit a cigarette and coughed long and slow, spacing the spasms out, clearing his throat and finally spitting something onto the ground and wiping his mouth. He took a couple of drinks and then capped the bottle. The wind was coming up a little. Faint flashes of lightning speared the earth miles away. He lay down on the seat with his cap over his eyes and his feet out the door. Before many minutes had passed he was asleep.

Soft droplets on his face woke him. He opened his eyes and looked at the cab roof over his head. He'd knocked his cap off and water was running down the inside of the door on him. His feet were wet. The windshield was blurred by rain and he could see only bleary forms of greenery through it. It was ten minutes after nine. He put his cap on and slid out the open door, put his feet into the mud already forming. The new ground was soft and he was under a hill, so he got in and cranked the truck and backed sliding and fishtailing through the red muck until he could wheel it onto a turnaround and point it out. He left it there and went down into the woods to see if he could find the hands.

It was a fine rain, a fragile mist that paled everything in the distance to a thin gray obscurity. The green woods, the dead red hills. He had to watch his balance going down into the hollow, catching at saplings on the steepest parts and easing himself down like an older man, the thousands of days of cigarettes wheezing in his chest.

At the bottom of the hill there was a small creek with tiny young cane and rocks and dewberries that he jumped in stride, landing heavily on the wet leaves and looking and finding the pink plastic ribbon tied to the tree. He walked around and found the fresh cuts on the live timber and stood looking at them for a minute. They'd never get the tract finished by the next day if the rain drove them out now. He knew they'd want to quit, even though the rain wasn't going to hurt them. He watched the sky, leaden and heavy with clouds. It wasn't going to clear off. It looked ready to set in for the day. He got in under a big tree and lit a cigarette and squatted, smoking, the smoke hanging in a small drifting cloud in front of him. It seemed as if the air itself had thickened.

He picked up a little stick and idly began breaking it into pieces, looking out at the woods from under the bill of his cap. At once the rain came harder and he made up his mind. He got up and went back toward the hill, across the creek again, bending to get through the underbrush, getting his cap snatched off once by a brier and picking it up and brushing the dirt from it before care-fully setting it back on his head.

He leaned on the horn for two minutes, until he was sure they'd heard it. He gave them ten more minutes and then blew it again to let them get their direction and cut off the distance by coming straight to him. It took them almost twenty minutes to get back. They arrived in a herd, laughing, wet, their clothes sticking to them, large red overshoes of mud encasing their feet. They stomped and kicked their shoes against the tires and the bumper, scraped them with sticks.

"Let's get in and go before it gets any worse," he said. "This road's slick as owl shit now."

They loaded up and settled in the back. They were happy and laughing, able to get by on two hours' pay. He heard somebody yelling just as he cranked the motor, and Shorty came around in a hurry, stepping high and wild in the mud, grinning.

"Let us get our stuff," he said.

The sacks were piled up on the seat and he handed them out the window. Shorty went back with them stacked up in his arms. The

rain was coming harder now and the wipers beat against the streaming water as he eased out on the clutch and felt the tires trying to
spin in the clay. The red ground was bleeding, little torrents of
muddy water already eating into the hillsides and funneling down
the road. Missiles of mud bombarded the fenderwells with hollow
detonations. He had to keep it in low and not risk missing second
all the way up the hill. The truck slid and almost bogged down
and tried to swap ends, but he kept cutting the wheel and finally
they crested over the top and trundled away peacefully toward the
highway, another day gone and wasted.

When he could steer with one hand, he reached and got the
bottle from beneath the seat and set it between his legs. He twisted
off the cap and searched on the seat for a Coke. It started raining
harder.

He had them all home by ten-thirty and he was back at the
house by noon. The dog met him, stood looking at him from
behind the steps, his broad white head lumpy with masses of scar
tissue and the yellow eyes peaceful and strangely human in their
expression of wistfulness. He spoke to the dog and went on in
with his two sacks. The house felt empty now, always. Loud and
hollow. He looked at the mud he was tracking over the carpet and
sat down on the floor beside the door, unlacing his boots and
standing them together beside the refrigerator. There was a pack
of hot dogs and a bag of buns and a dozen eggs and two six-packs
of Bud in one sack and he put it all in the icebox. He poured some
Coke in a glass and dropped in three ice cubes and filled the rest
of it with whiskey, then sat down at the table with a pencil and

some paper to do his figuring. Days and time and hours where he saw his profit coming through. Even with the bad weather he was making over two hundred dollars a day. He figured up what he would owe the hands if they didn't work the next day and drew it all up into individual columns and figured their Social Security and subtracted it and wrote down all their names and the amounts he owed them and then he was through.

There was a little watery stuff left in the glass, and he rattled the thin cubes around and drank it off. The rain was coming down hard on the roof and he thought about the dog in the mud, trying to find a dry spot in this sudden world of water. He got up and opened the back door and looked at the shed. The dog raised his head from his forepaws and regarded him solemnly from his bed of rotten quilts. Then he settled, whining slightly, watching the dripping trees and flattened grass with his eyes blinking once or twice before they closed.

He closed the door and thought about making another drink, but then he went into the living room and turned on the television and sat on the couch. Somebody was giving the farm report. He got up and changed channels. News and weather. The soap operas hadn't come on yet. There was a pale pink bedspread on the floor and he picked it up and pulled it over himself like a shroud and lay on his side watching the news. After a while he turned over on his back and adjusted his head on the pillow that stayed there. He closed his eyes and breathed in the stillness with his hands crossed on his chest like a man laid out in a coffin, his toes sticking out from under the edge of the bedspread. He thought about her and what she'd said that morning.

She was on the front desk now and that was better because he could go in like anybody else and talk to her if he didn't talk too long. He'd gotten at the end of the line and waited, watching her deal with other people, watching her smile. She looked better than he remembered, each time he saw her, as if leaving him had made her more beautiful.

The line moved slowly and he didn't know what he would buy. Stamps and more stamps, a drawer full of them at home already. Finally he stood before her, smiling slightly, averting his whiskey breath.

"You lookin good today," he said. "They keep you busy."

She kept her eyes on slips of paper in front of her, kept her hands busy with things on the counter. She looked up. Pain was marked in those eyes so deep it was like a color, old love unrequited, a glad sadness on seeing him this close.

"Hi, Joe." She didn't smile, this thin girl with brown hair and skin like an Indian who'd born his children.

"How you been gettin along? You all right?"

"I'm okay. How are you?" She still didn't smile, only folded her little hands together on the marble slab, her painted nails red as blood. He looked at her hands and then he looked at her face.

"I'm all right. We got rained out today and I done took everbody back home. What time you get off for lunch?"

"I don't know today," she said. Her eyes wandered, then came back to rest uneasily on him. "Jean's sick and Sheila's having her baby. I don't know when I'll get to go."

He coughed. He started to reach for a cigarette and then stayed his hand.

"I thought I'd see if you wanted to eat some lunch. Thought you might want to go out to the Beacon or somewhere."

"I don't think there's any need in that. Do you?"

"It wouldn't hurt. I'd just like to buy you some lunch."

She pulled a pencil from beside her ear and opened a drawer at her waist. But she closed the drawer and laid down the pencil.

"I'm not going out with you if that's what you want."

"I ain't said that. Why you want to do me like this?"

"Like what?"

"Won't talk to me. Won't even see me."

"This is not the place to talk about it. You're not gonna come in here like you did that other time. Mr. Harper'll call the police if you ever do that again." She leaned toward him and whispered: "How do you think that made me feel? Everybody in here saw you. I've got a good job here."

"I know you do. I'm proud you do."

"Then let me do it."

He raised his hands a little. "Hell, calm down. I just wanted to see you a minute."

"Well, this is not the place to see me. I've got to work."

"Where is?"

"I don't know. You want to buy something?"

"Yeah. Gimme a book of stamps."

She shook her head and reached under the counter.

"You use more stamps than anybody I know."

"I got me some pen pals now," he said.

She rolled her eyes and smiled a little. "Sure."

He pulled out his billfold. "How much is that?"

"Two-fifty for ten or five dollars for twenty."

"Give me twenty. You need any money?"

"Nope."

"I can let you have some if you need it."

"I'm doing fine. I got a promotion and a raise last week."

"Oh yeah?"

"Yeah."

"You been out with anybody?"

"None of your business. I wouldn't tell you if I had. There you are." She put the little booklet on the counter. He gave her a five dollar bill.

"Let me give you some money," he said. He had three fifties folded between his fingers and he put them on the counter.

She looked around to see who was watching.

"I'm not taking that. You'd think I owed you something then."

"You don't owe me nothin, Charlotte. I'd rather you have it as me. I won't do nothin but blow it. You don't want to go eat lunch?"

He had drawn his hands back and the money lay between them. He went ahead and lit a cigarette, turned his head and coughed.

"I can't right now," she said. Somebody had moved up behind him. An old woman, he saw, smiling and digging in her purse, shaking her head.

"I been doin real good," he said. "I ain't been out in about two weeks."

"That's good, Joe. But you can do whatever you want to now."

"Only thing I want is to see you."

"I've got to get to work now. Take this money," she said, and she held it out to him.

"I'll see you," he said, and he turned and walked out.

On the couch he turned his face to one side and saw the things happening on the television screen without seeing them and heard the words the actors were saying without hearing them. They were like dreams, real but not real. He closed his eyes and it all passed away.

They entered over a rotting threshold, their steps soft on the dry dusty boards, their voices loud in the hushed ruins. The floor was carpeted beautifully with vines, thick creepers with red stalks matted and green leaves flourishing up through the cracks. An ancient tricycle sat before the dead ashes of a fireplace whose old rough bricks, ill spaced and losing their homemade mortar, chip by sandy chip, seemed bonded only by the dirt dauber nests that lined the inside.

"Looky yonder," the old woman said, pointing to the tricycle. "Reckon how old that is."

In the vault of rafters overhead a screech owl swiveled its head downward like something on greased bearings to better see his invaders, then spread his small brown wings to glide soundlessly through the gable and out into the spring brightness.

They moved through the house with red wasps droning above them, to a back room where a nest anchored to the top log spanned sixteen inches, a mass of dull bodies with black wings crawling there like maggots, poised and vibrating. They backed away into the front room, quietly, carefully.

31

"Ain't nobody lived here in a long time," the boy said. He reached down and pushed the tricycle, which rolled woodenly across the floor, the pedals turning perhaps with weak remembrance from the feet of a long-dead child. He stood at a glassless window and touched two logs notched to within the thickness of a sheet of paper and wondered at what it had taken to raise hewed timbers a foot square and set them in place with such precision.

"We'll have to get somethin over them windows," the old man said. "And these vines got to be cleaned out."

"We better get that wasp nest down first," the woman said. The two girls had settled in a far corner with their sacks. They studied their father with a sullen recalcitrance.

"This old house is awful," the oldest one said. Her name was Fay and the little one was Dorothy.

"It's bettern a culvert," Wade said.

The old man stopped before a wooden safe weathered of varnish and blistered from a fire survived in some other household. He opened one of the doors and it protested with a thin yawning. On the dusty shelves inside were mice pills, the dry hollow husks of insects, tiny colored bottles with rusted caps.

The boy was fascinated by the logs. He touched their axed surfaces, felt the dried mud chinked in the cracks. He thought he would have liked living in times when men built houses like this one.

"Mules," he said. "I bet them people used mules."

The old man was picking up bottles from inside the safe, small blue ones and tall green ones of strange and flawed glass with bubbles of air trapped within the wavey walls.

"These old bottles liable to be worth some money," he said.

There was a little room attached to the side of the house. The ceiling joists were only six feet above a floor littered with leaves, scraps of newspaper yellowed and brittle, rotted bits of discolored fabric. The boy toed among the refuse, searching. He glanced at his father and mother. They were examining the bottles and arguing quietly over them. With his shoe he scraped twigs and dust away from the floor. The mold of untold years. He bent and picked up a shotgun shell soft with ruin, green with tarnish. He touched the crimped and swollen end and the faded paper flaked away in his hand. Small gray shot was packed loosely within, almost white now. He turned it up and poured over his shoes an almost soundless rain of lead. They were murmuring in the other room, talking. There was no furniture other than the safe, not even a chair. He looked out a window and saw a small shed tumbled down, windrowed with leaves, composed of green boards and cancerous wooden shingles. He saw a caved-in outhouse. And just beyond, a wall of pine woods was already gathering the day's coming heat. He looked around in the room. Whoever had lived here had been gone for a long time. He went back up front and joined his parents.

"Y'all can start pullin these weeds up," his daddy said.

Gary bent immediately and began tearing handfuls of them up through the floor, carrying them to the window and throwing them out.

"I wish I had a broom," his mother said.

"What we gonna do for water?" Fay said. "We ain't got no water."

***

33

"I imagine they's a creek around here if you'd look," Wade said. "Why don't you get up off your ass and see if you can find it?"

"Why don't you go find it your own self?"

The boy stopped what he was doing and looked at his sister. The old man was standing over her, the woman turning now and watching them. The girl got up slowly.

"They ain't even no bathroom in this place. Look at it. It's full of wasp nests, and weeds is growin right up through the floor. You don't even know who it belongs to."

The old man slapped her. A sound like a pistol shot, his hand suddenly exploding on her cheek, the dark hair flying around her head as her face was slapped sideways. The old woman moved and froze at once, sank down to the floor with her legs crossed and her hands in her hair. The girl doubled up her fist.

"Don't double that fist up at me," Wade said. "I'll slap the hell out of you."

She swung at his nose but missed by a good six inches. He caught her arm and twisted it up behind her back. He was trying to whip her with his open hand and she was trying to kick him. They danced in a demented little circle in the dust. The youngest girl watched with her hands caught at her mouth.

He tried to push her against the wall, but she whirled and kicked him hard in the balls. He went down with his teeth bared. She picked up a stick from the floor and commenced pounding him over the head with it, whipped him to the floor where he lay curled and groaning and trying to fend off the blows she was laying on him like someone beating a rug, him screaming for her to *Quit* it, that *Goddamn*, that *hurts*.

"How you like it?" she asked him. But Gary took the stick away from her and threw it out the window.

"That's enough," he said.

"You taking up for him now? What you taking up for him for?"

"Cause," he said. "All you gonna do's make him mad."

"I wish he'd die," she said. She bent over her father. "You hear me? I hate your guts and I wish you'd die. So we wouldn't have to put up with you."

The old man moaned on the floor with his eyes tightly closed. Through gritted teeth he said: "I'm goin to beat your ass till you can't sit down."

"You ain't nothing," she said. "I wish you's dead and in hell right now."

"You gonna wish you was somewhere when I get through with you," he told her.

"Y'all stop it," Gary said. "Here. Help him up."

He took hold of Wade's arm and pulled him to a sitting position. The hat had come off his head and his sparse gray hair was in disarray, coated with dust. He sat rocking back and forth, holding his belly. The girl was still circling him, looking for another opening.

"Get away from him, Fay," Gary said.

"You better get outa here," Wade said.

"If I had any other place to go I would."

"Get up off the floor, Mama." The boy bent to his mother and helped her up, one knee at a time. She was dazed and trembling, was pawing at her hair with her fingers as if she meant to comb it. The old man had one knee up and was forcing one of his hands against it in an attempt to rise. He showed his rotten teeth and struggled, finally made it up, and stood panting in the center of the room. He bent over and picked up his hat and dusted it off.

"I want this place cleaned up fore dark," he told Fay.

"You kiss my ass," she said. He lunged and got her by the throat. She didn't scream. She just closed her eyes and tried to force his hands away from her throat, the two of them stumbling against the logs. The boy tried to get between them, and the little girl and the woman joined in, all of them tugging at the hands clenched so tightly on her. She gagged and coughed and her face started turning purple until she said: "All *right*. Damn," and he turned her loose. She rubbed her throat and coughed some more. He weaved in front of her, raised one finger and put it in her face.

"You gonna do what I tell you," he said.

She didn't answer. The marks of his fingers were red spots on her neck.

"You hear me?"

Gary watched them and didn't move away. He could hear them heaving like runners after a race.

"One day," she said.

"One day?" The old man stepped closer. "One day what?"

"Nothin."

"All right, then. I don't want to hear no more of your smart shit. I'm tired of it. You hear?"

"I hear."

"Well, go on and do like I told you."

"What?" she said.

He gestured wildly with his hands. "Go on and start pickin this shit up. Get some of these sticks and leaves outa here."

They began picking up the leaves and trash that had blown in through the broken windows and carrying it all to the door and throwing it out. The old woman found a scrap of broom somewhere and they were soon obscured in the dust she raised attacking the floor. Wade started to say something, but then coughed and sagged against a wall. He leaned there coughing and then bent over gagging. His tongue came out. He was fanning at the dust with his hands. She swept harder, whipping the dust into a rolling cloud of brown smoke. The old man had both hands around his throat as if he might strangle himself. The dust plumed out the windows and rose to the rafters. Wade retched like a victim of tear gas, going to his knees on the wide boards. Gary helped him to his feet and led him outside, the old man hacking ferociously now, all but being carried by the boy. He allowed himself to be led to a fallen tree in the yard and he sat down on it, putting his head between his legs with his tongue hanging out.

"You gonna be all right?" Gary said. His father didn't answer, couldn't. He sat there choking, his shoulders moving in great spastic jerks.

"Maybe you need to get up and walk around," he said. He turned and looked at the dust billowing out into the yard. The dim figure of his mother inside was moving methodically through the room, the shaft in her hands sweeping back and forth. Fay stepped down from the house, coughing, and held onto the doorjamb with one hand.

"Hell fire," she said.

"Where's Dorothy?"

"I don't know. I guess she went out the other side if she ain't done choked to death. I don't see how Mama can stand it her ownself."

They went around to the other side of the house and the younger girl was there, beating the dust from her clothes.

"You okay?" he said. She nodded her head that she was. They stood together and watched the dust swirl and settle in the grass.

"She's crazy as hell," said Fay.

"Don't say that."

"Well, she is."

"You don't have to say it," he said. "If you don't quit smartin off to him . . ."

"I ain't scared of him."

"Ain't nobody said you were. It just don't do no good to aggravate him. All it does is just make it worse."

"He ain't worth killin," she said.

"Hush." He nodded with his chin toward the little girl. "She's listenin to you."

"I don't care if she is. How you think we gonna live out here? They ain't no water. Ain't even no windows in that old house."

"I'll fix em," he said.

"Horseshit. You can't fix up that old house. We don't even know who it belongs to. What we gonna do if whoever owns it comes up here and catches us?"

He thought about it for a minute. "Well, maybe we can find us someplace else."

"Where?"

"I don't know. He's sposed to know some people around here.

Maybe they know of a place. A place a little closer to a store or somethin. We got to have some way to get somethin to eat. Have we got anything left?"

"I doubt it. I don't think she's got nothin left. I don't know what we had to leave Texas for. At least we had a garden out there. There ain't nothin here." She looked around in disgust. "Back off in the woods. Poison ivy all over the place. I bet you couldn't find nobody in his right mind would live up in here."

"I wonder if he's got any money," Gary said.

"What do you think?"

"Naw."

"You know he ain't. If he did he'd of done found him a liquor store somewhere and spent it."

"Well, what we gonna do?"

She just looked at him.

"I don't know."

By noon they had most of the trash cleaned out but they were having to stay out of the room where the wasp nest hung. They were sitting under the shade of some trees in a yard that honeysuckle vines had taken over. Like foraging cows they had trampled them down and flattened them.

"Now how much money have we got?" the old man said to them. He looked hopeful.

"I ain't got none," Gary said.

"Don't look at me," said Fay.

"Where's your purse?" Wade asked her.

"I said I ain't got none," she told him. "What, you think I'm lyin?"

"I just want to check."

"I done told you I'm broke."

"Well, I just want to see."

"Well, you can just jump up my ass." She got up and started to pick up her purse, but he caught her by the arm. They fought briefly over it until he broke the strap and snatched it away from her. He upended it and dumped the contents on the ground while she cursed at him. A comb, a mirror, two sticks of gum, hair clips, lipstick. He shook it but nothing else came out.

"Now. You satisfied?" She knelt and started putting her things back in it, muttering under her breath.

"We got to have somethin to eat," he said.

"You oughta thought of that before you got us out here."

"You want me to slap you?" he said. She didn't answer.

"We gonna have to do somethin," Gary said. "Find us a job."

"Where you gonna find one at?" the old man said.

"I don't know. I guess I'll have to go look for one. How far is it to town?"

The old man looked around at the woods as if the trees bore road signs that marked the route to civilization.

"It's about ten mile, I guess."

"Ain't there a store no closer than that?"

"They's one over here at London Hill. Or used to be."

"Reckon they'd give us some credit?"

"They might. You could ask. They might give us credit."

"Well, why don't we walk over there and see? We got to do somethin. We can't set around here all day."

"You go. My legs is hurtin s'bad I can't hardly get up."

The old woman had not spoken but she was unfolding limp green paper in her hands. Each of them realized it gradually, turning one by one to look at her as she sat with her head down, her fingers trembling slightly as she fumbled with the wrinkled bills. She smoothed each one on her knee as she drew it from the wad.

"Where'd you find that, Mama?" Gary said.

"I had it," she said. Her hair was coated with dust and it hung limply around the sides of her head so that her ears stuck through.

"How much you got?" the old man said. He was taking it off her knee and counting it. "Eight dollars? You got any more?" She shook her head.

He got up immediately, his leg forgotten, and put the bills in his pocket.

"I'll go on over to the store," he said. "See what I can buy."

Gary got up. "Let me go with you," he said.

"Ain't no need for you to go. I can do it."

"Go with him, Gary," Fay said, nudging him.

"Just stay here. I'll be back after while."

"You gonna get some gas?" Gary said.

"Gas? What for?"

"For that wasp nest."

Wade shook his head, already starting off. "I ain't got nothin to carry it in."

"We gonna have to rob that wasp nest before we can stay in there."

"Well, if I find a jar to bring it back in I'll buy some." They stood and watched him stagger away through the hot woods. When he was out of hearing Fay turned on her mother.

"What'd you give him all that money for? He ain't gonna do nothin but catch a ride to town and buy whiskey with it."

"Leave her alone," Gary said. "She don't need you fussin at her."

At nine that night they were gathered around a small fire in the middle of the yard, mute in the thunderous din of crickets. The grasses and weeds were beginning to look like a bedding ground. They were cooking a meal of pork and beans in opened cans, and the old man was halfway through a bottle of Old Crow. They had foraged for firewood and had a pile nearby.

The faces around the fire were pinched, the eyes a little big, a little dazed with hunger. They sat and watched the blaze burn the paper off the cans. When the beans began to sizzle, the woman stooped painfully on her bad hip and reached for the cans with a rag wrapped around her hand. Clotted strings of hair hung from her head. She took five paper plates, set them out on the ground, and dumped the beans onto them, shaking them as she went, the way a person might put out dog food for a pet. She dumped the largest portion into the plate intended for the old man.

The breadwinner was sitting crosslegged on the ravaged grass, the whiskey upright in the hole his legs formed. He was weaving a home-rolled cigarette back and forth from his lips, eyes bleary, red as fire. He was more than a little drunk. His head and chest would slump forward, then he'd jerk erect, his eyes sleepy. Grimed and furtive hands reached out for the plates quietly, took them back and drew away from the fire into darker regions of the yard. The old woman took two small bites and then rose and scraped the rest of her food into the boy's plate.

The fire grew dimmer. The plate of beans before the old man steamed but he didn't notice. A candlefly bored crazily in out of the night and landed in the hot sauce, struggled briefly and was still. The old man's head went lower and lower onto his chest until the only thing they could see was the stained gray hat over the bib of his overalls. He snuffled, made some noise. His chest rose and fell. They watched him like wolves. The fire cracked and popped and white bits of ash fell away from the tree limbs burning in the coals. Sparks rose fragile and dying, orange as coon eyes in the gloom. The ash crumbled and the fading light threw darker shadows still. The old man toppled over slowly, a bit at a time like a rotten tree giving way, until the whiskey lay spilling between his legs. They watched him for a few minutes and then they got up and went to the fire and took his plate and carried it away into the dark.

Noon. The field bordering the road lay baking beneath a white sun, pale green rows of little plants that merged far away. The earth seemed to be smoking and it had no color, so dry was it, as if it had never known rain. It seemed dead as old bones. Down at the south end of the bean patch a tiny blue tractor was turning and coming back. It struggled against the immense flat landscape, crawling at what seemed an inch at a time, the dry soil not folding but merely breaking into dust across the plows. The old man scowled up at the blistering sky.

"Throw the rest of em out," he said.

The green metal Dumpster he stood beside was positioned off the blacktop on a bed of pit-run gravel as hard as concrete. The county workmen had bolstered up the shoulder of the highway and widened it, and bits of ground glass lay everywhere.

The boy was standing inside the rusty iron bin. He picked up another black garbage sack and slit it open with a knife; then, leaning toward the open door, mired to the knees in refuse, he dumped it out. A rain of cast-off matter cascaded: wet beer cans, egg shells, a half-pint whiskey bottle, cigarette butts and blowing ash. Unidentifiable bits of ruined fruit and fly-specked vegetables. Here a half-chewed weiner that a dog or a small child had worked over. All of it covered with wet coffee grounds. The old man bent over, pawing through it. He lifted three Diet Coke cans and fourteen Old Milwaukee cans from the rubble and put them into his tow sack.

"Ain't you gonna mash em?" the boy said.

Wade made a dismissive gesture with his hand. The boy bent to the piles of sacks behind him. He picked up another one and said, "If you'd mash em it'd make more room."

The old man just grunted. Each time he bent over, the boy could see a patch of loose belly flesh, pink and soft, in the gap where his overalls buttoned on the side. He tottered light-headed and delirious with hunger over mounds of garbage inside the smoked-up walls. He moved a newspaper. Green bottleflies swarmed up off a stringer of bream that somebody had thrown into the Dumpster. The fish were bloated, their eyes solid white. Their bellies were pale and their scales were gray. His stomach heaved but there was nothing to come up.

"Hurry up," the old man said.

The boy bent once more to his work. He knew his father was wanting to finish and get away from the road quickly, but before they had the tow sack half full, a pickup appeared far down the road. He raised himself up.

"Who is it?" he said.

"I don't know. You got any more in there?"

He didn't answer, only stood watching apprehensively as the

vehicle grew nearer and slowed. They looked at each other and Wade said: "Get outa there."

Gary climbed down from the Dumpster, holding onto the door. The pickup had slowed to a crawl and now a shield emblazoned on the door appeared, a county emblem like a Maltese cross. The truck stopped and the driver shut the motor off. They waited. A tall man with brown hair and khaki clothes got out. He didn't say anything at first, only studied them as if they were errant children whose unacceptable behavior he had suffered far past reason.

"Hidy," Wade said. "How you?"

The man put his hands on his hips and walked over to the Dumpster. He looked inside and shook his head.

"You don't care for us gettin these cans, do you? We didn't figger nobody wanted em."

The man kicked at the piles of trash they'd thrown on the ground, nudging at the mess with his toe as if he'd lost something in that stinking heap of offal. Then he looked up.

"You people are unbelievable," he said. "You really are." He kicked at the stuff again. "What do you think this Dumpster's for?"

"We ain't hurtin nothin," the old man said. "We just after these cans. Who are you, anyway?"

The man stared hard at him. "By God, I'm Don Shelby. I'm the supervisor of this beat. Who in the fuck are you?"

Wade Jones toed among the mosaic of ground glass and said nothing.

"Look at this mess," the man said. "Who do you think's going to clean it up? When we had a dump here and kept it bulldozed you wouldn't even drive down to the end to throw it out. And now I'll be goddamned if you're not throwing it out of the Dumpsters." He looked at Gary. "Do you know you can get put in jail for this?"

"Nosir," he said. He was wondering if he should run for it. The woods were pretty close.

"Well, by God, you can. It's a five-hundred-dollar fine for littering. Have you got five hundred dollars?"

"Nosir. I ain't."

"Well, that's what it would cost you. It's a state law." He looked at the pile of trash again as if he couldn't believe it was still there. "My hands can't run over here every fifteen minutes and pick this stuff up. They've got other things to do. Now you two pick up every bit of this mess and put it back where you got it. And I'm gonna stand here and watch you."

"Say you the supervisor?" said Wade.

"Damn right."

"But you ain't the law," he said doubtfully.

Shelby stepped up until he was in the old man's face. "Naw, I ain't the law. Smart son of a bitch. But I got a radio in that truck. And if you don't pick this shit up in the next five minutes I'll call the law out here and you can smart off to them."

Wade blinked. "Come on, boy." He nudged him. "Get down here and start pickin this stuff up. I told you not to make all this mess."

Gary bent and picked up an armload. "Ain't you gonna help me?" he said.

"I'm helpin," Wade said, tossing in a soup can, a rag, an empty potato chip bag. Nothing too heavy. A cereal box, a paper, an egg carton.

"I want it just as clean as it was before," Shelby said. He watched Gary for a bit, watched him bending over trying to pick up the myriad scattered lumps of trash. "Wait a minute," he said. He walked back to his truck and reached into the bed and brought out a new shovel with the price tag still attached. "Here," he said. "Use this."

"Yessir," Gary said. He started scooping. Wade stopped and raised one side of his hat, scratching at his head. He leaned back on the hood of the truck, the limp sack of cans tinkling faintly. He drew a handkerchief from his pocket and mopped his face. The man on the tractor was coming alongside them in the field and he had his head bent to see the wheel in the row. He and his machine were engulfed in dust, the thin silt rolling up on the tires and pouring like water off the cleats. They watched him pass, and as he came by he lifted a hand in greeting. The blades of the plow where they cut the earth were polished bright as chrome, rising and falling in the lifeless dust and the steady chug of the tractor echoing endlessly over the silence against the scrape of the shovel.

"He wants it clean, now," the old man said.

Gary nodded and kept at it. Shelby looked at his watch. The boy was pushing small piles of rubbish together, pushing them up against the wall of the Dumpster and using his hand to get it all in the shovel.

"I guess that'll do," Shelby said. Gary straightened and looked at him and then looked at this father. Wade nodded. The

---

49

supervisor held out his hand for the shovel and the boy gave it to him.

"I don't want to see this happen any more," he said. He tossed the shovel into the bed of the truck and it hit with a loud bong. He waited for Wade to unlean himself from his hood.

"My hands has got enough to do as it is. If you want cans you better get out and pick em up off the side of the road. That's where most of em's at anyway."

"Yessir," Gary said. Wade had his hands on his hips and was looking around like somebody deaf.

Shelby opened his door and stood with one hand on it, fixing them with a cold stare, each in turn. "I keep my eye on these things," he said. "I come by here just about every day."

Wade wouldn't even look at him.

"All right," he said. "You been told."

He got into the truck and cranked it and pulled away. They stood beside the Dumpster and watched him go up the road slowly, then pull off to the side and turn around. He was doing forty by the time he came by them again. They waved. He didn't. He went down the highway out of sight and finally even the sound of his tires vanished. It was hot and still where they stood, and the tractor was turning to make another pass.

"All right," Wade said. "He's gone. Get back up in there."

"What if he comes back?"

"He ain't comin back. It's dinnertime."

"He might, though. He might come back after while to see if we still here."

"You hear what I said?"

"Yeah."

"Then do like I told you."

"We done got just about all the cans," he said, but he was already climbing back up through the door.

A pattern emerged, one they discovered by employing a system of regular reconnaissance. The Dumpsters were emptied on Tuesdays and Fridays, which left the other five days of the week for harvesting the depths of them. They changed their salvage operations to night, covered safely by the cloak of darkness. Parts of each day were given over to walking along the sides of the highways, the boy down in the ditches throwing the cans up onto the road, the old man shuffling along and stuffing the sack. Often he would have to sit down and rest, and the boy would range far ahead and come back with his arms laden and his own sack full. They dumped the cans in a pile beside the house, and they would stand sometimes and quietly contemplate their growing wealth.

The old man made a trip to town one day, hitching a ride with a farmer who was going to the feed mill in a pickup. The farmer had a load of shelled corn, big sacks of it that swirled chaff into the face of the rider where he sat nodding in the back end.

When the truck stopped, he roused himself and got out in front of a barnlike building, its walls patched over with roofing tin and Purina signs. A rutted parking lot of gravel was littered with rusted farm implements, their moving parts frozen solid with corrosion and decorated with ten or fifteen cats. He climbed down from the back as the farmer came around.

"I sure thank you for the ride," he said. "Is it much further to town?"

The farmer was a man in denim pants and a T-shirt, a busy man hurrying toward his feed. "It's bout a mile," he said, pointing up the road with his chin.

Wade nodded. He looked, his eyes taking in the searing strip of asphalt lined with trees standing still under no breath of air and the sun overhead like a white coin in the sky. The farmer started lifting the sacks out and handing them across to a black man who had come silently from the depths of the shadows inside the building pushing a heavy two-wheeled cart.

"Well, listen," Wade said. He put a somber look on his face. The farmer in the truck stopped with both hands on the sewn ears of a sack and regarded him, the muscles in his forearms standing up like little ropes.

"You couldn't loan me a dollar or two, could you? I got a sick youngun at home and I done called about the medicine. They said it was five dollars and somethin and I ain't got but four dollars."

"A dollar?"

"Yessir. A dollar or two. I hate to ask you after I done caught a ride and all with you but she sure needs that medicine." He had one hand on the sideboards of the truck and his upturned face looked weak and ashamed.

"Why, hell," the farmer said, and looked ashamed himself. "Feller, I don't even know you."

"That's all right," the old man said quickly. "That's okay. I thank you for the ride anyway." He turned away and had taken but three steps when the farmer called out to him.

"Hey. Wait a minute."

He turned. "Yessir," he said. Waiting.

"Hell. Come back here a minute. You didn't say nothin about you had a sick youngun."

Wade scuffed his shoes among the little stones.

"I just hated to," he said. "You's good enough to give me a ride and all. I hated to ask you for anything else."

The farmer in the truck and the black man on the dock were watching him. The black man pulled the cart back and turned it and pushed it away into the dim stacks of feed and disappeared. The farmer got down from the truck and dusted his hands off. He approached his rider with a hurt look, his eyes downcast.

"Is she bad sick?" he said.

"Well. She stays sick pretty much. Been sick all her life."

The farmer nodded and rubbed his chin with a finger.

"How old is she?"

"She's four years old. Course the doctor's always sayin he's surprised she's lived this long. They said at first she would never live this long." He lifted his head and looked off into the distance, shaking his head slightly in awe. "She don't never complain, though. Just to look at her you'd never think they's nothin wrong with her."

"Well, Lord," the farmer said softly. "I got a granddaughter four years old." He had one hand in his back pocket and one hand rubbing his lower lip in indecision. It didn't take him long. He pulled out his billfold and opened it. He took some money out and thrust it at the old man as if it were burning his fingers.

"Take this," he said. "She might need somethin else."

Wade didn't look at the money but shook his head firmly. "I couldn't take that," he said. "I *can't* take that."

The farmer shook the money at him. "Go on," he said. "Hell fire. Take it."

"I sure hate to, mister. You done been so good already."

The farmer walked close and stuffed the money down in the old man's pocket. Wade stood with his head down, shaking it. He did that for about a minute. Then he turned and took five steps and stopped and looked back. The farmer was standing in the gravel watching him, his face touched with compassion or maybe something else.

"I got a bunch of stuff to do here or I'd carry you on into town," he said, and he seemed still ashamed. "But if I'm here when you come back by I'll be proud to give you a ride back home."

"I thank you," Wade said. "I reckon I better get on uptown and see about that medicine."

"Well. I hope your youngun gets all right," the farmer said softly.

The old man nodded and walked away.

In the air-conditioned cool of the supermarket he plucked a small bunch of grapes from the produce stand and had them all in his mouth by the time he got to the peanut butter. Squatting against the shining jars of jelly, he worked his mouth stealthily, firing the seeds down between his feet into a razored-open carton that he pulled from beneath the shelves. He went up front and got a cart and loaded the little section in the rear with dented cans of Vienna sausage and purple hull peas from a crate of damaged goods marked

down to quarter price. He was a careful shopper, a bargain hunter
adding figures in his head, carrying the ones. Like a blank-eyed
countryman, he stopped in the middle of the aisle with his face
up, as if the computations he performed so swiftly in his mind
were written on the ceiling panels. He paused beside the dairy
case, idly inspecting the merchandise, noting with disbelief the
price of real butter. When no one was looking he opened a plastic
half-pint of grape juice from the shelf and poured it down his
throat, placing the empty carton behind the full ones. A few feet
away, a boy in a green apron came pushing out from the double
metal doors that led to the back. He got a quick glimpse of baled
flour tiered to the roof, dog food on skids, block walls against
which pallets of beer and soft drinks were neatly arrayed. He
pushed his cart down to the meat case and examined the chickens
and pork chops. Leg quarters were on sale for twenty-nine cents a
pound but he passed them by. He picked up a package of sliced
smoked picnic ham, the meat so brown and delicately marbled,
the cooked hub of sawn bone in the middle. It was $6.97 for eight
slices. He dropped it in his cart. Through the glass he could see a
great hanging side of beef on a hook and butchers at work around
tables. There was a button to summon the meatcutters set into the
front of the case, and he pushed his cart down to it and pressed
it with his finger, watching them. Heads looked up, looked
back down. A young black man with a white paper cap on his
head stared at him with thinly veiled disgust and wiped his hands
on a paper towel before coming out to the front. He bent over the
meat case and rearranged sirloin steaks and chuck roasts as he
worked his way down to this customer.

"Can I help you," the butcher said, when he stopped in front of Wade.

"Y'all got any meat scraps?" Wade said.

"Meat scraps?" He looked out from under his cap, his hands moving busily and with trained efficiency over his goods. He stopped and rested his forearms over the back of the case and looked up the aisle.

"Yeah. Just some old bones or meat scraps for dogs. You got scraps to throw out, don't you?"

The butcher shook his head and he didn't look happy. "I don't know how much we got. Have to go back in the back and see. Ain't cut much today."

"I want some if you got some," Wade said. "I got some dogs at home."

"Well, we kinda busy," the butcher said. "I can go look when I get through with what I'm doin." Then while he shuffled the meat he mumbled about his own dogs and his daddy and his daddy's dogs, the full meaning of which Wade couldn't understand.

"Well, where's the manager?" Wade said. "I'll go ask him." He started looking around wildly.

The black man stood erect quickly. "Naw," he said. "Naw, don't go ask him. Hell, I'll go get it." He turned away and started toward the back.

"Y'all got a bathroom around here?"

The butcher pushed open one of the doors and jerked his thumb to the right. "Round back."

"Y'all care for me usin it?"

"Help yourself." He banged the doors when he went through.

The old man left his cart in the detergent aisle and stepped quietly through the swinging doors. He didn't see anybody back there among the cardboard boxes of ruined lettuce and black bananas, wet mops, sacks of potatoes, spilled cat litter. There were two massive white doors on the left. He walked all the way to the back of the room and looked to the right. He saw the door marked *Men*. The door was open and the light was off. He jerked his head left as the butcher came through with a box on his shoulder and went into the rear of the meat market, saying soft motherfuckers to himself. Wade went to the double doors and looked back out, toward the front. There was nobody out there. He knelt by the second freezer door and felt of the Miller tallboys stacked next to the white frost that oozed from the bad gasket at the lower corner of the door and crept across the floor, up the sides of the cans like a fungus. They were cold as ice, sweating thin beads of condensation. He took two from the plastic template that bound them and put in each pocket the champagne of bottled beer, then rose and made his way to the bathroom, where he turned on the light and locked the door.

When he emerged, belching, ten minutes later, he'd smoked two cigarettes in utter comfort and buried the empty cans in the trash bucket beneath wads of toilet paper he'd taken off the roll and stuffed in there. He retrieved his cart from the aisle and went down to the meat case. The same butcher looked up and saw him before he could press the button again. He came out of the meat market with a large cardboard box, marked on the side in heavy pencil NO CHARGE.

"Here," he said, and handed it across. It was a heavy box, the sides bulging. Wade just barely got it in his cart. He opened the flaps and looked inside. Bonemeal and bad briskets and the pink tails of pigs. He nodded.

"All right," he said, but the butcher had gone back inside. He glared as Wade pushed his cart away, then swung his meat cleaver down to the block with a vengeance.

Pork and beans were on sale, four cans for a dollar. A dozen went into his cart, along with two loaves of the cheapest bread. When he turned into the beer aisle he'd spent all he was going to on food.

He stopped and mentally added up his purchases. He considered the weight of his goods. Displays of beer were lined up on both sides of the aisle, the shelves stacked with many different brands. He ignored the imported and went straight for the domestic. Budweiser was $3.19 a six-pack for twelve ounce. Shit, he thought. He looked at a twelver to see if he could cut the cost. It was $5.99.

"Thirty-nine cents," he said, and a woman standing next to him jerked and looked at him and moved away. Busch was a little better at $2.98 but still he shook his head. The Old Milwaukee in cans was the best comparable buy he could see at $2.49 for fourteen ounces. But then he saw twelve-ounce bottles for $2.09. He stood there in a dilemma for three or four minutes trying to figure. For a fleeting moment he considered putting some of the bread back. Then he thought about the pork and beans. He was looking back and forth from his cart to the beer. And then he realized that he hadn't even considered cigarettes.

"*Shit*," he whispered. A boy sweeping the aisle was trying to sweep around him.

"What's the cheapest beer y'all got?" Wade asked him. The boy stopped and scratched his head. He looked around as if seeing it for the first time, since, in fact, he was.

"I don't know," he said.

"Well, see if you can help me. You got anything cheapern this Old Milwaukee? It's two forty-nine."

The boy went from display to display, checking prices.

"I guess we got this here," he said, tapping a stack of quarts. "It's sixty-nine cents."

Wade eyed it doubtfully. "What's that shit?" he said.

"Says. Misterbrow. Somethin."

"What'd that be for a case? Ten and two. Six ninety and . . . one thirty-eight. Be . . ." He looked at the boy.

"I don't know," the boy said.

"Be eight twenty-eight."

"Plus tax," said the boy.

"Plus tax. Which is . . . what? A nickel?"

"Six cents now."

"Six cents. Six eights forty-eight." He was wagging his head slightly from side to side. "Almost nine dollars."

The boy didn't say anything.

"But that's three gallons of beer," Wade told him. "Ain't that right? Twelve quarts to the case?"

"I guess."

"But I still got to get some cigarettes. And tax on all that . . ."

"I got to sweep this floor," the boy said.

"What'd I say while ago? Nine dollars. So a half a case'd be bout four and a half. Gallon and a half of beer. And this other . . ." He turned his head and looked back to the Old Milwaukee. "Two six-packs five dollars. Fourteen times twelve . . . ten's a hunnerd and forty . . . and twenty-eight . . . that ain't but a little over a gallon," he said. The boy had dropped all pretense of trying to sweep. He was just listening to him.

"Half a case of that's what I need," Wade said. "How bout takin six of them out for me?"

In the end he ditched six cans of pork and beans into the freezer section along with one of the loaves of bread, and wound up with five packs of generic cigarettes instead of a whole carton of Camels. He shoved into line and waited for the girl to set his things on the counter. He moved his head from his goods to the register like a tennis spectator as she rang it all up. He winced when she added the sales tax.

"Goddamn," he said. "Y'all the highest place in town, ain't you?"

She just leaned on one arm and tapped her nails on the counter and gave him a shitty look while he pulled out his money. A boy sacked the groceries and started to push the cart out the door.

"I got it," Wade told him, and went out onto the sidewalk. He had all his groceries in one sack, but the meat scraps alone were almost more than he could carry. He looked out over the parking lot as the sweat leaped out of him. He saw a parked cab and he pushed his cart down the ramp and went over to it. There was a ponytailed young white man sitting at the wheel.

"You got a fare?"

The man glanced up from his paper and flipped some ashes off

his cigarette down the door. He looked at his newspaper again
and turned a page.

"I's supposed to had one but if she don't bring her black ass out
here in about two minutes I'm fixin to go eat dinner."

"What'll you charge me to carry me out to London Hill?"

The driver looked up.

"London Hill? Hell, that's way out in the country." He shook
his head a little. "I don't know."

"What'll you take?" Wade said.

"How far is it?"

"It's bout ten mile."

He looked at his watch. "Let's see," he said. He looked up and
squinted from the sun. "I'll cut the meter off and run you out
there for ten dollars."

"All right."

The driver got out in a hurry and opened the back door, saying,
"Hurry up and get your stuff in fore that nigger woman gets out
here."

When the passenger was settled comfortably in the back seat
with his groceries around him, he dug into the sack and found one
of the hot quarts on the bottom. He pulled it out and twisted the
cap off, then turned the bottle straight up.

"Put that bottle down, damn. These cops in town see you they'll
have my ass."

He took it down. "What?" He was talking to the cab driver's
eyes in the rearview mirror.

"Hell, feller. You can't be drinking beer in my cab in town.
Don't you know that?"

"Well, you got a cup or anything?"

"Naw, I ain't got no cup. Just wait'll we get out of town." He picked up his mike. "Wait'll we get up on the bypass at least. I'm fixin to check out for dinner there, Ethel."

He pulled out into the street.

"You get that woman at Midtown?" said the radio.

"Did not there. I waited on her thirty minutes."

He went down the hill and turned east.

"Well, she called back there and said she's ready. Swing around and take her home before you go to dinner."

He put his knee up and clenched the mike, steering with one hand.

"I'm heading to the service station right now with one goin down. This thing's hot as a two dollar pistol, too. I might be able to get her in about a hour there. Maybe. Ten four?"

He stopped at an intersection and looked both ways, then pulled out. The radio sputtered, making the sound of frying bacon. He cut down the squelch and swung up onto the ramp and mashed the gas pedal to the floor. He met Wade with his eyes in the mirror.

"All right," he said. "You can get happy now if you want to."

He drove swiftly on the country road. Wade swayed slightly in the curves with his beer in one hand and a piece of the picnic ham in the other. Things were much changed from what he remembered from years ago. New houses, fields where woods once stood, a new county high school. Even the road was new.

"Say you live out there at London Hill?" the driver said. He didn't look around.

"Right the other side of it."

"You don't know old Joe Ransom, do you?"

The old man thought about it a while. He'd known some Ransoms at one time, back when he was much younger. Thirty or forty years before.

"I don't know," he said finally. "I used to know a bunch of folks out there. I been gone a long time, though. What's his daddy's name?"

"I don't know. You ain't never heard of him?"

"I don't reckon."

"I just wondered. He's supposed to live out there somewhere. I just thought you might know him."

"I don't guess I do," Wade said. He dug into the sack for another piece of meat.

He was halfway finished with the second quart when he told the driver where to turn off.

"How much further?" the driver wanted to know.

"It ain't much further."

"I got twelve miles on this thing already," he said, and he looked over his shoulder when he said it.

"I'll pay you."

Tractors were toiling their way through heavy clouds of dust. Trucks were parked in the fields with their loads of fertilizer and seed. The taxi sped by and left them behind.

"Bunch of farmers out here," the driver said.

"It's about another mile up here where you turn off. Big dirt road to the left and you go up this hill."

He slowed the driver down, and as they turned onto the dirt

road he pitched the second bottle out the window. The track was rough and the car bellied and bumped over the ruts.

"I ain't gonna get stuck up in here, am I?" the driver said.

"Naw. It ain't much further."

They went across a wooden bridge where a creek lay shallow within the banks, an eddy sluggish and brown and studded with stones showing their moss-grown faces, stepping stones for the coons and foxes and possums whose tracks dotted the sandy silt and went up the slopes of young cane, thick and nearly impenetrable, over the slides of beavers crusted with sun and broken open into jigsaw puzzles of hardened mud. Through fields of unnamed bushes and sagging wire, between oaks leaning to form a tunnel of shade, the dusty cab sped rocking and jarring, rocks flying.

"Damned if you don't live back in the sticks," the driver said.

"Here it is," Wade said, pointing. "Just drive right up in there."

The driver stopped and eyed the iron ruts left by tractors. He shook his head.

"This is far as I'm goin," he said. "I done come fourteen miles and you said it wasn't but ten."

"Hell, you can get up in there."

"Not in this car."

He shoved the shift into parking gear and got out. Wade climbed out on the other side and slid his box of scraps and his sack onto the ground. The beer bottles clinked.

"Owe me fourteen dollars," the driver said. Wade looked at him for a little while and then took the money out of his pocket and counted it. He had four dollars left after he paid his fare. He bent and stuck it into a sock and straightened. There was a cloud of dust far down in the field traveling along the rows. The driver put the money in his pocket and got back into the car. The old man had already started walking off with his hands empty when he leaned out and said: "You not goin to take this stuff with you?"

Wade turned around and looked at him. "I got somebody can carry it," he said.

urt Fowler was on his front porch taking the last sip from his last beer. He pitched the can into the aluminum boat that sat beside the porch just as a pickup with a camper bed came over the hill, the tires sucking gently in the mud. The truck slewed slightly as it swung into the yard and came to a lurching halt beside the single tree, where a rope hung. The door slammed and Joe got out and came around the front of the truck with five beers in his hand.

"What say, Curt."

He walked up to the porch and sat on the step.

"I knew somebody'd bring me a beer if I set out here long enough," Curt said. He helped himself to a beer and opened it and started pouring it down his throat.

"You ain't fishin today, Curt?"

"Naw, hell, water's too fuckin muddy, it rained like a sumbitch over here last night. You ain't workin today?"

Joe had on his sunglasses and a pair of knit slacks the color of cream and a new green velour shirt with tan piping around the collar. His shiny black loafers had mud on them.

"My niggers can't work in the rain. Afraid they gonna melt, I reckon. We's in a bad place, anyway, and I was afraid we wouldn't get out so we just come on to the house. It's been like that near every day. Where's that sorry-ass brother of yours?"

Curt shook his head. "I ain't seen him in about two weeks. I reckon he's gone back to Texas to hang sheetrock. Melba said she don't even know where he is."

"I wish to hell I knowed where he is. He owes me some damn money."

"He ain't never paid you that yet? Damn. I figured he'd done paid you by now."

Joe drained the can of beer in his hand and tossed it into the boat, which was fourteen feet long and already three-quarters full of cans. "I can't catch up with him," he said. "If you see him, tell him I want to see him."

"I'll tell him. What you fixin to do?"

"I don't know. Reckon Henry and them's got a game tonight?"

"I don't know. The sumbitch won't never tell me when they gonna have one no more. After I took a bunch of money off him he won't. Bastard's gonna make me mad sometime and I'm gonna whip his ass is what I'm gonna do."

"He might shoot your ass, too. George'll shoot you in a god-damn minute."

"They ain't gonna shoot nobody. They ain't gonna shoot me."

Joe got himself another beer and opened it. He pulled out his cigarettes.

"Let me get one of them off you," Curt said immediately.

"You the bumminest little fucker I ever seen," said Joe, but he gave him one.

"I just ain't had no way to get to the store."

"You just too lazy to walk, Curt. Where's Bobby?"

"Still in jail, I reckon. I heard you got into it with Willie Russell other night."

"Naw. He kept fuckin with me and I just slapped the shit out of him was all. He was drunk. Runnin his mouth. You know how he is."

"I'm surprised somebody ain't done killed him by now."

"Somebody will."

Curt sipped his beer and looked out across the yard.

"You know, though, I don't think he's been right at all since he mashed his balls off."

"Shit. I don't believe he mashed em off."

"You don't?"

"I don't. I've heard he's got one ball and I've heard he mashed em both off, but I don't know."

"Satch said he believes he's queer."

"I don't believe he's queer neither. I just think he's too fucked up for anybody to have him. That's why you don't never see him with a woman. Ain't no woman'll have him."

"I had a cousin one time like to lost his dick," Curt said. "Zipped it up in his zipper. You know how you'll do that when you're little."

"Oh, hell yes. It'll just about make you shit on yourself."

"He was grown, though. Zipped it up too fast and got some of the skin caught in it. And messed around and let it get infected before he went to the doctor. He like to went crazy over it. Thought they's gonna have to amputate his dick. They had to take him down to Whitfield for a while. His dick like to rotted off."

"Well, what'd they do?"

"His daddy told me they did a skin graft on it. Said they took some skin off his leg and sewed that on it."

Joe leaned back and sipped his beer and crossed his legs, gave off a little shiver.

"Off his leg? Why hell, it don't look like that would work. I don't believe I'd want no skin off my leg on my dick."

"You might if they's fixin to amputate it."

"They could amputate mine right now for all the good it does me," he said. He got up suddenly. "Reckon when Franklin'll be back?"

Curt was eyeing the three remaining beers mournfully.

"It ain't no tellin about him," he said.

"He probably don't even remember me letting him have it. Was drunk when he got it. I hate to have to chase down somebody that owes me money."

"I know it," said Curt. He started drinking faster. "When you seen old Van House?" he said, stalling for time.

"I ain't seen him," Joe said, and stepped down into the yard. "You tell Franklin when he comes back I want my money. I have to work for it just like everybody else and I ain't rich."

"I'll tell him. Let me get another one of these beers off you before you go."

Joe barely glanced at them. "Hell, get all of em. I got some more in the truck. Only reason I'm drinking beer's cause it's so hot."

He was almost to the truck when Curt came down the steps, two of the beers in one hand and another freshly opened in the other.

"You ain't fixin to go to town, are you?"

"I don't know," he said. He went on around and got in the truck. "I don't know where I'm fixin to go." He hated now that he'd stopped.

Unshaven, his hair wild, his clothes rumpled from sleeping in them, the man in the yard leaned in the open window of the truck to further detain this visitor, this rare company. "Let me ride up town with you," he said.

Joe looked at him, his eyes unreadable behind the dark glasses, his hand on the key and his foot on the clutch.

"You got any money? I ain't gonna buy your damn beer all night long."

"Oh, I got some money," he said. "I got a check I can cash."

He was already opening the truck door and sliding in. There were three packs of cigarettes on the dash and a little cooler in the floor. He slammed the door and sat there, ready for takeoff.

"Let's see it," Joe said.

"What?"

"Sumbitch, if you ain't got no money you ain't goin with me."

Curt set his beer in the floor and did a quick frisk of his pockets, grabbing himself all over with spread fingers.

"It's in the house," he said. "Let me run get it." He got out and started across the yard. "Wait on me!" he yelled back.

Joe sat shaking his head, thinking: Fuckass around here all evening waiting for him to get ready to go.

After a minute, Curt stuck his head out the screen door and said: "You got time for me to shave right quick?"

"Hell naw. You come get your ass in if you're goin. I'm fixing to leave."

He mashed the clutch and cranked the truck and revved the engine. Curt came flying out the door with a fresh shirt flapping around him, an envelope in his hand.

"I got it," he panted. He got back in and said: "I'm ready now. I got to stop somewhere and cash it, though." He picked up his beer and reached into his shirt pocket. "Goddamn. Left my fuckin cigarettes in the house. Wait on me just a minute."

He opened the door and Joe let out on the clutch. They went rolling through the yard.

"Wait a minute. I got to get my cigarettes."

"Just smoke some of mine. They's some up on the dash."

Curt grabbed a pack and closed the door as they moved through the yard and down the driveway and out onto the road. Joe looked at his watch.

"Don't start no shit and expect me to finish it, now. What kind of a check you got?"

"It's a goverment check," said Curt. "I can get it cashed anywhere. Grocery stores'll cash em."

"What you doin with a government check? What are you drawin from the government?"

"Aw, it's Mama's. I always cash hers for her."

"How much is it?"

"A hundred and thirty dollars. It's a pension check."

"Pension."

"Yeah."

"Your mama draws a hundred and thirty dollars a month?"

"Yeah. Plus, she draws Social Security and welfare, too."

"What's she doin lettin you have it?"

"She don't know I got it."

Joe shook his head. They went up the gravel road with the rich red mud squishing under the tires. Curt kept up a running commentary, expansive now with the promise of more beer and a night on the town. The woods thinned and opened up into green hills dotted with horses and cows and cultivated land gleaming wetly under the weak sun trying to break through the clouds. Tarpaper shacks and shabby mobile homes, actually no more than campers, lined the road, the yards full of junked autos and stacked firewood overgrown with weeds and pulpwood trucks with the windows smashed out and the rear ends jacked up and propped on oil drums, El Dorados with mud halfway up the sides parked before porches of rough sawmill lumber. Here and there were school buses fixed up with furniture and beds on the inside, the awnings made of splintered fiberglass, and new brick homes within sight of firetraps where carports were cluttered with dogs and three-wheelers and washing machines.

They turned onto the blacktop, and mud began slapping off the tires onto the undersides of the wheelwells. The bottomland lay untilled and dark with water, the brown rows of the past year's crop still standing in the new grass threatening to bury it. Stumps the size of Volkswagens had been bulldozed into piles in the corners of the fields.

"They gonna plant any of this this year?" said Joe.

Curt tossed his can out the window and reached for another

one. He felt of it. He looked at Joe. "You got any cold beers in that cooler?"

"They's a six-pack iced down in there. Goddamn, you done drank all them?"

"Naw. I'm gonna swap one out with you." He put the luke-warm beer in the cooler and took out a cold one and popped the top. "Hell, it's been too wet," he said. "It's rained on it just about ever week. They tried cuttin part of it about three weeks ago and mired the tractor and brought a dozer over to pull it out and mired it. I reckon it's still settin there if somebody ain't done stole it."

They turned at a crossroads and headed back up into the hills.

"I thought you's goin to town," Curt said.

"I am. I got to stop and see Henry first and see if they've got a game up tonight. I need to win me a little money if I can."

They crossed the bottomland, the long rows whipping past and wheeling by like spokes. Butterflies wafted and flitted through the lush growth at the roadsides, snake doctors hovered like gunships. The road brightened and the shadow of a cloud stood immense and dark and held part of the land in shade, a line of demarcation halfway across the fields.

"Look at that," Joe said. "We got to try and work tomorrow if we can. It's costin the shit out of me to lay out."

"Shit. If I had your money I'd throw mine away."

Joe grunted. He steered the truck between the holes in the road and tried to find some music on the radio. He'd been meaning to get a tape deck but he'd never gotten around to it. He punched a button and got WDIA.

"Damn it," he said. He twisted the dial around, and the radio snarled and whined while quick-speaking Spaniards exhorted their wares and somebody screamed CASH MONEY and twangy garbled country music flared and diminished amidst roaring and fuzz and static until finally he snapped it off. The road twisted through stands of pine, hills of hardwood timber green as Eden. They went down into a smaller bottom where one old unpainted house sat back from the road, with dead cotton stalks all around it, even in what should have been a yard. They pulled into a short driveway.

"You goin it?" Joe said, after he'd killed the motor.

Curt looked dubiously at the house.

"Naw. I don't want to go in. I'll just set out here."

"Suit yourself," he said, and he got out and slammed the door and went up the steps onto the porch. He knocked on the screen door and stuck his head inside.

"Henry? Hey, Henry." Somebody answered and he stepped into the hall. The house was built with a breezeway through the middle and rooms on each side. The old boards bowed and sagged under his weight. Joe opened a door on the right but there was nobody in there. Somebody said something again and he went to the back of the house. The door he opened belonged to the kitchen, and three men stood in there at a table, hacking and slicing on the carcass of a skinned deer, two holding, one cutting, all of them trying to keep it from sliding onto the floor.

"Now how'd y'all know I wasn't the game warden?" he said.

"Hell, they all out on the lake robbin trotlines," said Henry. "You know anything about cuttin up a deer?"

He looked at the thing doubtfully.

"I've cut up a few. I ain't no expert."

He leaned up against the wall and surveyed the mess on the table. It was covered with cut hair and caked with enormous clots of blood.

"What are y'all tryin to do, cut it up into steaks or what?"

Henry waved his knife. He was an old man with long white hair, overalls, no shirt or shoes.

"We just trying to get it so we can eat it. Thought we might cut it up in some roasts."

"I don't believe I'd cut it all up into roasts," Joe said. "Course you can do it any way you want to. I'd cut most of it up in steaks if it was mine."

"Well, you know how to do it? Stacy said he knowed how to cut it up and like to cut his fuckin arm off a while ago."

A drunk grinned and lifted a beer in a hand swathed with bloodsoaked paper towels. All the men were brothers.

"Hell, let George cut it up," said Joe. "George could cut it up if they give you enough time, couldn't you, George?"

"I could do as good as they doin," said the blind brother.

Joe unleaned himself from the wall and walked over to the table. "I hate to get a bunch of blood on these clothes. I'll cut the loins off for you and show you how to cut up the hams. You can make roasts out of the shoulders if you want to. That's about all they're fit for anyway."

They stepped back.

"Well, go to it," said Henry.

"You got a sharp knife?" he said, and laid his cigarettes down.

"I got a filet knife right here," said Henry.

"Let me see that, then."

He had them turn the deer on its side and then he tested the edge of the blade against his thumb.

"This is the best meat on it right here," he said, and he put the tip of the knife just behind the shoulder and sank it into the meat.

"Just hold it steady, now," he said. He pushed the knife down until he felt it stop against the first rib and drew it down, slicing the backstrap away from the vertebrae all the way down to the hip.

"Where did y'all get this deer?"

"It was hung in a fence up at Mr. Lee's old house a while ago," Stacy said. "Me and Henry was comin back from town and seen it. I come home and got George's pistol and shot it."

"What was it, a buck or a doe?"

"It was a doe. Big old doe."

He cut in deeply just behind the shoulder and just ahead of the hip, then took the knife forward under the meat and sliced toward his belly with the tip until he could grasp a corner of the loin and pull it up. He worked the blade back and forth against the ribs, pulling the meat up in a single strip and keeping the blade close against the bones. It came up smoothly, the white sinew wrinkling over the dark burgundy flesh until he passed the knife all the way down the ribs and held in his hand a thick strip of meat almost two feet long. He laid it on the table.

"That's some good stuff there," he said. "Look here."

He placed the top side down and cut and squared off the end and pushed the scrap aside with the knife. He cut off a loin steak two inches thick, then cut halfway through it again, so that when he spread it with his fingers it had doubled in size.

"That's how you do it. Butterfly steak. That's the best meat on it."

He put the knife down and went over to the sink and started washing his hands.

"Y'all can cut up the rest of it. Just saw the hams off and slice it all up in steak. I got to get on. When you gonna have another crap game?"

"We gonna have one tonight," Henry said.

"What time?"

"I don't know. When everbody gets here. We got to get through with this deer first. We got to get some freezer paper somewhere. Reckon John Coleman's got any at his store?"

"Yeah, he's got some. He keeps it."

"Well, just stick around. Stacy and George can finish this."

Joe picked up his cigarettes and lit one. He leaned against the sink.

"I got to go to town first." He grinned. "I got Curt out in the truck with me."

"What?" Henry said. "He scared to come in?"

"Said you's pissed off at him. Said he took a bunch of money off you other night."

"Why, the son of a bitch is lying."

"I figured he was."

"I'll tell you what he got pissed off about. He got pissed off cause I wouldn't loan him fifty dollars. Comes down here drunk, wantin to borry money off me to gamble with me. If I loaned him fifty he'd owe me a hundred. You ever heard of anything like that?"

Joe picked up his cigarettes and put them in his pocket. "I ain't surprised at nothin Curt would do. He's got his mama's pension check in his pocket right now. Fixin to cash it when he gets to a grocery store."

Henry shook his head.

"Him and Franklin have pissed away every penny that old woman had. When Jim died he owned two thousand acres of land and had way over a hundred head of cows. And I mean by God worked his whole life to get it. I can remember when he didn't have nothin. And now she ain't got nothin. Taxes. It's their own fault, I reckon. When them two boys was coming up they was a gallon churn used to set on the kitchen table. Was full of money, change. Quarters and dimes and nickels. Wasn't no pennies in it. Franklin and Curt would get ready to go to town and they'd go in there and just scoop up a handful. They always had plenty of money but they never had to work for none of it. No sir, I ain't loanin him no money."

"I'm fixin to take him uptown and get him drunk," Joe said. "He knows where Franklin's at, but he won't tell me when he's sober. I'll get about a six-pack in him and get some of them old gals to rub some of that leg on him. He'll tell me then."

"A drunk man tells no lies."

"You got that right. Well, I'll be back after while, Henry. You don't want me to bring Curt back with me?"

"I don't care. Leave him uptown and make him walk home if you want to. You can get you some of this deer meat when you get back if you want to. We ain't got much room in the freezer."

79

"All right," he said, and he went out the door. He closed it behind him and walked up the hall. He could see Curt sitting on the hood drinking a beer. He had his legs crossed, and was smoking a cigarette.

"Is Henry in there?" he said.

"Yeah. He said if you come in there he's gonna shoot your ass. Come on, get in and let's go." He was going down the steps as he talked, and he stopped beside Curt where he sat on the hood. A truck came around the curve and it started slowing as it neared the house. They turned to watch it come.

"I wonder who that is," Joe said.

"I don't know. Looks like it's comin in here."

It was. It slowed gradually and stopped beside the driveway, a white '78 Ford truck with a smashed fender and a driver screaming strangled curses as he dragged something up from the floorboards. Fried hair and a yelling mouth fifty yards away, a man with blood between his eyes.

"Is he talkin to us?" Joe said.

"God*damn!*" Curt threw one leg off the hood and slammed his beer down and Joe had started around the other side of the truck when the barrel came out the window and smoke erupted. Two concussions back to back sent hot lead flying as they labored with their hands up beside their chests, cartoon characters slipping and losing traction in the loose gravel. They were shot before they could move three feet. Joe fell and covered his head. Another shot went over his back and slammed into the house. Curt sobbed aloud and crawled behind the wheel of the truck, blood running from his shoe. Joe's ears were roaring and he heard the transmission of the truck grinding as the driver tried to shove it up in reverse. He got up and jerked the door open, hitting Curt in the head with it, and felt around among the beer cans under the seat for his pistol. His hand closed over it. He snatched it out and ran to the road. The pickup had backed into the field above the house and the driver was winding the wheel in a panic, looking out the window. Joe ran up the ditch, trying to shorten the range. The truck roared out, skidded, almost went into the ditch on the other side, and he stopped and opened up with the little .25, towtowtow, towtowtow! Two small medallions of paint leaped off the tailgate. As the truck pulled away, he threw the tiny gun after it. He slapped a hand up beside his ear and it came away slick with blood. His shirt had three holes in it that he could see, and more blood was coming from his arms and back. He wiped the blood away from his head and walked back to his truck. George and Henry and Stacy were on the porch, Henry with a 9MM Browning automatic in his hand.

"You all right?" Henry said.

"Hell yeah. I reckon. Where's Curt?"

They pointed to the truck. He knelt down and looked under it. Curt lay curled into a ball, his hands over his head.

Joe stood up. The hood and the left front fender had been ventilated. Later, he would count twenty holes in them, little puncture wounds that could have been in him.

"Come out from under there, Curt." He pulled up the sleeve of his shirt and saw the ragged hole in his bicep. "Shit," he said. It didn't hurt.

Henry and Stacy came off the porch. George stood back, both hands on a post.

81

"Get out from under there, Curt," he said again. "He's gone now. How bad you hurt?"

"Damn, Joe," said Henry. "You bleedin like a stuck pig."

"I'm all right. Little son of a bitch. I'll fix his ass. Get out from under there, Curt."

"I can't," said the small muffled whine in the dirt.

"Why not?"

"Cause," he said. He waited a moment. "I shit in my britches."

Joe looked at Henry and Stacy and grinned. "How you know I didn't shit in mine?" he said.

I t happened that the old man and the boy had been walking down a road with their bags of cans.

"I'm bout give out," Wade said.

"You want to stop and rest?"

"Yeah. Let's set down a minute and see if anybody comes by."

They sat and sat and sat.

"I don't believe nobody's gonna come by," Gary said.

"Just shut up. We need to get us a car."

"I'd like to have me a new car. I know what I'd buy, too. I'd buy me one of them SS Chevelles with a automatic transmission and tinted windows. And blackout mags. I'd run everybody around here."

The old man lay on his back and pulled his hat over his face.

"You know what?" the boy said.

"What?"

"If we'd get us a car I could get my driver's license."

The old man grunted and turned on his side.

"You can't get a driver's license. You don't know how to drive."

"If we had us a car I could learn, though. How much you reckon we could buy us a car for?"

"I don't know. It depends."

"Depends on what?"

"Depends on how much they want for it."

The boy pondered this and reamed out his ear with his finger, producing a crescent of brown wax on his nail that he wiped on his leg. He looked around.

"Let's walk on up the road. Ain't nobody gonna come by here. We might catch a ride up at the crossroads."

But the old man was sleepy and did not answer. The boy reached out and jostled his leg. His father moaned and turned in his sleep. He was lying in an ant bed. Ants were crawling over his shoes.

"You better move from there," Gary said.

His father's head collapsed onto an arm. He'd begun snoring.

"All right, then," Gary said. He sat there for a minute. He reached out and shook his father's leg. "You better move," he said. The old man pawed out at him, wheezing muttered words under his breath.

The boy sat and watched him sink deeper and deeper into sleep and fitfully begin a tortured turning and moving, as if his bones lay uneasy in his flesh. He whined once, sharply. His mouth jerked open and his nose twitched. He slapped groggily at his face and missed. The boy grinned. The old man bowed his back on the ground and stuck one hand inside his overalls and scratched. He panted gently, like a dog in labor, his face contorted. He seemed to nod vague agreement to some unspoken truth in his sleep. His limbs stopped moving momentarily and he lay on his side with one hand caught between his knees and the other arm pillowing his head.

It was as if a bolt of electricity suddenly penetrated him. His eyes snapped open and a look of such dread appeared in them that it was no surprise to the boy when he screamed.

"Haaaaaaaaaaaaaa!" he said. He was off the ground like a shot, running, jerking at the straps of his overalls and falling with a foot caught in his hands, trying to get his shoes off. But he couldn't even wait for that. He got one off and jumped up again and began a demented parody of aerobics or teenaged cheerleaders caught up in gymnastic attempts and twitched and hopped one-footed over the asphalt, making strange and meaningless gestures, emitting all manner of oaths, motherfuckers especially, a series of impotent ravings like one crazed with hydrophobia or loosed from a madhouse. He kicked one shoe flying and it sailed into a tree and hung there. The boy stood up and watched him.

"I told you to get up," he said.

The old man shucked clean out of his overalls and stood slapping them against the ground in his dirty shorts and T-shirt. He drew his shorts down to his knees so that his flaccid asscheeks and purple-headed penis were revealed among unbelievable amounts of short gray fur. Tiny red marks were all over his skin, as if he'd been sprinkled with a shotgun.

"Why didn't you tell me I's layin in a ant bed?" he said.

"I told you."

He started putting his clothes on, stepping into his overalls, but then he stopped and drew them back off and turned them inside out and inspected them minutely. He was still looking them over when they heard something up the road and saw a white pickup heading their way, coming across the bridge.

"Yonder comes somebody," said the boy.

"I ain't blind. Get down yonder and get my shoe out from that tree."

He got into his overalls and fastened the galluses and the boy went down into the ditch and picked up a stick and knocked the shoe loose, then tossed it up on the bank. The old man sat down in the road to put it on. The truck slowed and he watched it come. He was tying his shoelace when it pulled up beside him. He got up and looked through the windshield and went past the grille to the other shoe and picked it up and started putting it on. The boy came out of the ditch and stood beside the road. The driver of the truck was looking at them.

"What are y'all doin?" he said. He weaved behind the seat a little and turned up a Busch tallboy, and the old man homed in, going to the passenger window and hanging his arms down inside.

"We just messin around," he said. "You ain't got another one of them beers, have you?"

The man behind the wheel studied him carefully. He opened his mouth and let out an enormous belch, then threw the can out into the road. His face looked as if somebody had been ahold of it with a hatchet in years past.

"Where are y'all goin?" he said. He spoke very slowly and he could hardly speak at all.

"We just pickin up some cans," Wade told him. "You got one of them beers I could borrow off you?"

The man looked at him as if he couldn't figure out what he was.

He turned his head, slowly, steadily, and looked for the first time at the boy.

"What's he?" he said. "What's? Yonder's a can right there you can pick up," he said, pointing to the one he'd just thrown out. "Fuck it," he said. "I'll get it." He opened the door and held on with both hands and moved over to the can with his arms out for balance and bent over ever so slowly in the road and picked up the can.

"Where's you sack?" he said. "Where is your sack."

He leaned against the hood and turned the empty can up to his mouth. He wobbled when his head went back and then he took the can down. He stumbled backwards along the fender, trying to steady himself with his arm on the hood, but he didn't stop until his shoulder touched the windshield.

"Whoa," he said. He was offering the can. "That's one more." He ran his fingers up over his forehead and pushed his hair back. "Whew," he said. He looked owlishly about. He straightened back up and put both arms on the hood. The boy couldn't keep from staring at his face. The man saw him looking and said: "The fuck you lookin at?"

"I ain't lookin at nothin," Gary said.

"What are y'all doin?" he intoned again.

"Let me get one of them cold beers off you if you got another one," Wade said.

The man was trying to find a cigarette in his pocket and he finally found one. He turned it over in his hand a few times and stuck the filter in his mouth and then lit it. He smoked it for a moment, took it out and looked at it, then stuck it back between his lips.

"I tell you what I'll do," he said.

"What's that?" Wade was grinning, his eyes knowing, shining, as if they shared some secret.

"I'll give you a beer if you'll get me one while you in there, but first I got to tell you somethin."

"All right."

"Call him over here too."

"Who?"

"Him." He pointed to Gary.

"C'mere," Wade said.

Gary walked over and stood beside his father. He looked at a place on the man's neck.

"Look at me," the man said.

Gary looked at his face. "What?" he said.

"I said look at me." His eyes were dark and rimmed with redness. Gary looked. Looked deep at the hate burning in there, meanness ingrained but neutered by alcohol, impotent. Nothing to fear but still he feared something. He knew that he and his father would get in with this man and go wherever the road led as long as the beer held out. And he feared that.

"You see my face?" the man said.

"I see it."

"I went through a windshield at four o'clock one mornin and I don't give a fuck."

"Say you got a beer?" said Wade.

"I got a whole fuckin case."

"You want me to get you one?" said Wade, already heading for the cooler in the back end.

"Yeah. Y'all want a ride?"

Wade said that they did.

"Well, hop your fat ass in."

The boy was squeezed up between the two men with his feet on the hump, while Wade was freely smoking Willie Russell's cigarettes. Telling one lie after another. Russell had told them about ten times that he'd gone through a windshield at four o'clock one morning and didn't give a fuck.

"You want a cigarette?" he asked Gary.

"I don't smoke."

"Well hell, try one. You might get started."

"I don't want one," he said.

"Smoke one," Russell said.

"I don't want one."

"What, you a candy ass?"

"Naw."

The boy tried to sleep but he couldn't sleep with them talking. They went over roads he hadn't seen before. They pissed in the road and ran off the road. Russell opened the glove box and pulled out a Remington twelve-gauge shell and showed it to them.

"You see this?"

They saw it.

"I don't give a fuck who it is. He can't stand up to this. That's double-aught buckshot. You believe me?"

Wade was jovial, chuckling with a cigarette hanging out the corner of his mouth. Benevolent. A Samaritan to guide his driver over the sand hills and through the rough dirt roads, down the highways of patched asphalt lined with rusted wire and thickets of blackberries. Dark fat cows with white faces stood knee-deep in grass, their jaws so slowly working their tufts of fescue and their eyes fixed with such blank stares that they seemed stoned on a more potent weed. Willie Russell kept drinking, but he didn't seem to be able to get any drunker. In the watered ice at the bottom of the Igloo, Wade found a fifth of peppermint schnapps and they started passing it back and forth, talking like old friends, the ice water dripping on the boy's legs and soaking through instantly to his skin.

"I don't let no sumbitch slap me," Russell said.

"A sumbitch slaps me better look out. You know it?"

"Well," Wade said.

"Cause I'm fixin to kill him."

"Aw."

"But I ain't scared of the sumbitch and never have been. And I'll whip his ass if he fucks with me. Again. If he ever. Fucks. With me. Again."

Then why don't you do it stead of talking about it? the boy wondered. Drunk talk's all it is.

After an hour or so they turned onto a dirt road, the entrance to it overhung with great leaning trees and vines, the shade deep and strong like a darker world within the outer, a place of cane thickets and coon dens and the lairs of bobcats, where the sun at its highest cast no light over the rotted stumps and stagnant sloughs. The trees that bordered the road and spread out across the land beside it had closed their tops together, so long had they stood there admitting neither light nor shadow of hawk nor the blue smoke of chain saws. Old timber, and magnificent, the bark worn slick on the cypresses from the constant track of coons and the black mud richly marked with the feet of the things that lived there. They went down the road past the posted signs and stopped on a wooden bridge. Russell got out.

"I'm ready to go home," Gary told his daddy.

"Well, I ain't. They ain't a goddamn thing at home."

The boy sat on the seat for a moment and then slid out the open driver's door. He was tired of sitting cramped up and he wanted to stretch his legs. Russell was weaving on the edge of the bridge, waving a stream of his own into the stream below. Gary stepped to the edge and stood looking down. The water was twelve feet below, a thin trickle sliding over holes in the clay bottom where tiny fish hovered. He looked at Russell. He was pissing and holding a beer can straight upside down against his mouth.

Gary didn't know where he was and he was hungry and he knew there was no telling where they would wind up. They'd taken a lot of turns and gone over many roads and this place didn't look familiar. He saw the moccasin, immobile on the bank among the dried sticks and shriveled roots, a phantom appearing out of nothing. Without thinking he reached for the largest rock he saw and heaved it over. It made a great splash. Russell surged back and wavered on the precipice of the single two-by-eight that formed the border of the bridge and then, standing there with arms waving, dropped his beer and fell and caught himself by his arms and chin, hanging off the wood.

Gary went to him and grabbed the back of his shirt. Then he reached lower and caught his belt and heaved up on it.

"You little motherfucker," Russell said. Gary turned him loose and stood up. He looked at the hands clutching so desperately the splintered wood, the fingers so splayed and vulnerable, the nails just begging to be stomped.

"Goddamn, boy, what's the matter with you?" said Wade. He knelt and hauled on the back of Russell's shirt.

"Help me get him up."

"Let him get up by himself." He stood back and watched Wade trying to pull him up over the edge. Russell clawed at the boards, his chest, half-emerged, his eyes wild and his hands waving and slapping hard at the wood. He came shaken and panting onto the bridge and finally lay with his feet hanging out over the empty air but for a moment, and then he got up and took three fast steps and slammed the boy against the truck.

"Boy, I'll slap your face," he said. Wade didn't say anything. Gary looked at his father but he wasn't even looking at them. The boy tried to move, but there wasn't any use. The hands clamped on him were hard and ungiving.

"I ain't done nothin to you," he said. "Turn me loose."

"I seen you laughin at me."

"I wasn't done it."

"You throwed that rock at me."

"I throwed it at a snake. I wasn't throwin it at you."

Gary pushed one hand off him and jerked the other shoulder away. Russell shoved him hard and he fell to the bridge. Wade was drinking a beer and looking off into the trees as if this magnitude of land were his and he was pondering its worth. No help from that quarter, never had been, never would be.

"You a lyin little son of a bitch. I think I'll just throw your ass off in there and see how you like it."

Gary kicked at Russell at first while scooting backwards. But then he turned over and came up and they met beside the truck. Twice he was slammed against the quarter panel. He pushed, blind, striking blindly. Russell laughed at him. He was being slapped and, after the first blow, he couldn't even see where the hands were coming from. He didn't know where his father was and he didn't know why he wasn't helping him and more than anything he was afraid he was going to cry. He did the only thing he could do. He spied a rock between his feet, one about the size of his fist, and he bent over and seized it and drew back and delivered it to Russell's forehead. A steer in the killing pen goes down no sooner. He thought he'd killed him. A little droplet of blood squeezed out of the cut and ran down one side of Russell's nose. Gary stood over him. With his foot he rolled him over to send him for good into the creek. But the old man walked over with a hand up to halt him.

"Here now," he said. He pitched his empty can into the water below. While his son watched he robbed the still figure, turning out the pockets and taking the money. Russell lay on his back breathing raggedly, air and blood snuffling and mixing in his nostrils. The boy stood watching as his own breathing gradually slowed down, as his heart ceased its thumping. He heard the sounds his father was making in the truck after he turned away, but it wasn't until the old man started walking up the road without waiting for him to follow that he looked and saw the pockets of his parent crammed full of beer and the neck of the fifth of schnapps in his hand.

"What we gonna do with him?" he called.

Wade didn't look around when he answered, just kept walking.

"I ain't doin nothin with him."

"We gonna just leave him?"

"You better get the fuck away from him."

He looked down at Russell and saw the wisdom of this. But what of the future and the chance of meeting up with him again? It wouldn't be his father. It would be him.

After a while he went after the old man, keeping his distance, the bag of cans he retrieved from the back end rattling faintly against his leg.

J oe wouldn't let Curt sit on the front seat when he took him home. He made him ride in the back where the hands rode. After he left Curt's house, his arm started to hurt a little more, but he knew that was shock wearing off, knew it was natural because he'd been shot once before, with a .22. It was hurting like hell by the time he pulled up in front of his own house. He took the whiskey inside with him.

With his chest naked and the bloody shirt in the trash, he faced himself in the bathroom mirror and surveyed the damage. Two in the neck, one in each arm. Puckered and swollen craters of flesh, the blood already black deep in the meat. He picked up the whiskey off the vanity and took a drink. His face was unmarked and he couldn't imagine all that missing his head, three loads. The ball in his left arm lay blue against the skin, having come from behind, and it was the size of a pencil eraser and very hard. The two on the outside edges of his neck had passed through. He dabbed alcohol over the wounds, front and back, and stoppered them with Band-Aids.

It was sort of like being shot with an arrow in a Western. Home surgery was required. His knife wasn't sharp enough. He took it out and tested the edge with his thumb and put it back in his pocket. The piece of lead moved around under the skin of his left arm when he put his finger on it. There was a peculiar feeling of fever in both his arms. He felt around on the other arm and couldn't feel anything. There was just the hole in back. He found a hand mirror of Charlotte's and held it over his shoulder, looking at the wound in the mirror. He turned the bottle of alcohol up over it and doused it thoroughly. It burned a little and then quit.

He had to go back to the kitchen to find the tape and he had to look in three drawers before he found it, some half-inch stuff he'd bought a long time ago for masking a car's windows. He wrapped some of it around one side of a new double-edged razor blade and then he held himself still before the mirror. The blood started as soon as he began to cut, and he had to blow it out of the way, to see where to put the blade. The pellet looked to be just under the skin but it was actually in the muscle. He cut with the grain, separating the fibers of his body, tensing his shoulder as much as he could in the hope that it would pop out. But he had to widen the hole and grit his teeth and close his eyes sometimes as he bore down on it, until he felt the steel meet the lead. Then he squeezed it like a pimple, the black ball tearing itself out of the wound and forcing the tissue aside until it slid all slippery and skinned to the surface, where he picked it off with his other hand and held it in his palm. A little piece of lead, badly misshapen. He threw it in the trash.

He stood and let the blood flow for a while, then took up the bottle of alcohol and upended it against his arm, sealing the mouth of the bottle with the muscle of his bicep. Tiny boiling clouds of blood entered the bottle and he watched while the alcohol slowly turned pink. When he'd stood it for as long as he could, he took the bottle down and wetted a washcloth and bathed the blood off his arms and chest. He patted around on the hole with a dry tissue. The flesh around the lips of the wound was puffy. He put Band-Aids front and back.

The whiskey still stood on the sink beside him, and he picked it up and drank some of it, then shivered and shook his head. Blood was seeping out around his bandages. He turned off the light in the bathroom, staggering a little, and took the bottle with him. It wasn't even dark outside yet. There was no way he could go to town, bleeding the way he was. It would ruin another shirt if he put one on. He lit a cigarette and opened the back door and looked out into the woods behind the house where a matted little copse of honeysuckle surrounded the remnants of a treehouse he'd built once, now only rotten boards hanging from rusty nails. If he killed Russell they'd send him back. This time they'd keep him until he was old.

He called the dog a few times but he didn't come. He heard somebody going down the road on a three-wheeler and he looked past the corner of the house to see who it was. Some kid, his hair flying, who lived up the road toward London Hill.

He went into the kitchen and mixed a drink and sat down on the back steps with it. By dark he'd mixed two more.

He was on the couch with some music playing low when he heard the car pull up and stop. He lifted his wrist. Nine-thirty. A car door slammed, then another. He heard the dog growling under the house and he got up stiffly and went to the door. He called to the dog to be quiet when he saw who it was.

"Shut up," he said. "Y'all come on in."

"Will he bite?" one of them said. They were standing in the yard, just beyond the dim light cast by the living room lamp.

"He won't while I'm out here. He better not."

The dog rumbled a low warning in the dark beneath the porch. They didn't come any closer.

"Hold him, Joe."

"He won't do nothin."

"I'm scared of him."

"Why, hell." He went down the steps and squatted on the concrete blocks and whistled at the dog, trying to calm him down. "You better shut up under there. Y'all come on. He ain't gonna bite you, I promise."

As they stepped closer the dog was a white flash rocketing from under the house. They dropped their beer and tried to run but he nailed Connie and she fell. He had her boot in his mouth, but Joe grabbed an ear just as the dog tried to go up her leg. He pulled the ear taut and doubled his fist and gave him a lick on the side of his head. The teeth clicked like a steel trap as Connie snatched her foot away and got up.

"Son of a bitch, what'd I tell you?" he asked the dog. The dog tried to pull away from him toward the girls. They picked up their beer and stepped past him and went into the house and shut the door. The dog had his belly low to the ground, straining, and it was all Joe could do to hold him. He hit him in the head three times. The dog just closed his eyes and took it.

"When I tell you to shut up I mean shut up. You hear me?"

The dog straightened and stood balanced on all fours and looked

at him, his gaze clear and level and his eyes untroubled. He licked
the hand that whipped him, then turned his head and stood watching the house. Joe turned him loose.

"You go get under the house and you stay there. Go on, now."
The dog walked away until he was once again a white blob and
disappeared into the gloom by the steps. He settled there, invisible, a pale guardian who never slept.

Connie had her boot off and the leg of her jeans pulled up when
he went in. Her friend was on the couch beside her, her face a
little strained with fright.

"Did he get you?" he said. She shook her head.

"I think he just bruised it. It didn't break the skin."

"Hell, I should have held him, I guess."

"What if you hadn't been here?" the other girl said.

"If I hadn't been here," he said, looking carefully at her, "you
wouldn't have no business in my yard."

"I ain't hurt," Connie said. She pushed down the leg of her
jeans and started putting her boot back on. "We come to see if
you wanted to drink a beer. What you got those Band-Aids on for?
What you been into?"

"Nothin," he said, and got up. "I'll be back in a minute." He
walked down the hall to his bedroom and took an old work shirt
out of the closet and put it on. They were talking in low voices
with their heads together when he went back into the living room,
but they pulled apart and smiled at him.

"What are y'all up to?" he said.

"We just been riding around," Connie said. "We didn't know if
you'd be home or not."

"I didn't mean to be," he said. "Who's your friend?"

"This is Cathy. She lives down at Batesville. She knows Randy."

He looked at her again. She was thin and had long black hair.

"I don't really know him that well," she said. "I just know who he is. I see him sometimes out at D.J.'s"

"You do? I don't never see him. Tell him his daddy said hi next time you see him."

"Okay. I will."

"Is he still over there in that trailer on old Six with them other boys?"

"I think he is. We was supposed to've gone to a party over there a couple of weekends ago but we didn't go. This girl I was with had a wreck."

"Aw." He got up and took his glass to the kitchen and started mixing another drink. "Anybody get hurt?"

"No sir."

He looked at her and then grinned at Connie.

"I mean, no. She was fixing to drag this boy and run into him. But they got us for dragging. That's why we didn't get to go."

He went back to the chair and sat down again.

"Don't you want one of these beers?" Connie said.

"Naw. I drank some beer this afternoon. I don't want no beer. I was just about asleep when y'all pulled up."

"We didn't mean to wake you up."

"It's all right. It was time for me to get up anyway. I'm glad he didn't hurt you. Usually when he gets ahold of something he won't turn loose."

"What kind of a dog is that, anyway?" the girl Cathy said.

"He's a pit bull, ain't he, Joe?"

"He's half pit bull. Half pit bull and half treeing walker. Why his ears look like they do. I meant to have em trimmed at the vet's when he was a puppy but I never did."

"He's big," the girl said.

He lit a cigarette and Connie opened a beer. He wondered why she'd brought somebody with her and knew she probably wanted something.

"Can I talk to you for a minute?" Connie said.

"Talk."

"I mean . . ." She moved her head slightly toward Cathy.

"Oh. Well, come on back here." He got up and she followed him down the hall to the bedroom. He sat down on the bed and she shut the door.

"What you want?" he said. "A quickie?"

She smiled and slid down over him, pushing him back on the bed, running her hands over the mat of hair on his belly. She kissed him, but he turned his head away suddenly and coughed.

"Damn," he said. He put his fist over his mouth and coughed and coughed. "Shit." He wiped his mouth and sat up and took a drink of her beer. "I got choked for a second. I got to quit smoking one of these days."

"You all right?"

"Yeah." But he could feel the blood running under the Band-Aids, and when he looked, he could see it. He got up and stripped off the shirt and wadded it and threw it on the floor. The Band-Aids were peeling loose.

"What happened to you?" she said.

"Don't worry about it. I'm just gonna get a bath cloth and wash it off. I'll be right back."

He stepped into the bathroom and took a washcloth from the clean pile of towels in a chair and soaked it in hot water and washed the blood off again. It looked as if the wounds had scabbed over lightly once, but he'd torn them loose messing with the dog and with her. Now they bled freely, clear fluid seeping with the blood. She came to stand beside him and watch him watching himself in the mirror. His face was on backwards and the part in his hair on the wrong side. It made his face look twisted. She touched his shoulder. There was a Polaroid picture lying on the vanity and she picked it up and looked at it. Somebody who looked a little like him, only twenty years younger, with the sides of his head almost shaved, in a coat and a tie, holding a pretty girl in a white dress by the arm. Old happiness ingrained on their faces as they smiled at the camera, the future a bright promise on that day long ago.

"This is your wife," she said. She touched the picture almost reverently and put it back down. Then she moved it, so it wouldn't get wet, as if that time could be preserved by the image of its past existence.

"Was. Has it stopped?"

She looked at his neck, at his arms.

"Yeah," she said. "I think it has."

"Good. I ain't got no more Band-Aids, anyway. I was gonna go uptown after some but I never did go. I had me a few drinks and laid down. I should've went on."

"You want me to go get you some?"

"Naw, hell. I don't guess. If I could just get it to quit bleedin it'd be all right. What was it you wanted to ask me?"

"Nothin," she said quietly. "It don't matter."

"Hell, tell me."

"We just thought you might want to go out. She's wanting to meet Randy. We thought you might know where he is. He wasn't at home."

"You didn't have to come back here to ask me where he is. What else you want?"

She turned away from him and looked out at the black night beyond the back door. The little shed and the junk scattered around it were illuminated in the cold glow from the yard light.

"Frank's back. I don't want to stay at Mama's."

He stopped what he was doing and looked at her. Looked at her hair and her back and her tight jeans.

"I thought she run him off."

"She did. Two times. He called her beggin the other night and she told him he could come back if he'd leave me alone. He promised. I got my stuff and left."

"Why don't she just shoot the son of a bitch?"

"Aw, she says it ain't his fault and all this shit. Says I go around in front of him half naked and he can't help it. Every time I go in a room I look around and he's right behind me."

"He's wanting to fuck you."

"Hell. I don't know what for. You just as liable to walk in the door and catch em on the couch going at it as not. I'm sick of it. Sick of her, too."

He stepped back into the bedroom to pick up his drink but it wasn't in there. He got another drink of her beer.

"Well, they's another room here. You still work up at that cleaners?"

She turned around with her hands in her pockets.

"Yeah. I wouldn't need it long. Just till I save some money and get me an apartment. Or a trailer. I won't be no trouble. I won't tell her where I am."

He shook his head. "Shit. She'll know where you at."

"Who's gonna tell her?"

"Don't nobody have to tell her. She's called over here before looking for you. Wanting to know if I'd seen you."

"What do you tell her?"

"I don't tell her nothing because I don't figure it's none of her damn business. Hell, you're twenty-one, ain't you?"

"Three more months."

"Well. You old enough to where you can do what you want to."

"He's liable to come over here."

He laughed. "I hope to hell he does. I don't know why your mama supports the sorry son of a bitch. Long as I've known him he ain't never held a job. I put my old lady through a lot of shit but I always had a job. She'd have put me down pretty damn quick if I hadn't."

She'd been standing in the hall talking to him and now she came in and sat on the bed. She leaned up and got her beer and held it between her knees with both hands, watching him going through the closet.

"I don't want to get you in any trouble," she said.

"You ain't gonna get me in no trouble. You got a car, ain't you?"

"Yeah. That's mine out there."

"You got to carry her back home tonight?"

"Cathy? Naw. She's got her car uptown. I just have to take her to town."

He found another old shirt and put it on and closed the closet door.

"Why don't you let me ride up there with you, then, drop her off and take me to the drug store? I got to get some stuff to put over this. I'll ruin my sheets and everything else. All my shirts."

"You got it," she said. She got up from the bed and went to him. "I didn't know nobody else to ask."

"Hell, it's all right. You welcome to stay over here."

She kissed him, but he just patted her on the ass and gently pushed her away.

When they got out to the car, he made the other girl get in the back seat with the dog.

"Y'all start coming over here regular," he said, "you better get to know him."

They went back by Henry's for the deer meat, but she wouldn't go in. Cars and trucks were wedged against each other in the tiny yard with no possibility of exit for those hemmed in against the porch. They sat in the dark on the front seat for a few minutes while he tried to identify the vehicles of enemies who might have reason to challenge him in his weakened state.

"I won't be but a few minutes," he said. It was more like thirty. But later, in bed, he told her that he couldn't go in and not speak to anybody. He didn't tell her that he'd taken three hundred and twenty dollars out of the game during the time he was there. He didn't tell her about the eyes that shifted in the smoke when he walked in, the shadowed figures and drinkers spread out along the walls who paused in the moment a hush fell over the room. They saw him bleeding from the four holes and not a man asked the cause of his ills when he squatted with the money and the dice in the circle of light on the floor, the old boards and dust, the false teeth in his head gleaming like bones and his eyes bright with pain and liquor. He won the money and nobody asked him to stay and try to lose some of it back. But he thanked Henry for the tenderloin and even tried to pay him for it.

She was on her side now, breathing lightly and slowly with the glow from the yard lights coming through the crack in the curtain. Her long brown hair spilled in a rush over the pillow and under her back. He pulled his deadened arm out from under her neck carefully, and she mumbled something and drew up into a ball. He didn't wake her getting up.

The dog raised his head from where he lay on the carpet in a dim pool of light. Joe didn't turn the lamp on. He turned on the television and left the sound low and groped around in the half dark until he found the whiskey bottle and propped it between his legs on the couch. The dog lowered his head to his forepaws and lay still on the floor. The red glow of Joe's cigarette lived and died in the darkened living room. And the next morning she found him there, naked, sprawled beneath the faded bedspread like those revelers of old in cracked paintings whose names or makers she'd never known, would never know.

The boy was up and about with first light, creeping softly among the sleeping members of his family. He collected the scattered and crushed beer cans from where they lay in whatever places they'd been thrown and carried them outside and added them to the growing pile. The squirrels at the fringes of the yard clattered the pine bark with their claws at the sight of him and hid themselves on the off sides of the trees before clambering away over branches still wet from the rain. He was soaked to the knees after one trip through the yard. Beggar-lice clung to the cloth of his jeans in mats. He stepped back inside long enough to take just one of the frosted cakes from inside the safe. He looked at it for a moment. His little sister was in the corner next to Fay with a fishing seine thrown over her, her thin dirty legs drawn up almost to her chest, her hair in lumps of dust and spiderwebs and the tiny turds of mice. He took another package of the cakes out and went to her and eyed the old man in deep hibernation on the bed of leaves he'd made. The father had spent a half day gathering the leaves and had enlisted the little girl to help haul them up from the hollow in garbage bags recycled from the county Dumpsters. Don Shelby would shoot to kill if he could find them now. Fay was flat on her back with her head on one side, her hand drawn up over her eyes as she rocked and moaned through the bad dreams she made in her mind.

He shook his little sister until she woke. She seemed startled to see him there. With a finger to his lips for caution he showed her what he had in his hand and then slipped the little cellophane package beneath her minnow net and stood up and made motions with his hands. She stared dully at him, uncomprehending. But when he went out the door, she was sitting up and tearing softly at the plastic with her fingers, a silent child.

A path led down through pine woods. It was an old path in which needles had settled over the years, just the faintest impression of a trail. Soon he was out of sight of the house and treading quickly past an old cairn of rocks that he'd already dug among and abandoned. Such an abundance of squirrels fled before him that he wished for a gun to help stave off starvation. Some of them didn't know what he was and clung to the sides of the trees, barking like tiny dogs. To these he held out a finger and said *pow* silently. They inverted themselves and stood head-first and watched him go, their black eyes bright and hypnotic after him. He went down to the creek and stepped into the rock beds, where a thin trickle of water coursed musically over the shattered stones and fell from bench to bench ever lower into the hollow. A weak sun was trying to break through the tattered clouds. He probed into the clay banks with a long stick, testing for snakes, watchful of where he put down his feet. He'd seen the copperheads before, dull slow things brown as the leaves they pressed their cold bellies against, no more noticeable than the bark of one tree in a forest of trees. His eye caught a flicker of movement ahead and he walked closer to see a box turtle with patterns of yellow sunbursts on its back like the imprint of a kaleidoscope. He tapped the stick on its shell and watched the legs and head shoot inward and the door on the front of the lower shell come up like a drawbridge and close with a long slow hiss. He went on.

At the bottom of the hollow he turned west, keeping his feet out of the wet ground that seeped moisture in a wide track, going along beside it to a narrow wash that even in summer's months was never dry. He could see the springhouse now and he walked on up to it, a ramshackle structure long rotted and all but obliterated by wind, sun, rain and time. The delicate latticework lay soft with mold on the ground, the posts that once held the roof leaning inward across the pool. The boy knelt on one of the three wide flat stones covered with lichen and green with moss. From the center of the spring came a soft undulation that rippled the surface gently and kept grains of sand in motion, ceaselessly turning and resettling on the clean bottom. He bent and touched his lips to the water, much the way some foraging animal might. It was sweet with a faint taste of iron and so cold it made his teeth ache. There were two six-packs of beer in the bottom of the spring, the blue of Busch slightly distorted beneath. He drank again and caught his breath and then wiped his mouth and sat up and crossed his legs on the stone. The cake was a little stale, the icing partly melted from where he'd held it in his hand. He ate his breakfast slowly, looking around at the birds flitting and singing in the awakening woods. The spring sang to him a low and throaty warble. He wiped his hands on his pants when he'd finished and knelt once more and drank, then stood up and turned and stepped away from the spring.

There was a little white marble marker set in a clearing fifty yards away, a place kept free of vines and creepers for reasons he didn't know. Fan-shaped plants with thick green blades like knives were planted in a circle around the grave. He stood there and looked at it for a while. The marker was no bigger than a cereal box. He wondered why they'd chosen to bury him here, alone with the animals and the snakes and the deep green shade. Maybe only John Edward Coleman knew, ten years old for an eternity, dead and asleep with the worms these seventy-nine years. Perhaps he'd played here. Or died here. An old man now, Gary thought. If he'd lived that long.

He'd brought his little sister down and showed it to her and told her it was a grave and that there was somebody buried here, but she'd only looked at it. He could remember a time when she'd talked, but it had been a long time now since she'd said anything. If she cried there were only tears. In happiness only a smile played from her mouth. And few of those here lately.

He walked on, wandering aimlessly. He jumped a deer once, but there was only the brief flash of a long white tail bounding away through the trees and then it was gone. The timber here was second growth and sparse, not like what was close to the house. Fire had swept over it a long time ago, yet some of the trunks were still blackened. He came out on a bluff that overlooked a section of cane and thickets, the low tops showing in the distance more timber and a lazy coil of black smoke from a house somewhere just beginning its burn to the ground. Along the edge he walked, stopping to run his hands over the old knife scars of names and dates healed almost unreadable in the bark of a giant beech riddled with squirrel dens and half toppling out over the void below. A hollow tree, it was once burned on the inside by squirrel hunters, the flames from the bed of leaves running up it like fire within a flue. He looked up into the top branches. A fat coon stared down at him from a fork, then put its hands over its eyes and turned away, an obscure lump of fur residing most peacefully this fine spring morning.

He walked a fallen log on the ground and then walked it again, holding his hands out from his side and then stepping down. He turned.

They emerged slowly in the distance through the slanted trunks and matted tangles of briers, slashing doggedly at the trees and the nets of vegetation hung like the giant webs of spiders across their paths. Faint cries could be heard. They were a group of seven or eight black men, with their shirts tied around their waists, some with flashing silver tubes in their hands and some with bright orange, all of them spread out arms' width apart and traveling slowly to the trees, then around and around them, stabbing and slashing. He sat down on the log and watched them come. When they were almost abreast of him, he could see that there was one who moved among them holding plastic jugs in his hands, attending to them when they called out. They were shouting back and forth to one another things he couldn't make out, only a word now and then. Then, as he watched, the one nearest him threw up his hands and screamed. They all ran at first, scattering in all directions, but then they came back cautiously, tiptoeing over the wet leaves until they congregated at one spot on the ground and drew close in a circle and then with short cries and hysterical abandon began hacking and beating the spot with their sticks and poison guns, darting in and out like dogs on a bayed bear. They were all talking and shouting at the same time, a hoarse chorus of curses that echoed and disturbed greatly the solitude of the woods, and they seemed frantic in their fear of whatever lay so helpless in the face of this ferocious attack. Demented John Henrys beating something into the ground. When they finished with it they seemed still reluctant to approach too closely. One of the men thrust at the thing with a long stick and picked it up, and the boy could see the white belly of the snake rolled over on the stick and the twin lengths of its body hanging down either side. They shouted. The man flung it down and they beat it some more, the sticks whacking on the ground in relentless unison and sounding strangely hollow on the earth. They dragged it around on the ground some more and pushed its head into the dirt until they seemed to be satisfied that it was dead.

The boy sat watching them on the log and wondered at what they were doing in the woods. There seemed to be no logical purpose to their work. They were still grouped in a cluster, lighting cigarettes and jabbering loudly. Some of them had even squatted down when a white man came up behind them and said something. They turned and he said something else and came over to them. They pointed to the snake. He looked at it and stepped closer and took hold of its tail and pulled it out and studied it. He said something and they laughed. Now they began to stand up one by one and throw the cigarettes down and disperse back into their loose ranks. The man stood with his hands on his hips watching them and fished a cigarette from his pocket and lit it. With his hand on a tree he leaned and watched them go past. The boy could see a little white cloud of smoke hanging around his head, the grips of a pistol sticking out of his back pocket.

The man turned when he heard the boy coming down the bluff and he waited until he'd reached the bottom and made his way over to him.

"Hey," Gary said.

The man nodded, still leaning against the tree, studying him. There was a look of tolerant amusement about him. He wore a black cap with CAT written across it in yellow letters. He had a big diamond ring on one finger.

"Where'd you come from?" he said. "You ain't lost, are you?"

"No sir." He pointed. "I live right over yonder."

The man squatted and picked up a twig.

"Over yonder where? There ain't nothin but woods back in there that I know of."

Gary put his hands in his pockets and looked at the ground for a moment.

"We just live back in the woods over there. In this old log house. Where's that snake they killed?"

"Right there. Ain't he a nice one?"

Gary stepped closer and looked at it, a smashed loop of muscle as thick as his wrist slowly ebbing toward death in the torn leaves.

"Them hands said it was a highland moccasin but I asked em what was a highland moccasin doing down here in the lowlands. I'da hated to stepped on him."

"I would, too."

"You sure you not lost?"

"I'm just walkin around," Gary said. "I seen them fellers when they killed that snake. I saw a big old coon in a tree back up yonder a while ago."

"You did?"

"Saw a deer while ago, too."

The man nodded and didn't say anything else.

"What are y'all doin, cuttin wood?"

The man looked up. He shook his head.

"We deadnin timber. I ain't figured out where your house is yet. There ain't no houses back in here that I know of."

Gary pointed to the bluff. "It's back straight in through there, over about three or four hills."

"Yeah? Is it close to the highway over there?"

The boy thought and nodded his head slowly.

"Sort of. They's this road, this dirt road you go up and it's another road you cut off of and it goes up beside this big bottom where they got some beans planted. It's this old house sets up on top of this hill with a bunch of pine trees around it."

"Oh," the man said. "Who you rentin it from?"

The question seemed innocent but the boy didn't know what to say. He scratched his head.

"Well. We ain't really rentin it I don't guess. We just sort of stayin in it till we find us a place to live."

"We?"

"Yessir. My mama and my daddy and my two sisters. And me," he added. "Y'all kill these trees?"

"Yeah. We inject em. You see them guns they had?"

"Yessir."

"See where they've cut these? Look right here."

The boy walked over beside him. The tree he leaned against had cuts all around the base, and something like thin molasses dripped from the cuts.

"Poison," the man said. "You got that gun you inject it with. Then in about a week it'll start to die."

"What for?"

"Weyerhauser land. They kill the timber off so they can come in and plant pine trees on it. Next winter we'll come over here and put out little pines on it. All this'll die and be on the ground in about six or eight years."

"Why?"

The man looked at him as if he didn't have any sense at all.

"Well, this ain't good enough timber to log it. It's just scrub stuff, so all they want to do is get rid of what's on it so they can put pines on it." He unleaned himself from the tree. "I got to get on and see about these hands. They'll set down if I don't stay right on their ass."

He'd already turned away to go before it all came together for the boy.

"I'll see you," the man said.

"Them guys work for you?" Gary said.

The man stopped and looked back. "Yeah. You don't want to work, do you?"

The boy took three anxious steps forward. "Yessir. I need a job. My daddy needs one, too."

"Your daddy? How old's your daddy?"

"I don't know," he said, and he didn't. "But I want to work even if he don't. I need a job bad."

The man pulled his pants up slightly and coughed into his hand. "How old are you?"

"Fifteen. I'm just little for my age. When you want me to start? I can start right now if you want me to."

"Well," he said, considering. He looked at his watch. "You could get a whole day in if you started now. You want to?"

"Yessir. Just tell me what to do."

"You don't need to go back and tell your daddy?"

"Nosir. They all asleep, anyway."

"All right, then. Come on over here."

They walked across the floor of the woods maybe sixty feet and stopped beside a line of trees already injected. The man pointed.

"See this here? Where these trees done been poisoned? What's your name, anyway?"

"Gary Jones."

"My name's Joe Ransom. You got a Social Security card?"

"Nosir. I ain't never had one."

"You ever worked anywhere before?"

"Yessir."

"Where?"

"Lots of places. I picked a lot of produce. We been in Texas pickin tomaters but we left, Daddy said cause of the wetbacks. But I've worked all over. Georgia and Florida. I pulled watermelons in Georgia last year."

"I don't guess you're scared of work, then. I'll tell you what I do, now. I pay a day's pay for a day's work. We start in about six and quit at one or two. If we work to dinner and get rained out I pay for a whole day. That sound fair enough?''

"Fair enough," said the boy.

"All right, then. Just get on this line of trees and you can see where they've come this mornin. It's probably close to a half mile or so back to my truck. Stay on this outside line where they've injected and you can't miss it. You'll come out on a road over yonder and they's a big yellow dozer up on this bank. Go to the right, two or three hundred yards and you'll see my pickup. Old GMC. And the guns and stuff's in the back. They got a top that just screws on. Get you one and fill it up with poison and then come on back down through here just like you went out and you'll catch up with us somewhere. You got all that?''

The boy had already started off. "Yessir."

"You ain't gonna get lost, are you?''

"Nosir. I hope not." He started running.

"And bring one of those jugs of poison back with you."

"All right," he called back.

"We'll need it before we get through with this round," Joe shouted after him. He heard the boy answer back, some word, and the sound of his feet rapidly diminishing through the woods. Then he was gone. It was the first time he'd ever hired a hand who didn't ask what he paid.

J oe was asleep on the couch one Saturday afternoon when his daughter woke him up, knocking on the door. He got up and let her in and cleaned clothes off a chair and told her to sit down. He moved the whiskey bottle to the side of the couch after he saw her looking at it.

"I just thought I'd come by and see you," she said. "See how you are."

"Aw, I'm all right. I talked to your mama other day up at the post office. I tried to get her to go eat lunch with me and she wouldn't do it. I don't know what she's got against me."

"She ain't got anything against you."

He didn't agree with that but he nodded anyway. He was still sleepy and knew he probably looked bad. He lit a cigarette and sat back.

"You still smoke?" he said.

"Not much. The doctor said whatever you smoke or drink the baby gets too, so I just about quit."

He drew one leg up on the couch and rubbed his face.

"Yeah, I guess that's right. You listen to him. Take care of yourself. How much longer you got to go?"

She smiled for the first time, this child who had grown up so quickly in other houses with him, the one whose only defense against the things in him had been kindness and which kindness he felt he'd never repaid, never could.

"Five or six more weeks. I got the day marked on my calendar. If it's a boy we gonna name it after you."

"You don't have to do that."

"I want to."

"Well, that's good." He didn't know what to say to her now, never knew now. "That's good," he said again.

"Mama said you told her you'd been doin real good lately. Said you told her you hadn't even been out anywhere in two weeks."

He nodded without looking at her, but she was looking at the bottle.

"I'm gonna fix me a drink," he said. He got up and made one and brought it back to the couch. They sat uneasily in the room, in awkward silence that lasted while he tried to think of things to say.

"She gave me some of that money you gave her. She gave me seventy-five dollars. I bought some baby clothes and stuff. Some diapers."

"You better have plenty of them."

"I got two dozen."

"You better get four dozen."

"Mama said you wouldn't never change our diapers."

"Well. That's right."

"Why not?"

"I don't know. Didn't want to, I guess."

He bent forward on the couch and held the glass with both

hands. It was hard for him to meet her eyes. She remembered him as being too busy for her and her brother. When they cried he never heard. Charlotte was the one who took care of them and raised them, Charlotte was the one they cried for when they were sick. Not him. It was never him.

"You know she still loves you, don't you?"

The questions were in her eyes that she wouldn't ask, had never asked. Why did you do the way you did? Why did you run us all away?

"She don't love me," he said. "I don't blame her. She's give me enough chances. Maybe she'll find her somebody that can take care of her."

"She won't. She's afraid to."

"Why?"

"You know why."

"I don't."

"She's afraid you'd kill him."

He tried to laugh it off, but his face felt as if it might crack. He shook his head and finally looked at the floor.

"That ain't what's stoppin her. She knows better than that."

"But you might. You know you might. I know how you can be when you get mad." She paused. "Or drunk. I'm sorry, Daddy. But it's true."

"Listen. Your mama can do what she wants to. I ain't married to her no more. If she wants to remarry I won't say a word. Is she wantin to?"

"She ain't even had a date. Anybody that knows you won't date her."

"Is that what she said?"

"I know that myself."

"Well." He turned the glass in his hands, feeling the weight of her gaze on him. "Y'all don't know everything."

"I know you," she said.

"You sound just like your mama. Y'all ain't happy if you ain't fussin at me."

"I ain't fussin at you," she said, and he was startled to see that she was close to tears. Her eyes were wet and her mouth had set up that little trembling just like Charlotte's always had when she'd been forced to gather the strength to stand up to him in the past.

"Goddamn, don't start in cryin."

"I ain't cryin."

"You fixin to."

She didn't wipe at her eyes. She kept her hands clenched in her lap, her fingers twisted together.

"I didn't come out here to fuss at you. I came to see you cause I miss you. I just wanted to see if you were taking care of yourself."

"I'm okay," he said, and he took another sip from his glass. "Y'all don't need to worry about me."

"You know if you'd stop drinking she'd take you back."

He shook his head.

"We done been through all that. I quit drinking one time and carried her up to Memphis, to this nice restaurant up there. I ordered one beer and she like to had a goddamn hissy. I hadn't had nothin to drink in two months. Hadn't touched a drop. And then she wanted to make a big scene over one beer. I told her to just get her ass up and go get in the car. I was tryin hard but that wasn't good enough for her. Ain't nobody gonna run my life for me. You don't know what I've had to put up with."

"I know what she's had to put up with."

"Yeah?"

"I growed up in it. She's tried."

He settled back on the couch and slumped down and looked out the window, rattling the ice gently in the glass. How could he explain it to her? "I know she's tried. You can't live with somebody for twenty years and not know em like I know her. She's a big churchgoer and I ain't. She don't like to be around anybody drinkin, don't even like to smell it. I drink and I like to drink. That's it. If you have to argue with somebody day in and day out you're gonna get sick of livin with em. I don't care how much you love em. You can't fight all the time and not have it do somethin to you. There ain't nobody who can live like that. Me and your mama can't."

He stopped and shook his head. They could talk it over and over and it wouldn't change anything. She wasn't coming back. Nothing was ever going to change. He didn't know what Theresa wanted to come over here and start talking about it for. All it did was make him feel worse.

"Are you happy by yourself?"

"I'm used to it," he said. "That don't mean I like it. I can come and go when I get ready, and they don't nobody say nothin to me. Y'all wouldn't be here now even if we'd stayed together. When have you seen Randy?"

She smiled slightly and then winced as the baby kicked inside her. She grabbed her stomach and eased herself back, drew in her breath sharply.

"He kickin you?"

"Whew. Yeah." She smiled weakly. "He don't usually kick in the daytime. Mostly it's at night when I lay down. I'm all right. Can I get a drink of water or something?"

"Yeah, sure, what you want?" He set his drink on the floor and got up quickly and went to the icebox.

"Just anything," she said.

"You want some Coke? I got some orange juice or I can make you a cup of coffee."

"Just some juice if you got it."

He filled a glass with orange juice and brought it to her. He sat back down across from her and watched her drink it.

"You sure you ain't gonna have twins?"

"It's just a big baby, the doctor said."

"Say you ain't seen Randy?"

"Yessir. He come over to the house the other night and eat supper with us. Mama cooked us some steaks out on the grill and he worked on her sink some. He had to put one of them traps or whatever under there. And fixed the lock on her door. He didn't have a whole lot to say to me. I guess he ain't never got used to the idea yet. I guess he's ashamed of me."

"Well," he said. It was all he could think of to say. He knew she was probably right. He was almost glad his mother and daddy weren't alive to see this happening. Randy hadn't killed the boy and that was something to be thankful for, that he wasn't in the pen over it.

"I might still get married some time," she said. "This ain't the first time it ever happened to anybody, and it won't be the last."

"First time it ever happened to one of mine," he said.

"It's my baby. It ain't yours."

"It's your decision."

"That's right."

"If you want to keep it it's up to you. But it's gonna be rough on the kid and one of these days he's gonna ask you why. If it's a boy he's gonna have to learn how to fight. You know what other kids'll call him."

"I've done thought of all that."

"Have you?"

"I have. Me and Mama's talked about it. I can get a job later on. I want to go back to school later on. You can't get no kind of a decent job around here without an education. I used to couldn't see that. I see it now."

"Well, I'm gonna fix me another drink," he said. "You want some more orange juice?"

"I got to go," she said, and she got up and handed him the glass. He took it and then she put her arms around him and held him. He hugged her only a little, fearing to hurt the unborn child. She drew back and looked at him, the top of her head only level with his chin.

"I love you, Daddy," she said. "I'll see you."

She turned to go and he told her to wait a minute. He went back to the bedroom and got some money and brought it out to her.

"Here," he said. He held out a hundred and a fifty and some twenties. She looked at it and shook her head.

"I didn't come over here for money."

"I know you didn't. Take it. Hell. For doctor bills if nothing else. I know you got doctor bills."

"I can't depend on you for the rest of my life. Ain't none of this your fault."

"To hell with whose fault it is. Long as I'm able I'm gonna take care of you." He put the money in her hand and closed her fingers around it. "It ain't nothing but money."

But it was not money she was looking at now. He turned his head. Connie stood in the hall in a short blue bathrobe.

"Excuse me," she said, and went quickly back to the bedroom.

"Damn," he said.

"Yeah. Damn's right. She's the same age as me. You know that? She was in the same grade as me. You ain't never gonna change. Here. Keep your damn money. I don't want it."

She threw it in his face, and left. He didn't try to call her back.

Wade had been dubious of the job to begin with, and now he was trapped in a living hell of steaming green timber. The men around him were moving like beaters through the lush jungle, breaking through the undergrowth, flailing wildly at the trunks and vines. They'd call out for water or poison, and a man would come running, bearing his refills in plastic milk jugs. Like winos they staggered through the tremendous heat. There were no rests or breaks. But there were yellowjackets to be contended with, and poison ivy, and sullen copperheads, which lay motionless and invisible against the brown leaves, becoming an actual part of them, lethargic and sluggish until the moment they chose to coil and strike.

Joe watched his two new hands from the top of a ridge. The old man stopped every two minutes, looked around, and leaned against a tree. When the boy went ahead too far, he called him back. Joe noted that it took one man working nearly full time just to keep this reluctant tree-killer watered. He lit a cigarette and slapped at a gnat on his neck.

———

Down in the great green hollow the old man tripped and almost fell. He was approaching a creek. The boy had crossed on a log and was already attacking the young sycamores on the far side with a ferocity driven by the promise of money.

Wade mopped at his unfamiliar sweat and studied the flow of the stream. The banks were five feet high, clotted with vines and treacherous with mud. He walked upstream for twenty yards and stopped. It looked no better there. He went on up, fifty feet more, and paused. He stared back over his shoulder, searching, but Joe was crouched low beneath a young persimmon, silently watching him through the leaves.

The old man stepped behind a bush and sat down. The bossman closed his eyes briefly and shook his head.

At noon the hands walked out of the woods and congregated at the pickup. They piled their poison guns inside the camper hull, and a black dwarf began issuing the lunch sacks from a cardboard box on the seat. The boy was there and took his small parcel, his meal of Vienna sausage and crackers and a hot Coke and a Moon Pie, and sat on the ground and started eating. He could hear the thin tortured cries of his father coming up through the brush, could see not a shape but the mere suggestion of a body struggling, some crippled floundering going on down there among the vast interwoven tapestry of vegetation. Some of the men began to look about.

"Reckon at old man can get up outa there?" said one.

"Aw, he's all right," said Gary. "He just ain't used to workin is all."

Some had sardines and others potted meat. The radio was playing in the cab, and Joe had wandered off somewhere. From Prince Albert cans kept in back pockets against the sweat of their buttocks, they rolled cigarettes of homegrown dope and passed them around. They smiled, blew smoke in little streams, grew languid and happy. The boy munched his food slowly and sniffed at the air.

Finally the old man emerged from a slash, stumbling along in a strange gait, gone crazy, evidently, slapping at his head as if he'd slap it off. The more coherent ones among them could see the tiny dance of angry insects around his hat. Yellow-and-black, miniature dive bombers stalling their engines in midflight, poised, wings humming, stingers raised aloft before boring in madly, tail first.

"Don't bring em up here!" the dwarf yelled, but it was too late. They gathered up their drinks and cigarettes quickly, clutching sacks and fighting at the air, yowling like cats as they started getting popped. And within five seconds they were all jerking dementedly and slapping, running away in a drove.

Joe dropped these two off last of all. He pulled up at the entrance to their road and shut off the truck. He took a quick drink of the hot whiskey on the seat and shivered, then got out and walked to the back and peered into the camper. The boy was helping his father crawl across the spare tires, the poison guns and jugs, this elder moaning on all fours like a political prisoner newly released from a dungeon. He stood eyeing them and took off his cap. He knew the boy would work—he'd proven that—but the old man would hold him back. He swept one hand through his thick hair and resettled his cap and put his hands on the side of the truck.

"Can you make it out of there?" he said. He lit a cigarette.

"Aw. Yeah. I'll make it. I guess," Wade whispered. "Just help me over to the tailgate, son," he said in a broken voice. The boy had him by the arm, guiding him along. Joe watched him dispassionately and knew almost certainly that whatever the boy made, the old man would take from him. Probably every penny. He quickly figured in his head what he owed them, and had the money ready by the time the old man swung his legs over the tailgate. He counted it again and laid it down.

"What?" said Wade. He picked up his money. "You pay ever day?"

"Naw," said Joe. "I don't need y'all back no more. That's yours there, son," he said, nodding at the remaining bills.

"Well," Wade said, but that was all he said. Gary picked up his money and looked at it. Then he looked at Joe.

"I'd sure like to work some more," he said.

"Maybe later. I'll let you know." He started to say more, started to tell him to be out on the road at six in the morning ready to work, that he could always use somebody who worked as hard as he did. But he looked at the old man again. He'd gained strength suddenly, was already pushing himself off the tailgate, turning, starting to hurry the boy away from the road, not looking back. But the boy looked back. Joe could read his face. Panic. I need the money. Don't leave yet.

He got back into the cab and sat there. He took another drink of the whiskey and chased it with a sip of Coke off the dash. He wanted to see how long it would take, if he'd even wait until they were out of sight. He leaned across the seat, smoking the cigarette and thumping the ashes into the floor. They were going slowly up the dirt road. The old man held his hip, prodding it along. He stopped and looked back. Joe cranked the truck and pushed it up into reverse. He started backing, looking out at them standing a hundred yards away. The old man and the boy faced each other in the dust of the road, like boxers. Then the boy fell. He kicked the ground, on his back, holding his pockets. The old man bent over, pawing at him, but Joe didn't wait to see any more.

Their supper was cooked in a pot against the coals, and the blackening flames ran up the sides of the vessel as if they'd climb into the food. Nameless beans with a piece of rancid rind bubbling in the spring water, stale loaf bread in a bag. The boy's eye was closed and he kept soaking it with a wet rag. The old man had gone with the money. The four of them sat speechless in the yard with the dark trees all around. The youngest girl had her legs crossed beneath her dress, and she rocked, hugging her elbows in her hands. The old woman seemed entranced by the flames. Her face was like the faces of soldiers shell-shocked in the trenches whose minds had heard the enormity of the blast and could not accept it as real. Stunned into silence, remembering . . .

The car and the man and the woman. The music and the lights and how they weren't like them. How the cut grass smelled and the sounds of the children splashing in the fountain and the aroma of barbecue in the air, the lights strung from pole to pole and the microphones and the stage and the people milling everywhere and the quilts spread on the ground and the lawn chairs and coolers and picnic baskets they were eating from and how the bats soared briefly over the softball field and the heat and the children. She remembered him hitting her, although there was no memory of the pain, just the blackness she fell into and waking up later to find that Calvin was gone for good.

Careening softly and with his hands out before him, Wade went like a blind man down through the alley and out onto the street. Cars and trucks were parked nose to tail on both sides and others were cruising for parking places. He stood with his back against a wall and listened to the gigantic pounding of a great drum in the night that came from a brightly lit door in the alleyway where young people were walking in twos and threes, so many of them at the entrance they had formed a large group. A man at the door was checking them and herding them single file up a walkway like cattle. But it spoke of nothing if not the promise of drink. Wade pushed himself off the wall and went across with his arms dreamily coming up, astonished at the lightness of his feet. Past a beauty salon with padded chairs displayed in muted lights and big mirrors reflecting his movements as he glided past, a figure of unbalanced gait and slouchy posture. He eased up at the rear of the crowd, and they moved aside and made room for him so quickly that he felt welcome. Whatever lump of shabby currency his roving hand found first in the pockets of his overalls it drew out and clutched. Closer and closer to the magic door he drifted, the keeper of it already eyeing him and shooing the students in like chicks. Over their heads the bouncer watched this vision come forward with his tattered scraps of paper money. Music and smoke poured out the door into the alley, and the old man felt warm and safe and happy. As he drew nearer, such a deafening clash of sound emanated that the patrons and the keeper of the door shouted in one another's ears. He was alone suddenly, none behind him and none before him but the linebacker or whatever he was, a monster man, a giant blocking the way with his thick arms folded over his massive chest. His face was impassive and he did not speak. He blinked his eyes once slowly and heavily like some huge lizard and shook his head and stood his ground. Turn back, old man, begone. There is no room in the inn.

He turned away as he knew he must, down the boarded catwalk and past the white walls where someone patted his back. He did not turn to see the face. A black arrow pointed his way. He walked with great sadness in his heart past darkened cars and trash cans and a warehouse door studded with cracked windows. Into each life a little rain must fall but perhaps it monsooned in his. He trailed with his hand a yellow stripe at waist level and his shoulder scrubbed lightly at the brick. His feet tried to twist under him, and he told them silently to keep moving one ahead of the other until he stood with his hands in his pockets on another sidewalk. Cars went by, close, their exhaust fumes like rotten eggs. Across the street was a bank; and in a shop, darkened shoes in rows. He let another black arrow direct him west and walked until the street was bisected once more. Cars and buildings lined both sides of a roughly paved lane. There was a hole in a brick wall halfway down the left side that threw a square of yellow light onto the pavement, and he made his way toward it on his tired and wasted legs. He stepped past the corner of the doorway and stood there blinking at the stairs. What manner of establishment? He went up the stairs and peered in through a security door, cupped his hands around his face and watched what went on. Tables and chairs. Stools set up along a wooden bar and glasses shining in ranks overhead and the polished handles of kegs. All was not lost. Salvation lurked just beyond the glass. He opened the door and took himself inside.

Things got quiet when he presented himself at the bar. Pool cues rested, patrons turned and stared. The bartender ceased his whiskey-sour vibrations. The old man heard voices from below and craned his neck sideways to see concrete steps and the legs of people standing. Another world beneath this one. He slid off the barstool and made his way downstairs to find a beer bar and bearded drinkers with gold earrings and cutoffs and Harley-Davidson insignias on their skins and clothes. The floor was spotted with red paint, scuffed away by the shoes of many. He ordered Miller and was served immediately. He paid and lifted the bottle to his lips. Then he went back upstairs.

He tapped a cigarette out of the pack and lit it with a match, waving it slowly in his hand, dropping it on the floor. He crossed the room, sucking at the beer, and stopped to watch a game of eight ball. A thin boy dropped the ball in a corner pocket and another boy gave him a dollar. He moved on, deeper into the room.

He passed under some brick arches and out a door into an open room with no roof. He stood there and studied the stars in the heavens with the beer tilted up to his mouth. Everywhere around him loomed the walls of the old hotel. He finished the beer and set the bottle on one of the benches and opened the door at the far side of the room. He found himself on a landing above a cavernous room so packed with people and music and lights that it made his head sing for a moment. A girl sat at a card table in front of him with a cigar box full of money and a rubber stamp in her hand. He eased up to her and pulled out his green.

"How much?" he said.

She stood up and waved to somebody. Somebody waved back. She turned back around and watched him with eyes uneasy, not believing his ripped clothes, his gray whiskers, his black fingernails.

"Wait a minute," she said. She pinched her nose and deserted her post and went down the stairs. The old man pocketed his money and stamped the back of his hand with the rubber stamp and went down the stairs behind her. He was quickly lost in the milling crowd below.

Late that night the rain fell thinly in the streets around the square, slashes of water streaming diagonally in the air above the wet sidewalks. Passing cars sprayed it up from their wheels, and the blooming taillights spread a weak red glow across the pavement as the hum of their engines quietly receded into a night no lonelier than any other. The stained marble soldier raised in tribute to a long dead and vanquished army went on with his charge, the tip of his bayonet broken off by tree pruners, his epaulets covered with pigeon droppings. Easing up to the square in uncertain caution came a junkmobile, replete with innertube strips hung from the bumpers and decals on the fenders and wired dogs' heads wagging on the back shelf, the windows rolled tightly on the skull-bursting music screaming to be loosed from within. Untagged, uninspected, unmuffled, its gutted iron bowels hung low and scraped upon the street, unpinioned at last by rusty coat hangers, a dying shower of sparks flowing in brilliant orange bits. No taillights glimmered from this derelict vehicle, no red flash of brakes as it pulled to a stop. It inched forward in jerks, low on transmission fluid. The old man watched these things. Later that night he was thrown in jail.

A public drunk was reported, an inebriated senior citizen whooping out great obscenities on the county square, performing some unmetered step on the timeworn bricks. Two policemen in a dispatched cruiser picked him out, a sly sot now apparently dozing on a green bench. They threw the light on him. He tried to run. The cops left the cruiser idling in the middle of the street and took off after him. Their feet slapped loudly around the sidewalks as the old man hobbled down the steps to the street. Some drunken students from the university were going to their cars from The Rose, and they stopped to watch the fun.

But he was old and the police were young and they hemmed him up against the front of a jewelry store. He elected to make his stand against a backdrop of silver platters and bridal china, his eyes wild and red in the flashlight beams, his thin chest heaving from his exertions. The cops went closer and then suddenly stopped.

"Shit," said one.

"Goddamn," said the other.

They seemed loath to put their hands on him. A crowd of students had gathered by then, it being past midnight and the bars now closed, and they stood watching the feinting and dodging. One of the cops approached and the old man immediately tried to put a headlock on him. The cop flung him off like a bundle of rags and he dropped to the pavement and started moaning.

"Stop that," the cop said. "Get up here. Here."

The old man huddled into a wretched ball on the concrete.

"Go on and kick me, you sumbitches," he said.

They stood watching him, unsure of how to proceed.

"Put the cuffs on him."

"You put the cuffs on him."

"I ain't touching him. I ain't putting my hands on the stinking son of a bitch."

"What you gonna do? Walk him to the jail?"

"I'd rather, as to have him ride in my car."

"Listen, now. Get up from there. Get up off the ground. Ain't nobody going to kick you."

"I know how you do. Get me over to the jail and you'll whup the shit out of me. I been in jail before."

"Aw, no shit. Well, you fixing to be in jail again. Now you get your ass up from there and get over there in that car."

But he would not rise. He'd either passed out or was using a marsupial's ruse. They braced him up under his arms. His feet lolled, boneless. They staggered beneath the assault of his body odor. Chickens dead three days in the sun had never smelled so rank. Ruined elephants on the plains of Africa paled in comparison. The cops gagged and tried to lift him. He lay limp as a hot noodle, quietly exuding a rich reek, a giddy putrefaction of something gone far past bad, a perfect example of nonviolent protest. They went across the square in the dead of night, dragging their prisoner, hapless victims themselves of circumstance, booed and hissed loudly by the students, struggling along with his unwashed wasted carcass like exhausted mules.

City court. Wade sat on a bench with other defendants whose crimes against the town he did not know. He turned his hat in his hands idly. The windows were open in the high walls of the second-story room and the sounds of traffic on the square drifted in. A black uniformed bailiff was nodding himself to sleep in a chair beside the judge's podium, and Wade thought about just getting up and walking out. Everybody else seemed resigned to their fates. He got up and put on his hat and went to the door. Two lawyers in the room studying their documents looked up at him and looked back down. He opened the door and peeked. An empty hall, closed rooms. He tiptoed out, his feet soundless on the rubber tiles, and closed the door softly. From somewhere came the dull clack of typewriters. A girl turned the corner with a Coke in her hand. He started to ask her how to get out of the building, but he didn't want to arouse suspicion. When she went into an office, he looked around the corner and saw a blank wall. Halfway down the hall he opened a door and looked inside. A vacuum cleaner and dust mops. He thought about hiding in there for a while, but he knew that soon after capture was the best time for escape. He walked around the other corner and came to a bank of elevators. He punched a button and a soft little bell rang when the light came on. Sounds came to his ears of mechanical hissings deep somewhere in the entrails of the courthouse, sliding cables and turning gears. He waited. The bell chimed gently again and the doors slid open. He stepped forward. The two cops who had arrested him stepped forward to meet him.

"Where the fuck you think you going?" one of them said.

"I's lookin for the bathroom."

He waited a long time for his case to be called. They wouldn't let him smoke and nobody would sit close to him. The bailiff had given himself over totally to rest, mouth gaping and head back and eyes closed. Wade leaned back and listened as the judge droned on. Sally Bee Tallie, found guilty of assaulting Leroy Gaiter with a cowboy boot. She said the whole thing was her brother's fault. Roosevelt Higginbotham, a public drunk in his own yard, which he argued unsuccessfully was not a crime. The judge slammed his gavel and fined them or sentenced them to jail or set them mowing grass and picking up litter for the good of the public. People speeding, forty-five dollars a whack. The city making money hand over fist. The public defenders doodling on papers and staring out the windows like children longing for recess. The old man sat with his elbows on his knees, watching the proceedings uneasily with slowly shifting eyes. At last he was called and he stood up. The judge was a man not thirty years old, in a double-knit suit. He studied the papers before him carefully. The cops had long since resigned their chins to the cups of their hands. The judge looked up.

"They don't have any address for you, Mr. Jones. Where do you live?"

"I live out close to London Hill," he said. "I don't know what the address is. Ye honor."

Ye honor evidently didn't like that answer. He tapped his pen menacingly on the lectern. He looked at the bailiff but seemed reluctant to call the whole court's attention to the fact that he was asleep by waking him up. Indeed it was as if a glance at that peaceful face made him uneasy. He looked out over the room and raised his eyes until he was talking to a spot high on the rear wall.

"You've got to have an address, Mr. Jones, or we'll declare you a vagrant. You know what a vagrant is?"

"Oh, yes sir. I ain't no vagrant."

"You ever been declared a vagrant before?"

"Well. I been declared one. Shore have. They declared I was one in Oklahoma City one time, but they never could prove it."

The courtroom had almost emptied, and the cops sat regarding him with their arms crossed and their faces dull with boredom. The judge nodded somberly, chewing on his lower lip.

"Do you ever get any mail, Mr. Jones?"

"No sir."

"Well, just say you did. Where would the mail come to if somebody wrote you a letter?"

He thought and thought and at length said, "I don't believe nobody knows where I'm at."

One of the cops shook his head and the other one closed his eyes. The judge put the pen in his mouth and chewed on it and opened something in front of him. He read for a few minutes.

Then he wrote something down. He cleared his throat and looked down on Wade.

"Are you on a rural route, Mr. Jones? Are there any mailboxes around your house? You do live in a house, don't you?"

"Oh, yes sir, I live in a house. But they ain't no mailboxes around there nowhere. I ain't never seen one. Sir."

"All right, then. You might want to remember this. Your address would be General Delivery, London Hill, Mississippi, three eight six oh five. You're charged with public drunk and resisting arrest. How you plead?"

"I don't know what to do," he said immediately. "I'm afraid if I plead guilty it'll be a big fine, and I ain't got no money to pay it. What if I plead not guilty?"

"You mean, what'll happen?"

"Yessir. What'll happen?"

"Well then, we'll have to have a trial. You'll have to get you a lawyer and fight it."

"Yessir."

"But you'll have to go back to jail first. Or we'd have to set your bond. Can you make bond?"

"I don't know. How much is bond?"

"It'll be about a thousand dollars. Do you know a bondsman?"

"Naw sir," he said sadly, keeping his head down and shaking it. "I don't know no bondsman."

The bailiff jerked awake suddenly and gripped the armrests, his tipped chair slamming down hard on the boards. He glared wildly around.

"And, too, you'll have to pay an attorney and court costs. These two officers swore out the complaint against you. Why don't you just plead guilty and be done with it?"

"What'll it cost me if I plead guilty?"

"I can't tell you that until I sentence you."

Everybody was waiting to see what he'd say. Or waiting to get the hell out of there, one.

"What chance I got of winnin if I fight it?"

"Not much, I'd say."

"It's their word against mine."

"This court does not take the testimony of police officers lightly."

He knew they had him either way he went. But he was eating pretty good in the jail. Big plates of scrambled eggs and toast with coffee for breakfast and fried meat with two vegetables for supper.

"I reckon I'll plead guilty, then," he sighed. "Bad as I hate to."

"Mr. Jones, this court finds you guilty and fines you four hundred and fifty dollars, payable immediately." WHAP! went the gavel.

The old man staggered back, almost as if a visible blow had hit him.

"What!" he said.

"Of course, you can always work it off for the city if you can't pay the fine."

"Work it off? How long?"

"Oh, we'll round it off to about forty-five days."

"Do I have to stay in jail the whole time?"

"You certainly do."

"I don't guess I got no choice, then. What kinda work I'm gonna have to do?"

"Whatever needs doing, Mr. Jones. Bailiff, you want to take this man back to the jail? And maybe get a good night's sleep before court tomorrow?"

They set him to pushing a lawnmower the first day. There were rolling green hills of grass in the park, and against this immense backdrop he was a tiny worker toiling with exaggerated slowness in the early morning heat, a small wretched figure stopping every few minutes to wipe the sweat from his brow. Other captured felons with long knives whacked listlessly at weeds. The whole day and forty-four others just like it stretched endlessly before him. The park was deserted, baking, barren. Sober drunks with nails mounted in mop handles speared bits of trash and deposited them in garbage sacks tied around their waists. The mower blade was sharp and the motor ran smoothly. Wade talked to himself and cursed his luck with a sullen vindictiveness. Each pass he made was about three hundred yards long. They'd have cut it with a tractor and a bush hog if they hadn't had him, but they had him. He figured they had all kinds of things planned for him, painting curbs and hauling garbage, painting tennis courts and picnic tables. He had resolved to make his escape at the earliest opportunity, but he didn't know where he was. There was a line of woods rimming the east side of the park where he could conceivably hole up until darkness came, but at the rate he was going it would take him two weeks to get over there.

At midmorning the lawnmower sputtered and died. He stopped

and mopped at his sweat and stood looking around him. The city trucks were parked in the shade beside the pavilion and he made his way down to them. Two black boys were sitting in the shade when he got there, smoking cigarettes. They were park employees, kids hired for the summer maybe.

Wade rummaged around in the bed of a truck, looking for an antifreeze jug with gas. There were razorous joe-blades and green-stained weedwhackers piled up in there. He rooted among them, shoving things aside, sweat stinging his eyes. Finally he looked over at the boys.

"Y'all know where the gas is?" he said.

"They supposed to be some in there," one of them said.

He looked and looked. He found an antifreeze jug but it had antifreeze in it. He poured some out on the ground to make sure, and sure enough it was green.

"That ain't gas. That's antifreeze."

The boys looked at each other. One of them scratched his ear. "We supposed to have some," he said.

"Well, you *ain't* got none," Wade told him. He looked at him with what appeared to be barely controllable rage. His face was red and droplets of sweat were swinging on his jowls. "I can't cut the grass without no gas. By God, if I'm gonna work down here, y'all got to furnish me with some gas. I ain't gonna buy it myself."

"What you think?" one of them said.

"I don't know," the other one said. "I guess, run get him some."

"I'll get it," Wade said. He got in the truck and shut the door. They looked at each other.

"He supposed to be drivin that truck?"

He cranked it and pulled the shift down into low, popped the clutch and spun one small spurt of gravel from a rear wheel. They were without phone or radio and even though they chased him for a short distance, shouting and waving for him to come back, he was soon a small blue speck flying down the street. They stopped and stood looking after him as he disappeared from sight. They turned to each other.

"You gonna be in trouble."

"Me in trouble? It's you in trouble."

"It ain't me. It's you."

"They gonna put you back paintin that swimmin pool."

"I done painted that pool one time."

"You may paint it two times."

few days later the old man stood in front of the liquor store for a long time with his hands in his pockets. He eyed the rows of brown bottles within, Dickel, Daniel's, Turkey, and wetted his dry lips slowly, as if he were astonished at the taste of his own tongue. It was ten-thirty and the regular winos were briskly conducting their early-morning business, shapeless men in rumpled clothes who emerged from the front door looking neither right nor left. He stood there until one went in that he thought he could handle and then he walked down to a laundromat and waited, squatting on the cracked concrete against the bricks, idly watching the cars move about in the parking lot. He whistled a low and tuneless hymn. Next door in Shainberg's, some women were adjusting stacks of jeans and moving over the polished floors and talking in voices that had no sound. He picked up a scrap of wood and turned it in his fingers.

An old black man came out and turned down the alley between the stores and shuffled past with a nylon windbreaker over his arm. Wade didn't appear to watch him shamble around the corner. He waited a few more deliberate minutes. He got up and dropped the piece of wood and stepped around the corner. There was nothing but discarded tires and mop handles and a broken compressor with one wheel missing, all piled against the back side of the building. For a moment he lost the shuffling figure. Then he looked toward the bypass and saw him in the act of halting his climb up the bank, putting one hand down, easing himself to rest on the sparse grass of a red clay hill. Wade watched. The black man put his coat down and drew his knees up and opened the bottle he had and tilted his head back. Wade started across the parking lot. With his head down he lifted his eyes and marked the man's position, noted the stream of cars flowing past behind him, high on the hill. The parking lot ended abruptly in a choke of kudzu and honeysuckle.

He stopped at the ditch and looked up at the man forty feet above him, lifted one hand in greeting.

"Hey," he said.

The black man said nothing, didn't look. He capped his liquor and wrapped it in his coat.

"I's wonderin if you could tell me how to get to Water Valley," Wade said. "Wife's in the hospital down there and I just now got here."

The old black man raised one long bony finger and pointed due south. His face was the face of stone, sullen, the eyes red and malevolent, his countenance ruined with the scars of small drunken wars. He bore small scraps, perhaps of cotton, in the dark wool of his head.

"How far is it?" Wade said. He stepped across the ditch and stood there looking up. He had his hands in his back pockets but his eyes searched the ground. He stepped a little higher and the black man rose in a crouch. One hand rested on the ground, the other clutched his precious bundle tightly.

"That the highway goes to it?" he called up.

The scarred head nodded yes. Just once. Don't come no closer.

Wade stepped forward another five feet, grasping a sapling to aid himself. He stopped and looked behind him. A boy was changing a tire on a tiny car behind Otasco, and a freight truck was backing up to Big Star. Blue milk cartons were stacked higher than a man's head on the dock.

"I just wondered was I goin the right way," he said to the ground.

The head above him nodded again.

"You don't care for me comin up there, do you?"

The man shook his head, soundless wonder etched on his face. In his troubled gaze he seemed to hold some terrible secret.

The old man went up the bank like a mountain goat and squatted next to the drinker. The black man didn't look at him.

"What are you drinkin?" said Wade.

A demented smile crept onto the face of the wino, three long yellow fangs bared in the purple gums.

"Fightincock."

"You ain't drinkin some wine, are you?"

"I may," he said.

"Yeah? Why, hell. That's all right. Lot of folks think a feller ought not drink at all." He wasn't looking at him. He was smiling to himself, talking to himself, looking out over the parking lot. "Little drink never hurt nobody."

The black man was watching him carefully now, perhaps seeing him in a new light.

"That right," he mumbled.

"Shoot," Wade said. "I get me a little drink when I can but the old lady raises so much sand I don't drink much around the house. I just usually get me a drink when I'm uptown like I am now."

"You wife in the hospital?"

He paused for a moment, thinking. "Aw yeah. Well, yeah she is —today. I got to get off down here at Water Valley and go see about her. That's where I was headed. What it was, I's supposed to got paid this mornin but the feller that was supposed to paid me ain't never showed up. I's gonna get me a little somethin to drink and head off down here to Water Valley and see how she was doin."

The man drew his bottle up to his lips, arms still wrapped in his coat, and untwisted the cap. He sipped it as if it were something forbidden. He wiped his lips and his face.

"What all wrong with her?" he said.

"Got cancer," Wade said immediately. "Got cancer of the leg. Just eat up with it all over, can't even walk. Gonna have to put her in the rest home, I guess."

The black man was sucking bubbles from the mouth of the bottle. He put it down and said: "Aw."

"Yep. A feller don't know from one day to the next which one'll be his last."

The scarred head nodded mute agreement to this undeniable truth. But he didn't offer the bottle in commiseration. The old man watched each swallow, each sip, like a hungry child. Clouds were bunching up high in the east, a dark bank of them that loomed up suddenly to banish the sun. In their hillside glade the shadows bled together. Wade saw that the rain was not far off. He hunched his shoulders against it even as he scanned the ground around him. But he was sitting on something, a hard bump beneath his shoe. He moved one foot and nudged it with his toe and it rose up from where it was half buried, brown and heavy and coated with a brittle corrosion that flaked away as he worried it with his toe.

"I believe it's fixin to rain," he said.

He let his right hand drop and pulled on it and broke the dirt around it free, a ringbolt twelve inches long, buried where some construction worker, long ago laboring on the shopping mall below, had perhaps flung it one day.

"Yes," he said, "I believe it's fixin to rain some."

He whipped the bolt straight across his body without looking and it landed hard on the forehead of the black man, who was in the act of passing the bottle, and knocked him whimpering into the grass with his eyes full of blood. He curled up and began a spasmodic kicking, until the old man hit him again, and then he stiffened and quivered. A sodden thump, a hammer on rotten wood.

He rifled the pockets quickly. Thirteen dollars in cash, three U.S. Government food coupon booklets worth sixty dollars each.

And the bottle of Fighting Cock. He got that, too.

The sun had gone in too early and the sky looked like rain. The air was cooling and the wind shifted and moved among the stiff tops of the pines along the road. The ditches were rich with cans and Gary marked them to memory for later retrieval, for harder times. But these seemed hard enough. His eye was still swollen and black-looking but it didn't hurt. He could see out of it a little now, anyway.

He could hear the trucks and cars coming a long way behind him, but he moved to the shoulder of the road and did not turn and raise his thumb as they drove past. The mailboxes were slowly becoming more frequent, the land more populated, but the houses were too far from the road for him to want to ask directions. He kept walking, his stomach empty and hard and tight, his head light. It was all he could do to keep going. The road climbed and twisted through the land. At the tops of hills he could look out over green forests and hay fields far off in the distance, where barns and silver metal towers stood hazy under the gray and leaden sky. Beyond the last greenery he could see was another line, blue as smoke, the last trees of the horizon. Earlier he had come through a bottom where hawks hunted over the sagegrass or merely perched on limbs thin as pencils, watching over all that moved before them, but there were no hawks now. There were neat fenced pastures and deep oak hollows and muscadine vines growing beside the road. Posted signs, barred gates. Little gravel trails stretching away to nothing through lanes of pine trees. He kept seeing mailboxes and he watched for them to stop. He didn't know for sure if he was on the right road. He was just trying to do something, do anything. He didn't know how far he'd come but he guessed five miles.

In another thirty minutes there were more houses, closer together. The sun tried to peek back out but the clouds moved over it and hid it again. In two more hours it would be dark and his journey all for nothing.

It had been easy money to him and he couldn't understand why Joe Ransom had let them go. Maybe the man wouldn't even be home now. Maybe he wouldn't find his house.

The rain came, thin drops that spurted dust from the roadside gravel, small explosions of brown dirt. The sun was trying to shine. He could see the rain marching against the forest, bending the treetops with the wind it brought and waving the boughs wildly. He started running, looking, and when he saw the big rusted culvert, he went down the bank over the loose gravel and beer cans and slipped and caught himself with one hand and stepped down into gray muck that sucked his shoetop in. He pulled his foot loose and bent and stepped into the culvert, ducking his head and entering a cavern of corrugated blackness. In the round mouth of the thing he squatted and watched the rain beat the grass flat and slowly grow into a curtain of water that obscured the trees twenty yards away. He bent with his feet spread wide. Before long he felt the first trickle come between them and watched it pipe out in a spout over the lip of the culvert. He tried to put his feet up higher on each side of the barrel, but soon there was four inches of water racing down and rising. It flooded his shoes, then his ankles.

"Well, crap," he said. He braced himself up like a cat facing a dog until his back met the roof of the tunnel he was in. The roar was a din and the color of the water was like pure mud. One foot slipped, then one hand, and he flew out of the culvert and landed churning in the middle of a creek rising to an angry level, foaming with bits of straw and trash and sticks. He pawed his way through the brown water to the bank and clambered up over the edge of it, his knees coated with mud, his shirtfront and his hands slick with it. The water was cold and the wind was a solid thing he could push his body against and feel it push back. There was nothing for shelter. Leaves were wafting across the road as they were torn from the trees and sucked out of the woods. He tried to go up another bank slippery with mud, but it defeated him again and again. His ears were full of water. It didn't seem possible to him, but the rain doubled in intensity. The world was gone, nothing left but gray disaster. He squatted on the side of the bank and dug his heels in, covering his head with his arms and waiting for it to be over. He was washed clean by the rain. Every drop of mud ran from his clothes and shoes. He had never seen such a rain. He had never even imagined that such a rain could come.

ay would keep her own promises. The lights she dreamed of, the clothes she would wear, the distant cities shimmering in the highways of her mind.

"He ain't comin back," she said.

That old woman she had watched grow older and older until she was bent and wasted neither turned her face nor gave any sign that she'd heard. There was something bubbling before her in a lard can, set atop a niggardly fire banked with dirt on a rotten sheet of rusted tin in the floor. The smoke had settled comfortably in the ceiling, to drift at its leisure out the windows and shift slowly among the hewed timbers. They could hear the wasps dropping like lead shot on the floor in the other room. Not one penetrated that wall of fumes. By morning they would all be gone, scattered to the four winds, their paper home a fabled trophy for a small boy to prize.

"If he was comin back he'd of done been back."

The little girl paid no attention. She'd made a doll of sticks and rags and she was rocking it to sleep. On its burnt face she laid some sweet kisses that almost made the older sister stay. Fay watched her mother, perceiving not even the rise and fall of her chest to mark her breathing. Just the thin bubbling in the lard can, the wisps of steam playing below her face. She could almost hate her for staying with him for this long, never having a house to call her own. Nothing but squatting before a fire like this one for as long as she could remember. She couldn't remember now how long Tom had been dead. Maybe it was ten years. Maybe it was twelve. And Calvin. Wherever he was, if he wasn't dead, he was better off than them.

"I seen him in a dream," her mother said.

"Hush."

"He was in a car. Had the longest purtiest hair, like a woman's. Long and curly, down on his back. Like Absalom. Absalom was on a mule runnin away from his enemies and caught his hair on a limb. I member the picture from the Bible was in it. He was tryin to cut his hair loose with a sword. Things'll get better."

"Things won't never get better here."

"They can't get no worse."

"That's where you wrong, Mama."

She stood up. She slipped her feet into her shoes and she picked up her purse and she looked around in the room. She had the clothes she was wearing, a skirt stuffed into the purse, and that was all she had. She looked at her little sister once. She was curled up in the corner, talking silently to the stick baby.

"I'm gone," she said.

"If you goin to the store I wish you'd bring me back some Kotex," the old woman said.

She didn't look at her mother again. She stepped across the

floor and down the rickety set of steps and gingerly, dodging the briers, picked her way out of the yard and through the honeysuckle vines and only looked back once, at the ruined house and the smoke coming out of the windows and the tall black pines growing blacker as dusk fell.

oe almost didn't hear the dog for the rain on the roof. The sound of the growling was an undercurrent, an accompaniment, something that might have been there for a long time. The noise stopped, then it started again. It got a little louder.

"Is that that dog?" he said.

Connie was in the chair with just panties and a robe on, a beer in her hand. They'd been drinking since afternoon but he hadn't touched her. There were days she couldn't make him.

"I don't know," she said. "Is somebody out there?"

"I don't hear anybody. Ain't heard no car drive up."

"It probably ain't nobody. Ain't nobody with any sense out in this."

He nodded and lit a cigarette, coughing a little. "Why don't you fix me another drink, baby?" he said.

She got up and took his glass to the table and got out some more ice and Coke and whiskey. She didn't put much whiskey in it. She stirred it with her finger. When she handed it to him, he took a small sip and didn't look away from the television, just held out the glass and said: "I can't even taste that."

She took it back to the table and poured more whiskey in it. She gave him the glass again and got her beer and sat down in the chair.

"We gonna go anywhere tonight?" she said.

"I don't know." He looked at her. "Where you want to go?"

"I don't know. I just wondered if we was."

"I hadn't planned on it. Unless you want to."

"We don't have to."

He looked away. "I'm just sorta enjoyin settin here with the TV," he said. She had cleaned the house from one end to the other, washed all his clothes and ironed his shirts, cleaned all the bad food out of the refrigerator, feeding the scraps to the dog and trying to make friends with him. He guessed it wouldn't hurt to take her somewhere, but he hated to get up and take a bath and get dressed and drive to town in all this rain.

"I guess we could go eat," he said. "Get us a steak somewhere. Or would you rather have some seafood?"

"It's just with you. I don't have to go nowhere."

What the fuck'd you bring it up for then? he wondered.

"I don't guess we got anything here," he said.

"Hot dogs."

"I meant to give you some money and let you go to the store. I guess we need to do that before long."

She nodded. The dog kept growling under the house.

"Stick your head out the door and see what that damn dog's so unhappy about," he said. She got up and went to the door and opened it. It was dark out there. She looked.

"They's somebody out here."

"Hit the light."

She turned it on. A bright yellow glare lit up the mud and the streaming grass.

"Who is it?"

"I don't know. He's just standin out there by the road. What you want me to tell him?"

"Tell him to come on in."

She looked back at him. "He ain't gonna come in long as that dog's out there."

"Say you can't tell who it is?"

"Naw. I don't know who it is."

"Well, fuck. It's somebody either wantin a drink or money one," he said. "That's the only reason anybody comes to see me, anyway."

He got up off the couch with his drink and went to the door. He looked out. There was a thin dark shape standing out by the road, just standing there. He squinted.

"I can't tell who it is," he said. She pulled her robe closed and held it with one hand. The rain slanted brightly in front of the porch light, obscuring the form standing so still in the glistening road.

"Shut up," he said, but the dog wouldn't hear. "I wish I could tell who it is."

"Well, don't make him just stand out there in the rain all night."

"I ain't making him stand out there. Didn't even know he's out there."

"He's scared of that dog's what it is," she said.

"Well, go down there and hold him. He won't bite you."

"That's what you said last time."

"He knows you now, though."

"Shit."

"I don't want to get out. I ain't got any shoes on."

"I ain't either. I wouldn't touch that dog if I did."

"Aw, go on."

"Not me."

"I wish to hell I knew who it was," he said.

And then the little wet shape called out: "Would y'all hold that dog?"

"Aw, hell," Joe said. "Here. Hold this."

He went down the steps barefooted and snapped his fingers until the dog came out to stand beside him, then squatted in the rain and took him by the collar. He patted him. The dog strangled with his rage.

"Settle down, now. Ain't nobody messin with me," he said. He tightened his grip on the hamestring.

"I got him," he said. "Come on in."

"You sure you got him?"

"Who is it, Joe?"

"This boy I know. Come on, now, I'm gettin wet."

The boy stepped off the road and came slowly across the muddy yard, never taking his eyes off the dog. His feet were encased in gobs of red mud.

"Go on up the steps there," Joe told him. "Take your boots off."

The boy bent over and started fumbling with the sodden laces on his boots.

"Go on up the steps," Joe said. The boy straightened and looked at him, looked up at Connie.

"You can set down right here and take em off," she said. She moved back from the door, and he went up the steps and sat on the doorsill.

"Y'all hurry up," Joe said. "I'm gettin wet."

The boy got his boots off and set them together on the top step and stood and turned and walked to the center of the room, where he stood shedding water onto the carpet. Joe turned loose of the dog and shoved him under the porch with his foot and slammed the door going in.

"Damn, Gary," he said. "How long you been out there?"

"I don't know. A good while."

"Let me get you a towel," Connie said.

"Bring me one, too. Boy, you soakin ass wet. You liable to be sick from this. Why didn't you holler?"

The boy looked up, small, muddy, forlorn. Quietly dripping all over the floor. "I hollered one time," he said. "That dog almost come after me. I's afraid if I run he'd come after me anyway." He motioned helplessly with his hands. "I's sorta trapped," he said. "Couldn't get no closer and couldn't get no further away."

"What's you gonna do? Stand there all night?"

He thought about it. He shook his head. "I guess I would've. Fore I'da had him get ahold of me."

Connie came back with the towels and gave him one. He dried his hands and then started rubbing his head with it.

"He ought to get out of them wet clothes," she said. "He'll have pneumonia."

"Aw, I'm all right," Gary said. "I just wanted to talk to you about workin some more."

The bossman draped the towel over his shoulders and picked up his cigarettes. He smiled a little crooked smile, not unkindly. "Work? Boy, don't you see what it's doing out there? It's pouring down rain."

"Yessir," Gary said. He rubbed the towel over his head. He put a finger in it and drilled his earholes a little.

"Where's my drink at? Have you got some pants he can wear? What size waist you got, anyway?"

He looked down at himself. "I don't know what size," he said. "My mama gets my clothes for me. I just wear whatever she gets."

What he was wearing was a pair of khaki pants that were pinched up around his waist with a belt that was six inches too long. A Kiss T-shirt and a pipe welder's cap.

"I think I got some jeans he can wear," she said. "Let me go in here and see."

"Well, set down," Joe told him. "I didn't know you were out there. You oughta hollered."

"I figgered if I hollered again he'd nail me. I bet nobody comes messin around here when you ain't here."

"Why I got him. I ain't here much. Way things are now, some sumbitch'll back a truck up to your door and just load up what he wants while you gone to work. He won't bother somebody just walkin down the road, though. A dog's smarter than you think. Anybody comes in this yard they better have a gun. I got to be here when they read the meter. Long as you stayed in the road he didn't bother you, did he?"

"Nosir. He just growled was all."

"You could have walked on off and he wouldn't have done anything. The road ain't his. He knows what's his."

"Here," Connie said, and handed him a pair of jeans. "Try these on. I believe they'll fit you."

He took the jeans and looked them over and looked around.

"Bathroom down the hall," she said, pointing. "You can change in there."

"Yesm," he said, even though she wasn't four years older than he was. He found his way down the hall and went into the bathroom and shut the door. Then he groped around in the dark looking for the light switch. Feeling all over the wall. He turned it on and then he stood for a minute just looking at all the products scattered on shelves and around the sink and lined up beside the bathtub, a wide assortment of ointments and creams and shampoos and deodorants and colognes and aftershaves. He opened some of them and sniffed, and looked at their labels. Meaningless symbols printed there whose messages he could only imagine. In the mirror stood a wet boy-child whose hair was twisted all up over his head like a rooster's comb. He found a brush on the sink and pawed at his hair with it, slicking it down long over his ears. There was long downy hair all over his chin and neck that he'd never shaved. Finally he pulled the threadbare shirt over his head and unbuckled the belt and pulled the wet trousers down over his knees and stepped out of them and stood naked in the room, his balls shriveled and drawn from the cold and the wet. He dried himself all over and put on her blue jeans. They were almost a perfect fit except that her legs were longer than his, so he turned them up at the bottoms four inches and went back up the hall. They were sitting down in the living room when he walked back in. He stood there holding his wet clothes in his hand.

Joe got up. Worse than he'd thought. Wandering urchin wafted up on the shores of human kindness. Asking nothing but the chance to earn. Offering his hands not to take, but to make.

"You feel better now?" he said.

"Yessir. I sure do. I been wantin me some blue jeans for a long time. These is Levi's."

"You welcome to them," Connie said quickly.

"You walk all the way over here?"

"Yessir. I got caught in some bad rain about three miles from here. It come a storm over there."

"How'd you know where I live?"

"I didn't. I was just lookin for you. I'll work. I need a job bad. I'm tryin to save my money and get me a car. Or a truck. If I had me somethin to go in I could get me a regular job. That's what I need. But I can't get a car till I get a job. That's why I wanted to talk to you. My daddy don't care if he works or not. But I do."

Joe paused to phrase his answer.

"Well, son, I don't know when we'll get back to work. It just depends on the weather. We can't even get into the woods till the roads dry up a little. That'll be two or three days if the rain ever stops. But if it rains some more I don't know when it'll be. I wish I could tell you somethin but I don't know myself. I'd a whole lot rather be making some money than sitting around the house here."

"Yessir," Gary said.

"Would you work in the rain?"

"Yessir. It don't matter to me."

Joe smiled and reached for his drink.

"Well, I hate you walked all the way over here for nothing," he said. "Let me slip my shoes on and I'll run you back home. You ain't moved from where you were, have you?"

"Nosir. We ain't moved."

"Just let me go back here a minute. Come on, Connie."

When they got back to the bedroom, she shut the door and turned around to him.

"I feel sorry for that boy."

He sat on the bed and started pulling on his socks.

"I can't give him work when I ain't got none myself. He can work when we start back if he wants to. Long as he don't bring his daddy. That son of a bitch ain't worth killin."

"I'm gonna give him one of my shirts. I got some old tennis shoes in here he can have, too."

He looked around at her and picked up a shoe.

"Why don't you just go ahead and get dressed and we'll go to town and get us something to eat. If we going out we might as well go on and eat supper. We got plenty of time."

She sat down on the bed beside him and folded her hands between her knees. "You reckon they've got anything to eat?"

"I don't know. I don't know whether they have or not."

"Why don't you ask him?"

"Ask him? Hell, I don't want to ask him that. I don't want to embarrass the boy."

"Well, what if they ain't? What if he's waiting on y'all to start back to work before they can get anything to eat?"

"Shit," he said. "I don't know. Maybe they ain't. They livin up there in the woods. I ain't been up there but I know where they're at. I used to birdhunt up there and it ain't nothin but an old log house. Ain't nobody lived in it for fifty years, I bet."

"Fifty years?"

"Hell, it ain't nothin up there," he said, and got up to find a shirt in the closet. "Only people you ever see up there is either huntin or fuckin, one." He turned around and gave her a grin. "Or huntin a place to fuck."

"Reckon who hit him in the eye?" she said.

The bossman didn't bother to answer that.

The rain was streaming down the sides of the glass, the wiper blades hardly able to keep it at bay, when they pulled to a stop in front of the store. There was a watery visage of gas pumps and posts and a screen door, a yellow bulb on a cord illuminating the mosaic of bottle caps packed tightly into the red sand.

"I reckon he's still open," Joe said. "How about puttin about ten dollars worth of gas in the truck?"

The boy was sitting next to the window, and he got out wordlessly and went back to the pump and turned the lever, unhooked the nozzle and twisted off the cap. Joe went inside.

Cigar smoke hung from the ceiling in layers, wreathing the old man, who was leaning back against sacks of flour with his endless newspapers and magazines and Civil War books. The roar

of the rain on the roof shut out every other sound. He picked
up his cigar and looked at his friend.

"What you say, Joe?"

"Reckon it's ever gonna quit?"

"Four inches on my gauge. These farmers is gonna be in a
mess."

He didn't know if the boy would come in or not. If he did he
did.

"Would you ring up some stuff for me, John?"

"Sure."

He closed his paper and rose stiffly and went around behind the
counter and laid the cigar in an ashtray. Joe picked things that
didn't have to be refrigerated, or things that didn't need to be
cooked. Vienna sausage and canned chicken and soups and chili
and potted meat and Spam.

"Would you slice me up about two pounds of ham and a pound
of cheese?"

With the thunder cracking all around, the noise was near deafening. The old man went silently to the refrigerator, his hands
slow and orderly. The electric saw ran unheard and the meat fell
silently onto the tray with each pass. He got crackers and loaf
bread, mayonnaise and mustard. He piled the cans up in his arms
and carried them to the counter. The old man laid the wrapped
packages beside them and rang everything up.

"Have you got one big sack you can put all that in, John?"

"Ought to have. This rain's bad on y'all."

"Yessir, it is. Looks like every time I get a little ahead it starts
in again."

John Coleman laid his pencil down and looked up, touched the side of his glasses with a forefinger.

"Twenty-seven even, Joe."

"Ten dollars gas." He gave him the money.

"Out of forty. Three dollars. You don't want all that in two sacks?"

"This is fine," he said, sliding it off into his arms. "I'll see you, John."

"Don't hurry off."

He stopped at the door and looked back. "I'm headed to town. You want anything?"

John stood looking down, leaning one hand on the counter, scratching at the side of his neck.

"You going by the liquor store?"

"Yeah. What you want?"

"Get me. Get me two fifths of some good whiskey."

"What you want? You want some Jack Daniel's?"

"Naw. Don't get that. Get me two fifths of Jim Beam if they got it."

"They got it. You want some beer?"

"Naw, I got some beer. Curt and them brought me some beer today. I wouldn't mind having a drink of whiskey, though."

"All right. You gonna be up later on?"

"Yeah, I'll be up."

"All right then."

He went out and the screen door flapped hollowly behind him. He went around to the other side and opened the door and slid the sack in on Connie's legs. The boy was seated beside her once again, keeping close to the door.

"Boy, you gonna get wet again," Joe said.

"Yessir. Reckon I will."

It was no better when they stopped again. They sat for a moment, the wipers beating gloomily at the downpour. Joe was thinking that the sack would be all to pieces before he went a hundred yards. He pulled out the handbrake.

"Wait just a minute," he said.

He went blindly out into the rain and raised the door of the camper hull, cursing, getting mud off the tailgate on his clean pants, fumbling in the dark for what might not even be in there any more. But it was. His hand found it and pulled it out.

"Here," he said, when he opened Gary's door. The boy got out.

"What?" he said.

"Put this over it. Maybe it won't fall apart before you get home."

Connie put the sack down on the seat and he slid the plastic garbage sack upside down over the groceries while the rain lashed him. When he had it wrapped he gave it to the boy.

"I hate I can't take you no closer. You couldn't get up that road in a Jeep now."

"This mine?" the boy said. He acted as though he couldn't believe it.

"Hell, it's just some stuff. I'll come see you when it dries up. We got plenty to do when the weather gets right."

He didn't wait for an answer but shut the door on Connie and went around to the other side. He got in and shut the door, pushed in the handbrake and ground the transmission into first. He blew the horn and they pulled off.

In the black and howling night the boy stood there with his heavy sack in his hands and hugged it tightly, one dim red eye moving away from him and the sweep of white light boring a tunnel of rapidly diminishing size down the rain-slicked highway, the water flashing in front of the lights until it passed from sight, until the sound of it ebbed, until even the tires sang away to nothingness and he was alone.

He turned his face up to the streaming heavens and they answered. He was immersed. He let it pelt his face. Blacker nights he'd not yet seen. Ground bled to sky, woods to road. But he knew the way. He turned and started up through the mud.

The creeks were raging with dark water, angry and swollen. He stopped on the bridges and rested. The mud was thick and it made for hard walking in his new tennis shoes. The food was in his hands and no one would know if he stopped now and opened something and ate. But there was a black wall of nothing that somewhere held his family, and his home, and it was that he headed into with ever quickening steps.

The owner of the package store on top of the hill had the doors open at ten o'clock sharp. He was sandwiched between a pizza parlor and a hair salon, and it was a good location because business sometimes bled over from each flanking establishment. He kept his clocks exactly on time, so he knew it was not yet a minute past ten when the first customer of the day stepped inside and nodded. A patron of dubious financial stability who might have spent the previous evening in a ditch, judging from the amount of dried mud slathered on his boots and overalls and flaked on the side of his face. An old man with rolled-up sleeves and a battered hat and a nervous tongue that he dabbed across his lips. The owner straightened from his newspaper and looked at the first customer.

"Can I help you with something?" he said.

"I's just lookin," Wade said. He moved over in front of a shelf and stood there with his hands at his sides and studied the bottles. Looking at the prices, the owner decided. To see what he could afford. Probably had some quarters and dimes in his pocket, hoping it was enough. Or waiting for a chance when his back was turned to grab something off the shelf and run outside with it.

The owner took three steps and cut off his only escape route and stood between the door and the counter, idly studying an inventory list. He was low on the Turkey half-pints and the Popov fifths. Two cases each. He made little notations on his sheet. He glanced around at his customer. An unpleasant aroma was beginning to fill his immaculate little store. He narrowed his eyes at the man. The man didn't move, didn't look around.

They usually headed straight for the wine cooler, for the Thunderbird and the Boone's Farm and pure grain alcohol. He didn't like them loitering, had signs forbidding it, in fact.

"If you're looking for something in particular I can show you where it is," he told him.

"I don't know what I want."

"The wine's in the cooler."

"I don't want no wine."

"Well, what do you want?"

The old man turned just his head in an odd way. "I know what I want but I don't know what you call it."

The owner sighed. Dealing with these people over and over. With the depths of their ignorance. The white ones like this were worse than the black ones like this. Where they came from he didn't know. How they existed was a complete mystery to him. How they lived with themselves. He tossed his list onto the counter without ever thinking he might have helped make them the way they were.

"Can you describe it?"

The old man turned around. He looked at the bottles on the opposite wall. "Well, it's clear," he said.

"Is it vodka?"

"Naw."

"Is it gin?"

"Naw, it ain't gin. It's kindly thick-like."

The owner wiped a hand across his face. He could have sold the whole thing at a good profit to his son-in-law months before. He went back to the cooler and opened the glass door and reached in, brought out a cold half-pint of peppermint schnapps and held it out.

"Is this it?"

"I don't know."

He carried it to him, all the way to the front of the store. He handed it to him.

"Is that it?"

The old man was looking at it carefully, holding it close to his face and moving his lips.

"I don't know if this is it or not. It looks kindly like it. What is it?"

"Schnapps."

"What's it taste like?"

"I don't know. I don't drink."

The old man looked at him curiously. When he looked at the bottle his brain seemed to stop working. Finally he raised his head.

"I don't know if this is it or not. What if I buy it and this ain't it?"

"You mean, what if you drink some of it and then decide you don't want it?"

The old man nodded vigorously.

"Yeah. What if I do that?"

The store owner rubbed his temples.

"Well, in that case you simply bring back the unused portion and we cheerfully refund your money and put the rest of it back on the shelf."

"Aw yeah? I ain't never seen a place that would do that before."

The owner sighed and went around behind the counter. He unlocked the cash register with his key and rang it up.

"Two dollars," he said.

The old man hadn't moved. He was looking back toward the coolers. "Wait a minute," he said. "Have you not got this in a bigger bottle?"

"I thought that was what you wanted. I've already rung it up."

"I may want a bigger bottle."

The owner put both hands on the register and looked at his customer. I am a fool, he thought. I am a fool and I am going to make sixty-five cents profit by fooling around with this other fool. He walked out front and took the half-pint away from the old man. There were some fifths on the opposite shelf, hot ones, and he walked over to them and pointed.

"We have fifths and half-pints," he said. "No pints."

"Can't get it in a pint?"

"No."

"How come?"

The owner lied. "They don't make it in a pint."

"Why's that?"

He took a deep breath. Just a few more minutes. Just a few more minutes and he'd be gone.

"There's a reason for it," he said. "It costs more to make a pint bottle than it does to make a fifth or a half-pint bottle. It's not the liquor. It's the glass."

"Well, I be damn. I didn't know that."

"It's a little known fact of the liquor industry, actually," he said.

"Well, I be damn."

"Do you want this fifth of schnapps?"

"I don't know," Wade said. "How much is that?"

"Six twenty-five."

The old man didn't say anything. To the owner he looked as if he had lost what little brains he had. He held up a finger and pointed.

"A half-pint's two dollars, and a fifth's six twenty-five?"

"Right."

"Well, I's just kinda figurin," he said. He rubbed his chin whiskers a little. "Let me ask you somethin."

"Anything."

"How many half-pints would you say was in a fifth?"

"What?"

"How many . . ."

"I heard you. I don't know. How many would you say?"

"I'd say four or five. Or maybe a little over four."

"Maybe. But I doubt it. Now if you want this take it. If you don't I'm going to put it back on the shelf."

"I's just tryin to figure the best deal," he said. "If it's five half-pints in a bottle and at two dollars, that's about ten dollars worth at that rate in a fifth, right?"

"I don't know what you're talking about," the owner said. "I have no idea what you're talking about."

"I wish they made it in a pint. I bet a pint wouldn't be over about four dollars, would it?"

"I told you they don't make it in a pint."

"I wish they did."

"I wish they did, too. Now," he said. He was offering the bottle and its companion on the shelf like a sacrifice, a grail, a chalice. To take one of them or leave or whatever.

"Shit, just gimme the fifth," the old man said.

"Fine," the owner said. He went over to the shelf and got one and handed it to him. He still had the half-pint in his other hand. He headed back toward the cooler with it, to put it back inside, all the way to the back of the room.

"I think you'll be happy with your . . ."

But the door slammed the instant he opened the cooler, and he paused. He didn't even look around. There was no need. It was done.

He set the little bottle back inside the cooler, gently among its brothers, so as not to disturb them, knock them over. He shut the door a little sadly and stood looking over his goods momentarily. They were lined up in neat rows, perfectly straight. He checked his cooler about thirty times a day to see that everything was in order. He couldn't stand disorder, couldn't abide sloppiness.

After a while he went up to the front of the store and sat down in the high-backed chair behind the counter. He took out his pipe and reached for his tobacco and slowly put it in, tamping it lightly, sighing to himself with enormous lassitude. He lit it with a match, turned the match slowly in the flame, puffing lightly, until the whole bowl was glowing red and consumed in fire. He shook out the match and drew deeply, and turned in his chair to gaze out through the large plate of glass where the name of his own little business was written backwards in paint. He didn't know where the man had gone. There was nothing but kudzu across the road, an apparently impenetrable jungle of green vegetation that crept softly in the night, claiming houses and light poles, rusted cars and sleeping drunks, the old and the infirm, small dogs and children. He wondered if maybe the old man lived in there and had trails like a rat, like the slides of a beaver or the burrows of a rabbit. Perhaps it was worse than he thought. Perhaps there was a whole city of them under there, deep, sheltered from the rain and shaded from the sun, with tents and canopies pitched beneath, cooking fires, camps where the children played and where they hung their wash. Where else could they hide? Anything was possible. And they only came out once a month, when the welfare checks and the food stamps were issued, and they stocked up on everything, and disappeared back into their lair. Maybe one day he'd look. Maybe one day he'd lock the store and walk across the road and peer over the edge of the creepers and look down, to see if he could spot a wisp of smoke, to see if he could hear their radios playing, their TV sets. Maybe they had Honda generators and refrigerators. But he knew, really, that he wouldn't look. He wouldn't look because he didn't really want to know. He didn't want to be right.

The days went by and the rain would not stop. Or it would stop for a day or a day and a half and Joe would gather his crew and park on the highway and send them up the muddy slopes only to blow the horn for them an hour or two later when the drops began to pelt down on his truck, where he was sitting drinking whiskey. He hadn't gone after the boy because he hadn't wanted to walk up the muddy road. But the boy had walked it. He'd walked it every morning the sky wasn't cloudy and waited by the highway, pacing, studying the sky and listening as the cars and trucks came within hearing. The old GMC never showed. He gave up hope late each morning. He knew they wouldn't start at that time. There was nothing to do but go back through the mud to the log house and idle his day away. The food went rapidly. His mother would say nothing of Fay. After a while he stopped asking.

Joe stayed in the living room when Connie was at work, playing the same songs over and over on the tape player, watching game shows and soap operas. His needs were few and his money was stacked in sheaves. Some days he and John Coleman sat behind the stove and hid their whiskey from the women and children who came into the store. John told stories of dogfights over the African deserts, of wading rivers behind the German lines, of nightmare fights with knives and gunstocks. They ate pigskins and crackers and poured Louisiana Hot Sauce on their sardines. Sometimes in the afternoons the store would be closed without warning. They'd have the curtains drawn over the door and hear people knocking and see them trying to see in, dim figures with one hand cupped over their eyes as they leaned against the glass, wanting gas for their pickups or Kotex or a loaf of bread or a pack of cigarettes or a dozen eggs for breakfast.

John Coleman had returned from the war in 1945 a quiet man, a wounded man with shrapnel close to his spine and shrapnel beside the bones of his legs, and in his head that same torn steel. A man with few words for people, who had seen all of the world he wanted to see. Not sullen, just a somber aloofness that no one could see was sadness for what men did to other men. He had inherited the store from his father and had kept it open all these years and each day of the year. He was a prodigious reader, a drinker with capabilities near legendary, a man with plenty of money. He ordered rare volumes, collections, series of books and chronicles of war. He studied and memorized little-known facts. He stayed inside the store days and in his little house across the road nights and never went anywhere. Joe would not go to town most times without stopping and asking him if he needed anything.

The days of May drew by and the fields stayed wet and the woods dripped water. Joe fished in his tedium, cutting canes in the river bottom and rigging set hooks with cord and lead and jabbing them deep into the bank. Morning and evening he checked them, carrying a five-gallon bucket of live crawdads along the path, stopping to take off the fish and checking every hook to see that it was baited. Then back at the house by eight or nine, skinning the fish with pliers while they hung shivering on a post, stripping the living skin from their pale bodies and flinging the offal to the waiting dog, whose jaws snapped shut in midair over the flying morsels. One morning he eased up to the bank after baiting all his hooks, after standing around for a while to see if the fish were biting. He squatted at the lip of the bank and took a cigarette out of his pocket and lit it, smoking and watching the smoke drift across the slow brown water. Limbs in the current dipped and swayed, rose and fell. He looked down and thumped the ash with his little finger. And not a foot below him, there in a little cutback in the bank, lay a snake with scales the size of his thumbnail. He didn't say anything. He might have just sat down on the bank without looking and hung his legs over. It wasn't coiled, just lying there, and he couldn't see its head. So he just looked. He could even smell it now that he had seen it, a dry sour smell like dead vines in a garden or carrion that is almost wasted away, until the essence of its scent is almost gone. He only wished that he had his pistol and could see its head to shoot it because nobody would believe it without the evidence of its dead body. There was probably no safe way he could kill it. He watched until he grew tired of it, until he convinced himself that it couldn't really be as big as he thought it was. Then he got a stick and poked it. The head flew out in a blur, hard enough to jar the stick in his hands, and he drew back a little, not certain it wouldn't come up the bank. He leaned over and poked it again, but the snake bunched and moved and began to flow into the river, loop after loop of steel muscle sliding over the mud, an impossible girth of snake that ended in a stubby tail. He stood back and watched for it to surface in the water, but it never did, python, boa, anaconda of Mississippi. And he was careful never to run the hooks at that place again, to watch the ground when he walked near there.

Mornings he would park his truck off the road, hidden from view in a copse of trees close to the river and near the place where he got on the path. He was laden with fish one morning coming back to the truck, a stringer cutting into the flesh of one hand and the crawdads in the bucket sloshing sluggishly in stagnant black slough water in the other. He was tired of dressing fish and being out of work and his hands were tired of carrying these things for half a mile. He stopped within view of the bridge to rest his legs before the climb up the bank to his truck. He squatted in the wet weeds and smoked a cigarette, mopping at the sweat on his forehead with his arm and wrist. A rifle cracked suddenly, close, then again and again. He looked toward the bridge and saw a man standing there, facing away. But he knew him anyway. With one hand he caressed the healed holes in his neck, and then he hunkered down, keeping bushes and trees between them, went closer. The .25 was in the truck and was no good for even shooting snakes, you couldn't hit anything over six feet away with it.

The rifle spat from time to time as turtles floated up to see if it was safe and found it was not. He went closer and closer, silently up the overgrown bank next to the bridge until finally he could pull his head up over the bottom rail with most of his face hidden behind a post and examine this fool who had leaned his rifle on one side of the bridge while he drank a beer on the opposite. He went up over the side and walked carefully down the concrete curbing until he was within twenty feet of the gun. He grinned then. He walked to the gun and picked it up with no noise. Then he leaned against the side and held the rifle in his arms until the man felt him there behind him and whirled. The eyes were wide in the blasted face.

"Surprise, motherfucker," Joe told him.

Willie Russell dropped his beer when he saw the gun leveled at him.

"Don't shoot me," he said.

"Why not? Son of a bitch, you shot me."

"I's drunk, Joe. I didn't mean to do it."

"You know I could kill your ass right here and nobody would know it?"

He lowered the gun to waist level and took out the magazine and jacked the round out of the chamber. He dropped the gun and it clattered on the concrete.

"I ain't goin to walk around the rest of my life lookin over my shoulder for you," he said.

"I ain't gonna mess with you no more, Joe. I promise."

"I ought to beat your goddamn face in worsen it is. That's what I ought to do. I just hate to go back to the pen over a piece of shit like you."

"I'm sorry, Joe."

"You better be. You better listen to what I'm tellin you. You got it straight?"

"I got it straight."

"All right, then," he said.

Russell walked over immediately with his hand stuck out. "Let's be friends," he said. He caught a left with his nose and a right with his throat, went down strangling, his eyes enormous, blood running down his shirt. He knelt, choking, on his knees.

"That's for shootin me," he heard. "I ain't shakin hands with you, you son of a bitch."

Russell was trying to say something. He was trying to make some words come out of his mouth. He was crying silently and Joe left him there for people to see as they eased across the bridge in their cars and slowed and almost stopped and then went on. He walked back down into the woods and got into his truck, thinking no more of fish or the river and only of whether or not this would settle it and if he had done the right thing and knowing that he probably had not since he had left him alive.

The rain ended that day and the woods stood steaming as they slowly dried. He sharpened the poison guns with a file and rounded up plastic milk jugs and went to Bruce for more poison and, on the seventeenth day of May, went back into the woods with nine black men and one white boy.

When the old man came back to the log house he was drunk and disorderly. He staggered in through the door one Tuesday morning about nine o'clock and stood there staring dully about, his face cut by briers and lumpy with mosquito bites, the clammy legs of his overalls plastered to his shins. His wife looked up to see him and he said, "Goddamn you," and went for her. She rose like a cat with her fingers curved into cat's claws and they met in the center of the room in a rush of dust. He slapped at her face and she pushed him out the door. The steps were rotten. He stumbled. There was a splintering of wood and he crashed to the ground. He had to stay there a moment, lolling his head drunkenly, looking for a stick maybe, the young summer sun burning a hole in his head. He lurched up onto his knees and tried to throw one leg up onto the floor of the house as he clutched at the sides of the door frame, grunting, halfway in and halfway out. His eyes were maddened, his tongue sticking out between the gaps of his teeth.

"Come on," she said, motioning to him. "Come on in."

"I ever get up," he said. He pawed his way into the room on his hands and knees and grabbed a windowsill to pull himself erect. He opened his arms and waddled spraddle-legged across the room and enveloped her in what he must have thought was a crushing embrace. They waltzed around the room, little scrolls of dust leaping from beneath their feet. The little girl sat crooning to her doll and not watching them, changing paper diapers and smoothing paper hair. The woman pushed at his face and tried to take his arms from around her. This married couple of thirty-six years tumbled out the back steps and lay there groaning with their hurts in the hot grass, until she rolled over and tried to get away from him. He grabbed her leg. She fell on him. Kissing him all over his face and pulling at his clothes, jerking up his shirt.

"Make me a baby," she said. "We got to make Calvin again," she said. He tried to crawl away and she caught him by the leg, trying to take off her pants. He tried to get up, but she leaped on his back and rode him down. He was begging her to stop and all but crying for her to turn him loose. The little girl watched from the window, her thumb caught in her mouth, as her mother and father moaned and groaned and crawled in the yard half naked. Strange sights but not as strange as some she'd seen, others that kept her silent. Endless nights in bitter cold, shaking with no covers and drawing no warmth from the knees pressed against her chest and the wind screaming through the cracks, or summer days and them like desolation angels through a desert wavering with heat and the blacktop burning their feet with every step they took. But he was down now, she was holding him.

"I got him," her mother called. "Let's kill him."

The only thing in the room big enough to do it was a brick. The child grabbed it up and tore through the room and leaped out the door and across the yard. He saw her coming and tried to get away. He was up, jerking his leg, sliding his wife along the ground, trying to get into the protective woods. When the little girl got close she threw the brick. It missed. She ran back toward the house for another one. She was going to rob the fireplace, one at a time. She squatted beside the blackened bricks and tugged one loose, then another one. She gathered them up in her arms, but when she went back he had pulled himself loose and was leaning against a tree with a big stick in his hand, while her mother lay in the yard with her legs spread, calling out to him to come on and do it to her, him shaking his head, trying to find a smoke in one of his pockets.

It was past three when the boy returned. He came up the road with his shirt wrapped around him, his hands empty. They were sitting in the back yard and he looked at his father. The others went into the house.

"When'd you get back?" the boy said.

The old man had two or three hot beers spread in the grass beside him. He was drinking them slowly, cupping each one in his hands. He had no answer for this upstart of his loins. The boy stood there. His hands were cut and bruised, his eyes burning from the poison that had splashed up into them.

"Where's your money?" Wade said.

Gary shrugged. He squatted a ways off. "He ain't give us none yet." His mother leaned out the door and said that supper would be ready in a few minutes.

"Gimme some money," Wade said.

Gary looked at him, looked away.

"I ain't got none."

Something flickered over the old man's face. The boy had hard muscles in his arms. He was crouched lightly in the yard, the waiting over for a day that had seemed so far off in the future down the lonely roads of years past and was now here without warning.

"He ain't paid you?"

"He ain't paid me. He'll pay me Friday."

Wade sucked the last of the suds gently from the can and eased it to rest beside his leg in the grass.

"Gimme some money."

Gary didn't even look at him. "No," he said.

The old man reared up drunkenly.

"What'd you say?"

"I said no."

Wade came across the grass after him and caught him by the leg, and they rose, holding each other until the old man began to hit him in the head with his doubled fist. The boy clenched his father close and smelled the awful stench of him, pushed him back while receiving the blows on his face and neck.

"Now quit it," he said. His father's breath was coming harder. His arms were swinging, his knotted fists finding no target as his son pushed him away. He swung so hard at Gary that he turned all the way around and fell. He lay on his back, scrabbling at the ground like an overturned turtle. He made it up on one knee and pushed off with his hands.

"I ain't got no money," the boy said. "He ain't paid us yet."

"Pays ever day," said Wade, coming after him.

"Just cause he fired us that time."

He backed around in the yard. His father followed him, but his breath was beginning to go and his legs were shaking. His steps were wobbly. Drinking hot beer in the sunshine had given him an uncontrollable head. Finally he went to his knees, his tongue out. His eyes were rolled up almost white in his head. He pitched over face forward into the grass and then he didn't move any more. The boy looked at him. He looked back at the house. His mother and his one remaining sister were standing in the doorway watching.

"Drag him around in the shade and come eat," his mother said.

Joe began to drive them harder as the last days of May slipped away. He stayed with them constantly now, taking a gun himself and joining their ranks as he tried to finish the tracts he had contracted for. He hired more hands, a load of them that bellied the pickup down so that it scraped and dragged over every rough spot in the road and ran down the highway canted up, and still they were not enough. He could see now that June would catch him unfinished, a matter of a lot of money. He pushed them more and more, harrying them around their edges, shouting, prodding the slow, the lazy, the hung-over, his own head throbbing and pounding under the summer sun. Clouds of gnats enveloped them and the yellowjackets rose boiling from their nests in the ground, and they moved through the green and tangled veldt like zombies in a monster movie or the damned in some prison gang, until under their breath they cursed him and work and the heat and the life their ways had led them to. They began to quit one by one. Three quit one Saturday and he made them understand they'd walk back to the truck and wait until the working day was over before he'd take them back to town. They stood in a small group, muttering, their eyes baleful and lowered, watching him narrowly as he moved away with the rest of the crew.

"Hey!" one of them said.

He turned back. "What?" he said. He had sweat in his eyes and he was already angry over their quitting. He'd been stung five times that morning and all he wanted to hear was one wrong word.

Gary was listening but he wasn't looking back. He had his head down, making overtime. Taking all he could get and glad to get it.

"You need to take us back to town," a man named Sammy said.

"You want to go back to town you can walk," Joe told him. "I ain't got time to run you back to town." He turned to walk off again.

"I ain't walkin back to town."

"Then you gonna have to wait on your goddamn ride."

"Hey!"

Joe threw his poison gun down. He turned and walked back. "You got anything to say, say it. I got work to do."

Sammy must have thought the other two were going to back him up, but now they stepped away. He looked around at them.

"Y'all gonna let him do this to us?" he said.

"I ain't done nothin to you," Joe said. "I hired you to work and if you don't want to work when I need you, I ain't got time to mess with you. I ain't worked you no harder than anybody else. Look yonder." He pointed. "They all still workin." But they weren't. They had stopped and turned back to watch what happened.

"Ain't hired on to work no nine hours a day. Didn't say nothin bout workin weekends."

"You didn't have to get in the truck this mornin, Sammy. And I can't do nothin about the weather. I got till the first of June to finish up and if you don't want to help you can go set in the truck. But I don't want to hear no more of your mouth. You've laid on your goddamned ass all your life and drawed welfare and people like me's paid for it. That's why you don't want to work. Now shut your fuckin mouth."

He turned one last time to go away and be done with it and heard the quick movement behind him, stepped back and spun as the knife passed under his arm, coming up, the steel flashing bright and quick to make a burning red stripe on his tricep. He hit Sammy in the nose and Sammy's nose exploded. The knife fell. He went to his knees and Joe grabbed his collar and pulled him forward. Nothing was said, no sound but their gasping breath in the early morning stillness and the scrape of their feet in the leaves. Sammy swung wild, once, then closed his eyes when he saw the next one coming. It snapped his head back and then it was over. Joe stood over him, a thin trickle of blood winding down his arm like a red vine and, drop by drop, falling off his middle finger to spot the leaves crimson, little spatters on the floor of the woods, like the trail of a wounded deer.

He said: "If they's anybody else don't want to work, or got somethin to say, you better speak up now."

Nobody spoke. They stood immobile in the hush with the thin calling of tree frogs the only comment.

He said: "I don't give a fuck if ever one of you wants to quit right now. I'll load the whole bunch up and pay you off. Last chance."

Gary turned away and slashed at a small bush. He went up to a tree, stabbing, pumping the poison into it. He mopped his forehead with his arm. The rest of them turned away one by one and fell back to work. Joe walked over to his poison gun and picked it up. The two who had quit with Sammy looked at each other uncertainly, now that their mouthpiece had been silenced.

"What you want us to do with Sammy?" one called out.

Joe cut and slashed and checked the time by his watch. "I guess you better drag him back to the truck if you want to ride to town this evening," he said.

An hour later he noted that all three had fallen back into the ranks silently and were working beside everybody else. Nothing else was said but he paid those three off that afternoon.

It came up one day at lunch that Joe was going to get rid of his old truck and buy a new one when they got finished with their tracts. The boy chewed his bologna sandwich dry and worked up enough spit to ask him how much he wanted for the old one. Joe turned his head and looked at him.

"Why? You want to buy it?"

"I'd like to have it," Gary said.

"It needs some work done on it."

"I can fix it."

"You ever worked on a automobile before?"

"I can learn."

"Oh. Well, you might have to work on that one a good bit. I

spend about as much time workin on it as I do drivin it. Course it
ain't nothin major wrong with it. Just little shit. Old motor uses a
little oil. Needs some brakes on it. Needs that shifter fixed for sure."

"How much?"

He thought about it. They wouldn't give him anything for it on
a trade-in. Two or three hundred dollars at the most. The body
was beat all to hell, the tires were slick. The front bumper was
hanging loose on one end.

"I hate to price it," he said. "I ain't ready to get rid of it right
now."

"I won't need it long as I'm ridin with you," Gary said.

Joe lit a cigarette and stretched out on the ground. He looked at
his watch and called out to his workers: "Y'all hurry up, now, it's
almost time." They were only taking fifteen minutes for lunch
now, but everybody kept quiet about it. He was paying them time
and a half after two p.m. and double time on Saturdays and
Sundays.

"I couldn't guarantee it, now. That truck's old. Got a lot of
miles on it. You might do better to just try to find you one in town
somewhere. Or let me look around for you one."

"It wouldn't look too bad if it was washed up. I'd take that camper
bed off it. Fix that bumper. All it needs is a bolt in it probably."

He looked at the boy. Then he looked at the truck. It was old, it
was dirty, it was junky. But he guessed he wasn't looking at it from
the boy's side. The boy had probably never had anything to call
his own. He started to just say he'd give it to him.

"I'll take two hundred dollars for it when I get my new one," he
said.

Gary stuck his hand out. "That's a deal."

Joe took the hand, squeezed it, then got up. He put his hands on his hips and called out that it was time to start back to work.

The boy worried about how he was going to pay for it all afternoon. He had to have some way to hide part of the money while he was saving it, and he had to have the money by the time Joe got ready to trade, which wouldn't be far off. The end of the month. It presented other problems. Gas and oil to buy, and his job would be over. But he reconciled himself with the thought that he could find something else to do. There were jobs everywhere, he figured. You just had to get out and find them. And he needed a vehicle for that. He hit upon it as they were taking a break from the heat that afternoon.

"What if you was to hold some of my money out and keep up with it?"

Joe was taking a drink of whiskey and when the boy came out of nowhere with that, he didn't know what he was talking about. He squinched his eyes almost shut and searched for the Coke on the dash and grabbed it and took a swallow.

"What are you talkin about, son?"

"To pay for my truck. How bout if you hold out about fifty dollars a week and let me pay for it like that?"

"Well. We probably won't work but about two more weeks. Hell, they all ready to quit. They been ready. Only reason they've stayed this long's cause I had to hit Sammy that day."

The boy fell silent. He had fifty dollars hidden under a rock down in the woods behind the house. The whole family was living off him now. His father robbed his pockets at night until there was nothing left.

"Where were you born?" Joe said.

"I don't know."

"Where's the rest of your family at?"

"This is all of us, I reckon."

"Where were you raised?"

The boy looked down. He still remembered Tom falling off the truck and the truck behind them going over his head, how everybody gathered around in the hot Florida sun, looking at him sprawled there dead. Was he four or five? And Calvin. Little brother. Gone now too.

"Different places," he said.

Joe looked at him. He knew nothing of him except that he would work. But his work was almost over. It was a long time from June to December.

"We finish this tract," he said, "they'll settle up with me. They'll shut us off after this one. They won't be no more work I can give you until this winter."

"What do you do?"

"You mean when I ain't doing this?"

"Yessir. When you ain't doing this."

Fuck. Drink. Gamble.

"I get by," he said.

"You know of anything I could do until this winter? I got to keep a job."

"Y'all can't stay in that damned old house this winter, can you?"

Gary turned up the last of his hot Coke and drained it. He set the can on the ground and pulled out his cigarettes. He had taken to smoking regularly since he was making money regularly.

"How cold does it get around here in the winter?"

"Shit. It gets cold as a witch's titty. We had ice stayed on the ground four days last year. You couldn't even get out on the road. I stayed up at the store with John about half the time. It didn't do to try and drive on it. They was cars all up and down the road in ditches."

"What did people do about goin to work?"

"They didn't go. The ones that live out here didn't. It stayed below ten degrees for three straight days. People had water pipes froze and busted and couldn't get into town for parts to fix em with. We couldn't work. Ground was froze solid."

The boy sat there, studying the situation. "I got a little money saved up," he said, finally. "If we could work two more weeks I believe I can get enough up to pay you."

"Well. We'll worry about that later. We'll work it out. Let's get on up and hit it."

The other hands rose in a group like a herd of cows or trained dogs in a circus act when they saw the bossman stand up. They picked up their implements and thumped their cigarettes away. The whole party moved off into the deep shade with their poison guns over their shoulders, the merciless sun beating down and the gnats hovering in parabolic ballets on the still and steaming air. The heat stood in a vapor over the land, shimmering waves of it rising up from the valleys to cook the horizon into a quaking mass that stood far off in the distance with mountains of green painted below the blue and cloudless sky. Joe stood in the bladed road with his hands on his hips and watched them go. He surveyed his domain and the dominion he held over them not lightly, his eyes half-lidded and sleepy under the dying forest. He didn't feel good about being the one to kill it. He guessed it never occurred to any of them what they were doing. But it had occurred to him.

T he shelves in the old wooden safe that stood in a corner of the log house were now stocked with food. Gary couldn't remember when they'd ever eaten so well. There were proper pans to cook in and Joe had given him a little green Coleman stove that burned each evening with a cheery blue flame. Their windows were tacked over with Visqueen, which admitted, in brightest sunshine, a pale murky light, like half-light, that kept the interior in a gloom through which their restless figures moved without shadow. He'd chinked the cracks between the logs with old cotton found in a pen in a field. In the dead of night under their mildewed quilts recycled from the hands of the haves, these have-nots lay with their ears pricked in the darkness as the drone of the mosquitoes moved toward them like supersonic aircraft, their radar just as deadly, just as accurate. He bought poison and sprayed for ticks, whacked with a broken joe-blade the assemblage of overgrowth surrounding the house into some semblance of a yard. He kept an eye out for a castoff screen door, but these seemed hard to come by.

His routine was to charge his things and get Joe to drop him off by John Coleman's on Fridays to pay his bill. This Friday Joe put gas in his truck while the boy was inside and then followed him in to pay his own bills. The storekeeper was counting some money back into the boy's hands. The boy said thank you and went out and got in the truck.

"How about addin up my bill, John?" The old man reached for a pad of notes and a pencil. He started punching buttons on his adding machine, sucking on a cold cigar.

"Y'all bout to get wrapped up?" he said.

"We like about another week, I believe. We ought to done been through but we just had so much to do. All that rain early."

John rang it up. "Looks like twenty-two fifty."

"Thirteen gas, John."

Joe gave him the money and took his change back and stuck it in his pocket.

"Thank you, John."

"Thank you. Listen," he said, his eyes cut toward the door. "That boy there that works for you."

"Him? Yeah. I wish I had about ten of him. We'da done been through."

"Is he not that Jones's boy?"

"Who?"

"Wade. I know that was him come in here the other day and wanted to charge some stuff to that boy. Said they both worked for you. I wouldn't let him have nothin till I talked to you. But the more he stayed in here the more familiar he looked. If I ain't mistaken he lived here a long time ago."

Joe looked toward the door and pulled out his cigarettes.

"That boy's last name is Jones. His daddy's sorta fat and don't ever shave. I don't reckon he ever takes a bath, either. Smells like he ain't had one in about twenty years."

"That's him," John said. "I knew that was him. Have you not ever heard em talk about all that shit that happened down there on the Luster place a long time ago?"

They had leaned closer to each other over the counter and were talking in low voices like assassins plotting, like revolutionaries talking revolt.

"Seems like I heard Daddy and Uncle Lavert talk about it one time. It was somebody hung down there, wasn't it?"

"Hell yes. It was three years before I went to Europe. That boy's daddy was in on it, they said. He left out. Oh, it was a hell of a mess. It was Clinton Baker they hung. He was down there three days before they found him. Hangin in a tree and buzzards eatin on him."

"Aw hell." He had to think about that for a moment. "How come em to kill him?"

"Don't nobody know. J. B. Douglas was in on it, him and Miss Anne Maples's oldest boy. Buddy. And that boy's daddy, they said. But he run off. I thought that was him."

"Well damn," Joe said. He looked out at the boy. The boy was in the truck looking down at something, saying silent words. "What did they do to em?"

"Well, they all run around together, Clinton and Buddy and all of em. They had a old house they gambled in down there. After they found Clinton and went and got him down and all, they went over to J. B.'s house to talk to him, see if he knowed anything about it. Sheriff went over there. That was old Q. C. Reeves. He pulled up in the yard and started across and J. B. come out the door with a shotgun. And fore they could even decide what he was up to, he set down on the porch and stuck it in his mouth and blowed his brains all over his mama's porch. With her standin in there in the kitchen fixin to put dinner on the table. I never seen so many flowers at a funeral as his had. It was the worst thing to happen around here in a long time. Buddy Maples went to the pen but he died or got killed down there, I still don't think the truth was ever told about that."

"What, did he admit to doing it?"

"He admitted he was in on it. Or admitted enough to where they talked him into pleadin guilty to murder. Hell, they didn't even have a trial. But he never would tell how come they done it. That was the thing of it. They was every story in the world told about it."

"Like what?"

"Aw, hell, you can hear anything. It was told they poured gas on him and struck a match to him. I don't know if it's true or not."

"Goddamn," Joe said. "Well, could they not still get him? His daddy, I mean?"

"Shit, I don't know. It's been so long ago. I knew damn well that was him come in here other day."

Joe looked out toward the truck again. "I wouldn't let him have anything if I was you. That boy would be the one that would have to pay for it. He owe you any money?"

"Him? Not a penny. He's bought a good bit but he's always paid."

"Well." He looked up at John Coleman. "What in the hell would they want to burn him for?"

The old man lit the cigar and took a long slow puff of it and laid it in the ashtray. He leaned on his elbow and turned his head away.

"They's probably drunk," he said.

They coasted to a stop beside the growing cotton, where the honeysuckle blossoms hung threaded through the hogwire in bouquets of yellow and white, the hummingbirds and bees constant among them and riding gently the soft summer air. The boy held some money out.

"Here's half of it," he said.

"Half of what?"

He pushed the money at him. "A hundred dollars. You said you'd take two. You ain't changed your mind, have you?"

"Just keep it. You can pay me when I get my new one. I got to have this one to drive till then."

"I wish you'd go on and take it while I got it. Or keep it for me."

"Just hang onto it."

"I'm afraid I might lose it or somethin'll happen to it."

But Joe wouldn't take his money, and finally the boy put it back in his pocket. He got out and pulled his shirt off the seat and shut the door. He leaned in the window.

"I'll see you Monday," Joe told him. "Be out here at six, okay?"

"We ain't gonna work tomorrow?"

Joe looked up the road, then looked back. The boy seemed worried.

JOE

"Naw. I got to have a little break this weekend. You know what I mean?"

He was sure he didn't but the boy nodded that he did. He stepped back sadly. Joe shifted into gear and let out the clutch, tossing his best worker a wave of the hand. When he looked back through the camper glass he could see him walking across the road. Dark was half a day away. And it didn't matter what his daddy had done, what he did was all that mattered.

He reached under the seat for the whiskey and got it up between his legs and twisted the cap off. He laid it on the seat and took a drink. It was hot, he had no chaser, it burned going down. Summer was coming and soon it would be Friday night. And yes, they had probably been drunk when they burned him. A man did things he wouldn't normally do when those little devils were running loose in his head.

He called Connie from a pay phone outside a drug store that was just down the sidewalk from B&B Liquors. He was chewing gum and he had set his fifth on the concrete so he could dial. The telephone rang in his house three times and then she picked it up and said hello.

"What you up to?" he said. "Naw, hell, not right now. I just got some stuff I need to do." He listened to it a little while, not long. He never listened to it long.

"Well, I's probably drunk when I said it. You ought to know by now not to pay attention to me. I'm liable to say anything."

He coughed into the phone. A police cruiser crept at an idle around the parked cars and rounded the end of the lot and stopped.

"Listen, I got to go. They's a goddamn cop settin right here watchin me. I guess the sumbitch thinks I'm drunk. Me? Naw. Not yet. Hell, I don't know. Go shoot some pool or somethin. Go out to Vivian's. I might be out there later. I don't know what time. Naw, I ain't gonna promise. Well, suit yourself then." He hung up. "Goddamn women."

He picked up his bottle and walked straight as an arrow in front of the police car and got in his truck. He halfway expected the car to follow him. It did, for a while. It went out of the shopping center after him. But halfway up the hill it turned off and he went on about his business.

There was nothing but a porch light showing at Duncan's house. Joe parked the truck behind a green Grand Prix and got out and took a drink from the bottle. He put the pistol under the seat.

He could hear it raging behind the door when he knocked, its barking harsh, the growling a little hysterical. Then the sound of somebody cursing, a yelp of pain from the Doberman. The door opened two inches. He saw an eye, a chain, a black muzzle three feet above the floor, where ivory fangs drooled a ropy spittle.

"That son of a bitch bites me I'm gonna kill him," Joe said. "Go put him up."

The door closed. Other doors were slammed inside. Brown beetle-bugs bombarded him and the porch and the light. The door cracked open again and then it opened all the way. He stood there, waiting.

"You got that bastard put up?"

"He's in the kitchen," she said. "Come on in. He ain't going to bother you."

He wanted it made plain, though.

"I'm tellin you, now. That sumbitch bites me I'm gonna blow his fuckin brains out."

"He ain't gonna bite you."

"All right, then," he said, and stepped inside. There were women wall to wall, old and young and fat and skinny. They lay on couches and sat on the floor eating popcorn and watching movies from a video store. He guessed it was a slow night. He had to step over some of them. The worn dowager who had let him in went to the small bar she tended and waited there, her bosom like mangoes, her lips like blood.

"Can I fix you up with somethin, baby?" she said. She scratched absently at something in her hair.

Joe leaned on the bar and set his whiskey down.

"Come here and give me some sugar, Merle. I want you to lay them lips on me."

"Where you want me to lay em, honey?"

"I ain't decided yet."

She smiled and bent over to him. He kissed her for about a minute and then pulled away.

"Damn," he said. He picked up her hand and held it. "Why don't you just marry me, Merle? We wouldn't even have to fuck. Just kiss and cook supper."

"You asking?"

"Hell yes."

She laughed and went to the icebox and got a canned Coke out. She took a glass from the cabinet and scooped ice cubes from a tub in the sink. He looked at her sad rippled legs and the bra that cut into her back, and shook his head.

"I ought to asked you about twenty years ago," he said. "For real."

She mixed his drink using his own whiskey and set it before him. He held her hand again.

"What you got the blues over tonight?" she said. She reached for a barstool, still holding his hand, and drew it up close and sat.

"Hell, I don't know. I'm all right."

"I've heard you say that before. I believe you said that the night you shot that cop."

He lowered his head. "Well."

"Can you still fuck?"

"Not much. Just ever once in a while."

"You the only one I ever seen that would admit it."

"What you see is what I am. Last time I tried it I couldn't do nothin. Just bump up against it. I done got too old, I guess."

He picked up his drink and sipped it, and took some money from his pocket, the leaves of green not missed by the eyes that watched from the dark living room.

"Here," he said, and gave her a five. "Keep it."

As she put it in a drawer under the counter, the Doberman walked out of the hall and stood looking at him. Coal black, a chain of silver, sleek and lithely muscled, and the lips lifting ever so slowly from the white teeth that lined his mouth. The dog hated him, had always hated him, ever since he was a puppy. He wished for the pistol under the seat with a slight chilling of his blood and felt that something that hated so strongly for so little ought not be allowed to hate anymore. The dog stood ravenous and slobbering on the bright yellow linoleum, the flanks tense and the brown eyes not blinking. Joe looked into the animal's eyes and the eyes looked back with a deep and yearning hatred.

"Harvey," one of the girls called. "Harvey, settle down."

Joe watched him, watched him hear her voice and relax, all the muscles so keyed going slack at once, the hide sliding shiny and loose over the back and legs. The dog walked to a water dish and lapped three times and raised his head and looked at him again. He growled.

"Put the son of a bitch up," he said again.

Merle got down off her stool then and whistled the thing back, and Joe sat there sipping and hearing the toenails clicking down the hall, until she shut the animal away in a darkened bedroom and turned and came back to sit with him.

"What do y'all keep that goddamn thing around here for?" he said.

"Duncan says it's a good idea. Says it stands to reason that a deputy sheriff or anybody else we don't want in won't come in with something like that standing in the door, gives everybody else a chance to run out the back door and hide. I don't believe he likes you," she said.

"Hell naw, he don't like me. He'd like to eat my ass up is what he'd like."

It hit him then that there wasn't any reason for the thing to be here and there wasn't any reason for him to keep coming over here as long as it was because eventually it was going to nail him. Somebody was going to take it too lightly, one of the girls who could pet it was going to turn it out on him one night.

He looked down into his drink and heard the Doberman scratching at the thin door with its nails, whining and wanting out. He could imagine the dog in there in the dark, growling low, sitting on his haunches, leaning forward to gnaw and worry the wood. He lurched up suddenly.

"Where you going?" Merle said.

It smelled the Doberman when he opened the truck door and let it out in a flow of white liquid muscle. He told it to hush when it started whining and then he caught it by the collar. They dragged each other toward the door, him trying to drink from the bottle with one hand and hold his dog in the other. When they got up on the porch it barked and pawed at the door. Joe knocked, three thunderous blasts upon the flimsy wood. A pale girl opened the door and took one look and slammed it back, but he pushed it open before she could turn the lock. He went on in with the dog in tow. Only three of the girls were still up and they began to edge to the corners of the room. The dog had begun a low insistent growling and was straining forward an inch at a time, its toenails digging in the shag carpet.

"Where's he at?" Joe said, and then it got away from him. He grabbed for it and missed. It hurtled down the hallway to the room and bounced once against the door, and the Doberman spilled out in a rush of clicking teeth and flying saliva and slobbering outrage. In that tight little space they reared and sought each other's throats, the sounds they were making fearsome and out of control. The half-Pit came dragging him backwards into the kitchen, the blood already soaking into the white muzzle, where the Doberman was held, locked by the throat.

"Kill his goddamn ass," Joe said. The girls were screaming and going out the door. He pulled up a chair and sat down to watch it. There wasn't much to watch. The Doberman was shitting on the floor of the kitchen, while the half-Pit went deeper and deeper into his throat, mashing the blood out like water from a sponge, throttling and shaking him, droplets of blood flying over the clean walls and the table, the floor slick with it. The Doberman went down in the blood, his eyes glassing over slowly, the shine of life fading. The half-Pit turned him loose, licked curiously at him once, whined and looked back at its master, its face gore-stained and its tail wagging

"Good boy," Joe said, petting his dog.

They made it eight miles down the road before the deputy's car caught up with him. He wouldn't pull over. The dog had its head hung out the window, its long ears flapping in the breeze. He'd always liked to ride. Joe pulled over in the middle of the road with blue light flashing inside the cab. Through the side mirror he saw the car drop back, heard the big engine start to scream. It shot forward and tried to come around the left side, but he pulled over to the left, watched the car slide sideways and halt briefly with dust rocketing and swirling before the headlights. He could hear gravel flying behind him. He got another drink of the whiskey and closed one eye so that he could see how to stay in the middle of the road. Orange fire barked from the window of the deputy's car, shots aimed for the tires. He reached over and found a half-warm beer on the seat and opened it, started using it for a chaser while they reloaded.

They finished it where 9 runs into Calhoun County. A state trooper had his car parked sideways in the road and he was down across the hood with a shotgun to his cheek. Joe wouldn't have stopped for him, either, but he misjudged by two feet the amount of room it would take to go around the left side. His wheel dropped off a culvert and he turned down into the ditch, jerking the wheel to no avail. The brakes wouldn't stop the tires from sliding in the dewy grass. At five miles an hour he slammed into an oak tree three feet wide and broke the windshield open with his head. The dog went out the window and ran.

When he came to, the headlights showed dark green jungle depths and bugs danced in the halos of light they made. Far down and away through the black night came the wail of sirens faintly, like sirens singing, like souls lost in the sky. Through the trees, faint blue flashes of light.

When Joe woke the first time, it was to summer heat that held not a breath of air. Someone had taken a lighter and held it against the ceiling while kneeling on the upper bunks and writing strange fuck-slogans in smoke up there. There was a white man in T-shirt and skivvies and shower shoes sitting at a table with a black man in a rumpled suit and a red tie, playing cards. They regarded him as he came awake and then they ignored him. He slept again.

He woke to the sound of banging. If anything it was hotter. What he'd have given for a cold drink of orange juice. He couldn't believe where he was.

He felt of his pockets. Shirt, pants, back pockets. There was nothing on him, no money, no cigarettes. He rose up finally and sat on the edge of the cot, his shoes still on his feet. With his fingers searching carefully he found blood caked above his eye and a knot above his ear. No memory came forward to attest to the reasons for their existence. They were only there and had somehow come with the rest of it. The walls were green and there was a little fountain above the commode. If he wanted a drink, he'd have to drink from that. What he'd been lying on was a stained striped mat about an inch thick. Other men lay sleeping on other bunks throughout the cell. He looked at the card players.

"Has one of y'all got a cigarette I can have?"

The white man looked around. "I've got a Kool if you want a Kool."

He got up and went over and took one offered from the pack and stuck it in his mouth.

"I ain't got a light either. You gonna have to kick me in the ass to get me started, I reckon."

"Here's some matches. You want to sit in on a hand?"

"Thanks. No, thanks."

When he had his smoke going, he went back and sat on the bunk. From the heat in the cell he judged it to be afternoon. He remembered standing in the road at night and seeing the truck against a tree, the lights shining. He thought he remembered somebody pulling his hair while he was hitting somebody else. He touched his scalp with his fingertips. It was tender, sore. There were small bare places where some of his hair had been pulled out. He couldn't remember faces, complete events, just nightmare scenes that were vague and surreal, like glimpses of a movie he might have seen.

He finished the cigarette and dropped it on the cement and ground it under his heel. The door to the cell was solid steel, with a small rectangular hole large enough to admit trays of food. He got up and went over to it and bent down so that he could look out into the hall. There was nothing to see but another wall and nine or ten cases of beer stacked against it.

"Hey. Jailer." He rested his head on the cool metal ledge and thought he might throw up from the idiocy of it all. From not learning his lesson, from the subservience he'd have to effect. There was no telling what he'd done. Murder maybe. Mayhem, at least.

Steps sounded in the hall. A man bent over and looked in.

"What you want?" he said.

"I want to get out of here."

"No shit. I magine everybody in there'd like that."

"I get a phone call, don't I?"

"Yeah, you get a phone call. Who you want to call?"

He thought for a moment. Not Charlotte.

"I don't know yet. Can you let me out and let me get some cigarettes? Did I have any money when I come in here?"

"We got your money in the desk. You want me to take enough out to get you some cigarettes?"

"I guess so. What have they got me for?"

"I'll have to go ask. I wasn't here last night."

"You mind?"

"Naw. Just hold on."

The steps went away slowly. He heard a door open and close. Somebody was yelling in another cell. Down the hall a tray slot opened. "Hey. Hey! Somebody. You hear me? I'm sick. I want to go to the doctor. Open this door."

The door to the hall opened. A voice called down: "What you yelling about now?"

"I want to go to the doctor. I'm sposed to be takin medicine."

"I done told you you ain't going down there. All you wanting is some more dope."

"Naw, I ain't wantin no dope. I'm sick. I need to go see the doctor. I was sposed to done been down there."

"Go back to sleep, Roscoe. You got three more weeks."

"I can't stay in here three more weeks. I got to go see about my kids, you son of a bitch."

"You stop that goddamn cussing. You been yelling ever since you got here. I'm tired of hearing it."

"I don't give a fuck what you tired of. Now, goddamnit, open this door and let me out, you cocksucker."

"You better shut up."

"I ain't gonna shut up."

"I'll get that strap."

"Well, *get* the fuckin strap!"

He shouted some more things but the door closed on him and his words fell on no ears that wanted them. After a while he sobbed. The tray slot pulled back shut and there was silence. Joe rubbed the scabbed place over his eye and wondered if it had been stitched, or needed stitching. In a few minutes the hall door opened again and the steps came back to his door.

"You still on probation?"

"Naw. I been off probation three years."

"Well. They can't find a field officer. Said he was out feedin his cows."

"Hell, they don't need to talk to a field officer. I ain't on probation."

"They seem to think you are."

He groaned and held his head. He was trying to think of a name but now when he needed it most it wouldn't come to him. Bob or Bill Johnson or Jackson.

"What they got me charged with?"

"Shit. A heap. DWI and assault on an officer. Resistin arrest. Whole buncha stuff. You gonna need you a lawyer."

"Can you get me a bailbondsman?"

"I can try."

"They's a card in my billfold if you'll look in there. Did you get me some cigarettes?"

"You never did say what kind."

"Any kind. Salems if you got em. Anything. Can you get me a Coke?"

"I'll see."

The steps went away again. It was nearly an hour before they returned, but he wouldn't bum another cigarette. The jailer called him to the door and let him out. He stood with his head up in the hall while the jailer locked the cell behind him. The tray slot opened down the hall and a mouth came into view.

"Why's he gettin out? Huh? How come he's gettin out?"

"Knock it off, Roscoe," the jailer said. To Joe he said, "Walk in front of me. Now hold it. I got more keys than Carter's got little pills."

At last he stood in the dayroom with lounging cops and trustees with their feet up in chairs watching television. They eyed him warily.

"Where's my truck?" he said.

The jailer was dumping his personal belongings from a manila envelope onto the cluttered desk. Keys, a ring, change, his wallet and comb and pocketknife. He was presented with a typed list of items which he himself had signed for.

"Check to see that everything's here and then sign. Count your money."

He picked up the billfold and opened it. He didn't know how much he was supposed to have but there was nearly two thousand dollars in it. It tallied with the inventory sheet.

"It's all here," he said. He slipped it into his back pocket and picked up his other stuff and signed. He looked up. All the city police were watching him. All their eyes were hostile. One had a Band-Aid on his chin.

"You can't learn your lesson, can you?" this one said.

"You talkin to me?"

"There ain't nobody else standing here, is it?"

Joe ignored him, though he hated to, and turned to the jailer.

"You know where my truck is?"

The jailer had settled in a chair and was unwrapping a sandwich from waxed paper. It looked like egg salad with hot peppers and tomatoes, and the jailer was reaching for a bottle of Louisiana Red Hot sauce.

"I believe they took it to King Brothers," he said.

That would be about fifty-five dollars if he could even drive it home.

"Can I go now?"

"Not till you make bond. He'll be here before long."

There was nothing to do but wait on the bondsman. Nobody

ever got in a hurry about something like this. There was a water fountain on the other side of the room and he started walking toward it.

"Hey," the cop said.

He stopped.

"Yeah?"

"Ain't nobody said you could walk over there."

"Ain't nobody said I couldn't, either."

He went on and bent over the fountain, drank the cold water for a long time. When he finished, he wiped his mouth and turned around. Somebody was coming in, a man with a briefcase.

"There's my man," he said.

They had him on $2500 bond and he was surprised it wasn't higher. They hadn't set his court date and it took only a few minutes to get released. He paid the bondsman the money and they said he could go. He had his hand on the door to freedom when the cop with the cut chin spoke again.

"We'll see your ass in court, Ransom. You going back this time. This time they'll keep you."

Ten years before, it would have been different. Now he would not let himself say anything. He wanted away too badly. They'd had him once and he had promised himself they would never have him again. Now they had him. He opened the door and walked outside.

The cars moved along the streets in the hot sunshiny Sunday afternoon. Couples with children sat on the low brick wall in front of the jail, talking in quiet voices, plans made, promises promised, hands clasped and hearts maybe shuddering with fear. For some it was almost a home, but he wanted it for his home no more. He went down the concrete steps and across the narrow street, the bells in the courthouse tower starting to chime. They tolled two times and he marked each sound in his head and stopped for a car that was cutting through the parking lot of the bank. He was glad of not calling her and of her knowing nothing of this. As the car went past he raised his eyes to see the driver who had already seen him. He wasn't sure. She had on sunglasses. It might have been anybody. He watched the car until it went out of sight, but she never looked back.

Dawn on Monday found the boy waiting beside the road with his gloves in his hand, squatting in the pale dust, his ears tuned for the sound of a motor. Cars and trucks appeared as specks down the road and grew larger and gained form as they hurtled toward him and sped past but not one slowed or stopped. Not one was an old GMC with a wrecked camper hull.

He sat there until the mist burned off, until the sun rose and lit the fields and dried the dew from the cotton. It hadn't rained. He sat until the sun held the land in its grip for another day and he knew he wasn't coming. Then he got up and faced down the road where the black strip of asphalt curved away toward the crossroads, toward distance and futility and nothingness. Nothing stirred anywhere. No breath of wind nor any sound. A light sweat broke out on his back. It was five miles, but he had a little money, and good credit. There was nothing to go home to anyway. He started walking, that old familiar thing that made riding such a joy.

*

At midmorning he trudged up the last little hill and walked between two pickups just as two men came out the door. He stepped aside for them to pass and he nodded. The boards of the floor just beyond the door were patched with printer's tin and tacked insecurely and they crinkled when they were stepped on. He went inside and stood looking around. It looked empty. He waited. There was a single lightbulb in the ceiling, a yellow glare of illumination in a cavern of bad cereal and atrophied potato chips, long forgotten and stashed behind the bug spray. The coal stove sat at the rear of the room, lacquered with tobacco juice. Flystrips hung from the scorched ceiling with their victims mummified, handfuls of black rice flung and stuck, untouchables. There were crazy patches of tin all over the floor. He reached back and pushed the door open a little and let it fall to. The old man parted the curtains behind the counter and stepped out.

"Hey, Mr. Coleman," Gary said. He went over to the blue Pepsi box and slid the lid back. He felt among the cool bottles, examining the caps. In the dark water he found the letters R and C. The old man came from behind the counter slowly and eased himself down on the bench, the cigar cold and dead between his fingers. Gary closed the lid and went to the rack of cakes and got a double-decker banana Moon Pie.

"You ain't seen Joe, have you?"

He turned at the old man's question.

"He never did come by. You seen him?"

John Coleman leaned back and rubbed his forehead with his fingers. A crescent scar hung there, hung in flesh like an eighth of a moon. In his skull likewise lay the shrapnel he thought had killed him one day long ago. The boy could not know that it itched, it always itched, it never stopped its itch.

"He wrecked his truck the other night. I believe they've got him in jail."

"Jail?"

"I magine."

He looked down at what he had in his hands. His hunger seemed so small then, so stupid. He wrecked *his* truck the other night. He slowly opened the RC on the drink box and sat on the bench on that side, held the bottle between his legs while he opened the cake.

"I waited on him a long time," he said.

The old man sat like a statue. He seemed to read some bad news on the screen door. A car passed outside, a flash of red that went out of hearing. The air pump kicked on and it chugged and chugged. John Coleman stretched one leg out and reached into his pocket for his lighter.

"How bad did he tear it up?" Gary said.

"Tear what up?"

"That truck."

"Oh. I don't know."

The lighter snapped and the smoke flooded out of his mouth. He bent forward and stroked his knee absently with the silver rectangle. Finally he dropped it in his shirt pocket.

"I wished I knew," the boy said. "I was supposed to buy it. I hope he ain't tore it all to pieces."

The storekeeper offered no response. He seemed to hate to have anybody in there with him. The boy ate his Moon Pie and drank his RC and formed possible lines of conversation in his mind.

"Reckon when he'll get out?" he said.

The old man shook his head. He crossed his legs and put one hand on the bench. The wood there was smoothly worn, polished, shiny.

"Depends," he said, finally. "Last time they got him they kept him two weeks."

"You don't know what happened?"

"Had a wreck was all I heard. I think the highway patrol got him."

That was all he'd say about it. He got up and went back behind the curtain where secret things were that nobody ever saw. A cot, shelves of books, shoe boxes of old money both rare and near extinct. Hot Budweiser in cans that he'd drink when he took the notion. A framed photograph of an old man and an old woman, their faces like leather in a tintype portrait, poised uncertainly and fearful on the porch of their log house. Theirs was the one that lay near the spring house, entombed there after the first house burned down, far away now from where they slept their eternity away on the hill. He sat there for a while, until he heard the boy call out.

He'd laid a dollar on the counter when he stepped back out.

"I need to pay you for that," he said. "I had a big RC and a Moon Pie."

He put the burning cigar in the ashtray and punched the buttons on the register. He rang it open and said: "Sixty-five."

Going out the door the boy looked back at him. John Coleman seemed like something made of china, a being or mannequin with living flesh but wires for bones. His glasses caught the tiny sunlight and flashed it across the room.

"You come back," he said.

In the countryside by nights without the moon, there sometimes roamed an indigent, a recycled reject with eyes sifting the dark and sorting the scattered scents, walking beside deep hollows and ditches of stinking water. The hours he kept were usually reserved for the drunk and the sleeping. With his sloe-lidded eyes that in the daytime tried to hide from the sun, he spied treasures all over the land. No thing unlocked was safe from his grasp, he who could squat in the road and talk to the dogs and still their dying growls, all save one.

With his myriad transactions he would convert these Troy-Bilt tillers and battery chargers and bugwhackers to a small amount of money and show up at the store wet to the knees and clamoring for Pepsi and peanuts, tomato juice and Alka-Seltzer. He went in on John Coleman one day with a fistful of food stamps. The old storekeeper was lying back against a pile of flour with a book in one hand and a cigar in the other. He had gone to sleep, and now came a crafty assassin and thief whose feet toed soundlessly over the worn and creaky boards. The hand with the cigar had come to rest against his stomach and he held the book to his chest, his snores long, sonorous, drafty. He'd once drunk three big Pepsis poured into a pot on a dare of not stopping and all but died from it, long before rumors of war, before the talk around his father's store altered from general topics and became focused on one thing: war. He had been reading about the fallen on the field of Shiloh and about the retreat into the Hornet's Nest and about the bullets in the orchard cutting the peach blossoms like falling snow. He could only shake his head over it, a war like that, that long ago. But he had been drinking that morning, as he did some or sometimes many mornings, and the heat and the beer and the book had done him in.

Wade crept about the room and eyed the register warily, ready at any moment to assume the position of a customer just entered and just as surprised as the one he feared might wake. He reached out and tapped his knuckles on the glass pane of the candy case. He rapped three times. The slow sighing and tuneless whistling sawed through the air. He took two steps closer to the counter, then stood finally with his hand on it, regarding the merchant caught in his dreams. John Coleman's neck was wrinkled like a turtle's and a slow pulse beat steadily at the corner of his jaw. His glasses had fallen sideways on his nose and he appeared old, weak, vulnerable. But there against his leg lay an automatic pistol blued with rust, close to hand, the snout shiny with age and use. Wade put both hands in his pockets and nudged John's foot with his toe. The eyes opened like a child's with no sleep in them, and the first thing he did was straighten his glasses.

"Ho," he said, and he got up, the hand trailing the pistol now by his leg and behind the counter where it was placed in some strategic spot not known to anyone but himself.

"I hate to wake you up," Wade said.

"I wasn't asleep. Just had my eyes closed. What can I do for you?"

"Aw, I just need to look, I reckon."

He was eyeing the shelves, gripping with his hand in his pocket the wad of food coupons he had taken off the dead black man. He looked over the shelves and noted what was there, the bags and boxes and brightly colored cans. Nothing was marked, for the old storekeeper kept the prices in his head. If he didn't know the price he would immediately name one. He gave credit to the reliable and the unreliable alike, slow to ask for payment, didn't really need it. On the pagan holiday a masked drunk stooped, smiling, behind the counter, wearing a plastic face, the lights out, hearing the tiny cautious steps outside the door, the cars idling, the parents watching as the little ones came inside. He always lit a coal-oil lantern and set it in the floor. To the young it gave an awesome quality to the room, small glints of shine on the shelves, fearsome shapes behind the stove. It was one of their favorite places to go. He'd hear them stop, hear them whisper to each other, gathering their courage. He'd let them say it three times before he leaped out with the flashlight, a white-haired frog with wings of hair on the sides of his head ratted up with a comb, cackling like an insane rooster. He loaded up their bags and they came back every year until they were too old to come in costume any more. And he would not even touch one of these that he had so badly desired to sire. He could only watch them grow from year to year, become men and women over and over, send their own inside for trick or treat.

"What you need?" he said to Wade. He was sure now that the

one rumored was in fact the same. There was no smile on his face, nothing but a hard glare.

"Aw, I'm just lookin," he said. He stepped to the shelf and hefted a can of Viennas. "How much?"

"Fifty-five."

"Goddamn, you high, ain't you?"

"You don't like the price go buy it somewhere else."

Wade got three cans. He got three packs of cigarettes. John saw that he was shopping and stepped behind the curtain and opened the refrigerator. There was a bottle of Jim Beam half full in there, and he tilted it out and took the cap off and turned a good drink down his throat. He stuck an eye to the crack in the curtain and watched Wade slide a flat tin of sardines down in his overall pocket. I got my goddamn eye on you, he said to himself. Then he got another drink. He wanted something to chase it with then, so he brought the whiskey out and set it on the counter and came around and went to the drink box. From an eye corner Wade watched him get a small green glass Coke, open it on the box and drink about half it. Then he watched him walk over to him and reach into his overalls and take out the sardines and put them back on the shelf.

"You holler at me when you get through," John said, and he went back behind the curtain. Wade stood stunned. He didn't even try to use the food stamps. Half drunk like he was he just walked out the door.

When John Coleman stuck an eye to the curtain there was nobody standing inside. He came on out. There was no money on the counter. He locked the register, then unlocked it and rang it open. The money was packed in there, stuffed tightly, the tens, the fives, the ones. He slammed it shut and locked it again and got his pistol and put it in his pocket and went outside. The screen door slapped shut behind him. He strode quickly between the whittled benches and past the square red tank coated with oil and insects, with the pump handle on top to dispense the kerosene, and stepped over the board the red sand was shoveled against and walked to the middle of the road and faced left. There was nothing beside the slow figure going down the road trying to open a can of Vienna sausages except two houses on the right and an abandoned one on the left and Mr. Frank's barn that might or might not have a cow in it. He pulled the pistol from his pocket. Then he looked at the store.

"Well shit," he said. He rushed back inside. The whiskey was sitting on the counter where he'd left it. He rushed back outside. Wade had become a small target but an immobile one, his fingers holding each juicy sausage and moving them into his mouth rapidly. John Coleman in his sixty-sixth year jacked the action back on the Llama and let it fall to, slipped the safety and aimed. Nora Pinion, horrified suddenly, almost pulled up for some gas. Wade leaped when the first bullet furrowed the asphalt and droned off heavily into the catalpa trees on his left. He spun, and the second bullet sprayed his leg with supersonic grains of sand.

"God*damn*," he said. He could see the storekeeper, slightly squatted to steady his drunken hand, drawn down on him at the top of the hill. He raised his hands and everything fell out from under his arms. He hadn't thought to get a sack. The voice drifted down to him, slow, clear: "You bring that stuff back up here."

Wade gathered his purloined goods with one hand, one hand in the air. He wanted no misunderstandings. By the time he got back up to the top of the hill, John had put the pistol away. He held the door open for Wade and Wade marched to the counter and put two cans of Vienna sausage and three packs of crackers on the counter, the crackers broken, crumbled inside the cellophane, not desirable but edible.

John Coleman walked behind the counter and unlocked the register. He stared across until Wade unloaded the cigarettes.

"Don't come back in here," he told him.

The word traveled fast, it seemed. One fine morning the boy woke on the quilt he used for a bed and lay turned on his back to hear the live things around him: the wasps buzzing busily overhead in the hot air in their obscure comings and goings; the jays outside his window screaming their curses to the squirrels that shook the branches and the dew from them as they scurried about; the far-off voices of other birds deep in the woods and the high thin piping of tree-frogs so loud and ventriloquistic they could never be found. The sun was shining on him through the window and it became too hot to sleep any more.

He got up and put on his clothes and went through the house. The little girl lay like one shot dead, and his father and his mother were nowhere to be seen. In the pie safe and on shelves nailed together from boards there were cans of soup, dry rice, Granola bars. He got a Granola bar with raisins and almonds and munched it while scratching himself and wondering where his parents could be.

Going down the road later in the hot morning sun, he passed a field of hay being baled. There was a flatbed truck inching along the rows of hay, and men were walking beside it throwing the bales up to another man who stacked them behind the cab against a high wooden wall. He stopped in the dusty roadside weeds to watch them labor. Already the heat made the toiling figures hazy and vague in the distance. He could hear faint cries, the revving of the truck motor from time to time. The baler was working along with a steady drumlike sound, the red machinery pushing each bale out in stages until it leaned toward the ground and fell off the chute and another appeared behind it to follow.

He lifted a finger and drew it across the beaded sweat on his brow and flung it to the ground. He saw what looked like a boy his age and studied him. The boy was having trouble with the bales. Twice he saw him drop them. Once he broke the strings on one and the man on the truck yelled down something to him. They moved in a palpable mist of heat under a disastrous sun amid clouds of chaff. Gary tossed his can sack into the ditch and stepped down after it. He found a sagging place in the wire and stepped over the top strand.

He had to follow the truck for a while because it didn't stop at first. On the ground were two old black men and the white boy. A white-haired man at least sixty was on the bed of the truck. A hard unfriendly face, a visage carved from burnt leather looked out from under a shredded-straw cowboy hat that held his face in shade. Gary kept trying to talk to him, but he kept looking around and going back to catch the bales. Finally Gary ran and caught the back end of the truck and swung himself up onto it. The old man leaned around and hollered into the window and the truck stopped.

They all turned and looked at him. They had on long-sleeved

shirts and gloves. Their faces were encrusted with bits of hay and they were wet with sweat. The boy he'd been watching was red in the face and looked ready to drop. It looked as though they were putting on the first load.

The old man was chewing tobacco and now he leaned his head over the side of the truck and spat and hit the webs of his thumbs together twice in the gloves. He didn't look happy.

"What you want?" he said.

"You need any help?"

The old man looked dubious. He leaned back against the wall of hay and looked out over the field. Most of it was still in long raked piles all over the ground.

"I reckon we can handle it. Throw that damn bale up here, Bobby. What you waitin on?"

The boy on the ground had been listening. He was chubby and soft-looking. He bent and grunted up with the bale and said, "Well, you stopped." He just barely got it up over the edge of the bed and with a herculean effort at that.

"I'll be goddamned," the old man said.

A sharp voice inside the truck said a name.

"Well, any damn body fourteen year old ought to be able to pick up a bale of hay. Give it here." He snatched the bale off the bed and threw it over his head into place and then glared down at the boy. The boy wasn't looking at him. He was walking ahead. The two ancient blacks were each standing beside a bale but the old man didn't yell at them. They were both older than he was. One of them had a solid white eye and wore glasses, the lens cracked over the bad eye as if in simultaneous injury.

"I just thought you might need some help," Gary said. "Didn't figure it'd hurt nothin to ask."

"You ever hauled any hay?"

"Yessir. I've hauled a good bit."

"Where at? Who for?"

"Well," he said. "I ain't never hauled none around here. I've hauled a bunch in Texas. I hauled all one summer down there."

The old man worked his cud and looked at Gary's thick little arms and legs.

"Can you throw one up on the truck?"

"Yessir."

"Let's see you throw one then."

He got off on the side of the truck and walked to the bale nearest him. He bent his legs and muscled the bale up against his chest and walked to the truck with it. It was seventy or eighty pounds, felt like. He tossed it up over the side onto the stack and all the old man had to do was hit it on the side and settle it straight. He looked down on him.

"How old are you?"

"Fifteen, I reckon. I'm just little for my age." He was looking up and shading one hand against the sun in his eyes.

"You gonna work in that?" He was pointing to the black T-shirt Gary was wearing.

"Yessir. I ain't got no other shirt with me. It don't matter."

"That hay'll stick you."

"It's all right. I've hauled in a short-sleeve shirt before."

"You ain't got no gloves."

He worked his fingers open and closed once. "My hands is tough," he said.

"Well." He called down to one of the black men: "Come on, Cleve." Then: "All right. Get over here on the left and maybe you can help this boy keep up. We done had to crank the baler out twice cause he couldn't pick em up."

"Yessir. Thank you." He walked behind the truck and the old man leaned around the hay. "Let's go," he said. The gears clashed as it went into first and the truck started rolling. Gary walked fast alongside it and hurried on to the next bale, going by the fat boy who barely got his on before the truck moved past. When it came by Gary he handed a bale up to the old man. When he went by the cab again, he saw a woman with a straw hat behind the wheel, a brown stain of snuff on her chin. She had both hands in a desperate clench on the wheel, with the truck crawling about two miles an hour. The old man cursed every time the fat boy tried to put one up.

"How much does hay haulers make in Texas?" he said.

Gary handed another one up to him and he turned and stacked it. "It just depends," he said. "Who you work for. I worked with a bunch of Mexicans one day and got two cents a bale. I never did go back and work for that fellow no more, though."

"Well," he said. "I pay a nickel a bale and dinner. That all right with you?"

"Yes sir," he said. He could already envision the feast. "How much we gonna haul today?" He was working and hurrying and throwing the bales up while they were talking.

"They's another field down yonder," the old man shouted. "Other side of that creek. See yonder?"

Gary looked. He could see a pale green square of flattened grass shimmering in the distance.

"We got another truck comin after dinner and three more hands," he said. "We gonna haul till dark if we can. You think you can stand it?"

"I can stand it," Gary said. The baling twine had already made deep red lines in his palms. He hurried ahead and picked up a bale and stood waiting with it.

"Uh uh," the old man called. He put it down.

"Now see there. You havin to pick it up twice. Don't pick it up till the truck gets to you. Wait on the truck."

"Yessir."

"Now, come on with it."

He tossed it up.

"I thought you said you'd hauled before."

"I have. It's just been a while."

"How much of a while?"

"Aw. A year or two."

"Well. It's all the same. In Texas or Missippi. All you got to do's put it on the truck."

He walked past the other boy and stopped beside him just as he was starting up with a bale. He was bent over from the waist, his back bowed.

"Use your legs," he said.

The boy looked at him. He was white around the mouth.

"What?"

"Use your legs. Don't pick it up with your back. Look here."

He bent over a bale with his forearms resting on his thighs.

"See here?" He raised the bale with his arms like a weightlifter doing a curl and straightened his legs at the same time. When he came erect the bale was at chest level. When the truck passed he threw it up.

"See there? It's easier like that. It don't give your back out like that."

He smiled at the boy but the boy didn't smile back. When the old man went to the other side to catch the hay, he walked up next to Gary and said, "That's my granddaddy. Daddy makes me come out here in the summertime and help him. All he ever does is fuss at me, though."

"You get paid?"

"Shit," the boy said. "I wouldn't come out here and do it for nothin. What you think I am, crazy?"

"I don't guess."

"I wouldn't even be out here if I didn't have to.

"Aw."

"I don't care if I don't never make any money or not."

Gary didn't say anything to that.

"Plus I have to mow the yard and hang out clothes, too."

"Yeah?" Gary said.

"And they don't even pay me for that."

Long before dinnertime the old man saw the red welts forming on Gary's hands and gave him an extra pair of gloves. When they had the truck loaded they stopped and tied the load down, the old man on top crawling around and rigging the rope, Gary kneeling under the truck and throwing the free end of the rope around for him to take up the other side and tie off. They rode on top to the trees that held the shade at the fence and left that truck and took an old '65 Chevy pickup back out to the center of the field. The baler was finishing up and they had what looked like about two hundred more to pick up.

"We'll have a hundred and thirty-five on two loads," the old man said. They had water in plastic milk jugs that had been frozen solid and wrapped in grocery sacks. It was cold and sweet and Gary knew it would ruin him if he drank too much of it. The fat boy, Bobby, turned the jug up time and time again. They took a break under the shade when they had both trucks loaded.

"You smoke?" the old man said. He pulled a pack of Winstons out of a dry shirt he'd put on.

"Every once in a while," Gary said.

"Well, here." He gave him a cigarette and then gave him a light. They sat crosslegged on the ground and the man looked at his watch.

"Ten-thirty," he said. "Where you live?"

Gary drew on the cigarette and looked out over the field. He rested his weight on one arm. He tensed it, felt the muscle bunch, untensed it.

"We live up on Edie Hill," he said.

"Edie Hill?" The eyes were flat and gray. The boy could see the lifetime of hard work in them, the hundreds of days like this one still remembered and not banished by time.

"Yessir," he said. He flicked at the fire on his cigarette with his little finger. It was quiet on the ground there, the heat rising around

them and drawing the sweat effortlessly from them and already
dampening and darkening the old man's fresh shirt.

"I used to know some folks lived up around there," he said.
"Didn't know nobody lived up there now."

"We just livin in this old house up there," Gary said. "I don't
reckon it belongs to anybody."

"Is it back up there around a big pine thicket? Got some old
sheds and stuff around it? Old log house?"

He drew deeply on the cigarette and studied his feet. He didn't
look up. The burning air had twisted the hair on his neck into wet
locks that curled up and cooled his skin. "It's a log house," he
said.

"You one of them Joneses that moved back here?"

"Yessir."

The old man nodded and looked off into the distance, the blue
denim of his overalls tattered and faded. He waited a few moments before he spoke.

"How much you reckon's on them two trucks there?"

Gary looked. "I don't know," he said.

"A hundred on this one. Thirty on that one." The old man got
up, pulling his billfold from his back pocket. "Six dollars and
fifty cents."

The boy sat on the ground watching him, the cigarette smoking
between his fingers. "What is it?" he said.

The old man didn't answer. He stuck a thin thumb between the
leather jaws of his billfold and pulled out a five and a one. The
two paper bills fluttered to the ground like wounded doves and
were anchored almost immediately by two pitched quarters that

landed flat and soundlessly and pinned them to the faded green stubble in front of his feet. He looked up. The old man was staring down on him now with his eyes hard and unfeeling. He bent over and picked up the gloves the boy had been using. The woman and the fat boy were standing by the other truck. They had not spoken.

"Let's go," he said, and they climbed into the cab. The haymaster put one foot on the rear hub and gripped the bed with his dark and freckled hands and pulled himself up over it like a seal clambering onto an ice shelf. But there was no coolness in that field. Long after they had gone Gary sat motionless beneath the shade tree, watching their wavering figures struggling relentlessly over the parched ground, their toiling shapes remorseless and wasted and indentured to the heat that rose from the earth and descended from the sky in a vapor hot as fire.

S ometimes in the singing underbrush the boy could hear sounds that came only at night, strange rustlings and movings that lay dormant in the daytime and rose after the sun fell into the deep green beyond the creek faded to black, the hushed voices and far-off crying dogs that rushed and swept through the dark timber, the faint yellow lights moving across the bottomland. Sometimes he'd go down there to hear them better.

He could follow the path without a light and climb a hill behind the house and come out on a dirt road washed with shadows, where he could see little puffs of dust rising and falling beneath his bare feet. He'd stop on the wooden bridge and listen, squatting there in the warm night. He could hear men talking, the quick baying, the short rush of dogs through the woods.

One night he sat motionless on the bridge with the rough wood under him and heard the quick splash of little feet in the shallows. He knew it was a coon. He could hear the dogs far back, trailing. There was no sound around him but the slow musical trickle of the stream and the slow wind that rustled the cane. The little feet came closer, stopped. He saw the coon, one small dark blob on the creek bank, a scurrying shape bent south with humped and pumping legs. The dogs came upon him in a rush; it wasn't until he heard their feet striking the water that the first one opened again. Five dogs, mottled moiling shapes indistinct in the dark, splashed down the ribbon of water and flowed beneath the bridge with their voices like hammers, sudden shocks of noise that disrupted the peace and serenity of the night, tore it apart with their anguished cries, swept past the bridge and down the bank, their voices louder than he could have imagined, echoing up and down and back behind him, all around him, until the whole of the woods rang with the sound of the race. The boy heard them catch it, heard the angry sounds of the dogs and the high thin chittering of the coon as they pulled it apart with their teeth. He saw the yellow lights struggling up through the woods as the men who owned the dogs came to see after them, and he got up, and waited a moment, some longing deep within him he couldn't name, and went away before they came too close.

omebody was beating on something down the road. The boy had been walking for a long time and he could hear the sound of it now. It was midmorning and he was on his way to the store again, their supplies low, empty bellies all around him. He still had money saved back, hidden under a rock a long way from the house, but already he'd seen the old man in the woods, bending, stooping, looking. He knew he'd have to move it soon, maybe find a hollow tree or even bury it. There was a good bit in his pocket but he would hide that before he returned home.

The sound of banging was irregular, hollow and muffled, and as he got closer he could hear small random curses. It appeared to be coming from near Joe's house. He rounded the last curve and the old GMC was there, the hood up, the left front fender off, the bossman kneeling over it on the ground and attacking it with a ball peen hammer and a tire iron. The boy stood watching him for a moment. Then he smiled. He walked on up the road and turned into the yard. Joe was laying the flat end of the tire iron in the wrinkles in the metal and drawing back and whopping it with the hammer. He would hit a few licks and then pause to examine his handiwork.

"Hey," Gary said.

Joe looked over his shoulder at him and smiled.

"Hey, boy," he said. "What you doing?"

Gary walked up beside him and squatted. The fender was lying with the painted side down and he could see the edge of an anvil sticking out from under it.

"I's headed to the store. What are you up to?"

Joe laid the hammer down and sat back on his heels. He fished a cigarette out of his pocket and lit it. Sweat had soaked his shirt.

"Ah hell, I'm trying to beat some of the dents out of this fender. You still want this truck?"

Gary got up and went around to the front of it. The mangled grille was lying on the ground. He looked inside the engine compartment. The radiator had been pulled out, but what looked like a new one was lying on a piece of cardboard beside the truck.

"Is this all that's wrong with it?"

"Yeah. I done had a new windshield put in it. I got another hood and put on it."

Gary looked. The glass was new and it had a new inspection sticker in the corner. The hood was a pale green.

"How did you get it to the shop?"

"I had to go over to the junk yard where they towed it. They put that hood on for me and put that windshield in. I drove it home but the radiator had a leak in it. I got James Maples to bring me a radiator from town yesterday. I'm fixing to put it in quick as I get through with this fender. Come here and help me hold it down, how about it?''

The boy sat down and gripped the edge of the sheet metal. Joe put his tire iron on it and beat a wrinkle flat.

"It may not look too good but it'll beat not having one on it at all,'' he said.

"We gonna work any more?'' the boy said, in between licks.

Joe didn't pause with his hammering. "Nah. We through. I got to get cleaned up. And go to Bruce. Get my money. Try to find my dog. You want to go?''

"Yessir.''

"All right. We got to put this back on. Put that radiator in. I ain't been able to find a grille.''

The boy didn't know whether to ask him about being in jail or not. Maybe Joe knew what was on his mind. He stopped hammering and looked up.

"I guess you heard what happened to me.''

"Well.'' The boy looked down at the fender, looked back up, squinting against the sun. "Sort of. I heard you had a wreck.''

"That all you heard?''

"Nosir. I heard you got put in jail.''

"It wasn't the first time,'' said Joe. "Probably won't be the last. Did you know I'd been in the penitentiary?''

Gary shook his head slowly. "Nosir,'' he said.

"Well, I have. I did twenty-nine months for assault on a police officer. The motherfuckers pulled me over behind a shopping center uptown and thought they were gonna whip my ass. I wasn't doing nothing. Waiting on an old gal to get off from work. Now I was drunk, I'll admit that. But I wasn't fucking with them." He looked up and smiled grimly. "But I had put one of em in the hospital about a month before."

The twisted piece of metal in front of him was beginning to resemble a fender again, just a little.

"What I need are some dollies. I used to be a body man a long time ago."

"What's that?"

"Dollies?"

"Body man."

Joe glanced up at him briefly and then back down.

Sometimes it seemed that the boy didn't know a lot of things a boy his age should know. They'd been driving by the Rock Ridge Colored Church one day back in the spring and the boy had asked him who lived in that big white house.

"That's a guy that fixes cars after they're wrecked. You know. Put on new doors. New fenders. Or like this. Straighten the old ones. It's cheaper. Sometimes it don't look as good. You got to know what you're doing. I used to paint a lot but I started having nosebleeds and I had to quit it."

The boy nodded.

"I'll give you a job this winter. We'll start in setting pines about December. We'll work on that till March or April. You can make you plenty of money then. Planting pays more than deadening."

"You mean we're gonna set out trees?"

"Yeah."

"Well, how you do it? You have to dig a hole and everything?"

"Naw, naw, it ain't like that. Here, let's move it up a little this way. Make sure that anvil's under it. All right. Hold it right there. See if we can get this big crease out of it. No, we set em with a dibble. Little old iron bar. It's got a dull blade on it. You just kick it in the ground and it digs a little hole. You just stick your tree in and then close it up, stomp on it. Go on to the next one. Takes about five seconds."

"Five seconds? How big's the trees?"

"Oh, they're just little bitty things. Baby pines. About a foot long. Naw, but what I was telling you about them motherfuckers . . . see a cop can fuck over you if he wants to. Don't get me wrong, there's some good ones. But you live in a place and get on the wrong side of the law like I did. Like I do. They'll look for you. They find out where you hang out, they'll park and wait for you. That's what they did to me that night."

"You mean the other night?"

"What other night?"

"The night you had the wreck. Got put in jail."

Joe looked up at him and pointed to the fender with the hammer.

"You mean this?"

"Yessir."

"Naw, naw." He shook his head. "I'm talking about what I got sent to the pen over. Move it a little more that way. Hold it. Hell, I been out a good while. Stayed in two and half years. They tried to shoot me. After I whipped all three of them they did. Or one did. He went for his gun and I grabbed it. He was fixing to kill me. Told me he was. But all he did was blow his kneecap off. Hold it right there, now."

The boy watched him while he hammered, watched the muscle bunching in his bicep and the pellet hole there and the crooked nose and the dark hair curled in ringlets on the back of his neck. Watched the tanned hands and the scarred knuckles, outsized, knotty with gristle.

"Only way I got out light as I did was my lawyer got him on the witness stand and made him mad." He looked up, looked back down. "I told him they'd been fucking with me. He went and looked it up. They were gonna put me in as a habitual offender. You can get thirty years for that. They'd pulled me over seventeen times in sixty-four days. They'd arrested me once. That was when one of em hit me in the back with his stick and I put him in the hospital. My lawyer went to the police station. He looked at the arrest records. A good lawyer's worth his money. I got old David Carson up at Oxford. He's high but he's good. It took me two years to pay him off after I got out of the pen. But it would have took me a lot longer if I'd still been in."

He laid down the hammer and the tire iron and lit another cigarette.

"Let's see what she looks like now," he said. He raised the fender and turned it over. It resembled something of its original shape. "Hell, that ought to be good enough. Long as the bolts'll go in."

"What you want me to do?"

"Help me hang it back on the fenderwell. I got all the bolts over here in a hubcap. Hold it a minute."

The boy stood holding the fender in place. Joe stooped and picked up the hubcap and set it on the breather.

"Now just hold it until I can get one started," he said. He had a socket and a ratchet in his hand. "You just hold it and I'll put em in. Yeah, old David's a good lawyer. He's been out here and deer-hunted with me. I've got access to some good timberland. I get it about a year before they cut it."

The boy didn't say anything, just stood holding the fender while he started the bolts and ratcheted them down. When he had three in, Joe told him he could turn it loose. He stepped back and looked inside the cab. Mud was caked on the floormats. The seat had a huge rip across the driver's side. There was a rubber-coated gunrack mounted above and behind the seat. The dash was piled high with papers. There was a long brown sack with a bottle in it lying against the hump in the floor. Joe looked around the corner of the hood.

"You want to do something for me?"

"Yessir."

"Reach in there and get me one of them beers out of that cooler in the back. Damn if I ain't done got hot."

He went to the back and raised the camper door. It fell twice before he got it to stay up. There was a big yellow Covey cooler with a red top in the back. He pried the lid open and looked inside. There were eight or ten bottles of beer covered with ice and water. He got one and looked at it.

"This here?" he said, holding it out.

"Yeah," Joe said, without looking up. The boy walked back and handed it to him. He put the ratchet down and twisted the top off the beer and tossed the cap out in the yard. He turned the beer up and took a good third of it down, then looked at his watch.

Nearly eleven o'clock. Damned if he wasn't starting earlier every day. He set it down on the fan shroud and balanced it precariously there and picked up another bolt.

"You like beer?" the boy said.

"Yeah. Do you?"

"I ain't never had one."

Joe looked around at him and grinned. "Ain't never had one? How old did you say you were?"

"I think I'm fifteen. That's why I ain't never got a Social Security card. I ain't got no birth certificate."

"I thought everybody had a birth certificate."

"I ain't. My mama said the place I was born you couldn't get one."

"Why hell, I wouldn't worry about it, then. You won't even have to file income tax. Long as you don't hold a public job. You won't even have to register for the draft. You ever been to school?"

"Nosir."

They stood looking at each other across the ten feet that separated them.

"You can't read."

"Nosir."

He picked up the beer again and drank some of it. "There's worse things, I guess. How do you sign your name?"

"I ain't never had to."

He bent under the hood of the truck again. He couldn't understand how the boy could have come this far without knowing what a church was.

"Can I buy one of those beers from you?"

He leaned around again and looked at him.

"What?"

"I'm kinda thirsty. I was headed up to the store to get me something to drink. Can I buy one of them from you?"

Fifteen. Maybe. And never had a place to call his own, don't know where he was born. He'd go up to the house one day and get him. See what kind of shape they were in up there.

"I tell you what, son. You can drink one of them beers if you want it. I don't reckon your daddy would care, would he?"

"I don't reckon."

"But you can't buy one from me. Friends don't buy things from one another."

"Yessir."

"And don't say sir so much to me."

"Yessir."

Joe bent under the hood again.

"You still want to give me two hundred dollars for this truck?"

An hour later he had it running with the radiator full of water. He had changed his clothes and had most of the black grease washed off his hands. The boy had finished his third beer and was sitting in the yard.

"Come on and get in," Joe told him. "I need to go by the store and get some gas."

The boy climbed in the other side. He wasn't saying much. He'd already noted how good those cold beers were. He understood now what the old man was after on all those nights and weekends and weeks sometimes, what he went for and what he wanted to feel. Nothing mattered now, he knew it the first time he met it. He was with the bossman, who was going to take care of him, and he probably wouldn't even have to worry about walking back home. He was going to get the truck, some way, some day, and then he'd learn how to drive it.

Later he remembered stopping by the store and getting ice and gas, the long ride to Bruce and the long wait in the hot sunshiny cab of the truck at the Weyerhauser plant, the big chain-link fence and the piles of logs as far as the eye could see, the water spraying over the stacked lengths of them. Joe stayed inside nearly forever, it seemed, and he got sleepy in the truck. They ate somewhere, thick hamburgers and fries in little white cardboard containers. A roadside stand had T-shirts and the bossman bought him one, AC/DC, although neither of them knew their music; the shirt was for a boy who needed one because he didn't have one on and might need one wherever they wound up. Two kindred souls, one who sat on the tailgate drinking another beer while the other one kicked the bushes and stomped the clumps of grass beside the freshly skinned tree, whooping and hollering and looking all around. Many houses, many yards, one where Joe struck up a conversation with a pretty young housewife, making her laugh easily, admiring her with his eyes, her knowing it. No, but she hadn't seen the dog. And now she had his number if she needed to call him. There was an old man in a rocking chair in another one. Joe pulled up right beside the porch, where the old man had a cane planted firmly between his shoes, hand-rolling his cigarettes, the little bag and paper pinched up tight against his chest, nodding or shaking his head; the bossman was genial and deferential to advanced age, good natured, easy, but each time, he pulled away from a house, saying *Goddamn, I won't never find him*. Down dirt roads they drove, past houses off dirt roads, little yards enclosed by high woods and brush, enclaves carved out of the wilderness where deer came at night and sniffed at the children's toys. Once he thought he slept. They were miles removed from where they had been, Joe having given up on asking folks and just riding the roads in a dry county and drinking whiskey, trying to find his dog, telling Gary over and over what a good dog he was. *He wouldn't have done anything to you, maybe just nipped you a little*. Sometimes they met cruisers with uniformed deputies or even the real bad boys, the highway patrol, military, hardass, looking for people like them. *Don't never wave to them. They know you guilty of something when you wave*. Days and nights in the ring at Fort Jackson when Joe held the middleweight title for sixteen months and defended it successfully nine times—Gary heard about that. Women and divorce and rolling the bones, jail and a grandbaby coming, he'd raised that dog from a puppy, had been the only friend he'd had in a while. Everybody thought he'd gone crazy but he hadn't gone crazy. *They tell ever kind of lie on me it is. The bastards would hang murder on me if they could get away with it. You listen to what I'm telling you. A poor man ain't got a chance against the law. How can some rich son of a bitch do something and get off? And a poor man go to the pen? It's money. The rich ones know the judge and play golf and shit with him. Hell, go out to the country club and have a few drinks. Weighs about a hundred pounds. He's got long ears but a docked tail. Well yessir I meant to get around to doing that but I sorta did a halfway job on him.*

Oh, he's a unique looking dog, I promise you that. But if you happen to see him. It don't matter what time you call. Day or night. Yes sir. Thank you, sir. A deep green creek stirring beneath a steel and concrete bridge, the bossman wearing shades and holding his dick in one hand and a whiskey bottle in the other, grinning and saluting him where he stood pissing in the road. Having to jump in and zip up his pants quickly because somebody was coming. *You ain't drunk, are you? I used to know an old gal who lived around here. Now, son, you talk about some good stuff. I wonder where that damn dog is. He's got to be around here somewhere. Some where.* Stopping at a store for cigarettes, his head lolling out the window, pigskins to sober up on that were of the hot variety and made him drink more. He didn't have to be home at any particular time, he was sure. *Just drive yonder way,* the boy kept saying. *Just drive yonder way.* He got it in his head that somebody had stolen the dog, or that the police might be holding him against his will. And there he was finally, standing not fifty yards from the tree Joe had hit, then loping, staying out of the road, where the cars whizzed by at sixty, even when they saw a man trying to get his dog by the side of the road. *You got more sense than I thought you had. Get back there. Lay down and behave. We going home right now.* The sun growing gentler and the evening light changing, going softer, touching the horizon beyond the road faintly blue, the clouds rolled up high in white masses steadily changing shapes. Once again roads that he knew or had been on if even briefly. Here the bridge where the man he had to hit with the rock. *You point the motherfucker out to me. I'll settle his goddamn hash.* The same fat cows, the same lush grass. A doe deer feeding among them now, little wild cousin with lespedeza hanging from her working mouth, the heartprint hooves. Both of them drunk now, a roady buzz that would linger for a while. Lights beginning to come on in London Hill, the storefront lit, a flashing glimpse of the old man standing under the naked bulb where it hung from a cord in the soot-stained ceiling. *I'll drop you off if you're ready to go.* They stopped and let the dog out. Joe held him and made Gary pet him and the dog accepted it and licked his hand. The broad tongue raspy, pink, wide. The creased forehead with its knots of tooth-marked scars. *Yeah, but all them dogs is dead. You better sober up a little before you go home. Oh? You ain't ready to go home? Well, I could find some place else for us to go, yeah.* Late evening coming, little flocks of nine and ten doves sailing over the light wires or perched on the same with their feathers ruffled and squatting in deep composure. Meeting people with parking lights on, the air suffused with the smell of things living, the trees green and standing with their grapevines twisted about them and their roots knurled deep in the good earth. A warm late spring or early summer evening with the branches beginning to merge together, for things in the distance to grow less plain, finally until night fell and all the lights had to be turned on and the day was another event.

T he old man was shaking where he lay next to the house, nearly fetal with his clenched hands pillowing his head. The blacks inside had run him out again and now he didn't know what hour it was or day it had been or even where he lay. He would doze a little as sleep tried to close in on him, but always the fear he had of them kept his eyes opening and blinking him not to go to sleep, not here, where he feared they might cut his throat and lift the few bills he had and put him in the river for the turtles to feast on.

The underside of the house close to where he rested was strewn with broken beer bottles, odd lengths of pipe, here and there money fallen through cracks in the floor. A few feet away lay a dead cat, its bones showing through the rotten hide like yellow tusks. The old man heard feet walking on the wood above. A questioning voice raised a question. An answering voice answered it. An exclamation. Once in a while an angry word. And once in a while the electric strokes of a guitarist choking down a neck with fingers greased by skill, and there were no voices then.

He determined he would make it back inside and see what was

happening. If maybe there was anything to eat. He could see a dark cow in the dark pasture looking at him under the house and swinging her tail. He rolled himself over onto his belly and crawled out from under his hiding place. He had to beat the dirt off his clothes. It bounced out in large brown puffs. He thought there was a piece of a drink left somewhere.

He stumbled around in the back yard, which was littered with spare tires, grass grown up through the lug-bolt holes, with rotted wooden barrels sawn in half that had once held flowers. The back porch was of rough sawmill lumber and it leaned to the left. Screened in with rusty wire, patched with cotton thread. He lurched toward it feebly in the night. The cow raised her head and shook her horns, a gesture not lost on him. He'd already noted that the dogs didn't like him worth a damn.

There was his glass, left where he'd put it on the bottom step. He knelt and drank from it.

The lights were on low and now there were no unfriendly growls to make a man nervous. They had a movie going on the TV and VCR but the sound was low, too. It was warm and cozy and the girls were showing plenty of leg. Joe had the one named Debi in the corner, talking to her. Gary was alone in another chair in the corner, eyes shifting, drinking a tenth beer. It was four a.m.

Joe leaned over and poured another little shot of whiskey into her glass. "How late y'all stay open?" he said, then leaned over and kissed her again. She was a little chubby but marvelously assembled, no dog you couldn't take home to Mama. Her hair was blond on one side and brown on the other, just the reverse between her legs.

"Never past daylight. When me and you going back?"

"Hell, I can't do you no good."

"Since when?"

"Hell, I'm about too old to fuck. I wouldn't never get my money's worth."

"I'll give you your money's worth, baby."

She leaned around him and looked across the room. "How's your friend doing?"

"I think he's sobered up now. Goddamn, we been a long way today. He helped me find my dog."

She looked at him with a half smile.

"I'm surprised you even over here. You seen Duncan?"

"Naw, I ain't seen him. Why, he lookin for me?"

"I don't figure he is," she said.

He looked at the boy and saw him pretending to watch the movie, but saw each time he lifted the bottle to his lips the quick darting movement of his eyes toward the girls giggling and whispering on the couch. Three of them in their underwear, two fat, one skinny. Joe leaned toward the one he had his arm around.

"How'd you like to do me a favor?"

She smiled and gave him a kiss. "Sure."

He pointed with his drink.

"Break that boy in there."

She looked at the boy and then looked back at Joe. There was an amused little grin on her lips.

"Him?"

"Hell, he ain't never had none."

"How you know?"

Joe shook the ice in his glass and drank off the half inch of liquid that was there and sat up. He ran his fingers through his hair.

"Shit. I need to get my ass up and go on home. What time is it?"

"Little after four."

"A little after four."

"Yeah."

He set his glass on a table and leaned back on the couch. "Y'all got time to make it before daylight. Hell, it won't take him but a minute."

"How you know how long it'll take him?"

"Cause. I remember when I was fifteen. Go on and take him back."

She looked at the boy and shook her head doubtfully.

"I don't know," she said. "He looks mighty young. You sure he's fifteen?"

He reached in his pocket for a wad of money and peeled off a fifty and handed it to her. "Here," he said. "I need to get him home before daylight."

She looked at the money for a second, looked at the boy, then put the money in a little purse that was hanging on her wrist.

"Well, hell," she said. "What's his name again?"

"Gary."

She seemed to resign herself to it. "Gary. All right."

She got up and smoothed her chemise and her stockings and put her cigarette out. Joe saw the boy watching her. His face kept lifting as she got closer until finally she was standing over him and he was looking up at her. She put one hand on her hip and said something to him. He nodded and said something back. She sat on the arm of his chair and crossed her legs. Joe smiled to see that the boy couldn't take his eyes off her. She talked to him for a while and the boy kept nodding. She reached out and took his hand and pulled him up out of the chair. She started leading him out of the room, and he looked back at the bossman, his face terror-stricken, mute yet pleading, maybe for some words of instruction, explanation, until she pulled him out of sight.

He went down the hall with her tugging on his hand and followed her into a room with a parachute tacked to the ceiling. There was a lamp in the room and a bed and a chair and a bowl of water on the floor. The covers on the bed were rumpled, the pillows lumped together. She pushed him down on the bed and he sat there looking at her with wild eyes.

"You ain't never done this before, have you?" she said.

"Done what?"

She bent over him and he looked into the deep cleavage she had.

"This." Her mouth came down on his and then quickly pulled away. "Damn."

"What's the matter?" he said.

"Your breath is awful. Do you not ever brush your teeth?"

"Naw."

"Well, you need to."

He just looked at her. She opened a door at the back of the room and light spilled out over him. He rose up a little. He could see a mirror and a sink, and towels hanging from rings on the wall. She stepped into the room and started running the water, looking through drawers.

"Come in here," she said.

He got up and set his beer down and staggered into the bathroom. She held up a blue implement that was foreign to him, made of plastic and with white bristles. From a tube she squeezed a white paste onto it.

"Here," she said, and held it out to him. "Do me a favor and brush your teeth. I got some mouthwash, too. I ain't gonna fuck you if I can't even kiss you."

"What am I supposed to do with it?"

"You supposed to brush your teeth with it."

"Well, how you do it?"

She glared at him. "Shit, do you not know nothin? Here."

She showed him. He stood beside the sink with her, marveling at the foam that built over her lips. She turned the tap on and bent her head under the faucet and finally spat clear water into the sink and turned it off.

"Now here. I ain't got no germs, I don't reckon. I thought everybody knew how to brush their teeth. Where you been all your life?"

"Just around," he said.

"I'll be in here when you get through. Hurry it up."

She left him in the bathroom and shut the door behind her. He stood looking at himself in the mirror, holding the toothbrush in front of his mouth, puzzling over it. He put it in his mouth and touched his teeth with it. He turned the water on as she had done.

"Hurry up," she called, a muffled voice from beyond the door.

It felt strange and hard in his mouth. But he started brushing and it made his teeth feel good. So good that he kept on and on until she snatched the door open and stood there naked behind him. He turned with foam on his mouth, the handle of the toothbrush hanging slack.

"Well goddamn, are you coming on or what?" she said.

"I'm just brushin my teeth."

"Well, you done brushed em long enough. Come on and get it if you going to get it." She flounced her fine ass away and got on the bed, waiting for him.

He rinsed his mouth and turned off the water and put the toothbrush down. Looked at himself in the mirror and turned the water back on. He was still a little drunk and he wetted most of his face, rinsing his mouth out some more. When he had finished he shut off the water and looked at himself in the mirror again. In the mirror she lay behind him small on the bed, the dim lights showing her legs and stomach. Her red fingernails lay alongside her thigh. He cut off the light in the bathroom and went to her.

"Hey."

"Hey."

"I got em brushed."

"Well good. Now come on. Kiss me."

"Like that?"

"Naw. Open your mouth a little. Shit. Don't push so hard."

"I like that."

"Lay down with me. Just relax. You're nervous. Why don't you take your clothes off?"

"What for?"

She raised her head three inches off the pillow and stared at him. "What the hell you think I got mine off for?"

"Well, I didn't know."

She got up and threw the chemise over herself and found her cigarettes and lighter and lit one. Her face leaning to him in the lamplight was so young, so childlike and so smooth and so unwrinkled. She had a few freckles.

He reached over and got his beer and drank from it. He knew he was supposed to do something but he didn't know what it was. And what he was looking at between her legs was to him a strange and hairy puzzle.

She walked around the room for a while, smoking her cigarette, her arms folded.

"Take your clothes off," she said.

"We got to go in a little bit," he said.

"Shit." She went to the door and stuck her head out. "Joe!"

Gary lay on the bed and looked at her. She talked for a while with her head stuck out in the hall and then Joe leaned his head in.

"Boy, you all right?"

He waved his beer.

"I'm doin fine."

"Well, you better hurry up, now. We got to get you on home before long."

He heard her say something about giving him his fifty dollars back. There was some more arguing. After a while she shut the door and came back and sat down on the bed beside him.

"Listen," she said. "Do you want to do it or not?"

"Do what?" he said.

"Hell, boy, fuck. What do you think?"

He didn't know what to think. He had heard the word, from his daddy and Joe and the hands. Things were beginning to dawn on him.

"Shit," she said, and crawled down off the bed. "Take your pants off."

At first he thought she was going to hurt him and fought against her. He didn't want any teeth down there. But he understood soon and, like Joe said, he didn't last long.

When the light was turned on and Joe stuck his head back in, he was still lying back across the bed with his pants around his ankles. Debi was gone, had sought herself a darker nook.

"Boy, you all right?"

"Yessir, believe I am."

The boy walked up in the dust of the road and saw his mother standing in the yard, looking at him. The sun was high and she had a stick in her hand. He put his hands in his pockets and felt of the money there. He turned around and headed back the other way.

"You come here," she called after him.

"I'll be back in a minute."

"You come back here."

"In a minute."

"Now."

He didn't answer but walked around the curve of the trail out of sight of the house. Bees were buzzing in the patches of clover between some of the trees, and he looked back to see if anybody was following him. He looked to his pocket and brought the money out all wadded in his hand and started counting it as he walked. Money to him was something that was hard to make and hard to hold onto once it was made. But he enjoyed making it and he enjoyed saving it, and he began to look around for a good place to hide some more of it now that the work was over. The truck money was already hidden, but he never walked near it, would only walk there once more.

In front of the house the pines thinned away to scrub oak and bushes and sandy soil with scattered rocks. He looked back again and stepped off the trail, sighting on a big den tree where he'd seen coons leave in the evenings and return in the mornings, regular as bankers checking in and out of their offices. The woods were hot and dry and the leaves were noisy underfoot. He slowed down and stepped more carefully, as if he were stalking something. He had his first hangover and his head was not feeling good.

There was a creekbed that was nearly dry in the bottom of the hollow and he stepped across that and looked up at the coon den. A young one regarded him from his hole high in the tree, just his head poked out, then withdrew his face and was seen no more. The boy stood beside the tree, scanning the woods around him. He was tired from his night but he thought of the girl constantly, every second, never stopping. He had begun to feel a feeling for her that he could not describe even to himself.

When he had stood there for a minute or so, his eye picked out a small gray rock on a little hillside where pines had fallen long years ago and nature had weathered them down to their hard skeletal hearts. The rock lay among these lengths of prime kindling, and he walked over and knelt down beside it, looking back once to line up the den tree with his position. There was an old pay envelope in his pocket, and he pulled it out and put all the money in it except for one twenty-dollar bill. On both knees he scanned the woods around him, his eyes moving slowly, searching, noting particular trees and the clumps of honeysuckle and the matted nests of briers and the downed timber, listening for any sound there might be, but hearing nothing. When he had satisfied himself that he was alone, he carefully rolled the rock over and put the money beneath it and replaced it exactly as it had been for who knew how many years. There was a sudden feeling of eyes on him and he jerked his head up, both hands on the rock, but there was nothing, only the silent woods and the birds flitting through the tree limbs, the brief rattle of an Indian hen on a dead and acoustic trunk. His heart grieved with worry over the money, but the quiet woods lulled him with trust. He got up and moved away from the rock, careful not to disturb the leaves, and sighted back on it once more when he got to the den tree.

The rock sat in a bright patch of sunshine, streaked with pale veins and bearing small growths of velvety green moss. The sound of his steps receded through the woods and diminished, faded, was gone. The wind blew gently and the shadows wavered over the ground. The fallen pines lay around the rock, the woods warm, airy with light, flushed with sunshine.

After a time another noise appeared, a hushed step, a careful approach. The noise grew louder, a slow crunching of leaves underfoot, stealthy, heard only by one. A foot stopped beside the rock, an overall-clad knee came down to rest. A gnarled and shaking hand spread out over the rough warm face of the rock, trying to hold its secret there deep in the snakey woods.

The new pickup sat idling at the curb in front of the liquor store, and he came out of the door with three fifths of whiskey in his arms and got in it. He liked the way the new truck smelled. It had a V-8 with an automatic and the salesman had talked him into getting one with air conditioning. He was glad of it now. He rolled the window up and turned the air on. He had owned it for about an hour.

There was a new cooler in the floorboard with a case of Pabst iced down in it, and he shoved the top aside and got one out and put the top back on. The gas gauge was sitting close to empty but he figured he could make it to London Hill.

He met a sheriff's deputy not a mile out of town and looked in the rearview mirror to see if the deputy would hit his brakes. He did, briefly.

"Fuck you, sumbitch," he said, and turned his beer up. The truck had a good radio and he found a country music station and turned the volume up. George Jones was singing "He Stopped Loving Her Today." He sang along with George, at peace with the world. After another mile or two the black car appeared far down the road behind him, trailing him slowly.

"You motherfucker," he said. He watched it for a while and saw that it was slowly gaining. The blue lights were not flashing. He sped up a little, eyeing the gas gauge, muttering under his breath. He went into a curve, and once he got out of sight of the deputy's car and crested the hill, he drove onto another blacktop road that intersected Old Six, Camp Lake Stephens Road, pulling the wheel hard to the right and sliding the whiskey bottles across the seat. He mashed hard on the gas and drove to a small driveway about a hundred yards down the road and turned around. He sat there for thirty seconds and then roared back down the blacktop road. He pulled up to the highway and turned to the right again, then pulled out and took another drink of his beer.

He caught sight of the cruiser again within three more miles. The car in front of him slowed and he eased up behind it. He could see the deputy looking back at him through the rearview mirror. Joe waved to him but he wouldn't wave back.

He followed him down the road for another mile and the cruiser sped up and pulled off. It went out of sight up the highway around a curve. When he went past Manley Franklin's old store four miles later, it was pulled up on the other side of the building, facing the road, and it sped out after him, the blue lights flashing.

"I figured that shit," he said. He put on his blinker and pulled over on the shoulder and waited while the car eased up behind him. He dropped the empty beer bottle in the floor and lit a cigarette. The deputy took his time getting out. Joe rolled the window down and sat there.

The deputy walked up beside him, and he was a new man Joe didn't know, a stranger behind shiny sunglasses.

"Nice truck," the deputy said.

"Thanks."

"Noticed you ain't got a tag on it. You just get it?"

"About five minutes ago. I do something wrong?"

"Not that I know of."

"What'd you pull me over for then?"

The deputy rubbed his chin. He rested the knuckles of one hand on the butt of his gun. The leather holster creaked like a new saddle.

"How much have you drank?"

"I ain't drank nothing but one beer. I got three bottles of whiskey right here if you'd like to examine them."

"They told me you were a smartass."

"Who told you?"

"You think that was funny a while ago, trying to outrun me?"

"I wasn't trying to outrun you. I got off the highway and took a piss. Ain't no law against that, is it?"

He was a young man, with thin arms. The widest part of him was the belt and the gun around his waist. Joe pulled the gearshift down into drive and stepped on the brake.

"If you're through shootin the shit I'm ready to leave."

"I ain't through talking to you."

"I think you are."

He pulled off and left him standing there, reached in the cooler and got another beer. He watched through the rearview mirror as the deputy got back in his car and killed the blue lights. The car had not moved from beside the road by the time he lost it from view, and he didn't think about it or look back any more. Randy Travis was singing a song of love and heartbreak on the radio, and he was much more interested in that.

He pulled in at John's store and got out, took the gas cap off and locked the premium nozzle open so that it flowed slowly into the tank. He carried one of the fifths inside the store.

"Hey, John," he called.

He turned at a noise beside the door and the storekeeper was standing out there with his hand on the screen, looking at the pickup. He stepped inside, shaking his head.

"How about loaning me about ten thousand this afternoon?" he said.

Joe set the whiskey on the counter and pulled a wad of bills from his pocket, thumbing through them for a twenty. He pulled one out and put it beside the whiskey.

"I think I got a good deal on that one, John."

"It's pretty."

"Thanks."

"I like that color."

"I looked at a red one I started to get but I liked that one better. Come on and get in and we'll go for a ride."

He was just kidding, but the old man looked at his watch and said: "By God, I don't guess there's no reason I can't."

"Well hell, good, come on. Wait a minute."

He went out the door and released the lock on the nozzle and finished filling the tank, twenty dollars even. When he stepped back inside, the old man had put his money inside a bank bag and was holding his pistol and a couple of cigars taken from a box on the counter, and was standing there with another cigar in his mouth and the whiskey in his pocket.

"Twenty even, John."

The storekeeper nodded and said, "Let's hurry up and get out of here before somebody comes by."

"You taking that pistol with you?"

"Hell yes. I got about sixty thousand dollars in here."

"Damn. You got another gun I can borrow?"

"This one'll do."

Joe held the screen door open for him, then opened the door of the truck so he could pile his things on the seat. John Coleman walked back to the store on nimble feet, wearing socks and sandals. He locked the door and slammed it shut and started out to the truck but went back and unlocked it and reached in and cut off the power to the gas pumps and then locked it again. A car came down the road, slowing down hurriedly, swinging in.

"It never fails," he said, from where he stood beside the truck just about to climb in. He lifted the lid on the cooler and looked inside. "Lord have mercy, boy," he said. He looked up at Joe. "Let's go. Quick."

They got in and Joe pulled the shift down into drive.

"You don't want to wait on this guy?"

"Hell naw, don't wait on him."

But the driver of the car had already gotten out and was walking over to the truck. He had long black hair, a dirty T-shirt, and very greasy hands. He wiped his nose and leaned in the window of the truck. Joe noticed how close his hands were getting to the uphol-stery of his nice new nice-smelling truck.

"Mr. Coleman? How bout opening up for me?" he said. He shook his head and looked around inside the truck.

"I'm going somewhere," John said. "I'll be back after while."

"You ready, John?" Joe said.

"Yeah," John said. "I'm ready."

"I need to get a few things, Mr. Coleman," the man said, but Joe let off the brake and the truck moved. The man grabbed the outside mirror, printed the chrome with grease, and said, "Now wait a minute."

Joe put the brake on and shoved the shift into park.

"Let's go, Joe," the old man said. "Hell, he don't want to do nothing but charge something." He bent over and reached inside the cooler for a beer, and Joe saw something cross the black-haired man's face at the sight of the back of John Coleman's head.

"You better get them greasy goddamn fingers off my truck, boy," Joe said.

He acted as if he didn't even hear that, just kept holding onto the mirror and looking at John.

"All I want's five dollars worth of gas, Mr. Coleman. My wife told me she'd get paid next week, I promise you."

John Coleman leaned back in the seat and twisted off the top and turned the bottle of beer straight up in the middle of London Hill and took a good hit. He opened a bottle of the whiskey on the seat and did it the same way, then wiped his mouth. He didn't look at the man outside the truck when he spoke.

"You done promised me about twenty times. You ain't paid me nothing in three months and you just wasting your breath. Let's go, Joe."

The greasy hands went to the inside of the door as if to hold them from leaving, and Joe opened his door and walked around the back and right up to him.

"You get them hands off my truck."

The guy turned to him, looked him up and down.

"Fuck you," he said. "Who in the fuck are you?"

Joe didn't hit him but one time. The pickup wheels spun sand and gravel on him where he lay in front of the pumps.

They rode and drank. Joe sucked a cut knuckle and wished for his dog to lick it. John Coleman agreed that it would help.

"That boy," he said. "I've done him ever favor I could. Some folks you can't do nothing with. Just sorry. God knows I've done plenty of drinking and stuff in my time, but I be damn if I ever tried to cheat anybody out of any money."

It was late afternoon by then and they had the windows rolled down, the music turned down so they could talk. It surprised Joe that John Coleman would hear a song he recognized and, once in a while, turn the radio up, then turn it back down when the song was over. There were horses in pastures and hawks with their wings folded sitting high in the trees. One redtail hunted low over an overgrown field they passed, the land fallow, thick with cockleburs. It floated along, turning, rising, passing again, wings flapping for a thermal.

"I'm glad they protected them hawks," John said.

"I sure like to watch em."

The sun waned and drew down between the clouds and put the land in a soft light, cooled the air. The hair riffled on their forearms where they held their elbows on the doors. They saw dead snakes here and there. Flattened rabbits and marsupials, awkward buzzards lifting from carcasses on long and laboring wings.

"You ever hear that thing about a possum having a forked dick?" said Joe.

"A possum breeds through his nose."

"I've heard if you put a split in one's tail and stick a stick through it and put him in the river, he'll just go around in circles till he sinks."

They stopped on the Lynch Creek bridge to take a leak and stood there drinking their beers while they pissed. John Coleman had a dick like a horse.

"Are y'all through working, Joe?"

"Yessir. We're finished for this year, I reckon. I could have made a lot more money if it hadn't rained so much."

They got back in and the black car was there suddenly, lights revolving, the door opening almost before it came to a stop.

"Well, I will be goddamn," Joe said. He'd started to pull off but he slammed on the brake and put the gearshift up in park and got out. He walked to the back of the truck. The deputy was mad, his chest heaving. He strangled something out and Joe said, "What?"

He looked back at John through the rear glass. All he saw was the back of his head.

"You been riding around drinking ever since I saw you?" the deputy said.

He saw then what was going on, loss of pride, the simple stupidity of youth, the weight of the badge. But he still wouldn't let anybody mess with him, he didn't care who. And he was drinking.

The deputy held out a little contraption made of plastic and metal.

"You want to breathe in this?"

"Naw, I don't want to breathe in that."

He turned around and got back in his truck and asked John Coleman if he was ready for another beer. The deputy walked up beside the truck and held out the little thing. He had one hand on his gun.

"Are you gonna breathe in this or not?"

Joe didn't answer him. He pulled it into gear and mashed on the gas, being careful not to sling any gravel. The deputy stood in the road behind him growing smaller.

"I bet I pissed him off that time," he said.

John didn't answer. He was tracking the cruiser behind them in the fingerprinted mirror. The siren came on. Joe kept driving. They met several cars that nearly pulled over to the shoulders of the road but then went on past, the necks of the drivers craning to see. The car swung out behind him and came alongside. The deputy was motioning toward the ditch with his finger. He kept driving.

"What's the deal?" John said.

The car sped up and turned crossways in the road ahead of him, and Joe came to a stop this side of it. There wasn't any place to turn around. He put it up in reverse and hit the gas when he saw the deputy come out with his hand on his gun. He leaned out the window looking backwards and got it up to about forty, the rear end's high-speeded whining reminding him he'd never make it.

John Coleman sat sipping his whiskey and his beer. After a little bit he said, "I think he's gonna catch us."

Joe slammed on the brakes and the cruiser shot past, slewed sideways in the road with the tires barking. He started to take off again, keep him going like a runner between bases for a while, then said no.

He got out. He put his hands on the hood. The deputy walked up.

"I ain't done a goddamn thing," Joe said. "I ain't drunk. You better look for somebody else to mess with cause I ain't done nothing. You keep messing around with me and I'm gonna hurt you."

"Turn around," the deputy said. "Put your hands behind your back."

"You been watching too many goddamn TV shows, son."

The deputy came close with the cuffs in his hand.

Joe caught him by the neck and pushed him against the hood of the truck and got the pistol away from him without a shot being fired. All the while the boy's eyes watched him with a deep and maddened rage. Joe tossed the gun underhanded, lightly, saw it land in a clump of sagegrass on the other side of the ditch.

"I guess if I drive off now you're gonna get a shotgun out of the back and shoot my ass, ain't you?" he told him.

The deputy wouldn't say. They drove off and left him and he didn't follow them any more. Joe could see him in the rearview mirror, looking for the gun.

*

Later that night an unmarked Ford, a new dark blue one, was sitting beside his driveway, idling, when he pulled up. The sheriff himself. He stopped in the road for a moment and looked at the car and all it represented. Then he turned and pulled into his yard and killed the motor and got out and put the keys in his pocket. He was only a little drunk.

The sheriff had the window down and he was listening to country music on the radio. He turned the volume down and shook his head when Joe walked up beside his car.

"Get out and come on in, Earl," he said.

The sheriff picked up the microphone and spoke into it for a few moments and then he shut the car off. He opened the door and got out.

"You still got that badass dog?"

"Yeah, he's around here somewhere. Hold on a minute."

He walked across the yard and the dog came out from under the house. He caught him by the collar and pulled him over to the corner of the foundation and hooked him to a chain. Then they went in.

"I'd offer you a drink if I thought you'd take one," Joe said.

"I'll drink a Coke if you've got one."

"I've got one." He took it out of the icebox and handed it to him. "Have a seat. I'm gonna fix me a drink."

The sheriff settled himself on the couch and crossed his legs.

"How's your kids doing, Joe?"

"They all right, I guess."

"I heard you had a new grandbaby."

"Yeah. A boy. They didn't name him after me."

He finished mixing his drink and took it over to the table and pulled out a chair and sat down, lit a cigarette.

"All your kids about grown now, too, ain't they?"

"Yeah. One in college. The other one starts this fall. I reckon Johnny's thinking about getting married. I wish he'd wait. Get his degree."

"What's he going into, law enforcement?"

"Yeah."

"You got a new man working for you now, don't you?"

"Yeah I do," the sheriff said, and shook his head. He took a sip of his drink and waited a little, scratched the back of his hand. "I talked to the judge about you for a while the other day. He came to see me."

Joe picked up his drink and sloshed the ice around in the glass and took a good drink of it. "That fat sumbitch. What'd he 'low?"

"Well, I'll tell you. He 'lowed he was about tired of looking at you standing in front of him."

"Probation?"

"Aw naw. Hell naw. I had a little talk with my new man a while ago, too. I'm gonna let him shuffle some papers for a while. He was pretty hot. I asked him a few questions and pretty much figured everything out. He's a little gung ho, is all. A little overeager."

"Yeah, a little," Joe said.

"But he ain't what I'm worried about. Me and you been knowing each other a long time. I know how you are. He don't. He just made a mistake."

"He was just out looking for somebody to fuck with." The

sheriff looked at him for a few long slow seconds, and reached for cigarettes that were no longer in his pocket.

"Let me just ask you a question, Joe. Do you really want to go back to the goddamn penitentiary?"

He thought about it, shook his head. But he didn't answer.

"You can't go in people's houses and kill their dogs. It don't matter what else is going on. You can't fistfight with the Highway Patrol. Judge Foster won't put up with it. He don't have to put up with it. It's why they build prisons. He's wanting to give you three years with no parole for assault on a police officer. And I don't know if I can talk him out of it. He was mad as hell. And maybe I don't even need to talk him out of it."

The silence ticked by. They looked at each other in the little room and neither spoke for a while. The sheriff got off the couch and walked to the table and shook a cigarette out of the pack lying there and lit it.

"Now you done got me back smoking," he said. "Damn it. I been quit three weeks."

"I quit trying to quit. They's two cartons on top of the icebox if you want a pack."

The sheriff muttered something and walked over there and got a pack.

"There's some matches in the drawer."

The sheriff opened the drawer and got a box of them.

He pulled out a chair and sat down at the table beside him. Joe thought he looked old and tired. His hair was thinning, turning gray.

"How long you figure you and Willie Russell can keep shooting at one another before one of you winds up dead?"

Joe chuckled and picked up his drink.

"That bastard," he said. "Somebody ought to do the world a favor."

"I'm trying to do you one. You were thirty-five when you went to the pen the first time. What are you now, forty-two?"

"Forty-three. Fixing to be forty-four."

"You getting old, Joe. I ain't never mistreated you, have I? Tell the truth."

"Naw, you ain't, Earl. You've stuck up for me when you could."

"I used to be as wild as you."

"At one time you were worse."

"I can't tell you how to live. I ain't trying to. Charlotte never could do anything with you, it ain't no use in me trying. I've talked to her, too."

"I don't need you talking to her for me."

"She called me. I'm the sheriff. I had to go see her. She pays taxes in this county just like everybody else. She's got a right to talk to me. It ain't never too late till you're dead."

He didn't move, just looked at the cigarette smoking between his fingers, the brown nicotine stains.

"I been around for a while. I ain't dead yet."

The sheriff got up and clapped him softly on the shoulder, a reassuring pat between former friends.

"I'll see you, Joe. I hope you'll think about what I said."

Joe sat there while the lawman went out, while he went down the steps and started across the yard.

"Come back any time," he called out through the screen door, but the only answer was the car cranking and a brief squeal from a rear tire, the sound of the car rocketing down the road until it faded from hearing. The dog whined and he went out and unsnapped him from the chain.

There was no traffic on the road. The night lay hot and humid around him, and he considered going to town. Connie was gone, her clothes taken, only a broken comb left behind with a scribbled note he didn't bother to read. It was easier without her. He didn't have to listen to anything. But she'd made the bed feel better.

He went inside and changed his shirt and left again. The truck had plenty of gas left in it but he didn't want to go to town.

He backed out into the road and headed west, toward Paris and the Crocker Woods and the Big W, where there were dirt roads and big deer green-eyed in the night and no lawmen patrolling the old blacktopped roads. He got a beer from the cooler and opened it and rolled the window down and stuck his arm out. There was good music on the radio. The dark trees enveloped the road in a canopy of lush growth, and the headlights cut a bright swath through the night, exposing wandering possums, frozen rabbits, huge brown owls swooping low across the ditches.

He drove down from the hills and leveled out in the bottom where the young crops stood dark in their ordered rows and the smells of the night came fresh and welcome on the warm air.

He thought of the time the three blacks had hemmed him up and how someone had let them do it because his attitude was not good. Two of them were in for murder, but that didn't scare him and he didn't particularly respect that. Killings were different in that some were matters of honor and others simple acts of meanness committed during robberies against helpless victims and he didn't respect that. They came at him all at once and he broke one of the men's head against the side of a bunk and left the other two bleeding on the floor and kicked them a little as he talked to them and explained things and then fell on in line with the others in time for supper. That was the last time anybody messed with him. He'd done the rest of his time without incident.

It would be different now. He probably wouldn't know anybody in there, didn't want to know anybody in there. He hadn't made friends in there. He'd kept to himself and neither loaned nor borrowed. He didn't box. He read, slept, worked out with weights. He looked down now at the round ball of his stomach stretching the bottom of his shirt tight. But he couldn't argue with the man if he wanted to give him three years. And David Carson might not be so lucky this time. There was the matter of the dead Doberman. They'd have Duncan in court to testify, maybe. Duncan might listen to reason for enough money, or the right threat, or both. He smiled to himself, thinking of the look on the boy's face that night with the girl.

The figure struggling up out of the tunnels of night was overalled and walking like a person about to fall, his arms waving with some vague cadence and his legs slowly moving him along, the boy's daddy. Joe slowed and involuntarily moved the truck over when he turned and looked at what was coming toward him, as the old man cocked first a thumb and then moved toward the vehicle in an incoming rush with his arms out so that Joe had to wrench the wheel violently to keep from hitting him. He swept past him and slowed down even more, the figure in the brakelights' red glare receding behind him in the rearview mirror.

He drove very slowly and thought about walking home drunk in the dark for no telling how long and he wondered how it would be to be in that place.

He went another mile and then pulled into a driveway and turned around and went back up the road. The old man was about where he thought he'd be, plodding along with his head down and his arms swinging. He pulled across the road and slowed more and then stopped in front of him, the window down, his arm hanging out. The old man came closer, his steps heavy in the roadside grass, the crickets talking, a dead snake flattened in the road there in front of him. He walked beside the pickup window and never turned his head or gave any indication of anything and kept on walking and walked on past and Joe turned his head to see him growing darker as he stepped beyond the glare of the taillights. He knew he should let it go at that.

He went on up the road and threw the beer can into a ditch and got another one and smoked a cigarette. He hadn't been up around the old place where they lived in a long time, but there had been a time when seven coveys of birds could be stalked and shot at, a long time ago when he had good dogs, when the kids were little, before most of his troubles. There were Saturday afternoons when he could put the two dogs in the trunk and take his automatic and walk the fields in the stiff winter breeze and be one with the dogs, his eye steady on the barrel, the birds exploding from the cover on their dynamite wings, the brace, the shock of the shot, the birds dropping neatly, folding, the dogs already starting to move toward them. A long time ago, days he'd almost forgotten about. The house was in bad shape even then, the logs sagging in the middle and the vines climbing up their sides. It had been deserted for who knew how many years and was probably older than anybody he knew or had ever known. He couldn't imagine them living in it.

He thought about the boy's daddy taking the boy's money. A sorry motherfucker indeed.

He turned around in a churchyard and drove back down the road and turned the radio off. Wade was still going down the road when he pulled up beside him and stopped. The door opened immediately and he got in and placed his feet around the cooler and reached in nearly instantly and got himself a beer.

"Help yourself," Joe told him.

"Goddamn, I thought nobody never would stop."

"I tried to while ago and you just walked on past me. What are you doing out walking?"

"Well, I been flyin but my arms got tired. Damn that beer's good and cold. Can you take me home?"

"I don't know. I don't know if I can get up in there or not."

"Aw yeah, you can get up in there. Willie and them brought me home the other night."

"Willie?"

"Yeah. Willie and Flo. Aw, the sumbitches had been drunk, up at Memphis. Went up there and they had a bunch of money and they got off with some of them old stripper girls and went to this hotel in West Memphis, Willie said this old girl'd been rubbing his dick and everything so he said what the hell I'll fuck this son of a bitch, she went over there in the bathroom to do something and he passed out watching the television, come to she was going out the door, well, he jumped out of the bed and run grabbed her, had all her clothes on. Well, naturally she kicked him in the balls first thing and he grabbed her leg going out the door and she started in kicking him, him laying there hollering you mother-fucker and then she started slugging him with her damn purse in the head and liked to knocked him out again, so he grabbed her goddamn pants and pulled em off and said she took off out across the parking lot in her panties and he said she had a fine ass. Well, there was another son of a bitch in there he said done fucked and sucked everything in sight and she was passed out in the bed. Well, he said the old girl with his money was try-ing to get into a car out there and leave and his balls was about to kill him, so he runs out butt naked and she's cutting the top out of a convertible with a fingernail file and he just knocks the cold shit out of her with his fist and grabs her purse. The damn cops get there and one of em sticks a goddamn pistol right in his ear and says I'd love to see you breathe, and them cocksuckers take em to jail and it costs em twenty-four hundred dollars and he didn't even get a blowjob. I may go up there with em next weekend."

He turned his beer up and drained it with his throat pumping and rolled the window down and threw the can and puked down the outside of the door and rolled the window back up and got another beer. He opened it and started drinking it.

"Where you been?" Joe said.

"Over at some niggers'. They wouldn't give me no pussy. Black motherfuckin son of a bitches. Damn dog bit me."

He reached down and pulled up the leg of his overalls and ex-amined a wound there and let it fall back down over his wet shoes.

Joe could smell him, an odor of old sweat and puke and garbage. He turned the vent so that fresh air would blow in.

"Y'all still living up yonder where you were?"

"Yeah. We got it fixed up pretty good now. I won some money and bought some furniture. One of my girls run off, I reckon."

"One of your girls? How many girls you got?"

"I had about five at one time. I had three boys. Two of em's dead."

He never had heard the boy mention that. Or five sisters either. He guessed there were a lot of things about him he didn't know. Never would know. And might be better off not knowing.

"Aw, goddamn, she had to smartmouth everything I said. I got in a goddamn fistfight with her a while back. She stole some money from her mama and I tried to whip her ass and she picked up a goddamn board there bout long as your leg and hit me with it. I told her to get her ass out and she left. I don't know where she's at. Don't care, neither."

"How old's she?"

"Hell, I don't know. Seventeen or eighteen, I guess. You ain't got a bottle of schnapps in that cooler nowhere, have you?"

"Naw."

He was surprised that the old man had cigarettes, but he did, and his own lighter, and there was a bottle of something in a paper sack in his hip pocket, resting against the seat. They drove down through the bottom, and past the fields, and the cows stood behind fences or lay scattered over the pastureland in dark forms like black boulders against the emerald grass. He ran over a couple of snakes, lining the left front tire up with their heads and hearing the little pops when their heads exploded. Frantically writhing loops lashing the warm asphalt, left behind unseen in his wake.

"Your boy's a good worker," he said, finally.

"He'll probably grow up to be a smartass, too. That's the hardest fuckin work I ever done in my life."

"Give me one of them beers out of there," Joe said. "How many's in there?"

"I don't know," he said. He had his hand down in the cooler sloshing around. "How bout turning on the light?"

Joe reached up and turned the cab light on. The old man had a long scabbed cut down his jaw. Blood was caked on his chin. One sleeve of his shirt was torn nearly off.

"They's five or six in here, feels like."

"Well, hand me one."

The old man passed it over and put the top back on the cooler and reached for the bottle in his pocket. He opened it and Joe turned off the light and watched him out the corner of his eye turn the bottle up and pull steadily on it for a few seconds. He pulled it down and he heard his lungs rattle.

"Gadammmmmmmmmmm," he said.

"What are you drinking?"

"Damn if I know what it is. I thought it was schnapps when I bought it."

"Let me see it."

"I don't know what it is."

"Let me look at it."

He turned the light on again and the old man handed him the bottle. He looked at the label. It was a pint of Ron Rico 151.

"Goddamn," he said, and handed it back. "You could take a match and set that shit on fire."

"I believe you could."

He decided to drive down by the dirt road and see how far up it he could get. It was fairly dry now but he knew he'd never make it all the way. He turned off the highway and eased up the gravel road. The gravel was sparse and the fences were in bad shape. Small flash floods had swept over the road and it was rutted and washboarded. He hated to have his new truck on it. He went across a battered wooden bridge, and it creaked and moaned as he eased the weight of the truck over it. He looked down into the dark water where reptiles and amphibians lay unseen and where the coons walked and fed and listened for the hounds and lived their nocturnal lives.

"I heard that boy was going to buy that old truck off you," the old man said.

Joe glanced at him.

"Yeah. I reckon he is. I meant to get him today and help me bring it home but I never did get around to it."

"Where's it at?"

"Up at Oxford. Out there at Rebel."

"You gonna finance it for him?"

"He said he had the cash."

The old man was silent for a moment. A possum froze by the weeds and then trotted across the gravel with its tail high and went into a ditch and disappeared.

"I doubt if he's got enough money to buy a truck."

"He made plenty this spring. I think he saved a good bit. He supported your ass, didn't he?"

"I don't owe him *shit!*" the old man said, and Joe stopped the truck.

"What you stopping for? It's still a ways up there."

"This is far as I'm going. I'm turning around right here."

"Hell. Take me on up the road. I don't want to walk."

"Tough shit," Joe told him. He put it up in parking gear and looked at him. "That boy saved his money for a couple of months to buy that old truck. And let me tell you something. It's his. I could give a shit whether he pays me the money or not. I piss away that much gambling in one night. But he wants that truck. And if I find out something's happened to his money, I'm going to whip whoever's ass had something to do with it. Now get out. Before I knock your ass out."

The old man was silent. He opened the door and got out and shut it. He walked to the front of the truck and stood illuminated in the headlights, blinking like some huge grounded owl. He went on up the gravel road drinking the beer, stopping to look back once in a while, the wet legs of his overalls flopping around his legs. Joe watched him through the windshield, fading back into the darkness he had come out of, walking along with his head down like some draft animal strapped into a lifetime of hard work with no choice but to keep walking a row. The new truck hummed with precision, the clean dashboard, the bright dials and gauges. The wind lifted and moved a few strands of Joe's hair. He kept sitting there.

"You sorry son of a bitch," he said.

There was a dim light showing inside Henry's house and one vehicle was parked in the yard, an old Pontiac Tempest. The cotton around the house was small and stunted and the whole place looked as though it had settled into an era of decay. He pushed the headlights off and sat with the parking lights on for several minutes but nobody came to the door. He was a little drunker now and he wanted to gamble. Most of the beer was gone but there was some whiskey under the seat. He lit a cigarette and pushed off the parking lights and killed the engine. Henry didn't have a dog. With the house so close to the road, his dogs kept getting run over. He got out and went across the yard and mounted the steps and knocked lightly on the door. No sound came from within, only the soft murmur of a radio playing. He opened the screen door and stuck his head in.

"Henry. Hey, Henry."

No answer. All asleep?

He stepped into the hall and opened the door on the right. The room was dark and unoccupied. The door on the left was closed and he knocked gently before he opened it. A wan blue light from a silent television screen filled with snow cast the room in a shadowy glow, a vague inconsistent light where sleeping figures sprawled. There was an old army cot against one wall and Henry was piled up in it naked but for his underwear, his arm over his face. Stacy was in a battered recliner with a quilt thrown over him, his head back, eyes closed, mouth wide open. And George, the blind brother, sat in a straightback wooden chair with the 9MM in his hand and a dead woman at his feet, whose blood had come out of her body and made a dark rug on the floor around her. He held the pistol in one hand and a glass of something in the other. His hair was white, shaggy, disordered. The radio played country tunes softly.

He said one word: "Joe?"

But his visitor had no wish to be verified, and he did not answer. He let himself out as quietly as he had let himself in and got back in his truck and drove home through the black night, into oak hollows, past standing deer with eyes like bright green jewels, who raised their ears and stared as he passed by them and beyond.

There was a knock on the door the next morning and it took him a moment to realize and remember what he had seen, the milky blue opaque eyes dead and lifeless and unblinking and the woman undeniably dead, too, so still, so quiet.

He lay in the bed with the sheets twisted over him and stared at the ceiling until the knock came again. He looked at his watch and saw that it was nearly seven. Probably the boy.

His pants were lying on the floor and he got up and yelled that he was coming, then stepped into them and found his cigarettes and lit one and went up the hall to the kitchen and crossed to the door with just a little irritation toward the boy for waking him up so early. He unlocked it and swung it open and there stood Charlotte in her uniform, the dog fawning over her like a puppy.

"Well," he said. "Surprise, surprise."

She looked up at him and smiled that little smile. Then she stopped smiling.

"I ain't coming in if there's a woman here," she said. He stepped back from the door.

"Come on in. Ain't nobody here but me and the dog."

She came in and he closed the door behind her, wishing he'd combed his hair, and wanting the house to be a little cleaner. He saw her looking at the mess, clothes piled up, dirty socks on the floor. His muddy boots sitting in the kitchen, empty cans on the table.

"I didn't know if he'd remember me," she said.

"Shit. Him? Get you a chair and sit down. Let me go comb my hair. Why don't you make us some coffee? It's up there in the cabinet. I'll be right back."

"Okay. I can't stay but a little bit."

He went back to his bedroom and put on some clean blue jeans and a white shirt that he buttoned halfway up. He combed his hair and brushed his lower teeth and his denture, her asking him things, saying yeah or naw until he finished. When he went back into the living room she was sitting on the couch and she had folded some of the clothes.

"Don't worry about that stuff," he said. "I'll get it later. You put the water on?"

"Yeah."

He busied himself picking up cans on the table, pouring what was left in some of them down the drain, putting the cans in the overflowing garbage can inside the broom closet. He looked at her and she looked awfully good to him. She'd fixed her hair differently, and she'd gained a little weight.

"You look good, baby," he said.

"You don't."

"Well hell, I just woke up. What's the occasion?" She looked down at her fingers and moved a little ring with a red stone in it. She looked back up and she looked uncomfortable.

"I just wondered were you going to see the baby. He's been home for a couple of weeks now. Theresa would like for you to come see him." She waited a moment. "And I'd like for you to come see him. If you want to. I think he looks like you."

Years ago she would have broken and started crying. But that vulnerability in her eyes was gone now, all that cheerful hope. She was forty-seven now.

"I forgot your birthday," he said, and got down two cups from the cabinet, set out the sugar, got milk from the icebox.

"I don't want no coffee, Joe. I've got to get on to work anyway."

He got the coffee pot and poured two cups of water and then looked over his shoulder at her.

"Hell, you don't have to go to work till nine, do you? You got time to drink a cup of coffee I know."

He fixed it for her and carried it to her and retreated back to the kitchen table so that there was at least a barrier of distance between them. He didn't know what kind of thoughts she had about him now.

"Thanks," she said. She pulled out her cigarettes and he got up and got her an ashtray.

"I thought you quit," he said.

"I've cut way down. I don't know if I could quit completely. Working up there helps. We can't smoke inside the building any more. I don't smoke but five or six a day. I feel a lot better."

"You gained a little weight."

"A little."

"It looks good on you."

She didn't answer. For a while they sat in uneasy silence.

"I shouldn't have come over," she said. "I didn't call first. I didn't see no other vehicle outside. When did you get that new truck?"

"Yesterday."

"I like it."

"I do, too."

She smoked nervously, like someone who didn't know how to. After the first sip she didn't touch her coffee again, just set it back on the small table out of the way.

"He's got black hair."

"Oh. The baby."

"Who'd you think I was talking about?"

"I didn't know."

"Are you going to go see him? He's your grandson. It looks like you'd want to. He's cute as he can be."

He picked up his cigarette from the ashtray and sipped his coffee.

"Last time I saw Theresa she wasn't too happy with me."

"That don't mean she don't want you to see your grandson, for God's sake."

"I'd rather see the little fucker that got her pregnant. I'd still like to have a talk with him."

"And do what? Randy's done had a talk with him. That was bad enough. My God. It's a wonder I wasn't pregnant when we got married. You ain't forgot what it's like to be young that quick, have you?"

He didn't answer any of that. He sipped his coffee and looked out into the back yard, smoking his cigarette.

"All she wants is for you to go over sometime and see him."

"Well. I didn't know if she wanted me to or not. I didn't want to be in the way or nothing. Is she doing all right?"

"She's doing fine. She's going back to school to get her GED and then she's going to start out at Ole Miss part-time and work part-time."

"Who's gonna keep the baby?"

"Mama and Miss Inez. I'll keep him at night if she needs me to. I don't never go anywhere."

"You want some more coffee?"

"No."

"Well." He got up and fixed another one for himself, scratching his arm where the lead itched sometimes. He'd thought about seeing if he could have it taken out. He wondered if she'd heard about that.

"Are y'all working now?" she said.

"Naw. We through."

"How'd you do?"

"We did good. For all the bad weather we had."

"I guess you paid cash for the truck."

"Yep. That's usually the easiest." He stood at the sink with a fresh cigarette between his fingers, looking at the floor. "We've got plenty to do this winter. I got enough left to tide me over for once."

"If you don't lose it."

"I don't bet nothing but what I can afford to lose."

"You used to not worry about it."

"I'm more careful now. I don't bet the grocery money no more."

"That's nice to know after all them baloney sandwiches we used to eat."

"I had to eat em, too."

"Yeah. And the kids did, too."

The words seemed to hang in the air for a moment and he saw that she regretted them. After having to monitor him for so long it was a hard habit for her to break, he guessed. She looked at the door.

"I didn't come over here for this," she said.

"What did you come over here for, then?"

She got up from the couch and picked up her purse.

It had a long strap and she put it over her shoulder.

"I just wanted to tell you to come see that baby. Theresa ain't mad at you. She's just hurt because you ain't been over. We don't ask much no more."

"That's all you come over for?"

She turned her eyes to his face and said: "Not quite."

"You need some money?"

"No."

"What, then?"

She waited a long moment and then she walked to him, taking the coffee from his hand, undoing the top button of her blouse. He put his hand in there and touched her.

"You sure we ought to be doing this? We ain't married, you know."

He was smiling but she wasn't.

"I need it," she said.

"Okay."

He took her hand and led her down the hall.

T he boy woke in the hot sunshiny hush of the old house and opened his eyes and looked upon his chest to see money piled there, looking as if it had just come out of a washing machine, all crinkled and twisted and per-verted and jumbled into a wondrous pile of twenties and fifties and ones and fives.

He looked at it, with the happiness slowly growing on his face, and his hands moved up from his sides and captured it, lifting it above him, releasing it little by little, the crushed bills dropping and fluttering, caressing his face, brushing his eyelids, rustling softly in the air, like leaves in the fall that slip and twist and turn, dancing to the earth, dying in the light.

He was squatting on his haunches in the side yard painting a metal chair when the bossman came around a curve in the road, whistling, and put up his hand and waved. He'd been sitting there painting and thinking about the girl and thinking about going back to see her after he got the truck. He was the only one at home and he didn't know where the rest of them were. All their missions were of a certain furtive nature, like those of dope smugglers or bank robbers.

"Hey," he said loudly, and dipped his brush. He'd found the chairs at the dump and they were perfectly good, just rusted a little, and John Coleman had given him a small can of black paint and a tiny brush when he'd told him of his needs.

Joe walked up in the yard, stepping around the briers, looking in the grass for snakes. He was dressed as if he were ready for a dance or something, clean blue jeans and pale Tony Lama boots and a red striped shirt.

"So this is it, huh?" he said, and the boy grinned and kept painting.

"This is it. I'm painting me some chairs."

"I see that. Got em looking pretty good, too."

His friend squatted next to him and pulled out his smokes, looking all around.

"Damn, I ain't been up here in years. They ain't no telling how old that house is. Was that old tricycle still in there?"

"Yeah."

"Is it still in there?"

"Naw. Daddy sold it to somebody for a antique."

Joe smiled and sat down and leaned back, then stretched out on the grass and lit his cigarette.

"I got me some cigarettes inside," the boy said. He put the paintbrush on the lid of the can and got up. "Let me go in here and get em and I'll smoke one with you. You want a Dr. Pepper? But we ain't got no ice. We run out last night."

Joe held up a hand. "I'll pass. Here, smoke one of mine."

He was already headed in, going up the steps. After he got inside he poked his head out a paneless window and grinned again and said, "It ain't no need in me smoking yours when I got some in here. I just keep em hid so Daddy won't smoke em all up." He drew his head back in.

From where he lay Joe could see under the house and could see the sandstone foundation, the logs resting on strategic rocks maybe chipped flat by some pioneer with high boots and a muslin shirt. The logs had long cracks and they were huge and they bore on their sides many axe marks where the round sides had been hewed away. He couldn't imagine the weight of them, of how men had lifted them and put them into place, master builders turned to dust by now.

The boy came back out and sat down beside him and carefully pulled a cigarette from his pack and lit it with a gopher match, shaking the match out and taking a drag with his eyes closed. He smiled again.

"What you in such a good mood about today?" Joe said.

"I don't know. I just am. When we gonna go see them old girls again?"

"What old girls?"

"The ones we saw other night."

"Oh. Them? Boy, you better leave that old gal alone. She's liable to hurt you."

"Hurt me?"

"Hell yeah. She might squeeze you in two with them legs she's got. What are you doing today, anything?"

"Naw, I ain't doing nothing. You need me to help you?" The bossman sat up and crossed his legs.

"I thought we might go get that old pickup if you wanted to. I need to get it off their lot. I thought I'd drive you up there and you could drive it back home. You can drive it, can't you?"

"Sure," he said. He got up immediately and put the lid on the paint can. "Let's get out of here before they come back."

"Who? Your daddy and them?"

"Yeah."

"Where they at?"

"I don't know. I guess they left sometime last night. They was all gone when I got up this morning."

"What? They just take off and don't tell you where they going?"

"Yeah. It's always been like that."

Joe sat there for a moment longer and then he looked at the boy.

"I talked to your daddy a little while the other night. He said one of your sisters run off. Is that right?"

Gary was wiping the brush on a nearby pine tree. He nodded and stuck his cigarette in his mouth.

"Yeah. Fay took off. Shit, she's been gone for a good while."

"Where'd she go to, reckon?"

"No telling."

"Y'all didn't go look for her?"

"Naw."

"Why not?"

He gave Joe a little smile, lifted his shoulders in a small gesture of fatalism.

"I don't know."

He sat looking at the boy, watched him while he poured a little gas from a jug into a jar and put the brush in it and swished it around.

"She got mad at Daddy," he said. "She didn't like this place. Thought we's gonna get in trouble staying here. You the first one that's come around."

"What y'all gonna do if the owner comes around and runs you off?"

"Move, I guess. I'm ready to go if you are."

Joe waited just another moment.

"You ain't missing none of your money, are you?"

"Not a bit. I'm ready to go if you are."

The old truck was parked beside a new van, and Joe looked through the tinted windows, admiring the blue upholstery and the woodgrained paneling inside it.

"Boy, you could do you some crackin in this thing," he said. Gary was standing beside him with his hands cupped around his face, looking with him.

"Hell fire. I could live in this thing," he said. "Reckon how much it costs?"

Joe stood back and looked around.

"Shit. Probably about twenty thousand. You ready to go?"

"Yeah."

"Let me walk over here and crank it up and see how much gas it's got in it," Joe said, and he pulled the keys out of his pocket and opened the door and got in. The motor turned over slowly and caught, then died. He sat there pumping the gas pedal.

"Always give it a little gas before you try to crank it," he said.

The motor spun again and caught and he revved it up, little spurts of blue smoke coming from the tailpipe. The boy looked up and down the road in front of the auto dealership. Traffic was fairly heavy. He imagined the pedals under his feet and the wheel and the gearshift in his hands. Late afternoons of joyous tranquility on country roads with the radio playing, the girl beside him languishing on the seat, smoking a cigarette, her legs crossed, laughing with him. No more walking up and down the road.

Joe pulled on the handbrake and got out. The truck sat there shuddering and vibrating, idling with a rough stutter.

"You got plenty of gas to get home," he said. "You might want to stop at John's and put some more in it if you're going to ride around some, though."

The boy reached in his pocket and pulled out his money and held it out in a folded wad.

"Here," he said.

Joe looked at it. "What's that?"

"I got the money," he said. "Count out what's yours."

"Hell, I ain't worried about that. Just stick it back in your pocket. I got to find the title when I get home and sign it over to you anyway. You'll have to get you some insurance. You know that, don't you?"

"Insurance?"

"Yeah. It's a law in Mississippi. Can't drive without insurance. It's got insurance on it now. It's still in my name. After I sign it over to you it's yours. I'll show you what all you need to do some-time. Just come out to the house one day before long and we'll find the title and get it fixed up. I'm gonna go on. You gonna be all right?''

"Sure."

"You want me to follow you?"

"Naw. I'll be fine."

"All right, then. I'll see you later."

He walked over to his new truck and got in and cranked it up and pulled out. Gary put his money in his pocket and went to his truck. The door was open and he got in and sat down, looking at everything. He knew that certain pedals had to be pushed. He'd watched Joe drive it over and over. He closed the door. It sat there idling. He stomped the clutch and threw it violently into reverse and let out on the clutch and it died. He pulled it back down into neutral. It cranked easily now that it was warmed up, but he choked it off three times before he noticed the lever sticking out beside his left knee. He unlocked it and pushed it in and managed to back the truck up three inches before he choked it off that time.

By the time he managed to back it out of the parking space, two salesmen from inside had come out, maybe to make sure he didn't run over a new car on the lot. He could see them watching him and it made him nervous. He tested the brakes, jerking to a stop, then pulled it down into low and leaned far over the steering wheel and drove down the hill toward the road. He slammed it to a halt and let out on the clutch and it died again. He sat there cranking on it with one hand tight on the wheel. He looked both ways. Cars were coming both ways. He'd meant to watch Joe to see which way he went, but in all the excitement he'd forgotten to. He thought he might have gone left, so he turned his wheel to the left, too.

Cars were still whizzing by. He waited patiently for five minutes, until the road was completely clear, revved the engine up to a controlled screaming whine, and dumped the clutch. The truck shot out into the road and he cut the wheel so that the body slanted over on its springs and he missed second and then dropped it down into third, but it had plenty of torque by then and he went flying toward the first traffic light. Nobody had told him anything about that and he went through it on red. A new Firebird coming across squalled its tires and nosedived with smoke flying into a Volkswagen that had already been wrecked once. The boy weaved to the right and went around them, craning his neck to see. The drivers were looking at him and yelling inside their cars. He went on down the road. He made it through two yellows and one green, but at the next intersection cars were turning onto the street and he had to come to a complete stop. He wondered why the Firebird had come out of a side road like that and just plowed into another car. He felt a little better now, felt that he was starting to get the hang of it. He managed to glide to a fairly smooth halt and get it back down into low. As he sat there waiting and looking around, a police car with siren screaming and blue lights flashing came out of the pack of cars ahead and passed by him at fifty or so, gaining speed. The light turned green and he went on.

He turned the radio on low. The music was comforting, something low and sweet by a woman with a voice full of anguish. He had lots of plans, new clothes and a wash job for the truck, regular trips to the grocery store with his mother and sister in tow. No more walking to John Coleman's. Just drive up there and have a cold drink when he felt like it. Ice cream for little sister before it could melt.

He went halfway through town without incident and then, seeing a beer sign he recognized outside a store, he turned right suddenly without signaling. Somebody behind him blew a horn. He blew his in answer and drove on up to the store, parked and left it in neutral. He pulled out the handbrake, leaving the motor running.

Inside the store there was air-conditioned coolness. Five or six older black men were sitting around a table playing cards in the relative dimness of the rear of the building.

"Hey," he said to everybody. Another old man was almost asleep behind the counter, propped in a high chair with his jaw in his hand. The coolers were on the far wall and the boy walked over and stood looking through the glass. All kinds of brands, all of it cold. He picked a brand that had a colorful label and opened the door and reached in and got a six-pack. He walked back up to the counter with it and set it down.

"I need some cigarettes, too," he said, and started pulling his money out.

The black proprietor came awake groggily and looked at the beer and put his hand on it and looked at the register and blinked and yawned. He looked at the child standing before him and said: "What kind?"

"Winstons," the boy said. "I need me about two packs, I reckon. And some matches, too."

The storekeeper hit some buttons on the register and pulled the cigarettes out of a rack over his head and bent beneath the counter for the matches. He pulled out a sack and put the beer in it and dropped the other stuff in on top.

"You ain't workin for the man, is you?" he said. The boy stopped and looked at him.

"I used to," he said. "I just bought his truck." He pointed out the window. "See it out there? I got to wash it, though."

The man shook his head.

"I think you could use you a new fender, too. Seven eighty."

The police car went screaming back by as he walked out of the store with the sack in his hands. He wondered what all the excitement was about. Bank robbery maybe.

He drove out of town slowly, sipping happily on a cold beer, digging the music, the world as fine as he could remember it being in a lifetime.

there was a woman Joe saw sometimes who lived in a small community twenty miles south of London Hill, and he rode down there one Friday evening to see if she was home. She lived alone and she had a lot of money that she liked to spend on him. He never saw her out anywhere at all and she never mentioned other men, never called, never bothered him, was always glad to see him. Whenever he got with her they would drink for days and wind up in hotels in Nashville or Memphis or Jackson, Mississippi, ordering room service and driving her white Cadillac around and mixing drinks in the car.

The road to her house wound down through low hills and farms with ponds scattered throughout the green pastures. The evening he went, there were bats about and swifts coursing the coming night on their sharp-tailed wings. The earth lay doused in the cool of the approaching night and hay wagons with their loads of tiered green blocks churned slowly over the land with the helpers throwing the bales up. He breathed in the good scent of freshly mown fescue and slowly lifted a beer to his mouth.

The road was white stone and the tires sang slowly as he eased into the night. Silage barns stood in the distance and he saw a bobcat enter its run and disappear through the bordering bushes. Catfish ponds lay faintly green in the gloom, and on one bank, a farmer stood, throwing out feed by the handfuls.

The night moved in and he had to turn his parking lights on. He had to slow down once for a dog that was lying in the road. The dog got up grudgingly, it seemed, looking back over its shoulder as it walked to one side.

"That's a good way to get run over," he told the dog.

He sped up once he got on the state highway, his radio fading as he headed south. He changed to another station but it was no better. Finally he shut it off. He pulled his headlights on and the bugs swarmed in small knots ahead of him, blasting into the windshield and sticking there. The window was rolled down, his arm hanging out, and the wind was moving through his hair. The beer between his legs was empty so he pitched the bottle over the roof of the cab with a hard upward swing of his arm and looked back to see it sail into the ditch. He got another one from the cooler in the floor and twisted the top off, drank deeply and set it between his legs.

Near a small road sign that advertised a steak house he turned right and went slowly down a patched asphalt road where trailer homes and Jim Walter homes sat side by side, their yellow lights glowing, the people reduced to dim forms in the yards, tires hanging from scrubby trees with ropes. Just past this, kudzu lay solid on both sides of the road as far as the eye could see, claiming every hill, every light pole, every tree. Eventually it thinned away and there were trailers once again. A mile past the last one a fine brick home sat back from the road, a long low structure with a well-kept yard and a white wooden fence that ran around all four sides of the property. He slowed and turned into the driveway, a gravel lane between pine trees whose limbs nearly brushed the sides of the truck. He crept down the driveway with the rocks crunching under the wheels. When he came out of the trees there was no car in the carport and no lights on in the house. He stopped.

"Well shit," he said. He sat there looking for a moment, knowing he should have called first. It was nearly dark. He shoved the gearshift up in park and got out, walked up the little brick pathway, looking at the flowers she had planted there, and stepped up on the small stoop and knocked on the door. From somewhere came the faraway yap of dogs. He knocked again and then turned and went back to the truck and got in and turned around in front of the house and went back out the driveway. A car was coming down the road, slowing as it passed him. A man was driving, with a woman sitting beside him, and they looked him over as they went past. He didn't wave. He turned the wheel and lifted the beer to his lips and drove quickly back to the state highway and turned the wheel east, toward Lee County, toward Tupelo and a bigger city and more bars and more policemen available to get after him. Knowing it as he sped that way, not really caring.

Full darkness descended and he kept drinking, tossing the bottles out over the roof and reaching for fresh ones in the floor. Later he stopped at a liquor store just inside Tupelo and bought a bottle of Crown Royal and checked in at the Trace Hall and pocketed the key without going to the room and got back in the truck and drove to a honky-tonk a few miles away. He hid his pistol under the seat and locked his truck. A sign outside the door promised the appearance of George Jones but he doubted it.

There was a long bar inside, and of all the faces reflected in the glass, there was not one he knew. He took a stool and ordered whiskey and Coke and drank the first one within three minutes. When he motioned for a refill the bartender shrugged and poured.

A hefty bouncer with a black shirt and cold eyes watched him from a corner. Joe looked up and saw him watching and locked eyes with him until the bouncer looked away. The bar was dark and country music floated through the smoky air. Couples danced to the slow ones under turning lights. He saw a woman down the bar looking at him, smiling at him, whispering to her friend, turning back to smile again. He picked up his drink and moved that way.

He woke in a strange bed, in a room filled with daylight. He rolled over and rubbed his eyes, his tongue like a thick pad of cotton. He was naked under satin sheets, his clothes hung carefully over a chair. His shoes were on the floor together, neatly, beside the chair. His wallet and keys and change and comb and pocketknife were on a table beside the bed. He dozed, slept again. Settling in peace he dreamed of the cotton fields of his youth, the shimmering rows spread out before him as he worked, the little plants falling away cleanly from the sharp blade of the hoe as he thinned them and dragged out the grass, the brown dirt turning darker as he chopped and stroked with the hoe, working his way toward the end of the row and the shade where the water bottle and his lunch waited. He worked an endless row in his dream and his mouth was dry in the dream and he came awake with a great thirst and sat up and rubbed his face and reached for his underwear and pants.

When he opened the bedroom door, there were some framed pictures of teenaged children in a paneled hall and he knew none of them. The house he stood in was quiet. He could hear a lawnmower running somewhere. To the right was what looked like a kitchen and he had orange juice on his mind if there was any to be had.

There were three plates smeared with the remains of eggs sitting on a bar, before three stools lined up next to the refrigerator. He moved to a double glass door and looked out into a back yard with lawn chairs and a gas grill and an above-ground swimming pool where children's rings with the heads of horses and ducks floated on the bright water. There seemed to be nobody about. He went back to the refrigerator and opened the door, then shut it and read the note addressed to him: *Joe, I had to go to the airport. Fix yourself some breakfast if you want it. I'll be back by eleven, Sue*

The night came back in a rush and he looked at his watch. It was ten-thirty. He opened the door again and pulled out a quart bottle of Tropicana and rummaged through the cabinets until he found a glass and poured it full. He stood at the bar and drank it down quickly and immediately felt better. He couldn't remember exactly what she looked like, and he hated to stick around any longer.

He was buttoning his shirt in the bedroom when he heard the

front door slam. An unfamiliar voice called his name. He heard the sound of her heels clicking on the parquet flooring in the kitchen, then the muffled sound of her footsteps on the carpet of the hall. He turned toward the door. The steps paused. A vision of loveliness there at the door, an approving grin which he returned.

"Hey," he said.

"Hey yourself." She put her purse down and walked over to him and put her arms around him. She kissed him, a small good fragrance in his nose. Her breasts flattened against him and he held her by the shoulders. She kicked her shoes off and moved her hands down the front of him, reaching, touching. He kissed her neck. She pushed him backwards toward the bed. He didn't protest.

That afternoon they lay in the sun on chaise longues with a small cooler of beer beside them, rising to slip into the pool and float on air mattresses, bumping into each other with the warm rays on their bodies. She'd found an old pair of pants with a waist that fit him and she'd cut them off with pinking shears. Her body was tanned in a black one-piece, her brown hair just turning to gray. She was forty-one and she'd been divorced for two years. He learned that her two children had just left that morning for a two-week visit with their father in Orlando.

There was a high wooden fence around her back yard and she lay with her eyes closed, floating on the air mattress with a small smile on her face. Joe watched her in wonder and kissed the tiny freckles at the tops of her breasts. When the sun went straight overhead she took him back to the cool sheets of her bedroom and rocked and swayed over him, that dreamy smile growing to a shuddering twitch of lips with her breath catching harshly in her throat, their bodies in total harmony with each other, the only one ever except Charlotte. She folded herself over him and kissed the side of his throat and stroked his arms and chest with fingers soft and sure. They talked in low voices and when the sun started down she drove him back to the bar for his truck.

That night they had drinks on a patio she and the children had built themselves, porterhouses sputtering while small yellow flames leaped in the gas grill. She kept a careful eye on the steaks and cooked them just the way he liked them, bleeding red juices when she cut them with the knife. He held hands with her at times, something he hadn't done in a long time, and had thought he'd never do again.

Long after midnight he held her in the bed while her head rested on his chest. He listened to the slow measured sound of her breathing and wondered how any man could give up something like her. The sculpted ivory of her torso where the sun had not touched it made her legs and arms look black in the darkness of the room. Her lacquered fingernails rested lightly on his stomach. He dreamed again, but not of childhood fields. He dreamed of the prison yard and of clearing the roadside grass with sickles and the horses the guards rode standing over him drooling their slobber down on his bare back and of enduring it all, watching the days tick off the calendar one by one and the hot Mississippi sun bearing down on the truck patches, him on his knees pulling tomatoes and beans and peas, of the heavy wire mesh fences that fenced in the inmates, of the smoky lights that loomed in the darkness outside the camps, where in the black towers the unseen guards with their rifles sat watching for movement in the packed dirt beside the buildings. He twisted in his sleep, his legs moving. Near dawn he got up and put on his clothes and gathered up his things and let himself out of the house quietly, locking the door firmly behind him, not looking back, getting in his truck and turning on the parking lights, backing out of the driveway slowly, easing into the street, pulling the headlights on and reaching down for the last lukewarm beer in the cooler, eyeing the whiskey that was still on the seat. The gas tank was half full, more than enough to get home.

The old GMC with the battered fender was parked near a wooden bridge on a gravel road three miles from London Hill, and the old man was sitting on a downed tree with his shoes and socks off, paring his toenails with a pocketknife. From time to time he looked over the lip of the creek and watched a big perch that was riffling over the shallow water, flitting here and there above the sand bottom on feathery fins. Once in a while he rubbed his swollen knuckles.

He could see the youngest girl moving in the back beneath the camper bed, the truck rocking slightly each time she moved on the cot and turned uneasily. There was a good breeze easing the heat underneath the massive oaks and he fanned at his opened shirt with his hat. From time to time he lifted a bottle in a paper sack and drank from it, watching up the road, waiting.

After a while a slowly growing noise began to creep its way into the uncertain realm of his bad hearing, and he cocked his head to determine from which direction it was coming. He saw it round the curve, a plume of dust rising close behind it like a small brown tornado that was content to stay in the middle of the road. It was a white Ford pickup. Soon he could hear the rocks speaking beneath the tires.

The girl sat up on the cot.

The old man nodded, putting his hat back on his head, getting up with studied slowness and crossing the ditch to lean against the fender.

The truck slowed, pulled up behind and stopped. Willie Russell was driving and another man was with him. They didn't get out. They sat there on the seat like mutes or idiots, looking back and forth at one another and at him leaning on the fender.

"Hell," the old man said. "Cut your motor off."

Russell cut it off. Wade walked over to the Ford and put his hand on the side mirror.

"Where's she at?" said the driver.

The old man motioned with a cocked thumb over his shoulder.

"Thirty dollars," he said. "Apiece." The one on the passenger side already had his money out. The mutilated driver bent forward in the seat, struggled with his back pocket for a moment, and drew out a cracked brown billfold. He pulled money from it, worn bills greasy and soft as chamois. They paid the old man the combined sixty dollars and he counted it and nodded and pocketed the money. He turned without speaking and walked up the road to sit on the roots of a big tree in the shade about a hundred and fifty feet away.

They got out of the truck together and looked both ways up the road. They entered through the back door of the camper. The door came down. It closed with a rattle, rattled again, then slammed hard.

The old man fanned himself with his hat, lifted his whiskey from a pocket, and looked off into the distant fields burning under the sun.

After a while the truck began rocking, the worn springs creaking mildly as if in some weak protest or outrage.

Gary was in the woods, by the spring. He held his knees and rocked there, back and forth, the wet rag he had soaked in the spring water pressed to the eye already swollen shut. The day was hot and the sun lanced down between the trees and he felt it on the back of his neck like a warm hand. The spring bubbled gently and the leaves whispered quietly and he saw before him not unlike a dream the *seven states they had lived in, transient, rootless, no more mired to one spot of territory than fish in the sea, Oklahoma, Georgia, California, Florida with tall and black-haired Tom falling off the truck and the truck behind them running over his head. That was in 1980. He could see other states, other days, mild ones, mountains in the distance, the little tarpaper shacks where they had once lived. Miles and miles of blacktop highway, the bundled clothes, the mildewed quilts after a night of sleeping on the side of the road. All his life he'd been hungry, all his life waiting behind the old man for whatever scraps of food were left, watching the quick champ of his stubbled jaws, the food disappearing rapidly from the plate, the lowered eyes of his mother as if she hadn't noticed that something was wrong. They'd never furnished an answer for Calvin but he remembered him clearly because he had carried him. He had white hair, white as cotton. They had been living in a camp outside Oklahoma City. There were tents pitched everywhere, and everybody did their cooking outside over fires. But they had little to cook. His father stayed gone most of the time, and when he came in, it was late at night, and there was always trouble, and arguing, and Calvin crying for something to eat, sucking at the meager breasts of his mother even after there was no more milk, and she would shush him, rocking him, both of them crying together in their emptiness. He remembered all that. Finally there was no work for them. The Mexicans had come in a flood and the old man cursed about them, saying how they'd taken all the jobs to where a white man couldn't get work.*

There was a city they walked into one day. They went to a park and located a water fountain, sat down in the shade that Fourth of July. Children raced over the grass, chasing balloons, and people were sitting on the ground eating from picnic baskets. His mother went among the happy people, stooping and bending, saying things to them, getting something here, pointing back to them, getting something there, and he sat with his father and the girls and Calvin in the shade until she returned bringing them chicken legs and biscuits and sandwiches. He took a chicken salad sandwich and broke off little pieces of it, pinched small bits off and fed them to his little brother, watching him gum the bread and meat. He found a cup and filled it with water and gave him small sips.

He ate a little himself. He made sure his little brother got all he wanted. He rocked him in his lap, mopped the sweat from his forehead with his shirttail, crooned him to sleep. And when he slept, he laid him on the soft grass and turned him on his side.

One couple kept watching them. An older couple, white haired, with nice clothes and diamond rings. They came closer finally.

The man pulled at the crease of his trousers before he sat down. His wife lingered nearby.

"That's a beautiful baby you have," the man said.

His father turned and frowned. "Hey," he said.

The man came forward in a parody of a duckwalk, inching along. He had steelrimmed glasses that flashed and caught the dying sun. They began talking. The woman eased herself down on the grass and smiled and smiled. On a plywood stage a band had formed to play bluegrass, boys and men made up in western shirts and jeans and boots, scarves knotted around their necks. There was a fiddler among them and he stepped up and bent to the microphone, bending his arm and keeping his chin tucked. They started playing.

He sat in the grass and heard them and watched them and it seemed like everything would be better in his world if they could find one place to stay. He knew even then that they were different, his people, this family that traveled all night sometimes. The sky grew darker and the lights came up and the people sat on the hillsides and watched the bands come up and make their introductions and then take the stage and do their numbers. There were four bands that played that night, and when the last band ended its final set it appeared that something had been arranged.

He had never ridden in such an automobile. He sat in the back seat of the Lincoln with the girls and his mother, Calvin asleep in his lap. His father was in front, with the man and his wife. There was whiskey. He could smell it. He'd learned the smell of it early. His father and his mother passed the bottle back and forth and she drank heavily, the only time he ever saw her do that. They talked like old friends, his father in his torn overalls and the man and the woman in their nice clothes.

They drove for miles in the night through strange country, some of it barren, flat, gray as stone. Later there were oaks and beeches and river bottoms, plowed dirt black as night. He slept some. And when he woke they were still talking, still passing the whiskey bottle, but his mother and the girls were asleep. And Calvin. By leaning up over the seat he could see him cupped in the woman's arms, his bland face and closed eyes a picture he wouldn't forget. There was a look of radiance on the woman's face such as he had never seen on the face of anybody. There was joy there, the purest sort of happiness. He could see his little brother's face blue in the dashlights, the crown of hair around the woman's head shot through with light. It had been puffed up, made to look thicker than it was. He could see her scalp.

When he woke again it was to early morning darkness. The woman and the man and Calvin were not with them. There was a Greyhound bus parked at the curb, gouts of smoke curling from the tailpipe. His mother was having some kind of fit. She had her face in her hands, clawing at it, backing away from the car, and his father was talking to her from behind the wheel. Then he got out of the car and took her roughly by the arm and tried to fling her in through the open door, but she caught herself against the frame and pushed back with her arms, saying no in a high chant. His father wrenched her around by one arm and doubled his fist and hit her in the face and she sat down in the seat. He bent over and caught up her legs and put them inside the car. He started to slam the door but she came back out. He kicked her and she flew back, moaned, and fell half over in the floorboard. His father slammed the door on her and walked around and got in. The boy he was then looked out the window, saying nothing, watching the huge trembling bus idling at the curb with the dark figures of sleeping passengers inside. And the car began to slide away. Window by window they left it, the long gray dog emblazoned on the side moving backward, the nose and the outstretched feet, then lamp posts and storefronts and closed shops and sidewalks and finally empty streets, ghostly intersections where red lights slowly blinked and no people stood. He turned around in the seat on his knees and felt of the rich upholstery of the car and felt the quiet power that began to pick up speed and bear them nearly noiselessly through the night. He watched the town grow smaller behind them until it was only a dim blaze of lights at the end of two black lanes of highway marked on each side with a white strip, the dots and dashes of centerline emerging ever quicker from beneath the trunk, the red glow of the taillights skimming and a yellow sign receding to a small bright dot.

The morning was only a few hours old but the whiskey bottle was half empty. He wasn't weaving badly, and he almost made it to his house. But then he saw the boy going down the road walking, and he pulled over. The boy stood there a moment, looking away with his hands in his pockets, then turned his head to face him with the big purple bruise over an eyelid that was completely closed, the lid stretched tight like the skin of a ripe plum.

"Get in," Joe said.

The boy shook his head. A car came up the road, slowed, and drove between them. The boy stood there looking with one eye across the short distance that separated them.

"Get in, Gary."

He seemed to hold back from taking some final step. Whatever there was in his face was something he hadn't shown before. But finally he walked across the little asphalt road and stepped down into the ditch briefly and opened the door and got in.

"Look here."

The boy turned and showed it to him. It looked even worse up close.

"Your daddy's left-handed, I see," he said, and the boy drew back before he could touch him and eased back against the seat. He looked like a joke but he wasn't a joke.

"How you know he did it?" he said.

"Who else would? Where's your truck?"

The boy said nothing. Joe looked up in the rearview mirror and saw something coming and sat there until it went past. Then he pulled out.

"I should have done give you a boxing lesson."

"I don't need no boxing lesson. I'm gonna bust his damn head open is what I'm gonna do."

"That might cure it. I ain't going to ask you if it hurts. Why don't we stop by the house and get some ice for it? It might take some of the swelling down."

"I had some cold water on it. I don't guess it done no good."

"Ice is about the only thing that'll help it. It's probably too late to help it much."

"Where you been?" the boy said. "You all dressed up."

"I been over at Tupelo. I just got in a while ago. Here, take you a drink of this whiskey. That'll make your head feel better. It always does mine."

The boy picked it up and twisted the top off slowly, tilted the neck toward his nose and sniffed and moved it to his mouth all in one motion, taking just a tiny sip, then another, then he took a full swallow while Joe watched him and drove at the same time. He didn't make that bad a face.

"Get you a Coke out of the floor there. I put two quarters in a Coke machine at a gas station in Pontotoc a while ago and three of them son of a bitches come out."

The boy reached for one of the cans in the floor and held the bottle up.

"You done drank all this this morning?"

"Yeah. I started early today. Listen, you got any idea where your truck might be? When did he get in it?"

"Early this morning. I was asleep and heard him crank it up."

"You didn't hide the keys?"

"Naw. I didn't think to."

Joe slowed the truck as they came within sight of his house, and he reached and got the whiskey. He put on his blinker and pulled into his driveway and parked the truck. The dog watched from under the house. Joe lifted the whiskey and pulled hard on it, took it down, and turned to face the boy for a moment.

"You want another drink?"

"Might as well," he said. They sat there in the truck with the sun steadily climbing. "I don't guess it matters what time of day you drink, does it?"

Joe gave him a little wave of his hand.

"It don't to me. I reckon one time's good as another."

The boy opened the Coke and took a drink of the whiskey, then turned up the Coke. He did that twice.

"Damn, you need to quit hanging around me, boy. Give me that bottle back."

He was grinning when he said it. He nearly tousled the boy's hair, but turned instead and looked at the house. It looked like they might as well go find the old man and see if they could untangle things.

"I reckon he's got Dorothy with him."

————

"Who's Dorothy?"

"That's my little sister. The one that can't talk."

"Can't talk?"

"Won't. She used to would. She just quit one day and ain't never said another word."

"You shittin me."

"Naw."

"How old's Dorothy?"

"I don't know. I guess about twelve or thirteen."

"He ever took her off before?"

"Not that I know of."

A dark thought moved in his mind and he looked at the boy carefully. He put the top back on the whiskey.

"Tell you what," he said. "I'll run in here and grab some ice and a towel. You had anything to eat?"

"I don't want nothing to eat."

"All right. Just hold on and we'll ride down the road and see if we can see your truck anywhere, okay?"

"What if we find it?"

"I hope we do," he said, and got out. He lit a cigarette, said something to the dog, and went on in. He was back out in a few minutes with a towel and some ice. The boy watched him while he laid the towel out on the seat and started cracking the ice in the tray, not saying anything else.

When they backed out into the road, Gary had a large wad of towel pressed against his eye. Joe drank some more of the whiskey and then ran one hand through his hair. Part of his shirttail was hanging out of his pants and the truck was low on gas.

"I come by other day and I didn't see your truck," the boy said. "I was gonna see about that title or whatever."

Joe was mostly looking out the window while he was driving. Somebody was building an addition on Jim Sharp's house and a concrete truck was backed up against the house, the huge cylinder turning, men working in high rubber boots.

"Yeah," he said absently. "Yeah, we got to get that fixed up one of these days."

He turned off onto the first gravel road and reached for the whiskey again.

"You ought to just move in with me is what you ought to do," he said. "Hell. At least you wouldn't have to worry about him stealing your goddamn truck."

He took a drink and passed the whiskey back to the boy. The road was dry but spotted here and there with mud holes and he splashed through most of them. The cows stood back from the road like statues as they passed. The sun was bright, the pastures laden with dew shining in the early morning light. Bobwhites dusted themselves in the road before running single file into the weeds.

"Move in with you?"

"Hell yeah. You could find something to do this summer. Shit, paint houses or something. I know you could find you a job. You could probably get on a crew and do some carpenter work or something. It's lots of stuff to do, you just got to get out and find it."

"What would I do about them?"

"What do you mean?"

"Well. I'd kind of hate to just go off and leave em."

"Why? What in the fuck have they ever done for you?"

"I just kind of hate to go off and leave em."

"Stay with em, then."

They went across the first bridge and it rattled underneath the truck as they rolled over it. He could see the old GMC from there, parked beneath the oaks that shaded the next bridge. The other truck was parked beside it, the white Ford, but he already knew what they would find. He slowed the truck. The sun was climbing higher. He thought about the old cons in the pen who would take the young and pretty boys down and how they would muffle their screams while they raped them. How everyone turned their heads and looked away because it didn't concern them and it wasn't them.

"Listen. If anything starts happening, you get your little ass out of the way. You hear?"

"What do you mean?"

"I mean get out of the goddamn way. Put the cap on that whiskey."

A man was leaning against the fender of Willie Russell's truck. He'd seen him before, but he didn't know his name. He hung around the Dumpsters sometimes, driving a wrecked car full of feral children.

"Stay in the truck," he said, and stopped and reached under the seat for the pistol. He saw Wade stand up quickly and walk across the road and climb with a wild and pawing energy the brier-infested opposite bank, look back once and pile headlong over the fence to vanish in the tangled growth there. When he had the gun in his hand, he stomped on the gas and sped across the bridge and slammed on the brakes, and was out the door with the pistol almost before the truck had stopped moving. The man on the fender started backing away with his hands out in front of him, then he turned and started running. Joe let him go.

When he stepped around the end of the GMC and looked inside and saw what was back there, saw the blood on the little girl's legs, he backed up a step and waited. She was putting her clothes back on. Russell was fastening his pants and trying to talk to him. Joe didn't answer him. Gary had gotten out and was suddenly standing beside him, looking in.

"Dorothy," he said, the only word he said.

"Get her out, Gary. Get her out and get her in my truck and you go home."

She pulled her dress down and quickly got off the cot, and slid out over the top of the tailgate. Gary took her hand and led her away. She wasn't crying. She wasn't making any noise at all. Gary put her in the truck and went around and got behind the wheel, and Joe looked at him for a moment. Their eyes met for the last time and then the boy looked down at the gearshift. After a few seconds he pulled the lever down and took his foot off the brake and they went rolling past. Joe realized too late they'd taken his whiskey. The truck went on down the road and when the sound of it finally faded away, he walked close with the little gun out in front of him and pushed the safety off with his thumb. It made a tiny click and Russell closed his eyes and covered those eyes with his hands. Waiting. Joe started to tell him a few things first, then decided there was no need of that.

EPILOGUE

———

That winter the trees stood nearly barren of their leaves and the cold seemed to settle into the old log house deep in the woods. The old woman felt it seep into her bones. Each morning the floors seemed colder, each day it was harder to crank the truck. The boy piled wood for colder days to come. At odd times of the day they'd hear the faint honking, and they'd hurry out into the yard to see overhead, and far beyond the range of men's guns the geese spread out over the sky in a distant brotherhood, the birds screaming to each other in happy voices for the bad weather they were leaving behind, the southlands always ahead of their wings, warm marshes and green plants beckoning them to their ancient primeval nesting lands.

They'd stand looking up until the geese diminished and fled crying out over the heavens and away into the smoking clouds, their voices dying slowly, one last note the only sound and proof of their passing, that and the final wink of motion that swallowed them up into the sky and the earth that met it and the pine trees always green and constant against the great blue wildness that lay forever beyond.

———

JOE

An Affair of Honor: Larry Brown's *Joe*

This essay was written by Cleanth Brooks in recognition of the publication of Larry Brown's *Joe.* Cleanth Brooks is generally recognized as one of the most influential American literary critics of the twentieth century. His distinguished career spanned more than six decades of American life and letters, and produced many of the century's seminal critical studies of modern poetry and fiction. Along with John Crowe Ransom, Allen Tate, and others, he helped establish the "New Criticism," which revolutionized literary studies during the 1930s and 1940s. With Robert Penn Warren, he coauthored *Understanding Poetry* and *Understanding Fiction*, two cornerstones in the practice of teaching and reading literature that have been considered essential texts in many colleges and universities. He was without question the single most influential American critic of the fiction of William Faulkner; his two studies, *William Faulkner: The Yoknapatawpha Country,* and *William Faulkner: Towards Yoknapatawpha and Beyond*, remain milestones in the study and understanding of America's most important modern fiction writer. Brooks died in 1994.

An Affair of Honor

Larry Brown's *Joe*

by Cleanth Brooks

Larry Brown's hometown is the same a William Faulkner's, Oxford, Mississippi. But his novel, *Joe*, is not imitation Faulkner. Brown has his own style
and is quite comfortable in it. Nevertheless, the Beat Four district of Yoknapatawpha County peeps through here and there. But it is Beat Four forty or fifty
years later than, say, that of *Light in August* or *As I Lay Dying*. There are still
plenty of buzzards, hawks, and owls in the countryside, probably more deer
there now in the 1990s than Jewel Bundren ever saw there earlier, and more
possums. But the mules are gone, replaced by tractors, and on the now hard-
surfaced roads there are pickup trucks and in the towns, supermarkets. The
people, however, at least the rural whites, have not changed too much. They
now listen to country music on their radios and some of them drink whiskey—
quite a lot of it—with Cokes for chasers.

Brown's style is rather simple and straightforward. His descriptions are
exact. A field being plowed by a tractor looks like this: "The dry soil [is] not
folding but merely breaking into dust across the plows." The imagery quietly
adds substance to the action in question. Thus, when old Wade Jones strikes
his wife to the ground, she "[falls] over on her back in the dirt and [lies] with
her arms outspread like a witness for Christ stricken with the power of the
Blood." This echo of a violent and ecstatic religious service, one with which
the woman was probably familiar in her youth, supplies just the right note,
and it helps account for our sense of her present victimage.

Simple and habitual actions are often described in almost minute detail,
so that we actually see them and almost participate in them. Here is an old

man drinking a can of beer. He "opened the can and foam exploded from it. It ran down over the sides and over his hand and he sucked at the thick white suds with a delicate slobbering noise and trembling pursed lips. He tilted the can and poured the hot beer down his throat . . ." The prose, as here, is alive. The reader keeps experiencing the scene at virtual firsthand.

Joe is a very fine piece of fiction. For all its seriousness, Larry Brown's novel is thoroughly readable, not because it has a good measure of sex and blood and thunder in it, but because the author knows how to write, has a real story to tell, and knows how to tell it. The events related are circumstantial, the characters credible, and what the characters do to each other seem to be inevitable actions. The dialect is sound. I know it, for I grew up in the same cultural subsection. Most of the people in this novel say "naw" for "no" and "go find it your ownself," not "go find it yourself." But the dialect constitutes no barrier for the general reader, who will understand the work easily enough.

One of the characters, Wade Jones, is a man "who rarely drinks water," though he is usually hard put to it to get his whiskey and beer. Wade will remind the reader, at least a little, of Faulkner's Anse Bundren, who is a lazy beggar, who preys upon his children for money and favors, and who makes absurd promises that he depends upon his children to fulfill. Anse is a completely worthless man, and yet there is something a little comic about him. He is the utterly shameless scrounger.

There is nothing comic about Wade Jones, however. He is wickedly malignant. He sells one of his infant children to a wealthy childless couple. His teenaged daughter runs away from her house because she despises her father and can no longer live there; and in the novel we are allowed to watch Wade kill an old black wino in order to rob him. Wade Jones will do anything to get his whiskey.

There are others in this novel who rarely drink water. Joe Ransom, whose first name provides a title for the novel, is also a great drinker, who loves whiskey and fortunately is able to buy all that he needs. But Joe Ransom is forged of very different metal than is Wade.

He loves to gamble, and is rather successful at it. He makes sufficient money easily. His divorced wife lives in the town. He respects her—in a curious way, he still loves her—but she knows from hard experience that she and Joe are truly incompatible. Yet she does not mean to marry anyone else, and her daughter tells her father that if her mother ever did marry another man, he would kill him. Joe tries to dismiss this possibility with a laugh, but obviously his divorced wife is indeed in some sense still precious to him.

He enjoys the society of women. He is apparently quite attractive to them, and there are in this novel two instances in which a woman who has some wealth invites him in. Yet, as much as Joe frankly enjoys such sexual adventures, he does not confuse them with love. In the second episode he simply steals away early in the morning without even leaving a note.

Joe Ransom is a man who insists on running his own life in his own way. He refuses to be controlled by anyone else or even be gainsaid by a woman whom he loves. Living his life on his own terms makes him a good many enemies, though that fact daunts him not in the least. Yet his is not the arrogance of the bully. He lives by his own code of honor. To shape and present this special kind of character convincingly is a formidable test of any author's powers. It is a test that Larry Brown easily succeeds in passing, for most of his readers will accept Joe's essential reality.

If there are a few skeptics who find him not quite convincing I can help them, I think, by recommending that they read Bertram Wyatt-Brown's *Southern Honor,* published in 1982. A substantial treatment of southern ethics and behavior, Wyatt-Brown's study focuses on the antebellum South, but it makes plain that honor, as a powerful directive of personal conduct, did not expire with the Civil War. Neither was it ever a feature limited to the conduct of the planters of the Virginia Tidewater or the South Carolina Low Country. Honor was a powerful element throughout the culture of the South. Even the poor white was usually jealous of his personal honor.

I am not arguing that Larry Brown ever read Wyatt-Brown's book. As a sensitive observer who grew up in the South, he did not need to read a book in order to create a character like Joe Ransom, and to have that same character distinguish between killings that "were matters of honor and others [that were] simple acts of meanness committed during robberies against helpless victims..." These latter Joe did not respect; a killing for honor was something else again.

Yet why all this talk about honor and about the rather special character of Joe? How is it relevant to this novel? Because, in the latter part of this novel, Joe does some things that are rather unusual. He meets Gary Jones, a fifteen-year-old boy who exhibits several traits of character that are themselves out of the ordinary. The son of Wade Jones, Gary has never gone to school, cannot read or write, and has begged to be given a job, not even asking what the wages are. Joe takes him on, and finds that he is an excellent worker.

Joe Ransom does something else unusual. Though he has been shot by a man named Russell, he has made no retaliation. Russell's gun was of small caliber, Joe's wounds were superficial, and Russell had been very drunk at the time. Earlier, Joe had been in the penitentiary for two and a half years. He has been told that if he kills Russell he will be sent back to the penitentiary for a long stay. He didn't like it there the first time, and now, in his forties, he will like it very much less if he has to go back. "This time they'd keep him until he was old." Yet as the book closes, Joe is evidently preparing to kill Russell. He aims his gun and flips back the safety. "Joe started to tell him a few things first, then decided there was no need of that."

The final chapter ends there. We don't hear the gun bark or see Russell fall, or learn what happened later on to Joe. Instead there are two more paragraphs that constitute what is called an "Epilogue." The time is now evidently winter. The wild geese are over the house, streaming south toward the Gulf marshes. We are told that "they"—but not who "they" are—stood looking at the geese go over. But if we have read this novel (or let the novel really talk to us), we do not need to be told. We know who "they" are, and that the lack of a happy ending is unimportant. The way that Larry Brown's *Joe* ends is right, the sufficient conclusion of a very fine novel. A story has been fully told to us, a story that is significant.

TOM RANKIN

Larry Brown is the author of nine books—five novels and two collections each of stories and personal essays. His work has received many awards and prizes, including two Southern Book Critics Circle Awards for fiction, the Mississippi Institute of Arts and Letters Award for fiction, the Thomas Wolfe Award, and the Lila Wallace–*Reader's Digest* Writer's Award. He died in 2004.

Additional Books by **Larry Brown**
Available Wherever Books and E-books Are Sold

Facing the Music, stories

These ten stories confront, head-on, the dark side of the human condition. This is the work of a writer unafraid to gaze directly at characters challenged by crisis and pathology. But for readers who are willing to look, unblinkingly, there are unusual rewards.

"Ten raw and strictly 100-proof stories make up one of the more exciting debuts of recent memory—fiction that's gritty and genuine, and funny in a hard-luck way." —*Kirkus Reviews*

Stories • Paperback • ISBN 978-1-56512-125-6 • E-book ISBN 978-1-56512-731-9

Fay, a novel

In this taut, seductive novel, seventeen-year-old femme fatale Fay Jones hitchhikes her way down Mississippi Highway 55, with just the clothes on her back, two dollars, and a pack of cigarettes, and leaves bodies and broken hearts in her wake.

"Brown's magic is to make the reader wonder at this plucky heroine, then care about and finally root for her as she winds toward the novel's gripping conclusion. Spellbinding." —*People* magazine

Fiction • Hardcover • ISBN 978-1-56512-168-3 • E-book ISBN 978-1-56512-732-6

Dirty Work, a novel

Larry Brown's shattering first novel is the story of two men—strangers—one black, the other white. Both were born and raised in Mississippi. Both fought in Vietnam. Both were gravely wounded. Now, twenty-two years later, both men lie in adjacent beds in a VA hospital. Over the course of one day and night, each recounts his story to the other.

"The writing, the characters, and the plot are so compelling that you can't help but stay with the book until its conclusion."
—*The Washington Post Book World*

• A *USA Today* Book of the Year

Fiction • Paperback • ISBN 978-1-56512-563-6 • E-book ISBN 978-1-56512-724-1

A Miracle of Catfish, a novel

Larry Brown's posthumous novel is the story of one year in the lives of five characters—an old farmer with a new pond he wants stocked with baby catfish; a bankrupt fish pond stocker who secretly releases his forty-pound brood catfish into the farmer's pond; a little boy from the trailer home across the road who inadvertently hooks the behemoth catfish; the boy's inept father; and a former convict down the road who kills a second time to save his daughter.

"*A Miracle of Catfish* yields so many pleasures, it hurts to say so."
—*The New York Times Book Review*

Fiction • Hardcover • ISBN 978-1-56512-536-0 • E-book ISBN 978-1-56512-696-1

Other Larry Brown E-books

Father and Son, a novel
ISBN 978-1-61620-206-4

Big Bad Love, stories
ISBN 978-1-61620-205-7

On Fire, a memoir
ISBN 978-1-56512-808-8

Billy Ray's Farm, nonfiction
ISBN 978-1-56512-709-8

"For detox to work and take hold, it needs to address the 'whole self.' I am excited to see that my colleague and friend, Dr. Deanna Minich, has written *Whole Detox* for this very reason. Quite frankly, I think that she is the perfect person to talk about detox in this new 'whole' kind of way. Truly, 'detox' needs to keep up with the evolving science, and I think that's what we have *Whole Detox* here to do."

—Mark Hyman, M.D., *New York Times* bestselling author and director of
the Cleveland Clinic Center for Functional Medicine

"Within her book, *Whole Detox*, the reader will find the best of Dr. Minich and an opportunity to improve their health through the wisdom she provides from both her extensive research and clinical applications. This is the book in which the approach to detoxification offers the whole picture in a program that is tried and proven to be successful."

—Jeffrey Bland, Ph.D., founder and president of the Personalized
Lifestyle Medicine Institute

"I love the approach of *Whole Detox*, which looks at you as a whole person—a complex body, mind, and spirit comprised of interrelated systems that, when in balance, provide the key to complete health and wellness. Deanna shows you how to address your whole self to heal, detoxify, and change your life!"

—Sara Gottfried, M.D., *New York Times* bestselling author of
The Hormone Reset Diet

"*Whole Detox* is an empowering, enlightening read—a practical manual for cleansing, healing, and thriving."

—Dr. Frank Lipman, *New York Times* bestselling author of *The New Health Rules*

"*Whole Detox* redefines detox in a colorful, holistic way that heals not just the body, but the whole being. Deanna has brought together her scientific mind and her creative soul to develop a 21-day program that can change lives and transform the human spirit."

—Alejandro Junger, M.D., *New York Times* bestselling author of
Clean, *Clean Gut*, and *Clean Eats*

"You'll never think about detox in the same way again after reading and experiencing *Whole Detox*. It's mind–body medicine meets nutritional detoxification through the spectrum of color. Genius, creative, and inspiring."

—Amy Myers, M.D., *New York Times* bestselling author of
The *Autoimmune Solution*

"*Whole Detox* offers up a comprehensive and integrative program that paves the way for reestablishing health, disease resistance, and vitality. Deanna Minich guides with knowledge, expertise, experience, and most importantly, compassion. Her dedication to the art of healing is evident in every word."

—David Perlmutter, M.D., author of the #1 *New York Times* bestsellers
Grain Brain and *Brain Maker*

WHOLE

DETOX

A 21-DAY PERSONALIZED PROGRAM TO BREAK
THROUGH BARRIERS IN EVERY AREA OF YOUR LIFE

DEANNA MINICH

HarperOne
An Imprint of HarperCollinsPublishers

This book contains advice and information relating to health and is not meant to diagnose, treat, or prescribe. It should be used to supplement rather than replace the advice of your physician or other trained health-care practitioner. If you know or suspect you have a medical condition, have physical symptoms, or feel unwell, it is recommended that you seek your physician's advice before embarking on any medical program or treatment. All efforts have been made to assure the accuracy of the information contained in this book as of the date of its publication. Neither the author nor the publisher accepts any responsibility for your health, how you choose to use the information contained in this book, or your medical outcomes resulting from applying the methods suggested in this book.

Names and identifying details have been changed to honor people's desire for confidentiality.

FIRST HARPERCOLLINS PAPERBACK EDITION PUBLISHED IN 2017

Designed by Yvonne Chan

Library of Congress Cataloging-in-Publication Data is available upon request.

ISBN 9780062426802

22 23 24 25 26 LBC 8 7 6 5 4

To my father, who is healing the ancestral threads, and to my niece, Eleanor, who is creating healthy patterns for the future.

To the healing of past, present, and future generations from the effects of *all* types of toxins and with hope for a planet filled with the full spectrum of health and vitality.

You are not a drop in the ocean. You are the entire ocean in a drop.

—RUMI

CONTENTS

FOREWORD

I get the questions all the time from my patients: "Why detox?" "Isn't detoxing just a fad?" Of course, "detox" is a word that means different things to different people, which is why sometimes it can cause confusion. Most people relate detox to juicing, fasting, or eating lots of cruciferous vegetables and drinking lots of lemon water. There is definitely a food component to detox. I talk extensively about how to do a detox diet right within my book *The Blood Sugar Solution 10-Day Detox Diet*. Sure, it's taking out sugar, gluten, dairy, and caffeine. Equally important, it's about including whole, colorful foods in the diet, which are chock-full of nutrients. It's that tender balance of avoiding unhealthy foods and including nourishing foods in our everyday eating. I believe strongly in living the age-old principle of "food as medicine" and starting here first and foremost.

The other part of detox—lifestyle—gets less recognition than food, but I believe it's very important to consider. I'm a huge believer in the power of community, in sociogenomics, and in how our social networks can add or take away from our health. We need to be looking at the root of whom we are personally connected to, because as the research shows, their habits can become ours. We also need to be examining other lifestyle toxicities, like going to a toxic job every day that doesn't nourish our soul; having toxic emotions stored within, thinking recycled toxic thoughts that limit our potential; and being exposed to environmental toxins through home, school, and work.

For detox to work and take hold, it needs to address the "whole self." I've seen this time and time again in my patients. If they change their food, many times they change their lives. However, when they see detox as a temporary deprivation, only to thrust themselves back into a toxic lifestyle and do it again, then detox doesn't have the full potential it could. I am a huge advocate of lifestyle change, and I see detox as being a short-term reset button to fuel long-term changes.

I am excited to see that my colleague and friend Dr. Deanna Minich has written *Whole Detox* for this very reason. She sees detox much like I do—that it needs to focus on the whole person, incorporate whole foods, and look at the whole-systems approach we embrace within Functional Medicine. In fact, we know each other through our work with the Institute for Functional Medicine. In 2014, she collaborated with the Institute to launch and lead the seventy-thousand-person worldwide Detox Summit and then had thousands of people do the detox in the Detox Challenge. Similar to the results I find in my clinical practice, she found a 50 to 60 percent reduction in symptoms just within twenty-one days. Furthermore, she is also faculty for the Institute, teaching specifically the food and lifestyle aspects of detox.

Quite frankly, I think she is the perfect person to talk about detox in this new "whole" kind of way. Deanna is a scientist and clinician who is keen on looking at the psychology, eating, and living features of someone's life. I especially enjoy the fact that she uses so much color in her teaching and draws upon her talent as a visual artist.

It's very promising to see that we are redefining detox in the twenty-first century. The Father of Functional Medicine, Dr. Jeffrey Bland, introduced nutritional detoxification (metabolic biotransformation) in the twentieth century and brought important concepts to the foreground. Now, decades later, with the emerging areas of mind–body medicine, we've come to realize that toxins cross over between the body and the mind. Physical toxins, like heavy metals, can create psychological effects, and psychological toxins, like stress, can have physical manifestations. Truly, "detox" needs to keep up with the evolving science, and I think that's what we have *Whole Detox* here to do.

Mark Hyman, M.D.
Director of the Cleveland Clinic Center for Functional Medicine

FOREWORD

For decades, the word "detoxification" was narrowly defined to refer to pharmacogenomics, which is the manner in which specific inherited traits influence the way that drugs are metabolized and eliminated from the body.[1] In 1980, as a university professor trained in nutritional biochemistry, I started to wonder if the detoxification of drugs was influenced by the food and its associated nutrients that we ate. I had the fortune of meeting Dr. William Rea, a physician in Dallas, who had specialized in understanding the relationship between chemical sensitivity and individual differences in detoxification.[2] I began to understand that the metabolic pathways utilized in drug detoxification could be influenced by nutrients and foods.[3] For example, grapefruit juice was known to change the activity of some drugs that went through a cytochrome enzyme known as CYP3A4.[4] There were also certain herbs, like St. John's-wort, known to alter these hepatic enzymes and thus became contraindicated by pharmacists to patients if they were on specific drugs.[5]

Based on what I observed within the context of my background in nutritional biochemistry, I decided to go further down the path of exam-

1. Q. Ma and A. Y. Lu, "Pharmacogenetics, Pharmacogenomics, and Individualized Medicine," *Pharmacological Reviews* 63, no. 2 (2011): 437–59.
2. W. J. Rea et al., "Chemical Sensitivity in Physicians," *Boletín Asociación Médica de Puerto Rico* 83, no. 9 (1991): 383–88.
3. H. F. Woods, "Effects of Nutrition on Drug Metabolism and Distribution," *Comprehensive Therapy* 4, no. 10 (1978): 49–53.
4. K. Fukuda, T. Ohta, and Y. Yamazoe, "Grapefruit Component Interacting with Rat and Human CYP3A4: Possible Involvement of Non-Flavonoid Components in Drug Interaction," *Biological and Pharmaceutical Bulletin* 20, no. 5 (1997): 560–64.
5. J. W. Budzinski et al., "An In Vitro Evaluation of Human Cytochrome P450 3A4 Inhibition by Selected Herbal Extracts and Tinctures," *Phytomedicine* 7, no. 4 (2000): 273–82.

ining how nutrition, especially protein and certain plant extracts, could alter metabolism and change one's health. In 1995, I published a paper in the *Alternative Therapies in Health and Medicine* journal to detail some of our clinical research on the role of nutritional intervention in detoxification.[6] We found that patients who were chronically ill with what had been diagnosed as "chronic fatigue syndrome" and were given a medical food formulated with specific nutrients to enhance detoxification pathways in conjunction with a "clean," low-allergy, calorie-controlled diet did significantly better and had a greater reduction of health complaints (52 percent reduction) compared with those who were administered the same diet without the addition of the medical food (22 percent reduction in symptoms). We were able to show that symptom reduction was associated with the normalization of liver enzymes involved in detoxification that might have otherwise been impaired. Additionally, we were able to statistically increase reserves of sulfur and glutathione in these patients, both of which are essential compounds for biochemical pathways of detoxification. At this time, we recognized from the research of Drs. Rosemary Waring and Glyn Steventon that the onset of Parkinson's disease is often associated with insufficiencies in a patient's detoxification system, particularly in glutathione metabolism.[7]

From this beginning I came to recognize that the metabolism or detoxification of alcohol by the liver was very dependent upon nutritional status,[8] as was the metabolism of common over-the-counter drugs like acetaminophen and ibuprofen.[9]

This study sent me further in the direction of researching detoxification from biochemical and nutritional perspectives. I continued doing research into the role that various nutrients had on the metabolic detoxification processes. My colleagues and I utilized a number of specific tests to evaluate the detoxification potential of the individual, including the caffeine and

---

6. J. S. Bland et al., "A Medical Food-Supplemented Detoxification Program in the Management of Chronic Health Problems," *Alternative Therapies in Health and Medicine* 1, no. 5 (1995): 62–71.

7. Adrian Williams et al., "Xenobiotic Enzyme Profiles and Parkinson's Disease," *Neurology* 41, no. 5, suppl. 2 (1991): 29–32.

8. C. S. Lieber, "A Personal Perspective on Alcohol, Nutrition and the Liver," *American Journal of Clinical Nutrition* 58, no. 3 (1993): 430–42.

9. K. D. Rainsford and J. Bjarnason, "NSAIDs: Take with Food or After Fasting?" *Journal Pharmacy and Pharmacology* 64, no. 4 (2012): 465–69.

benzoate clearance tests.[10] In 1991 Dr. J. O. Hunter, a well-respected medical research professor at Cambridge University Hospitals, authored an article that indicated that the adverse reaction some people have to specific foods may be a result of their inability to detoxify the natural substances found in the food.[11] All of these studies proved to us that nutritional status and specific nutrient supplementation programs could have a significant influence on detoxification of both foreign chemicals and endogenous toxins produced by normal metabolism.[12]

It was at this point that I was very fortunate to have Dr. Deanna Minich join our research group at MetaProteomics in Gig Harbor, Washington. From the day she joined our research team the focus on nutrition and specific nutrients took a step forward. She was a superb researcher who helped pioneer the understanding of nutrition in supporting the detoxification processes of the body. Her work on the role of the alkaline diet in detoxification was a major advance in the development of a dietary program to support improved detoxification.[13] The recent paper on detoxification that she and her research colleague Romilly Hodges have had published is a landmark review paper that clearly defines the role of foods and food-derived components in metabolic detoxification.[14]

Over the past thirty years in the field, I have come to recognize that "detoxification" is a term that means more than nutritional detoxification. The use of the word often implies something quite different from how we had used the word within my research. The term now describes the metabolism of drugs, metabolites from gut bacteria, pollutants, metabolic byproducts, and even "toxic" experiences, relationships, and thoughts.

10. T. Wang et al., "Caffeine Elimination: A Test of Liver Function," *Klinische Wochenschrift* 63, no. 21 (1985): 1124–28; J. Soto, J. A. Sacristan, and M. J. Alsar, "Use of Salivary Caffeine Tests to Assess the Inducer Effect of a Drug on Hepatic Metabolism," *Annals of Pharmacotherapy* 30, nos. 7–8 (1996): 736–39; and M. Takayama and S. Yamada, "Clinical Usefulness of Benzoate Tolerance Test in Patients with Liver Cirrhosis" [in Japanese], *Rinsho Byori* 40, no. 12 (1992): 1303–6.

11. J. O. Hunter, "Food Allergy—or Enterometabolic Disorder?" *Lancet* 338, no. 8765 (1991): 495–96.

12. W. R. Bidlack, R. C. Brown, and C. Mohan, "Nutritional Parameters That Alter Hepatic Drug Metabolism, Conjugation, and Toxicity," *Federation Proceedings* 45, no. 2 (1986): 142–48.

13. D. M. Minich and J. S. Bland, "Acid–Alkaline Balance: Role in Chronic Disease and Detoxification," *Alternative Therapies in Health and Medicine* 13, no. 4 (2007): 62–65.

14. R. E. Hodges and D. M. Minich, "Modulation of Metabolic Detoxification Pathways Using Foods and Food-Derived Components: A Scientific Review with Clinical Applications," *Journal of Nutrition and Metabolism* (2015): e760689.

With this broad definition of detoxification, I come back to what we know of the relationship of diet and specific nutrients to support the specific inducible metabolic processes associated with detoxification. This concept of detoxification has become one of the seven core physiological processes within the functional medicine concept. There is now irrefutable evidence that toxic burden contributes to many chronic diseases, including type 2 diabetes,[15] cardiovascular disease,[16] arthritis,[17] and neurodegeneration.[18]

I am so impressed with how Dr. Minich has incorporated into her book *Whole Detox* the expansive, evolving science of nutritoxigenomics into a sensible program for improving the body's detoxification program that the average non-scientist can successfully apply in their own lives.

For more than ten years I have observed Dr. Minich in her role as a senior leader of our research and development team, in which she provides consultation to patients in the Functional Medicine Research Center. Deanna is not only an expert in the science of nutrition as it relates to detoxification but also a holistic systems thinker who is able to understand the broader personal and lifestyle issues related to detoxification. Her knowledge about how people develop and then respond to detoxification programs is not theoretical but rather derived from years of clinical experience with hundreds of patients. In addition to her background as a functional medicine nutritionist, she has integrated elements of personalized lifestyle medicine, determining what felt right for her patients specifically and how to tailor their detoxification to their specific needs.[19] Deanna is able to make the sometimes technical aspects of lifestyle medicine more consumer friendly through her artistic use of images and color. She teaches with metaphor and creativity, which allows for a well-rounded approach to all she does.

15. K. W. Taylor et al., "Evaluation of the Association Between Persistent Organic Pollutants (POPs) and Diabetes in Epidemiological Studies: A National Toxicity Program Workshop Review," *Environmental Health Perspectives* 121, no. 7 (2013): 774–83.

16. M. Porta, "Persistent Organic Pollutants and the Burden of Disease," *Lancet* 368 (2006): 558–59.

17. A. I. Catrina, K. D. Deane, and J. U. Scher, "Gene, Environment, Microbiome, and Mucosal Immune Tolerance in Rheumatoid Arthritis," *Rheumatology* (Oxford) 23 (2014): 469–75.

18. V. Nicolia, M. Lucarelli, and A. Fuso, "Environment, Epigenetics, and Neurodegeneration: Focus on Nutrition in Alzheimer's Disease," *Experimental Gerontology* 68 (2015): 8–12.

19. D. M. Minich and J. S. Bland, "Personalized Lifestyle Medicine: Relevance for Nutrition and Lifestyle Recommendations," *ScientificWorld Journal* (June 26, 2013): 129841.

Within this book *Whole Detox*, the reader will find the best of Dr. Minich and an opportunity to improve their health through the wisdom she provides from both her extensive research and her clinical applications. This is the book in which the approach to detoxification offers the whole picture in a program that is tried and proven to be successful.

Jeffrey Bland, Ph.D.
President of the Personalized Lifestyle Medicine Institute

INTRODUCTION: WHY WHOLE DETOX?

My patient Sandy was frustrated.

"Dr. Minich," she said, "I'm *really* hoping you can help me. I feel like I've tried every detox under the sun, and they all work, but only for a little while. I've heard that *your* detox does some really great things and that it will change my life, and I really hope that's true. Because, honestly, I'm starting to lose hope."

I could well understand Sandy's frustration. Like many of my patients, she was looking for a way to lose weight, feel great, and boost her energy. She was also struggling with brain fog and some mild anxiety. Some of my other patients suffer from aching joints, sleep problems, depression, listlessness, or fatigue. For many, I'm not the first stop on the health-care trail; they've tried conventional medicine, a number of supposedly healthy diets, a wide range of fitness programs, and at least one or two cleanses. Many even improve—for a while. Then, like Sandy, they start to drift back to the same set of problems that sent them searching for help in the first place.

Does that sound like you? Are you also frustrated that those five or ten or twenty pounds keep coming back after you've worked so hard to lose them? Do you wish there was a way to regain your lost energy and sharpen up your brain? Are you struggling with sleep problems, anxiety, or depression that you'd prefer to treat naturally? Do you feel as though you keep running into the same brick wall?

If so, I hear you. I've spent enough of my life seeking answers for my own health problems to know just how frustrating and sometimes scary that can be. When I began as a functional medicine nutritionist, I was thrilled that I'd have the chance to translate my years of science and research into practical ways of giving people access to the vibrant health that is our birth-right. At that point, I had a lot of faith in good nutrition as the royal road to health—the way to living well and feeling great.

Over the years, though, I, like Sandy, became frustrated. I began to see that for many patients, the wonderful nutritional suggestions I was making simply didn't "take."

Maybe they would for a while. The patients would be incredibly excited as they finished the consultation, thrilled with their jump-start to a healthy life. They had shed pounds and lost inches. Their brain fog had cleared. Their anxiety had calmed. Their depression had lifted. Detox had given them a glimpse of just how great life could be when they felt this good, all the time.

And then a month, two months, half a year later, many of those same patients would return, discouraged, maybe even defeated. They had started to regain the weight. Their aches and pains were back. They no longer felt the energy, the hope, the vibrant health they had once enjoyed.

What had gone wrong? Why would an approach that had worked so well stop working?

I struggled with this problem for several years, and then finally I got it.

The reason most detoxes have so little staying power is that they treat only a part, but not the whole.

They deal with part of your body, not your whole body.

They tell you what to take out, but they don't focus on what to put in.

They deal only with your physical body, not with your whole self.

And as a result, they often fail.

WHY MOST DETOXES DON'T LAST

They Don't Deal with Your Whole Body

Most detoxes pick one single part of your body—your liver, perhaps, or your gut. But very few programs look comprehensively and systematically at your whole body and make sure that your entire physical self—from your feet through your belly through your heart to your brain—has every bit of support it needs to expel all your toxins.

This whole-body approach is essential, especially given that the latest developments in medicine focus on the activity and interrelationships of your body's networks: not just your gut but your digestive system; not just your digestive system but the interaction between it and every other organ and system in your body. Your liver doesn't work separately from your gut; they work *together*. (The scientific terms for this type of thinking are "network medicine" and "systems biology.")

They Focus on What to Take Out, Not What to Put In

Most detoxes zero in on reactive foods, industrial chemicals, and other environmental toxins. They tell you how to protect yourself from these toxins, and maybe they even offer you a few weeks' worth of meal plans. Or they focus on a few potentially toxic foods—caffeine, sugar, and gluten, perhaps, or maybe soy, peanuts, and artificial sweeteners. Some detoxes are more restrictive, with an even longer list of things to cut out. But none of these approaches gives enough attention to your *whole* body, comprehensively, systematically making sure that every one of your vital systems is getting the full spectrum of nutrients it needs.

They Focus on the Body, Not the Whole Self

Most detoxes tell us how to avoid reactive foods and industrial chemicals, which is great. But do they help us shed toxic thoughts, let go of limiting beliefs, or cope with the stressful situations that frequently make us ill? Not that I've seen.

Every time you encounter an upsetting relationship, a frustrating personal situation, or a depressing day at work, your body is flooded with biochemicals that have the power to sabotage your health. I'm talking about stress hormones like cortisol, which cues your body to put on the pounds, disrupt your sleep, and drive up your blood pressure, potentially sending you down the road to obesity, diabetes, autoimmune conditions, and cancer. I'm talking about the shattering experience of heartbreaking grief, which research has shown can literally disrupt the workings of your heart. I'm talking about lives that seem plagued by loneliness and boredom, which numerous studies have shown are characterized by more chronic health problems and also end sooner than lives full of passion, meaning, and community.

We now have volumes full of research showing that stress, boredom, frustration, and heartbreak aren't simply psychological states. Rather, they are *physical* conditions that profoundly affect your health: through your hormones, your blood pressure, your neurotransmitters, and, ultimately, your entire biochemistry. A happy, relaxed person is biochemically different from an angry, sad, or fearful one. Your body affects your thoughts and feelings . . . and your thoughts and feelings affect your body. This interaction is straight out of Human Biochemistry 101. It can be a significant disrupter of your health—or a profound tool for healing.

Yet most detoxes ignore this life component and stick strictly to nutritional advice. Even when they pay lip service to "stress relief" or "taking time for yourself," they fail to offer any concrete, workable program to actually get rid of your life toxins. As a result, most detoxes are sadly incomplete, because if you don't heal the whole person, you'll just see the same problems coming back again and again and again.

DETOX'S NEW FRONTIER

I didn't want my patients to keep suffering. I didn't want them to follow up the brilliant initial success of their detox with a disappointing fizzle a few weeks later. I didn't want a detox that worked only briefly, randomly, or occasionally, and I didn't want a detox that addressed the body alone.

So I began searching for a program that would allow us to remove every single toxic barrier that keeps us from total health and vital, fulfilling lives. I drew on my years doing academic and professional research into the biochemical and nutritional properties of food, and on my experience as a clinician who had worked with thousands of patients. I wanted a detox that spoke to every facet of our bodies and our lives—a clear, actionable program that even the busiest and most stressed of my patients could follow.

The culmination of this process was Whole Detox: the first comprehensive, systematic approach to breaking through *all* the toxins that hold us back. But first, I had to rethink what I meant by "toxin."

REDEFINING "TOXIN"

Okay, we all know that "detoxification" means, literally, to get rid of toxins. But what exactly are toxins? We're used to speaking of them in purely physical terms. My research and my clinical practice have taught me that they are much, much more. Toxins are better understood less as poisons than as barriers—obstacles to the life and health we truly want.

On a physical level, this is pretty clear. If we look at the thyroid signaling system, for example—the complex network of glands and hormones that regulate thyroid function—we see that poor thyroid function makes the whole body more vulnerable to environmental toxins, interfering with our ability to detoxify. At the same time, the increasing toxic burden disrupts the thyroid signaling system, making it more difficult for different parts of the system to communicate with one another. These toxic barriers to communication further depress thyroid function, creating a vicious cycle that can sabotage our entire quality of life. Depression, weight gain, brain fog, exhaustion, memory problems, and, potentially, heart disease are only some of the chronic conditions that can result.

Yet when you remove the toxic barriers, communication resumes. Thyroid function improves, and we suddenly have a new lease on life.

Slowly I came to see that the very same principle applies to life toxins. If mental, emotional, or spiritual challenges are standing in our way, they can block our progress—and undermine our health. I began to see that when I helped my patients release their life toxins, their health improved as well.

For example, my patient Marqueta had struggled for years with a limiting belief: she felt she couldn't be a successful, empowered woman and also retain her femininity. Marqueta's mother had grown up in a very traditional religious household, and she had tried to instill those same values in her daughter, including the notion that women were supposed to be quiet, timid, and sexually passive.

This limiting belief was keeping Marqueta from pursuing relationships with men who really interested her. Any time she found a man she liked, she worried that she was being "too sexual" and "too forward." She also worried that the man would be put off by her success as the administrator of a local hospital.

When she came to me, she was suffering from crippling menstrual cramps. She also described herself as "dried up—my brain just won't work." Once a creative, vital person, she was clearly struggling with many toxic barriers. Her physical symptoms expressed her life issues; her life issues were shaped by her physical problems.

Enter Whole Detox. I addressed Marqueta's hormonal issues in a variety of nutritional ways: healthy fats, better hydration, some herbal supplements. I also worked with her to identify the limiting belief that functioned as such a daunting obstacle. I encouraged her to foster her creativity, even in such little ways as how she dressed or how she decorated her office. I asked her to write in her journal about the women she admired and wanted to emulate, and to identify the qualities in herself that resembled those women. Through a wide variety of modalities—diet, supplements, lifestyle, self-exploration, journaling, and creative activities—I helped her get rid of the toxic barriers that were holding her back.

Once Marqueta understood how to identify and overcome all the toxins in her life—from reactive foods to limiting thoughts to frustrating relationships—she was able to reclaim her health. Because she wasn't following an abstract system but rather identifying her own personal toxins, she was empowered far beyond what partial detoxes could achieve. Thanks to the tools she had learned through Whole Detox, she would be able to target and defeat her personal toxins for the rest of her life.

Even after a few weeks, the results were astonishing. Soon after we began working together, Marqueta transformed her wardrobe from dull grays and beiges to brilliant oranges and yellows, which suited her much better. She began to feel creative and "flowing" again, no longer "dried up" and "stuck." She started a new relationship, slowly and tentatively, but with more passion and excitement than she had previously allowed herself. Her menstrual cramps disappeared. Her hormones were in balance. The culmination came at her last appointment, when she showed up with a haircut so dramatic and different from her previous style that I honestly almost didn't recognize her.

This, to me, is the essence of Whole Detox. Marqueta had broken through the toxic barriers that were limiting her life so she could finally savor the full spectrum of her whole self.

DISCOVERING WHOLE DETOX

When I developed Whole Detox, I had been working for nearly a decade as a nutritionist. I had done graduate research into the nutritional properties of the carotenoids that give foods their color, as well as into the biochemical properties of fats.

I had also explored other ancient healing arts, including Traditional Chinese Medicine (TCM), Ayurveda, and many others. A single yoga class I took more than twenty years ago first turned on the lightbulb in my head, illuminating the many healing truths available to us, even if they are often neglected by conventional practitioners.

So in my quest for detox's new frontier, I went back and searched my library for every discipline I had ever studied: nutrition, neuroscience, epigenetics, physiology, and psychology as well as yoga, Ayurveda, TCM, and traditional healing. Odd as it might sound, I also explored color and drew on my background in the visual arts. After all, color has long been associated with emotion and mood as well as with the phytonutrients that make fruits, vegetables, herbs, and other plant foods such a crucial part of our diet. Color plays a role in East Indian healing too.

Working with this rich array of influences, I came up with a new approach to detox. Its power was astounding. As I introduced this approach to my patients, I saw how deeply mind, body, and emotions all affect one another. Remove a toxic food from your diet, and you might also free yourself from depression, anxiety, or helplessness. Eliminate a toxic thought, and you might also rev up your metabolism and lose some unwanted weight. Tear down the barriers to your sense of purpose and connectedness, and you might also revitalize your immune system and restore your optimism.

The opposite was also true. Hold on to a toxic belief, and the healthiest diet in the world might not free you from troublesome symptoms. Remain mired in a stressful life, and even without caffeine, sugar, and refined flour, you might still feel wired, anxious, or depressed. A raging hunger for meaning or community might keep you dissatisfied and on edge even when your body is fully nourished.

Every one of us is a complex biochemical structure in which every factor affects every other factor in an endless synergistic loop. Sometimes this synergy works against us: Negative thoughts can impair our health; poor health can breed negative thoughts. As your health gets worse, your thoughts get bleaker; as your thoughts get bleaker, you move less, crave more sugar, and send more stress hormones coursing through your veins. You feel even sicker . . . and your thoughts spiral further down into depression. Talk about a vicious cycle!

But with Whole Detox, you can transform the downward spiral of disease into an upward spiral of vibrant health. By addressing nutrition, exercise, thought patterns, and many other factors at the same time, you can break through toxic barriers and create an energized, full-spectrum life.

WHAT WHOLE DETOX WILL DO FOR YOU

Whole Detox integrates Western science and Eastern medicine. It is a systematic way of overcoming every barrier that keeps you from health, energy, and fulfillment. So welcome to Whole Detox, because it will change your life:

- You'll begin to heal the parts of your body that are struggling under their toxic burden, including your endocrine system, digestion, heart, bones, and brain.
- You'll shed pounds, boost your energy, heal your aches and pains, and recover from debilitating symptoms, feeling calmer, more vital, and more energized than you have in years.
- You'll detoxify your relationship with your community, your family, and yourself.
- You'll detox through food and also through movement, new thought patterns, and emotional expression.
- You'll break through conflicts and creative blocks, which will free you to pursue long-deferred dreams for work, love, and personal satisfaction.
- You'll feel nourished, not deprived, because sometimes the best detox is not cutting something out but rather bringing in more of what you need!

Most important, Whole Detox is a *personalized* approach. You'll zero in on the parts of your body—and your life—that most need cleansing, healing, and revitalization. You'll also acquire the lifelong ability to target your personal barriers by using the Whole Detox Spectrum Quiz. As a result, Whole Detox is the fastest and most effective way to become your healthiest, most energized, and most fully realized self.

THE POWER OF WHOLE DETOX

To illustrate the power of Whole Detox, let me share with you the story of George, who came to me frustrated and helpless about six months after completing a detox with another practitioner. George's problem was that he couldn't sleep—an aching frustration that had been with him ever since his sophomore year in college.

Now in his midforties, he was paying a heavy price for his insomnia. He often found himself short-tempered with his children as well as his wife. Since his father had been a short-tempered, angry man, George hated the feeling that he was repeating his father's version of family life.

At work, too, George struggled to remain calm and centered. The owner of a small tech company, he frequently had to travel on business, working with clients in various parts of the country. He knew that a sleepless night before an important meeting could jeopardize a vital relationship, yet he hated to depend on sleep aids.

Sleep problems were ruining his life, he told me frankly the first time we met. His despair was all the greater because he had recently completed a detox that, for a few sweet months, had finally seemed to heal the problem. On that program, he cut out caffeine, sugar, white flour, and unhealthy fats. He drank water with lemon juice to flush the toxins out through his urine, and he took yarrow pills to support his liver's detox function. He got a water filter, an air purifier, and blackout curtains to keep "light pollution" out of his bedroom. Anything that could interfere with his sleep, he got rid of. And for a time it worked. George's sleep quality improved until finally, after less than two weeks, he was sleeping deeply throughout the night. For the next few months, he felt as though he had witnessed a miracle.

Then, slowly but surely, the old sleep problems began creeping back.

When a loud noise in a hotel corridor woke him up one night, he tossed and turned for hours. When a difficult client meeting loomed the next day, he couldn't fall asleep till nearly five A.M. When his ten-year-old daughter came down with a high fever one night, he lay rigid beside his sleeping wife, imagining all the terrible ways her illness might play out.

"What's the problem?" George asked when he eventually came to see me. "Once I started sleeping again, why couldn't I *keep* sleeping?"

"I think three things might be going on," I suggested. "First, there may be some toxins that are personal and specific to you—some reactive foods or problematic chemicals that are disrupting your body. Most detoxes are cookie-cutter—one size fits all. They can be a great first step, but they don't necessarily identify the toxins that are disrupting your system."

George nodded, beginning to look more hopeful.

"Second, although your previous detox focused on what to cut out, you didn't really find out what to put in. Healthy fats are really important for sleeping. So are complex carbohydrates. There may be some other imbalances we will discover as we work through your entire body, systems in your body that are not getting all the nourishment they need."

George nodded a second time, seeming even more hopeful.

"Finally—and maybe most important—we can't just look at your body. We have to look at your whole self."

Now George was startled. "You mean there's something wrong with me, with my personality?" he asked.

"Not at all," I said quickly. "But your body and your mind aren't really separate. They're both part of the same system. Your thoughts and feelings are biochemical events that have a profound effect on the rest of your physiology. We can work only on the body level, as your previous detox did. But this is Whole Detox, and I think it would help you to work on the life level as well."

George and I had many long talks about what might be keeping him awake. As he thought about his bad-tempered father, he recalled many late-night arguments his parents used to have. His father had worked until midnight at the restaurant he owned, and when he came home, he expected George's mother to offer a sympathetic listening ear and a plate of hot food. George's mother, for her part, was exhausted after a long day of working at an office downtown and then making dinner for her children. George's father frequently woke her up, and the two fought, waking George. The sense that night was the time to be alert, on edge, ready to protect the people he loved yet helpless to do so, had never really left George.

He had also held on to the sense that to be a truly successful businessman, like his father, he had to stay up late, worrying about his business. Without realizing it, he had adopted that same worry, as though by falling into a deep sleep he was neglecting his business and letting down his clients. Of course, the exact opposite was true. His sleep problems were actually interfering with his ability to be a good family man and an effective businessman.

Certainly, he had found it helpful to cut out the foods and beverages that had disrupted his sleep, and he also benefited from adding in the supportive foods I suggested. But George was a whole person, and he needed a whole detox, one that included both health *and* life issues. To solve his sleep problem, he had to identify *all* the toxic barriers that kept him up at night, not just the nutritional ones.

YOUR 21-DAY PROGRAM

The Whole Detox George embarked on with me is what you're about to begin, too.

In chapter 1, I'll give you an overview of the cornerstone of Whole Detox: the Seven Systems of Full-Spectrum Health. These are seven clusters of physical and life issues that can be supported, healed, and detoxed in similar ways.

Once you've learned about each separate system, chapter 2 will help you see how all of them work together. It's called "The Power of Synergy" because synergy—the extra benefits you get from many systems all working in harmony—is truly the force behind Whole Detox.

Then, in chapters 3 through 9, I will provide an in-depth look at every system so that by the time you begin your Whole Detox, you'll be able to see your body, your life issues, and your goals in those terms.

This approach offers you two striking advantages that make Whole Detox more effective and longer lasting than any other detox I've seen.

First, these seven systems target every aspect of your body and your life: every anatomical system and also every life issue (work, love, community, spirituality, etc.). When you target each of the seven systems, you guarantee yourself a truly *whole* detox, identifying every single barrier that stands between you and optimal health, between you and a wholly inspired and fulfilling life.

Second, working with the seven systems enables you to create a truly *personal* detox—one that zeroes in on the specific barriers that are most troublesome to *you*. The Whole Detox Spectrum Quiz helps you work through every one of the seven systems, identifying each specific physical, mental, or emotional issue that stands in your way. What most people discover is that one or two systems are more out of balance than the others, while one or two other systems are areas of strength and power. When you identify your strengths and weaknesses, you can find ways to immediately support the strengths and improve the weaknesses, which will improve your physical, mental, and emotional well-being.

THE SEVEN SYSTEMS OF FULL-SPECTRUM HEALTH

Here are the seven systems that encompass the health of your entire being:

The ROOT: adrenal glands, immune system, DNA, bones, skin, survival, community

The FLOW: ovaries/testes, reproduction, fertility, urinary system, colon, partnerships, creativity

The FIRE: digestive system, blood sugar, work–life balance, energy production

The LOVE: thymus, heart, blood vessels, lungs, compassion, expansiveness, service

The TRUTH: thyroid gland, throat, mouth, ears, nose, speaking, choice, authenticity

The INSIGHT: pituitary gland, brain, neurons/neurotransmitters, sleep, mood, thoughts, intuition

The SPIRIT: pineal gland, electromagnetic fields, circadian rhythms, connection, purpose, meaning

---

These seven systems might seem a bit counterintuitive at first—why should adrenals, the immune system, and community all be part of the first system while ovaries, creativity, and the colon fit together in the second? But I promise, by the time you've finished reading chapters 1 through 9, these seven systems are going to seem intuitive and even a little obvious. And by the time you've finished your twenty-one-day program, you won't remember thinking any other way.

As a clinician, I found that these seven systems of health were my keys to the kingdom: through them, I could see that seemingly disparate issues—usually separated into nutritional, anatomical, psychological, and spiritual—did actually benefit from being treated together.

For example, the first system of health includes, among other things, immune function, bone health, identity, rootedness, and security—all the things that ground us and define us in a physical way. I could address immune function by giving my patients an immune-healthy diet, but I could also help them to create a strong sense of personal boundaries. They could enhance their bone health through supplements but also through yoga exercises that help them feel grounded. Meanwhile, a healthy immune system and strong bones could create a feeling of rootedness, safety, and security. In other words, treating one ROOT issue opens the door to a whole new world of improvement.

During your twenty-one-day program, every three days you'll detox another system of health, starting at the ROOT and working your way up to the SPIRIT. By the end of the three weeks, you will have addressed every toxic barrier in your life.

I'll be with you every step of the way. I'll tell you exactly what to eat each day (the recipes are simple, colorful, and delicious!). And I'll guide you through each day's activities: affirmations, meditation, visualization, journaling, explorations of limiting thoughts, and recommendations for healthy movement: a whole spectrum of ways to break through your personal toxic barriers. The instructions are clear and unambiguous—all you have to do is follow directions.

I've provided every single thing you need to complete this program successfully, including mouth-watering recipes, most of which can be prepared in thirty minutes or less. I've also shared shopping lists and some suggestions for how to lay the groundwork in the week before you start.

Whole Detox may be one of the most exciting journeys you'll ever take—and it doesn't end after twenty-one days. I've also included a section on how to maintain Whole Detox for life, so you can be sure to keep removing barriers and creating fabulous results.

DETOX FOR THE TWENTY-FIRST CENTURY

I'm thrilled to share Whole Detox with you, because I think it's high time we found a new definition for "detox." We need a detox that employs the whole spectrum of ancient and modern knowledge, and one that treats the whole spectrum of who we are. As a functional medicine nutritionist, I believe that "food is medicine," but I've also come to believe that this approach is not enough. Most people cannot heal on food alone. Yes, health requires a foundation of good eating, but good eating will not necessarily solve our emotional woes or stop our limiting beliefs and toxic self-talk.

The Seven Systems of Full-Spectrum Health have been recognized by ancient healing traditions for thousands of years. They still hold true in the present day. Our physiologies are so intricate and complex, and so are the ways each of our bodies interacts with our entire being. No two of us are alike, yet each of us contains these seven systems, this spectrum of color that helps define our bodies and our lives.

Whole Detox empowers us to remove not just physical toxins but *all* the barriers that impede our growth. Whole Detox is a twenty-one-day program, yes, but it's also the beginning of a *whole* new way of life.

CHAPTER 1

WHOLE DETOX FOR YOUR WHOLE SELF

My patient Padma was confused—and skeptical.

"I came to you for nutritional advice, and to detox," she said with her faint flavor of an Indian accent. "But you are talking to me about all sorts of other issues besides food. I am a person of science—a sociologist—and I want to focus on science and the facts."

I smiled. I had heard these objections before, but seldom did my skeptical patients express their opinions so bluntly, and so soon.

By being so clear, Padma allowed me to be clear in response. "I am also a person of science," I told her. "And what I've learned in more than fifteen years of research and clinical work is that the most scientific approach to healing doesn't ever focus on just one small part of the human body, let alone ignore the role of thoughts, beliefs, and emotions in our health. You get the best results by addressing the whole person. That's what this program is all about."

Padma still looked doubtful.

"Padma," I went on, "you think that beliefs and emotions are separate from the physical body. But, in fact, every time you have a thought or feeling, it is expressed biochemically, as a cascade of neurotransmitters, hormones, or cellular responses. Therefore, your physical condition can have an enormous impact on your mood, your ability to think clearly, and your overall outlook on life—just as your mood, thoughts, and beliefs can affect your physical condition. Mind–body medicine isn't some mystical mumbo jumbo. It's Human Biochemistry 101."

Most of us are used to making distinctions between our body and our emotions. We believe that "I feel hot" or "My foot hurts" or "My doctor tells me I'm at risk for a heart attack" are fundamentally different types of state-ments from "I feel scared" or "My heart aches" or "If my boss keeps me late one more night this week, I'm going to go through the roof."

Of course, in some ways, those *are* different statements. While we can't measure the subjective experience of heat or pain, we can take our tempera-ture with a thermometer, x-ray our foot for broken bones, and run a whole range of tests to assess our risk for a heart attack. Fear, grief, and anger are harder to measure. And even though we turn to physical metaphors to express our emotional states, we know we don't mean them literally. Your heart doesn't *really* ache. Your blood isn't *literally* boiling. You aren't *actually* about to explode.

Yet in a very real sense, the contrast between mind and body is what my old professors used to call "a distinction without a difference"—a distinc-tion that, at the end of the day, isn't really very useful. Because, in fact, there isn't really any such thing as "body," "mind," "sensation," "emotion"—those are just the names we've come up with to make sense of our experi-ence. What we *really* have, when we look at our human lives, is biochemistry: one big interactive network of hormones, neurotransmitters, synapses, and glands whose job is to respond to the challenges and opportunities of our environment. These responses all happen through electricity and chemistry, and all of them are always *both* physical *and* emotional. That is, any thought or emotion is reflected in a biochemical event, and any biochemical event has its mental and emotional dimensions.

If someone runs up to you with a knife, for example, you might expe-rience the emotion known as fear. Or you might feel anger or determi-nation or some other emotion. You are likely to think, *This doesn't look good* or *I wonder if I can run fast enough to get away.* Whatever thoughts and emotions you might have, you'll also experience an immediate, measurable physical response: the stress response. Your muscles will tense, your blood will begin to flow toward your muscles and away from your stomach, your heart will beat faster, your pupils will contract, your palms will sweat, and you'll start to breathe quickly. And behind both the mental and the physical responses is a flood of stress hormones—cortisol, dopamine, adrenaline, noradrenaline, and many others—triggered via a complicated chemical cascade initiated in your hypothalamus and passing on to your pituitary and your adrenals. Your mental, emotional, and physical experience—the thoughts, feelings, and sensations you experience—all show up in biochemical events.

And guess what? It doesn't really matter if you *actually* experience danger or if you just think you *might* be in danger . . . or even if you *remember* a time ten years ago when you actually were in danger. Memory, imagination, fantasy, anticipation—all of these produce the same physical response. A hypnotist can convince you that you're scared and produce in you a stress response. So can a powerful speaker alerting you to a political or social threat. So can a movie, a roller coaster, or even a really scary novel. Or a dream. You might think the attacker with a knife is real and the nightmare is unreal, and of course that is an important distinction, but an equally important point is the fact *your body doesn't know the difference.* The biochemical responses and electrical impulses that trigger the chemical cascade are the same whether they are generated by an actual physical event or a mere thought.

Now, what does this mean for those of us who want to lead healthy, fulfilling lives? It means we need to be aware of the complex ways in which our bodies and minds interact—in which the categories we like to call "physical," "mental," and "emotional" are often blended and blurred. If you feel depressed and I suggest you eat more fiber, and in a few weeks you've cheered up, then your body has measurably affected your mind. If you feel stressed and you then have trouble digesting your food (because, among other things, stress lowers your stomach acid), your mind has measurably affected your body.

When I realized this truth, I understood that I needed to incorporate it into my work as a functional medicine nutritionist. I couldn't just tell my patients what to eat; I had to help them detoxify from *all* the factors that might be adversely affecting their health.

This insight cut two ways. Patients with seemingly intractable psychological issues—anxiety, depression, stress—frequently got spectacular results from changing their diets. At the same time, patients with seemingly incurable physical issues—joint pain, cardiovascular issues, thyroid problems, and ulcerative colitis, to name only a few—got their own spectacular benefits from letting go of some limiting beliefs, nourishing their creativity, and otherwise supporting their minds and emotions.

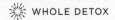
We tend to think of the boundary between mind and body as a kind of seawall—a rigid, firm barrier clearly marking out the difference between water and land, wet and dry. In reality, the boundary is more like a wide patch of damp sand over which the tide ebbs and flows: now water, now land, now a mixture of both—and constantly changing.

HORMONES: WHERE MIND AND BODY BLUR

One of the quickest ways to understand the interplay between our emotions, thoughts, and physical selves is to consider our hormones.

A hormone is a signaling molecule that helps to regulate the body's physiology and behavior. Hormones are produced by glands, which are part of our endocrine system, the system of hormones and glands that regulates immune function, stress response, fertility, digestion, circulation, metabolism, cognition, mood, the sleep–wake cycle, our circadian rhythms, and many other aspects of ourselves.

Unfortunately, hormones in popular culture have been blamed for female "craziness"—the kind of insanity that women are supposed to feel when they are PMSing, pregnant, or undergoing menopause. The fact is, we all have hormones, and every single one of us—of every age and gender— is profoundly affected by them. When our hormones are in balance, we are sexually vital, vigorous, clear-headed, calm, motivated, and energized. When our hormones are out of whack, so are we: anxious, obsessive, wired, and insomniac . . . exhausted, listless, "foggy," and depressed . . . or, for a double whammy, some of both.

Please don't misunderstand me: I am not saying that our hormones rule our lives (though it can often seem that way!). I am saying that they are the middle, overlapping ground between what we usually think of as "mind" and "body." If you are terrified by thoughts of losing your job, you'll have very high levels of stress hormones. That thought—*I'll lose my job and I won't be able to support myself or my family*—is enough to measurably alter your anatomy. (Yes, there is research in which scientists measured blood levels of hormones after asking subjects to think about upsetting situations.) If you listen to music, your stress hormones may decrease, and you may find yourself able to think more calmly and rationally about whether your job is really at risk or how you'll respond if you do lose it. (Yes, there is research about how music lowers your stress hormone levels.) If you drink caffeine, your cortisol levels will rise in response to the physical stimulus—and these rising hormonal levels might cause you to start feeling anxious about your job again. If you meditate or just breathe deeply, you might once again lower your cortisol levels and find yourself in a calmer state. Your thoughts might reflect that calm feeling, moving from *I'll never work again* to *I'll call Judy on Monday and see if she's hiring*. This positive thought might make you feel even calmer . . . and your stress hormones will fall a little bit more.

Do you see how quickly mind and body flicker back and forth? Whether the stress hormone spike is caused by something physical (caffeine) or mental (the prospect of being fired), you experience a measurable physical response (rising hormone levels). That physical response—whatever its cause—affects your mind.

Likewise, whatever caused your stress hormones to go up (caffeine or fear), you can lower those hormones through something physical (a warm bath) or mental (meditation). And when your stress hormones have fallen—for whatever reason—you will experience different thoughts and emotions.

CASE STUDY: STRESS HORMONES

What Produces Stress Hormones?

Physical: caffeine, blood sugar spikes and crashes, hunger, environments that are too hot or too cold, physical danger (facing an attacker, skydiving, bungee jumping), physical challenges (hiking rough terrain, rowing a boat, lifting weights)

Mental: a tough puzzle to solve, a difficult math problem, an unfamiliar language, note-taking as a speaker talks too fast, a phone call on a bad connection where you can't quite hear the other person

Emotional: a troubled child, a sick parent, a challenging relationship, worries about health or finances, anxiety about public speaking

As you can see, the lists under each category could go on and on. What I want you to notice is how seemingly unrelated events—bungee jumping and worrying about bills; public speaking and working out at the gym; a fight with your spouse and white-water rafting—all stimulate a release of hormones.

Now, here's where it gets even more interesting. How you think affects how you feel, and, consequently, how you feel affects your stress hormones. If you learn you are about to be fired, you might experience any of several different responses, for example:

- *I'll never get another job.*
- *There are plenty of jobs out there. Guess I'll polish up my résumé and start hunting.*

- *My family will think I'm a failure.*
- *My family will come through for me. I can't wait to see them on Sunday to tell them all about it.*

- *I really screwed up this time.*
- *Sometimes things just go wrong. This really isn't such a big deal.*

Can you guess which thoughts on this spectrum are more likely to raise your stress hormone level and which are more likely to lower it? This is why working with belief patterns and limiting thoughts is such a crucial part of Whole Detox.

The problem gets still more interesting—and more urgent—when I tell you all the ways that excessive stress hormones can adversely affect your body:

Symptoms
- Acne and skin problems
- Anxiety
- Brain fog
- Depression
- Imbalanced blood sugar
- Increased blood pressure
- Increased likelihood of PMS, menstrual problems, menopausal problems
- Indigestion
- Insomnia—can't fall asleep, can't stay asleep, or both
- Lowered sex drive and/or sexual function

Disorders
- Autoimmune conditions
- Cancer
- Cardiovascular conditions
- Diabetes
- Obesity

We've taken only a brief look and only at one group of hormones. Your body contains dozens of other hormonal groupings that profoundly affect you as well! Each time you examine one of the Seven Systems of Full-Spectrum Health, you'll learn some of the endocrine glands and hormones associated with that system. You'll be able to see in sharper detail just how your hormones mediate between your body, thoughts, and feelings. You'll realize how hormonal—and overall—health is supported by altering what you eat, yes, but also by exploring what you think, feel, and believe.

A CLOSER LOOK AT THE SEVEN SYSTEMS OF FULL-SPECTRUM HEALTH

We have just seen that our biochemistry crosses the boundaries between body, mind, and emotion. The next step is to ask *how* we can best treat common physical, mental, and emotional problems. That's where the Seven Systems of Full-Spectrum Health come in: seven clusters of physical, mental, and emotional issues that are best addressed together.

My notion of the seven systems is informed by science and inspired by the combined healing traditions of medicine, spirituality, and yoga. Each system is based in an endocrine gland, moving from the base of the spine up to the crown of the head, and each one represents a nexus of anatomy, physical function, and biochemistry as well as a group of emotions, thoughts, and life issues. It's a very sophisticated and elegant way of integrating body, mind, and emotions—far more nuanced and specific than any other approach I've seen.

In fact, the more success I've had with the seven systems, the more dissatisfied I've become with the notion of "body-mind-spirit." Rather than the sum of these three parts, we are a spectrum of many. Why talk about "body" in such general terms when we could make precise distinctions between the immune system and adrenals (part of the first, the ROOT, system of health), the urinary tract, kidneys, and reproductive system (part of the second, the FLOW, system), and the digestive tract plus the pancreas (part of the third, the FIRE, system)?

The Seven Systems of Full-Spectrum Health give us a way to focus our thoughts about different issues, through nutrition; lifestyle, which includes mental, emotional, and spiritual concepts; and color, which allows us to access the powerful emotional and physical effects of each color as well as the various nutritional properties embodied in the colors of food.

System	Nutrition	Lifestyle	Color
The ROOT	Red foods Protein Minerals	Identity Groundedness Family Tribe	Red
The FLOW	Orange foods Healthy fats Hydration	Creativity Fertility Letting go and being in the flow	Orange
The FIRE	Yellow foods Complex carbohydrates Healthy sweeteners	"Fire in the belly" Ambition, drive Work–life balance Self-esteem	Yellow
The LOVE	Green foods Leafy vegetables	Love Expansiveness Service Grief	Green
The TRUTH	Liquid foods (e.g., soups, stews, sauces, juices) Iodine-rich foods Moist fruits	Verbal expression Authenticity Choice	Aquamarine
The INSIGHT	Blue-purple foods Nutrients that modulate mood and cognition Foods that help with sleep	Imagination Intuition Dreams and sleep	Indigo
The SPIRIT	White, detoxifying foods Fasting Pure foods	Spirituality A sense of being part of some- thing larger than oneself Meaning and purpose	White

Using the seven systems approach gives me and my patients a powerful set of tools to identify toxic barriers and come up with solutions. If I know that you're having trouble with immune function—say, you're frequently coming down with colds and flu—that suggests you might have some toxins in your first system of health. You might need to eat more red foods or up your intake of protein and/or minerals. And/or you might need to consider your sense of personal boundaries—refusing to take on other people's problems or not allowing loved ones to blame you for their own shortcomings. And/or you might want to think about how to improve your relationship with your "tribe," the people who give you your primary sense of identity.

Likewise, if you tell me you feel "ungrounded" or you "just can't settle down to anything" or you frequently feel anxious and unsafe, I might also diagnose first system issues, which I might also address with a combination of physical, mental, and spiritual approaches. Using these seven systems allows me to get more specific than just "body," "mind," and "spirit." And when you have mastered them (and you will, I promise!), you'll be able to get equally specific and equally powerful at overcoming toxic barriers.

These seven systems may seem counterintuitive at first. You might not see why leafy green foods belong in the LOVE system along with your heart, or why blue-purple foods, like blackberries, belong in the INSIGHT system alongside the pituitary gland. But bear with me, because once you grasp the nature of each system of health, it's going to start making a whole lot of sense.

What follows is an overview so you can start to see how these seven systems account for all the physical, mental, emotional, and spiritual issues we experience. They cover the whole spectrum of human experience—another reason I call this program Whole Detox.

To ground each system for you in practical terms, I've included a few specific Whole Detox suggestions, just so you can see how these concepts might translate into real life. Don't worry about following them now or even remembering them; they're just to give you a taste of how this approach works. When you follow the actual twenty-one-day program, I will tell you *exactly* what to do on each day.

SYSTEM 1: THE ROOT
Adrenal Glands, Immune System, DNA, Bones, Skin, Survival, Community

The ROOT part of us represents our most basic sense of safety and survival. As psychologist Abraham Maslow taught us, if we don't meet our survival needs or feel safe, it's difficult even to think about anything else: we are constantly on edge until we feel rooted. So Whole Detox starts by addressing your ROOT, emphasizing the core elements of survival and identity, including family and community.

The ROOT also speaks to our basic identity as a physical person. If we're going to be fully present in our body, we need to feel rooted, grounded, and safe. Our adrenal glands kick into action whenever we feel threatened, releasing stress hormones at the least sign of danger. At the same time, our immune system keeps our inner boundaries secure. DNA and genetic expression—all the essential biochemistry that creates our core identity (and that is inherited from our family and community)—is also part of the ROOT. Finally, the ROOT includes the anatomical structures that define our body and keep us planted firmly on the earth: bones, feet, joints, legs, muscles, skin, and rectum.

Red is the color of the ROOT. For example, red foods, such as red bell peppers, strawberries, and tomatoes, are rich in the vitamin C our bodies need to manufacture stress hormones. Red blood cells feed on ROOT foods' iron, copper, and calcium. Proteins of all types, including animal protein like red meat and vegetable protein such as black beans, assist in stabilizing our bodies' energy by helping us to balance our blood sugar and by supplying the necessary iron for the red blood cells to carry oxygen.

When you detox your ROOT, you will focus on eliminating foods that stress your adrenal glands and immune system while eating the protein, minerals, and red foods that support all core issues of your ROOT. You will also consider your relationship to family, community, and tribe.

SYSTEM 2: THE FLOW
Ovaries/Testes, Reproduction, Fertility, Urinary System,
Colon, Partnerships, Creativity

Moving up from the ROOT, we address the second system of full-spectrum health, the FLOW. As Mihaly Csikszentmihalyi has shown in his landmark book *Flow*, being in the flow is crucial for creativity, whether we're talking about art, scientific discovery, or innovative ways to solve problems. When we enter this space, we become capable of sustaining a profound relationship with our work, colleagues, friends, and intimate partners.

Accordingly, the FLOW centers on the parts of the body that enable us to create new life—our ovaries (for women), testes (for men), and entire reproductive system—as well as our ability to produce new cells. Meanwhile, our kidneys and bladder literally govern the body's water fluxes, helping to balance our consumption of liquids and regulating our hydration. When we are in the flow, it means taking in and letting go with ease. The large intestine is also part of this system, since it allows us to pull out the water we need from the waste products we eliminate.

The FLOW also includes the still or turbulent waters to creativity, emotions, and relationships. I've had more than one patient who found herself able to become pregnant after releasing blocked emotions in a relationship or making more room for creativity in her life.

Orange is the color of the FLOW. Orange foods, like carrots and sweet potatoes, get their color from carotenoids, such as beta-carotene, which are associated with hormone levels and ovulation. Maybe that's why I've noticed that a lack of orange-colored, carotenoid-rich foods seems to be linked to infertility. Other types of orange foods, such as citrus fruits, contain bioflavonoids that keep our blood vessels open, preventing the stagnation of varicose veins and allowing our blood to flow. Finally, both carotenoids and bioflavonoids help to prevent cancer, keeping our bodies from engaging in unhealthy types of growth and reproduction.

When you detox your FLOW, you will focus on staying hydrated, removing the substances that disrupt your reproductive hormones, supporting your FLOW with healthy fats, and rekindling your creativity. You will also look at ways to keep your emotions flowing.

SYSTEM 3: THE FIRE
Digestive System, Blood Sugar, Work–Life Balance, Energy Production

Moving further up the body, we reach the glands and organs associated with the third system of health: the FIRE. Our pancreas, liver, gallbladder, small intestine, and stomach all burn the food we ingest, transmuting it into the energy we need to survive, just as a fire burns fuel to produce life-giving warmth. Accordingly, nutrient absorption, biotransformation, blood sugar balance, and digestion belong to this system of health.

The FIRE ignites our drive to work, achieve, and compete. A healthy FIRE is full of energy, power, and confidence. An overactive FIRE might lack work–life balance, losing the joy of accomplishment in the burning need to do more and more and more. An underactive FIRE might feel simply "burnt out." My research and clinical experience have shown me that this system of health tends to be out of alignment for just about everyone, with nearly 80 percent of my patients and students showing some imbalance in this system. An imbalanced FIRE is truly the bane of our busy, burnt-out modern lives!

Just as a fire must burn in balance—neither starved for fuel nor choked by too much green wood—so do our bodies need balance: the right types of food to keep our blood sugar stable; the right amounts of rest and stimulation to keep our energy stable. Likewise, we must all find the balance in our lives, between situations in which we "go with the flow" and situations in which we take charge, assert ourselves, and blaze forth with our goals, projects, and achievements.

Many of the glands and organs associated with the FIRE are located in and around the solar plexus—the area at the pit of the stomach—so I find it interesting that when we talk about someone who has a lot of energy and drive, we say that he or she has "fire in the belly." When our energy is depleted, we're "burnt out" or "fried to a crisp," possibly because we've been "burning the candle at both ends." We can also be "fired" from a job. These common expressions speak to our intuitive recognition of this third system of health, and to the way both our bodies and our life issues are components of the same system.

Yellow is the FIRE's color, and it's also the color of quick-burning refined carbohydrates. The diet that has become increasingly common in the modern world tends to include far too many of these high-energy, yellow foods, which perhaps is part of the fuel for an overactive FIRE. A more balanced FIRE is fueled by slow-burning, low-glycemic, high-fiber carbohydrates, such as those found in whole grains and legumes. The FIRE also requires a whole team of B vitamins, such as thiamin (B1), riboflavin (B2), niacin (B3), pyridoxine (B6), folate (B9), and cobalamin (B12), all of which are crucial for generating a healthy metabolism and extracting energy from our foods.

Detoxing your FIRE has you loading up on high-fiber carbohydrates and fiery yellow foods, such as ginger and turmeric. You'll also look at how to create your own personal version of work–life balance and harness the "fire in your belly"—your ambition, energy, and drive.

SYSTEM 4: THE LOVE
Thymus, Heart, Blood Vessels, Lungs, Compassion, Expansiveness, Service

Moving up from the belly and into the chest, we arrive at the LOVE, the fourth system of health, which resides in the kingdom of the heart and lungs. Here we open up to compassion and service as well as expansion, in the way that love in all its forms makes us feel larger, more generous, a "bigger person," someone whose warmth and good feeling radiate outward into the world. The LOVE can also expand through an embrace, an apology, a feeling of gratitude, or the simple, comforting touch of a loved one's hand. Central to this fourth system is the thymus, the organ that governs our adaptive immune system. Also central is the magnificent heart, which is far more than just a pump. Science suggests that it is also a neuroendocrine gland, affecting hormone balance as well as blood flow.

Just as love and compassion enable us to respond to a wide variety of threats, so do the thymus and heart help the body distinguish between various challenges. Meanwhile, the blood vessels, lungs, and lymphatic system serve us by spreading nourishment and oxygen throughout the body, while the lymph carries toxins away. You might see the LOVE organs as providing compassion and self-care to our entire being while helping us overcome the obstacles to growth and healing.

One of the challenges of the LOVE is to make sure that we are giving it to ourselves. Many of my patients find that their LOVE has become imbalanced, always expanding out to children, parents, friends, spouses, and perhaps even clients or colleagues, but rarely directed inward toward themselves. Forgiveness—of both ourselves and others—is an example of a way to balance the LOVE. The Western tradition associates love with the heart, while TCM views the lungs as the seat of grief. Indeed, when the LOVE is out of balance, it often manifests as overwhelming grief—"heartbreak" that refuses to heal. Too much pain can also cause us to shut down our hearts, closing off our urge toward compassion, service, and love.

Green is the color of the LOVE. The color green represents healing and nourishment, so it's no wonder that green foods are "heart-healthy." All green foods contain chlorophyll, which acts as an antioxidant and blood purifier, promoting robust circulation. Green detox foods include spirulina, chlorella, leafy greens, and cruciferous vegetables like broccoli, Brussels sprouts, and kale.

Detoxing your LOVE focuses on green leafy vegetables and expansive aerobic movement, which allows your cardiopulmonary system to function at its best. You will also consider how to expand your sense of compassion, gratitude, generosity, and self-love.

SYSTEM 5: THE TRUTH
Thyroid Gland, Throat, Mouth, Ears, Nose, Speaking, Choice, Authenticity

From the heart, we go up to the throat area, where both the voice box (larynx) and the thyroid gland are located. Now we are in the fifth system of health, which I call the TRUTH.

The TRUTH includes an array of sensory organs that provide us with inputs to integrate: ears, nose, throat, and mouth. We need to take in information and choose what to do with it—decide what's true and what isn't, make authentic decisions, and truthfully express our responses. Listening and speaking are therefore part of the TRUTH.

Smelling and chewing are also integral to this system, along with the thyroid gland, which helps us metabolize the food we take in, finding the body's authentic rhythms and, ideally, its healthiest weight.

The TRUTH also guides the image you present to the world—your sense of who you are. Words like "authenticity," "choice," and "voice" are all part of the TRUTH—"voice" in both the physical sense of speaking and the metaphoric sense of your unique self-expression. If you can tell the world your truest thoughts—if you can share your most genuine and authentic self— you have taken a powerful step to support your TRUTH.

Many of my patients struggle to face their personal truths and express them to the world. People who feel their metabolism "won't let them" lose weight are often afraid to speak their truth. Maybe they've been told all their lives to shut up, to be polite, or to lower their voice, literally or metaphorically. Maybe they don't believe they have anything important to say. But I'm struck how finding the voice to speak your own truth can be a powerful, liberating force for thyroid function and the creation of a healthy metabolism, especially when you are also supporting your thyroid gland with the right foods and supplements.

Aquamarine is the color of TRUTH. When you detox your TRUTH, you'll consume delicious sea vegetables and lubricate your throat with fruits, soups, sauces, and juices. You'll bring more awareness to your daily habits so you can begin to make the choices that serve you best.

SYSTEM 6: THE INSIGHT
Pituitary Gland, Brain, Neurons/Neurotransmitters, Sleep, Mood, Thoughts, Intuition

The sixth system of health—the INSIGHT—includes your pituitary gland, which some consider the "master gland." The pituitary is like a busy train station, constantly receiving and transmitting signals throughout the entire brain and body. This central hub of your physiology and psychology is well recognized in ancient traditions of healing as a pivot point for meditation.

The pituitary is also sometimes called the inner eye, as it maintains surveillance over a wide range of activity throughout your entire biochemistry. Your physical eyes belong to this system too. In other words, both outer and inner sight are part of the INSIGHT. Similarly, the INSIGHT includes all your neurons, neurotransmitters, and brain cells, which process and interpret what you see, perceiving metaphorical and abstract truths as well as literal, physical ones.

Mood, thoughts, and sleep are all part of this system of health, as are visualization, imagination, reflection, and intuition. If you've ever felt that a bad night's sleep, a foggy brain, or a depressed mood was keeping you from seeing things clearly, you've experienced how crucial this system can be.

And if you've ever felt that your vision cleared after a good night's sleep, a nourishing meal, or a comforting talk with a friend, you know the potential of detoxing the INSIGHT and seeing truly once more.

When I treat patients whose INSIGHT needs Whole Detox, I marvel at the deep, intimate relationship between body, thought, and emotion. You simply can't think clearly when you're getting the wrong foods, and you're all too likely to be depressed, anxious, or overly emotional as well. Likewise, when you see the world clearly, you have the passion and energy to commit to your health, because you understand better what your body needs.

Indigo is the color of the INSIGHT, so we support this system of health with blue and purple foods: blueberries, blackberries, purple kale, purple asparagus, purple cauliflower, purple grapes. Berries and grapes in particular are good sources of resveratrol, the powerhouse antioxidant that helps protect your brain and nerves. Blue and purple foods also promote neuronal plasticity, which is the scientific way of saying that they improve your brain's ability to create new pathways, improving your cognition, learning, and memory.

Detoxing your INSIGHT involves loading up on blue and purple foods, keeping a dream journal, and learning to listen carefully to that "still small voice" within. You will support both your brain matter and the workings of your mind.

SYSTEM 7: THE SPIRIT
Pineal Gland, Electromagnetic Fields, Circadian Rhythms, Connection, Purpose, Meaning

Finally, we come to the seventh system of health, the SPIRIT, which includes some of the biggest issues we ever wrestle with: connection, purpose, and—for want of a better term—what we might call soul. This system enables us to experience that we are both microcosm and macrocosm, both individual beings and indistinguishable from the whole, both individual drops of water and participants in one big ocean. The SPIRIT is where you connect to meaning in your life, to your life's calling, to the values, beliefs, and activities that most profoundly embody what you consider important.

Grounding the SPIRIT in the body is the pineal gland—a receiver within our brain that distinguishes between light and dark, day and night, sunlight and moonlight. If your circadian rhythms are off—if you can't get into a regular sleep pattern, if you can't make an easy transition between seasons, if you can't function optimally while doing shift work, or if you feel lost and disconnected—your seventh system needs Whole Detox.

This is the system in the body that regulates your vitality and your ability to age gracefully. When you feel you are declining in health faster than most or you are aging too fast, it's often your seventh system—governing your "life force"—that could use some support. You might need more time in the sunlight, some nutrients to help your cells remain vital, or perhaps a different room in which to sleep. You might even be feeling drained because you don't know your life's purpose—you don't have a reason to get up in the morning. A sure sign of a "toxic" seventh system is feeling out of touch with the significance of events and commitments that get you through the day.

White foods help cleanse and clarify the seventh system. When you think of the color white, you might think of purity or clarity. This system holds within it the high path of enlightened, good clean living. Sometimes it's not as much about what we eat as the manner in which we eat, at what time we eat, and whether we eat too much. That's why one element of the SPIRIT is abstinence of food through a variety of fasting approaches.

Now, let's be clear: "White foods" doesn't mean processed foods full of white flour or white sugar. When it comes to the SPIRIT, it refers to foods that embody the ultimate healing properties for multiple organs: ripe pears (especially good for moistening the lungs), cauliflower (cleansing for the liver), coconut products (an accessible energy source for the intestines), onions and garlic (cleansing for the blood and liver), cabbage (cleansing for the liver and, when fermented, excellent for the gut), and white beans (high in fiber).

The SPIRIT detox focuses on naturally white foods, healing light, and journaling about your life's purpose. You will also have the opportunity to reflect on the "miracles" in your life—the tiny bits of awe that keep you feeling the juice of what it means to be alive.

WHOLE DETOX IN PRACTICE

When you go through your twenty-one-day program, you'll look at each system of health separately, so you can make sure to fully address each one. But as you carry Whole Detox into your life, you'll work with the whole spectrum, just as I do with my patients. To give you an idea of how Whole Detox and the full-spectrum approach works in real life, let's go back to my patient Padma.

Padma taught urban sociology at a university, a job she generally enjoyed but also found rather stressful. During her first year of college, she suffered from crippling panic attacks as well as stress-related headaches. An M.D. prescribed some antianxiety medication, which Padma used very judiciously, fearing she would become addicted. As she saw that she was capable of getting good grades and pleasing her professors, she became less anxious and was able to stop taking the meds.

Now, however, her panic had returned, set off by rumors of funding cuts at her university. Although she was one of the senior members of her department, she was beset by fears that her research funding would cease. Although she wasn't having panic attacks, she did feel far more anxious than she would like, and her headaches frequently caused her to miss classes and appointments.

As with all my patients, I looked at the full spectrum of Padma's physical, mental, and emotional life. When she told me that she drank several cups of coffee throughout the day, I knew that was at least partly responsible for both her anxiety and her headaches.

But Whole Detox delves into more layers. I wanted Padma to identify her own personal toxins, whether in the form of food, relationships, thought patterns, or other issues, so she could either remove them or develop the strength to live with them more gracefully. I knew that, either way, Whole Detox could allow her to find the vitality and resilience she needed to overcome any barrier that held her back.

I began by giving Padma the Spectrum Quiz I give to all my patients. (You'll get to take this quiz too.) As we analyzed her results, we discovered that she had weaknesses in three systems of health: the ROOT, the FLOW, and the TRUTH.

As a child of immigrants, Padma had always felt a kind of disconnect between her Indian identity and her American one. Although she admired innovative thinkers, she always felt too fearful to let her own creative impulses flow or to "think outside the box." She felt nervous, too, about expressing her true opinions, for fear of alienating others who already saw her as foreign and perhaps a little strange.

At the same time, she tended to eat irregularly, and not in a particularly healthy way. A vegetarian, she wasn't making sure to get the full spectrum of vitamins and minerals her body needed. Instead, she lived largely on lentils and rice, with few fresh, moist fruits or vegetables. She rarely drank water or even tea, which meant she was fairly dehydrated. She was beginning to develop a thyroid condition, which was at least partly responsible for her anxiety and her headaches, and was at least partly caused by an iodine deficiency.

Here are some of the ways Padma's problems manifested across the spectrum:

	Physical symptoms	Nutrition	Lifestyle
The ROOT	Headaches	Too much caffeine Not enough protein Not enough minerals Not enough red foods: beets, cherries, watermelon	Struggles with ethnic identity while living in a foreign country A feeling of ungroundedness Uncertainty of her tribe
The FLOW	Anxiety	Not enough fluids Not enough orange foods: carrots, sweet potatoes, oranges/citrus	Not allowing herself to be creative A feeling of being "outside the flow of life"
The TRUTH	Thyroid dysfunction	Not enough iodine Not enough ocean foods: sea vegetables Irregular eating	Fear of "speaking up" Not wanting to appear different Reluctance to present new ideas

Diagnosing Padma's concerns was not a simple matter of cause and effect. Anxiety, poor thyroid function, low iodine levels, and a reluctance to speak her truth—Padma struggled with all these issues, and who is to say which had come first or which were most important? The bad news was that they were all making each other issue worse. The good news was

that any steps Padma took—even small changes—could create a healing
momentum that might operate on many levels at once.

Accordingly, I encouraged Padma to undertake a spectrum of physical,
emotional, mental, and social activities:

- cut back on caffeine;
- hydrate regularly throughout the day;
- eat more sea vegetables in soups and broths, more protein, more
  fresh fruits and vegetables;
- do some grounding yoga poses; and
- spend some time journaling about what "speaking her truth"
  meant to her.

This last point was not completely clear to Padma, so I asked her to think
of some people in history or in her life who spoke their truth—who made
it clear through words and deeds exactly what they believed in and what
they stood for. Padma identified Gandhi, the writer Toni Morrison, and
Marisa, a friend from childhood with whom she was still close. "You always
know where they stand," she told me. When I asked her whether that was
true for her as well, Padma slowly shook her head. "I am more secretive,"
she told me. "I don't want people to know so much about what I believe."
I asked her to think about whether that was something she might want to
change, and, if so, to imagine how she might make this shift in her life. I
also suggested that Padma explore ways to identify her tribe—whether cul-
turally, by being part of an Indian community, or professionally, by finding
social scientists she respected and with whom she felt safe expressing her
ideas. As you can see, the full-spectrum approach allows for a wide variety
of responses to a problem while helping each response enhance the others.

Sometimes we need to detox by letting go of foods, habits, or relationships. Sometimes we need to get more of something. Padma, for example, had
to let go of excessive caffeine while also getting more iodine, protein, and
fresh produce. She had to let go of her fears of what others might think while
also enriching her life with more community, rootedness, and connection.

Within a few weeks, she began feeling the benefits of Whole Detox's
full-spectrum approach. She looked better, felt better, thought better,

worked better. She enjoyed the glow of health. She celebrated the richness of her complex identity. She slept better. She spoke out more at faculty meetings. She had more energy. She began to write an article that she felt was much closer to her "true voice" than any of her previous publications. "I can feel the barriers melting away," she told me on our last visit. It's a thrilling feeling—and one that I want for you too!

Let's get started. The next seven chapters will take you, one by one, through the Seven Systems of Full-Spectrum Health. The more you get acquainted with each one of them, the more clearly you'll be able to see how these systems operate in your life and how to make Whole Detox work for you. As soon as you begin your twenty-one-day program, you'll realize how quickly Whole Detox pays off. The great thing is, it just keeps getting better and better.

THE WHOLE DETOX SPECTRUM QUIZ

Welcome to your Whole Detox Spectrum Quiz! You will have the opportunity to focus on each system of health, targeting the physical, mental, and emotional barriers that are holding you back from optimal health and a wholly fulfilling life. In each system, you will identify the issues in five areas: two relate to food and your bodily symptoms, and the other three concern life issues.

These questions and categories may seem powerful and exciting, or they may not seem to make much sense. You may find it inspiring to answer these questions, or perhaps you'll find yourself feeling anxious, sad, or even a little angry. Many of my patients feel some or all of these things as they move through each question.

Whatever your responses, I promise that you will learn a lot, and you will set yourself up for a powerful detox journey. Go ahead and fill out the quiz. Allow yourself at most about ten to fifteen minutes to complete it, so that you don't belabor any one question but rather go with your first impulse. When you've finished, I'll tell you how to make use of the results.

I recommend doing the Whole Detox Spectrum Quiz three times within three days under different circumstances. For example, on Sunday, when you might be relaxed and not working, then again on Monday, perhaps during the

day or during a break you have at work, and then finally on Tuesday evening, when you come home from work. Having three points of reference will help you see what is *consistently* imbalanced rather than a simple situational response.

For each statement, answer either *yes* or *no*. When you are done, tally the number of *no* responses for each system. Write down the number in the box provided at the end of the quiz.

THE WHOLE DETOX SPECTRUM QUIZ

THE ROOT

Do you feel "comfortable in your own skin"?	Y N
Do you feel it's acceptable to say no to others?	Y N
Do you feel safe in your body?	Y N
Do you feel safe in your home?	Y N
Are you free from pending danger or harm?	Y N
Do you find it easy to deal with daily stressors?	Y N
Are you capable of working well under pressure?	Y N
Is surviving in your everyday world easy?	Y N
Do you go with your instincts?	Y N
Do you trust others?	Y N
Do you spend quality time in supportive communities?	Y N
Could you go to your community for help when you need it?	Y N
Are your social networks positive and uplifting?	Y N
Are your family and/or close friends supportive?	Y N
Are you in harmony with your family of origin and/or upbringing?	Y N
Do you remember to eat when stressed?	Y N
Do you eat protein with most meals?	Y N
Do you avoid foods that disagree with you?	Y N
Do you eat natural, whole foods that are red in color (e.g., apples, cherries)?	Y N
Do you feel grounded after eating?	Y N
Do you have a strong constitution?	Y N
Are you usually "the last one to get sick"?	Y N
Are you at a healthy body weight?	Y N
Is your skin clear?	Y N
Are you free of joint pain and inflammation?	Y N

THE FLOW

Do you express your emotions to others with ease?	Y N
Do you readily go with the flow?	Y (N)
Do you express yourself when you feel something is "off"?	Y N
Do you refrain from eating emotionally?	Y (N)
Are you generally in touch with your feelings?	Y N
Do you take a creative approach to life?	Y (N)
Do you generally put your ideas into action?	Y N
Do you have unique perspectives on situations?	Y N
Do you have a healthy "creative side"?	Y (N)
Do you enjoy being your creative self?	Y N
Do you make time for play?	Y (N)
Do you consider yourself playful?	Y N
Do you aim to have fun in all you do?	Y (N)
Are you comfortable with your sexuality?	Y (N)
Are you able to create a healthy, fulfilling partnership with another person?	Y N
Do you eat some healthy fats and oils every day?	Y N
Are you eating natural, whole foods that are orange in color (e.g., carrots, pumpkin, oranges)?	Y N
Do you regularly eat tropical fruits (e.g., mango, papaya, coconut)?	Y N
Do you drink purified water?	Y N
Do you drink fluids throughout the day?	Y N
Is your sex drive good?	Y (N)
Are your bowel movements of a normal consistency (no diarrhea or constipation)?	Y N
Do you feel adequately hydrated?	Y N
Do you engage in activities that make you sweat?	Y N
Are your hormones balanced, to the best of your knowledge?	Y N

THE FIRE

Do you think you have a good energy level?	Y N
Does your daily life energize you in a healthy, stimulating way?	Y N
Does being around people give you energy?	Y N
Do you feel energized after eating, as though you are full of energy to be active and to move?	Y N
Do you take on a reasonable number of goals without overreaching?	Y (N)

Are you confident yet not egotistical?	Y N
Are you ambitious in achieving your goals yet never lose sight of priorities in your personal life?	Y N
Are you focused on your goals but also flexible in your process to achieve them?	Y N
Do you feel satisfied with your performance on projects or tasks?	Y N
Do you keep your ambitious goals in check with enjoying life?	Y N
Do you maintain work–life balance?	Y N
Do you make time to have fun away from work?	Y (N)
Are you realistic about taking on work that you can reasonably do?	Y N
Do you handle a busy schedule without fretting?	Y (N)
Do you only say yes to things you can comfortably do?	Y N
Do you avoid consistently eating sweets or desserts?	Y (N)
Do you avoid consistently eating meals high in processed starchy foods (e.g., breads, pastas, pretzels)?	Y N
Do you avoid quick-energy, caffeinated drinks?	Y (N)
Do you avoid overeating when you are stressed?	Y (N)
Are you more likely to take time to prepare meals than eat out?	Y N
Do you digest your food well?	Y N
Do you have healthy blood sugar levels?	Y (N)
Are you free of digestive complaints or conditions?	Y N
Does your stomach feel comfortable after eating?	Y (N)
Are you trim in your belly area?	Y N 8

THE LOVE

Have you been able to release past events that hurt you?	Y N
Are you able to easily let go of grief?	Y N
Are you quick to forgive?	Y N
Are you able to give to and receive from others equally?	Y N
Is your heart open but with select boundaries that are healthy?	Y N
Are you physically active?	Y N
Are you physically fit?	Y N
Do you make time to be in nature?	Y N
Do you breathe deeply?	Y N
Do you do some aerobic activity on a regular basis, such as walking, biking, or running?	Y N

Do you make time for *you*? Y N

Do you let others help you if you are in need? Y N

Do you take care of yourself to the same extent you are able to take care of others? Y N

Are you living out your heartfelt passions? Y N

Are you routinely setting aside time in your schedule to do what you *feel* like doing
rather than do what you feel obligated to do? Y (N)

Do you eat plant-based foods every day? Y N

Do you eat cruciferous vegetables (e.g., broccoli, kale, Brussels sprouts, cabbage)
at least three times per week? Y N

Do you eat leafy green salads at least every other day? Y N

Do you feel grateful for your daily meals? Y N

Do you love eating vegetables of all types? Y N

Are your hands and feet comfortably warm? Y (N)

Can you breathe without difficulty? Y N

Is it easy to breathe while you exercise? Y N

Is your blood pressure normal? Y N

Is your heart rate normal? Y (N)

3

THE TRUTH

Are you true to yourself no matter what? Y (N)

Do you enjoy your uniqueness? Y N

Do you feel free to be you? Y N

Are you consistent in living according to your values? Y N

Do you feel open in giving your opinion when asked? Y N

Do you speak your truth in a clear and conscientious way? Y N

Are you comfortable expressing yourself verbally? Y N

Do you find it enjoyable to converse with others? Y (N)

Do you enjoy talking things out as a way of processing an event or issue? Y N

Do you speak up if there are issues you feel strongly about? Y N

Are you confident in your decision-making ability? Y N

Can you easily make a decision even when there are many choices? Y (N)

Are you able to choose what is important to you? Y N

Do you usually walk away knowing you made the best choice you could? Y N

Are you comfortable making decisions? Y N

Do you chew your food well? Y (N)

Do you eat an adequate amount of food (not too little, not too much)?   Y N

Do you have a normal, healthy appetite?   Y N

When you eat, do you only eat and not multitask?   Y (N)

Do you choose foods you know are healthy for you?   Y N

Does it seem that you have a normal metabolism?   Y N

Is your thyroid healthy, to the best of your knowledge?   Y N

Does your throat stay moist and free from soreness?   Y N

Do you have healthy teeth?   Y N

Is your jaw loose and relaxed?   Y N

THE INSIGHT

Do you consider yourself to be smart or able to easily understand concepts?   Y (N)

Are you good at solving problems based on what you know?   Y N

Compared to most people, do you consider yourself a "thinker"?   Y N

Do you like learning new things?   Y N

Are you a quick learner?   Y N

Do you consider yourself intuitive?   Y N

Do you get impressions about things yet to happen?   Y (N)

Do you have a good sense of discernment?   Y N

Do you listen to your inner knowing?   Y N

Do you allow your intuition to help guide you through life?   Y N

Do you sleep all through the night?   Y (N)

Do you regularly sleep seven to eight hours per night?   Y (N)

Do you have a consistent, healthy sleep pattern?   Y N

Do you fall asleep easily without the use of sleep aids?   Y N

Do you wake in the morning feeling refreshed?   Y (N)

Do you avoid drinking too many caffeinated drinks?   Y N

Do you avoid eating too much chocolate?   Y N

Are you free from food addictions?   Y N

Do you abstain from drinking excessive amounts of alcoholic drinks?   Y (N)

Are you able to focus your attention without relying on external substances
(e.g., caffeine, alcohol)?   Y (N)

Are you able to clear your mind before bedtime?   Y N

Are you attentive to tasks on hand and mindful of your actions?   Y N

Is your memory good?   Y N

Are your moods stable?   Y N
Do you meditate or engage in a mindful practice of some sort?   Y N

THE SPIRIT

Is your life full of meaning?   Y N
Do you feel connected to life in ways that invigorate your spirit?   Y N
Are you concerned with greater planetary causes (e.g., ending hunger, world
    peace)?   Y N
Do you feel you have a special mission or a calling by which you live?   Y N
Do you find yourself inspired to commit to changing the world?   Y (N)
Do you live a spiritual life?   Y N
Do you have faith that everything works out as it needs to?   Y N
Do your spiritual views direct your life decisions at a high level?   Y N
Do you feel strengthened through your spirituality?   Y N
Do you believe in something greater than yourself?   Y N
Do you have regular exposure to sunlight?   Y N
Do you feel that you radiate an inner glow?   Y (N)
Do you sleep during the nighttime hours and stay awake during the daylight hours? Y N
Do you have access to bright white lights in your living space?   Y N
Does life feel "light and wonderful" rather than "heavy and dark"?   Y (N)
Do you regularly detox your body?   Y (N)
Do you regularly eat certain foods that are known to be good for detoxification? Y N
Do you eat fresh organic food over fried food?   Y N
Do you avoid plastic containers (e.g., for food, water)?   Y N
Do you avoid using toxic personal care products (e.g., chemical-laden lotions,
    hair-care products, makeup, deodorant)?   Y N
Do you take precautions in minimizing your exposure to excessive electromagnetic
    fields (EMFs)?   Y (N)
Is your nervous system healthy (e.g., no pain, numbness)?   Y (N)
Are you resilient and recover quickly from any illness?   Y N
Do people say that you look younger than your age?   Y N
Do you think that your life force, or constitution, is stronger than most others? Y (N)

SCORING YOUR QUIZ

Note the number of *no* responses within each system:	
The ROOT	4
The FLOW	8
The FIRE	8
The LOVE	3
The TRUTH	5
The INSIGHT	7
The SPIRIT	7

INTERPRETING YOUR SYSTEM SCORES

- If you answered *no* to fewer than ten questions within any system, this system is likely to be balanced.
- If you answered *no* to between eleven and fifteen questions within any system, you have a *moderate* imbalance of that system.
- If you answered *no* to more than fifteen questions within any system, you have a *severe* imbalance of that system.

Your scores help you identify systems that include your core strengths as well as systems that are out of balance. You'll learn more about each system in the next several chapters, and in your twenty-one-day program, I'll work with you in detail to heal each one.

You might be tempted to skip right to a particular system, but I urge you to read through every chapter. Every system works with every other system—that is the power of synergy—and to heal one, it helps to understand them all.

For any system where you have a strong imbalance, take a look at the questions to which you answered *no* and see whether you can detect a pattern or similarity. For example, if your *nos* in the ROOT all relate to food, you should pay particular attention to proteins, minerals, and red foods. Or if all your *nos* in the TRUTH concern your voice and self-expression, you'll know to pay special attention to those issues and how you can speak your truth more fully and easily. One of the wonderful things about Whole Detox is the way it allows you to target personal concerns and fine-tune your responses. Remember that no matter which system you focus on, you are focusing on the whole of who you are. Everything is interconnected, as I explained earlier.

What if your scores indicate that *all* your systems are balanced? Well, that may happen, similar to when you get your blood work done and find that your number fit within the range of what is considered healthy. For example, your thyroid hormones may check out normal, but you still have issues of thyroid imbalance. I would encourage you to look at the scores in a more personalized way: you might be at the top or bottom of that range. If all your scores come in as balanced, you have two ways to target your personal barriers and take advantage of opportunities for growth. You can do either or both:

- Pick the system with the most *nos* and focus some extra attention there. For example, maybe your FLOW is balanced with fewer than ten *nos*, but out of all your systems, it's the one that has the most number of *no* responses. That would indicate you need to put your energy here. Even if you are generally balanced in that system, a single *no* indicates a potential barrier that might be keeping you from enjoying your fullest spectrum of health, wellness, and fulfillment.
- Scan the questions and note the *nos* to which you have the most intense, anxious, or sad response:
  - *Oh, I could never do that!*
  - *I wish I could do that, but it's not gonna happen.*
  - *Other people can do that, but not me.*
  - *I don't even want to do that—why are you asking me about it???*

If you had a strong reaction to a particular question, that might indicate a barrier that is holding you back. As you move through your twenty-one-day program, be open to the possibility of removing or overcoming that barrier.

Whatever your score, it is essential to think about how each system operates in your life. Continue to ask yourself how you can make the most of your current strengths. What can you do to remove your current barriers? And, most important, what can you do to make sure each system helps you achieve your overall purpose, bringing you to a richer and more inspired life?

CHAPTER 2

THE POWER OF SYNERGY

Before you look at each of the seven systems separately, I want to introduce you to the synergy that animates each system and binds all seven systems together. This is your chance to think further about how Whole Detox affects your body and your health. What does a healthy balance look like for you?

Because each of us is a unique individual, your healthy balance will look different from mine. Because you are on a lifelong journey, each system will likely take on different meanings at different times in your life. And because life resists simple solutions, your greatest strength may resemble your greatest weakness.

The one constant in this process is synergy: different elements working together to create a whole that is greater than the sum of its parts. Synergy can work negatively, as when excess weight, a struggle with anxiety, a stressful job, a neglected love life, and an overwhelming sense of perfectionism all make each other worse. (Can you see that these elements are all part of an imbalanced third system—an excess of the FIRE that has quickly led to burnout?) Synergy can also work positively, as when high-fiber carbohydrates, a joy in work, some refreshing meditation, and a self-loving attitude create a steady supply of fuel to support your health and well-being.

In fact, the greatest strength of Whole Detox is the way it reverses negative synergy and replaces it with positive synergy. This is why my patients enjoy such swift and powerful results. Each element of Whole Detox—food choices, exercise, affirmations, journaling, and other activities—works in concert with the others to create an ever-widening upward spiral: a veritable healing cyclone!

So in this chapter you're going to take a closer look at synergy: within each system, between all seven systems, and throughout the course of your life. This perspective should enable you to further personalize your approach to Whole Detox as you identify and overcome the barriers in your life.

WHEN YOUR STRENGTH LOOKS LIKE YOUR WEAKNESS

Roberto is the kind of solid, reliable guy everybody can depend on. He married his college sweetheart, went into the family business, and is raising two children, who are doing well in school. He lives just a few miles from his parents, and most Sundays he and his family join his relatives for a big, raucous dinner with everybody's favorite foods and long games of touch football, soccer, or cards.

Roberto is proud of his work and family. Sometimes, though, he wonders whether his life lacks adventure. And while he knows his marriage is stable, he has the feeling that his wife would like a little adventure too.

———

Zenia has had, by all accounts, an extraordinary life. A talented photographer, she has spent most of her life traveling from one assignment to another: a battle in rural Afghanistan, a presidential inauguration in Buenos Aires, an art opening in Stockholm, a fashion show in Milan. She has always had an unusual ability to adapt to whatever circumstances in which she found herself, and now, in her sixties, she can look back upon an impressive body of work, several satisfying romances, and a network of friends and colleagues around the globe.

In this latest phase of her life, however, Zenia is beginning to crave a little stability. She wonders whether her scanty savings will be enough for her old age. Does she need a new retirement plan? She wonders, too, whether it's time to pick a home and put down roots, maybe even look for someone steady in her life.

———

Jared has a forceful, fiery energy that has taken him to the top of his marketing company in a remarkably short time. He works long, hard hours and is amazingly productive. He loves his work, is proud of his accomplishments, and, in his midthirties, looks forward to more.

But Jared frequently feels stressed and burnt out. His long-suffering girlfriend has just given him an ultimatum. And he wonders where he could make room in this demanding life for the children he has always wanted.

––––––––

Leah has the gift of empathy. Close friends, new acquaintances, and even total strangers seek her advice, her listening ear, her open, loving response. She always seems to know what another person might think or feel, and she has a seemingly boundless ability to step up with comfort or help.

But Leah finds it so easy to see another person's point of view that she often loses sight of her own. And she is so willing to give to others that she finds it challenging to nurture herself.

––––––––

Brandon is a truth teller. A natural leader, he has the ability to take charge of a situation, speak honestly about what the problems are, and offer workable solutions. His colleagues, employer, friends, and family all depend on him to cut through the "noise" with clear, useful answers.

Sometimes, though, Brandon is so preoccupied with his own vision of the truth that he forgets to listen to others. Or maybe he doesn't *forget*; he might simply not see the need. As a result, he occasionally makes mistakes that might have been avoided—and he sometimes alienates those who feel ignored.

––––––––

Solange is one of the most intuitive, insightful people her friends have ever met. If you have a problem that makes no sense to you, Solange is the one to speak with. She has the uncanny gift of seeing through the surface and penetrating right to the heart of a matter.

Sometimes, though, Solange feels overwhelmed by her own mind, buried under all the thoughts and insights that seem to keep coming and coming and coming. Although she usually enjoys her insightful vision, she does sometimes wish she could just empty her head and give her mind a rest.

––––––––

A calm and generous professor of religious studies, Matthew is considered by his community to be very spiritual. He always seems to be operating in another dimension, inspired to a higher purpose and connected deeply to his students, his research, and his ascetic lifestyle.

One winter, however, Matthew picks up the flu and he just can't seem to shake it. When he comes to me, I realize that Matthew is severely malnourished and underweight. Although he has been feeding his soul, he has neglected his body, with potentially dangerous consequences for the future.

These seven portraits all illustrate the challenges of creating a positive synergy and a balanced, healthy life. In every case, the person's greatest strength is also their "fatal" weakness; their heroic achievement is also their tragic flaw.

I share these stories not to criticize these seven people, all of whom I appreciate and admire. Rather, I want us all to see how hard it can be to make the most of our gifts, each of which has both a bright and a dark side. As you take your own journey through the seven systems, I hope you will treat yourself with patience and compassion, recognizing that there are no easy answers and no one right way of navigating these dilemmas. Instead of pursuing one final resolution, I invite you to view these contradictions as opportunities for growth.

System	Positive attributes	Negative attributes
The ROOT	Steady, solid	Stuck, stagnant
The FLOW	Creative, expressive	Dramatic, chaotic
The FIRE	Ambitious, achieving	Workaholic, perfectionistic
The LOVE	Caring, compassionate	Self-sacrificing, people pleasing
The TRUTH	Authentic, free	Resistant to authority, paralyzed by choices
The INSIGHT	Intuitive, intellectual	Moody, thought-obsessed
The SPIRIT	Purposeful, seeing the big picture	Fragmented, languishing in the physical world

A LIFELONG JOURNEY

One powerful way to view the seven systems is as a lifelong progress, with each system characterized by the issues of a different phase in life:

1. The ROOT: As infants and children, we seek stability and rootedness in our family, our community, and our tribe. We are primarily preoccupied with issues of safety and identity, wanting to know at the most basic level who we are and how we can protect ourselves (or who will protect us). A solid ROOT enables children to explore and grow, venturing beyond the security of the family circle and out into the wider world. An unstable ROOT can create a lifelong quest for identity, safety, and/or a primary family.

2. The FLOW: As teenagers, we enter into the turbulent FLOW of hormonal life, feeling creative, sexy, generative, and ready to go where life takes us. Our identities are fluid as we explore the possibilities that have newly opened up, and we meld into the networks formed with friends and peer groups. Although many adolescents yearn for solidity and certainty, the teenage years are almost inevitably a time when everything is uncertain, open, and flowing, and the best we can do is accept the instability, embrace the excitement, and enter into the waves of emotions.

3. The FIRE: In our early twenties, we burn with drive and ambition, on fire with the desire to make our mark on the world. Youth is as restless as a runaway fire, reaching as high as a leaping flame. For those young people who have chosen a life's work or profession, youth can be a time of burning joy as well, in which every new achievement explodes like a burst of fireworks, lighting up the night and illuminating the way ahead.

4. The LOVE: Our late twenties and thirties are often a time for focusing on the heart, as relationships turn into marriages and twosomes turn into families. This is a time to nurture our partners and our children, expanding into a love and service that go deeper than any we have yet known.

5. The TRUTH: In our forties, we have begun to understand our own truth and to find our own voice. At the halfway mark in our lives,

we have reached the time for big decisions and clear choices. Do we continue on our present course or switch to a new way of life? Either decision is momentous and requires a clarity about our inner truth and our path.

6. The INSIGHT: Turning fifty brings a new depth of wisdom and understanding, the chance to see the world in our own way and to make sense of all we have learned. "Insight" is the watchword for this half-century mark, as we finally learn to trust our intuition and inner knowing.

7. The SPIRIT: In our sixties and beyond, we begin to think more of the spirit than of the body; we become preoccupied with meaning, connection, and our place in the larger scheme of things. As we grow older, we prepare to leave behind our bodies and the physical world, embracing the spirit as the next phase of our existence.

In this view of the seven systems, the synergy emerges over time. Each system modifies and deepens the ones that came before it as wisdom deepens and perspective grows. From this viewpoint, a lifetime is not enough to make use of all the seven systems have to offer. But at each stage of life, we can appreciate where we are now, what has come before, and the new stage that is still to come.

BALANCE ACROSS THE SEVEN SYSTEMS

One of the challenges of Whole Detox is for each of us to customize our own approach, pursuing our unique goals in our own special way. The point is not for all of us to end up with identical versions of health and wellness but rather for every one of us to craft a unique path.

Here are three examples of patients who created lives that worked for them, each with a different balance among the seven systems:

Leila is an ambitious professor of literature who works slowly but steadily toward her goals. In her midforties, she has published two books—about average for her field.

Leila wonders if she might accomplish more if she put more

time and energy into her work. But she is unwilling to focus on work at the expense of the other things she enjoys: attending yoga classes, cooking healthy meals, and sharing a warm, close relationship with her husband.

———

Danny married his high school sweetheart as soon as they both finished college, and he never looked back. Together they have four children, and while life is hectic sometimes, they both really enjoy their family life.

Danny works as a CPA in a local accounting company, a job he doesn't love but doesn't mind. His favorite thing about it is that he's able to finish at five P.M. each day, so he can head home to spend time with his family.

Recently, he has started volunteering at a local homeless shelter. He gets a lot of satisfaction from helping people who really need it, and sometimes he convinces one of his kids to come with him and give a few hours as well. Danny sees his highest purpose on earth as taking care of others—whether his clients at work, his family at home, or the folks at the shelter. Sometimes he's bored, and sometimes he's frustrated, but mainly he's satisfied.

———

Kira has been a dedicated tennis player since she was a little girl. Every spare minute goes into improving her game, and her professional results bear witness to her impressive efforts. Now she is approaching the age when she'll have to step back from the highest levels of the game, and she's trying to decide what she'll do next. Coach? Start a sports-related business? Take some time off and travel the world? Kira has been focused on tennis for so long that she has no idea what her next move should be.

Leila, Danny, and Kira are each trying to craft a life that fits them—a life that balances all the different things they want. If we look at each life in terms of the Seven Systems of Full-Spectrum Health, we might come up with something like this:

	Leila	Danny	Kira
The ROOT	Strongest	Very strong	Weak
The FLOW	Moderate	Weak	Weak
The FIRE	Moderate	Weak	Strongest
The LOVE	Very strong	Strongest	Weak
The TRUTH	Moderate	Weak	Weak
The INSIGHT	Moderate	Weak	Weak
The SPIRIT	Moderate	Moderate	Weak

What conclusions can we draw from these three very different people?

First, it's nearly impossible to end up with strength in all seven systems. We just don't have the time and energy. You can have moderate strength in many systems or outstanding strength in a few systems or another balance of weakness and strength, but there simply isn't room in a single human life to have strength in all seven systems at the same time.

Second, each of us has different needs and capacities, and our systems reflect that. To Leila, living a balanced life is very important, so perhaps it is not coincidental that all of her systems translate into being rather equal. Even though she doesn't achieve exact strength in all seven systems, she comes close. Kira, by contrast, is happiest focusing all her attention on the FIRE. If her single-minded focus on tennis ends, she'll have the chance to decide whether she'll direct her FIRE toward another goal, go with the FLOW for a while, commit to the LOVE or the SPIRIT, or make a completely different type of choice. These choices would leave Leila and Danny feeling adrift and dissatisfied, but they work for Kira.

Finally, as we have already seen, things change over a lifetime. Having established a strong family life and a well-balanced LOVE system, Danny has the room to strengthen his SPIRIT system. Having spent many years focused on the FIRE, Kira might be ready to experiment with a different type of life. Leila might at some point decide to put more energy into her work or to open up her life still further and find new ways to go with the FLOW. Different choices are right for different times.

AWARENESS IS YOUR FIRST STEP

My goal in teaching you about Whole Detox and the Seven Systems of Full-Spectrum Health is not to prescribe a certain type of life for you or even a certain route to health. Rather, it's to give you the tools so you can make the choices that are best for your life and your health. If something isn't working—if you're struggling with toxic barriers that are creating symptoms, frustration, or pain—it's often helpful to look at which system or systems are out of balance or perhaps need more attention. But if your life is fulfilling and your health is optimal, that's an excellent sign that you're following the path that's right for you.

My guidance to you is to be aware of all the possibilities and to not sell yourself short. Far too many people live lives of quiet desperation, resigned to borderline health, frustrating jobs, and unsatisfying relationships. If something in your life isn't bringing you joy, you can use Whole Detox and the seven systems to diagnose where the problem is and come up with a solution. If something that worked for years has now stopped working, you can use the principles of Whole Detox to figure out where to go next. And if you know something is wrong but you can't quite put your finger on what, Whole Detox is there to help you find awareness.

That's why I'm excited to introduce you to the Seven Systems of Full-Spectrum Health. When you've understood each one, you'll have a very real and concrete sense of the possibilities in life—how good you can feel, how fulfilled you might be. In that sense, Whole Detox is a great adventure, inviting you to celebrate the full spectrum of life. So turn the page and let's get started! A rainbow of opportunity awaits.

CHAPTER 3

THE ROOT

Consider a tree for a moment. As beautiful as trees are to look at, we don't see what goes on underground—as they grow roots. Trees must develop deep roots in order to grow strong and produce their beauty. But we don't see the roots. We just see and enjoy the beauty. In much the same way, what goes on inside of us is like the roots of a tree.

—JOYCE MEYER

UNDERSTANDING THE ROOT	
Anatomy	Adrenal glands, immune system, DNA, skin, bones
Functions	Identity, defense, fight-or-flight response
Living	Safety, survival, community, tribe
Eating	Protein, minerals, red foods

THE SCIENCE OF THE ROOT

The ROOT includes a number of seemingly disparate concepts: immune system, adrenal glands, protein, community, and tribe. Intriguingly, a growing body of scientific research associates these issues as well. As you will see, the elements of the ROOT concern our core identity plus our sense of safety, self-defense, boundaries, and belonging.

- Our immune system protects us from foreign invaders, such as bacteria and viruses, and helps us restore body integrity after an injury or a wound. It distinguishes between self and non-self at the most basic level.
- Our adrenal glands protect our survival by triggering the fight-or-flight response—our body's primary reaction to any type of challenge, including illness, stress, and danger.
- Protein is a building block of our whole structure, from our DNA and enzymes to our bones and muscles to our skin, hair, and nails. Protein is fundamental to our physical self. It also provides our adrenal glands with balanced fuel during a stressful event and can assist us in feeling stabilized.
- Community and tribe help create our understanding of who we are and whom we "belong to" ("an American," "a Southerner," "a New Yorker," "a Catholic," "half Portuguese, half Italian," "a member of the Rodriguez family," "a Green Bay Packers fan").

Many of us are used to thinking of these elements separately. But each affects the others, in both negative and positive ways. Excess stress on the adrenals can weaken the immune system. Loneliness and isolation lead to stress. Having a strong tribe can make us more able to resist both stress and illness. All of these ROOT issues affect our sense of identity and well-being, and when we deal with them together, we can unleash a powerful synergy.

Let's take a closer look.

IMMUNITY AND STRESS

Many of us think of immunity and stress as separate issues, but in fact, they are closely intertwined. When you experience stress—whether physical (a wound, an illness) or emotional (a deadline, an argument), your immune system frequently takes a hit. When you experience constant stress—again, either emotional or physical—your immune system is significantly challenged. Understanding the biology of how stress and immunity affect each other will help you better care for your ROOT.

Let's begin by looking at the stress response, which is generated by your adrenal glands. In fact, stress is one of the biggest toxins we confront on a daily basis. When you face a challenge of any type—physical, mental, or emotional—your body triggers a cascade of energizing chemicals that fire you up, make you more alert, and help you mobilize your resources for the task at hand. One of these stress chemicals is cortisol, which is great at the right levels but becomes a huge health hazard when your levels are chronically elevated.

Healthy cortisol levels leave you feeling energized and focused. When levels are too high, too low, or fluctuate in unhealthy ways, you might feel wired, anxious, sleepless, and jumpy; drained, exhausted, foggy, and unfocused; or a confusing mixture of both. This is known as adrenal dysfunction, though some of us just call it exhaustion!

If you have one single challenge to face in a day, you can often rise to the occasion, mobilize your resources, respond appropriately, and then relax. One stress at a time, followed by a period of relaxation, allows your adrenals to remain healthy and strong because you haven't overloaded them and you've given them time to recover.

However, in our modern world, many of us live with continuous stress. Some of us face major challenges that never seem to go away: a sick parent, a troubled kid, a debilitating relationship, a frustrating job. Others face a set of smaller challenges that also never seem to subside: constant errands, never-ending housework, driving the kids from lesson to lesson, a job that never seems to leave you time for lunch or even a coffee break.

Continuous stress is where the problem begins, because that type of stress creates chronically high levels of cortisol and adrenaline. These high levels of stress hormones affect you in all sorts of ways—often unhealthy— including an overactive immune response. After all, stressors mean challenges, and challenges often mean danger. So when your cortisol levels are chronically high, your immune system responds with alarm, resulting in inflammation.

Unfortunately, the same problem can result when your cortisol levels are chronically low. At this point your immune system sees that you don't have enough cortisol to respond to a challenge—those times when you feel foggy, exhausted, and seriously in need of a break—and once again, it mobilizes a protective response, i.e., inflammation.

When your chronically unbalanced cortisol gives rise to chronic inflammation, and this chronic inflammation in turn alarms your adrenals, it triggers yet another flood of cortisol. Thus a vicious circle is born, as these two integral aspects of the ROOT work to undermine your health:

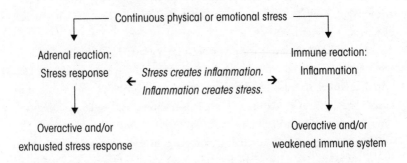

Stress weakens the immune system in a number of ways. When pregnant mothers are stressed, for example, the immune systems of their offspring suffer, making them more susceptible to infection. Children from families in which there is a lot of psychological stress show low immune activity, and they tend to overreact to the toxins in some vaccines compared with those who are not stressed. A person who faced traumatic stress in childhood is more likely to be hospitalized with an autoimmune disease later in life.

If you have an autoimmune condition, you may already have discovered that daily stressors can play a role in setting off your symptoms. That's because of the way cortisol and inflammatory chemicals interact: excess cortisol triggers an inflammatory response, which in turn produces symptoms. Even if you don't have an autoimmune disorder, excess cortisol can trigger a whole host of symptoms, from acne to achy joints to PMS / hot flashes to sexual dysfunction to frequent colds and flu, as well as more serious disorders and risk factors (see page 60).

Fortunately, healing your ROOT with Whole Detox can help you reverse this process, creating a healthy synergy between your stress response and your immune function and supporting your optimal survival in the physical world.

IMMUNITY AND COMMUNITY

Stress isn't the only factor that affects your immune response. So does your community and your tribes. In fact, several studies have shown that people with strong social networks tend to be hardier and more robust. Most clinicians will tell you that people who feel supported by their social networks experience a greater sense of safety and enjoy generally lower stress levels. As a result, their immune systems are far less challenged by continual bursts of cortisol.

By the same token, people who have weaker social networks tend to be more stressed—and less healthy. Research done with university students found that those who reported themselves as lonely and those with smaller social networks tended to have lower immune function as measured in their response to a vaccine. Loneliness was also associated with a number of other symptoms, such as less quality sleep—and higher circulating levels of cortisol. As we just saw, constantly high blood levels of cortisol are very bad for your health, disrupting a number of other organs and putting you at risk for a wide variety of disorders.

One of my favorite studies was conducted in 2003 and published in a journal called *Psychological Science*. A group of 334 healthy men and women were exposed to the virus for the common cold and then monitored for symptoms. The volunteers who described themselves as "most sociable"—who spent the most time with people and seemed to have the closest social relationships—were far less likely to come down with the cold. To me, this study makes a lot of sense when you know that community and immune function are both part of the ROOT, both part of what keeps us feeling safe and secure.

THE POWER OF RED

Research associates the color red with some attributes related to the ROOT:

- Alertness
- Anger and aggression related to survival and danger
- Avoidance of a threat
- Self-control, ego
- Vigor

For example, a 2014 article published in the conference proceedings of the Engineering in Medicine and Biology Society found that when participants were put in a room with red light, they had a higher level of brain activity associated with "alertness, agitation, mental activity, and general activation of mind and body functions." They also were more likely to feel anger and "vigor."

A 2015 study reported in the *Personal and Social Psychology Bulletin* associated red with anxiety, to such an extent that reading words in red type—or even the word "red" printed in black type—could "impair cognitive performances." In other words, red stressed people so much that they had trouble focusing on their reading.

An article in a 2014 edition of *PLoS ONE*, the journal of the Public Library of Science, intriguingly titled "Red—Take a Closer Look," suggested that the color red made people more attentive to both happy and angry facial expressions; that is, red made people more alert to the possibility of either reward (a happy expression) or threat (an angry expression). A 2013 study in *Emotion* came to a similar conclusion: in the words of the article's title, "Red Enhances the Processing of Facial Expressions of Anger." In the study, when subjects viewed faces on a red background, they were more easily able to identify angry facial expressions. Once again, it seems that the color red has a subtle but striking effect upon our adrenal system, which alerts us to potential threats and danger.

A 2012 study discovered that red plates and cups actually caused people to eat and drink less than when the plates and cups were blue or white; the authors suggested that the color red acted as a subtle stop signal. Or perhaps, on a subconscious level, the color made the subjects more alert and aware of what they were eating. When we don't notice our food, it's much easier to overeat. Red can wake us up to attend to our surroundings and ourselves.

Now that you're aware of the power of red, how can you take advantage of it? I'll tell you what I tell all my patients and students: Start tuning in to the effects of the color red (and all other colors) upon *you*. Notice what you choose to wear and ask yourself if you've chosen those colors for a particular reason. Become sensitive to the ways the colors in a room affect you: the colors of the walls, the curtains, the tablecloth, the plates. Does red rev you up to feel alert and focused? Does it provoke your anxiety or perhaps your sense of excitement? Does it help you to feel grounded, rooted, more down to earth?

One of my patients told me that when she's feeling "up in the air," she wears a red T-shirt to bed, "so I can get grounded while I sleep." Another patient who had systemic inflammation didn't realize that she was wearing the color red all the time—as far down as her underwear and as far up as her lipstick. When I asked her if her clothing was reflecting what was happening on the inside of her body, she had an aha moment. She began wearing light blues and greens to create a different experience in her everyday life, one that was more calm and relaxed.

Her experience was supported by the comment of a dermatologist who knew nothing about my Whole Detox approach. He once said to me, "Why is it that women that come to me for inflammatory skin conditions like acne and rosacea seem to also be wearing red much of the time?" I don't know whether the color expresses the problem, causes it, or both, but I do know that color can have a powerful healing effect. Becoming aware of how color affects *you* is an eye-opener within Whole Detox, as you learn to invite all the colors of the spectrum into your life.

GET TO KNOW YOUR ROOT

Identity and the Immune System

As we just saw, the ROOT represents our relationship to the physical world: how we distinguish self from non-self and how we respond to threats to our physical survival—safety, home, food, and money. Because our immune system defines our boundaries—what we let in, what we reject—you might say that it represents our identity: who we are within a complex environment. If we don't have a basic sense of self—what's good for us, what's bad for us, what supports our body, and what threatens it—it's very difficult to feel safe.

The immune system defines us and protects us by identifying threats and developing responses. Of course, your immune system is constantly encountering entities it doesn't recognize, most of which are harmless. So your adaptive immune system learns to identify the threats and then develops antibodies—biochemicals that signal your immune system to go on alert when a previously identified danger enters your body.

Some of these dangers are toxic bacteria. That's why, after you've been exposed to a bacterium—either through actually getting sick or via a vaccine—you have antibodies that alert your adaptive immune system to keep that bacterium from attacking you again.

But sometimes your immune system overreaches, tagging common foods like milk, cheese, eggs, bread, pasta, and soy as dangers. This reaction can occur because of a common disorder known as leaky gut, when the lining of your intestinal wall becomes permeable, depriving your immune system of a safe boundary. Instead of tightly holding in all the food you're trying to digest, that permeable lining allows some partially digested food to leak through. Your immune system fails to recognize this undigested food and may come to consider it a toxic invader, tagging it with antibodies. Then the next time you eat that type of food, your immune system produces its standard defense: inflammation.

As we saw earlier, inflammation is intended to be a healing response, but it does have side effects. And when inflammation is chronic—when your immune system is continually responding to invader foods—you get symptoms:

- Anxiety
- Brain fog, trouble focusing
- Depression
- Digestive issues: reflux, nausea, feeling too full, indigestion/ heartburn, constipation, diarrhea
- Frequent colds, flu, sore throat
- Headaches
- Listlessness
- Muscle and/or joint pain
- Restlessness
- Skin problems: acne, rosacea, eczema
- Sleep problems

This is why Whole Detox begins at the ROOT, pulling out all the foods that might be causing this type of immune system response:

- Alcohol
- Caffeine (chocolate, coffee, soft drinks, tea)
- Dairy products (cheese, milk, yogurt)
- Eggs

- Gluten (barley, spelt, wheat, and, in some cases, oats)
- Peanuts
- Processed carbohydrates
- Processed meats
- Shellfish
- Soy
- Sugar and sweeteners (includes artificial ones)

After a twenty-one-day Whole Detox, your immune system calms down, many antibodies disappear, and you can reintroduce foods back into your diet. Some people never really lose the antibodies and will have to keep some foods out permanently. Other people can eventually reintroduce foods after several months. When you have finished your twenty-one-day program, you'll learn how to figure out which foods you can reintroduce (see chapter 12).

Self-Defense and the Adrenal Glands

If the immune system takes care of your internal response to danger, the adrenal system manages your external response. Your adrenal glands are designed to put you on high alert whenever your body perceives a potential threat. If your immune system interprets partially digested food as a threat, your adrenals will be on high alert far too much of the time.

As we have seen, your adrenal glands generate your body's response to stress—anything that challenges you to greater exertion. Stress can be physical (hiking, working out at the gym, lifting your groceries up onto the counter) or it can be emotional (a sick child, a difficult boss, a troublesome relationship). Stress can also take the form of minor but significant demands on your body—the kinds of little things we tend not to notice but that nonetheless take their toll:

- Exposure to toxins—the kinds normally found in our external environment: air, food, water, and items found in our homes, including many types of furniture, carpet, cleaning products, and personal-care products
- Inflammatory foods—the ones that challenge our immune system
- Lack of sleep

All of these forms of stress trigger an adrenal response: the body mobilizing itself to respond to danger.

Ideally, your stress response is followed by a "relaxation response," allowing your mental and physical resources to restore and replenish before the next big challenge. But when the stress never really stops, you never get enough of a relaxation response. Instead, you get more or less constant stress—and your adrenal glands start to feel the strain.

Constant stress can come from a state of mind: you're always worried about work, family, relationships, or life in general. It can also come from physical stressors: you never quite get enough sleep, you're eating too many foods that stress your body. For many people it's both. This unremitting stress creates a constant drip, drip, drip of stress hormones into your system. As a result, you often feel edgy, anxious, wired. You might have trouble sleeping. You might also have the opposite reaction: feeling draggy, listless, unfocused. Some people have both reactions: sometimes feeling wired, other times feeling exhausted. Often, sleep cycles get messed up, so that you're wide awake late at night but can't keep your eyes open in the afternoon.

Some version of this adrenal distress happens to many of us, as we skimp on sleep, stress over grades or job performance, or worry about career and security. These are all ROOT issues: adult identity, financial safety, ability to survive independently, and ability to take care of our loved ones.

Although we may not be in any actual physical danger, our adrenal glands know only one response to stress: the fight-or-flight mode, during which a cascade of stress hormones gears the whole body up for danger. And because we aren't countering that stress response with a relaxation response, our adrenals start working overtime.

Luckily, with Whole Detox, we have a number of ways to support our adrenals:

- Addressing issues of identity, family, and survival
- Finding ways to relax
- Getting enough sleep
- Supporting adrenals with clean proteins and red foods
- Removing problem foods

BALANCE YOUR ROOT

Our goal with Whole Detox is to achieve a kind of balance—not necessarily "more" of the ROOT but rather "the right amount" of the ROOT.

Of course, "imbalance" can mean either too much or too little. A person with an underactive ROOT might be anxious, spacey, or ungrounded. A person with an overactive ROOT might be stubborn, a creature of habit, or stuck in a rut.

The right amount of ROOT will look different for each of us. For one person, it might mean going to work in the same place at the same time, day after day. Another person might flourish in a community of friends who are available by phone, e-mail, or Skype. For yet another person, it's about staying close to their biological family in the town where they grew up. The right amount of ROOT might also look different at different points in our lives, as our need and capacity for different types of stability evolves.

We are also complex creatures who often possess many contradictory traits. As you look at the following lists, you may find indications that your ROOT—or that of someone you know—is sometimes balanced, sometimes overactive, and sometimes underactive.

So, bearing in mind that these indications are provisional—meant to point you toward your own definitions rather than simply adopting mine—here are some portraits of ROOT balance and imbalance.

A person with a healthy ROOT
- has a well-functioning immune system, with no autoimmune issues and rarely, if ever, gets colds or flu;
- has a strong social network of friends and/or family members;
- is free of adrenal issues, feeling neither tired nor wired, with a deep reserve of energy to respond to the stresses and challenges of their life;
- feels "at home" in their body, rarely, if ever, feeling physically unsafe or threatened;
- eats moderate amounts of protein throughout the day to stabilize their blood sugar, support their body, and fuel their energy;
- feels comfortable and settled yet also flexible and able to move out of habitual ruts if needed; and
- eats a variety of red foods to support immune and adrenal health.

A person with an underactive ROOT

- frequently gets colds and flu, and might suffer from an autoimmune condition;
- struggles with adrenal issues, frequently feeling tired, wired, or both;
- eats little protein but a lot of carbohydrates, especially refined carbohydrates, perhaps to compensate for the low energy that results from exhausted adrenal glands;
- feels easily thrown or bowled over by the stresses of daily life;
- feels a deep sense of insecurity about their physical safety;
- has the uneasy sense that they don't have a right to exist like everyone else, that their very survival is a burden or at risk;
- has trouble "settling down," whether in a home, a relationship, a career, or simply to focus on completing a task;
- feels "lost" without a tribe or community to support their identity;
- feels isolated, exiled, outcast, or emotionally homeless;
- might have given up on their physical survival, might neglect themselves physically;
- might be struggling with challenges to their survival, such as homelessness or unemployment;
- might be or have been anorexic; or
- might be fragile, thin, and jumpy, feeling that life is always "coming at me" in insurmountable ways.

A person with an overactive ROOT

- has difficulty adapting to change of any kind;
- seems stuck in a rut or set in their ways;
- takes everything literally;
- feels heavy and stuck in their life;
- stubbornly resists changing a custom or long-standing way of doing things;
- rarely changes their opinion;
- can't imagine making a decision or even having an opinion that might upset their family or go against their community;
- can't imagine an identity separate from their family or community;
- might eat too much red meat;

- might be overweight and/or thick in their lower body;
- might have varicose veins or hemorrhoids;
- might have gout, arthritis, or joint inflammation;
- might say yes to every potential moneymaking endeavor because they never feel they have enough money to survive;
- is on constant alert, possibly paranoid about issues of privacy or being controlled; or
- might stock their kitchen pantry full of food because "you never know when disaster might strike."

RE-GROUND YOURSELF:
HOW THE ROOT DETOX WORKED FOR ROB

My patient Rob was struggling. A law student in his midtwenties, he had always been ambitious and hardworking. He'd gotten top grades at a top college, won admission into a prestigious law school, and become an editor of his law review. Thanks to his commitment and dedication, his future seemed assured.

Then, suddenly, Rob was plagued with a set of mysterious symptoms. He was drained of energy, listless, and unmotivated. He either felt so exhausted that he had to take an afternoon nap or so wired that he couldn't fall asleep till the sun came up. Previously able to depend on his laser-sharp mind, he suddenly found himself unfocused and foggy.

He also had the feeling that, as he put it, he just "couldn't settle down to anything." When he tried to read, he couldn't finish an assignment. When he began to write, he had trouble completing a thought. When he started work on one class, he found himself switching to the assignment for another. "Whatever I'm doing, it seems like I should be doing something else," he explained. Underlying this restlessness, he noticed a kind of creeping dread, as though something was really wrong that he just couldn't put his finger on.

He was at his wit's end, so he began to look for help. His first stop was to see a doctor, who suggested a combination antidepressant/antianxiety medication. But Rob was fairly certain he wasn't depressed, just tired and foggy. And while he often felt anxious, he hated the idea of taking a medication to, as he put it, "erase my feelings."

Then his mother, whom he described as "sort of a health nut," suggested that he eat more fresh vegetables. Rob tried to remember to grab some lettuce from the salad bar and to snack on carrots and celery while he studied, but he didn't really notice much difference.

His girlfriend thought maybe he needed to see a therapist to work on whatever psychological issues were dragging him down. But somehow, that idea just didn't click with Rob, who couldn't really believe that the problem was "all in my head."

When Rob came to me, one of my first thoughts was how piecemeal and partial the other responses had been. Conventional medicine, nutrition, and psychology can all be extremely helpful, but none of these disciplines typically treats the whole person. We need a comprehensive, systematic approach. In most cases, you can't just add a few things into your diet and hope that fixes the problem. And while therapy can open up important areas for exploration, it might miss some nutritional issues that are helping to create the problem. By contrast, Whole Detox addresses the whole person.

Rob's inability to settle down and focus, as well as his lack of motivation, led me to believe that he might be wrestling with his ROOT system. I wondered if he was questioning his identity in some way. Maybe some of his lack of focus and motivation had to do with a feeling of being ungrounded—being literally unable to "settle down."

It turned out that Rob's parents had recently retired, selling the house he'd grown up in and moving into a nearby retirement community. Somehow, the loss of those childhood roots threw Rob into a state of confusion. When his family home was intact, he had felt grounded and settled. Having a firm foundation had freed him to pursue his goals. But with the loss of that grounding, his whole identity seemed "up in the air." He began questioning what he was doing in law school, whether he had chosen the right path for himself or whether he had forged forward on this path because of ingrained, early-imprinted family stresses around being successful and having enough money. He worried about paying back his huge loans after he graduated and whether he could create for himself the life he wanted. With his parents moving on to a different stage of their lives, he realized that he, too, had arrived at a new stage, and he felt overwhelmed by his new adult responsibilities.

At the same time, he wasn't getting the nutrients he needed to support him in this struggle: the grounding, energizing support of healthy proteins and red foods. The immune system and the adrenals are the foundation for the ROOT, and I knew that Rob's brain fog, anxiety, listlessness, fatigue, and sleep problems were common symptoms of immune/adrenal issues.

Using a Whole Detox approach, he could address the full spectrum of his ROOT: the diet, lifestyle, and psychological exploration he needed to feel grounded and well defined once more. Let's take a closer look at the ROOT and see how I helped Rob through the first system of health.

PROTEIN TO SUPPORT YOUR ROOT

When I think about identity and defense, I immediately think of protein. We are literally made of protein. Our bodies, after all, are made of a protein-based structure, and our systems run on the proteins known as enzymes. And our DNA, the core genetic material that makes up our identity, is composed primarily of protein. When our DNA is activated by an outside signal—such as food, sunlight, toxins, or stress—it starts to churn out proteins that act as messengers in our body.

The protein matrix of the bones is packed with sturdy minerals to give us our defining structure and the bulk of our being. Our muscles hug our bones tightly, enabling us to move and function. On a finer level, our skin, which gives us physical boundaries, is made of proteins like collagen.

Even deeper within the body lie the building blocks of protein, the amino acids, which we need to fortify our immune responses. Protein is also crucial for the effective function of our adrenal glands and its production of hormones.

As you can see, protein literally constitutes our identity. Protein is who we are at the most fundamental level of our existence.

Protein also is crucial to our liver, which needs a constant supply of quality proteins in order to rid our body of toxins. Without protein, we simply can't get the poisons out of our body.

Not surprisingly, then, protein is our primal defense—our ancestors' go-to food to defend against starvation and loss of body fat. Early humans might often have been desperate for a bit of meat or fish to build up their body fat against the long, cold winters or to sustain them in treks across the desert. Even now, when we don't feel safe, most of us turn to protein, the food that originally made us feel grounded and secure.

While I don't want to encourage you to overconsume protein, as so many of us do, I do want you to remember this simple equation: protein equals survival. If you ever find yourself craving an extra-big helping of meatballs, a thick, juicy hamburger, or a succulent steak, you might well ask yourself, "Am I feeling threatened?" or "Do I feel the need to be more 'rooted' in this moment?" Certainly if you want to feel grounded, go for a high-protein food rather than one high in carbohydrates or sugars. Protein will stabilize your blood sugar and give you the sensation of satiety deep within.

In recent years, between the Paleo movement and committed vegans, it has become rather difficult to talk about protein. Some people maintain that animal proteins are best suited to the human physiology; others insist that animal proteins are unhealthy and perhaps even immoral. Since you know I'm an advocate of personalized medicine, it probably won't surprise you to learn that I won't choose sides! Some people do better with animal protein; others do better with a vegetarian or vegan diet. Be open to choosing whatever you need at any particular moment rather than following a generic diet. Your body will change over your lifetime, so what works at one time might change at another. Only you know what works best for you—and the more grounded in your ROOT you are, the better you will know. Some people do well with lots of animal protein, some with moderate amounts, some with none. While legumes are healthy choices for many, some people simply do not do well on them, even if they soak and treat them overnight, perhaps because of various phytochemicals, such as lectins, or maybe because their digestive system is not working optimally.

However, if you do eat meat, don't overdo it: no more than once a day for animal proteins and no more than once or maybe twice a week for red meat, unless you are able to find high-quality, grass-fed sources. Overeating poor-quality meat can create inflammation, which once again stresses your immune system and overworks your adrenal glands. Do your very best to eat clean meats, from animals that have been fed organically grown food and been pasture raised. Factory farms are full of industrial chemicals and antibiotics, and inhumanely raised meat is loaded with toxic stress hormones.

One potential health concern with meat is the way heterocyclic amines—a type of carcinogen—form during the cooking process. You can offset that danger by including green leafy vegetables rich in chlorophyll with your meal. In other words, make sure you prepare a hearty spinach salad (with an avocado for some extra healthy fat!) to accompany your grilled grass-fed buffalo burger.

On the other hand, if you're a vegetarian or vegan, make sure you're not skimping on the vegetable protein and you're supplementing properly with B12 if your levels are low.

Whether you prefer animal or vegetable protein, you do need protein, no ifs, ands, or buts! Besides acting as one of your body's building blocks, protein also helps to stabilize your blood sugar. Think of how quick-burning refined carbohydrates throw you onto a blood-sugar roller coaster. When you're constantly careening from sugar high to sugar crash, you feel flighty, dreamy, out of your body. Solid, healthy proteins—lentils; beans; wild-caught fish; organic, grass-fed, pasture-raised meats—keep you anchored in your physical body in a healthy, grounded way.

HEALTHY PLANT-BASED PROTEINS FOR YOUR ROOT

Different types of proteins contain different amino acids, and your body needs all of them. That's why I highly recommend that you frequently change up your protein sources, especially if you're a vegetarian or vegan. Here are some plants that are rich sources of protein:

Food	Serving size	Protein (grams)
Lentils	1 cup, cooked	18
Black beans	1 cup, cooked	15
Chickpeas	1 cup, cooked	15
Kidney beans	1 cup, cooked	15
Hemp seeds, shelled, whole	¼ cup	10
Quinoa	1 cup, cooked	8
Almonds	1 ounce	6
Brown rice, long grain	1 cup, cooked	5
Spinach	1 cup, cooked	5
Chia seeds	1 tablespoon	3

METALS VS. MINERALS

Heavy metals are a huge source of toxic trouble, whereas minerals are vital to our detox—and to our overall health. I've found that many people become confused about the difference, so let me set the record straight.

"Heavy metals" generally refers to those metals that result in health problems for humans, chiefly aluminum, arsenic, cadmium, lead, and mercury. While we want minerals to ground us and support our ROOT, heavy metals ground us too much, creating a host of problems that undermine our health and well-being.

WHERE DO HEAVY METALS LURK?

- Dental amalgams, which contain mercury
- Drinking water, which is often contaminated with a variety of metals
- Certain types of fish, which contain mercury
- Impure fish oils, which contain mercury
- Food that has been contaminated with pesticides and/or grown in contaminated soil
- Hijiki, a type of seaweed, which may contain arsenic
- Certain types of rice, particularly brown rice and rice grown in Arkansas, Louisiana, or Texas, which are high in arsenic; brown or white basmati rice grown in California, India, or Pakistan and white sushi rice contain far lower levels of arsenic
- House dust, which has a wide variety of contaminants
- Some red lipsticks as some of them are known to contain lead
- Some deodorants that contain aluminum

Heavy metals are established carcinogens that bind to different proteins in our body, preventing them from proper function. They tend to accumulate in the kidney, liver, bone, and brain, where they can produce neurological problems: tremors, trouble focusing, and other nervous system disorders. They can also disrupt gastrointestinal and cardiovascular function. Even small increments of lead in the bloodstream can raise your blood pressure, while heavy meal toxicity can also alter your white and red blood cell counts. Finally, heavy metals can create skin lesions or hyperpigmentation—a bluish or darker skin tone.

How should you protect yourself? Here are a few suggestions:

- Have any mercury-laden dental amalgams replaced by a dentist who understands the correct, nontoxic procedure for removal.
- Test your drinking water or check with your local area's water department to see if test results are available, and then, if necessary, install a water filter (see Resources).
- Keep your house as free as possible of dust.
- Choose lower-mercury forms of fish and only pure fish oils.
- Choose organically grown foods.
- Choose a natural, aluminum-free deodorant and organic cosmetics.
- If you think you are suffering from heavy metal poisoning, get a blood test and, if necessary, work with a functional medicine practitioner to detoxify your system (see Resources).

Minerals, by contrast, are crucial detox elements that help ground, strengthen, and protect us:

- Zinc is a constituent of a protein known as metallothionein that helps to upregulate this protein, which in turn binds heavy metals and helps facilitate their removal from the body.
- Selenium is required for the efficient function of glutathione, a major antioxidant and detox compound.

You can take supplements of these two minerals, or for your selenium, you can eat Brazil nuts (best source!), seeds, fish, grass-fed meats, and eggs, and get your zinc from some of the same sources: nuts, seeds, seafood, and grass-fed meats. You'll note that all of these sources will also provide you with another ROOT essential: protein.

RED FOODS AND YOUR ROOT

The ROOT represents the red segment of the spectrum. While I didn't make that association myself—I got it from East Indian medicine—I was fascinated to discover the wealth of science anchoring the color red to the ROOT.

As we saw in the beginning of this chapter, the color red provokes urgency in our survival, revving up the stress response and gearing us to fight or flee. Besides the four studies I quoted, other researchers have found that the color red triggers our stress response in various other ways. Because red captures our attention, setting off the heightened alertness that is part of the stress response, it's a useful color for stop signs, danger warnings, and other situations in which we need to focus quickly.

The scientists who made this association might have been interested to learn that certain red foods are full of vitamin C, which properly balances the production of the stress hormone, cortisol. In other words, without vitamin C, we can't mobilize a proper stress response. We also need this important vitamin for proper immune function—to defend against colds, flu, and more serious ailments. These vitamin C–rich foods include red bell peppers, chili peppers, strawberries, tomatoes, cranberries, watermelon, goji berries, raspberries, and cherries.

Red apples provide vitamin C too, along with other nutrients. They also contain the phytonutrient quercetin, which bolsters immune function and reduces inflammation. Just remember that apples are one of the most pesticide-laden fruits, so buy the organically grown variety!

Red teas are another great way to detox your ROOT. Herbal teas are one of my favorite beverages for a detox, with a lot of pivotal research suggesting that teas support our detoxification pathways. My red-colored favorites are rose hip, hibiscus, and rooibos teas, all of which have minerals, flavonoids, and other phytonutrients to help reduce inflammation and improve immune function.

Iron is essential for the ROOT since it is one of the central components of red blood cells, which carry oxygen and give us the energy to exist. Of course, the most abundant source of iron is red meat. Iron can be both good and bad for us. In the right quantities, iron stabilizes our red blood cells for better oxygenation, helping us to feel invigorated and alive. However, too much iron can be toxic and cause a form of rancidity or rusting to occur in the body, known as oxidative stress. To keep your iron levels optimal, you'll want to balance plant and animal sources of red foods, both during and after your detox. You'll get a feel for how to do this in the first three days of your Whole Detox, which should help you balance your red foods afterward.

Another type of red food nutrient is lycopene, a red carotenoid found in tomatoes, pink grapefruit, and watermelon. Recent research shows that lycopene is a strong supporter of your ROOT, helping to build strong bones, with possible protective benefits against cancer, heart disease, and other age-related disorders.

MAKE THE MOST OF YOUR TOMATOES

Cooking your tomatoes is a nutritious choice, because you make the lycopene more "bioavailable"—that is, more available to your biochemistry. In other words, when you eat raw tomatoes, your body absorbs less lycopene than when you eat them cooked or processed. And if you cook them with olive oil, you get even greater benefit. Cooked tomatoes are likewise superior to raw because the heat makes it easier for you to absorb phytonutrients like naringenin (a potent antioxidant, especially for liver health) and chlorogenic acid (which positively impacts sugar and fat metabolism).

So besides adding protein to your diet, add some red foods of all types: a healthy ROOT likes variety! Choose beets, cherries, red apples, pomegranates, strawberries, raspberries, goji berries, watermelon, and some red herbal teas, and watch your immune system and adrenal glands flourish.

SUPPORT YOUR ROOT WHILE YOU EAT

We will fully address ROOT issues during the first three days of the twenty-one-day program. But if you're feeling in the need for some immediate support for your ROOT, here are a few quick tips on how to cultivate rootedness while you eat:

- Eat on the floor rather than in a chair.
- Eat with your hands or use wooden or ceramic utensils rather than silverware.

- Eat in nature, outside on a sunny day.
- Eat barefoot, with your legs uncrossed.
- Follow your instincts on food choices.
- If you are having trouble making healthy choices, ask your body what it needs in that moment.
- Do a simple guided imagery to get rooted in your body before preparing or eating food.

GET GROUNDED—LITERALLY

A number of studies have discovered several benefits in making direct contact with the earth, by walking barefoot outside or, if that's not possible for you, being mechanically wired to a device that transfers the earth's electrons into the body. This practice, known as earthing or grounding, seems to decrease pain and inflammation, improve sleep and mood, and reduce blood viscosity and clumping. As Dr. Gaétan Chevalier and his research team have said, "The research done to date supports the concept that grounding or earthing the human body may be an essential element in the health equation along with sunshine, clean air and water, nutritious food, and physical activity."

Since grounding is so beneficial, why not find as many ways as possible to maximize the connections between your body and the earth? As I mentioned above, you might want to try eating barefoot, close to the ground, using your hands rather than silverware. When the weather is nice, maybe take your meal outside and enjoy it under a tree.

LIFE ISSUES: IDENTITY, SAFETY, SURVIVAL, COMMUNITY

Let's return to my patient Rob and what he needed to do to strengthen his ROOT. On a physical level, his body perceived that his safety and survival were at risk; hence, the overreaction of his immune system (to defend him from "dangerous" foods) and his adrenal glands (which kept putting him in fight-or-flight mode in response to the "danger"). This affected his psychology as well. You can't have your body in a fight-or-flight state and not feel anxious, revved up, on edge; that's what that state is for. So if you frequently find yourself feeling anxious and on the brink of feeling like you are falling apart, you might consider whether there are physical or nutritional reasons for your stress as well as psychological ones.

Of course, Rob was also facing a number of stressful issues. His parents had sold his childhood home. He was in a challenging program, about to face a highly competitive career. For the first time in his life, he would be responsible for his own finances, and he was taking on that responsibility while saddled with an enormous amount of debt. There were very good reasons for him to feel at risk.

On the other hand, the stress response—preparing for a fight-or-flight situation—isn't always upsetting. Sometimes it's exciting, thrilling, or full of pleasurable anticipation. A team getting ready to play a big game, a musician about to perform a major concert, a person about to go on a romantic date—all of these people are stressed in a physical sense, but they experience those stress hormones as positive, even enjoyable. So one of the ways I worked with Rob was to see if he could reinterpret his feelings of dread and unsettledness as excitement and anticipation. Yes, his identity was changing rapidly. Now, instead of being a child who lived with his parents, he was an adult preparing for an adult career. That certainly might seem scary, but wasn't it also an adventure? After all, he had chosen this career, he'd done very well at school, and he'd been quite excited about becoming a lawyer. We worked in various ways on his choice to perceive "unsettled" and "uncertain" as potentially exciting states as well as frightening ones.

Besides the challenges in his work life, Rob faced challenges to his core sense of self. When his parents sold his childhood home, his very identity seemed to be in question—his primary relationship to his community. Instead of being a son, a child, someone to be cared for, he was about to become an adult, a man, an independent person. Instead of his primary tribe being other young people his age—the friends he hung out with, the girlfriend he dated—he was about to join a new tribe: lawyers. So we worked on helping him to further define his tribe and his new identity, as a lawyer, as an adult, as a man in a serious relationship with a woman, as the adult child of aging parents. Yes, he was losing one identity, but he was also forging another. Focusing on his new identity helped him feel less "unrooted" about losing his old one.

At the end of an extensive ROOT detox, Rob felt focused, clear, and determined. While he couldn't eliminate the uncertainty in his life, he could shift his relationship to it, celebrating what he was going toward even while, perhaps, mourning the stage of life that he was leaving. He could support himself with the kinds of foods that kept him grounded, alert, and best able to handle stress. He could avoid the foods that made his life challenges more difficult, and he could make sure to get the sleep and relaxation he needed.

Rob also liked knowing that he had learned so much about himself and his ROOT. He knew that if he ever again felt unsettled and ungrounded, he had the tools to identify what was going on and to remove any barriers in his way.

DETOXING YOUR ROOT: WHAT TO CHOOSE
- Clean, lean proteins to support your adrenal glands and immune system
- Organically grown red fruits and vegetables, such as beets, cherries, apples, pomegranates
- Body awareness to balance your stress response and keep yourself in the moment
- Community—contact with people who reinforce the identity you have chosen

DETOXING YOUR ROOT: WHAT TO AVOID
- Toxins that stress your immune system, such as heavy metals, genetically modified organisms (GMOs), artificial dyes, foods with additives or preservatives
- Foods that cause your immune system to be reactive—maybe take a temporary break from dairy, gluten, eggs, and soy
- Situations in which you often feel you have to defend yourself
- Situations that stress your adrenals, such as when you do too much, say yes when you'd rather say no, or lose your sense of healthy boundaries
- Negative attitudes and limited beliefs about safety, survival, and money, for example,
  - *If I don't have a lot of money, I'll never get anywhere.*
  - *It's a man's world—a woman might as well give up before she starts.*
  - *There's no room in this world for someone like me.*
  - *I can never survive without my family's support.*

STRENGTHEN YOUR ROOT

I'm excited for you to go through the twenty-one-day program of Whole Detox—the same program I've shared with thousands of students and the same approach I use with my patients.

But to me, Whole Detox is just the first step. The real benefit is how the program helps you become aware of the role each system of health plays in your life and the ways in which each color affects you. The more you learn about Whole Detox, the more options you will create to support your health—and your life.

We could easily spend an entire book just on the ROOT, but I want you to get to know the other six systems of health as well! So let's move on to the second system of health: the FLOW.

CHAPTER 4

THE FLOW

Life is a series of natural and spontaneous changes. Don't resist them—that only creates sorrow. Let reality be reality. Let things flow naturally forward in whatever way they like.

—LAO TZU

UNDERSTANDING THE FLOW

Anatomy	Ovaries/testes, large intestine (colon), urinary system
Functions	Fluid balance, reproduction
Living	Emotions, creativity, partnerships, sexuality
Eating	Healthy fats and oils, water, orange-colored foods

THE SCIENCE OF THE FLOW

The ROOT is all about grounding to the earth and anchoring ourselves in the physical world. The FLOW, by contrast, represents our fluid, flowing, dynamic emotions. The FLOW calls upon us to let "e-motions" (energy in motion) move freely through our bodies so they don't stagnate and end up diseased.

If you feel "stuck," "dried up," or "blocked," chances are that something has disrupted your FLOW. Likewise, if you feel "swept up" in your feelings, "flooded" with emotion, "dissolving" in grief, or emotionally out of control, you might be struggling with an overflow of the FLOW. Whenever you feel moody, overly emotional, numb, infertile, or uncreative—and especially if you are having problems with sex or reproduction—you would do well to take a Whole Detox approach and consider your FLOW.

On a physical level, the FLOW refers to the parts within the body that help water ebb and flow: our cellular fluid, urinary system, and large intestine, which controls the uptake of water from the undigested matter running through us.

urinary system for detox

The urinary system is what enables us to balance the fluid in the body. It's a complex array of organs, including the bladder, which holds the urine; the ureters/urethra, which channel urine out from the body so it can be excreted; and the kidneys, which govern the whole process.

Most of us don't think twice about urination unless something goes wrong, but in fact, it's a hugely important bodily function. Throughout the day, we accumulate physical toxins—from food, air, water, home items (furniture, carpet, mattresses), cleaning products, and personal-care products (shampoo, moisturizer, cosmetics). Getting rid of those toxins on a daily basis is a crucial factor in our health.

The body has natural ways of getting physical toxins out: through urine, bowel movements, tears, and sweat ("pee, poop, cry, and sweat," as I usually say to my patients). If we can't properly excrete toxins through our urine, they build up inside us with problematic consequences, including weight gain, fatigue, and other symptoms: headaches, skin problems, digestive issues, and frequent colds, flu, and infections. In some cases, the toxic buildup causes even more serious problems, making us vulnerable to autoimmune conditions and cancer. Keeping our FLOW in good shape is one way to stay healthy and strong.

What's the best way to support your urinary system? I can tell you in three words: hydrate, hydrate, hydrate. Take half your body weight, convert it to ounces, and drink that much purified water every day throughout the day. If you drink coffee, tea, or any other caffeinated beverages, add some more water to cover the diuretic (water-releasing) effects of caffeine. If you're physically active or live in a hot climate, add several more ounces to cover that too.

Most of my patients are dehydrated when we start working together,

55 oz

usually without even realizing it. Our thirst monitors—evolved during a prehistoric era when we couldn't be certain of getting clean water on demand—tend not to kick in until we're already well past the point of dehydration. In other words, by the time you feel thirsty, you've already stressed your body—and your urinary system. Remember in chapter 3 when I told you that chronic stress can result from not sleeping enough or eating too many inflammatory foods, and that this stress can have terrible consequences for your adrenals and immune system? Well, dehydration is another type of chronic stress that can burden your body, so you may be surprised to discover what a calming, healing effect proper hydration can have. Your goal is to drink enough water to prevent yourself from ever getting thirsty.

If you're not used to drinking lots of water, you might have a little trouble at first getting yourself to drink enough. Within two or three days, though, you'll find yourself naturally craving the water your body needs. You'll know that you're drinking enough water when your urine always comes out light yellow or almost clear, even first thing in the morning (unless, of course, you are taking certain vitamins, which can turn your urine yellow).

The Creative FLOW

We've looked at the physical FLOW, but there are other considerations as well. One is creativity, evoking our playfulness, openness, pleasure, and sensuality. Our reproductive organs—ovaries and testes—help us create life, making them part of this second system of health. The FLOW is also associated with each cell's ability to replicate and grow.

Our physical creativity depends upon our ovaries (if we're female) or testes (if we're male). Whole Detox is crucial to support these glands, which are under an increasing amount of pressure from the environment, thanks to the ever-growing number of toxins to which we are exposed. I'm saddened but not surprised to see that we have a growing infertility epidemic among both men and women. After all, plastics contain toxins that are endocrine disrupters; that is, chemicals that disrupt our endocrine system, or our hormones. (These toxins are often referred to as "xenoestrogens," from the prefix xeno, meaning "foreign.") Endocrine disrupters can block or alter pathways in the body that are regulated by estrogen, creating hormonal imbalances in both sexes. It can also cue both men and women to manufacture too much estrogen, leading to a condition known as estrogen dominance: basically, when you've got too much estrogen relative to your other reproductive hormones.   *[handwritten: rH toxins]*

Estrogen dominance can have disastrous results for both men and women. Females with too much estrogen suffer from menstrual and menopausal issues as well as weight gain, mood swings, and other symptoms. Men don't have the menstrual problems, but they do face all the others. And both sexes struggle with sex drive and fertility.

Infertility can also result from stressful emotions, and infertility can lead to emotional distress. As we discussed previously, stress—especially extreme stress and most especially continuous stress—produces an excess of stress hormones, particularly cortisol. Cortisol, in turn, disrupts male and female hormones, which, when you think about it from a biological perspective, makes sense. For our ancestors, stress meant either starvation or life-threatening exertion—treks across the tundra, enduring the arctic cold or the desert heat. Those were hardly the times when the community would be served by the birth of new members. The resources of the body were thus directed not toward conception, pregnancy, and breast-feeding but toward basic survival and caring for the children they already had. In our own time, we see this phenomenon when young female athletes lose their periods or never get them in the first place—another example of the body's primal effort to hoard its resources for survival in the face of "life-threatening" exertion.

Now you can see why Whole Detox begins at the ROOT. Before we can meet any of our other needs, we need to know that basic survival has been assured and the needs of the community have been met. Frequently, when someone comes to me with a fertility or hormonal issue, I'll make sure we address the ROOT as well as the FLOW, so the two systems of health are not working at cross purposes.

Another factor in sexuality and reproduction is a person's own attitudes about being a man or woman. We live in a society with very firm and even rigid ideas about what male and female is. Many of us don't fit the ideal we've been given, and as a result, we might run into physical problems as well as psychological ones.

While I don't have scientific research to support this, I do have my own clinical observation and that of my fellow practitioners. We often see situations in which someone comes for treatment about a sexual or reproductive issue and is helped by diving into their own sense of being masculine or feminine.

For example, I've observed many women who feel they have no time to be feminine or they don't even know what it means to be a woman other than being stressed and juggling multiple roles. I've actually struggled with these notions myself, and I know that in both myself and my patients, female struggles can manifest in "female problems," including difficult menstrual cycles, challenging entry into perimenopause or menopause, infertility, and endometriosis.

Another common result of female stress is polycystic ovarian syndrome (PCOS), a syndrome in which women who are highly driven in a stressful environment develop high cortisol and high testosterone. This hormonal imbalance produces a number of symptoms, including irritability, hirsutism (the growth of hair), and an ovary that isn't quite fertile.

Men also wrestle with gender identity. Our culture equates manhood with violence, overwork, and competitive sports. Men pursuing an alternate version of masculinity—supportive, nonviolent, collaborative, with the goal of becoming a leader who inspires and empowers—might encounter ridicule, harassment, or even physical aggression.

Whole Detox, with its full-spectrum approach to the second system of health, can help to resolve these issues in both physical and emotional ways. When our creative FLOW is released, we can enjoy a rich fertility, as when a river overflows its banks to nourish the surrounding soil.

Another dimension of creativity, of course, is nonbiological: the creation of art, stories, new ideas, interesting ways of preparing a meal or arranging a room. Looking at the FLOW in all its dimensions, we can see that being creative is a healing force, helping us to resolve biological issues as well as emotional ones. As you'll learn later in this chapter, many of my patients have renewed their FLOW—biologically and emotionally—by giving themselves permission to be creative. And many who had felt their creativity was blocked have recovered their inspiration and creative vision by addressing the physical nature of the FLOW.

In all of these voyages toward healing, color is extremely important. The color orange has a remarkable ability to unlock biological fertility as well as intellectual and emotional creativity.

THE POWER OF ORANGE

The science on the color orange is fun and fascinating. A wide variety of research has linked orange to the FLOW via its relationship to fertility and hydration.

First, it seems that orange is a mating color, one that alerts members of the animal kingdom to go with the flow of their reproductive urges. Researchers in the Department of Marine Ecology at the University of Gothenburg, Sweden, found that when some fish engage in courtship—including when females are competing for the attention of males—"a rapid increase in orange coloration . . . gives the belly an intense 'glowing' appearance" that attracts potential mates. A study from the Department of Ecology and Evolutionary Biology at the University of Toronto found that certain guppies are so attracted to the color orange that prawns have developed orange spots on their pincers to entrap the sexually excited fish with a "sensory lure." Moreover, as scientists from the University of Padua have discovered, orange correlates to guppies' fertility, specifically "with faster and more viable sperm . . . suggesting a possible link between dietary carotenoid intake and sperm quality." Thinking about the FLOW, I like to remember that what we're talking about here is the ability of sperm to swim, to negotiate the reproductive fluids that enable the creation of new life.

The color orange is linked to reproductive health in birds as well. According to a group of Swiss researchers at the University of Bern, male birds with brighter plumage have sperm that is better protected against oxidative stress. Researchers wondered whether beta-carotene—the compound that turns foods orange—offers that protection. Their hypothesis was confirmed when they gave less colorful males carotenoid supplements and improved their sperm quality. Of course, you don't have to take carotenoid supplements; you can just eat more orange foods!

Another fascinating area of animal research indicates that beta-carotene concentrates in the corpus luteum (a developing egg in the ovary), where it may play a role in ovulation by assisting with the production of progesterone. Animal studies likewise suggest that beta-carotene supplementation supports ovarian activity and progesterone synthesis in goats. As I've said, I've noticed a similar effect in my human patients, who sometimes seem to have hormonal shifts when consistently increasing their intake of beta-carotene-rich, orange-colored foods. Indeed, Polish scientists have discovered that uterine tissues contain beta-carotene, while a 2014 study published in the journal *Fertility and Sterility* suggests that when women boost their beta-carotene intake, their chances of becoming pregnant seem to improve.

Finally, a study in the *Journal of Urology* found that men who drank orange juice enjoyed a reduced risk of kidney stones, linking orange both to kidneys and to the image of fluids freely flowing through the urinary system. After all, aren't kidney stones a particularly painful form of stagnation that impedes urinary flow?

To bring of the creative flow of orange into *your* life, try drinking your water in an orange-colored glass. Place an orange-colored object in any space where you'd like to ramp up your creativity: your workspace, your home office, perhaps even your kitchen. And on days when you'd like to generate more inner flow—emotional, creative, or relational—slip into an orange sweater or put on a pair of orange socks or earrings. Your FLOW will love you for it.

GET TO KNOW YOUR FLOW

The FLOW of Relationship

The FLOW represents the relationship between opposites—the movement that flows back and forth between male and female, mind and body, yin and yang. Just as the ROOT brings out the need for community, the FLOW allows us to appreciate the need for another person. Thus we can see the power of the FLOW in our partnerships or the relationship between two people. In any important relationship—work and friendship as well as romantic—we are always growing and creating through the dynamic dance with others. Sometimes we have blocks to commitment and we flow from one relationship to another, never quite arriving at what we need. Other times we begin to stagnate within the framework of a comfortable relationship that might not suit who we are, yet we don't feel like we have an escape available.

The FLOW teaches us both the beauty and the bane of interdependence. In a healthy relationship, the FLOW creates enhanced personal growth for each individual. In an unhealthy relationship, we encounter the shadow of codependence as each partner leads the other into a downward spiral of fear, anger, and pain, bringing out the worst in each other and moving each other in a negative direction.

The FLOW reminds you to ask how your relationships and choices are creating who you are in every moment, for better or for worse. When my patients reach this phase of Whole Detox, I see them questioning their toxic relationships, marriages, and business partnerships. They begin to see that the FLOW offers them possibilities and potential. The FLOW is a constant reminder to avoid the stagnant water of unhealthy partnerships and move into those that bring us into the rushing current of life, where creativity is always possible.

FLOWING WITH SMALL MOVEMENTS

A Native American teacher once told me that when we stop dancing and telling stories, we stop living—that is, we cease feeling full of life. Life is movement, and when we are not tapping into our gift to move, we stagnate. Our chi, prana, or life force starts to create stagnant pools in various parts of our bodies—often in our joints or muscles, which ache from the toxic accumulation. This type of stagnation can cause pain and lack of function in organs as well.

Luckily, we can start our bodies flowing again by embracing movement, even seemingly small and insignificant movement. Walk a few steps farther in the parking lot instead of parking close to the entrance of a building. Take the stairs instead of the elevator. Every hour or two, walk briskly to another floor in your office building or grab a ten-minute walk on your lunch break.

You can also embrace therapeutic movement. If you choose a type of movement that you feel passionate about, you will most likely stay in the flow, so experiment a bit and find something you really enjoy. Here are some moving ideas to start you flowing:

- An afternoon walk in the park
- Gardening
- Yoga of all types: hatha, kundalini, Bikram, ashtanga, etc.
- Tai chi
- Qigong

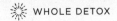

- Aikido and other martial arts
- Kayaking and water sports—especially great for flow because of the water element!
- Dance classes: Zumba, ballet, free form, Nia, etc.

The Emotional FLOW

The physical FLOW, the creative FLOW, and the relating FLOW regulate our urination, reproduction, and relationships. For the FLOW to operate freely, however, we need to consider one final dimension: the emotional.

Water has long been a symbol of emotions in many mythologies and many types of traditional medicine. And no wonder. When we are flooded with grief, water comes out of our bodies in the form of tears. When we are awash with fear, water comes out of us as urine and watery diarrhea. The moon—which both science and mythology link to emotions, mood swings, and periods of "lunacy"—has the magnificent ability to shift large bodies of water on our planet. Emotions bring together the symbols of water, urination, fertility, and creativity. And, indeed, when our emotions are unexpressed, fertility and creativity are frequently blocked as well. Biologically, we can imagine that stuck emotions are stressful—either caused by or causing stress, or both—and that the excess stress leads to too much cortisol, which disrupts mood, cognitive function, and, as we've just seen, our ability to feel sexual and to reproduce.

Problems can result from unfelt emotions and thwarted creativity, including unwanted creative proliferation within our bodies. Perhaps unhealthy bacteria or yeast will multiply in the gut, creating digestive problems. Maybe emotional distress will lodge in the gut, creating diarrhea, irritable bowel syndrome, Crohn's disease, and related disorders. We might even view cancer as the overproliferation of cells in response to a physical or emotional obstacle that the body could not overcome or release.

Whenever I think of the emotions, I also think about food, which is one of the most emotional issues I know. If one of my patients feels their eating is out of control, the FLOW is where I always start. Indeed, experts estimate that as much as 75 percent of overeating can be attributed to emotions, since when we feel unable to process our emotions, many of us are tempted to stuff them down with food.

What's exciting about these findings is the multiple solutions they allow us to consider: hydration, nutrition, emotion, creativity, or some combination of these. Addressing each of the issues supports the others, toward an end result of greater health, freer emotions, unblocked creativity, and greater sexual and reproductive function. Whole Detox draws much of its power from the power of synergy: the way each feature of a system of health supports and heals every other one.

Support Your Flow by Crying and Sweating

As we release water through our eyes or our pores, we often release emotion as well: sorrow or joy with our tears, anxiety or excitement with our sweat. Both the physical and the emotional release can have highly beneficial effects.

Crying is a form of detox in which we let go of our stored emotions and inner pain. It also literally eliminates inflammatory compounds: cytokines and chemokines. People who cry easily in response to emotion might even have fewer symptoms and better health than those who restrain their tears. Interestingly, healthy fats that embody a fluid, flowing structure—the omega-3s—can help heal dry eye, suggesting an additional close partnership between the characteristics of this second system.

Sweating is another primary way to release toxins, including PCBs, phthalates, bisphenols, and other compounds. In some cases, sweating is an even more efficient form of elimination than release via blood or urine. That's why I want you sweating through physical activities or in a sauna during your Whole Detox. Keep those toxins flowing *out* so you can allow more of the healthy creative FLOW in.

BALANCE YOUR FLOW

Balancing each system of health can be tricky; sometimes you may have "not enough" and sometimes you may have "too much." Everyone has their own personal definitions for "not enough," "too much," and "just right," and these definitions will likely change over the course of a lifetime. But again, bearing in mind that these are just provisional images, let's consider what balancing the FLOW might look like.

A person with a healthy FLOW

- has a healthy reproductive system, with the ability to be fertile at the appropriate age;
- has a healthy urinary system and the ability to resist urinary tract infections and other urinary problems, such as stones and inflammation;
- is able to excrete fluids effectively by sweating, urinating, and crying;
- has healthy levels of gender- and age-appropriate hormones, such as progesterone for women and testosterone for men;
- feels open to "going with the flow," remaining unconstricted when things don't go their way;
- has a creative approach to living, responding to challenges with some innovative solutions;
- has the capacity to be playful and open;
- can accept the ups and downs—the "flow"—of life;
- accepts his or her sexual orientation and gender identity, whatever they define it to be;
- is open to partnerships and relationships of all types—sexual, creative, emotional—and
- is comfortable eating healthy fats, chooses a healthy variety of fats, and avoids unhealthy or excessive fats.

A person with an underactive FLOW

- has edema or swelling somewhere in their body;
- might be going through premature menopause;
- might be prematurely infertile due to low levels of hormones;
- might have reproductive issues that involve stagnation or blocks, such as a blocked fallopian tube (hydrosalpinx), vaginal dryness, or impotence;
- might be losing their vitality at an early age, such as declining testosterone in men or declining progesterone in women;
- might avoid consuming dietary fat because they think they will get fat;
- might believe they are fat when they are not;

- might have issues with codependence;
- might have difficulty expressing or even realizing their emotions;
- might have difficulty "going with the flow" and/or might appear overly serious; or
- might be constipated or have infrequent or hard bowel movements.

A person with an overactive FLOW
- might be overly dramatic and emotional;
- always comes up with new ideas, but rarely puts them into motion;
- is prone to emotional eating;
- has many fleeting relationships with partners but is unable to sustain them;
- has high body fat relative to muscle mass for their age and gender;
- has reproductive issues that involve overactivity or inflammation, such as heavy cramping or bleeding with periods, prostatitis, cysts, or fibroids;
- has high levels of estrogen;
- has high exposure to xenoestrogens / endocrine disruptors;
- excessively urinates or feels the urge to urinate;
- has frequent bouts of diarrhea;
- is constantly thirsty;
- eats salty foods;
- eats high-fat foods; or
- indulges excessively in life's pleasures.

FIND YOUR FLOW:
HOW THE FLOW DETOX WORKED FOR MY PATIENTS

Because the FLOW manifests in so many different ways, I'd like to share with you five seemingly diverse patient stories. Each of them, however, has one thing in common: they all relate to an imbalance of the FLOW.

Merissa felt out of sorts and, as she approached her midforties, she began gaining weight. Her hormone levels were starting to decline, and she suffered from vaginal dryness, painful periods, and almost a complete loss of interest in sex. She was also frustrated by mood swings, which seemed to come at her "out of the blue," and depressed by the thought that her sexy, sensual self had, as she put it, "sort of evaporated." "I feel like I've just dried up and I have nothing to offer anymore," she told me.

She clearly needed some support for her hormonal imbalance—more healthy fats and orange foods; fewer unhealthy fats; a cleaner diet, generally; and some FLOW-inducing exercises of the type you'll be doing in days four through six of your twenty-one-day program. But Merissa also needed support for her sexuality and creativity.

We started gradually, with a class in water aerobics and one in Zumba to get her flowing in the water and in her body. But I also suggested that she try dressing differently. Every time I saw her, she was in the same old sweats and T-shirt with a messy ponytail on the top of her head. Her outward appearance reflected her inner doldrums.

When it's difficult to change the inside, what I like to do is change the outside. So I asked her to treat herself to a little shopping spree, even at a secondhand store. Her eyes somewhat lit up at the idea, and when I saw her next, she wore gold bracelets, her hair was flowing over her shoulders, and she was all decked out in a flowery dress! She was smiling and loving her new look, clearly radiating her beautiful feminine energy. Whole Detox had affected both her inner and outer being—through nutrition, yes, but also through helping Merissa renew her relationship with her feminine self.

Although Jorge was a successful accountant, he harbored a deep frustration: he had always wanted to be an artist. In college, he had studied graphic design and dreamed of working in that field full-time, but his father, a struggling small businessman, had urged Jorge to choose a more secure life, "where you work for someone else and always have bread on the table." Jorge had come to me because his wife was concerned that, as he told me, "I just sort of shut down. I feel numb all the time, like I just can't feel *anything* anymore. I'm doing fine at work, the bills are getting paid, nothing is really *wrong*, exactly. But I'm just going through the motions."

Like Merissa, Jorge benefited from eating orange foods and healthy fats. But he also needed to come to terms with his personal creative flow, which he had more or less dammed up after graduating college in order to placate his father. As Jorge came to realize how deeply he longed for a more creative and authentic life, he found the courage to leave his profession and commit to his once-abandoned life as an artist. Taking a huge leap of faith, he started a graphic design business, which to his great delight became a successful enterprise. He was thrilled to discover that his emotional life opened up at the same time, allowing for better communication—and better sex!—with his wife.

Ariana is one of those people who seem to live at the center of a perpetual drama. A highly emotional person, she feels everything deeply. She explained to me that she struggled with irritable bowel syndrome (IBS), which she had noticed was likely to flare up at her most intensely emotional times, hitting her with severe bouts of watery diarrhea.

"I feel like my emotions just wash through me and sweep me away," she told me, dabbing at her eyes. "I don't want to be one of those people who keeps it all inside, like my husband. What is life if you can't feel anything? But I don't want to keep getting sick either."

What Ariana really needed was to work not just on her overactive FLOW but also on her underactive ROOT and lack of boundaries. I could clearly see that she needed some quality protein to feel more stabilized and she needed to take out the sugar that was contributing to her ups and downs. I also encouraged her to map out her emotions each day, using my simple Whole Detox Emotion Log (see pages 381–83).

Through her work with the Whole Detox Emotion Log, Ariana discovered that she was not just overly emotional; she was very, very sad. Her sorrow stemmed from her pain over her mother's death, made even more painful by Ariana's unwillingness to deal with the full spectrum of her emotions about her mother. Since these emotions had not been resolved before her mother had died, Ariana was left with a potent cocktail of rage, guilt, and grief, and so her sorrow continued to bubble up again and again, a wellspring that refused to be suppressed.

When we realized this, I asked her to create a grief timeline that might help us identify her unresolved sorrow. We also looked at how she had subtly but continually changed her eating habits and lifestyle after each grief event.

Whole Detox helped Ariana begin a long process of recovery, which included additional counseling as well as nutritional support. Now, years later, she is still a deeply emotional being, but she has much better boundaries and far more effective coping mechanisms to still the turbulent tides within her.

At age forty-two, Chuck had what he considered a deeply shameful secret: he suffered from erectile dysfunction and, as he told me, "couldn't perform as a man." This was a relatively recent problem; throughout his twenties, he had had an active sex life, which he told me was satisfying sexually although, he later revealed, not so satisfying emotionally. Two of his girlfriends had cheated on him, and one had been so withholding that "I felt like I could never do anything right." He owned a small marketing company, and he was concerned about his work life also. "I feel like I've just run out of ideas," he told me. "Like the well has just run dry."

Like many of my other patients, Chuck's issues were both nutritional and something more. His diet was certainly lacking in good-quality fats and oils. He tended to eat carelessly and even to skip meals if no food was easily available. Although he had been an avid runner and weight lifter in his twenties, he had long since stopped exercise of all types.

His FLOW was gone because he was not flowing: no food or poor food, and little exercise. He needed some basics, so I got him going with regular vegetable and fruit smoothies every day, with plenty of orange fruits and vegetables along with healthy fats. He wasn't so thrilled with this new concoction at first, but then he started to get into the groove of his morning smoothie. The energy they gave him inspired him to start running again, until gradually, he was running several miles and feeling fit.

Fitness and energy helped make Chuck more confident, and so he began flowing at work too. He landed some new projects he was really excited about, and he felt encouraged by his success.

Months later, he met Lorraine, a wonderful woman who valued and supported him in every way. With Lorraine, he was able to heal the sense of his doing nothing right that his previous girlfriends had reinforced, and also to develop a satisfying sexual life. Together, they have taken up a daily running practice, keeping each other motivated and on track.

————

Elaine was a financial analyst in her midthirties who showed up at our first meeting in a sober gray suit and white blouse. "It's my work uniform," she told me, making a face. "If I didn't dress like this, they wouldn't take me seriously, but I do get tired of it sometimes."

During this first visit, Elaine told me that she was frustrated, almost desperate: after two years of trying with her husband, she still hadn't gotten pregnant. The tests on both of them hadn't turned up any problems, but for some reason it just wasn't happening. Neither one was open to the idea of IVF or other fertility techniques, but they did want to conceive their own child. "Is there anything I can do to get things moving?" Elaine asked me.

Elaine was one of those perfectionists who always did everything "right." She had already been to all the well-known functional medicine practitioners, followed all the diets, and taken all the supplements. She was whip smart and determined to do whatever she needed to, but for the first time, her determination just wasn't paying off.

I saw at once that she was a high achiever, used to achieving her goals through sheer determination and will. Her testosterone was up, from working in a corporate environment full of competitive men. She was trying to blend in, but she was missing something. She had lost her sense of being feminine. She never indulged in anything fun. And the last thing on her mind was being creative, which she considered "a waste of time."

As with Merissa, I knew we had to take it one step at a time. First, I suggested that she take a leisurely Hawaiian vacation with her husband. Reluctantly, she agreed, but she returned from her trip more open and relaxed.

Then I asked her to sign up for a creative journaling class. "I don't have the time," she snapped.

"Okay," I answered. "Then let's dial it down. Do something creative just five minutes a day. After all, it's for your health. And it's just five minutes."

She let out a sigh of irritation but agreed to try.

A few weeks later, Elaine showed me a collage of images that represented her goals. I was excited to see that the collage was filled with color, flowers, and positive words. This small movement in the direction of her creativity opened her up to other endeavors, and eventually, she began writing poetry.

She had made peace with the idea of not having biological children, so she and her husband eventually adopted Khloe. Six months later, Elaine was ecstatic to find out that she had gotten pregnant! Getting back into the FLOW had brought her a sense of fun, creativity, and joy.

HEALTHY OILS AND FATS TO SUPPORT YOUR FLOW

You stabilized the ROOT with protein and red foods. You will nourish the FLOW with the right balance of quality oils and fats as well as orange foods.

I love encouraging my patients and students to reintroduce healthy fats into their diet, not least because I spent four years studying essential fatty acids as a doctoral student, and I'm always amazed at what an enormous boost the right types of fats can provide. Essential fatty acids come by their name honestly: they are literally essential to every cell in our bodies. Our cell walls are made of fat, meaning that we need fat to enable nutrients to flow in while toxins and waste products flow out. Moreover, our brains are mainly composed of fat, so we desperately need healthy fats to think clearly and balance our emotions.

I've noticed over the years that many of my patients become emotional about eating fats. They believe that fats are not good for them and that eating fats will make them fat. This thinking has been fostered both by conventional medicine and by poorly informed journalists, but it is a toxic notion that creates more problems than it solves. What we're after is *balance*: not no fat or too much fat, but the right proportions of the right types of fats. Your goal is to load up on the healthy fats while letting go, as much as possible, of the unhealthy ones. You also need to balance your intake of different types of healthy fats.

Reproductive health also depends on healthy fats. Animal studies have shown that unsaturated fats in the right proportion are associated with fertility. In humans, omega-3 fatty acids are important nutrients in the growth, development, and health of the fetus and newborn infant. Including high-quality sources of omega-3s in the diet, such as wild-caught salmon, and perhaps also taking purified omega-3 fish oil supplements might be helpful for increasing healthy fats in the newborn, leading to reduced inflammation and allergies.

SYMPTOMS FROM NOT CONSUMING ENOUGH HEALTHY ESSENTIAL FATS

- Cognitive and mood imbalances
- Dry skin—lack of hydration and flow
- Hair loss
- Infertility
- Inflammation—too much heat without the cooling watery flow

Two types of healthy fats are known as omega-3 and omega-6. Omega-3s are typically found in plants, nuts, seeds, and fish, while omega-6s are found in meats as well as in some types of plants, such as avocado. Grass-fed meats, dairy products, and eggs also contain some omega-3 fats.

The typical modern diet—heavy on the corn-fed meats and animal fats; light on the fish, nuts, and seeds—contains far too many poor-quality omega-6s. Compounding the problem is the way that body fat—whether animal or human—becomes a toxic sinkhole for all those fat-loving industrial chemicals like PCBs, which dissolve in fat and are stored there. So when we consume too much animal fat—especially from factory-farmed animals—we end up with an overdose of toxins.

There's another type of fat problem that applies to both animal and vegetable fats: metabolic endotoxemia. Basically, whenever we eat a high-fat meal, we get a loosening of the tight junctions that hold together the cells of our intestinal wall. The result is the leaky gut we talked about in chapter 3—a version of too much FLOW as partially digested food passes through our gut walls.

To make matters worse, excess fat stimulates our gut bacteria to produce toxic substances that can then leak into the blood ("toxemia" literally means "toxic blood"). If you feel nauseous, gassy, or bloated after a high-fat meal, it's at least partly due to the unhealthy bacteria dumping their toxic products into your blood via your leaky gut. Yuck.

If you get your fat from olive oil, fish, and avocados, you're far less likely to encounter this ugly effect than if you consume the unhealthy trans fats and industrial oils that are part of so many packaged, processed, and fast foods. It's a lot easier to overdose on the unhealthy fats too, since they saturate the chips, French fries, and pizza that so many people snack on, as well as lurk in many other store-bought and restaurant foods spreading in popularity around the globe. No wonder we are looking at a worldwide fat and oil problem!

The solution? Here are a few suggestions:

- Avoid processed, packaged, and fast foods unless you know they contain only healthy fats.
- If you eat fish, choose wild-caught.
- If you eat animal meats or animal products, choose organic, humanely raised, and free-range or pasture-raised.

- If you eat dairy products, choose organic and those free of hormones and antibiotics.
- Moderate your consumption of animal and dairy products, and make sure to balance them with omega-3s, from fish, flaxseed meal, green leafy vegetables, nuts, and seeds.
- Consider supplementing with omega-3 fats, such as two fats that are found in fish: eicosapentaenoic acid (EPA) and docosahexaenoic acid (DHA). Make sure, however, that you buy only the cleanest fish oils, or you'll just end up with concentrated mercury.

Two other categories of fat are saturated (usually solid) and unsaturated (usually liquid). Every cell in your body contains a fat layer around its perimeter. As you might imagine, the composition of this fat layer determines how the cell functions: the nutrients and other substances it takes in and toxins and waste it lets out. Adding these precious unsaturated, flowing fats to our diet can lead to significant changes in the fluidity of our cells and their ability to receive and transport more efficiently when it comes to detox.

FISH AND WATER

If you're looking for the perfect FLOW food, you couldn't do better than the slippery, silver salmon: it lives in water, has a brilliant orange color on the inside, and is rich in omega-3 healthy fats. Also, salmon is relatively low in mercury compared with other fish choices, which, as we saw in chapter 3, is a major health hazard.

Regrettably, methylmercury is frighteningly common in seafood. If you want to learn more about the healthier choices at the fish market, check the Resources section for websites that can keep you current.

The Environmental Working Group can also help you find a filter for your water source so you can hydrate in peace of mind (see Resources). Meanwhile, avoid plastic containers for water as much as possible, since the plastic likely contains substances that disrupt your creative reproductive hormones. Stick with glass and stainless steel.

WHICH FISH HAVE THE HIGHEST LEVELS OF THE FLUID OMEGA-3 FATS?

Food	Serving size	EPA (grams)	DHA (grams)
Crab, Dungeness, raw	3 ounces	0.24	0.10
Herring, Pacific, raw	3 ounces	1.06	0.70
Salmon, Chinook, raw	3 ounces	0.86	0.62
Salmon, sockeye, raw	3 ounces	0.45	0.60
Sardines, Pacific, raw	3 ounces	0.45	0.74

BE FLUID IN YOUR FAT CHOICES

Have you ever noticed how people start to think that if a food is good for you, then you need to have more of it? For some time everyone seemed to focus on extra-virgin olive oil. Now coconut oil is all the rage. Coconut this, coconut that. After being told for years that coconut oil was bad for us, we now understand that it is quite healthy—but we need to consider the overall quantity. I am sure the tide will shift again at some point. Changing up your oils is your best alternative, and you will see several different types of oils in my Whole Detox recipes.

Meanwhile, check out some of my favorite fats for you to focus on:

Essential Fatty Acids

- *Sesame* oil is naturally rich in sesamin, a plant compound that improves your liver's fat-burning efficiency.
- *Hempseed* oil contains a mixture of both omega-3 and omega-6 fats. It is also rich in an anti-inflammatory fat called gamma-linolenic acid (GLA).
- *Flaxseed* oil is an abundant source of one of my favorite omega-3 fats, alpha-linolenic acid (ALA).
- *Fish* oil is another great source of omega-3s and essential fatty acids, especially when you take it in concentrated form as a supplement.

Helpful Fats

- *Coconut oil* isn't an essential fat, but it provides an abundant source of short- and medium-chain saturated fatty acids, which your liver and gut can quickly burn for energy. I've incorporated coconut oil into your Whole Detox to give your liver, gut, and brain the energy boost they need. Some newer research on coconut suggests it is also beneficial for giving the brain fuel, in addition to being antifungal, antiviral, antiparasitic, antimicrobial, and protective for the liver.

- *Extra-virgin olive oil* is known to contain some potent phytochemicals that act as antioxidants and anti-inflammatories. Plus, it's delicious! When you purchase olive oil from the store, look for not just "cold-pressed" or "extra-virgin" on the label but also "unfiltered" so you are getting the dense, cloudy oil full of those medicinal agents.

- *Avocado oil* is a relatively new oil that is good for cooking at higher heat. It has some health benefits, such as improving the function of mitochondria, the energy-producing organelles in the cell.

Packaging Matters

When thinking about fats and oils, don't forget how they are stored! Go for glass or stainless steel containers, and avoid plastic if you don't want endocrine-disruptive plastic molecules to migrate into your food. Fats and oils go rancid in heat, light, and oxygen, so make sure the container lids screw on tight and that you're keeping everything far away from the heat of the stove as well as from direct sunlight. Consider storing oils that you don't use very often in the refrigerator to extend their freshness. And of course, make sure to cook each fat at its correct temperature, or you will have toxic fats in your meal.

GO NUTS!

A super way to support Whole Detox is to eat nature's own combination of protein and healthy fats: nuts and seeds. Not only do you get lots of healthy omega-3s but you also combine the grounding of the ROOT protein with the FLOW of healthy fats. Your liver needs protein to properly rid your body of physical toxins, while your cells need healthy fats to defend against toxins and to excrete any waste and toxins that make their way into the cells.

Nuts and seeds give you a two-for-one that is especially important for vegetarians, who need to work a bit harder than carnivores to make sure they consume enough balanced protein and fat. Nut butters are an excellent way to add some protein and healthy fat to your smoothies as well.

Of course, many people can't digest nuts and seeds, responding with allergies or food sensitivities. If that's you, try rotating them every three or four days, which might enable you to tolerate them better. In fact, this type of rotation is a healthy choice even if you're not intolerant.

If you have difficulty digesting nuts, you may want to try sprouting them or soaking them in purified water for four to six hours before eating. Allowing their structure to soften means they can flow more efficiently because your digestive tract breaks them down more easily.

Several of the recipes on your twenty-one-day program call for nuts, especially on the vegetarian track. Please avoid them if you have an allergy or sensitivity.

ORANGE FOODS AND YOUR FLOW

Ah, the wonders of orange foods, from the deep sunset-colored blood orange to the pale, creamy orange of a slice of cantaloupe. Some orange foods are sweet, some tart, and some savory, but they have one important thing in common: the carotenoids that give them their color. I spent years studying this class of plant-based compounds during my graduate research at the university, which has given me an abiding appreciation for their contributions to our health and the FLOW, with particular admiration for their role in ovulation and hormone levels.

Just as fats can go rancid on your kitchen shelf or on the stovetop, so can they go rancid within our bodies, but this process is impeded by the carotenoids, which make their way into our cells. Some animal research suggests that beta-carotene—which converts to retinol, or vitamin A—also concentrates in the corpus luteum, the developing egg in the ovary. There it may play a role in ovulation by assisting with the production of progesterone, a hormone that is vital to fertility, a smoother menstrual cycle, and overall hormonal balance.

Insufficient progesterone results in estrogen dominance as well as a number of other mood and cognition problems: brain fog, mood swings, anxiety, depression, and sleep problems. Eating orange foods and healthy fats makes you feel better in so many ways!

ORANGE FOODS THAT NOURISH YOUR FLOW

- Apricot
- Bell pepper
- Cantaloupe
- Carrot
- Curry powder
- Kumquat
- Mango
- Nectarine
- Orange
- Papaya
- Peach
- Persimmon
- Pumpkin
- Squash (acorn, buttercup, butternut, kabocha)
- Sweet potato
- Tangerine
- Turmeric powder, turmeric root
- Yam

Beta-carotene dissolves in fat, so if your body is going to absorb it properly, you need to consume a little fat with your orange foods. Some research also suggests that heat might be essential to ensure that the fibrous structure of a plant breaks down enough to let the beta-carotene flow and become available for absorption.

What's your takeaway? Add some fat to your orange fruits and vegetables—just a bit—and, if possible, cook them lightly.

COMBINING ORANGE FOODS AND FATS: A FEW SUGGESTIONS

- Sauté your orange bell peppers in sesame oil at a very low heat until they are just slightly softened.
- Add a light coating of extra-virgin olive oil to some steamed squash, maybe with a touch of lemon or vinegar.
- Cut your carrots into matchsticks and steam them lightly in some coconut milk or clarified butter, until just slightly soft.
- Dress your baked or steamed sweet potatoes with a bit of coconut milk and a dash of ground nutmeg.

I've noticed that many infertile women don't seem to be getting their daily dose of orange foods, which means they're probably not getting enough beta-carotene. Could this be why they have trouble with ovulation and conception?

Other orange foods contain different types of phytonutrients, such as the bioflavonoids we find in oranges and tangerines. Getting a wide variety of bioflavonoids is helpful for keeping our blood vessels wide open, so they easily accommodate blood flow, keeping blood from stagnating into varicose veins and similar conditions. Finally, carotenoids and bioflavonoids have been shown to help prevent cancer—imbalanced FLOW triggering the body's excessive creativity, perhaps?

TROPICAL FOODS TO SUPPORT YOUR FLOW

Have you ever lived in the tropics or been there on vacation? Why are these glorious destinations where people often choose to relax? The sunshine, warmth, and foods embody the elements of relaxation, delight, joy, pleasure, and freedom. Bringing more of these foods into our lives, especially when they are in season, can enhance our playful inner child, who wants to have fun with food, as well as our adult self, who wants to tap into sensuality. Banana, coconut, fig, kiwi, mango, orange, papaya, and pineapple are all luscious options.

SUPPORT YOUR FLOW WHILE YOU EAT

You'll learn all about how to get yourself flowing in days four through six of your twenty-one-day program. But here are a few quick tips to get you started. Use any that appeal to you and keep the rest in reserve for a day when you'd like to get things moving:

- Drink enough water so your hunger and thirst signals are not mixed. Sip fluids throughout the day.
- Drink some warm water seasoned with cooling herbs like fennel and mint.
- Pay attention to how you feel when you eat. If you're blocking your feelings, ignoring your food, or eating while stressed, you'll lose the flow of hunger and fullness, making you vulnerable to emotional eating.
- Give your inner child time to create a meal, playing with the experience, making full use of colors and textures, and experiencing your emotions about cooking and sharing food.
- Sip some coconut water, eat some young coconut meat, or take a spoonful of coconut butter to satisfy hunger urges.
- Create some playful, colorful water by adding slices of lemon, lime, strawberry, fresh mint leaves, or cucumber, or drink some orange-infused water.
- Eat high-water orange fruits, like melon, papaya, and mango.
- Make a meal of an "avocado taco": cut the avocado into two halves, pry out the pit, and with each half, squish the meat up from the skin. Mmmm, healthy, filling fats and a delicious taste besides!
- Drink smoothies containing carrot, mango, tangerine, and/or orange juice instead of soft drinks.
- Choose an orange-yellow yam over a white baked potato.
- Add turmeric powder into smoothies, into a vegetable stir-fry, and into hamburger meat patties.
- Enjoy an apricot, cantaloupe slice, clementine, kumquat, orange, tangerine, nectarine, or peach as a snack.
- Prepare puréed carrots, butternut squash, and/or pumpkin.
- Make a tropical fruit smoothie containing frozen, cubed mango, papaya, and orange in a base of coconut milk and topped with ground cardamom and cinnamon.

- Put together a trail mix by blending different nuts (cashews, almonds, walnuts) with dried orange-colored, non-sulfated fruits (apricots, mango, papaya).

DETOXING YOUR FLOW: WHAT TO CHOOSE
- Healthy fats and oils, such as extra-virgin olive oil, sesame oil, flaxseed oil, hempseed oil, coconut oil, avocado oil, fish oil, wild-caught fish
- Nuts and seeds as a source of protein, rotated frequently to avoid triggering intolerance and sensitivity
- Orange foods, such as carrots, mangoes, melons, orange bell peppers, oranges, tangerines, sweet potatoes, yams
- Tropical fruits, such as banana, coconut, fig, kiwi, mango, orange, papaya, pineapple
- Purified water
- Emotional "flow," nurturing your full emotional range without feeling emotionally out of control
- Creativity, expressing yourself in your own way
- Sensuality and sexuality, allowing your sexual, sensual side to emerge and "flow" freely

DETOXING YOUR FLOW: WHAT TO AVOID
- Impure water
- Water and foods in plastic containers
- Excessive amounts of animal fats, such as fatty meats, butter, and cheese
- Unhealthy fats, such as trans fats
- Storing emotions within rather than expressing them creatively and freely
- Repressing or denying creative expression

DIVE INTO YOUR FLOW

My patients tend to make two unhelpful assumptions when it comes to the FLOW.

One is that emotional expression and FLOW involves always expressing every single emotion or telling every person close to you exactly what you are feeling at all times. This is not at all what I mean by letting your emotions flow! Often—perhaps even most of the time—sharing our feelings instantly and unedited is not the best idea. In some relationships, tact, silence, and detachment might be much better choices than free expression. In just about every relationship, it's usually better to express your emotions when you have some mastery of them, especially if you're angry, anxious, or feeling needy. Giving yourself some time to think about your feelings and make rational decisions about how to share them is frequently the best plan.

Regardless of how you choose to express your emotions to others, however, you can always choose to let them flow freely within yourself. Knowing what you feel and allowing your feelings to bubble up without censorship or control is often a good first step. If you're in a situation in which you need to be more guarded, make sure you give yourself some space later on or at the end of the day to cry, laugh, shout, write out your feelings, or otherwise feel what you feel. And of course, in many intimate relationships, it is important to express anger, fear, and grief as well as to let other emotions flow freely "in real time" rather than controlling their expression. You've got a lot of choices about how to behave with others; just always make sure to let your emotions flow for yourself.

Second, with regard to creativity, I've noticed that many patients and students hear that word as meaning "being an artist." On the contrary, you can be creative about how to be creative! Sure, creativity can express itself through writing, music, painting, sculpture, or dance. But it can also come out through creative problem solving, a new way to arrange your furniture, or an impulsive day of unexpected adventure. Any time you come up with something new, you've tapped into your creative side—and you have found your FLOW.

CHAPTER 5

THE FIRE

The most powerful weapon on earth is the human soul on fire.

—FERDINAND FOCH

Success isn't a result of spontaneous combustion. You must set yourself on fire.

—ARNOLD H. GLASOW

UNDERSTANDING THE FIRE	
Anatomy	Digestive system: pancreas, stomach, liver, gallbladder, small intestine
Functions	Digestion, assimilation, transformation
Living	Energy, empowerment, achievement, ambition, work–life balance
Eating	Carbohydrates (simple sugars and complex grains), fiber, yellow-colored foods

THE SCIENCE OF THE FIRE

The FIRE is one of the most challenging systems of health for just about everybody I work with. At least 80 percent of my patients and students struggle with an imbalanced FIRE, most commonly feeling burnt out with too much stress.

Another huge FIRE issue is unhealthy foods—the fast-burning refined carbohydrates and sugary sweets that set us up for a huge flare-up of energy followed by a swift, exhausting burnout. Think about the way a carefully tended fire blazes sky-high when you throw paper or dried leaves on it— and how that quick-burning fuel seems to be gone in an instant, leaving your flames starved and exhausted. That's exactly what happens when you eat refined carbohydrates and sweets: a rush of quick-burning energy followed by an exhausted crash and the desperate need for another quick burst of fuel.

Whether the problem is too much work or too many carbohydrates, imbalanced FIRE energy creates blocks and imbalances, resulting in belly fat, obesity, and type 2 diabetes—health challenges that are nearly as common among my patients as stress and burnout.

The FIRE and Your Digestion

The stress that comes from overwork creates a "fire in the belly" that ravages our delicate internal ecosystem. Increased stress depletes the digestive enzymes we need to absorb nutrients from food. With poor digestion, we can become malnourished even as we continually overeat, consuming nourishment we cannot receive.

Stressful jobs and imbalanced lives also disrupt our microbiome, the community of microscopic creatures living in our intestines and throughout our body. The microbiome is a crucial factor in our health, playing an important role in mood, mental focus, and energy levels as well as in digestion, heart function, and many other systems. Just twenty-four hours of stress can alter the composition of this bacterial community, transforming it from a friendly, positive presence into a source of toxins and inflammation.

What happens when too much work and too little play disrupt our enzymes, our microbiome, and our gut? We lose our fire, burn out, and flame out, feeling uninspired, unmotivated, and exhausted. We also set ourselves up for a host of disorders, including obesity, high blood pressure, diabetes, and metabolic syndrome.

The link between belly fat and a stressful job has been dramatically demonstrated in a number of large-scale population studies conducted in England and Japan as well as many smaller-scale studies around the globe. Time and time again, researchers came to the same conclusion: working at a high-stress job was a significant risk factor for obesity—specifically, larger waists and belly fat ("abdominal adiposity"). The association between an imbalanced work life and the belly—the center of the third system of health—couldn't be clearer. And when you throw in "fiery" yellow foods—processed carbohydrates, sugar, and fried foods—the triangle is complete.

The FIRE and Diabetes

Another intriguing body of research suggests that pressures at work are linked to diabetes in both men and women. A 2014 study published in *Diabetes Care* found that "job strain is a risk factor for type 2 diabetes in men and women *independent of lifestyle factors* [emphasis added]." In other words, even when you're not eating high-carbohydrate and high-sugar foods, a difficult work life creates blood sugar issues and an imbalanced FIRE.

A similar study in *Psychosomatic Medicine*, covering more than 5,300 workers aged twenty-nine to sixty-six in Augsburg, Germany, found that "men and women who experience high job strain are at higher risk for developing [type 2 diabetes mellitus] *independently of traditional risk factors* [emphasis added]." Once again, a problematic work life seems to create the conditions for diabetes even apart from poor diet. Several other studies come to similar conclusions.

Tending Your FIRE

By contrast, work–life balance can keep your FIRE burning with a steady, warming glow—and certainly, the right foods can help. When you bring food into your stomach, it's like making an offering to your internal altar. The flames of digestion gradually transform the food into the energy you need while your mitochondria—the powerhouses located in each cell—create cellular energy. This slow, healthy burning creates good digestion and a healthy weight.

Every one of us has a FIRE within. Sometimes it burns brightly enough to shed light on our goals, lighting up the areas where we need to put our energy. Other times, we overextend ourselves and burn out. Or perhaps our FIRE rages out of control with too much to process: information overload, racing thoughts, overthinking, a tendency to overpromise and underdeliver. The result is often chaos.

Yet it is possible to keep our FIRE burning at an even flame. Once we cherish that spark of willpower that originates in our solar plexus—the original "fire in the belly"—it can keep us moving joyously forward toward our goals, on a journey where both process and destination are bright with meaning.

THE POWER OF YELLOW

Strikingly, a number of studies bear witness to the power of yellow generating energy. A study conducted in Oxford, England, found that yellow mustard bran helped a group of young, active men have a better post-meal response to glucose after eating potato and leek soup compared to eating the soup by itself. Likewise, a Canadian study found that whole yellow pea flour—a complex carbohydrate—helped overweight people improve their use of insulin.

You can find lots of ways to brighten up your life with yellow. If you work in an office with fluorescent lights, see if you can bring in your own lamp with a soft yellow bulb, so you can enjoy the cheery and balancing effects of yellow. When you need a break or a moment to balance work and life, try lighting a candle—perhaps even a yellow candle—so you can focus on the slow, steady yellow flame and enjoy the healing, energizing properties of fire. You can also decorate your workspace with yellow, uplifting images, like a yellow smiley face, to remind you of work–life balance and to steer you away from burnout. Open yourself to the joys of yellow as you seek to balance your own personal FIRE.

GET TO KNOW YOUR FIRE

Burning Ambition

We live in a power-hungry, stress-filled society that is always expecting us to give more and more. Our ability to maintain balance in the midst of chaos becomes increasingly difficult when demands and responsibilities begin to pile high. We try to accommodate and stay in control by saying yes when we really mean no, and after a short while, we feel burdened with life, while everyday events become drudgery. Finally, we collapse in utter exhaustion, unable to integrate all that fiery energy into our core self.

Yet when we can harness the power of burning ambition, we can achieve great feats! The FIRE energy helps us reach our goals, fueling our drive and commitment. Besides food, many things can fuel the FIRE energy: conversations, inspirational movies and TV shows, dreams of achievement, visions of greatness.

The third system of health is also associated with the ego—our sense of self. An unhealthy or imbalanced ego is either overconfident or under-confident, sometimes both. A healthy ego, by contrast, is fueled by confidence and empowerment. Think of the powerful, almost glowing presence of those charismatic leaders who exude certainty and inspire an eager, productive response. Their radiant energy is lit by an inner FIRE—and it often ignites the FIRE of others.

IMPROVE YOUR DIGESTION

If you're having trouble with indigestion or struggling with blood sugar spikes and crashes, try eating smaller meals and snacks. Think of a fire that has become overloaded with fuel: it can't burn properly if it's smothered in green wood. Eat less, or if you want to keep eating large portions, eat slowly, so your stomach has time to empty itself.

I also suggest making your meals less complicated, containing perhaps just one or two foods. And please make sure you're not stress eating. The more relaxed you are when you eat, the better your ability to digest carbohydrates. Besides, people who are more anxious tend to reach for food in times of stress, and stressful eating can result in craving more sugar.

Burning Out

When we pursue our goal with energy and excitement, we make good use of "fire in the belly." But when we "burn the candle at both ends," we run the risk of burnout: feeling uninspired, overwhelmed, or "blah."

Many of us labor under the idea that we can keep putting out more and more energy, that it's just a matter of willpower and our limits are self-imposed. But our bodies, minds, and emotions do have natural limits, and if we don't respect them, our FIRE runs out of fuel. I was fascinated to read a series of psychological studies that measured the effects of stress. The studies showed that psychological energy—the energy we use for self-control, for example—is a limited commodity, in much the same way that physical energy is. Just as you can't lift an infinite amount of weight or lift weights for an infinite amount of time, you can't exert an infinite amount of psychological or mental energy.

For example, if you have to cope with a rude clerk in a coffee bar, you might normally be able to brush off the annoying treatment and respond politely. But if you've been stressed by a major deadline, an uncooperative coworker, or a sarcastic boss, your resources for coping with the clerk might be depleted. The more demands you have on your energy, focus, and self-control, the fewer resources remain. People who are trying to raise families while working at demanding jobs know from experience that there is only so much energy to go around. If work is taking too much of it, the rest of your life is bound to suffer.

Of course, to some extent, challenges provide a kind of self-sustaining fuel: the more challenges you face, the greater your energy becomes to deal with them. That happens in physical situations too: the harder you exercise, the more strength and energy you develop. However, in both cases there comes a point of overload, where too much exercise exhausts you and too many mental or emotional demands deplete you. Many of my patients have reached the point where their work and life are seriously out of balance, where the demands of their jobs begin to undermine their ability to savor the joys of life.

Over the years, I've seen the issues of overload and burnout grow almost exponentially. To some extent, the problem is economic: the work week is getting longer, vacation time is getting shorter, and many people feel so anxious about being replaced that they don't even take the vacation they do have. To some extent, the problem is electronic: e-mail, social media, and the omnipresent cell phone mean that we're on demand 24/7, overloaded with work obligations, messaging friends, keeping up with a constant stream of information. At what point are you off duty? When do you turn inward instead of outward? A fire that never stops burning is in genuine danger of running out of fuel.

Often I see a close tie between burnout and unhealthy eating habits. When too much work seems to have drained life of all its sweetness, you might want to reward yourself with a sugary treat. But when sugar becomes a compulsion and perhaps even an addiction, you can lose the joy in sweetness too.

Whenever I see someone with a roll of fat around the middle, I know they've got a FIRE imbalance that is disrupting their metabolism, along with elevated blood sugar levels and unhealthy body fat. I can almost see the stagnant energy and congested fire that come from not fully digesting food, metabolizing glucose, and transforming dietary nutrients into energy. The saddest thing is when people are overweight yet their bodies believe they are starving—because they are not able to get fuel into their cells for energy, a condition known as being overfed and undernourished. Hunger for what we really need keeps us eating, even as our weight creeps up to an unhealthy level and our blood sugar rises into the danger zone.

One of my patients, Mollie, exemplified this problem. Feeling that her life had been drained of sweetness, she turned to sugary treats and eventually developed type 2 diabetes. Working two jobs and raising five kids, she felt fried by the effort of juggling all her competing obligations. "I need something sweet to keep me going, to give me energy—just a taste of something good," she told me. I wanted to help her find more sustainable fuel—and more sustainable sweetness as well. Later in the chapter, I'll tell you more about how I was able to help her find her own personal "sweet spot."

A Burning Joy

I've been speaking of work, drive, and ambition as sources of depletion, but I want to acknowledge that they are also sources of joy. When you love your work so much that you can't wait to get back to it, that's a brightly burning fire that warms you, energizes you, and lights your way forward. When a job is exhausting but also inspiring and fulfilling, you can discover new reserves of energy, like a phoenix rising from the ashes. When you love the journey as much as the destination, even a grueling work session can be illuminated by joy.

Of course, the most joyous work requires some kind of balance. You need downtime, sleep, relaxed meals, time for your body, mind, and emotions to recover from the fiery exertions that consume you.

But if you can find the sweetness in your work and your obligations, if you can feel the spark of inspiration or the flames of desire as you go about your daily routine, then you have found a remarkable resource indeed. When you are able to maintain a healthy balance of energy taken in and energy expended, you generate the radiance of "presence." When you are the master of your own energy, you can enjoy confidence, endurance, empowerment, and achievement in their highest forms.

BALANCE YOUR FIRE

Healthy FIRE energy will look different for every one of us, and it will probably look different to you at different times of your life. Still, we can set out some general guidelines that are clues to "too much," "too little," and "the right amount" of the FIRE.

A person with a healthy FIRE
- has a robust digestion so they can eat almost anything and feel energized afterward;
- has a healthy functioning pancreas that is able to produce adequate levels of enzymes to properly break down foods and enough insulin to take care of all the sugars they eat;
- has a normal blood sugar level;
- uses carbohydrates to sustain themselves rather than as a quick fix;
- feels inspired by goal setting and the prospect of achieving their goals; and
- strives to be their best without giving up if they can't "do it all."

A person with an underactive FIRE
- prefers spicy foods;
- selects warm or hot foods over cold foods;
- avoids cold drinks;
- often lacks an appetite;
- might end up snacking through the day since larger meals tend to deplete their energy;
- often gets tired after eating;
- has blood sugar that runs low;

- has a slightly inverted belly due to a concave, hunched posture;
- often has a sluggish liver and problems with detoxification;
- frequently has undigested food in a stool;
- may struggle with poor self-esteem;
- often shows a lack of initiative and might be perceived as unmotivated or even lazy;
- is less interested in work than in personal time;
- might feel that they can't keep up with competitive, ambitious people, so they just give up;
- might settle for being average;
- might be resentful of those who are successful and see them as "selling out";
- might have a victim mentality, feeling that someone else is responsible for their situation in life; or
- might feel that life is unfair and therefore gives up easily.

A person with an overactive FIRE

- binges on sweets or has a sweet tooth;
- needs to be in charge or in control almost all the time;
- tends to be excessively busy;
- may be overly confident of their abilities, perhaps arrogant or egotistical;
- is often fiercely competitive;
- might be a perfectionist;
- fixates on his or her goals to the exclusion of almost everything else;
- must be a high achiever in almost anything they undertake;
- refuses to accept failure even when energies would be better served elsewhere;
- has difficulty balancing work and life, is a classic workaholic;
- says yes to everything because they believe they can "do it all";
- is tightly wound with high expectations of themselves and others;
- is overly concerned with work and social status;
- is bombarded with too much information;
- overthinks and ruminates over everything;

- might have excess weight in the upper belly area or a distended, protruding abdomen;
- might have metabolic syndrome or type 2 diabetes, or be taking medication to lower their blood sugar;
- might have overactive liver dysfunctions or be on medications for liver-related issues, such as high liver enzymes, hepatitis, fatty liver, high triglycerides;
- is plagued by fiery digestive complaints after a meal or emotional events, such as ulcers, an acidic stomach, an upset stomach, esophageal reflux, GERD, or burping;
- feels hot or flushed after eating;
- forgets to eat due to being busy;
- eats sweet foods as a reward for working hard;
- eats on the run whatever is convenient and accessible;
- eats based on their work schedule, often rushing or working through meals;
- might be a stress eater;
- often multitasks while eating;
- eats when triggered by energy crashes;
- eats foods high in sugar and simple carbohydrates;
- might not eat enough fiber;
- often adds sugar or artificial sweeteners to foods;
- eats highly processed, convenient foods and/or fast foods;
- is sensitive to spicy foods;
- might consume energy drinks or caffeinated beverages;
- tends to prefer cold drinks and foods; or
- is drawn to sweet and refined yellow foods, such as bananas, corn, corn chips, or popcorn.

BURN BRIGHTLY: HOW MY PATIENTS HAVE USED THE FIRE TO TRANSFORM THEIR LIVES

For years, Simon had issues with his digestive system: nausea, bloating, gas. He also struggled with high blood sugar to the point where his doctor told him he was at risk for diabetes. Simon had a high-pressure job as a day trader, which he enjoyed but often found overwhelming. Once he'd had a doctor's appointment right after returning from vacation, and he was amazed to discover that his blood sugar reading was much closer to normal. For him, high blood sugar was an issue of both stress and diet: while he was working, he tended to snack constantly on starchy, sugary foods— donuts, bagels, muffins, cookies—simply because that was what was available in the break room at work.

Simon began switching to slow-burning, high-fiber carbohy-drates—quinoa, brown rice, lentils, garbanzo beans—which pro-vided him with a steadier, healthier source of fuel. He also began doing some vigorous exercise after work to "blow off steam." Finally, he committed to doing something genuinely fun for at least part of every weekend—some activity that he enjoyed so much, he was able to forget about work. Within a few months, his digestive symptoms were gone, he had lost a few pounds, and his blood sugar was consistently at a healthy level.

———

Jillian was overworked and fatigued. Her job as an IT executive often left her feeling depleted, and on weekends, she collapsed on her bed in exhaustion. Slowly but surely, she began to develop symptoms: Her skin broke out. She gained weight. She had trou-ble sleeping. She started to struggle with depression. Jillian needed help.

Inspired by her experience of Whole Detox, she eventually decided to take some downtime: a week's vacation at a women's writing retreat on the Oregon coast. The chance to walk in the woods, mull over her thoughts, and simply enjoy the quiet was a revelation to her. When she returned, she realized she wanted more balance in her life—"more of life and less of work," she told me. She decided to leave her current high-powered job for one that was less taxing and began to live a healthier, more balanced life. Within a few weeks, her symptoms were virtually gone, and she looked more radiant than she had in years.

———

Peter had suffered from GERD for the past decade. As we explored his history, he realized that his symptoms had begun just after he had started working a double shift as a cab driver. "I need those extra hours to support my family," he told me. However, the acid reflux had become so bad that he often had to pause while driving, getting out of the car to breathe deeply; otherwise, he doubled up in pain.

My "prescription" for Peter was deceptively simple: make some time on Saturday mornings to take guitar lessons, which he'd told me he'd always wanted to do. Within a few weeks, he was writing songs, expressing his emotions in ways he couldn't do before. Although he still leads a high-pressure life, that weekend music break was a huge relief, and soon, his GERD disappeared.

BURNING FUEL

Does food ignite your energy or does it burn up your inner power? Either way, food is closely linked to the FIRE through the digestive system. Or, put another way, the FIRE is represented in the body through the act of transformation: your digestive tract transforms your food into energy, and your organs transform the plants and animals you consume into you.

The digestive transformation begins in your stomach, but your liver, gallbladder, small intestine, and pancreas are all part of each eating event. Your liver produces bile, an acrid, yellow-colored substance that helps you absorb fat. Your gallbladder stores the bile. Your pancreas helps to break down and assimilate sugar (glucose) through the activities of enzymes and insulin, respectively. And your small intestine transfers nutrients from the digested food into the bloodstream, where it nourishes every single one of your cells. All of these organs are therefore part of the third system of health, helping to create the transformative power of the FIRE.

Although protein can give our bodies a needed boost, the fuel that gets us through the day is glucose. All fruits, vegetables, grains, and legumes are ultimately broken down into glucose and other sugars. In fact, we are wired for sweetness, which is why even newborn babies will always prefer the sweeter formulas if given the choice. On a primal level, our bodies under-

stand that sweetness equals energy. And because for most of human history we couldn't ever count on getting enough food, we are wired to want more and more and more.

Here is where we run into the contradictory nature of the FIRE, because we crave sweetness, but it isn't always good for us. Sugary sweets are FIRE foods because they are the quickest type of fuel there is. Refined carbohydrates—white flour and the pasta, baked goods, and snacks made from it—can often be sweet. Even when they are not, they burn quickly and create cravings. Fresh, organic corn is a naturally sweet and healthy food (although note that I have you avoid all corn during the Whole Detox program), but the chips and tortillas made from refined corn likewise burn too hot and are not generally healthy (not to mention that corn is predominantly genetically modified). And of course, one of the least healthy foods on the planet is the sweetener made from corn—high-fructose corn syrup—which is added to sodas and many processed foods, even the ones you wouldn't necessarily expect to be sweet, like soups and condiments. This overload of sweetness dulls our appreciation for it, so we need ever larger portions of sweet foods to be satisfied.

The color of the FIRE is yellow, and many of these unhealthy choices are yellow foods, but I don't want you eating them. Nor do I want you eating quick-burning fast foods—such unhealthy fuel for your inner FIRE! Significantly, fast and processed foods are often the cuisine of choice for people with too much FIRE, because they offer quick bursts of energy and ongoing support for a lifestyle in which you work overly long hours and neglect the rest of your life. Just listen to our language: "fried" foods that make you feel fried; "fast" foods that make you feel rushed. Grabbing food on the run or gobbling it down at your desk creates major digestive problems and pushes your stress levels through the roof. I can't tell you how much healthier it is to slow down, eat with pleasure, and enjoy your meals in a relaxed atmosphere.

Applying fire to food transforms it from raw to cooked, and this, too, is a double-edged sword. Sometimes slow-cooked food is easier to digest than raw, and nutrients often become more bioavailable when a food is cooked. But when you cook a food too long, the burnt, brown, or crisp part contains compounds known as advanced glycation end products, or AGEs. These fiery foods are aptly named, because AGEs speed up the aging process faster than any other compound in food I can think of. How do they do it? By creating inflammation—that is, they set your body on fire.

By contrast, a modest amount of heat can help break down some foods and make them easier to digest. Cooking also makes some valuable nutrients more bioavailable.

What's your happy medium? Eat some raw foods and some cooked. You will see in the Whole Detox program that I incorporate raw smoothies with a cooked dinner, and the lunch is half raw and half cooked. My guidance is when you need to cook, cook slowly, over low heat, and don't cook your foods to the point when they turn medium or dark brown, as in grilling, frying, toasting, or baking. Moderate heat will keep you warm, but high heat will only AGE you. So please avoid browned, crusty, and crispy foods. Inundated with AGEs and yellow foods, we risk premature aging, obesity, diabetes, and metabolic syndrome—all of which have become epidemic among people who eat a standard Western diet.

I do want you eating *some* yellow foods, the healthy variety: yellow summer squash, yellow bell peppers, wax beans, Asian pears, lemons, pineapple, and bananas. Yellow plant compounds include lutein and zeaxanthin, two carotenoids that are needed for healthy eye function. And lemons contain compounds like bioflavonoids, which support your liver through all phases of detox.

I also think it's good to eat slow-burning carbohydrates on occasion: quinoa, brown rice, and other whole grains. These FIRE foods offer you long-burning fuel whose flame reaches every part of you. Some of you prefer no grains whatsoever, which is fine; however, I have found that some people actually need this sustainable and high-fiber fuel source. Copious studies support the inclusion of whole grains in a mixed diet. The goal is not to let them have "power" over you but to make thoughtful choices about when to include them for your energy.

Another type of healthy FIRE nutrient is the team of B vitamins that are found in many of those slow-burning carbohydrates. Please note that when you supplement with B vitamins, your urine might turn yellow.

B vitamins also help extract energy from your food. They are crucial in glycolysis, the conversion of glucose into energy in your body, as well

as for the Krebs cycle, breaking down sugars, amino acids, and fatty acids. Meanwhile, B vitamins help you relax and de-stress so you can maintain a healthy work–life balance.

HEALTHY YELLOW FOODS

- Complex, unrefined carbohydrates, such as quinoa, millet, amaranth, sorghum, and other whole grains
- Soluble fibers—dietary fibers that will support your digestion and give your pancreas some relief by slowing down the release of sugar—found in oat bran, nuts, seeds, beans, lentils, peas, and some fruits and vegetables
- Ginger, a soothing yellow spice that can ease digestive problems like stomach upset and nausea
- Lemon juice and zest to spark healthy detox pathways in the liver and assist with alkalinization of an over-acidic, fiery eating pattern
- Herbs and spices, used in cooking, that add some "heat" to a dish and stimulate digestion, such as chili pepper, paprika, black pepper, cardamom, horseradish, cinnamon, garlic, and ginger
- B vitamins, to help relax and balance stress, and which can be found in many different foods, such as fruits, vegetables, whole grains, and legumes

YELLOW FOODS AND YOUR FIRE

Some FIRE foods are healthy; some are less so. Once you know the range of FIRE foods—many of which are yellow—you can make the wisest choices to fuel your inner flame. Here's a rundown of the main fiery yellow foods with my best recommendations for what to eat and how to eat it.

Carbohydrates

Notice how many carbohydrates you eat at each meal and over the course of a day. To empower yourself with the energy you need, you have to keep checking in with your fuel gauge, balancing the different carbohydrates in your diet. One day you might need oatmeal and lentils; the next day you might crave quinoa and black beans. One day you might carbo-load; the next day you might be completely uninterested in starchy foods. Learn how to tune in to your FIRE to know what type of fuel it needs.

PROCESSED CARBOHYDRATES

We typically grab these foods when we are burnt out and don't have the energy to cook. Ironically, they actually drain our inner FIRE, producing a quick energy rush followed inevitably by a crash. Processed carbohydrates also deplete our bodies of the valuable B vitamins and other nutrients we need for proper digestion and metabolism. It is best for you to let go of these foods as much as you can. Don't let them take your FIRE!

WHEN YOU NEED SOME SWEETNESS

A good general rule is to stick as closely as possible to a sweetener's natural form. Unhealthy, overly processed choices:

- Artificial or synthetic sweeteners
- Brown sugar
- Evaporated cane juice
- Granulated or powdered sugar of any type or color
- White sugar

Natural choices that are healthy in small doses and in combinations with other foods to blunt their glycemic effects:

- Applesauce
- Bananas
- Blackstrap molasses
- Honey, preferably raw and organic
- Juice concentrate
- Maple syrup
- Medjool dates

Try to combine a sweet food with some protein. That combination will modulate your blood sugar response, preventing those deadly spikes and crashes that set you up for cravings, constant hunger, weight gain, and diabetes.

SUGARY SWEETS

I'm sure you've heard this before, but let me say it one more time: sugar is ungodly toxic. It shuts down your detox pathways rather than revving them. It's tough to detox from sugar, but you can do it—your willpower is fiery! And if you can detox from sugar, you can detox from anything!

Now, how did we end up craving sugar in the first place? Through the years, I've observed that people gravitate toward sugar when they feel depleted and need some sweetness. So I would say that craving sugar could be a sign that you need some more joy in your life. If sugar truly made you joyous, I'd have a hard time telling you to avoid it, but the problem is that it's a quick-burning joy that disappears almost as soon as it shows up—again, think of the way a fire flares up quickly to consume a few sheets of paper or a handful of leaves. And the crash after the flare-up leaves you feeling worse than before.

Enough is enough. Finito. No more toxic sugar. There. I said it.

AVOID ARTIFICIAL SWEETENERS

The naming games give it all away: How can we expect anything artificial to spark our natural inner FIRE?

In fact, artificial sweeteners are ugly, toxic chemicals that your body doesn't recognize and therefore can't respond to. As a result, these chemical concoctions generate metabolic changes, disrupt the friendly bacteria in our gut, and might even create *more* weight gain than eating sugar. (But please don't eat sugar either!)

One of my least favorite artificial sweeteners is, ironically, packaged in *yellow*: sucralose. Each molecule is loaded up with three chlorine atoms, and when you recall that chlorine is used to disinfect swimming pools, you can imagine how little you want it in your body. But, honestly, the other artificial sweeteners aren't much better. Just avoid them.

COMPLEX CARBOHYDRATES

Ahhhhh, what a relief to leave toxic foods behind and focus on those that truly nourish our inner FIRE. I know a lot of books out there warn you against carbohydrates, but I don't want you to jump on that bandwagon, because legumes, gluten-free grains, and starchy vegetables are a powerful source of energy that keep your blood sugar steady, in addition to providing you with healthy phytonutrients and fiber.

All carbohydrates contain long chains of sugars. When carbohydrates are refined, these sugars hit your bloodstream too quickly, creating those spikes and crashes. But when carbohydrates are complex (unrefined), they also contain fiber, which turns a fast-burning carbohydrate into a slow-burning one. They also contain many other detoxifying phytonutrients, including lignans, lignins, ferulic acid, and many others. So please don't eliminate carbohydrates from your diet unless under specific guidance by your health-care practitioner—just choose the right ones in the right amounts.

CHOOSE COMPLEX CARBOHYDRATES FOR A STEADY SOURCE OF FUEL

Legumes
- Beans (adzuki, black, chickpea/garbanzo, fava, mung, pinto, white [cannellini, Great Northern, navy], and others)
- Lentils (green, orange, orange/red, yellow)
- Peas (black-eyed, green, snap, snow, split)

Gluten-Free Grains
- Amaranth
- Gluten-free oats
- Millet
- Quinoa (black, red, white)
- Rice (brown, purple/black, red)

Nuts and Nut Butters
- Almonds
- Brazil nuts
- Cashews
- Macadamia nuts
- Pecans
- Walnuts

Seeds and Seed Butters

- Chia seeds
- Flax seeds
- Hemp seeds
- Pumpkin seeds
- Sesame seeds and tahini
- Sunflower seeds

Starchy Vegetables

- Parsnips
- Potatoes (purple, red, yellow fingerling)
- Squash
- Sweet potatoes
- Turnips
- Yams

Low-Glycemic Fruits

"Glycemic" refers to how sugar is released from a food. A low-glycemic fruit releases less sugar within a set time period into your bloodstream than a medium- or high-glycemic fruit. Here are a few examples of low-glycemic fruits suitable for Whole Detox:

- Apples
- Berries
- Cherries
- Grapefruit
- Kiwi fruits
- Nectarines
- Pears

Grains, Gluten, and Digestion

Over the past few decades, an increasing number of people have been having trouble digesting grains and legumes, particularly those that include gluten, a group of proteins found in wheat, rye, barley, and some other grains. Because gluten is used in most processed foods and is added to make many bread products fluffier and lighter, we've all been massively overexposed to it.

The number of gluten-related digestive problems has skyrocketed. The most severe form of gluten problems is celiac disease, which only about 1 percent of the population has. However, it is thought that a much higher percentage have gluten intolerance (referred to as nonceliac gluten sensitivity, or NCGS), a less intense but still problematic response that can generate a number of symptoms, including headaches, acne, indigestion, fatigue, weight gain, and vulnerability to autoimmune conditions. I have it myself, so I know it well. For years, I had pain, swelling, and redness around my finger joints. I consulted with a health practitioner, who thought it was the soap I was using to wash my hands or a lotion I put on my skin, but I knew that couldn't be right. It was truly systemic, and when I removed gluten from my diet, the joint pain and swelling went completely away! I'm proud to say that I am as gluten-free as I possibly can be to this day.

There are many different theories about why gluten intolerance is on the rise. Some of the problems with gluten and with other grains and legumes might be due to the rise of industrial agriculture. The toxic burden in our environment is probably diminishing our digestive and immune functions as well. Consequently, gluten, grains, and legumes have gotten a bad rap, since many people have trouble digesting them or tolerating their effects.

This is a real shame, because whole grains and legumes impart some wonderful phytonutrients and can be high in B vitamins, fueling the metabolic cycles in your body. If digestion is an issue for you, I suggest that you avoid or minimize your consumption of gluten. You can also sprout legumes, which makes them easier to digest. If you use canned beans (not ideal, but I know this is most practical), make sure you buy organic, bisphenol-free brands and drain and rinse them to remove the nondigestible carbohydrates.

COLORFUL GRAINS

Did you know that grains come in many colors? The greater variety you sample, the more different types of carbohydrates, fiber, and phytonutrients you consume. Let your body "taste" the rainbow!

Quinoa: black, red, white

Rice: black (also called purple), black Thai, brown basmati, long-grain brown, short-grain brown, wild

Warming Spices

Flavorings can add a hint of fire to your meal while igniting a healthy digestion. We each have a different tolerance for "hot" foods, so tune in to your own fire as you choose your spices:

- Black pepper
- Cardamom
- Chili pepper
- Cinnamon
- Garlic
- Ginger
- Horseradish
- Paprika
- Turmeric

Beverages

As I mentioned in the previous chapter, I want you to stay hydrated. But I don't want you to drink too much during a meal because the liquid can dilute your stomach acid and cause your stomach to work harder. Iced beverages can also have a chilling effect on the flames of digestion.

If you're drinking a caloric beverage—soda, milk, juice, wine—you're increasing the amount of energy you consume. You might want to moderate energy consumption throughout the day by choosing water or herbal tea.

If you're concerned about excess weight or overeating, use fluids to your advantage: drink 16 ounces of water thirty minutes before a meal to reduce your food intake—as much as 13 percent, according to some research. Over time, this practice can lead to greater weight loss when combined with a lower-calorie diet.

TIMING IS EVERYTHING

According to Ayurvedic tradition, noontime is when our "metabolic fire" burns brightest. We can harness that energy by eating our largest meal at noon. Breakfast and dinner should be moderate meals because your energy is just revving up or winding down. Temper your eating accordingly during and even after your Whole Detox. Follow another traditional principle of detox by eating more cooling foods in warmer weather and warmer, cooked foods in cooler temperatures.

SUPPORT WORK-LIFE BALANCE WITH MIND–BODY MEDICINE

As you learned in the ROOT chapter, stress is one of the major culprits behind chronic disease. Stress at work can easily overwhelm our lives, leading to fiery confrontations with friends, family, or colleagues. When we feel our inner flames burn too hot, we might become inflamed or have redness, pain, or swelling.

That's why keeping stress in check is essential for good health. And mind–body medicine is one of the best ways I know to bring some cool, soothing relief to a hot head and a flaming heart. Such techniques as hypnosis, guided imagery, biofeedback, progressive muscle relaxation, yoga, meditation, and tai chi have been found to be helpful for reducing chronic diseases and symptoms like depression, insomnia, anxiety, irritable bowel syndrome, nausea, and pain, and for managing diabetes and hypertension.

You can also create your own mind–body medicine. Choose one meal a week to eat mindfully—slowly, joyously, savoring every bite. Take a long, slow walk in a beautiful environment. Sit peacefully in an indoor or outdoor space that soothes your jangled nerves and transforms your raging fire into a quiet glow. I've heard it from my patients time and time again: one of the most powerful changes they ever made was to take up meditation, even if it was just finding five minutes each day to sit in peace and stillness.

SUPPORT YOUR FIRE WHILE YOU EAT

It's not just *what* we eat, but *how* we eat that adds to our health. In days seven through nine of your twenty-one-day program, you'll learn how to keep your FIRE in check. Since this is the system that can most easily go out of balance, the following tips will help you maintain your own internal Zen mode even if the outer world seems chaotic and frenzied:

Breathe into your center. Before your first bite of food, take a deep breath into your solar plexus. Engaging your relaxation response will help you better digest your food. I find deep breathing easiest when I am sitting comfortably in a chair with my spine erect, my shoulders back, and my hands in my lap. Then I take three or four deep breaths to center myself into my inner power before beginning to eat.

 • *Get in touch with your hunger gauge.* Often we lose sight of our innate sense of physical hunger and our bodies' physical cues to eat. The demands of a busy life may lead us to forget to eat, or to undereat or overeat without realizing it. Staying in touch with your internal eating rhythms—and eating regularly—helps you keep your internal power rather than giving it over to irregular eating times and over- or under-eating. Sometimes this takes a bit of retraining! Many of us "think" our way into hunger, or assess it intellectually, rather than connecting to the power of our digestive system as the ultimate gauge. Try rating your hunger before and after eating to tap into how well you are maintaining your fuel reserves. If you find yourself "stuffed" after a meal, you may have inundated your energy input, placing an additional burden on your digestive system to process. Aim for about 80 percent fullness, or a point at which you are not stuffed, but also no longer hungry. Aim for the level at which you are able to take a light walk after eating.

• *Know your fuel.* Eating is meant to energize you rather than deplete your reserves. Some foods give you the punch of power you need, while others seem to drain you of your power. Do you find yourself eating foods that you *know* might "run you down"? When you do, you risk unbalancing your FIRE. Sugar is one such food, and added sugars are ubiquitous in the food supply, even in such unexpected places as salad dressings, ketchups, and sauces. Although they provide an initial burst of energy, in the long run, they will rob you of your energy through the roller coaster of blood sugar spikes and crashes. Stay on an even keel by balancing your sugar intake with dietary fiber and avoid artificial sweeteners, which can set you up for additional cravings and metabolic imbalance.

• *Schedule regular eating times.* Many of my patients find it helpful to create a regular eating schedule of small meals four to six times a day. This might be a good way to retrain yourself to get in touch with your eating rhythm: studies have shown that eating more frequent meals throughout the day (compared to a few large meals) helps us to maintain our blood sugar, and, therefore, provides more energy. However, your eating balance needs to be personalized to your needs: you might need to nibble and graze, or you might need a few large meals.

DETOXING YOUR FIRE: WHAT TO CHOOSE
- Complex carbohydrates
- Soluble fibers
- Yellow foods, such as yellow vegetables, whole grains, ginger, lemon, legumes
- Foods that give you sustained energy over time
- Work–life balance
- A healthy separation from work

DETOXING YOUR FIRE: WHAT TO AVOID
- Processed, highly refined carbohydrates
- Fast and convenient foods
- Foods that are tough to digest and assimilate
- Foods that create excessive bloating, discomfort, distention, or gas
- Eating more at one time than you can digest
- Foods high in sugar or those that unbalance your blood sugar
- Artificial sweeteners of *all* types
- Overcooked foods high in AGEs
- Situations where you feel like you are giving more energy than you are receiving in return
- Feeling that you have to "do it all," so you end up feeling depleted
- Focusing more on the goal than on the journey
- Workaholism—feeling so obsessed with work you can never let it go
- Perfectionism—focusing on trying to get every detail perfect rather than seeing the big picture

TEND YOUR FIRE

Each of the systems of health is a very personal affair—a reflection of your values, personality, genetics, and vision of life. Nowhere is this individuality more apparent than when you consider your relationship to the third system of health, the location of the ego and personal ambition.

Let's go back to my patient Mollie, whom I was telling you about earlier in the chapter. On her first visit, she was slumped in her chair and let out a huge, exhausted sigh.

"I feel totally burnt out," she told me. "I'm just fried. I feel like I'm just going through the motions—no fire, no spark."

I was fascinated by her language, because it so beautifully captured the paradox of the FIRE: too much, and you feel "burnt to a crisp"; not enough, and you lack that essential spark of passion and inspiration.

I began working with Mollie by exploring all the different ways that the FIRE burned in her life. Here's the list she came up with:

- Fiery inspiration sheds light on my goals.
- Energy fuels me and keeps me going.
- When I do too much, I burn out.
- When I have too much to process—information overload, over-thinking, stress, chaos—I feel like my flame is choked and my fire goes out.
- When I'm doing work I really love, I feel like I'm burning with an eternal flame.
- When I've been on overload and I take a break—long enough to feel really refreshed—I feel like a phoenix rising from the ashes!

I love the range of Mollie's images because the FIRE can be so empowering and joyous when it's in balance, and so toxic when we have either too much or too little. It can be hard to forge your own authentic relationship to your FIRE because of all the conflicting cultural and familial messages. Men are supposed to be ambitious; women are supposed to be less interested in worldly achievement than in tending to a home and family. All of us are supposed to work 24/7, endlessly on demand to bosses, clients, colleagues, and social media. Yet many films, TV shows, and popular songs demonize the overly ambitious character, presenting work not as a source of joy and inspiration but as something that interferes with the "true" happiness of love and a fulfilling personal life.

I know many people who find extraordinary inspiration and joy in devoting themselves to their work—indeed, I am one of them! Pretty much any time I'm awake, I'm thinking about the full spectrum of Whole Detox: wondering about the different colors in the spectrum, studying new research about food and light, endlessly fascinated as to what new things I can learn and what new ways I can help my patients, students, and readers. Even my recreation is color based: I paint in deep, saturated shades that make color real and palpable to me. This immersion in my working life isn't a cause of burnout to me, but rather a deep wellspring of joy.

My husband, by contrast, loves his work as an acupuncturist, but when the working day is over, he's delighted to let it go. He comes home and plays music, watches a movie, prepares a delicious dinner. He likes a variety of interests and tasks; unlike me, he isn't drawn to unify and deepen a single, all-absorbing focus.

I believe that both my husband and I have a healthy relationship to the FIRE, but look how differently each of us expresses it! What I hope for you, in every system of Whole Detox, is that you will get to know your FIRE, your ROOT, your FLOW, so you can nourish your entire being.

CHAPTER 6

THE LOVE

Love is the total absence of fear. Love asks no questions. Its natural state is one of extension and expansion, not comparison and measurement.

—GERALD JAMPOLSKY

UNDERSTANDING THE LOVE	
Anatomy	Heart, thymus, cardiovascular system, respiratory system
Functions	Circulation, oxygenation
Living	Compassion, expansiveness, loyalty, service
Eating	Leafy vegetables; raw, living greens; green foods

THE SCIENCE OF THE LOVE

The fourth system of health, the LOVE, is based in the heart and the lungs. The heart is an especially fascinating organ about which current medical opinion is evolving rapidly. For many years, conventional medicine considered the heart as little more than a pump—a mechanical device rather than a dynamic organ. Of course, even as a pump, the heart is a pretty amazing instrument. Every day it moves thousands of liters of blood through every inch of your body, disseminating the life force to your lungs, muscles, bones, eyes, ears, and brain, supplying every one of your cells with life-giving blood.

Recently, however, cutting-edge research has brought us to a more advanced view, seeing the heart not just as a pump but as a complex participant in the neuroendocrine system, producing hormones that activate the body in a variety of ways. Indeed, a group of scientists at the University of Ottawa have advanced a new specialty: cardiovascular endocrinology, the study of the biochemical effects of the heart. If the heart is a core player in the endocrine system, that means it affects thought, perception, and emotion as well as providing our cells with blood.

Recent research has also taught us that the heart is related to our emotions. All those metaphors about "let your heart guide you," "a heartfelt emotion," and "being heartbroken" have an actual physical component. When you are stressed or distressed, your heart beats faster, your blood pressure rises, and stress hormones inflame your system, putting you at risk of heart disease, stroke, and other cardiovascular ailments, which we now know are sparked and fueled by inflammation. When you are calm and full of joy, your heart beats at a healthy rhythm and your blood courses through your arteries at a healthy pressure.

Grief, Loss, and Your Heart

Grief, too, affects the heart. When someone is overcome with grief, their heart might even stop beating; researchers have documented cases of loss or rejection producing literal ailments of the heart. Just a glance at some press releases on recent research yields a host of evocative titles: "In Young Women, Depression Can Mean Literal Heartbreak," "Literal Heartbreak: The Cardiovascular Impact of Rejection," and "Why a Broken Heart Literally Hurts."

Other research shows that the loss of a beloved spouse can harm the heart of an elderly person. A study of more than ninety-five thousand Finns found that widowed men over sixty-five were at greater risk for ischemic heart disease. Puerto Rican researchers also concluded, "From clinical experience, we observed that the psychological category 'experience of loss' was associated with the onset and development of coronary heart disease." Research results supported this clinical observation.

Finally, a suggestive body of research has found numerous associations between bereavement and heart disease—a medical explanation of the broken heart. Bereaved spouses are at greater risk for heart disease. Even child-hood losses can affect adult cardiovascular function, according to a study conducted at Duke University's Psychiatry and Behavioral Sciences department.

The Cardiovascular Benefits of Love and Compassion

Love as well as grief can affect the heart. One study found that training women to have compassion for themselves modulates heart rate variability (HRV) as well as reduces anxiety and evokes a cardiac parasympathetic response—that is, a relaxation response in the heart. In other words, having compassion for yourself literally eases your heart.

Likewise, in 2015, a group of researchers tested the effect of a loving-kindness meditation on nitric oxide, a compound affecting blood pressure and heart health. The results suggested that the relaxing effects of medita-tion may well be the result of biochemical changes related to nitric oxide.

Heart and Lungs

Of course, we can't view the heart in isolation from the lungs; our blood must be oxygenated as it circulates throughout our body. If the lungs don't draw in enough air, the circulatory system is affected: red blood cells get less oxygenation and we end up having less energy. Most people breathe shallowly, not having the full benefit of expanding the lungs wide and open to release old toxins. Keep in mind that you can detox simply by taking a deep breath—it's free and fuels both your heart and lungs, supporting the two primary functions needed for survival.

Just as the heart and blood have a literal and a metaphoric power, so does the air we breathe. Air, after all, is the staple of our life force. Breathing deeply calms us; shallow, rapid breathing can make us anxious. Put more scientifically, deep breathing activates the parasympathetic nervous system (responsible for the relaxation response), while shallow, rapid breathing activates the sympathetic nervous system (responsible for the fight-or-flight reaction, or the stress response).

When we expand our lungs, our chest expands too, and as it relaxes, so does our heart. And when our body expands in that fashion, we feel more open to love, compassion, and service, extending outward to care for others as well as inward to care for ourselves. As we consider the fourth system of health, we'll be looking at both the physical and the emotional sides of your loving heart and your expansive lungs.

THE POWER OF GREEN

You might have thought that red would be associated with the heart; however, green is the color of the fourth system of health. Researchers have discovered some fascinating links associating this color with the heart. For example, an Austrian experiment found that exposing people to green fluorescent light seemed to have a soothing effect on their hearts, affecting heart rate variability (HRV). People who endure continual worry and anxiety seem to have decreased HRV, which is also associated with a number of disorders, including congestive heart failure and depression. If exposure to green light increases HRV, we can imagine that has heart-protective effects and might help to heal grief—precisely the associations suggested by the fourth system of health.

To bring more of the LOVE into *your* life, take a walk in the woods or on some green grass. Breathe in the loving breath of nature and revel in the expansiveness of greenery.

If the weather is against you or if the nearest green space is too far away, bring the green to you in the form of plants at home or at work. Even a small representative of something green—living, growing, sprouting—can bring the expansiveness of love and compassion into an everyday world that may feel like it's collapsing down on you. Consider an herb garden in your kitchen window or a potted fern on your desk—anything to which you can direct love and feel love coming back in return.

Plants and nature not your thing? Go the other way with some green money. Spend something on self-care in the form of a massage, a funny movie, a bottle of scented lotion—something that makes you open up and remember just how wonderful you are.

GET TO KNOW YOUR LOVE

Love is perhaps the greatest nourishment that exists. Human beings thrive on it. We feed ourselves with heart symbols plastered on T-shirts, bumper stickers, books, and cards. As Mother Teresa said, "The hunger for love is much more difficult to remove than the hunger for bread."

Sometimes we use food to show love. We prepare a beautiful dinner for a loved one. Or we invite someone we love to eat with us. One of the oldest human traditions is "breaking bread" with family, community, and even with strangers whom we choose to welcome, while we refuse to eat with enemies and people we don't trust.

We're used to thinking of love as a relationship between two people. Love, however, starts with the self, and that includes the way we feed ourselves. By eating healing meals, we express love for our bodies. When we love ourselves, we know, intuitively, what kind of food our bodies need—we "follow our hearts" in choosing what to eat. When self-love is starved, or blocked, it's harder to choose the right foods or to stop eating when we've had enough.

Focusing on the fourth system of health can be a challenge for many of us, especially when we confuse self-care with selfishness. Getting the nutritional support for our fourth system can be overlooked as well, since many of us don't recognize the crucial importance of loving green foods and minerals for both heart health and emotional health.

If we move from the physical nature of the heart to its metaphorical symbolism of love, we must then consider the nature of love itself. I like M. Scott Peck's definition, from *The Road Less Traveled*: "The will to extend one's self for the purpose of nurturing one's own or another's spiritual growth." If that's our definition, we can see at a glance why love must always include self-love. How can we become capable of nurturing another's growth if we neglect our own?

As we have seen, conventional medicine associates the heart and lungs because of the role of the lungs in oxygenating the blood and supporting the heart. In TCM, the heart is the source of love, while the lungs are the seat of grief.

At first glance, this might seem odd: How could love and grief be related? And indeed, in some ways, they are polar opposites. Love makes us feel expansive, caring, and larger than we were before. Grief can make us feel constricted, wounded, shrunken, or hunched over in pain. Love moves us to care, for others and ourselves. Grief can lead us to frozen indifference, stony numbness, a refusal to care lest we get hurt again.

And yet any time we love, we open ourselves to the grief and pain of loss, just as any time we experience grief fully, rather than resisting it, we allow that painful emotion to pass through us, leaving us open and ready for love. Hence, the heart (love) and the lungs (grief) work together as yin and yang, sunlight and shadow, exhalation and inhalation, diastolic (the heart expanding outward) and systolic (the heart contracting inward). If we see love and grief as two aspects of the same journey, we may become more able to both honor our grief and let it go, so we can expand into love once more. This is why I believe so deeply in the power of the heart. The heart is the inner fulcrum, or the sovereign organ, that brings together our earthly self and all the contraptions of survival, emotion, and power, with our higher will, intuition, and soul. Those who have truly tapped into their wellspring of self-love will let their passions be their guiding principle for decision making. In other words, they will follow their heart, connecting in the highest way to related qualities of forgiveness, gratitude, love, and service.

BALANCE YOUR LOVE

You might think, *The more love, the better,* and if you mean the experience of love, you would be right. When it comes to the topic of love within our Seven Systems of Full-Spectrum Health, however, the LOVE can most definitely be out of balance, just like any of the other systems.

A person with a healthy LOVE
- is full of passion for issues that are close to their heart;
- can love in a balanced way of caring, but not feel overly committed;
- is a natural "healer" type of person;
- is empathic and tuned in to others' feelings, but doesn't get dragged into them;

- has emotional wisdom;
- knows how to balance the head and the heart;
- is generous, but not to the point of draining themselves;
- has an open heart with healthy boundaries;
- gives and receives in equal measure;
- has normal breathing;
- has hands that are slightly warm, not cold;
- has normal blood pressure and overall good heart health;
- is open to sharing their meals and enjoys family-style eating; and
- loves eating vegetables and engages in plant-based eating.

A person with an underactive LOVE
- has difficulty forgiving themselves and others;
- has the feeling that their heart is shut down due to hurt and trauma, and can't be healed;
- tends to dwell on past events;
- might lack passion;
- tends to focus on their suffering and pain;
- is often not in touch with others' feelings since they tend to be overwhelmed by their own;
- might be perceived as cold or uncaring;
- might hold back love because of painful feelings;
- has a head that rules their heart;
- has shut people out of their life;
- might have become stingy, jealous, and bitter;
- doesn't like to be touched;
- tends to take more than they give;
- has trouble taking care of themselves;
- feels paralyzed by deep past hurts;
- breathes heavily and erratically, and might have asthma or sleep apnea (their breathing stops or is interrupted during sleep);
- has cold hands and a stagnant circulation;
- might have low blood pressure;
- might have a low heart rate;
- might have blockage and/or calcification in their arteries;

- prefers not to share;
- avoids vegetables;
- rarely eats or likes eating leafy greens and salads; or
- might have become numb because of a series of disappointing, painful events in childhood or because of a childhood lack of love.

A person with an overactive LOVE
- is often a martyr type or feels they have to sacrifice themselves;
- might feel overly hurt at the slightest sense of pain inflicted toward others and may even feel their pain for them;
- is a people pleaser;
- seeks others' approval for their sense of self-love;
- overextends themselves repeatedly;
- neglects their self-care;
- might be frustrated or angry about not being nurtured but has trouble asking for nurturing;
- might care more about others' feelings than their own, which might create bitterness;
- is often anxious, especially when it comes to ensuring that others are content;
- tends to extend care outward, rather than inward;
- might make dinner for everyone else and leave themselves out or eat standing up;
- might be very touchy-feely and likes to give hugs;
- is extremely loyal, but might resent it when they perceive others aren't equally loyal;
- might be overly devoted to a cause to the extent they neglect their own needs;
- is effusive with passion;
- has a heart that rules their head and might not use logic;
- breathes quickly and shallowly, and is subject to hyperventilation;
- might have high blood pressure;
- might have warm hands or red palms;
- might flush in the face or chest area easily;

- might have a high heart rate and abnormally fast heart rhythm, and might be subject to anxiety and heart palpitations;
- might have a personal history of breast cancer or of cysts or lumps in the breasts;
- expresses love by making food for others, but can become offended if the food is not eaten; or
- tends to eat lots of green leafy salads or vegetables and not be as balanced in getting quality protein.

PRACTICE SELF-COMPASSION:
HOW THE LOVE DETOX WORKED FOR HALEY

Haley was a woman in her early fifties who described herself to me as "brokenhearted." She had just ended a long, painful relationship with a married man, a relationship that she told me had been sometimes loving but which often had left her feeling "starved" and "heartsick."

She told me that as her relationship was ending, she found herself weeping frequently. She also felt anxious, waking up in the middle of the night with her heart racing. During the day, she sometimes got heart palpitations, "until it feels like my heart is jumping out of my chest."

Haley had always been a somewhat anxious person, but when these panic attacks struck, she felt as though nothing could ever console or calm her. "I feel that I'm the only one who will ever be there to take care of me," is how she put it, "and what I can offer to myself is just not enough."

Haley and I agreed that our work would begin by looking at the issues of self-nourishment and self-love. She seemed to have a lot of compassion for others and I wanted her to extend some of that compassion to herself. These issues are often viewed as psychological, but I see them as nutritional also. According to the fourth system of health, plant foods are LOVE foods, and I thought that by eating more green vegetables, Haley could support the process of healing her heart. I also thought that magnesium—used for establishing a healthy, regular, heart rhythm—would ease the palpitations and anxiety.

Haley was skeptical that simple changes in diet and a few supplements could shift her outlook, but she agreed to give my suggestions a try. To her amazement, the green foods and magnesium did indeed make a difference, and within a few weeks, she felt much calmer and more optimistic.

I also taught her some mindful breathing techniques that I believed could ease her pain and soothe her anxiety. I explained that she could focus on her breathing when she felt anxious but also when she felt alone and uncared for. Because both the lungs and the heart belong to the fourth system of health, breathing deeply and mindfully is good for the heart, physically and metaphorically. Slowing the breath allows the physical heart to find its healthy rhythm, while connecting to the breath enables us to transform the constricting emotions of grief and despair into the expansive feelings of love and compassion.

Fortified by these physical approaches, Haley was ready to take a more emotional journey, exploring all the ways in which she nurtured others before she took care of herself. Like many people—and particularly like many women—Haley had been brought up to believe that self-care was selfish, that a good person put others first. Longing for love and nurturing, she had generously cared for the other people in her life, but she felt guilty, anxious, and ill at ease whenever she tried to care for herself. At the same time, she admitted, she frequently felt frustrated and even bitter at the lack of balance in her relationships. "I would like more of a two-way street," she told me. "But the care seems to go only one way."

Over time, she came to see that if she always put others first, she was likely to find that other people were only too happy to receive without giving back. If she wanted more balance in her relationships—both at home and at work—she needed to tip the balance herself by finding ways to turn her love inward as well as outward.

When I reminded her of M. Scott Peck's definition of love, she readily agreed that she felt love for her ex-partner, for her two sisters, even for some of the coworkers at her job. She wanted what was truly best for them and was committed to helping them get it. But when I asked her how this related to her—what she had done lately to ensure her own growth into the best possible version of herself—she was at a loss. "I don't think of having a duty or obligation to *myself*," she said finally, "but I guess I do."

"I'm struck that you use the words 'duty' and 'obligation,'" I replied. "Is that how you think of love toward others?"

Haley took a surprised breath. "No," she said slowly. "I give to others because I want to, because I feel the rightness of it."

"Then why can't you give to yourself in the same way?" I asked.

Haley felt uncomfortable with the idea of giving to herself, but she could see how loving and caring for herself might be what she needed right now. She could also see how self-love and self-care might help to dissolve some of the bitterness and frustration she felt over "always giving to others and never really having them give back to me." Together we made a list of five things she could do in the coming week to turn her love and generosity inward:

- Get a massage at a local spa, and take a walk in the botanical gardens afterward.
- Clean up her home office, bringing in some flowers and an inspiring poster, so her personal workspace felt like a lovely, healing, serene place.
- Go to a funny movie she'd never quite made time to see, which starred two of her favorite actors and seemed like it would be a fun night out.
- Make sure to use a nontoxic, rose-based moisturizer twice a day, so her skin felt cared for.
- Spend five minutes at the end of every day breathing deeply and allowing herself to review what was good about herself and what was right about her life rather than always focusing on where she and her expectations had fallen short.

Haley was surprised at how difficult these seemingly pleasurable activities were to perform. I asked her how hard it would have been had they been for someone else—had she been booking a massage, setting up a movie date, or buying moisturizer for her ex-partner, one of her sisters, or a close friend. She agreed, "Nothing could stop me," if her care had been directed at somebody else. I urged her to extend that same commitment to herself as the best possible way to heal her LOVE.

FOREST DETOX

The power of green takes on a new dimension with "forest bathing"—time spent walking or sitting in a forest environment. In another example of how fourth-system elements come together, time in the greenery has significant implications for heart health and hypertension.

This therapeutic technique originated in Japan, where it is known as *shinrin-yoku*, or "taking in the forest atmosphere" or "forest bathing." Recent research has ratified the cardiovascular benefits of this green practice. In the words of one research team,

> The results show that forest environments promote lower concentrations of cortisol, lower pulse rate, lower blood pressure, greater parasympathetic nerve activity, and lower sympathetic nerve activity than do city environments. These results will contribute to the development of a research field dedicated to forest medicine, which may be used as a strategy for preventive medicine.

GREEN FOODS AND YOUR LOVE

Just as the heart brings together our physical and emotional selves, vegetables unite the rootedness of the earth and the literal and symbolic blossoming into an expansive space. Green foods are particularly nurturing—luckily, nature has provided us with a lot of them! In fact, green is the color most predominant in nature, offering us many chances to heal.

I associate the color green with the elements of healing and expansion. Just as the leaves on a tree open naturally, green represents an unfolding of love, service, and gratitude from within.

Within food, green indicates the presence of chlorophyll, king of the antioxidants. High-chlorophyll foods, such as spirulina, wheatgrass, alfalfa grass, barley grass, and chlorella, cleanse the blood and promote good circulation. Chlorophyll can also help bind heterocyclic amines—the carcinogens that develop when meat is cooked. I highly recommend pairing meat with green foods rich in chlorophyll because of the ways chlorophyll can bind carcinogens.

Besides chlorophyll, vegetables—green and otherwise—supply our body with several thousand varieties of phytonutrients, plant compounds that impart color and special functions to a plant:

- red, orange, and yellow carotenoids and xanthophylls
- yellow-green chlorophyll, catechins, isoflavones, lutein, and zea-xanthin
- blue-purple anthocyanidins, hydroxystilbenes, and phenols
- tan-white allicin, lignans, lignins, and tannins

Other vitamins and minerals can also support your LOVE:

- *Magnesium, potassium,* and *calcium* keep heart rhythms regular and reduce anxiety.
- B *vitamins,* especially *folate* (B9) and *cobalamin* (B12) maintain healthy blood flow and lower homocysteine, a compound associated with blood clots, heart attacks, and strokes.
- *Phytosterols,* a class of compounds in plant foods, help to reduce levels of "bad" (LDL) cholesterol, keeping the cardiovascular system healthy.
- *Phytoestrogens*—isoflavones, coumestans, stilbenes, and lignans—support your heart, balance your estrogen, calm your mood, and promote your health.

I never cease to be amazed by the impact of leafy green foods and green supplements upon a cardiovascular condition. For example, my patient Samuel was told by his cardiologist that he had a 70 percent blockage in his carotid artery, a condition usually requiring an intervention to open up the artery. Unwilling to engage in such a drastic procedure, Samuel was in desperate hope of a dietary solution. At my suggestion, he began eating leafy green salads every day for lunch and exercising on a daily basis, along with stopping his smoking habit, and within months, his blockage was nearly gone.

Likewise, Luke had been struggling for years with high blood pressure, for which he was taking several medications by the time he came to me. His wife—a longtime patient of mine—begged him to come see me, and finally, frustrated with his medications' many side effects, he agreed. I convinced him to start eating more green vegetables—broccoli, Brussels sprouts, kale, collard greens, spinach, chard, and escarole. He had always hated vegetables, but his wife found a number of creative and healthy ways to cook these greens: lightly sautéed with garlic, steamed in coconut milk, garnished with pine nuts and currants. Within two months, to his doctor's astonishment, Luke was able to significantly reduce his medications, and after six more weeks, he was off his meds entirely.

As I said, green foods—the LOVE foods—are some of the most potent medicines I know. So come with me on a tour of these healing foods to support your heart, lungs, and sense of LOVE.

PHYTOSTEROL CONTENT IN SELECT FOODS*

Food	Serving size	Phytosterols (milligrams)
Sunflower seed kernels, dried	½ cup	374
Rice bran oil	1 tablespoon	162
Sesame oil	1 tablespoon	118
Sesame seeds, whole	1 tablespoon	64
Avocado	½	57
Almonds	1 ounce	39
Sunflower seed butter	1 tablespoon	33
Asparagus, raw	1 cup	32
Olive oil	1 tablespoon	22
Pickles, sour	1 cup	22
Lettuce, green-leaf	1 cup	14
Sunflower seed oil	1 tablespoon	14

*It is thought that the diets of early humans contained an average of 1,000 milligrams of phytosterols per day because of the high intake of plant foods.

IF YOU ARE TAKING BLOOD THINNERS

If your health-care provider has prescribed you warfarin, Coumadin, or any other blood-thinning drug, talk with them about your intake of leafy green vegetables. As we have seen, vitamin K helps prevent blood clots—a potentially

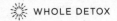

dangerous effect if you're taking a blood thinner—and you might need to avoid many green vegetables while you're on that medication.

If that is your situation, consider buying some liquid chlorophyll from a health-food store, and put ¼ teaspoon into an 8-ounce glass of water. Sip it throughout the day to get the benefits of this detoxifying plant compound. Chlorophyllin, a stabilized form of chlorophyll, is another substance that will bind toxins in the body coming in from foods like grilled meats. My patients have even told me that taking chlorophyll improved their body odor after a while—perhaps because the chlorophyllin binds the toxins that can create an unpleasant smell.

Phytonutrients

Phytonutrients are biochemical compounds found in plants—literally, since the word phyton means "plant" in Greek. They support the plant's health in various ways, and they support our health too.

Compared to everything else we consume, phytonutrients are a mere drop in the nutritional bucket. On average, you probably eat about 200 daily grams of carbohydrates, about 100 daily grams of protein, and more than 50 daily grams of fat. Yet even if you've loaded up your plate with fruits and vegetables, your daily phytonutrient consumption probably totals less than 1.5 grams—less than 1 small teaspoon each day.

Welcome to the power of the tiny, because this small, seemingly inconsequential amount can bring about significant changes in your metabolism. Welcome, too, to the power of diversity: a 2006 research study shows that you get far better health results eating small amounts of several different phytonutrients than large amounts of just a few. Combining plant compounds seems to maximize their synergy, with each expanding the power of the others. I think this is a wonderful symbolic image of service: giving to others makes you stronger, but you also need others to give to you.

You've probably heard that our goal should be nine to thirteen servings of fruits and vegetables each day—and, preferably, these are widely varied servings, covering the full spectrum of colors and the broadest possible range of phytonutrients. Unfortunately, the average American barely makes it to 3.6. I have to believe that the "phytonutrient gap"—the deficiency in rainbow compounds—is at least partly responsible for the skyrocketing rate of heart disease in the United States, which has become the number one killer of people in industrialized countries, with Canada, Europe, and Australia also high on the list. When I think of Samuel and Luke, whose vegetable consumption made their heart problems disappear, I wish I could convince every person to reach for the vegetables.

I'm so happy I could at least help my father, who for years struggled with a heart condition and high blood pressure. He now proudly touts his green smoothie every day as his mainstay, and indeed, Whole Detox has improved his blood pressure considerably and even allowed him to reduce his medications. What a relief!

So reach for those greens and enjoy your morning smoothie. If my father can do it, I know you can too.

Phytodetoxification

This intriguing new term has just made its way into the scientific literature, although my nutritionist colleagues and I have been familiar with the concept for quite a while. It describes the ability of plants to detoxify organisms like human beings—to help bind industrial chemicals, heavy metals, and endocrine disrupters so they cannot damage our bodies. As you can see, we need plants desperately. We simply can't do without them if we expect to stay clean in a toxic world.

Plants don't simply rid your body of toxins, however. They also open your heart and your circulation with their chlorophyll and vitamin K. As if that weren't enough, plants help us better connect to nature. If you've ever grown your own herbs in your kitchen windowsill or maintained a garden of any kind, you have experienced the love that results as you shower your beloved plants with the care and nourishment they require to survive, thrive, and nourish you right back.

Although I've met many nutritionists who would fight over meat, dairy, and even fish, I've never met a health expert who says we should not eat plants. Plants just make people . . . happy!

So when it comes to taking care of yourself, focus on plants of all types. Grow some, eat lots, and let them teach you about giving yourself more love, in all its forms. After all, no matter what diet we follow—Paleo, vegan, or flexitarian—we are all eating plants. Truly, plants are the great unifier!

Phytoestrogens

As the name suggests, "phytoestrogens" are the plant form of estrogen, but they are from one hundred to one thousand times weaker than the estrogen in the body. Phytoestrogens can be healing for your heart by assisting with an open circulation, and they provide a way to smooth out hormonal fluxes, especially for women approaching perimenopause and menopause, when the body's own estrogens are in decline.

A common source of phytoestrogens is soy, which has the potential to be a healthy food when not genetically modified. You won't find any soy in your twenty-one-day program, because many people have an allergic response to it. However, if your health-care provider hasn't cautioned you against eating it based on your physiology, you can do your heart a favor by enjoying a moderate amount of fermented, organic, non-GMO soy products in the form of miso or nattō.

Another phytoestrogen that is even more potent than soy is flaxseed. Studies suggest that getting more flaxseed in your diet might improve your heart health by reducing cholesterol and other blood lipids, in addition to potentially being protective against some hormonal cancers.

GOOD SOURCES OF PHYTOESTROGENS

Food	Phytoestrogens (μg/100g)
Flaxseed	379,380.0
Soybeans	103,920.0
Tofu	27,150.1
Soy yogurt	10,275.0
Sesame seeds	8008.1
Flax bread	7540.0
Multigrain bread	4798.7
Soy milk	2957.2
Hummus	993.0
Garlic	603.6
Mung bean sprouts	495.1
Dried apricots	444.5
Alfalfa sprouts	441.4

Dried dates	329.5
Sunflower seeds	216.0
Chestnuts	210.2
Olive oil	180.7
Almonds	131.1
Green beans	105.8
Peanuts	34.5
Onions	32.0
Blueberries	17.5

Note: If you have a hormone-sensitive cancer or are taking drugs for hormonal issues, check with your health-care professional about your intake of high-phytoestrogenic foods.

Heart-Healthy Crucifers

The word "crucifer" means "cross," which refers to the cross pattern you can see in the arrangement of the four petals of these plants' flowers. Crucifers include broccoli, cauliflower, collard greens, mustard greens, cabbage, bok choy, arugula, and Brussels sprouts, all of which support your heart as well as offer your entire body antioxidant protection against toxins and inflammation. In a large study conducted with Chinese adults over more than ten years, scientists discovered that eating more vegetables—and especially more cruciferous vegetables—led to improved heart health and increased longevity. Crucifers might also have an anticlotting effect that can keep blood flowing smoothly and help to prevent stroke.

That stinky smell shared by crucifers means they contain sulfur, an essential compound for guarding the body against toxins. Sulfur-containing compounds, such as the sulforaphanes found in broccoli and cauliflower, help to detox the body, supporting the work of the intestines and liver in ridding the body of contaminants. If you want to get the maximum detox, antioxidant, and anti-cancer benefit from your crucifers, chop them up with some garlic and onion and then let the raw vegetables sit for about five minutes before cooking. This short period of time gives "plant actives"—the bioactive compounds that protect against illness—a chance to form.

Sprouts and Leafy Greens

The raw, living, active components of young sprouts (broccoli, alfalfa, or mung) and leafy greens (romaine, red leaf, butterhead, escarole, and arugula) provide us with the vital, healing nutrients that move us into expansion. These foods offer our body substances that assist with the circulation of blood throughout the vascular system as well as provide us with protective compounds, such as indoles and chlorophyll. If you are following a low-oxalate diet due to kidney or gallbladder issues, remember that several green leafy vegetables contain oxalates:

- Beet greens
- Beet root
- Collard greens
- Kale
- Okra
- Parsley
- Spinach
- Swiss chard

Heavy metal accumulation in the body, such as lead, cadmium, and mercury, has been connected to high blood pressure and cardiovascular disease. Chlorella and, to a lesser extent, cilantro may be helpful in binding heavy metals, as has been shown in animal studies.

MAKE YOUR OWN SPROUTS—IT'S EASY!

You can make your own sprouts using a widemouthed glass jar and screened lid. Most health food stores will sell you seeds: alfalfa, broccoli, garbanzo bean, lentil, mung bean, mustard, radish, red clover, and sunflower. Make sure you wash your sprouts extraordinarily well, because dirty sprouts have been implicated in foodborne illness outbreaks. Also, if you have an autoimmune condition, avoid alfalfa sprouts, which contain a compound called canavanine that might cause inflammatory flare-ups in sensitive individuals.

Microgreens

Microgreens—the edible seedlings of vegetables and herbs—are some of the most nutrient-dense foods I know. Sprouts and microgreens are different: sprouts germinate in water, usually within forty-eight hours, and form roots, stems, and undeveloped leaves, whereas microgreens need soil and sunlight, and take about seven days to grow before they are ready to eat.

The tiny leaves of microgreens are usually very pungent in taste and have vibrant hues. They can be served as a main salad or as a garnish on a salad or sandwich. In an analysis of twenty-five microgreens, those that scored highest in vitamins and phytonutrients (vitamin C, tocopherols, carotenoids, phylloquinone) were red cabbage, cilantro, garnet amaranth, and green daikon radish.

GETTING THE MOST FROM YOUR GREEN TEA

Green tea is another heart-healthy food rich in antioxidants. What I recommend during the Whole Detox program is decaffeinated green tea. Steep green tea for eight to ten minutes to maximize the release of the anti-cancer compound epigallocatechin gallate (EGCG). Black pepper helps EGCG linger in your body, so try pairing some green tea with a dish that contains freshly ground pepper, like soup or a salad. One of my nutritionist friends doesn't like the taste of green tea, but she knows how good it is for her, so she uses it as the base for her morning smoothie—a great way to hide the tea but get the benefit!

Whenever you can, choose water with minerals for your tea, rather than distilled water. The minerals in water bring out the tea's flavor a bit more, and it's actually healthier.

SUPPORT YOUR LOVE WHILE YOU EAT

As we have seen, there are so many ways in which plant foods add to the quality of your health. In days ten through twelve of your twenty-one-day program, you'll learn what you need to do to support your LOVE. Meanwhile, here are some quick tips on how to expand your LOVE into your everyday meals:

- Before starting to eat, take a couple of seconds to move from your busy head into your beautiful heart. You can easily do this by thinking of a time when you felt loved. Let your heart go to that feeling of being filled with

love. Imagine that this feeling infuses your food. Sit in that loving space for twenty to thirty seconds.

- Have a heart image visible in your space. Eat from heart-shaped bowls, and put heart stickers on your refrigerator, blender, kitchen cabinets, and drinking containers, to keep the spirit of love alive in the places where you cook and eat.
- Give thanks for your meals: to the person who prepared it (even if it's yourself, which is one step closer to self-love!) and to the animals and plants that gave their lives so you would be nourished. Research suggests that gratitude has lasting health effects. Think of how it might help you to appreciate the meal and even digest it better.
- Share meals with others whom you love. Eating is the ultimate unifying experience—we all need to eat as human beings, so what better way to "feel the love" than to eat together.
- Sing while preparing food; invite the element of air to honor your lungs, which work so closely with your heart to oxygenate the blood.

DETOXING YOUR LOVE: WHAT TO CHOOSE
- Cool, leafy, raw greens that can soothe and open the heart with vasodilators, agents that promote the expansion of blood vessels
- Taking good care of yourself
- Giving yourself time to love yourself, through "me time" or other healing practices
- Breathing deeply
- Being in nature, especially the forest ("forest bathing")

DETOXING YOUR LOVE: WHAT TO AVOID
- Foods that clog the arteries: meat and poultry, which contain too much toxic animal fat
- Foods that cause vasoconstriction or high blood pressure: excessively salty foods
- Foods that cause breathing difficulties due to an allergic reaction
- Life events or situations that cause high blood pressure
- People-pleasing behavior
- Being the martyr or feeling that you have to rescue people

EXPAND INTO YOUR LOVE

As you look over the lists portraying a healthy LOVE, an overactive LOVE, and an underactive LOVE (see pages 137–140), you can see how complex the relationship is between love and grief, and how challenging it can be to keep your heart open, but not too open. The LOVE opens us to connection and intimacy, but it can also make us more vulnerable to abuse and neglect. Compassion and service to others can enrich and deepen our lives, but they can also lead us to neglect the crucial work of self-compassion and care for ourselves. Grief and loss can cause us to harden our hearts, but they can also be the inspiration that softens our hearts and makes us appreciate the loved ones who remain.

This is why I see Whole Detox as such a personal journey, and as a never-ending one. Your vision of a balanced LOVE is likely to evolve over time, appearing very different to you with every passing decade. The first step on this journey is awareness, so you can identify and overcome every barrier that keeps your LOVE from flourishing as you deserve.

CHAPTER 7

THE TRUTH

That inner voice has both gentleness and clarity. So to get to authenticity, you really keep going down to the bone, to the honesty, and the inevitability of something.

—MEREDITH MONK

UNDERSTANDING THE TRUTH	
Anatomy	Thyroid gland, ears, nose, mouth, throat
Functions	Speaking, chewing, hearing, smelling
Living	Speaking one's truth, choice, decisions
Eating	Mindful eating, varied flavors, moist and liquid foods, sea plants

THE SCIENCE OF THE TRUTH

If you move up from the heart and the fourth system of health, you reach the base of the throat: home of the voice box, the thyroid gland, and the fifth system of health, the TRUTH. This system also encompasses the ears, nose, and mouth, so it oversees hearing, smelling, and your sense of taste.

The thyroid is an incredibly important gland whose impact is often underestimated in conventional medicine. Through its effects on your metabolism, your thyroid gland helps to regulate your weight as well as regulating your mood, mental sharpness, and overall well-being. Even a slightly underperforming thyroid can produce significant symptoms, including depression, fatigue, listlessness, brain fog, and weight that seems impossible to lose, while an overactive thyroid can cause rapid and erratic weight loss as well as anxiety, sleeplessness, and a racing heart.

Underactive thyroid is a widespread problem in the United States, especially for women over forty. However, conventional tests for thyroid tend to target only the most serious problems and miss many of the smaller ones. That's why giving your thyroid the comprehensive support it needs is so crucial for Whole Detox. Many of my patients are amazed at how much clearer, sharper, calmer, and happier they feel once they start detoxing the fifth system, and many also find that it suddenly becomes surprisingly easy to lose weight.

Taste, Variety, and Your Health

Weight loss may be helped by a healthier thyroid, and it may also be related to an enhanced sensory experience of food. Yes, you heard that right: smell, taste, and texture can make a huge difference in how your body responds. If you eat monotonously, your body will crave variety, leading you to overeat, in search of the food or taste you didn't get. I've also seen patients who avoid sugar suddenly become obsessed with sweetness, finding it nearly impossible to resist their sugar cravings.

Conventional medicine tends to ignore taste, but cutting-edge research has discovered what I and my colleagues always knew: taste is pivotal to food, weight, metabolism, and appetite, and we neglect it at our peril. In fact, research suggests that our taste is impacted by our emotional state. Researchers at Cornell University assessed taste and emotions of 550 people who attended hockey games. There were a total of eight games, four wins, three losses, and one tie. Findings revealed that positive emotions during the winning games correlated with enhanced sweet and diminished sour intensities while negative emotions lead to heightened sour and decreased sweet tastes. In other words, when life is "sweet," you taste things sweeter, and, when life is "sour," you taste them that way, too. It's a novel concept in nutrition to say that how we taste says something about our lives! Recent studies have identified taste receptors in our intestines, airways, brain, and even in the testes and sperm. Bitter taste receptors seem to play a unique role in our gut function, metabolism, thyroid function, and body weight—so begin to fight weight gain and indigestion by steaming up some bitter leafy greens!

You'll also want to examine food type, and here, too, your body seeks balance. For example, if you consume a high-protein breakfast, you're likely to find yourself craving carbohydrates for lunch. And if you tell yourself, "I'm never eating carbs again," the cravings might become overwhelming. This wish for balance isn't caused by a sweet tooth or lack of willpower; it's fundamental to human biology, confirmed by research showing that sweetness is an inherent taste that attracts us from birth.

The solution? Make sure that you sample the whole spectrum of tastes every day and, ideally, at every meal. Get some sweetness from carrots, sweet potatoes, pears, and berries. Savor the sourness of citrus fruits and tart green apple. Enjoy the bitterness of greens and eggplant. Take in the wonderful taste of sea salt or pink Himalayan salt sprinkled on your stir-fry. Pique your taste buds with savory (umami) seaweed, tamari, and miso (organic only, please!). This variety of tastes will awaken your mouth, nose, and throat to the stimulating scents and flavors, spurring your thyroid to optimal function and revving up your metabolism. Just by stimulating your olfactory sense through the smells of food, you begin the digestive process.

I also urge my patients to add modest amounts of natural sweetness into their diets with sweet fruits (dates, figs, raisins, prunes) and natural sweeteners (raw honey, molasses, maple syrup). When I traveled to other countries, like Taiwan and Nepal, I noticed that small amounts of savory and sweet sauces, pickled foods, and other delicacies are part of almost every meal, which reflects the principles of traditional medicine.

A Full Voice for a Whole Self

We use our mouths to consume food, but we also use them to speak. Accordingly, life issues for the fifth system include authenticity, choice, and finding your voice. If you can tell the world your truest thoughts—if you can share your most genuine and authentic self—you have taken a huge step to support your TRUTH.

Some fascinating research suggests that we ignore our personal truth at our peril. In 2014, a group of German scientists published a study with the intriguing title "Lying and the Subsequent Desire for Toothpaste." They were curious about the relationship between a person's sense of doing something wrong and his or her wish to be cleansed, which they called the Macbeth effect, after the famous scene in Shakespeare's *Macbeth* in which a murderous queen dreams over and over that she cannot wash the blood from her hands. The scientists asked a group of subjects to commit either a moral or an immoral act—that is, either to tell the truth or to lie. Then the subjects had to rate the desirability of various products. Lo and behold, the people who lied gave higher ratings to cleaning products while a functional MRI revealed increased activity in the sensorimotor areas of the brain—the parts of the brain that experience taste and smell. "The results demonstrate neurobiological evidence for an embodiment of the moral-purity metaphor," the scientists wrote. "Thus, abstract thoughts about morality can be grounded in sensory experiences." Or, put another way, the fifth system of health brings together our sensory experience of smell and taste with our inner sense of truth and authenticity.

We also use our mouths for singing, and a growing body of evidence suggests that singing benefits our immune system by lowering stress and reducing inflammation. A 2004 study in the *Journal of Behavioral Medicine* found that people who listened to choral music responded with a drop in secretory immunoglobulin, a common marker of inflammation, as well as in the stress hormone, cortisol. However, *singing* choral music had even more beneficial effects. Finding our voice, it seems, is good for our health as well as our happiness, since subjects reported increased well-being after just one sixty-minute rehearsal. "These results suggest that choir singing positively influences both emotional affect and immune competence," the German researchers concluded.

A Swedish team came up with similar findings in a 2003 study entitled "Does Singing Promote Well-Being?" In this experiment, amateur and professional singers were given a singing lesson while scientists used an electrocardiogram (ECG) to record their cardiovascular activity. The researchers also analyzed subjects' blood, looking for biochemicals that indicate stress (primarily cortisol) and inflammation as well as measuring HRV.

As might be expected, the professionals revealed increased "arousal" during the lesson; that is, they were more worked up, anxious, and excited. To them, singing was serious business, and their test results reflected that tone. However, the amateurs found the lessons an occasion for "increasing joy and elatedness." Unlike the professionals, they weren't worried about their results, so they simply relaxed and enjoyed the experience of using their voices. As the researchers put it, "The amateurs used the singing lessons as a means of self-actualization and self-expression as a way to release emotional tensions." Both amateurs and professionals felt more "energetic and relaxed" after the lesson, however, suggesting that tapping into the power of the fifth system of health is good for immune function and stress.

Finally, a 2010 Hong Kong study divided people aged sixty-five through ninety into two groups. One group was given thirty minutes a week to rest; the other spent the same amount of time listening to music. Researchers found that quality of life improved significantly among the music listeners compared to the control group.

The Hong Kong study tested only listening—and indeed, the ears are part of the fifth system—but I have to wonder what might have happened if, like the German subjects, the Chinese participants had also been given the chance to sing. A 2015 study of 258 older English adults answered this question. They found that community group singing favorably affected quality of life in these seniors: they had less anxiety and depression. My takeaway from the research is that it is healthy to be listening and vocalizing.

I have wondered whether these messages shut down not only one's unique voice but perhaps thyroid activity too. I have seen associations between women with hypothyroidism (low thyroid activity) and an inability to speak freely. Maybe this is just coincidence, but I find it fascinating to watch patterns of how what we say (or, in this case, don't say) translates into bodily symptoms and complaints.

THE POWER OF AQUAMARINE

Aquamarine is the color of the TRUTH, and we nourish our mouth, throat, and thyroid with sea vegetables that come out of shining blue-green oceans—foods that connect us to the ocean just as root vegetables connect us to the earth. The iodine on which our thyroid depends comes from such sea plants as nori, dulse, arame, and kelp. These foods are also rich in selenium and zinc, deficiencies of which are a common cause of thyroid problems.

To tap into the power of aquamarine, turn your head and look up at the sky or out at the expanse of the ocean, allowing that vast blue perspective to help you gain *your* perspective. If you don't have access to a broad vista, keep a blue stone—turquoise or lapis lazuli—on your desk or bedside table. Quiet your mind, gaze at the blue, and allow the right decision to emerge.

You can also lubricate your throat with warm, soothing tea or soup sipped from an aquamarine mug. Drink in the color along with the heat and the nourishment.

Finally, when you want to focus on the power of your voice, slip on an aquamarine scarf, tie, or necklace. Bring that color to your TRUTH center and amplify the force of your personal truth.

GET TO KNOW YOUR TRUTH

One of our gifts as humans is to express our personal truths through words. Our throat is a meeting place for the passions of our heart as well as for the thoughts and insights of our mind.

Julian is an accomplished musician, a classical flautist who also teaches a select number of students. He sent me the following e-mail after doing some work on his TRUTH:

> I'd like to share an increase in my awareness while playing my flute yesterday. I have a few students, and during lessons yesterday I felt there was an unusual ease of playing. My throat was relaxed, I was able to play technical passages easily. I think your approach has freed my creativity in that I was very excited how quickly and clearly I could play and how resonant my sound was. It was so refreshing that I practiced an hour after I finished teaching. It was rejuvenating and I felt free.

Julian's message speaks to the close connection between our bodies and the whole of our lives. Set free to express his own particular artistic truth, Julian was able to reach a new level of physical performance. Just as Padma's thyroid issues and her ability to speak her truth were interrelated, so was Julian's creativity profoundly affected by his physical self—and vice versa.

BALANCE YOUR TRUTH

Balancing your TRUTH means finding a healthy relationship between speaking and listening; accepting your uniqueness and becoming obsessed with it; and holding fast to your inner truth and remaining open to the truths of others. Here are some factors to keep in mind as you think about balancing your TRUTH:

A person with a healthy TRUTH
- is true to themselves;
- accepts their uniqueness;
- feels free;
- lives a life that seems to fit who they are;
- feels comfortable speaking what is on their mind in whatever way is most effective for the situation;
- speaks and listens to others in equal measure;
- has a strong voice and sense of presence when speaking their truth;
- expresses themselves well in many ways, not just verbally;
- makes prompt decisions, but not hasty ones;
- doesn't violate the freedom of others;
- is comfortable speaking, even publicly, but doesn't necessarily seek out attention by speaking loudly or shying away;
- has healthy mouth, gums, teeth, neck, and nasal passages and normal throat moisture and mucous;
- eats the amount of food their body requires with an average appetite;
- is generally able to make time for regular meals away from other activities and focuses on enjoying the scents, tastes, and textures of each meal;
- makes time to eat with awareness, without engaging in other activities or becoming distracted by visual cues or noises; and
- eats moist fruits and drinks soups, sauces, and juices on a regular basis.

A person with an underactive TRUTH
- is often soft-spoken and feels uncomfortable exposing who they are, a shy person who doesn't like to speak up;

- is often embarrassed about speaking their views and might even cover up their true opinions;
- might gossip, start rumors, blackmail, or lie;
- speaks slowly, perhaps with a stutter or pausing to search for words;
- makes decisions slowly and might even be paralyzed by making decisions;
- often lets others make decisions for them;
- after a decision is made, often feels they have made the wrong choice;
- likes to fit in with everyone else;
- might project a sense of inferiority or exaggerated humility;
- embraces a "victim" mentality, feeling shackled and imprisoned by what they are told to be because it doesn't fit who they are, yet they are reluctant to speak up;
- prefers to process their thoughts and emotions through writing rather than speaking;
- has a phobia about public speaking;
- might have dry lips, mouth, throat, or nose;
- might be subject to bouts of laryngitis;
- might have a neck sore to the touch;
- might have lost teeth;
- might have jaw soreness or TMJ (temporomandibular joint);
- has a slow metabolism, low thyroid activity, and perhaps even hypothyroidism;
- might have a small mouth proportionate to their face and brittle, small teeth that tend to break easily, with lots of spacing in between;
- might have hearing loss;
- might feel they are vulnerable and likes to wear turtlenecks and scarves to protect their neck;
- might have a soft voice;
- might feel like they have a lump in their throat ("plum pit" in TCM);
- sometimes has an issue with swallowing or tasting;
- has a weak appetite and might not eat enough food;
- eats slowly in long, drawn-out meals;
- might experience challenges in their ability to communicate

with others in an authentic way, often with respect to their food choices and/or how they eat;

- might keep secrets when it comes to health and eating, such as eating snack foods in private;
- might not get enough liquids or "water foods," whether fruits, soups, sauces, or juices; or
- might have lost their sense of taste or have impaired taste.

A person with an overactive TRUTH

- is vocal and outspoken;
- might use foul language consistently;
- would rather talk than listen, and would rather be the object of attention;
- doesn't necessarily know what is true for them, and may be using excessive chatter as distraction from what is true;
- makes decisions quickly;
- sees themselves as special and different from everyone else;
- might project a sense of grandiosity or superiority;
- values their freedom and may have strong resistance to authority;
- might be so concerned with their own point of view that they violate others' sense of freedom or overstep their bounds;
- processes thoughts and emotions verbally;
- tends to overload the senses by doing too many things at once, such as always playing music in the background or talking on the phone while watching TV;
- might speak too fast;
- might have inflammation surrounding the mouth, gums, teeth, jaw, neck, or nasal passages;
- is prone to sore throats;
- might have shooting neck pain;
- has a fast metabolism and perhaps excess thyroid activity or hyperthyroidism;
- might have acute hearing or even ringing in the ears (tinnitus);
- is prone to vertigo;
- might have a high-pitched voice;

- has a strong appetite and might eat excessively without gaining weight;
- eats in a hurry and frequently on the run and/or while doing other things, such as listening to the radio, talking with others, watching television, driving, or working;
- might be eating constantly;
- might get hiccups after eating;
- might be overly drawn to fruits, soups, sauces, juices, and might even prefer to drink their meals rather than chew them because it's faster and more efficient; or
- always has something in their mouth, such as food, a pen, gum, mints, or candy.

LEARN TO SPEAK YOUR TRUTH:
HOW THE TRUTH DETOX WORKED FOR IRIS

Over the years of dealing with my own health and that of others, I have seen again and again how important it is to be true to ourselves in all arenas of our lives, including foods, eating, and our health. If we can't say no to the demands of others, we might also find it hard to say no to the foods that don't really serve us. The throat is a place of self-expression, but it's also the gateway for food to enter our body. When we come from a place of healthy expression, speaking clearly and truthfully, and eating mindfully, we can more easily choose the foods that our body truly wants and needs.

This was a challenge for my patient Iris, a faithful churchgoer who struggled every Sunday with the donuts, pastries, and brownies served as part of the after-service coffee hour. If one of Iris's friends offered a home-made cookie or "just a taste of my favorite cake," Iris felt unable to say no, even though she knew that sugary foods gave her migraines. Somehow, she just couldn't speak up for herself, preferring the agony of a day-long head-ache to the prospect of speaking the truth.

When she came to me for help, we quickly identified sugar as one of her food triggers, but then I realized she already knew that. Unlike some of my patients, she had long ago figured out which foods were good for her and which were not. The problem wasn't *knowing* her truth but *speaking* it.

Iris had other symptoms that led me to think her fifth system needed some support. She suffered from a dry throat, especially in the evenings. She had subclinical hypothyroidism—an underperformance of her thyroid gland—which didn't show up on conventional medical tests but revealed itself in a multitude of symptoms: fatigue, brittle nails, constipation, always feeling cold, brain fog, and an extra fifteen pounds that just wouldn't go away. She also suffered from TMJ, a pain in the jaw that comes from clenching the mouth shut and grinding the teeth. She told me that for years she had worn a mouth guard while she slept, but the soreness had persisted.

I was struck by the image of a clenched jaw, as though Iris was biting down on her words and refusing to release them. Indeed, as we talked, I noticed how reluctant she was to use her voice. She spoke so softly that I could barely hear her, and she frequently apologized, corrected herself ("Maybe that isn't true . . ."), and offered to defer to me ("I mean, I don't know. What do you think?").

She clearly needed support for all of her fifth system. For her chronically dry throat, I suggested a soothing cup of licorice tea after dinner. To address the hypothyroidism, I recommended she cut out gluten, a protein found in many grains, including wheat, rye, and barley. Gluten is often responsible for "molecular mimicry," a process whereby the immune system confuses gluten molecules with the molecules of your thyroid gland. A sensitive immune system releases "killer chemicals" to zap the gluten molecules, but the mimicry causes them to attack thyroid tissue as well. Cutting out the gluten resolves this process and allows the thyroid gland to operate more effectively.

For further thyroid support, I suggested she get more iodine and potassium into her diet by eating the sea vegetables that are part of the fifth system: dulse, hijiki, and nori. I urged her to choose warm, soothing foods that would feel comforting and nourishing in her mouth and throat.

I also gently asked her about her soft voice and her fear of public speaking. She told me that as a child, whenever she expressed an opinion, someone in her loud, raucous family would tease her, often to the point of ridicule. If she objected, she would invariably be told, "Stop being so sensitive" or "You don't know what you're talking about!" Iris had learned that it was easier to suppress her truth—her opinions and her feelings. She had carried this suppression into her adult life.

As she recounted these experiences, her voice got a bit stronger and I heard the beginnings of anger. "How did you feel about all that teasing?" I asked her.

"I hated it!" she burst out—and then looked surprised. I wondered if this bottled-up anger was behind her painfully clenched jaw.

Over the weeks I worked with Iris, her throat discomfort vanished, her jaw pain subsided, and her excess weight began to come off. A combination of emotional support for speaking her truth and nutritional support for her throat and thyroid had helped her detox her fifth system of health.

INTEGRATE THE TRUTH

I like to refer to the fifth system as the seat of integration, where we unite many diverse elements to create something new.

For example, we combine thoughts from our mind and passions from our heart to create expression through our throat. Or when we cook, we bring together fire, metal, and air (on our stovetop) with earth (food) and water (broth) to make a miraculous new entity called a soup. And, once again, you combine these elements in your throat: breathing in the fragrant scents that trigger your taste buds and bringing the vegetables and liquid into your body's cells. The fuel that warmed your soup also becomes part of your body, as does the warm air that radiates from every bite.

MOIST FOODS FOR YOUR TRUTH

Foods for the fifth system support your throat and thyroid. They are often warm, moist, and soothing as well as rich in the minerals and nutrients your thyroid needs. Here are some of the main types of TRUTH-full foods:

Sea Plants

Sea vegetables embody the symbiotic relationship between the elements of water and earth. Many of my patients haven't ever tried sea vegetables when they come to me, and perhaps this is your experience as well. I urge you to go on an "ocean journey," exploring all the different ways you can incorporate sea plants into your diet. Here are a few suggestions to get you started:

- Sprinkle dry dulse flakes on top of a salad.
- Add any sea plant variety to soups, stews, or broths. Nibble on dry dulse as a snack.
- Use a sheet of nori to make yourself a wrap.
- Instead of a salt shaker, keep a seaweed (kelp) shaker on your dinner table.

MEET SOME SEA PLANTS

- *Arame:* This species of kelp is frequently used in Japanese dishes. Its dark-brown strands have a firm texture and a mild, almost sweet flavor. You can add it to a wide variety of dishes, include pilafs, soups, casseroles, and even some baked goods, such as muffins. Arame is rich in a wide variety of minerals, including calcium, iodine, iron, magnesium, and vitamin A.
- *Dulse:* A red algae that grows on the northern coasts of the Atlantic and Pacific, dulse is dried into a texture something like jerky or a fruit roll-up to make a super snack food. When ground into flakes or a powder, it becomes a useful flavor enhancer for meat dishes, chili, soups, chowders, sandwiches, salads, pizza dough, and bread dough. You can also pan-fry dulse into chips, bake it in the oven covered with cheese or salsa, or microwave it briefly and then eat it with butter, as they do in Iceland. Dulse is a great source of iodine.
- *Kombu:* This type of kelp is used to flavor broths, stews, and rice dishes. It's also eaten as a vegetable and a snack, while transparent sheets are used to wrap rice and other foods. You can use kombu to soften beans during cooking and to chemically alter the beans to reduce flatulence. Like most sea vegetables, kombu is a good source of iodine.
- *Nori:* You might know nori as the seaweed used to wrap sushi. You can throw some into your soup and noodle dishes or eat it in the form of a soy-flavored paste. Nori is rich in B12, making it an excellent food for all of us but particularly for vegans, who frequently need to supplement with this vitamin.

I'm always excited to recommend sea plants to my patients, because these tasty vegetables benefit multiple body systems with an abundance of nutrients, including minerals, alkaloid antioxidants, and sulfated poly-saccharides. Alkaloids and antioxidants are types of plant compounds that have a wide variety of protective effects. Sulfated polysaccharides are like-wise protective against inflammations, bacteria, viruses, microbes, and tumors while supporting immune function and the digestive system. One such compound, fucoidan, appears to have anti-cancer, anti-inflammatory, cholesterol-lowering, and even anti-obesity effects.

Sea plants are especially good for the thyroid gland, supplying such cru-cial minerals as iodine, selenium, and zinc. While all sea plants are bathed in iodine, the brown sea plants seem to have the highest amounts, especially arame, kelp, kombu, and wakame. However, the mineral content—and par-ticularly the iodine levels—can vary greatly depending on where and when a plant was harvested.

When we look at getting iodine from sea plants, we don't just measure the plant's levels of that mineral; we also look at how bioavailable the iodine might be. This factor varies greatly depending both on the type of seaweed and on your body's iodine level.

Iodine is a crucial mineral. If you have a thyroid condition, especially an overactive thyroid, check with your health-care practitioner before intro-ducing large amounts of sea plants into your diet, because these can be contraindicated for hyperthyroidism.

Another cautionary note: sea plants' proficiency at absorbing minerals means they also tend to absorb heavy metals. This can vary depending on the type of plant and where it was grown—that is, how contaminated the water was. Check the label or ask your supplier whether they have tested their batches for heavy metals. Hijiki has been known to contain higher amounts of arsenic than other types. Choose certified organic options when available.

Finally, some species of sea plants may modify hormone metabolism. In a small case study series, three premenopausal women were given the edi-ble brown kelp Fucus vesiculosus (bladderwrack). In response, their menstrual cycles were lengthened by five to fourteen days. One woman saw a drop in estrogen while her progesterone levels increased, often a beneficial effect. The researchers suggested that this may be why estrogen-sensitive cancers are lower in populations like Japan's, in which sea vegetables are part of the everyday diet.

Moist Fruits

Fruits tend to be high in water content, so they are a perfect food to lubricate your throat. Some of my favorites are cantaloupe, watermelon, oranges, kiwi, nectarines, peaches, honeydew melon, and grapes. You can just imagine their moist, soft texture as I name them and feel how soothing they will be when you actually eat them. When your throat is moist and open, you'll find speaking more comfortable, and perhaps you'll be more likely to use your voice.

Make sure to choose fresh whole fruits rather than those that are in toxic cans or have added sugars. Your best bet is to consume whole fruit, including its fiber, rather than fruit juices, which can be very high in sugar. If you would like to choose a fruit juice, select those with no added sweeteners. Change up your fruit and fruit juice choices regularly—make sure you're getting a wide nutritional variety.

WATER + FRUIT = SUPER-HYDRATION

Hydration is crucial to the second system of health, while keeping your throat moist and relaxed is important to the fifth system. Both systems of health are concerned with expression: creativity for the second and verbal expression for the fifth. When we feel in the flow of being creative, our channel of TRUTH can open wide to let it out!

You can use a combination of water and food to enhance hydration. Add sliced cucumber, strawberry, melon, lemon, or orange to give your water a tangy twist. You'll drink more, and the time you spend savoring the subtle flavors will make your taste buds happy.

Soups, Stews, Sauces, and Smoothies . . . Oh My!

Liquid foods keep your throat moist and lubricated, quench your thirst, and load up your body with detoxifying nutrients. I especially like to recommend soups and stews during Whole Detox because true nutritional synergy occurs when you put diverse ingredients together with a little heat: sometimes you get improved bioavailability of nutrients, and often the ingredients just taste better and more interesting in combination, especially on the second day! Preparing soups and stews can also lead to olfactory stimulation, creating pleasant aromas that can affect your appetite. One study conducted in the Netherlands showed that healthy women exposed to a concentrated tomato soup aroma ate 9 percent less of a bland soup base than when they hadn't had such concentrated exposure.

Of course, I would much prefer that you toss ingredients into a large saucepan with water or broth to make that soup rather than get it from a can. A study at Harvard University showed that "consumption of 1 serving of canned soup daily over 5 days was associated with a more than 1000% increase in urinary BPA [bisphenol A]." Get the soup, but lose the bisphenol A coating in the can!

Soups can warm and open up the throat area and create more ease in eating. Spooning in warm soup takes longer than gobbling up your food, which might help you to slow down and savor each moment of your eating experience. Research also suggests that soup is good for weight loss: consuming any type of low-calorie soup before a meal can reduce the amount of food intake by as much as 20 percent.

Sauce can enhance a meal by making a vegetable tastier or pulling a dish together. Sauce can also cue us to release saliva and other digestive fluids and enzymes, promoting smoother digestion. Another benefit is the healthy fat in an oil-based savory sauce enables us to absorb carotenoids and fat-soluble vitamins; you miss a lot of nutritional benefits from vegetables and salads when they are fat-free! A vinaigrette or mustard dressing is always a delicious choice, but my favorite is sesame tahini made with sesame oil, so you'll have the chance to taste quite a bit of this super-creamy sauce in the Whole Detox recipes.

Smoothies and juices made of fresh fruits and vegetables can be another efficient way to consume the nutrients we need. Even my father, who is not the healthiest eater, can get his green smoothie down for breakfast every day. It's a great way to get in a load of nutrients first thing in the morning, which is why the Whole Detox meal plans consist of a smoothie a day.

I suggest you use a fruit and vegetable pulverizer, such as the Nutri-Bullet, Vitamix, or Ninja (my personal favorite) to get the whole food rather than just the juice. Oh, and one more thing: chew your smoothie. That's right! Keep that smoothie in your mouth rather than chugging it down, so the microbes and enzymes in your mouth can begin the process of digesting and utilizing nutrients. Green plants like arugula and spinach contain dietary nitrates that convert into nitric oxide, which allows your blood vessels to open wide. Your saliva helps in the process. So slow down when drinking smoothies!

Herbal Teas

I recently co-authored a scientific review paper on foods that influence detox pathways. You might be surprised to find out that one of most influential detoxers is tea, including black, green, honeybush, chamomile, dandelion, peppermint, and rooibos.

While herbal teas can be medicinal, with potent effects on your body, they can also contain heavy metals. Many people ask me about radiation in some of the green teas coming from Japan. The best rule of thumb, as with everything, is to choose from a varied selection, rotating your teas every three to four days. Choose organic tea leaves, and ask the manufacturer of the tea if they are checking for heavy metals and other contaminants in the finished product.

One of my favorite things to do is add a little bit of raw honey (the best is manuka honey or get a source of local honey) to herbal tea to coat my throat and boost my immune function. I remember when I had a bout of laryngitis some years ago. The tea and manuka honey seemed to make all the difference in getting my voice back, or at least soothing my throat until I could recover!

Foods with a Cultural Flair

With five tastes and five senses to honor as part of the fifth system, it's important to open up our exposure to a variety of foods. I like to have people expand their culinary horizons by engaging in various cultural foods, traditions, and practices around eating. Choosing to eat just one way all the time does not expose you to the full truth of the eating experience—a landscape that can be exploratory and healing. You will see that I have brought along some ethnic recipes within the Whole Detox, sometimes via such spices as tandoori and curry.

Food can often be the gateway to cultural insights. Why is the Mediterranean diet so popular and so healthful? Perhaps it's the food, but it could also be the Mediterranean way of eating: relaxed meals that take place over hours, usually in the company of family and friends.

So find out how people in Thailand eat coconut curry. Discover how Costa Ricans feel about their staple dish of rice and beans. Let your curiosity usher you into a mealtime adventure! It might be as medicinal as the food itself.

SUPPORT YOUR TRUTH WHILE YOU EAT

- Go slow, with slow-food restaurants, slow eating, and especially slow chewing. Eating too quickly can pack on the pounds. Research with children has associated fast eating (more bites per minute) with greater body weight.

- Put your awareness into eating so you get the most from the experience and don't feel like overeating. Studies show that cultivating a daily practice of mindfulness can help to reduce stress, binge eating, and emotional eating.

- Choose truthfully. Check out every choice about food that you are presented with and make sure it resonates with your inner truth.

- Become aware of the truth of your portion sizes. Do you remember that phrase "The eyes are bigger than the stomach"? Cup your hands together so you can get a sense of how big your stomach is, then use your innate awareness to stop eating when you've genuinely had enough. And watch out for those large portions, which cause us to eat 16 to 26 percent more than we would have normally.

- Expand your range of choices: look wider and broader, explore and discover, be adventurous. Shake up your food routine and try some foods you might not normally eat: perhaps Indian, Middle Eastern, European, or Ethiopian.

- Keep a food log to identify food ruts—habits that restrict your self-expression through food.

- Allow yourself to be free of dieting. Research shows that the more we feel restrained in our eating, the more likely we are to feel anxious, depressed, or unsettled.

DETOXING YOUR TRUTH: WHAT TO CHOOSE
- Iodine-rich sea vegetables to support your thyroid and supply you with needed minerals
- Soups, sauces, and juices that will lubricate your throat, as well as fruits that contain a lot of water: melons, grapes, tropical fruits, peaches, and plums
- A wide variety of tastes, which will make your tongue and taste buds sing!
- Humming, singing, or chanting to discover the true contours of your authentic voice
- Greater awareness of your daily habits, including your food choices, schedule, and tasks, in order to make the choices that truly serve your body, your spirit, and your purpose

DETOXING YOUR TRUTH: WHAT TO AVOID
- Environmental and food-based toxins that impair thyroid function, such as those that have chlorine, bromine, and fluorine (chemicals frequently used as pesticides, preservatives, and flame retardants)
- Gulping foods down, making them difficult to swallow and, ultimately, to digest
- Silencing your truth by not speaking up when you feel the need to
- Speaking in a truthful but cruel, insensitive, or uncompassionate way
- Gossiping, lying, swearing, threatening, exaggerating, or becoming cold and unresponsive

SPEAK YOUR TRUTH

Learning how to manifest your inner truth—how to express yourself authentically and make choices that align with who you are—is a lifelong process. There is no one right way to speak your truth, and there is certainly no easy way. Venting your thoughts without a filter is not necessarily the best way to speak your truth, but nor is clenching your jaw and biting down on every word that might possibly displease someone. Remaining in a relationship, a job, or a personal situation that violates your sense of inner truth is not good for your fifth system, but nor is breaking a commitment at a moment's notice or flitting from one "shiny object" to another. Knowing and speaking your truth can be a challenging process, but such an incredibly worthwhile one!

I myself struggled for years with questions about how to manifest my inner truth. As a scientist working in laboratories and academic settings, I wasn't always sure how to bring in the part of me that loved yoga, meditation, and alternative approaches to healing. I certainly never told my scientific colleagues about my abstract, vividly colored paintings! My career continued to progress, but I paid a heavy price. Because I wasn't speaking out of my deepest sense of inner truth, I'd return from a day's work or a scientific conference completely drained of energy, feeling dried up and shriveled, as though I might completely disappear. Perhaps I had more room to be "different" than I thought. Yet my childhood experience of a "health-conscious" mother, who also held strong religious beliefs, made me very anxious about not fitting in.

Then one day I noticed something curious. I nearly always wore either a scarf or a turtleneck, something to cover my neck and throat. I remember once before a TV appearance, I was determined to wear a high-necked sweater. My agent tried to talk me into another outfit, and I just froze with fear.

"Deanna, why can't you wear something that reads better on camera and is more flattering?" she asked me.

"I feel exposed," I told her. And then I started to wonder: What was I hiding?

Now I'm fortunate to have a career in which I can manifest all my inner truth: not just the scientist but also the yogi, the artist, the person who believes that psychology and spirituality are just as central to our health as nutrition and biology. It took me a long time to arrive at this place of truth, but it was so, so worth it. And the turtlenecks are gone, although I still like to wear scarves every once in a while!

How will you manifest your inner truth? What silence might you break? What knowledge will you bring to light? How will you make your voice heard?

Your answers may be slow in coming—or they might be right at the tip of your tongue. Either way, I invite you on your journey to detox your own TRUTH.

CHAPTER 8

THE INSIGHT

There is a universal, intelligent life force that exists within everyone and everything. It resides within each one of us as a deep wisdom, an inner knowing. We can access this wonderful source of knowledge and wisdom through our intuition, an inner sense that tells us what feels right and true for us at any given moment.

—SHAKTI GAWAIN

Intuition and concepts constitute . . . the elements of all our knowledge, so that neither concepts without an intuition in some way corresponding to them, nor intuition without concepts, can yield knowledge.

—IMMANUEL KANT

UNDERSTANDING THE INSIGHT	
Anatomy	Pituitary gland, brain/neurotransmitters, eyes
Functions	Seeing, thinking, intuiting/imagining, sleeping/dreaming
Living	Cognition, visualization, sleep
Eating	Stimulants (caffeine), depressants (wine), mood-altering foods (cocoa-based foods), blue-purple foods

THE SCIENCE OF THE INSIGHT

One of the most mysterious, fascinating organs in the body is the human brain. Scientists, philosophers, and mystics have all puzzled over the workings of this organ, trying to grasp the interconnections between mind and body, matter and spirit, thought and action, biochemistry and intention.

I don't pretend to have solved these age-old mysteries. But I do have an approach to healing, supporting, and sharpening your brain. Use Whole Detox to remove barriers in your sixth system of health, and watch your mood improve, your thinking sharpen, your understanding expand, and your sleep become deep, restful, and restorative.

As you already know from reading chapter 1, your brain is a biochemical marvel. Composed of fat, powered by electricity, and animated by a wide variety of chemical compounds, your brain processes thoughts, feelings, perceptions, and sensations, all while making sure your heart keeps beating, your lungs keep breathing, and your stress and relaxation responses fire off as needed. Oh, and let's not forget the brain's role in regulating digestion, hormonal activity, immune function, and countless other bodily functions. We can view these activities in biochemical and electrical terms, as integral facets of personality and worldview, in spiritual terms, or in some combination of the three. My purpose in this chapter is not to sort out which is which—far from it. I want you to see how important it is to support your brain in all dimensions—through revitalizing foods, vivifying activities, helpful thoughts, and practice in mindfulness—so your brain is in shape to perceive the world clearly, experience the full range of emotions, and make good decisions to advance your life.

A common challenge in supporting the brain, however, is that different disciplines tend to focus on their own areas of expertise—either physical or psychological—without seeing how all of these factors interact. A related challenge is that brain scientists tend to focus on brain chemicals, not realizing the extent to which other biochemicals affect the brain.

For example, a rich new area of study concerns the way insulin influences the physical structure of the brain. Insulin is the hormone that helps you metabolize glucose, or sugar; it's not usually considered a brain chemical. Yet, medical researcher Dr. Suzanne Craft has demonstrated that people with insulin resistance may be prone to more rapid aging in the brain and greater vulnerability to Alzheimer's and dementia. This phenomenon has been referred to as type 3 diabetes.

The brain, after all, is known to use a lot of sugar, which is why you might become ravenously hungry after a long, sedentary session of writing, reading, or thinking hard. But when there's too much insulin in your system, your brain shuts down its insulin intake, putting it at risk of an insulin shortage. We need insulin in our brains to metabolize glucose and to counteract a substance known as amyloid protein. Too little insulin, and the amyloid builds up, the threat of glucotoxicity grows, and inflammation goes wild, putting you at a significantly increased risk of dementia.

The brain has receptors for other hormones too. Estrogen receptors play a role in mood and cognition, which is why your moods go haywire and your brain gets foggy when estrogen levels drop, whether during the menstrual cycle or in menopause. Thyroid receptors help regulate metabolism, mood, and cognition, which is why even subclinical changes in thyroid can make you feel anxious, listless, or depressed (see chapter 7). The list goes on and on, since just about every important biochemical in your body has a role in the health of your brain.

Fortunately, the first five phases of Whole Detox have helped balance and support these hormones. And now, in phase six, we'll focus on the brain itself. Whew! Get ready for clearer thinking, improved mood, and better sleep.

Using the INSIGHT to Create Health

A scientific study by researchers at the HeartMath organization has defined intuition as "a process by which information normally outside the range of conscious awareness is perceived by the body's psychophysiological systems." Intuition is elusive; it appears on its own timetable and by definition resists submitting to our conscious control. The impromptu nature of its appearance makes it hard to test and even harder to measure, though a growing number of neuroscientists and other brain researchers have tried. The result is an exciting set of studies that suggest you can often harness your mind to heal your body.

For example, a 2013 study published in *Pain Research and Management* indicates that when children aged ten to fourteen years are taught the techniques of "mindful attention," they can better cope with pain. Rather than trying to ignore a painful stimulus, children seemed to do better by learning new ways to pay attention to it.

A 2012 article in *Psychology and Health* suggests that guided imagery and relaxation training can improve the lives of patients with inflammatory bowel disease, a painful and distressing condition that typically erodes quality of life. The notion that "brain training" can ease the pain of this condition offers exciting possibilities for managing other chronic conditions.

In fact, studies show that relaxation and guided imagery techniques can be useful for a wide variety of conditions that cannot be easily treated by conventional medical means: the discomfort of pregnancy's last trimester, the pain of giving birth, and the distress of chronic tension headaches, among others. I look forward to seeing further scientific exploration for this rich resource in health care.

THE POWER OF INDIGO

Indigo—the glowing color that comes between blue and violet in the rainbow—is associated with many elements of the INSIGHT: creativity and insight, alertness and improved cognitive function, and better sleep. Here are just a few examples of the power of indigo:

- A 2009 article in *Science* suggests that blue light helps people perform better on creative tasks.
- A 2008 British study found that exposing workers to blue-enriched white light improved self-reported alertness, performance, and sleep quality.
- An Australian experiment discovered that exposure to blue light made experimental subjects less sleepy as they tried to complete prolonged tasks during the night.
- Swiss researchers found that exposure to morning blue light seemed to improve daytime cognitive performance and well-being as well as help to modulate levels of melatonin (the hormone that helps you sleep) and cortisol (the stress hormone that helps you wake up).
- When motorists were exposed to blue light in their cars at night, their driving seemed to improve, according to a 2012 French study.

To access the power of indigo, stare into the vast nighttime sky, so deeply blue that it appears black. Quiet your mind and feel your insight awaken.

Intuition often comes to us through dreams, so consider indigo sheets for your bed or perhaps an indigo towel to wrap yourself in after your nightly bath. Better yet, keep a dream journal with an indigo cover and allow your inner voice to speak to you through its pages.

GET TO KNOW YOUR INSIGHT

The INSIGHT and Intuition

The INSIGHT includes both our physical eyes and the "in-sight" that draws upon our inner vision. Our intuition, often referred to as the "sixth sense," integrates all of our prior experience to produce insights that often seem mysterious and that frequently help us bridge the gap between our tiny individual selves—the microcosm—and the macrocosm of life. If we can harness our intuition effectively, we can use it to guide our lives.

Intuition can come to us directly—through what we see, hear, and feel. It can also come through dreams or via that quiet inner voice that speaks only in stillness. Remarkable as it may seem, nourishing the sixth system of health with balanced amounts of unsweetened cocoa powder, spiced foods, and blue-purple foods can often help us tune in to our cognition and even modulate our moods, which may ultimately open the gateway to our intuition.

Many of the foods that may spark our brain are tiny: spices, a teaspoon of cocoa powder, a few grains of coffee (although note that on your twenty-one-day Whole Detox, you will avoid caffeine). The notion of small substances making a large impact fits well with the concept of intuition: one of its functions is to connect the small to the big, the microcosm to the macrocosm. Have you ever noticed a tiny detail—perhaps the twitch of someone's mouth or an unusual word they used—and thought, *Oh, I get it—she's jealous* or *Now I see what's going on—he's planning to fire half the department*? Just as tiny stimulants and spices can spark your brain, so can seemingly insignificant details inspire your intuition.

Even the most logical, rational scientists have relied upon intuition and other types of knowing; the history of scientific discovery is full of insights born during dream time. Dmitri Mendeleev, the chemist who first organized the periodic table, struggled for hours to arrange the different elements in a logical order and then fell asleep at his desk. When he awoke, he had the solution: organize the elements according to their atomic weight. His INSIGHT had operated via an intuition his conscious mind could not access.

Likewise, August Kekulé could not seem to graph the structure of the benzene atom. Then he dreamed of a snake devouring its own tail, and he awoke to understand that the carbon atoms in benzene are arranged in a series of rings.

Daphne had a similar experience—though in our case, we actively worked to support her INSIGHT through nutrition. A web designer who routinely created beautiful, functional websites supported by elegant systems of computer code, Daphne had been stuck on a particular issue for several days. She had skipped meals, worked late into the night, "overdosed" on milk chocolate, skimped on sleep, and generally depleted her sixth system in a desperate attempt to force a solution. She began to feel as though the more she struggled, the less able she was to solve the problem.

She had worked with me several years prior, so she finally gave me a quick emergency call. I suggested that she lay off all the milk chocolate and start to load up on blue and purple foods—blueberries, blackberries, purple kale, purple cabbage—because I knew that the purple-pigmented proanthocyanins supported the brain's plasticity by reducing inflammation. "Maybe you can open up a new neural pathway that will lead you to your solution," I said, only half joking. Knowing how crucial sleep is to the brain, I also told her to get a good night's sleep.

Reluctantly, she agreed. She continued to address the changes in her diet and routine, and finally, weeks later, she woke up with a new idea that proved to be just what she'd been looking for. "I can't believe I solved the problem in my sleep!" she told me, laughing. Supporting her sixth system of health had given Daphne's brain the resources it needed to find her breakthrough.

If we harness our intuition effectively, it can guide our lives, helping us to make choices that best serve ourselves and others. And the better we get at knowing how to evoke our intuition, the more we can make use of this powerful ally. Sometimes we perceive our intuition outright, cued by something we see, hear, or experience; sometimes we receive its messages during stillness, contemplation, or dreams. Either way, intuition can often point the way to optimal health and a fulfilling life.

BALANCE YOUR INSIGHT

As with the LOVE and the TRUTH, it's difficult to see how you could have too much INSIGHT. Your first impulse might be "Bring it on! I'll take some more insight any day." Yet, as with all good things, you can indeed have too much INSIGHT, or rather, an INSIGHT system that is overactive, causing you to be wired, plagued by too many thoughts, and unable to stop thinking. Schizophrenia, bipolar disorder, multiple personality disorder, obsessive-compulsive disorder, and ADHD are only the most extreme examples of an overactive INSIGHT system. A person without a clinical diagnosis might also feel "I can't turn my mind off" or "Once I get started down a train of thought, I find it almost impossible to stop."

An underactive INSIGHT, by contrast, might cause you to feel slow, foggy, tired, and unable to think deeply. A balanced INSIGHT might be a better goal, although, as with all the systems, each of us will have our own version of it.

Yet sometimes an excess of the INSIGHT can be associated with genius, vision, or the kind of extraordinary insight that lights up new areas of knowledge. Perhaps a little obsessiveness, a little extra drive, can lead us to conceive new ideas that are truly valuable. And perhaps an underactive INSIGHT might be our opportunity to slow down, reset, and recharge, to take it easy for a while, to "go soft" and unfocus.

So explore the following lists, but allow your intuition and deeper sight to guide you. This is your opportunity to find out what type of INSIGHT is right for you.

A person with a healthy INSIGHT
- spends a healthy amount of time in reflection and contemplation relative to action and doing;
- enjoys healthy, positive thought patterns;
- is able to quiet their mind and redirect their thoughts as needed;
- is balanced in intellect and intuition rather than relying solely on either;

- is receptive to their intuitive voice, bodily senses, and instinct;
- can see the underlying meanings of situations;
- is able to bridge the practicality of daily living with the deeper themes of meaning and purpose, aware of both real details and symbolic images;
- has good attention to tasks;
- sleeps well, probably seven to eight hours per night on average;
- feels rested and refreshed upon waking;
- enjoys even, stable moods;
- has a sharp mind and good memory;
- doesn't overdo any food or beverage stimulants or depressants; and
- is not currently struggling with food addictions.

A person with an underactive INSIGHT
- might rely upon caffeinated beverages to help with focus, concentration, and thinking;
- looks to food and substances to *stimulate* their mind and thinking;
- oversleeps or sleeps a lot, frequently more than nine hours;
- doesn't remember dreams or claims they don't dream;
- feels fatigued early in the night;
- goes to bed early, but may wake up throughout the night;
- falls asleep throughout the day and likes short naps;
- has moods that shift slowly and can get stuck in one mood;
- lacks mental sharpness and often has a poor memory;
- might experience problems with blurry vision;
- might often feel that their mind "goes blank";
- tends to think through problems more slowly;
- might have difficulty being logical and/or learning new concepts;
- is not very good at thinking on their feet;
- is out of touch with their intuition;
- doesn't feel imaginative and doesn't consider themselves to be a visual person (has difficulty with guided imagery exercises); or
- finds it difficult to "see" into the future and tends to focus on the past.

A person with an overactive INSIGHT

- craves chocolate and is often a classic "chocoholic";
- has their moods quickly changed by foods;
- might have food addictions;
- might drink alcohol to calm down and is often particularly fond of red wine;
- can be an overly intuitive or an overly intellectual eater, either ignoring logic or ignoring their own instincts;
- might not be able to easily focus, becomes hyperactive easily, or might even have attention deficit hyperactivity disorder (ADHD) or tendencies in that direction;
- suffers from insomnia or restlessness during sleep;
- might sleep fewer than six hours per night;
- experiences volatile moods and quick mood shifts;
- seems to remember everything and might even have a photographic memory;
- might be prone to eye infections or inflammation;
- might get migraines or other types of headaches;
- thinks quickly on their feet;
- tends to overanalyze their life choices;
- is a visionary and thinks in the future more than in the past;
- dreams vividly;
- can be very moody or just shifts moods quickly;
- eats foods or takes substances to reduce their mental anxiety and overthinking; or
- is "always thinking," making it difficult to reflect, sleep, or meditate.

SPICE UP YOUR LIFE:
HOW THE INSIGHT DETOX WORKED FOR JANELLE

When I first met Janelle, she was at her wit's end.

"I'm a mess," she told me frankly. "I feel like my brain has just stopped working." And indeed, Janelle had a long list of frustrating symptoms: frequent migraines, sleep issues, memory loss, and a general sense of being foggy and unfocused.

A successful entrepreneur in her early sixties, Janelle worked long, hard hours to keep her business running in a challenging economy. She had been married for forty years to her husband, Edward—"steady Eddie," she called him with a sigh, describing him as "a wonderful man, but after forty years, you know. Not much magic left."

I had some nutritional prescriptions for her. I suggested that she eat a cup of blueberries each day, to benefit from their anthocyanins, a class of antioxidants found in blue-purple foods. As you'll see in what follows, anthocyanins can have a remarkable ability to restore brain health. Other patients had enjoyed significant improvements in memory and focus after increasing their consumption of blue-purple foods, and I expected Janelle to derive similar benefits.

I also recommended that she stop drinking her habitual glass or two of red wine before bed, since that seemed to be disrupting her sleep as well as triggering her headaches. While red wine can have some nutritional benefits, it can be challenging for many people because of the sugar content, alcohol, sulfites, and tannins.

Finally, because Janelle's life seemed so stressful, I suggested she take up meditation. I thought meditation would also help with her migraines, memory problems, and sleep issues.

But what concerned me most about her situation was the sense of boredom and "blah" that underlay the stress. "I feel like life has lost its savor," she said at one point. "When I was younger, everything was so exciting. Now it's as though nothing interesting will ever happen again."

I looked at my notes about her diet. I realized that she had loaded up her daily choices with highly spiced foods, like copious cups of black chai tea; additional infusions of caffeine from coffee, soda, and energy drinks; and lots of chocolate, which also contains caffeine. The excessive caffeine and chocolate were probably triggering headaches and creating sleep issues, and even the spices might have been too stimulating to let her relax and sleep at the end of the day. What struck me, though, was the possibility that she was responding to her sense of "blah" with spicy and stimulating foods. The problem wasn't really with her diet; she needed to spice up her life.

As we talked through these issues, Janelle realized that she had a few more choices than she had previously thought. Although her business required hard work and devotion, she could make the most of her free time by choosing new and interesting activities: a visit to a local Zen temple, a walk in a nearby botanical garden, a daylong whale-watching trip. She could also spice up her marriage by choosing some new activities with her husband.

"Eddie and I loved to visit amusement parks," she told me. "Isn't that silly? Our favorite was the roller coaster." Sharing even the small thrill of a scary ride seemed like the chance to rediscover some of the lost excitement in her marriage. Janelle also decided to take a salsa class with her husband, although initially he wasn't too keen on the idea. Eventually learning some sensual dance moves offered another chance to spice things up and recover the zest in their relationship.

Janelle's situation was a reminder of the power of Whole Detox. Neither the nutritional advice nor the life advice was enough on its own. Janelle needed to choose the right foods and avoid the wrong ones so she could support the biochemistry of her brain. But she also needed to look at the life issues that were driving her food choices, weighing down her thoughts, and draining her emotions. Nutrition, meditation, and life choices all worked together to remove the barriers to Janelle's INSIGHT and restore the savor to her life.

FOODS TO SUPPORT YOUR INSIGHT

INSIGHT-full foods can help clear your head, lift your mood, and give you access to your brain's intuitive capacity. If you're feeling foggy, depressed, unfocused, or anxious, the right foods can help to balance and support your brain:

- Whole foods and a Mediterranean diet (lots of fruits and vegetables, fresh fish, healthy fats, and whole grains) have been shown to reduce cognitive decline and to help the brain regulate energy expenditure, so both brain and body feel energized and strong throughout the day.
- Flavonoid-rich foods significantly reduce anxiety. They actually work in similar ways to the class of relaxants known as benzodiazepines (a type of tranquilizer that includes valium).

- Low-glycemic and low-sugar meals support cognition; by contrast, high-glycemic foods can impair your ability to think, reason, and focus within hours of eating. As we saw earlier, high-glycemic foods also generally lead to excess production of insulin, which can put you at greater risk of dementia over time. A growing number of studies show a close connection between type 2 diabetes and lower cognitive performance, cognitive decline, and/or dementia, suggesting a relationship between high-glycemic foods, excess insulin, and several related challenges to your brain.

- Natural sweeteners, such as raw honey and maple syrup, are the preferred choice. A number of animal studies have suggested a link between artificial sweeteners—particularly aspartame—impaired memory performance, and increased brain oxidative stress.

- Low-heat cooking and steaming help you avoid advanced glycation end products (AGEs), the crispy, crusty parts of food that result from high-heat cooking and frying.

- Low toxin loads from organically grown produce contain more phytonutrients, the vitamins and other nutrients found in plants. These phytonutrients support the health of your entire body, including your brain. And the herbicides and pesticides that cling to nonorganic produce have been shown to disrupt hormonal function and metabolic pathways (creating weight gain).

- Coconut oil has been shown to attenuate the effects of amyloid-beta, a brain-based protein associated with dementia. Coconut oil also seems to support the function of mitochondria, the cells' powerhouses, making coconut oil extremely supportive of brain cell health.

Generally, the more you can reduce inflammation—through both food choices and cooking methods—the more you promote gut and immune health, which in turn creates the biochemicals that your brain needs to generate a calm, optimistic mood and focused, sharp thought.

benzo-like

HIGH-FLAVONOID FOODS THAT HELP REDUCE ANXIETY

- Acai berries
- Arugula
- Bilberries
- Blackberries
- Black raspberries
- Black tea
- Blueberries
- Cacao beans
- Carob flour
- Cocoa, unsweetened
- Concord grapes
- Cranberries
- Currants
- Elderberries
- Green tea
- Kale
- Kumquats
- Mustard greens
- Parsley
- Radicchio
- White tea

Mood-Lifting Foods

Every meal you eat has the ability to put you into an uplifting mood or a downward spiral. The modern Western diet of processed and sugary foods is associated with a negative affect, which can be fearful, upset, nervous, or distressed, whereas a diet based on fresh fruit and vegetables, whole grains, fish, and healthy fats is associated with a positive mood, which can be inspired, alert, excited, enthusiastic, and determined.

Of course, no one diet is right for everyone. But once you're aware of how diet can affect your mood, you can tap into your intuition, your experience, and your knowledge to choose the foods that will best support you.

Sometimes hormonal changes, such as the menstrual cycle, lead us to crave certain foods, most likely in an effort to balance out a deficiency or an excess. Choosing foods that support the sixth system of health can help to balance both mood and hormones. The recipes for these three days of Whole Detox will give you a good start, pointing you toward the consciousness you need to create an effective, seamless dance between food and mood. Throughout Whole Detox, I counsel you away from unhealthy, processed foods, but who knows? Perhaps giving in to an occasional craving might be just what you need once in a while. Harness your intuition, honor your experience, and absorb the nutritional information in this book. Then you'll be able to choose—meal after meal, day after day—the foods that are right for you.

Foods That Contain Caffeine

As I mentioned earlier, caffeinated products (teas, coffee) are not part of Whole Detox. However, I do want to cover some basics about caffeine that you can use after you complete the program. Some people seem to be unaffected by caffeine, while others get jittery and nervous after ingesting it. Caffeine is metabolized in the liver, so if you want to know whether you can tolerate caffeine—and how much—your liver will let you know. Go with your physiological responses initially. If you feel wired for hours after a morning cup of coffee, your liver is a slow metabolizer and caffeine is probably not for you. If moderate amounts of caffeine give you a mental boost and an emotional lift—and if you are sleeping well each night—your liver is probably a fast metabolizer and you can handle and even benefit from some caffeine.

In fact, an increasing body of research suggests that caffeine could have numerous mental benefits. Studies show that it might prevent cognitive decline, reduce the incidence of dementia, and perhaps even be used to treat such neurological conditions as dementia and Parkinson's disease.

Of course, caffeine can have its downside, especially when we consume too much of it. For many people, caffeine disrupts sleep, provokes anxiety, and promotes headaches. However, as your detox continues, your liver becomes stronger and more efficient, and that might also affect your tolerance. On the other hand, too much caffeine can stress your liver, disrupting its ability to detox.

What's your takeaway? Once again, each of us is unique. Some substances—like white sugar and tobacco—are pretty much bad for everyone. Caffeine, though, has more varied effects. So when it comes to caffeine after your twenty-one-day Whole Detox, use both your mind and your intuition to know how much is good for you! And, when in doubt, just stay off it for the most part, having it only on an occasional basis.

Foods That Contain Cocoa

Certain foods lift our mood and maybe even re-create the bliss of being in love. Yes, I'm talking about chocolate, or, more specifically, foods that contain cocoa, which has a remarkable effect on our neurotransmitters and is one of the most powerful psychoactive foods.

What gives cocoa its power? A class of compounds called methylxanthines. The most common of these, theobromine, may work together with caffeine to create an enhanced effect when you consume dark chocolate. To make matters even better, the polyphenols and flavonols in the cacao plant help protect both brain matter and the cardiovascular system. Cocoa also contains flavonoids, a type of antioxidant that can help to open up the blood vessels, lowering blood pressure and inducing relaxation.

As you just read, a certain amount of caffeine can be good for us, stimulating the brain and sharpening our focus. A 1.5-ounce piece of dark chocolate contains 30 milligrams of caffeine—about a third of what you would find in a cup of coffee. Once again, use your own judgment about what relationship to chocolate works for you.

If you do tolerate chocolate, you will love the delicious, unsweetened cocoa-containing recipes in this phase of Whole Detox. After your twenty-one-day detox is over, you can also fight that late-afternoon slump with a small square of dark chocolate, which can help revive your brain and bliss out your mood. I suggest approaching your cocoa/chocolate experience with a clear intention, such as This chocolate is infused with joy or When I have finished this chocolate, I will feel relaxed and joyous. A study by researchers at the Institute of Noetic Sciences found that when people ate chocolate laden with intention, they experienced a better mood than those who ate chocolate with no intentions attached. A similar study, entitled "Metaphysics of the Tea Ceremony," had two groups of participants drink tea twice a day for seven days.

One group's tea had been "treated" with good intentions by three Buddhist monks, while the other group's tea was untreated. The groups were then asked to rate their mood and to indicate which group they thought they had been in. Those who had been given treated tea saw far greater improvements in mood. Those who believed their tea had been treated experienced even greater improvements in mood, but only if they actually *had* been given the treated tea.

If you are going to make hot chocolate, be sure you buy organic cocoa, because the conventional kind is laden with pesticides. Cocoa can also be high in heavy metals, such as lead, cadmium, and nickel, so contact your cocoa manufacturer about the heavy metal levels in their products.

COCOA + COCONUT = BRAIN POWER

Coconut has a number of brain benefits, especially in the form of young coconut water, a delicious drink that you can add to your juices, smoothies, and sauces as well as enjoy fresh. This beverage is full of electrolytes, like potassium, and might even help prevent Alzheimer's disease in menopausal women. Try mixing green tea or blueberry juice with coconut water and adding shredded coconut, flaxseed meal, or nut milks.

For an extra brain boost, mix cocoa and coconut. Both foods are well known for their brain benefits, and they add delicious flavor and texture to frozen treats, smoothies, puddings, and even granola. Mmmm, healthy, tasty fuel for your brain—what more could you ask for?

Foods That Help Your Brain to Remember and Learn

If you're concerned about keeping your brain sharp, these foods can help:

- Omega-3 fatty acids, which are found in wild salmon, flaxseeds, chia seeds, berries, tropical fruits, squash, and walnuts
- Turmeric in powder and raw root forms
- Flavonoids from cocoa, green tea, ginkgo biloba, citrus fruits, red wine, and dark chocolate
- Short-chain saturated fats from foods like coconut oil

- B vitamins, found in plant sources
- Vitamin B12, found in animal sources or taken as a supplement
- High-quality proteins that provide vitamins and minerals for the brain, including nuts, seeds, and whole-grain cereals

Now, at this point you're probably wondering where I stand on red wine after your twenty-one-day Whole Detox, since I suggested that Janelle cut out her late-night habit of having a glass or two. As with caffeine and cocoa, it depends. Some people have bad reactions to all of these substances; others do very well with them; still others have a varied relationship, able to enjoy some quantities of some substances at some times. So, once again, I refer you back to your own intuition. Your body will tell you whether, when, and how much you can consume these mood-altering foods. Just be aware of your body when drinking wine rather than mindlessly drinking—this is often when we get into trouble.

SPICE SAVVY

Turmeric contains a potent anti-inflammatory compound called curcumin. Black pepper contains piperine, an alkaloid with various protective properties. And when these two spices are paired together, there is synergy: more curcumin gets into the body than it does by itself. Try grinding some black pepper and mixing it with turmeric powder. To create a magical trio, add in some fat, like coconut oil or extra-virgin olive oil, because the fat helps the absorption too.

Foods That Contain Healthy Fats

I don't want to call you a "fathead," but I will tell you that about 60 percent of your brain is composed of fat! You want that brain fat to be nourished by the healthiest possible dietary fats, including lots of unsaturated omega-3s. Healthy fats keep your neurotransmitters flowing fluidly, supporting a good, positive mood. Studies have shown that people who are depressed may be influenced by the amount of omega-3 fats in their diet. You can feed your brain more healthy oils as well as magnesium by including more nuts in your meals. For example, blend walnuts with fresh herbs and sea salt to form a crumble and add it on top of salads, soups, and wraps. Don't go nuts—eat nuts!

Some other fabulous fats are the short- and medium-chain triglycerides. Coconut oil seems to have some therapeutic application for people with faulty memory, because it provides them with a suitable energy source when their brain cannot use glucose. Like other food items, however, please don't overdo it; coconut oil should never be your sole source of dietary fat! Make sure that you get the full spectrum of oils available on the market for the different cooking applications and tailored to your Seven Systems of Full-Spectrum Health. As we discussed in the TRUTH chapter, remember that variety is paramount in nutrition. Always shake things up a bit: the spices you use, the oils you cook with, and the vegetables you prepare. Variety helps keep neurons flexible and plastic!

Herbs and Spices: Jewels of the Plant Kingdom

You might recall that we discussed spices in the FIRE chapter, because several spices can help with digestion and warming a meal up for better metabolism. Similarly, we bring in spices here since they connect to brain function too. In fact, perhaps that is no surprise, considering there is a direct link between the gut and the brain (the FIRE and the INSIGHT).

Healing diets in the Mediterranean, India, North Africa, and elsewhere use an abundance of herbs and spices to restore the body and brain: oregano, dill, tarragon, ginger, black peppercorns, rosemary, and turmeric, to name only a few. Herbs and spices have been referred to as the "jewels of the plant kingdom" because they have a multitude of properties that cheer us up, pique our taste buds, and support our health, including anti-inflammatory, anti-cancer, and free-radical-quenching effects.

Even modest amounts of a spice or an herb can have a potent effect on your palate, your body, and your brain. You may not need large amounts to see substantial impact.

Curries are especially good for your brain, because they include curcumin, among other spices. Populations that eat more curry tend to have better scores on cognition tests. That shouldn't surprise us, because curcumin is well recognized for its antioxidant and anti-inflammatory action that reduces the buildup of the protein known as amyloid-beta, which is found in greater concentrations in demented brains. You will see curry and turmeric throughout the Whole Detox recipes so you can benefit from the way these two spices support your body and your mind.

Another healthy spice is <u>cinnamon</u>, which helps your body respond to insulin better (it is referred to as an "<u>insulin sensitizer</u>"). As you've already seen, excess insulin can disrupt brain function and put you at risk for dementia.

So tap into your kitchen pharmacy of herbs and spices! Sprinkle some saffron threads over your favorite dessert. Add a dash of ground cinnamon to your morning coffee. Put some zing in your salads by sprinkling them with crushed herbs and black pepper. Add fresh mint to your tea or a sprinkling of nutmeg on your steamed green beans. Spices can partner well with vegetables, legumes, whole grains, and meats—let your intuition guide you!

BLUE-PURPLE FOODS AND YOUR INSIGHT

As Janelle discovered, berries can have a remarkable power to heal the brain. Animal studies have found that berries—particularly the deep blue-purple kinds—help animals learn and improve their memory. When wild blueberry juice was given to nine older adults with memory changes, they demonstrated improved learning, word recall, and even a trend toward better mood after twelve weeks compared with those who drank a berry placebo beverage.

We used to believe that berries had their brain-healing power simply because they were concentrated antioxidants. And indeed, both berries and purple grapes are excellent sources of several antioxidants. Most notably, you have probably heard of resveratrol, a revered antioxidant in deep blue-purple foods that boosts energy and fights aging through its effects on our metabolic pathways.

Over and above the antioxidant effect, however, berries do support cognitive function. Recent research has shown that blueberries and strawberries influence various types of learning and memory, with berry compounds targeting specific regions of the brain.

Blueberries in particular have extraordinary effects on brain function.

They promote neuronal plasticity; that is, they help the brain change and grow in response to the demands made upon it. The more you make a conscious effort to learn and remember, the more your brain alters in response to this activity, and the tiny blueberry provides chemical support for that response.

Blueberries also have cell-signaling effects; that is, they play a role in how cells respond to inflammation. And they are engaged in the communication between neurotransmitters, the brain chemicals that modulate thought and emotion. Here is just a small sample of the exciting research into blue foods and the brain:

- Blueberries support neuronal and cognitive function, protecting the brain against the effects of aging and stress.
- In animal studies, blueberry extracts seemed to improve spatial memory and possibly helped to reverse age-related cognitive and behavioral decline.
- Concord grape juice seemed to support brain function in older humans, improving memory in those with mild memory decline or other types of cognitive impairment.

SUPPORT YOUR INSIGHT WHILE YOU EAT

- Use your eyes. See the colors of the food you purchase and the food you eat. Give yourself an eyeful before you begin to fill your belly.
- Eat intuitively. The hunches you have about what you need might be wiser than any nutritionist.
- Stay out of ruts. Habits are the enemy of insight and intuition; when you go on autopilot, you aren't really paying attention. Notice your body's signals and let them guide your choice of food.
- Meditate before a meal. It helps you clear the mental clutter and come into a place of peace.
- Notice your mood. See which foods change how you feel—whether they bring you calm, joy, or focus or make you more depressed, anxious, aggressive, wired, or foggy.

SUPPORT YOUR INSIGHT WHILE YOU SLEEP

One of the most important things you can do for your brain is to get lots of healthy, restorative sleep. While everybody needs different amounts of sleep, most of us need between seven and nine hours. You might also find that your need for sleep varies depending on what you're eating, how much exercise you get, and how much stress you're under. Most people underestimate their need for sleep—and most people don't get enough. I strongly urge you to make time for at least nine hours of sleep each night for a week and notice how long you actually sleep. Then commit to getting that much sleep every night.

A sadly common myth is that you can skimp on sleep during the week and then make up for it on the weekend. Unfortunately, our brains don't work that way. They are harmed every time you get insufficient sleep, and you don't restore that harm by sleeping longer one or two days a week.

If you're having trouble getting restorative sleep, completing Whole Detox is likely to help. Here are some suggestions to get you started:

- Cut out stimulants, even early in the day. No caffeinated coffee or tea, no chocolate, and no energy drinks.
- Avoid sweet foods and alcohol, especially after dinner.
- Unplug the electronics—computer, TV, and phone—at least two hours before bedtime.
- Make sure you are sleeping in a dark, cool room with no distractions. Blackout curtains and/or a sleep mask can help you shut out even the tiniest sliver of light, which will deepen your sleep and have you waking up refreshed.
- Invest in a good, comfortable mattress, one that is the right degree of hardness or softness for your taste. Many mattresses are loaded with chemicals and flame retardants, which give off toxic fumes you absorb while you sleep. Make sure you have a nontoxic mattress.

DETOXING YOUR INSIGHT: WHAT TO CHOOSE
- Blue-purple berries, which reduce inflammation in the brain
- Spices like turmeric and curry, which protect the brain from damage
- Deep, quality sleep, which fuels your dreaming and restores and heals your body
- Respect for your intuition through attending to your feelings, mood changes, and dreams
- A journaling practice to capture the wisdom of your inner world

DETOXING YOUR INSIGHT: WHAT TO AVOID
- Foods that disrupt sleep, especially excessive alcohol, caffeine, and processed sugar
- Foods that impair cognition, such as too much processed sugar or high-glycemic-index foods
- Too many stimulants, whether in your food or in your life
- A busy mind cluttered with too many thoughts

ENVISION YOUR INSIGHT

We each have our own unique INSIGHT—and our own unique way of supporting it. For some of us, stimulants are helpful sources of inspiration; others need to avoid stimulants or face anxiety, brain fog, and depression as the brain goes on a roller coaster full of exhausting peaks and crashes. For most of us, there is some kind of happy medium, the degree of stimulation that is helpful to us, although that happy medium might change depending on what kinds of stress we face and what kinds of mental, emotional, and creative demands we encounter.

Likewise, each of us has our own ways of accessing our intuition. Some of us are skilled at understanding the messages in our dreams and even at evoking dreams to tell us what we need to know. Others rely on meditation. Still others seem to know how to find quiet times—a walk, a long shower or bath, a drive in the car—to tune out the chatter of daily life and make a still space for our soft inner voice to speak.

Do you know how your intuition best speaks to you? If you do, I urge you to make enough time for yourself to benefit from this priceless resource. If you do not, I encourage you to explore your relationship with this special part of your being. Supporting your INSIGHT could be the wisdom you need to enhance both your health and your life.

CHAPTER 9

THE SPIRIT

Never underestimate the power of dreams and the influence of the human spirit. We are all the same in this notion: The potential for greatness lives within each of us.

—WILMA RUDOLPH

The new physics provides a modern version of ancient spirituality. In a Universe made out of energy, everything is entangled; everything is one.

—BRUCE LIPTON

UNDERSTANDING THE SPIRIT

Anatomy	Pineal gland, nervous system
Functions	Electromagnetic fields, life force
Living	Cleansing, circadian rhythms, purpose, meaning
Eating	Fasting, cleansing foods, natural white foods

THE SCIENCE OF THE SPIRIT

The SPIRIT as "Energy"

The SPIRIT begins with the life force that animates us into motion and invigorates every cell in our body. That life force goes by many names: cellular intelligence, vitality, chi, qi, prana, perhaps even electricity, which radiates through the network of interlacing nerves that threads through the spinal column out to every square inch of our flesh.

Sometimes the word "energy" is used to evoke the SPIRIT, such as "My energy is off today" or "I could feel the energy in the stadium mount as the home team began to win." That is a popular and unscientific use of the term "energy," yet it evokes a palpable presence that is both invisible and strongly felt. We can feel the energy even though we can't quite define it. And in recent decades, a growing number of scientists have tried to define it.

For some scientists, quantum physics seems to offer a way to grasp the notion of the SPIRIT. Quantum physics is the study of invisible particles involved in an interaction, such as generating a signal or charge. We can't see subatomic particles, but we can measure their effects. Likewise, we can't see the energy we might derive from looking up at the stars or imagining the human family, but is there something real about that energy nonetheless, something that materially affects our bodies and their biochemistry? Is there some force out there—some type of energy—that affects our minds and bodies?

I'm far from the only one asking these questions. This is one of the hottest new domains of physics, and slowly—very slowly—this research is beginning to make its way into modern medicine. Little by little, the notion of an "energetic field" is beginning to gain currency.

The SPIRIT and Light

Another way to explore the SPIRIT is via research into light. Fascinating new studies now reveal that living matter either conserves or releases light, depending on its health state. For example, foods that are decaying or under stress tend to give off more light, as measured in photons (the particles of light). It's as though the stress causes the food to release its vital energies— its light. By contrast, the practice of meditation or relaxation leads to the conservation of light—to the preservation of vital energies.

On some level, we know this intuitively. You can look at a friend—or at yourself in the mirror—and when the person is healthy, you see an almost literal glow. A person who is sick, depressed, or simply exhausted looks duller, more subdued. It is fascinating to imagine that these observations are not simply intuitive readings of facial expression or body language but actual perceptions of the amount of light being emitted.

Slowly but surely this insight into light and photon emission, too, is entering conventional medicine. Light medicine therapies are now finding their way into mainstream medical offices, with lasers of red, green, or blue light being used to achieve a wide variety of medical goals.

The SPIRIT and Electromagnetic Fields

Yet another approach to the SPIRIT is to consider electromagnetic fields (EMFs), invisible but potent clouds of charged particles that both respond to the environment and affect it. These fields can be sensed and measured, but not seen.

Some electromagnetic fields seem to help reduce pain and inflammation, with beneficial effects on such conditions as osteoarthritis, fibromyalgia, depression, and high blood pressure. Others may be harmful to human (and animal) health, particularly the ones emitted by high-voltage power lines and possibly also the cumulative effects of EMFs from appliances, electronic equipment, and the environmental effects of electrical production, telecommunications, and broadcasting.

Over the past two decades, our exposure to these fields has skyrocketed, as we surround ourselves with computers, cell phones, and other forms of electronics that are with us night and day, not to mention the environmental increase of power stations, broadcast facilities, cell phone towers, and Wi-Fi. While electromagnetism in small doses might actually have positive effects, as seen with pulsed electromagnetic field (PEMF) therapy, some scientists believe that this massive and continuous exposure increases our risk of cancer and other serious disorders. Moreover, the twenty-four-hour electronic daylight disrupts our circadian rhythms and has been shown to interfere with healthy sleep.

The flickering blue light of our computer screens disrupts the pineal gland and interferes with our production of melatonin, the hormone that makes us sleepy and keeps us in deep, restful sleep. Melatonin puts us to sleep, while cortisol, the stress hormone, wakes us up. An overexposure to electronics, especially after sundown, disrupts our melatonin–cortisol balance and plays havoc with our sleep patterns.

EMFs, meanwhile, potentially disrupt the tiny electrical currents that activate our biochemistry. Much of human anatomy, including the heart, is dependent upon electricity. Exposure to external sources of electricity—especially given how much of it we are exposed to—could disrupt our internal electrical "wiring."

POTENTIAL SOURCES OF EMFs

- Household and office wiring
- High-tension electric cables and towers
- Electric power lines
- Substations, transformers
- Radio and television transmission towers
- Cell phone masts/towers
- Cell phones
- Bluetooth and headphone devices
- Cordless phones, baby monitors
- Wi-Fi routers and wireless devices
- Wi-Fi hot spots
- Computers, laptops
- Microwave ovens
- Electric clocks, razors, blankets, hair dryers
- Fluorescent and compact fluorescent lighting
- Airport radar and telecommunication equipment
- Airport body scanners
- Military radars, radio frequencies, and extreme low frequencies
- Smart meters

EMFs affect humans in a variety of ways, depending on the type of field. Scientists have found some correlation between EMFs and a number of disorders, including childhood and adult leukemia, neurodegenerative diseases (such as amyotrophic lateral sclerosis, or ALS), miscarriage, and clinical depression although the results are inconclusive.

NEGATIVE EFFECTS OF EMFs

- A meta-analysis investigating studies published on EMFs between 1993 and 2007 showed slight increases for risk in brain cancer and leukemia compared with past studies.
- A meta-analysis conducted in 2008 by *Occupational and Environmental Medicine* analyzed a huge body of research and concluded that "EMFs may have a small impact on human attention and working memory."
- A 2006 study entitled "Mobile Phone Emissions and Human Brain Excitability" discovered that cell phones do significantly affect human brain excitability.
- Another study from the same year found a correlation between geomagnetic storm activity and the rates of suicide, suggesting that "perturbations in ambient electromagnetic field activity impact behaviour in a clinically meaningful manner. The study furthermore raises issues regarding other sources of stray electromagnetic fields and their effect on mental health."

However, as I touched on earlier, a particular type of EMF—a *pulsing* electromagnetic field (PEMF)—seems to offer exciting new benefits for people with chronic diseases. Here's a quick sampling of this research:

POSITIVE EFFECTS OF PEMF THERAPY

- A 2014 study in *Biological Psychiatry* found "rapid mood-elevating effects" resulted from low-field magnetic stimulation of subjects with depression.
- Another 2014 study discovered that PEMF therapy could be helpful when administered to patients with shoulder impingement syndrome.
- A 2013 study concluded that PEMF treatment "might be linked to improvements in peripheral resistance or circulation."
- In 2009, an article in the *Clinical Journal of Pain* found that low-frequency PEMF therapy "might improve function, pain, fatigue, and global status in [fibromyalgia] patients."
- A study reported in the *Journal of Alternative and Complementary Med-*

icine in 2009 reported that magnetic field therapy, specifically Bio-Electro-Magnetic-Energy-Regulation (BEMER), had beneficial effects on the energy levels and other functioning of patients with multiple sclerosis.

- A 2009 study conducted in India suggests that PEMF therapy might be a viable treatment for arthritis.

So, what should we conclude?

First, I think it's significant that PEMFs offer an unseen and yet powerful way of treating a number of chronic disorders that don't have good conventional treatments, including autoimmune conditions like fibromyalgia, multiple sclerosis, and arthritis. The potential benefit of PEMF therapies suggests that work with the SPIRIT offers an exciting new frontier in medical practice.

At the same time, I can't believe that constant overexposure to EMFs is good for us. I can't give you a definitive answer here, but I can give you my best recommendation, which is to reduce your exposure as much as you can. Every few months, do a "techno detox": unplug all electrical appliances, giving yourself a break both from electromagnetism and from the constant barrage of demands on your attention—even a day off periodically might make a difference. At the very least, your SPIRIT will benefit from the peace and quiet of uninterrupted living.

The SPIRIT and the Endocrine System

Grounding the SPIRIT in the body is our pineal gland, which distinguishes between light and dark, day and night, sunlight and moonlight. The pineal gland is the part of our brain that responds to light, and it may be involved in seasonal affective disorder (SAD), the depression that can result from insufficient exposure to light during the winter months.

Significantly, when the pineal is nourished with sufficient doses of bright light, SAD may ease or even dissipate altogether. Clearly this intangible—light, made only of photons—nonetheless has an important role in nourishing our physical selves. Since white is the color associated with the seventh system of health, I find it fascinating that bright white light is so healing to the pineal gland. (For more on white light and its medical uses, see "The Power of White," page 204.)

On the other hand, if your pineal gland is exposed to white light at the wrong time of day—if you see bright white light during the nighttime hours or have your sleep broken with bright light—it is prevented from producing sufficient quantities of melatonin, a hormone that helps regulate our sleep–wake cycle and is also an integral antioxidant.

People who don't get enough melatonin often develop health problems. For example, female shift workers tend to have greater rates of breast cancer, perhaps because they are working at night and sleeping during the day—exactly the opposite of what our bodies evolved to do. And indeed, cancer cells appear to proliferate in the absence of melatonin, while melatonin's protective effects seem to be extinguished by short-term exposure to bright white light at night. Ideally, you'll follow the rhythms of nature, but taking melatonin supplements, wearing a sleep mask, and darkening your room as much as possible can help reduce stress on your system during late nights and travel.

When your circadian rhythms are in sync with the planet's cycle of light, you can more readily maintain a sense of vitality and renewal. And when you feel "off," unbalanced, out of sync, out of sorts, it's often the seventh system that needs some support. Maybe you need more time in the sunlight (low vitamin D has become a widespread epidemic). Perhaps you need a darker room in which to sleep. Or perhaps you need some time to reflect on your life's purpose—the reason you get up in the morning, the relationships and commitments that get you through the day. As we have seen throughout this book, bringing together the different dimensions of a system can have transformative effects. The same is true of the seventh system, with its components of pineal gland, circadian rhythms, meaning, and purpose.

The SPIRIT and Well-Being

Fundamental to the notion of the SPIRIT is the profound connectedness that links us with all other humans and, indeed, all forms of life. It is this feeling of connection and integration that gives us our sense of purpose and meaning: because we are part of something larger than ourselves, what we do *matters*. And evidence shows that healing outcomes are dramatically improved among people who experience a deep connection with others or who believe strongly in some kind of greater purpose. This outlook seems to be particularly important for those with life-threatening diseases, including cancer.

Traditional religion is one way to access this larger sense of connectedness and purpose—but only one. Meditation, walking in nature, or any experience that takes you out of yourself can be an opportunity to feel that connection and enjoy its health benefits. You can dwell within the SPIRIT through the simple act of looking up at a nighttime sky in awe at how immense our universe is, or snorkeling in the ocean to discover the divine mystery of a whole other world that lives below us. Humans seem to have an innate attraction to being part of a greater whole, which is why Whole Detox is essential. Zooming out to see our lives from a distant vantage point—our place in the grandest possible scheme of things—will ultimately help us to zoom in and address any toxic barriers that keep us from becoming our fullest and most satisfying selves.

A growing body of research has demonstrated the links between mental health and spiritual awareness. For example, a 2014 Brazilian study found a correlation among patients undergoing dialysis. While "the stress of living with a terminal disease has a negative effect on . . . mental health," the researchers found that spiritual well-being was "the strongest predictor of mental health." Significantly, those dialysis patients who experienced that connection were also likely to sleep better and to have less psychological distress.

THE POWER OF WHITE

Throughout this book, we've explored the specific attributes of each color of the rainbow. White light, however, contains all the colors of the spectrum, much like the SPIRIT includes the entire spectrum of our lives and life itself.

Significantly, white light seems to be therapeutic in treating various types of depression. The SPIRIT is all about connection, and I view depression as the condition of being disconnected—from your emotions, from the people you love, from the web of life itself. It will be interesting to see what further research discovers about the benefits of white light, but here's a quick rundown of some of its successes so far:

- In 2011, a team of Swiss researchers found that five weeks of bright white light treatment improved depression during pregnancy.
- A 2001 study published in the *Journal of Investigative Medicine* revealed that bright light could be used to treat "circadian phase disturbances"—that is, irregular wakefulness and sleepiness—among the elderly.
- In 2011 Dutch psychiatric researchers found that both blue-enriched white light and bright white light might possibly be effective in treating SAD.
- Furthermore, a 2004 Danish study affirmed that bright light could perhaps be a helpful treatment even in *nonseasonal* depression when used in conjunction with antidepressants.
- A University of California, San Diego, study also found that bright light therapy combined with antidepressants and "wake therapy" could be effective in treating depression. Wake therapy is basically waking up depressed patients on the theory that too much sleep makes the depression worse. As you can see, there are close links between depression, light, and circadian rhythms—as you might expect from the themes of the seventh system—but we are only beginning to develop the research to fully understand them.
- Even bulimia nervosa might benefit from light therapy, according to a 1994 article published in the *American Journal of Psychiatry*. Some bulimics feel worse and binge more during the winter months, but the study found that "bright white light therapy [might possibly be] . . . an effective short-term treatment for both mood and eating disturbances associated with bulimia nervosa."

Would *you* like to benefit from the power of white? Spend at least ten minutes each day outdoors in the sunlight, or if you live in a wintry, cloudy climate, invest in a full-spectrum lamp and spend ten minutes a day basking in its glow. Immersion in full-spectrum light will help adjust your circadian rhythms, ground you on the planet, and support your nervous system.

GET TO KNOW YOUR SPIRIT

Although it can be challenging to define the SPIRIT, I'd like to suggest a few elements of this crucial system of health. Indeed, many of my nonreligious patients are surprised to discover that they do in fact have a fulfilling spiritual connection, and this connection sustains them in their efforts to cope with health and life challenges.

One aspect of the SPIRIT is the sense of *connectedness*: to all humanity, to our planet, to the universe itself. This bond extends outward to these grand dimensions, but it also extends inward, to a sense of the tiniest atomic particles and the deepest, most inward thoughts.

This connectedness can be a great comfort, especially in times of sorrow. When we feel lonely, hurt, or rejected, our sense of SPIRIT can remind us that we are never truly alone, that we are always a beloved member of the human family, kin to all living creatures, woven into the fabric of the universe. The sense of a human family inspired heroes like Nelson Mandela, who survived three decades in prison because his relationship to a larger world gave purpose and meaning to his plight.

Purpose and *meaning* fall under the SPIRIT, as they sustain us throughout life's challenges. Purpose—the sense that we are pursuing something larger than ourselves—gives us the motivation to continue when the going gets tough. Meaning—the sense that there is a reason, a value, to our efforts—gives savor to both good times and bad, so that we become larger than ourselves.

The challenge of this openness to the world, however, is that we can become overwhelmed by the pain and misery that is so prevalent on our planet. If I feel truly connected to all humanity, how can I enjoy my dinner when I am keenly aware that others are starving? How can I eat a living creature that perhaps was raised and slaughtered in pain? How can I find peace, joy, and meaning on a planet whose air and water and soil are slowly being poisoned? Feeling overwhelmed by the world's sorrows can lead some people to shut down, willing to disconnect rather than to feel the pain of connection.

These are not easy issues, and I don't pretend to have the answers. What I will say is that both scientific research and my own clinical experience show me the undeniable value of a spiritual life, whether you find that life through meditation, family, community, politics, religion, science, or any other means. If a scientist marvels at the intricacy of the atomic structure and the vastness of the ever-expanding universe, that sense of awe and wonder provides a gratifying sense of the SPIRIT, as much as the mystic who speaks to a Higher Power, the activist who plugs into history, the artist who is devoted to their creations, or the individual who simply savors a quiet walk in the woods. Although opening to the larger world can be painful, it also transforms our anatomy, flooding our body with relaxation chemicals, awakening us to our own possibilities, and giving us a reason to live.

If this notion appeals to you, I invite you to look for where the SPIRIT appears in your life and, if necessary, to unfold your daily life into more spiritual opportunities. Meditate. Spend some quiet time in a beautiful place, indoors or outdoors. Plunge into an activity you find absorbing, that takes you out of yourself. Open yourself to the possibility of connectedness and allow yourself to be refreshed, in body as well as SPIRIT.

When you balance your inner world with the outer, your reward is an increase in harmony and health. Medical researchers Dr. Nicholas Christakis at Yale University and Dr. James Fowler at the University of California, San Diego, have demonstrated the scientific validity of what they call being "connected." Their research suggests that our connections to other people can have a powerful effect on our body weight, our eating habits, and our happiness. That's the exact message of the seventh system of health: none of us is only an individual. Rather, we are the sum of all our precious connections, to our social networks and to our environment.

BALANCE YOUR SPIRIT

Of all the challenges in balancing each system, perhaps the trickiest to navigate is balancing the SPIRIT. How do we balance being grounded firmly in our body, on this planet, in the present moment, and also feel the pull of dissolving into the SPIRIT, into infinity and eternity?

And yet, as anyone who meditates will attest, it is this balance—this partaking of both body and SPIRIT, both now and forever, both here and everywhere—that can refresh the SPIRIT, rekindle our purpose, and keep us facing life's challenges with serenity and strength. During good times, we can plunge fully into the pleasures of the moment—while remaining aware that they will not last forever and we should savor them to the fullest while we can. During bad times, we can honor our grief—while knowing that "this too shall pass" and we are part of a larger whole that can sustain us through our individual sorrows.

This type of balance is not easy to attain, but it can ground and stabilize

us even while it helps us rise into the airy realms of the SPIRIT. Review the following descriptions of a SPIRIT that is balanced, underactive, or overactive, and consider what balance looks like for you.

A person with a healthy SPIRIT
- is both grounded in earthly matters and open to the spiritual nature of their life;
- appreciates a spiritual orientation to their life;
- is aware of their body's needs, their individual growth, and the larger world;
- knows how to put spirituality into perspective in their life, equally integrating it with other areas of living;
- makes time for meditation, prayer, or simply opening to the silence;
- feels connected with all of life but is not overwhelmed by the world's misery;
- sees everything in life as a divine lesson, but is not preoccupied or doctrinaire;
- is aware of others' states of being;
- has a strong sense of the meaning and purpose in their life;
- reflects upon the meaning of life;
- is seen as peaceful, humble, and thoughtful;
- is free from chronic, severe neurological complaints;
- is generally vital;
- is open to the use of energy medicine and other techniques for healing;
- is aware of their surroundings and moderately but not overly affected by them;
- feels connected to both their physical body and their spiritual self;
- is in generally good health;
- eats the right amount of food for their body and rarely forgets to eat;
- lives and eats based on an awareness of their interconnection with all of life;
- sees eating as a beautiful, divine miracle that nourishes body and soul; and
- will eat organically grown foods when possible.

A person with an underactive SPIRIT

- is relatively insensitive to their internal and external environments;
- feels connected to the physical body and disconnected from the soul;
- might appear overly gruff and judgmental;
- doesn't connect with people well;
- is not particularly drawn to natural settings;
- expresses doubt about the existence of something greater than themselves or a divine presence;
- is not especially interested in spiritual issues;
- sees life more as work or a chore than as a meaningful, special experience;
- lacks faith in others and themselves;
- sees life as physical and for our physical enjoyment, even to the point of excess;
- acts more than reflects;
- lacks a sense of purpose or calling;
- might feel lost or lonely;
- is unconcerned with toxins in food and regularly eats foods known to be toxic;
- tends to overeat rather than undereat and enjoys indulgent meals;
- might eat in response to toxic emotions and thoughts;
- has a dull sense of pain or is impervious to pain;
- might be numb or have dulled sensations; or
- is not fond of energy medicine modalities: has an "If I can see it, I believe it" mentality.

A person with an overactive SPIRIT

- might be acutely sensitive to pain;
- might suffer from neurological issues, such as tremors, epilepsy, neuropathy, pain, or Parkinson's disease;
- is drawn toward energy medicine modalities;
- is extremely sensitive—maybe even hypersensitive—to everything in the environment;
- feels detached from their physical body;

- might have let their health suffer due to neglect;
- might appear ungrounded, flighty, fragmented, or like someone who lives in their own world;
- is so concerned with spirituality that their bodily needs may be neglected;
- enjoys spending much of their time in meditation or prayer;
- feels so connected to all life and the planet that they are affected by everything;
- is overly sensitive to others' states of being;
- sees everything in life as divine and as a lesson to be learned;
- sees everything they encounter as full of meaning and purpose;
- is strongly purpose driven, to the point of being overly narrow and controlled by their mission rather than truly living it;
- spends time preoccupied with deep reflection on the meaning of life;
- might be overly concerned with toxins in food and will choose only organically grown foods;
- might be obsessed with cleanliness and purity;
- might have a large number of food sensitivities;
- might forget to eat; or
- sticks to simple meals, often not involving pleasure or joy.

BALANCE BODY AND SPIRIT:
HOW THE SPIRIT DETOX WORKED FOR MY PATIENTS

My patients' experiences make clear how challenging it can be to balance the SPIRIT—and how rewarding. Here are three examples of how detoxing the SPIRIT can transform a person's health—and their life.

Lucy was suffering from ulcerative colitis when she came to me. Her vitamin D was low and she had excessively high levels of her homocysteine and high-sensitivity C-reactive protein—all indicators of serious inflammation.

I knew that any conventional nutritionist would focus on Lucy's diet and intestinal health, prescribing probiotics to replenish her intestinal bacteria, glutamine to repair her gut wall, and supplements to support her immune system and bring down inflammation. And surely, I believed that the right foods and supplements would help her. But I didn't think they were enough.

Lucy struck me as someone who felt a bit lost or adrift. There was a vague, helpless quality to the way she described herself and her symptoms, but I felt that a ravaging anger was simmering underneath. When I asked her about her childhood, that anger began to seep through.

She told me that her mother had been ill with breast cancer all through Lucy's childhood and had died when Lucy was just fourteen. It fell to Lucy to be "the little mother" to her two younger brothers. Although she frequently felt inadequate to the challenge of being a parent, the one thing she could do, she told me, was cook for her family. "That was the one time I felt like I had anything to give." I was struck by the way she believed she could give material things—hot meals and nourishing food—but not spiritual or emotional nourishment.

Lucy told me, she did indeed feel adrift now, purposeless. It was as though her life had stopped when her mother's did, as though it had fallen to her to fulfill her mother's role at an age when she had been far too young to do so. I wondered if she felt disconnected from the SPIRIT, able to focus only on the physical, a choice that might have seemed the only option when she was young but was costing her dearly now.

When Lucy completed her Whole Detox Spectrum Quiz—the seven-part form that by now you have completed too—the area that came up extremely low was the SPIRIT. I knew that if I only worked with her on diet and supplements, I would be shortchanging her. She might get a little bit better, but without addressing the seventh system of health, she would never be truly well.

She and I had many long talks about finding purpose and meaning, about tapping into something larger than the body and the mundane tasks that needed doing to keep the body alive. Slowly and reluctantly, she began to take a yoga class and attend a meditation workshop. To her great surprise, she enjoyed this other way of relating to her body and she found the meditation far more satisfying than she had expected. "It's as though I've been thirsty all my life and finally someone handed me a glass of water" is how she put it to me.

Now Lucy is looking at what kind of life she truly wants—what work will satisfy her, what relationships will bring her joy. "I still don't have any of the answers," she told me in our last appointment, "but at least I've finally started to ask the questions."

———

Nathan was a once-vigorous man in his early thirties, prematurely gray and wrinkled. A night manager at an all-night restaurant, he was used to starting work at ten P.M. and going to bed at ten A.M. This "reverse life" wore on him, and his diet didn't help: it was full of sweet and starchy "quick energy" foods that he felt he needed to keep him going.

When he came to me, we talked about the well-established toll that shift work takes on the human body. Our bodies are meant to connect to the planet in a profound way, awake when the sun is up and asleep when the sky is dark. Violating this relationship can seriously disrupt a person's health.

Nathan began to realize that his night work was destroying his health. He got a job with normal hours and struggled to establish a more regular day–night pattern. Getting in tune with his circadian rhythms made a world of difference for him. He lost his belly fat, got his energy back, and felt ten years younger.

———

Magda was a tall, thin woman who was struggling with a severe case of asthma. When I met her, I thought she was almost too thin; there was a gaunt, starved look about her, and indeed, she told me she often forgot to eat or simply "didn't feel like it." She wasn't anorexic and she had never been diagnosed with an eating disorder; she just wasn't very interested in food.

The more we talked, the more I thought Magda fit the profile of someone with an overactive SPIRIT. She seemed almost obsessed with turning everything into a lesson or an occasion to "practice being my higher self." She worried continually about suffering children, abused animals, the destruction of natural habitats, feeling each story as though it were happening to her.

I admired her intense spiritual commitment. But I was concerned that her focus on the SPIRIT appeared to come at the expense of her body. I thought that small, regular meals would help her to feel grounded—rooted. (Yes, we've come full circle, from the SPIRIT to the ROOT!) I also thought that a steady, reliable source of high-fiber, healthy food, with lots of fresh fruits and vegetables ("the fruits of the earth"), would help to soothe the anxiety that so often triggered her asthma and would give her a solid, strong home for her overactive SPIRIT.

Magda saw her spiritual connection as the foundation for her life, but she agreed that maybe it was time for a bit of balance. She decided to take a class in West African dance—a physical, grounded form of movement that was also a way of celebrating the SPIRIT with every fiber of her body. Losing herself in dance was a spiritual experience for her, but it was also a way to relate more fully to her body and to feel love for her muscles, bones, and sinews as well as the less physical parts of herself. Dancing brought her a profound joy that balanced the sorrow she felt for the suffering planet.

Of course, I also suggested dietary changes and several supplements for Magda, and I know they helped alleviate her asthma and restore her immune system (asthma reflects a severely challenged immune system). But, as with Lucy and Nathan, just looking at food and supplements would have been only a partial solution. We are whole beings, and we need a whole detox—an approach that speaks to every single one of our Seven Systems of Full-Spectrum Health. When my patients removed their seventh-system barriers, their detox took a great leap forward, and their health took off.

FOOD TO FEED THE SPIRIT

Whatever your notion of the SPIRIT, I invite you to think about the ways in which something in you seems to reach beyond your immediate circumstances to more meaningful relationships—with your family, your community, your planet. I invite you as well to consider the ways that "SPIRIT-filled" foods can boost your health and inspire your life.

Cleansing Foods

The SPIRIT is about purification and clarification—getting clear of the physical fray so we can focus on what is really important. In detox, this means getting clear of any "noise" that interferes with our system—any preservatives, toxins, or problem foods that disrupt our body's harmony and keep us from feeling clear.

As a result, I place an even greater emphasis on cleansing foods as we venture into the SPIRIT. Of course, our bodies are meant to cleanse themselves—not unlike a self-cleaning oven! But we live in a world with such an enormous toxic burden that sometimes we need to give them a little help. Even before we are born, we take on some toxicity from our mother's toxic burden, and our own toxic burden only grows from there, thanks to pollution, unhealthy foods, and lack of activity.

Let's turn that process around! Lay down your toxic burden and shed the toxic barriers that are holding you back. To achieve this noble mission, however, you need the help of your primary detox organ: the liver.

Feed your liver with such herbs as milk thistle as well as with the spectrum of compounds in whole plant foods. In particular, alkalizing greens (such as parsley, fennel, kale, and cilantro), lemon, and sesame products (such as tahini) help the liver do its job. For the gut, insoluble fiber is ideal for sweeping toxins out of the body, via nonstarchy vegetables, berries, and legumes. You won't believe how good these cleansing foods can make you feel!

THE BODY AS A WHOLE: THE MANY PATHS OF TOXIN EXCRETION

- *Breathing:* Deep breathing or vigorous aerobic activity helps to expel toxins from your lower lungs.
- *Defecating:* Voiding the bowels at least once a day rids your body of waste and eliminates all the toxins that go with it. Ideally, you should be clearing your bowels two or three times a day.

- *Urinating:* Passing toxins through the urine we expel is another way to detox. But if the kidneys are stressed by environmental toxins and an unhealthy diet, they won't do an optimal job of getting rid of the daily burden of poison our food and environment thrust upon us.
- *Sweating:* Perspiration allows you to release toxins through your pores. But if your skin is layered with too many personal care products, and if you aren't exerting yourself enough to break a sweat, you miss out on this opportunity for detox.

Intermittent Fasting

Our bodies need food to restore and replenish themselves. But paradoxically, intermittent fasting can actually help your cells revitalize and rejuvenate. Occasionally depriving your cells of food—say, for twelve to sixteen hours at a time one day a week—can support better function of the mitochondria, the powerhouse that generates energy for the cells. Food restriction also helps your body lower the rate of cellular death.

Fasting of this type can significantly improve metabolic efficiency. You don't need as much sleep and your body begins to need less food. It's as though you're practicing, one day a week, for a time when you need no food at all and can live entirely on the SPIRIT.

As long as we live and breathe, occasionally going without food can actually be good for the body as well as the SPIRIT. Here's a small sampling of research on the benefits of fasting and calorie restriction:

Prolonged fasting seems to reduce levels of a hormone called IGF-1 (insulin-like growth factor–1), a substance that contributes to aging and perhaps to some cancers. Researchers believed that by reducing IGF-1, fasting contributed to cell renewal and regeneration.

Similar research found that fasting supported stem cell regeneration. We used to believe that stem cells were irreversibly destroyed by the aging process. Apparently, calorie restriction helps to reverse the effects of aging.

Fasting seemed to improve the mood of depressed and aging men. Researchers observed "significant decreases in tension, anger, confusion, and total mood disturbance and improvements in vigor."

DETOX SUPERSTARS

Detox superstars help the liver in multiple ways, through all the phases of detox. These foods include pomegranate, green tea, curcumin, cruciferous vegetables, and artichoke hearts. And medicinal mushrooms like reishi should be incorporated into some regular meals for their immune-modulating ability.

Make sure to give your mushrooms and vegetables their daily dose of light. Exposing cut, sliced mushrooms to sunlight increases their vitamin D content. Vegetables actually have their own circadian rhythms, so placing them in contact with sunlight rather than leaving them in a dark refrigerator promotes the formation of phytonutrients, according to a recent study.

Pure Foods

As you rid your physical body of toxins and debris, you strengthen it to allow for more openness to your SPIRIT. One way to lessen your toxic burden is to avoid taking it on in the first place! To support your SPIRIT, stay away from foods that have been contaminated with artificial ingredients or additives, including artificial sweeteners, dyes, preservatives, and coloring. When we load ourselves up with these synthetic ingredients, we challenge the nervous system, which is really quite sensitive and one of the first body systems to be impacted by toxin burden. If your nervous system is challenged in this way, you might develop neurological symptoms: headaches, hyperactivity, and the inability to focus on a task.

Instead, aim for clean, pure food: organically grown fruits and vegetables, meat from free-range animals, and wild-caught fish. Both your body and your SPIRIT will be relieved.

Clarifying Broths

The detox process gives your organs a chance to heal and restore, so look for foods that won't tax them unduly. Broths are easy to digest, nourishing, and soothing—an ideal support for a weary SPIRIT. Additionally, broths tend to be alkalizing due to the presence of electrolytes from vegetables, so they will help your body to naturally detox through a gentle shift in pH.

WASH YOUR ORGANIC VEGETABLES!

Even organically grown produce needs to be washed—and thoroughly. And thick-skinned fruits—avocados, oranges, lemons, limes—need to be washed so any residue from growing or transport is kept out of your kitchen. Get a U-shaped vegetable brush—they don't cost much—and scrub away the waxes, pesticides, insecticides, and herbicides that so frequently coat food. Make sure you rinse the brush well, and replace it or disinfect it with a white vinegar rinse every two to three months. Buy a brush with natural bristles and a wooden handle so you can recycle it when you're ready to replace it.

WHITE FOODS AND YOUR SPIRIT

By this time, you know when I say "white," I don't mean white rice, white flour, and certainly not white sugar. I'm talking about foods that are naturally white, not pale as the result of their natural fiber being processed away. The white color in refined foods indicates that the food has been drained of its life force—so how could it ever nourish you?

It never ceases to amaze me how our food culture strips bountiful nutrients away from foods that were already perfect in nature and then adds human inventions like preservatives. Why not leave the foods in their delicious, healthy, natural state? Are we trying to outwit Mother Nature? Do we actually think we can improve upon the original food?

Healthy, whole, white foods help cleanse and clarify the seventh system. Think ripe pears (especially good for moistening the lungs), cauliflower (cleanses the liver), coconut products (good, accessible energy sources for your intestines), onions and garlic (cleanse the blood and liver), cabbage (cleanses the liver and, when fermented, is excellent for the gut), and white beans (high in fiber).

SUPPORT YOUR SPIRIT WHILE YOU EAT

- Invite your SPIRIT to the table. Take a few moments to meditate, to feel gratitude, or to think about the purpose of this meal (to replenish your body, prepare you for a challenging task, share time with loved ones).

- See the cosmos in your plate. Your food began as a seed, planted in a field, tended by a caring farmer and workers, bathed in sunlight and moonlight, and visited by a multitude of insects. The seed transformed into a vegetable, which was eventually picked by someone's loving hand and then transported to a store or farmers' market. Someone chose the vegetable and then prepared it—perhaps you or someone at the restaurant where you ate. Savor the interrelationships that come along with the food.

- Get some exposure to the sun (indirectly or directly). The healing power of the sun is immense; it radiates and provides nourishment to all life. Before eating, allow your plateful of food to bask in the sun for a couple of minutes so it becomes invigorated with the high photonic energy of solar radiance. If you, too, bathe in the sun, even for a short time, you'll boost your body's production of vitamin D.

- Breathe deeply. Oxygen is the major component your body uses to access the energy in the glucose molecule, and every cell in your body depends upon glucose. Moreover, breathing into the low belly rather than shallowly helps to clear the body of toxins while delivering the raw material to burn food for energy. As you breathe, imagine yourself harnessing all the energy within the food.

- Experience love. The more we consume it, the more it grows, enabling others to be fed. The more love we are able to receive, the more we feed both the SPIRIT and the body. Enjoy love in all its many facets: love of the self, of others, of nature, of the planet, of whatever you perceive as larger than yourself.

- Cleanse your environment. Allow yourself to notice the people, situations, places, tasks, and events that are toxic for you—that create barriers to your total health and fulfillment. Then do whatever you can to remove or avoid these environmental toxins.

RESTORE YOUR SPIRIT WITH ENERGY MEDICINE

Energy medicine is recognized by the National Center for Complementary and Alternative Medicine, which is part of the National Institutes of Health. Although for years this approach to healing was scorned by conventional practitioners, energy medicine is now rapidly gaining acceptance within hospitals, clinics, and institutes. For example, many premier cancer centers now offer acupuncture and other alternatives to supplement conventional treatments. As a matter of fact, I would say that "alternative" medicine is not alternative anymore!

ENERGY MEDICINE THAT ADDRESSES THE SPIRIT

- Acupuncture
- Distant healing
- Flower essences
- Healing Touch
- Homeopathy
- Qigong
- Reiki
- Tai chi

As interest in energy medicine has grown, so has research into various alternative techniques. So far, much of the research is inconclusive, but some intriguing studies and some promising results suggest that addressing the SPIRIT in the form of energy may have significant effects.

In a 2009 study conducted at Kaiser Permanente, the giant Californian health-care organization, a group of people were offered treatment by Healing Touch, which, as the name suggests, involves the transfer of healing energy from a certified practitioner's hands. Many participants found that the frequency, intensity, or duration of the pain lessened after only a few treatments, and, perhaps even more important, they also "experienced profound shifts in their view of themselves, their lives, and their potential for healing and transformation." The researchers concluded that "energy healing can be an important addition to pain management services." Other research has found that Healing Touch can reduce pain in older adults, improve pain and mobility in people with arthritis, and soothe pain for those suffering from spinal cord injuries. Healing Touch might even have some effect upon the symptoms of cancer.

Another form of energy medicine is Reiki, a Japanese healing practice that involves being touched on the skull, shoulders, chest, and back. Numerous studies have suggested that Reiki creates health benefits, including relaxation, improvement in symptoms, prevention of symptoms, better mood, greater well-being, and a decrease in salivary cortisol levels, indicating a reduction in stress. Some research indicates that Reiki changes the functioning of an autonomic nervous system—the part of the nervous system that produces stress and relaxation responses—shifting the balance from unhealthy stress to a healthier state of relaxation.

Perhaps the most well-studied form of energy medicine is acupuncture, a centuries-old Chinese practice that involves stimulating energy pathways (meridians) with tiny needles. Dozens of published studies indicate acupuncture's effectiveness in treating chronic pain as well as many other conditions.

I find the emerging field of energy medicine to be quite exciting, especially for those domains in which conventional medicine has not been entirely effective, such as relieving chronic pain. The success of these therapies is yet another indication of the power of the SPIRIT, and the necessity of incorporating the SPIRIT into our quest for health.

DETOXING YOUR SPIRIT: WHAT TO CHOOSE

- Rest and rejuvenation for a wired nervous system
- A sense of awe regarding something larger than yourself: nature, the human family, the cosmos, or whatever moves you
- Regular cleansing practices
- Bright white light in your living space
- Peaceful contemplation and reflection on your life's calling or your path
- Quality time in nature: in a forest, on a beach, in the mountains, in the desert

DETOXING YOUR SPIRIT: WHAT TO AVOID

- Disruptive electromagnetic fields
- Activities that change subtle nerve function, such as too much use of your computer or cell phone
- Overeating or forgetting to eat
- Disruptions in your sleep–wake cycle
- Anything that causes physical pain
- Situations that make you chronically nervous

CONNECT TO YOUR SPIRIT

One of the most helpful books I've ever read was Dan Buettner's *The Blue Zones: 9 Lessons for Living Longer from the People Who've Lived the Longest*. Buettner decided to search the planet for the healthiest, longest-lived people and figure out what their secret was. Not surprisingly, the nine healthiest communities he identified ate clean, natural food; lots of fresh fruits and vegetables; significant amounts of healthy fats; and low amounts of animal proteins. They tended to be vigorous and physically active as well.

Perhaps more surprisingly to people used to thinking of health in strictly physical terms, the Blue Zones people enjoyed strong communities and a deep sense of purpose and engagement. They were part of something larger than themselves—a community as well as a spiritual world, which included ancestors and a whole system of belief—and this larger world both called forth their best efforts and ensured support when they faltered. Clearly, this spiritual dimension was an integral part of their long lives and optimal health. I invite you to detoxify the SPIRIT in your life—to remove the barriers to your SPIRIT—and complete this final phase of your Whole Detox.

CHAPTER 10

HOW TO GET THE MOST FROM YOUR WHOLE DETOX

Now that you've read all about the Seven Systems of Full-Spectrum Health, you're ready to start putting your knowledge into action. In seven three-day segments, you'll dive deeply into each one of the seven systems. Each day has its own unique theme:

DAILY DETOX THEMES

The ROOT	
Day 1	Body Awareness and Instinct
Day 2	Community
Day 3	Protein
The FLOW	
Day 4	Emotions
Day 5	Creativity
Day 6	Fats and Oils
The FIRE	
Day 7	Stress
Day 8	Thoughts
Day 9	Carbohydrates and Sugar
The LOVE	
Day 10	Self-Care
Day 11	Movement
Day 12	Vegetables

The TRUTH	
Day 13	Truths
Day 14	Affirmations
Day 15	Liquid Foods
The INSIGHT	
Day 16	Moods and Cognition
Day 17	Visualizations
Day 18	Spices
The SPIRIT	
Day 19	Connection
Day 20	Meditation
Day 21	Fasting

Each day, you'll address the day's theme using seven different approaches:

- Following the Whole Detox meal plans
- Keeping the Whole Detox Emotion Log
- Recording your limiting thoughts in a journal
- Engaging in physical movement
- Speaking specific affirmations
- Visualizing certain imagery
- Meditating

In fact, each approach corresponds to one of the Seven Systems of Full-Spectrum Health:

1. The ROOT: meal plans
2. The FLOW: Whole Detox Emotion Log
3. The FIRE: limiting thoughts
4. The LOVE: movement
5. The TRUTH: affirmations
6. The INSIGHT: visualizations
7. The SPIRIT: meditations

Let's take a closer look.

1. MEAL PLANS

Every day you will eat delicious, nourishing, colorful meals that support one of the seven systems. For the first three days of your detox, you'll focus on red foods and foods that support the ROOT: protein and minerals. For the next three days, you'll focus on orange foods and foods that support the FLOW: healthy oils and fats, tropical foods, and hydrating foods. For the three days after that, you'll focus on yellow foods and foods that support the FIRE: whole grains, legumes, and yellow spices. And so on.

The exciting thing about the Whole Detox meals is that they give you the chance to really explore each of the seven colors. You'll have the opportunity to experience for yourself how eating red foods, proteins, and minerals strengthens your ROOT, how consuming orange foods and healthy fats helps your emotions to FLOW, how eating the right kinds of yellow foods helps rebalance your FIRE.

When your Whole Detox is over, I'll want you to consume the rainbow: to include some of each of the seven colors every single day. But during your detox, you'll take it one color at a time, so you can have a good long visit with each. Think of these twenty-one days as a journey into the rainbow, where you can explore each color's effect on your mind, body, and spirit.

2. THE WHOLE DETOX EMOTION LOG

Every night before you go to bed, you'll complete the Whole Detox Emotion Log, noting the emotions you experienced that day. This is a simple exercise—you can take a look at the log on pages 381–83 to see just how simple—but its effects can be profound.

First, checking in with your emotions can be a transformative experience. Many of us focus so much on just getting through the day that we forget to pause, breathe, and ask ourselves how we feel. Our emotions get pushed aside, buried, or dumped into stagnant swamps, an underlying current of anger, sadness, anxiety, or frustration that we barely notice anymore but that saps our vitality and creativity nonetheless. We rush by the moments of excitement, satisfaction, and joy too, ignoring how we feel in favor of what we must do. The Whole Detox Emotion Log will help you to slow down a bit each day to reflect on your personal FLOW.

Second, by tracking your emotions on a daily basis, you'll have the opportunity to notice the patterns that shape your emotional life. Do you spend most of your days angry, frustrated, or sad? What makes you happy? What brings you peace? Are there activities or people who uplift you? Do certain situations routinely annoy you or bring you down? Becoming aware of how you feel over time can be a profound awakening.

Once you are aware, you can start asking questions. What can you do to spend more time feeling excited, inspired, or content? Do you have opportunities to alter patterns that aren't serving you? Is there an emotional message you've been unwilling to hear, such as *I thought Margo was my friend, but I really don't enjoy my time with her* or *Every time I take a walk, I feel happy and uplifted*? Learning how you feel gives you the opportunity to take the actions that serve you best.

The Whole Detox Emotion Log also gives you the chance to connect feelings to food. Do you find yourself craving sugar after a stressful day? Do you seek comfort food after a rough time with a friend? Do you finish your workday drained and dehydrated? These are the insights that begin to emerge from the simple act of noting your emotions.

3. LIMITING THOUGHTS

One of the things that sap our energy is limiting thoughts: *If someone else needs help, I can't say no. Nobody cares what I think. I'm not good at learning new things.* These—as much as heavy metals, pesticides, and xenoestrogens—are toxic barriers that weigh us down, sapping energy that might be used for better things.

Every day of your Whole Detox you have the chance to identify one of these toxic barriers and break through it. Each day I suggest three possible limiting thoughts relating to that day's theme. You can choose the thought that rings the most true for you or identify one of your own. Then you have the chance to spend five minutes journaling about that thought: how it has limited you, when you first began to think that way, what your life might be like without that toxic barrier.

I remember hearing years ago that we have from sixty thousand to eighty thousand thoughts each day—and a majority of them are negative! Imagine how those limiting thoughts are choking your internal flame and how much more brightly you would burn with better fuel. After all, we don't have infinite energy. Limiting thoughts weigh heavily upon us, putting out energy that could otherwise be used for better things.

As always, the first step is awareness: identify a thought that has been holding you back and give yourself a little time to reflect upon it. As you let go of limiting thoughts, you'll be able to replace them with expansive, positive, empowering thoughts—thoughts that better fit your current reality and serve you for a more fulfilling future. For many of my workshop participants, this has been one of the most exciting approaches within Whole Detox. I am eager to see what it brings for you.

4. MOVEMENT

Each day, you'll engage in some gentle movement. This might be a yoga pose, a walk in the woods, or some other type of movement that connects you to the day's specific theme. On your first ROOT day, for example, you'll take a walk, feeling the earth beneath your feet. On your first FLOW day, you'll go for a swim and flow with the water. On your first FIRE day, you'll do a tai chi "push hands" movement, designed to connect you with your solar plexus and your fiery drive to define your space. Through using your body, you will connect more intimately to each system.

Moving allows you to expand your lungs, keep your circulation flowing, breathe deeply, and engage your heart. Movement keeps nutrients circulating throughout your body, nourishing your organs, bones, muscles, and nerves. It expands your sense of possibilities, freeing you to go where you will and to carry your burdens lightly. It is a profound form of self-love—it's no accident those endorphins released by exercise leave you feeling happy and well cared for!

Many of us have difficulty making time for the self-care involved in daily movement. Although we spend hours rushing around to serve others—boss, clients, coworkers, family, friends—we find it hard to move just for ourselves. So for twenty-one days you'll have the chance to practice moving in ways that are primarily designed to benefit you and no one else.

Accordingly, for every movement I prescribe, I want you to do only as much as you feel comfortable with—no pain, no strain, no suffering, just small movements that allow your body to expand and breathe at its own pace. Do make time for the movement, but don't push it. Just allow your body to enjoy the movement that is your birthright.

If you've already got your own exercise program—whether yoga, running, weights, or anything else—that's terrific. You're welcome to continue whatever activities you choose. Just don't neglect the movement assignments in your Whole Detox, because each one has a very specific purpose, and I'd hate for you to miss any of them. The goal with these movements is not fitness or weight loss; it's a bodily recognition of each day's theme and each of the seven systems. Believe me, I've chosen each day's movement very carefully, and you'll get the full benefit of Whole Detox by completing each type of movement on the day it's prescribed. Allow yourself to be surprised by what you discover throughout the twenty-one days.

5. AFFIRMATIONS

An affirmation is a simple statement affirming a positive attribute of your life: "I am rooted fully in my physical body," "My moods are balanced and my thinking is clear and precise," "I am fulfilled with the abundance of life." When you fully engage with an affirmation, you find that it begins to become true for you, subtly transforming negative self-talk into positive and empowering truths.

Each day, I provide you with an affirmation you can use to identify with that day's theme, or you can feel free to write one of your own. Just be sure that you use only positive language: "I am free" rather than "I am not restricted." Be sure, too, that you phrase your affirmation as a fact, not as a wish, a hope, or a future possibility: "I am free" rather than "Someday I will be free" or "I want to be free."

I've used affirmations for years with patients and workshop participants, and I've always been surprised at how effective and transformative they can be. Science has begun to validate those perceptions with a growing body of research on the positive effects of affirmations. They are an integral part of many therapeutic techniques, and I am excited to include them as part of Whole Detox.

Many of my patients have asked me how they can repeat a statement that does not seem true to them. "What if I don't feel fully rooted in my body?" one of my patients asked me, regarding the Day 1 affirmation for the ROOT. "It's not true, so how can I say it is?"

My answer is that we are mining another possibility, another version of the truth. If you lived in the least toxic, most positive version of your life, the affirmation would be true. By asserting that it is true ("fake it until you make it"), you create the opportunity for it to *become* true.

If you find yourself feeling unsure or skeptical, why not experiment for twenty-one days and find out just how well affirmations might work for you? Say the words out loud, see how they affect your body and your emotions, and live in the vision they inspire. Use your voice to speak this truth, and see how healing it can be to connect to this alternate vision of yourself. Give yourself a chance to reprogram toxic beliefs into healing truths, and discover what possibilities begin to open up.

6. VISUALIZATIONS

The process of visualization is simple. Each day, I provide you with a brief description of an empowering image related to the day's theme. Using that image as a starting point, let your mind's eye conjure up the details, allowing your insight and imagination to take you on a visionary journey. You might be invited to visualize colors, places in your body, or even images of nature. Spending some time engaged with healing imagery can be a rich opportunity to explore a facet of yourself, your life, or your future.

Most of us spend at least some time daydreaming, fantasizing, or projecting our hopes, fears, and wishes into the future. Visualizing is no different, except that each day I give you a specific image with which to begin. Take the image and run with it—let your mind flesh out the vision and see where your insight and imagination take you. Before you can manifest what you want in your life, you have to envision it, so your twenty-one days of visualization will give you some good practice in using this effective tool.

As with affirmations, there is a huge body of research confirming the benefit of visualization as a transformative technique. My patients and workshop participants have confirmed that this approach unlocks new insights, sometimes inspiring major life changes, other times allowing for a richer and more satisfying experience of the lives they already have. In fact, next to all the recipes they love, this is their favorite part of Whole Detox. Leverage this technique just a few minutes a day to show you a new vision, and you might be amazed at the possibilities that open up.

7. MEDITATIONS

You will meditate, taking a few minutes each day to be in solitude and silence to allow meaning and purpose to surface. Many of us think of meditation in a somewhat limited way: sitting, eyes closed, motionless. That is one way of meditating, but not the only one, and within Whole Detox I give you a much more varied buffet of meditation choices. Once again, each day's meditation embodies the system and theme of that day, allowing you to explore them more deeply.

A great deal of research supports the many benefits of meditation and also indicates that meditation has the greatest benefits for those who practice regularly. My hope is that your twenty-one-day habit of daily meditation will enable you to become a consistent meditator so you, too, can enjoy these benefits.

If you are already engaged in a meditation practice, you can continue or not throughout this time, but either way, please follow my daily prescription. I want you to have the full spectrum of Whole Detox, and every meditation has been designed to give you the most complete, tailored experience.

One of the most intriguing findings in recent years has been the discovery that these mind–body practices actually transform genetic expression. While we can't change the composition of our DNA, we can absolutely change the way our genes manifest in our bodies and our lives—and meditation is one of the most effective tools for doing so. (Diet, exercise, and other lifestyle choices also have this effect.) And so we come full circle, as the spirit meets the body. We leave the body and the self to come back fortified, energized, and inspired, ready to pursue our life's purpose and to savor the meaning of life.

THE POWER OF SYNERGY, PART II

As you saw in chapter 2, Whole Detox draws profoundly on the power of synergy, making the most of how our seven systems constantly affect one another. I've designed your twenty-one days of Whole Detox to maximize the benefits of synergy, so every one of your seven systems is engaged on every day.

Many of my workshop participants start Whole Detox believing that the most important component is the food. Yes, of course the food is important—but the other six modalities are equally important. For the investment of about thirty minutes each day in addition to your meal preparation activities, you can benefit from the full spectrum of the seven systems, detoxing not just one part of your self but your whole self. I urge you to take full advantage of your twenty-one days by following the entire prescription—and allowing yourself to be surprised. Welcome to Whole Detox! You're in for a wonderful, colorful rainbow ride.

A DAY OF WHOLE DETOX

Feel free to organize your day as best suits your schedule. You can get into a routine for twenty-one days or make each day different—whatever works best for you. Here's one possible version of a Whole Detox day just to get you started:

Morning
- Begin the day with your *affirmation*. That way you can repeat it to yourself throughout the day.
- If you can, take a few minutes before breakfast to complete the *visualization* exercise. This imagery, together with your affirmation, will set the tone for your day.
- *Breakfast*

Midday
- *Lunch*
- On your lunch break, take a few minutes to identify and journal

about a limiting thought. For the rest of the day, notice how that thought appears and imagine how you might break through it.

Afternoon

- Snack

Evening

- Before you eat dinner, complete the movement portion of your day.
- Dinner
- As the day winds down, take time to meditate.
- As you prepare for bed, note the day's emotions in your Whole Detox Emotion Log.

FOODS FOR WHOLE DETOX: AN OVERVIEW

Foods	Yes to these	No to these
Fruits	Organic whole fruits, unsweetened, fresh and frozen	Fruit products with added sugars
Vegetables	All raw, frozen, sautéed, fermented, steamed, roasted vegetables	Corn; breaded, fried, or creamed vegetables
Legumes	All fresh, frozen, or dried beans/peas; hummus	Soybean products: soy milk, soy sauce, soybean oil in processed foods, soy yogurt, tempeh, tofu, textured vegetable protein
Animal proteins	Organic, free-range game and poultry; organic, grass-fed, pasture-raised lean beef; wild-caught fish	Breaded fish sticks, canned meats, pork in all forms (e.g., hot dogs), shellfish
Nuts and seeds	Nuts, unsweetened nut milks, and unsweetened nut butters; seeds and unsweetened seed butters	Peanuts and peanut butter

Foods	Yes to these	No to these
Protein powders	Hemp, pea, rice, and whey (whey protein powder for omnivores only)	Soy
Grains	Gluten-free grains: amaranth, arrowroot, buckwheat, millet, gluten-free oats, quinoa, rice (brown, purple/black, wild), tapioca, teff	Barley, cornmeal and corn starch, Kamut, oats, rye, spelt, triticale, wheat
Dairy and milk alternatives	Unsweetened milk alternatives: almond, cashew, coconut, hazelnut, hemp, rice	All dairy products, including yogurt
Eggs	Egg replacer	Eggs
Oils	Almond, avocado, flaxseed, grapeseed, hempseed, extra-virgin olive, pumpkin, rice bran, safflower and sunflower (high-oleic preferred), sesame, walnut	Butter, margarine, mayonnaise, processed oils, salad dressings, shortening, spreads
Sweeteners	Blackstrap molasses, dates and date syrup, honey (raw preferred), pure maple syrup, ripe fruits and fruit concentrates, stevia	Agave nectar; artificial sweeteners; evaporated cane juice; high-fructose corn syrup; refined, white, and brown sugars
Herbs and spices	All herbs and spices	Gluten-containing herbs and spices, herbs and spices with fillers
Other	Apple cider vinegar, balsamic vinegar, raw cacao and cacao nibs, unsweetened cocoa powder, coconut aminos	Barbecue sauce, chocolate, chutney, ketchup, relish, salad dressings, soy sauce, teriyaki
Beverages	Unsweetened fruit and vegetable juices; uncaffeinated herbal teas; filtered, distilled, mineral, and seltzer water	Alcohol, coffee and other caffeinated beverages (try to avoid decaf too), soft drinks

THE WHOLE DETOX MEALS: ADDITIONAL SUPPORT

Some Detox Challenges

By the time you finish Whole Detox, you're going to feel terrific. But some people experience a few challenges during the first few days of the program as their bodies adjust to the switch in food.

If you do experience transition issues, you'll probably have the most difficult time during the first two to three days, with another week or so of minor challenges. You can make the transition easier, however, by letting go of caffeine and processed sugar gradually over four to five days before beginning the program. Each day, cut back a little on your caffeine and sugar intake until you are down to zero. If you drink caffeinated coffee or tea, you might cut it with decaf, going from one-quarter decaf to half decaf to three-quarters decaf to all decaf.

Letting go of caffeine and sugar can produce headaches and irritability. Other withdrawal symptoms you might experience on Whole Detox include sleep problems, changes in temperature (feeling hotter or colder), lightheadedness, mood swings, joint or muscle aches, changes in your bowel habits, and changes in your body odor or breath. They won't last long, though, and as the program continues, you'll feel better and better.

Get Ready for Whole Detox
- Read through the program. Get a quick overview so you know what to expect.
- Check out the list of food staples on pages 239–40 and make sure you're well stocked. The list of where to get foods and some basic kitchen equipment, located in Resources, will also help you prepare. Ideally, you'll have plenty of glass containers and stainless-steel cookware.
- You might want to avoid any strenuous physical activity, since your body might need some time to adjust to the dietary changes. Judge for yourself and adjust accordingly.
- Relax and enjoy the process. Listen to your body, get some rest, and don't let the detox be "toxic" for you!

Omnivore or Vegan?

I've created Whole Detox meals with two options:

- The omnivore approach focuses primarily on clean, lean meats and seafood, vegetables, and fruits, with very few legumes, whole grains, nuts, and seeds.
- The vegan option includes vegetables, fruits, legumes, whole grains, nuts, and seeds.

I personally embrace all eating paths since everyone's needs are so different. You should feel free to choose; for any given meal, pick from either column. (However, the shopping lists have been organized for each plan separately, so if you want to mix and match, make sure you buy the right foods.)

TIPS FOR THE OMNIVORE APPROACH

- Choose organic, 100-percent grass-fed meats; organic, free-range poultry; and wild-caught fish. Avoid fish that contain high levels of mercury (see Resources).
- Don't overcook your meat; you'll lose too many nutrients.
- Trim any visible fat, which is a ready-made repository for toxins.

TIPS FOR THE VEGAN APPROACH

- If you are eating beans/legumes from cans, make sure to rinse them well, and choose brands stored in bisphenol-free cans.
- Rather than buy food in cans, it would be best if you could buy dry legumes and whole grains in bulk and soak them to reduce their cooking time.
- Check out the section below for a simple way of making beans.

WHOLE DETOX, BEANS, AND LEGUMES

Sure, it's quicker to open a can, rinse the beans, and eat them. However, when you cook them from scratch, you avoid the potential toxins that reside in most canned foods, along with the extra salt, sugar, and other preservatives (e.g., sulfites) that are often added. If you plan ahead, you can have beans in your freezer in serving sizes, ready to defrost and add to one of your recipes. Or you can just cook what you need for the next three to six days and store them in the fridge. All it takes is a little upfront work to make your life easier through Whole Detox.

Here are some simple instructions for cooking beans (makes about 5 cups cooked beans):

1 pound dried beans, any kind (the least expensive option is to buy them in bulk and rinse them well); this amount of beans will provide you with about 5 cups of cooked beans.

Optional: 1 bay leaf, 1 to 2 whole garlic cloves, ½ onion, and/or chopped carrots and celery

2 to 3 teaspoons sea salt, plus more to taste

The night before you plan to cook the beans (or during the day if you will cook them in the evening), pick through them and discard any shriveled ones. Then place the beans in a large bowl and cover them with a few inches of water. Leave them on the counter to soak overnight (or for 6 to 8 hours). Soaking will reduce their cooking time and help them cook more evenly. (Note that lentils and split peas need no soaking. Just rinse them and they are ready to cook.)

By the next day, the beans will have absorbed much of the water and nearly doubled in size. Strain them and rinse them gently. Discard the soaking water.

Transfer the beans to a heavy cooking pot, such as a Dutch oven. Add any of the optional ingredients you like and cover the beans with about 1 inch of water. Bring the pot to a boil over medium-high heat, reduce the heat to a gentle simmer, and cook the beans partially covered for about 1 hour. You may need to add more water, so check them frequently. Soaked beans can take 1 to 2 hours to cook, but they average about an hour. Cooking time depends on their size and variety.

Add the sea salt when the beans are just barely tender yet still too firm to eat. Try not to add the salt too early as it will lengthen the cooking time and toughen the beans. Continue simmering the beans until they are as tender and creamy as you like them. Add more salt to taste.

Cool the beans and transfer them in their cooking liquid to storage containers in portion sizes for your recipes. In general, beans will keep for one week refrigerated, or they can be frozen for up to three months.

Please note: If you intend to use your beans in a soup, it's best to slightly

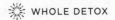

undercook them initially and finish cooking them in the soup itself. Once you've scooped up all your beans, this liquid makes a great base for soups and quick sauces.

Allow Time to Prepare

Each recipe involves only thirty minutes of cooking time, and many of the recipes require less. I have made it as efficient as possible by having you make enough for leftovers and then incorporate the leftovers into your next day's meals. For some people following Whole Detox, the recipes provide too much extra food. Feel free to scale back if you find that you need less. Conversely, feel free to proportionally increase the recipe if you need more. You may have extra food left over before the end of the twenty-one days; in those cases, you may use the extra food in place of recommended snacks or meals.

Don't Go Hungry

This isn't a diet program, and I don't want you counting calories or going hungry. I also don't want you eating more than your body needs. I've provided serving sizes for each recipe, but you don't have to follow them. Make more if you find yourself hungry; make less if you feel like you're eating too much.

Rotate Your Protein

You'll notice that protein powder is included in every smoothie. I've provided you with a list of suggested protein powders, and feel free to use any of them, but don't use one type for all twenty-one days. The more you rotate your food choices, the healthier you'll be. Repeating food choices can create food reactions. And practicing diversity ensures that you get a broader spectrum of nutrients.

Keep It Fresh

Select fresh foods rather than canned or frozen whenever you can. Also whenever possible, choose organically grown fruits and vegetables to reduce your toxin load. And even with organic produce, wash your fruits and vegetables thoroughly with a scrub brush and biodegradable soap.

If you must buy some conventionally grown produce, focus on organic choices for the following items:

- Apples
- Celery
- Cherry tomatoes
- Collard greens
- Cucumbers
- Grapes
- Hot peppers
- Kale
- Nectarines
- Peaches
- Potatoes
- Snap peas
- Spinach
- Strawberries
- Sweet bell peppers

Why these items? Because the Environmental Working Group says they are currently the most contaminated. So if you must buy conventionally grown produce, at least avoid these items on EWG's "Dirty Dozen Plus" list. This list is updated every year, so make sure you check in periodically—they even have an app for your phone (www.ewg.org/foodnews/).

Know Your Oils
Read oil labels carefully, and choose only those that are obtained by a cold-pressed method.

Drink Purified Water
Drink about half your body weight in ounces, up to 100 ounces each day. Make sure your water is filtered and please avoid plastic containers.

Be Comfortably Active
Physical activity is part of your Whole Detox program. If you already have an exercise plan, you can stick to it if you have the energy to do both, or you can just follow the recommended activities for twenty-one days. Whatever you do, don't stress or strain. This is a time for rest, recov-

ery, and healing. You'll be rewarded with boatloads of energy when your detox ends.

Choose the Right Blender

Make sure you have a high-speed blender for your morning smoothie. See Resources for suggestions regarding equipment.

What About Supplements?

I don't prescribe supplements during Whole Detox. However, if your health-care provider has asked you to take supplements, make sure you work with that person to determine whether you need to continue taking them during the program. Usually, people continue with their typical supplement routines, and if they want to add in dietary supplements tailored to detox, they check in with their health-care provider.

ALMOST THERE!

There are just a few more things to do as you prepare for Whole Detox:

- *Get your house ready.* Clear your kitchen so you have room to cook. Make sure the places you plan to eat and serve food are clear and uncluttered as well. Ideally, you would clean up your entire house to keep your mind clear and your body ready to detox, but if that feels like an overwhelming chore, just focus on the cooking and eating areas.

- *Get your network ready.* Let your friends and family know you'll be trying a new way of eating for twenty-one days. Ask for their support and encouragement. You might even invite them to do Whole Detox with you!

- *Get your mind ready.* Think your way through the next three weeks. Will you be taking food to work? When will you go shopping? Are your Emotion Log and journal by your bed? What do you need to do to make Whole Detox go as smoothly as possible? Envisioning your twenty-one days will help you anticipate and solve any challenges that might arise.

Shopping for Whole Detox

I strongly recommend shopping every three days for Whole Detox, buying just the foods that you need for your next phase. Your foods will be extra fresh and delicious, and you'll have the added benefit of focusing specifically on each phase.

If every three days just isn't practical for you, you can combine two phases into one trip and shop every six days instead. The following are your Whole Detox meal plans and shopping lists, organized phase by phase, with an initial Whole Detox Staples list for pantry items that will serve you all the way through.

SHOPPING LIST: WHOLE DETOX STAPLES

Many grocery stores stock organic foods. If you have trouble finding any ingredient in a recipe, there are several websites that carry organic foods and some unusual items as well. Fresh produce should be organic when possible, and if you need to, as I mentioned before, refer to EWG's "Dirty Dozen Plus" list of the most pesticide-laden produce that it's most important to purchase as organically rather than conventionally grown.

The following staple nonperishable foods will be used frequently during your Whole Detox. Regardless of which type of meal plans you follow, have these products on hand before you start your detox:

- Garlic bulbs, approximately 2 to 3 bulbs
- Ginger, fresh, about a 6-inch root
- Lemons (about 8–10 medium) and limes (about 2–3)
- Apple cider vinegar, organic
- Balsamic vinegar, no sugar added (contains natural sugars)
- Coconut oil, virgin, organic
- Flaxseed oil, cold-pressed, organic (store in the refrigerator)
- Olive oil, unfiltered (if possible), extra-virgin, organic
- Sesame oil, cold-pressed, organic
- Almond milk, unsweetened (boxed variety, or about 32 fluid ounces)
- Coconut milk, full-fat, 2 bisphenol-free cans, 13.5 ounces each

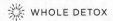

- Coconut milk, unsweetened, 2 boxes, 32 fluid ounces each
- Coconut water, unsweetened, 1 carton, 32 fluid ounces
- Coconut aminos
- Honey
- Chia seeds, about ½ cup
- Hemp seeds, about ¼ cup
- Flaxseed meal, about ¾ cup
- Protein powders (Ideally, as I touched on earlier, you will rotate protein powders, using as many different types as possible. Buy enough for a total of twenty-one servings. Serving sizes vary with each brand of powder, but aim for about 12 to 15 grams of protein per serving. Be sure there are no added sugars.) Choices include the following:

Hemp	Rice
Pea	Whey (for omnivores only)

- Spices and herbs, dried (These should be purchased in small amounts either in bulk or in small containers. Choose organic when possible.)

Bay leaves	Nutmeg, ground
Black pepper	Onion powder
Cardamom, ground	Oregano, ground
Cayenne pepper, ground	Paprika
Chili powder	Parsley flakes
Cinnamon, ground	Pumpkin pie spice
Cloves, ground	Red pepper flakes, crushed
Cumin, ground	Rosemary
Cumin seeds	Sage
Curry powder	Sea salt
Dill	Tandoori seasoning (typically includes
Fennel seeds	a combination of garam masala,
Garlic powder	garlic, ginger, onion, and cayenne
Ginger powder	pepper)
Lavender buds	Thyme
Mustard seeds	Turmeric powder

- Vanilla extract

YOUR DAILY PLAN

Breakfast: a high-protein smoothie with fruits and vegetables

Lunch: a salad with protein

Afternoon snack: fruit or vegetable paired with nuts or a protein spread

Dinner: a warm meal with vegetables, protein, and a small amount of grain (if applicable)

Your morning smoothie is quick and easy to make, so you should have plenty of time to prepare it, even on a day when you're heading off to work while helping your family get ready for their days too! If you want to have your smoothie later in the day instead and prepare one of the meals for breakfast, you may consider that too. However, I like smoothies first thing in the morning due to their ease and the ability to get a lot of nutrients in one sitting first thing in the morning. I suggest preparing your lunch salad and protein at the same time. That way you'll have it with you at the office; or if you work at home, you'll be able to relax during lunchtime, enjoying the fruits of your morning labors!

CHAPTER 11

WHOLE DETOX 21-DAY PROGRAM

DAY 1: THE ROOT—BODY AWARENESS AND INSTINCT

I think that what we're seeking is an experience of being alive, so that our life experiences on the purely physical plane will have resonances within our own innermost being and reality, so that we actually feel the rapture of being alive.

—JOSEPH CAMPBELL

Meal Plan

	Omnivore	Vegan
Breakfast	Rooty Toot-Toot Shake	Rooty Toot-Toot Shake
Lunch	Terra Salad and Beef Burger	Terra Salad and Kidney Beans
Snack	Apple with Almond Butter	Apple with Almond Butter
Dinner	Tandoori Chicken with Kale and Red Bell Pepper	Tandoori Chickpeas with Kale and Red Bell Pepper

Whole Detox Emotion Log

At the end of the day, track any emotions that you had on the Whole Detox Emotion Log.

Thought Pattern Activity

The following are some limiting thoughts that relate to the ROOT:

I am unprotected.

My body is a burden, and I wish I didn't have to take care of it.

I am out of touch with my bodily instincts.

Pick the limiting thought that seems to ring most true for you. If none of the examples feel true, write down your own limiting thought as it relates to the ROOT.

Next, set your timer for five minutes. Spend that time journaling on that thought, how it has affected your life, and how you feel when you have that thought.

Movement

Take a fifteen-minute walk outdoors. If you have a dog, take her or him with you. Breathe in the fresh air. Survey the landscape. Feel the earth beneath your feet.

Affirmation

Spend three minutes saying aloud the following affirmation:

I am rooted fully in my physical body.

Feel how your body responds to these words. You can also create your own statement. Feel free to write it on a beautiful notecard or a plain Post-it note and put it in your immediate environment for the day.

Visualization

Set a timer for three minutes. During that time, close your eyes and visualize yourself being completely rooted in your physical body. Imagine your body is like a tree, spanning its roots down through your feet and having your arms wide and open to the possibilities of your physical world. Feel yourself being stable and grounded.

Meditation

For three minutes, meditate with your eyes closed while standing with your feet firmly planted on the earth and your hands at your sides.

DAY 1 RECIPES

Breakfast

ROOTY TOOT-TOOT SHAKE
Dedicated to my father
Serves 1

¾ cup purified water

Juice of 1 small lemon, about 1
   tablespoon

½ medium raw beet, diced, unpeeled
   (save the other ½ for tomorrow's
   lunch)

2 to 3 beet green leaves

½ medium red apple, sliced (keep the
   peel on; save the other ½ for today's
   snack)

½ tablespoon chia seeds

1 scoop protein powder of your
   choice (hemp, pea, rice, or whey for
   omnivores)

⅛ teaspoon turmeric powder

Dash of ground black pepper

1 to 2 ice cubes (optional)

Put all the liquid and whole food ingredients into a high-speed blender first, followed by the dry ingredients, then blend everything until a fluid consistency is reached. Add more water if needed. Drink immediately.

NUTRITION INFORMATION PER SERVING

Calories	Protein (g)	Carbs (g)	Fat (g)	Sat Fat (g)	Unsat Fat (g)	Fiber (g)
226	27	23	7	4	0.2	2

Lunch

TERRA SALAD AND BEEF BURGER *(OMNIVORE)* **OR KIDNEY BEANS** *(VEGAN)*
Serves 1

FOR OMNIVORES:

1 Beef Burger (recipe follows)

FOR VEGANS:

¾ cup cooked kidney beans

2 handfuls roughly chopped red- and
   green-leaf lettuce, about 2 cups
1 tablespoon diced red onion

4 radishes, sliced
1 tablespoon unhulled sesame seeds

3 tablespoons balsamic vinegar
3 tablespoons extra-virgin olive oil

8 red raspberries
½ teaspoon crushed red pepper flakes

Place all the salad ingredients in a serving bowl.

With an electric hand mixer or food processor, mix together all the vinaigrette ingredients. Spoon half the vinaigrette over the salad. (Save the other half for tomorrow's lunch.)

Vegans, serve the salad with the kidney beans on the side or tossed in with the greens.

Omnivores, serve it with the following Beef Burger.

BEEF BURGER

⅓ pound organic, grass-fed ground
   beef
2 tablespoons diced red onion
¼ teaspoon turmeric powder

½ teaspoon dried rosemary
Dash of ground black pepper
Dash of sea salt
1 teaspoon extra-virgin olive oil

In a bowl, mix together the ground beef, onion, turmeric, rosemary, pepper, and salt until everything is well combined. Form the mixture into a hamburger patty.

Heat the olive oil in a pan, and pan-fry the burger from 7 to 10 minutes on each side.

NUTRITION INFORMATION PER SERVING

	Calories	Protein (g)	Carbs (g)	Fat (g)	Sat Fat (g)	Unsat Fat (g)	Fiber (g)
Omnivore	441	33	12	29	5	19	3
Vegan	436	15	42	24	3	17	12

Snack

APPLE WITH ALMOND BUTTER
Serves 1

½ medium red apple (leftover from breakfast), sliced
2 tablespoons almond butter

Spread the apple slices with almond butter and enjoy!

NUTRITION INFORMATION PER SERVING

Calories	Protein (g)	Carbs (g)	Fat (g)	Sat Fat (g)	Unsat Fat (g)	Fiber (g)
243	5	18	19	2	16	4

Dinner

TANDOORI CHICKEN *(OMNIVORE)* OR CHICKPEAS *(VEGAN)* WITH KALE AND RED BELL PEPPER
Serves 2

FOR OMNIVORES:

2 4-ounce organic, free-range, boneless, skinless chicken breasts, cubed

FOR VEGANS:

1½ cups cooked chickpeas

FOR BOTH:

1 tablespoon coconut oil
1 tablespoon tandoori seasoning
Dash of ground black pepper
½ teaspoon sea salt
1 garlic clove, minced
2 tablespoons diced red onion
¾ cup unsweetened, full-fat coconut milk

4 handfuls roughly chopped kale, about 4 medium to large leaves
½ large red bell pepper, thinly sliced into strips
Juice of ½ lemon
1 teaspoon extra-virgin olive oil

Melt the coconut oil in a frying pan set over medium-high heat. Add the tandoori seasoning, pepper, and salt, and stir the spices for a few seconds before adding the garlic and onion. Continue to stir the mixture until the onion becomes soft and translucent. Add the coconut milk, and mix it in well before stirring in either the chicken (*omnivore*) or chickpeas (*vegan*). Cover the pan and let the mixture simmer on medium heat for 7 to 10 minutes.

Meanwhile, in a saucepan, steam the kale and the red bell pepper until the kale becomes wilted and bright green (don't let it lose its color!). Remove the vegetables from the heat, and transfer them to a serving plate. Drizzle them with lemon juice and olive oil.

When the chicken or chickpeas are ready, spoon half of them onto the serving plate with the vegetables. (Save the other half for tomorrow's lunch.) Serve immediately.

NUTRITION INFORMATION PER SERVING

	Calories	Protein (g)	Carbs (g)	Fat (g)	Sat Fat (g)	Unsat Fat (g)	Fiber (g)
Omnivore	461	33	20	30	23	5	4
Vegan	507	14	46	33	23	7	10

DAY 2: THE ROOT—COMMUNITY

The power of community to create health is far greater than any physician, clinic, or hospital.

—MARK HYMAN, M.D.

Meal Plan

	Omnivore	Vegan
Breakfast	Red Berry Smoothie	Red Berry Smoothie
Lunch	Beet and Swiss Chard Salad with Tandoori Chicken	Beet and Swiss Chard Salad with Tandoori Chickpeas
Snack	Red Bell Pepper with Paprika Hummus	Red Bell Pepper with Paprika Hummus
Dinner	Grounding Chili	Grounding Chili

Whole Detox Emotion Log

At the end of the day, track any emotions that you had on the Whole Detox Emotion Log.

Thought Pattern Activity

The following are some limiting thoughts that relate to the ROOT:

I don't feel connected to people around me.
My family doesn't understand me.
I don't belong anywhere.

Pick the limiting thought that seems to ring most true for you. If none of the examples feel true, write down your own limiting thought as it relates to the ROOT.

Next, set your timer for five minutes. Spend that time journaling on that thought, how it has affected your life, and how you feel when you have that thought.

Movement

Do some physical activity that involves you being in a community setting; for example, go to a class at the gym or walk with friends.

Affirmation

Spend three minutes saying aloud the following affirmation:

I belong to communities that are nourishing.

Feel how your body responds to these words. You can also create your own statement. Feel free to write it on a beautiful notecard or a plain Post-it note and put it in your immediate environment for the day.

Visualization

Set a timer for three minutes. During that time, close your eyes and visualize yourself being completely surrounded by people who nourish, protect, and love you. See roots connecting you to each of them.

Meditation

Engage in a full-length mirror meditation by focusing on your image in a mirror without judgment. For three minutes, meditate on your physical self and see how your features, expressions, posture, and clothing reflect your community, family, tribe, and social network.

DAY 2 RECIPES

Breakfast

___

RED BERRY SMOOTHIE
Serves 1

½ cup strawberries

¼ cup red raspberries

¾ cup unsweetened coconut milk
(boxed variety)

1 scoop protein powder of your choice
(hemp, pea, rice, whey for omnivores)

1 tablespoon bee pollen granules
(optional)

Water and ice as needed

Put all the liquid and whole food ingredients into a high-speed blender first, followed by the dry ingredients, then blend everything until a fluid consistency is reached. Add more water if needed. Drink immediately.

NUTRITION INFORMATION PER SERVING

Calories	Protein (g)	Carbs (g)	Fat (g)	Sat Fat (g)	Unsat Fat (g)	Fiber (g)
247	28	18	6	4	0.1	4

Lunch

___

BEET AND SWISS CHARD SALAD WITH TANDOORI CHICKEN *(OMNIVORE)* OR CHICKPEAS *(VEGAN)*
Serves 1

2 handfuls finely chopped Swiss chard,
about 2 medium to large leaves

½ medium raw beet, grated, unpeeled

4 strawberries, sliced

1 tablespoon raw sunflower seeds

Toss together in a serving bowl all the salad ingredients with either the chicken (*omnivore*) or chickpeas (*vegan*). Pour yesterday's remaining raspberry vinaigrette over the bowl's contents and serve.

NUTRITION INFORMATION PER SERVING

	Calories	Protein (g)	Carbs (g)	Fat (g)	Sat Fat (g)	Unsat Fat (g)	Fiber (g)
Omnivore	576	38	38	34	23	6	10
Vegan	622	19	64	37	23	7	16

Snack

RED BELL PEPPER WITH PAPRIKA HUMMUS
Serves 1

½ cup hummus
½ teaspoon freshly squeezed lemon
  juice

½ teaspoon paprika
¾ large red bell pepper, cut into thin
  slices

Stir into the hummus the lemon juice and paprika, then use hummus as a dip for the red pepper slices.

NUTRITION INFORMATION PER SERVING

Calories	Protein (g)	Carbs (g)	Fat (g)	Sat Fat (g)	Unsat Fat (g)	Fiber (g)
229	10	23	12	2	9	9

Dinner

GROUNDING CHILI
Serves 2

FOR OMNIVORES:

½ pound organic, free-range, lean
  ground turkey

FOR VEGANS:

1½ cups cooked adzuki beans
¼ cup purified water

FOR BOTH:

1 tablespoon extra-virgin olive oil
½ medium red onion, diced
2 garlic cloves, minced
1 teaspoon ground cumin

1 teaspoon chili powder
1 teaspoon paprika
Dash of sea salt
Dash of ground black pepper

6 shiitake mushrooms

1 cup chopped cauliflower

1 carrot, scrubbed and chopped

2 medium tomatoes, diced

2 tablespoons uncooked quinoa (red variety preferred)

2 cups low-sodium tomato juice

1 cup purified water

In a large soup pot set over low to medium heat, heat the olive oil and sauté the onion and garlic until the onions become soft, about 2 to 3 minutes. Add the cumin, chili powder, paprika, salt, and pepper.

Omnivores, add the turkey and brown it for about 5 to 7 minutes.

Vegans, add the adzuki beans plus about ¼ cup water, so the beans don't burn, and cook the mixture for about 2 to 3 minutes.

Both omnivores and vegans, then add the mushrooms, cauliflower, carrot, tomatoes, quinoa, tomato juice, and additional cup of water. Cook the mixture for about 8 to 10 more minutes, stirring consistently. Season to taste.

Spoon up half the chili and serve warm. (Save the other half for tomorrow's lunch.)

NUTRITION INFORMATION PER SERVING

	Calories	Protein (g)	Carbs (g)	Fat (g)	Sat Fat (g)	Unsat Fat (g)	Fiber (g)
Omnivore	417	28	36	18	4	12	9
Vegan	469	21	79	9	1	6	21

DAY 3: THE ROOT—PROTEIN

*Our cells engage in protein production, and many of those proteins are enzymes
responsible for the chemistry of life.*

—RANDY SCHEKMAN

Meal Plan

	Omnivore	Vegan
Breakfast	Sunrise Smoothie	Sunrise Smoothie
Lunch	Beet Root and Greens Grounding Chili	Beet Root and Greens Grounding Chili
Snack	Avocado and Walnuts	Avocado and Walnuts
Dinner	Ginger-Garlic Beef on Quinoa	Ginger-Garlic Black Beans on Quinoa

Whole Detox Emotion Log

At the end of the day, track any emotions that you had on the Whole Detox
Emotion Log.

Thought Pattern Activity

The following are some limiting thoughts that relate to the ROOT:

I am ungrounded.
I feel unstable in my body.
My surroundings don't support me.

Pick the limiting thought that seems to ring most true for you. If none
of the examples feel true, write down your own limiting thought as it
relates to the ROOT.

Next, set your timer for five minutes. Spend that time journaling on
that thought, how it has affected your life, and how you feel when you have
that thought.

Movement

MOUNTAIN POSE (TADASANA)

1. Stand with your body relaxed. Your feet should be shoulder-width apart.
2. Bend your knees slightly.
3. Tilt your pelvis slightly forward.
4. Keeping your body balanced, evenly distribute your weight over the soles of your feet. Feel the ground solid beneath your feet.
5. Maintain this position for three minutes. As with all yoga poses, go to your comfortable limit. Nothing should be painful.

Practicing this barefoot and outdoors adds a connection to nature and the earth (but is not required, especially if you live in a cold climate).

Affirmation

Spend three minutes saying aloud the following affirmation:

I am anchored in my beautiful, strong, physical structure.

Feel how your body responds to these words. You can also create your own statement. Feel free to write it on a beautiful notecard or a plain Post-it note and put it in your immediate environment for the day.

Visualization

Set a timer for three minutes. During that time, close your eyes and visualize yourself feeling strong and stable in your skeletal structure. See your bones as being packed with the necessary minerals they need. Imagine your muscles as being fibrous, fit, and flexible, working well with your skeleton.

Meditation

For three minutes, invigorate and stimulate your bones with a weight-bearing, meditative activity. Take a leisurely walk outside, and as you do, contemplate each step. See each step as significant, strong, and strengthening. Make the movement your sole focus and meditation.

DAY 3 RECIPES

Breakfast

SUNRISE SMOOTHIE
Serves 1

- 1 small red apple, sliced (leave peel on)
- 1 small carrot, scrubbed and diced (leave peel on)
- 4 pink grapefruit sections (save the rest of the grapefruit for today's lunch)
- 1 teaspoon freshly squeezed lemon juice
- ½-inch piece fresh ginger, chopped
- 6 red raspberries
- ½ cup unsweetened coconut milk (boxed variety)
- 1 tablespoon flaxseed meal
- 1 scoop protein powder of your choice (hemp, pea, rice, whey for omnivores)
- Water and ice as needed

Put all the liquid and whole food ingredients into a high-speed blender first, followed by the dry ingredients, then blend everything until a fluid consistency is reached. Add more water if needed. Drink immediately.

NUTRITION INFORMATION PER SERVING

Calories	Protein (g)	Carbs (g)	Fat (g)	Sat Fat (g)	Unsat Fat (g)	Fiber (g)
402	28	41	17	11	1	9

Lunch

BEET ROOT AND GREENS WITH GROUNDING CHILI
Serves 1

- 1 small to medium raw beet, grated, unpeeled (totals about 1 cup)
- 2 beet green leaves, finely chopped
- 7 red grapes

FOR THE DRESSING:

- 3 tablespoons grapefruit juice (from the leftover grapefruit from breakfast)
- 2 tablespoons extra-virgin olive oil
- 1 teaspoon ground oregano
- Dash of sea salt
- Dash of ground black pepper

Combine the beet, beet greens, and grapes in a bowl. Stir or whisk together all the ingredients for the dressing, then pour the dressing over the salad.

Warm up yesterday's leftover Grounding Chili to serve with the salad.

NUTRITION INFORMATION PER SERVING

	Calories	Protein (g)	Carbs (g)	Fat (g)	Sat Fat (g)	Unsat Fat (g)	Fiber (g)
Omnivore	634	31	57	32	6	24	14
Vegan	469	24	100	23	3	18	26

Snack

AVOCADO AND WALNUTS

Serves 1

½ avocado (leave the pit in the other ½ and save it for tomorrow's lunch)
½ teaspoon freshly squeezed lemon juice

Dash of sea salt
1 scant handful (about 8) walnut halves (red variety preferred)

Drizzle the avocado with lemon juice and sprinkle it with salt, then eat it with the walnuts.

NUTRITION INFORMATION PER SERVING

Calories	Protein (g)	Carbs (g)	Fat (g)	Sat Fat (g)	Unsat Fat (g)	Fiber (g)
266	4	11	25	3	21	8

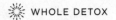

Dinner

GINGER-GARLIC BEEF *(OMNIVORE)* OR BLACK BEANS *(VEGAN)* ON QUINOA

Serves 1

FOR OMNIVORES:

- 4- to 6-ounce organic, grass-fed flank steak, cut into strips

FOR VEGANS:

- ¾ cup cooked black beans

FOR BOTH:

- 1 teaspoon sesame oil
- ½ teaspoon minced fresh ginger
- ½ garlic clove, minced
- 2 tablespoons diced red onion
- 1 tablespoon extra-virgin olive oil
- 1 teaspoon chili powder
- 1 teaspoon ground cumin
- 1 teaspoon paprika
- 1 teaspoon ground oregano
- ½ teaspoon garlic powder

- ½ teaspoon onion powder
- 1 teaspoon sea salt
- 1 teaspoon ground black pepper
- 1 medium turnip, diced
- 1 medium carrot, cut into bite-size strips
- 1 cup chopped broccoli
- 1 large portobello mushroom, sliced
- ½ cup cooked quinoa (red variety preferred)

In a wok or heavy skillet set over medium heat, warm the sesame oil. Add the ginger, garlic, and onion, and stir-fry the mixture for 30 seconds.

Omnivores, add the beef strips, olive oil, chili powder, cumin, paprika, oregano, garlic powder, onion powder, salt, and pepper to the skillet, and continue stir-frying until the beef strips are cooked through, about 7 to 10 minutes.

Vegans, add the black beans, olive oil, chili powder, cumin, paprika, oregano, garlic powder, onion powder, salt, and pepper to the skillet, and continue stir-frying for 4 to 5 minutes.

Both omnivores and vegans, then add the turnip, carrot, broccoli, and mushroom, and stir-fry for another 2 to 3 minutes. Season to taste. Serve over the cooked quinoa.

NUTRITION INFORMATION PER SERVING

	Calories	Protein (g)	Carbs (g)	Fat (g)	Sat Fat (g)	Unsat Fat (g)	Fiber (g)
Omnivore	657	50	44	32	7	21	10
Vegan	543	19	72	21	3	17	18

SYSTEM	ENDOCRINE GLAND	ANATOMY	PHYSIOLOGICAL ACTIVITIES	CORE ISSUES	FOODS
THE ROOT	**Adrenals**	• Blood cells • Bones • DNA • Immune system • Joints • Legs and feet • Muscles • Rectum • Skin • Tailbone (coccyx)	• Enzyme activity • Flight-or-fight response • Gene expression • Protein production	• Safety • Survival • Tribe	• Dietary proteins • Immune-enhancing foods • Insoluble fiber • Mineral-rich foods • Root vegetables • Red-colored foods
THE FLOW	**Ovaries/Testes**	• Bladder • Hips • Kidneys • Large intestine • Reproductive system • Sacrum	• Cellular replication • Fat storage • Reproduction • Water balance	• Creativity • Emotions • Relationships	• Dietary fats and oils • Fermented foods • Fish and seafood • Nuts and seeds • Tropical foods • Water • Orange-colored foods
THE FIRE	**Pancreas**	• Gallbladder • Liver • Small intestine • Stomach	• Assimilation • Biotransformation • Blood sugar balance • Digestion	• Balance • Energy • Power	• Dietary carbohydrates • Healthy sweeteners • Legumes • Soluble fiber • Whole grains • Yellow-colored foods
THE LOVE	**Thymus and Heart**	• Armpits • Arms • Blood vessels • Breasts • Hands • Lungs • Lymphatic system • Shoulders • Wrists	• Breathing • Circulation • Oxygenation	• Compassion • Expansion • Service	• Leafy vegetables • Microgreens • Phytonutrients • Sprouts • Vegetables (especially green)
THE TRUTH	**Thyroid**	• Cheeks • Chin • Ears • Mouth • Neck • Nose • Throat	• Chewing • Metabolism • Hearing • Smelling • Speaking	• Authenticity • Choice • Voice	• Fruits • Juices • Sauces • Sea plants • Soups • Teas
THE INSIGHT	**Pituitary**	• Brain • Eyebrows • Eyes • Forehead • Neurons • Neurotransmitters	• Mood balance • Sleep • Thought processing	• Intuition • Reflection • Visualization	• Caffeine • Chocolate/cocoa • Mood-modulating foods • Spices • Blue-purple foods
THE SPIRIT	**Pineal**	• Electromagnetic field • Energy meridians • Nervous system	• Circadian rhythms • Cleansing • Light sensitivity	• Connection • Purpose • Soul	• Fasting and detoxification practices • Photons • Toxin-free foods

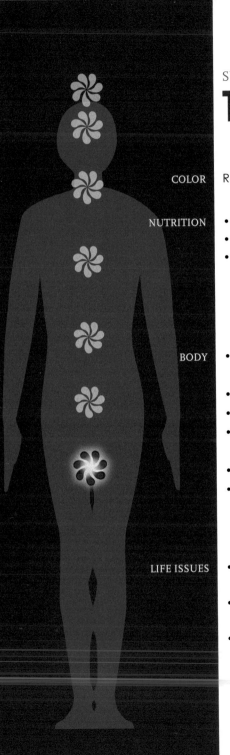

THE ROOT

COLOR Red

NUTRITION
- Protein (animal and vegetable)
- Minerals (e.g., calcium, iron, zinc)
- Red foods (e.g., cherries, pomegranate, apples)

BODY
- Protein-containing structures (e.g., muscles, skin)
- Mineral-containing structures (e.g., bones)
- Immune system
- Adrenal glands and stress hormones (e.g., cortisol, adrenaline)
- Lower body from legs to feet
- DNA: individual identity, genetic identity, inheritance, and blood

LIFE ISSUES
- Safety and the ability to survive in a physical world
- Connections to people and social networks: family, communities, "tribes"
- Rootedness, groundedness: relationship to the physical earth

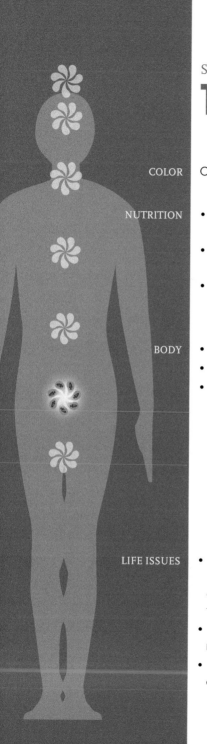

THE FLOW

COLOR Orange

NUTRITION
- Fats and oils (unsaturated and saturated fats)
- Orange foods (e.g., carrots, sweet potatoes, citrus fruits, salmon)
- Water

BODY
- Reproductive system: ovaries, testes
- Urinary system: kidneys, bladder, urethra
- Large intestine, which pulls water from waste products

LIFE ISSUES
- Creativity: art, scientific discovery, problem-solving, new ideas, making a home beautiful, new recipes, foods from different cultures
- Fertility: producing new life, new ideas, new energy
- Partnerships or relationships with one other person

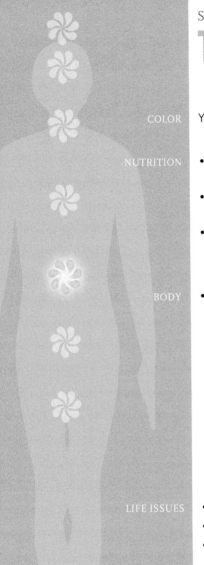

THE FIRE

COLOR   Yellow

NUTRITION
- Carbohydrates: quick-burning sugars and starches, high-fiber foods
- Yellow foods (e.g., ginger root, yellow summer squash, banana)
- Whole grains and legumes high in fiber and B vitamins

BODY
- Digestive system: stomach, pancreas, liver, gallbladder, small intestine

LIFE ISSUES
- Drive and ambition
- Energy, power, and confidence
- Work-life balance vs. issues of burnout

THE LOVE

COLOR Green

NUTRITION
- Vegetables
- Green foods (e.g., spirulina, chlorella, leafy greens, broccoli, Brussels sprouts, kale)

BODY
- Heart and cardiovascular system: circulation of nutrients to care for the entire body
- Lungs and respiratory tract: associated with expansiveness and also with grief
- Thymus: adaptive immune system (responding to threats appropriately)
- Lymphatic system

LIFE ISSUES
- Compassion and service
- Self-care
- Expansion: feeling larger, more generous
- Grief
- Movement (e.g., aerobic activities like walking, dancing, jogging)

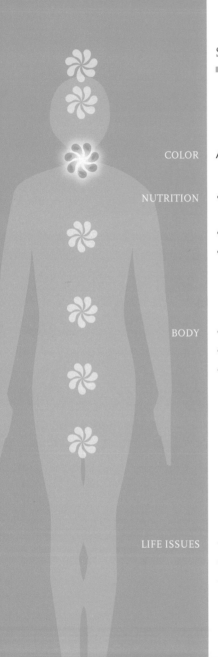

SYSTEM 5
THE TRUTH

COLOR
Aquamarine

NUTRITION
- Sea plants (e.g., nori, wakame, hijiki, dulse)
- Fruits
- Liquid foods (e.g., smoothies, soups, sauces, broths, stews, teas)

BODY
- Voice box (larynx) and throat
- Thyroid gland
- Sensory organs: ears, nose, throat, and mouth

LIFE ISSUES
- Authenticity
- Voice: speaking your truth
- Choices

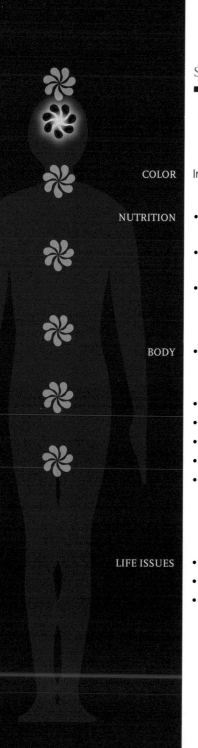

SYSTEM 6
THE INSIGHT

COLOR | Indigo

NUTRITION
- Blue-purple foods (e.g., blueberries, blackberries, kale, grapes)
- Mood-modulating foods (e.g., caffeine, chocolate, alcohol)
- Spices

BODY
- Pituitary gland, which organizes biochemicals necessary for thought and emotion
- Eyes
- Sleep
- Neurons, neurotransmitters, and brain
- Cognition and thought processing
- Mood

LIFE ISSUES
- Insight and intuition, the "inner eyes"
- Visualization
- Reflection and discernment

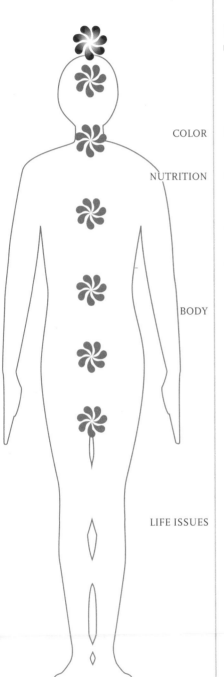

SYSTEM 7
THE SPIRIT

COLOR | White

NUTRITION
- White foods (natural, not bleached) (e.g., cauliflower, coconut products, onions, garlic, cabbage, white beans
- Cleansing, purifying foods (e.g., lemo organically grown foods)
- Fasting

BODY
- Pineal gland, which modulates circadian rhythms
- Response to light
- Electromagnetic field

LIFE ISSUES
- Spirituality
- Sense of purpose and meaning
- Feeling connected to something larg
- Awe, wonder, and gratitude

DAY 4: THE FLOW—EMOTIONS

We all know that being able to express deep emotion can literally save a person's life, and suppressing emotion can kill you both spiritually and physically.

—LISA KLEYPAS

Meal Plan

	Omnivore	Vegan
Breakfast	Tropical Smoothie	Tropical Smoothie
Lunch	Shredded Carrot and Cabbage Salad with Mediterranean Cod	Shredded Carrot and Cabbage Salad with Nut-Seed Pâté
Snack	Nectarine and Macadamia Nuts	Nectarine and Macadamia Nuts
Dinner	Wild Salmon with Tangy Apricot Sauce and Greens	Creamy Carrot Coconut Curry Soup

Whole Detox Emotion Log

At the end of the day, track any emotions that you had on the Whole Detox Emotion Log.

Thought Pattern Activity

The following are some limiting thoughts that relate to the FLOW:

How I feel isn't important.
My emotions need to be controlled.
I fear becoming lost in my emotions.

Pick the limiting thought that seems to ring most true for you. If none of the examples feel true, write down your own limiting thought as it relates to the FLOW.

Next, set your timer for five minutes. Spend that time journaling on that thought, how it has affected your life, and how you feel when you have that thought.

Movement

Enjoy a swim or some water aerobics! Depending upon your geographical location, you may opt to take a dip in an indoor pool. However, if you have the option, natural bodies of water are best. Swimming puts minimal stress on the joints and strengthens the cardiovascular system. Even if you don't consider yourself a great swimmer, the backstroke is one of the easier, more relaxing swimming strokes. If you don't have access to a pool of any type, making large swimming motions with your arms to engage your cardiovascular system.

Affirmation

Spend three minutes saying aloud the following affirmation:

> I am open to my fullest, healthiest emotional expression.

Feel how your body responds to these words. You can also create your own statement. Feel free to write it on a beautiful notecard or a plain Post-it note and put it in your immediate environment for the day.

Visualization

Set a timer for three minutes. During that time, close your eyes and visualize yourself being in the flow of your emotional expression. Imagine any happy feelings dancing inside you and creating healthy movement. Let these happy feelings visit the places within you that feel stuck and stagnant, allowing for greater movement and ease.

Meditation

For three minutes, sit still with your hands cupped in your low belly region. Close your eyes and do a scan of your body from top to bottom, looking for stored, stuck emotions. If you find any, meditate on that place. Create a dialogue with the emotion using a journal.

DAY 4 RECIPES

Breakfast

TROPICAL SMOOTHIE
Serves 1

1 cup peach slices
1 small banana
1 cup unsweetened coconut milk
  (boxed variety)
1 tablespoon flaxseed meal
1 tablespoon unsweetened coconut
  flakes

½ teaspoon ground cardamom
½ teaspoon ground cinnamon
1 scoop protein powder of your choice
  (hemp, pea, rice, whey for omnivores)
Water and ice as needed

Put all the liquid and whole food ingredients into a high-speed blender first, followed by the dry ingredients, then blend everything until a fluid consistency is reached. Add more water if needed. Drink immediately.

NUTRITION INFORMATION PER SERVING

Calories	Protein (g)	Carbs (g)	Fat (g)	Sat Fat (g)	Unsat Fat (g)	Fiber (g)
390	28	42	13	8	0.1	7

Lunch

SHREDDED CARROT AND CABBAGE SALAD WITH MEDITERRANEAN COD *(OMNIVORE)* OR NUT-SEED PÂTÉ *(VEGAN)*
Serves 1

FOR OMNIVORES:

1 tablespoon extra-virgin olive oil
½ teaspoon ground oregano
3 ounces wild-caught cod
Juice of ½ medium lemon

FOR VEGANS:

¼ cup raw sunflower seeds, soaked for
  several hours and rinsed
¼ cup raw pine nuts, soaked for several
  hours and rinsed
2 tablespoons tahini
⅛ teaspoon ground cumin
Juice of ½ medium lemon

FOR BOTH:

½ cup shredded carrots

½ cup shredded red cabbage

1 handful mixed greens, about 1 cup, cut into bite-size pieces

½ avocado (saved from yesterday), cubed

Sea salt and ground black pepper to taste

FOR THE DRESSING

2 tablespoons orange juice

1 tablespoon high-oleic sunflower oil or extra-virgin olive oil

¼ teaspoon parsley flakes

In a small bowl, combine the carrots and cabbage. In another small bowl, whisk together all the dressing ingredients, then pour the dressing over the carrots and cabbage. Set the salad aside.

Omnivores, heat the olive oil in a skillet set over medium-high heat, then stir in the oregano. Gently add the cod to the skillet and squeeze the lemon juice on top. Let the cod cook until it's firm, about 5 minutes on each side. While it's cooking, arrange the mixed greens and avocado on a serving plate. Place the cooked cod on the greens, and top the cod with the salad (or put it to the side if you prefer). Season to taste.

Vegans, in a high-speed blender or food processor, blend the sunflower seeds, pine nuts, tahini, cumin, and lemon juice, adding water as needed for consistency. Arrange the mixed greens and avocado on a serving plate. Spoon the salad on top of the greens, followed by the nut and seed blend. Season to taste.

NUTRITION INFORMATION PER SERVING

	Calories	Protein (g)	Carbs (g)	Fat (g)	Sat Fat (g)	Unsat Fat (g)	Fiber (g)
Omnivore	535	19	22	44	6	46	10
Vegan	720	18	32	64	7	40	11

Snack

NECTARINE AND MACADAMIA NUTS
Serves 1

1 medium nectarine (or orange if you prefer)
1 scant handful (about 10) macadamia nuts

NUTRITION INFORMATION PER SERVING

Calories	Protein (g)	Carbs (g)	Fat (g)	Sat Fat (g)	Unsat Fat (g)	Fiber (g)
245	3	19	20	3	16	4

Dinner

WILD SALMON WITH TANGY APRICOT SAUCE AND GREENS *(OMNIVORE)*
Serves 2

1 tablespoon plus 2 teaspoons extra-virgin olive oil
1 8- to 10-ounce wild-caught salmon fillet

2 handfuls arugula or other leafy greens, about 2 cups
1 teaspoon freshly squeezed lemon juice
1 teaspoon dried dill

FOR THE SAUCE:

3 apricots, pitted and diced
3 tablespoons balsamic vinegar
1 teaspoon minced fresh ginger
1 tablespoon sesame oil

4 tablespoons orange juice (fresh-squeezed preferred)
1 teaspoon orange zest

In a skillet set over low heat, warm 1 tablespoon of the olive oil. Place the salmon in the oil with its skin side down. Cover the skillet and let the salmon cook.

Meanwhile, make the sauce. In a small saucepan set over medium heat, combine the apricots, vinegar, and ginger, and stir the mixture for about 2 to 3 minutes. Reduce the heat to low, and add the sesame oil, orange juice, and orange zest, combining everything well. Then pour this heated mixture on top of the salmon, continuing to cook until the salmon is done, turning it on each side for a total cooking time of about 7 to 10 minutes.

In a bowl, lightly toss the greens with the remaining olive oil, lemon juice, and dill. Transfer them to a serving plate, then dish half the salmon alongside them. (Save the other half of the salmon for tomorrow's lunch.)

NUTRITION INFORMATION PER SERVING

Calories	Protein (g)	Carbs (g)	Fat (g)	Sat Fat (g)	Unsat Fat (g)	Fiber (g)
470	36	14	29	5	23	1

CREAMY CARROT COCONUT CURRY SOUP *(VEGAN)*
Serves 2

2 teaspoons coconut oil

½ medium yellow onion, chopped

8 medium to large carrots, scrubbed, cut into ½-inch-thick rounds

2 teaspoons curry powder

¼ teaspoon ginger powder

1 cup purified water

2 cups organic vegetable broth

3 tablespoons almond butter

½ cup unsweetened, full-fat coconut milk (canned)

Sea salt and freshly ground pepper to taste

In a large saucepan or soup pot set over medium heat, melt the coconut oil. Add the onion, sautéing it 3 to 4 minutes, or until it becomes soft and translucent. Add the carrots, curry powder, ginger powder, and water, and let the mixture cook, stirring it constantly, for another 30 seconds. Pour in the broth, raise the heat to high, and bring the soup to a boil. As soon as it reaches a boil, reduce the heat to low and partially cover the pot. Simmer the soup about 15 minutes, preferably until the carrots are somewhat tender. Add the almond butter and the coconut milk, stirring for an additional 30 seconds, allowing the nut butter to melt slightly.

Carefully transfer the soup in batches to a high-speed blender or food processor, or use a wand mixer in the pot, and blend the soup until it's smooth. Season it with salt and pepper.

Ladle half the soup into a serving bowl and eat it while it's hot. (Save the remaining half of the soup for tomorrow's lunch.)

NUTRITION INFORMATION PER SERVING

Calories	Protein (g)	Carbs (g)	Fat (g)	Sat Fat (g)	Unsat Fat (g)	Fiber (g)
445	8	38	32	16	14	9

DAY 5: THE FLOW—CREATIVITY

Creativity involves breaking out of established patterns in order to look at things in a different way.

—EDWARD DE BONO

Meal Plan

	Omnivore	Vegan
Breakfast	Mango-Peach-Ginger Smoothie	Mango-Peach-Ginger Smoothie
Lunch	Kale and Carrot Salad with Orange Cardamom Dressing Wild Salmon with Tangy Apricot Sauce	Kale and Carrot Salad with Orange Cardamom Dressing Creamy Carrot Coconut Curry Soup
Snack	Orange Bell Pepper with Walnut Pesto	Orange Bell Pepper with Walnut Pesto
Dinner	Rosemary Lamb and Herbed Quinoa	Rosemary Lentils and Herbed Quinoa

Whole Detox Emotion Log

At the end of the day, track any emotions that you had on the Whole Detox Emotion Log.

Thought Pattern Activity

The following are some limiting thoughts that relate to the FLOW:

I'm not very creative.
I rarely have good ideas.
Creativity is for artists only.

Pick the limiting thought that seems to ring most true for you. If none of the examples feel true, write down your own limiting thought as it relates to the FLOW.

Next, set your timer for five minutes. Spend that time journaling on that thought, how it has affected your life, and how you feel when you have that thought.

Movement

The FLOW is centered in the area just below your waist and stomach—the area where your reproductive organs, kidneys, and bladder are located. Get your energy flowing by working your hips: Spin a hula hoop around your waist for three minutes. If you don't have a hula hoop, sit on the floor, open your legs as wide as you comfortably can, and stretch with a flat back (as best you can) over to each foot. Make sure your back is as straight as you can make it—don't let it curve—as you keep your neck aligned with your back. Reach from side to side, pulling out of your hip area and giving yourself a maximal stretch forward, to the level of comfort only.

Affirmation

Spend three minutes saying aloud the following affirmation:

I am highly creative in my actions and thoughts.

Feel how your body responds to these words. You can also create your own statement. Feel free to write it on a beautiful notecard or a plain Post-it note and put it in your immediate environment for the day.

Visualization

Set a timer for three minutes. During that time, close your eyes and visualize yourself feeling the flow of the creative force. Imagine that it, similar to a waterfall, cascades over you and enters every cell of your being, making you feel more vibrant and playful in all you do and think.

Meditation

For three minutes let yourself do a flowing meditation by sitting quietly in a chair while you move your upper body in a slow, circular motion.

DAY 5 RECIPES

Breakfast

MANGO-PEACH-GINGER SMOOTHIE

Serves 1

½ mango, cored and diced (save the other half for tomorrow's smoothie)

1 small peach, sliced

2 Medjool dates, pitted

1 teaspoon grated fresh ginger

½ teaspoon ground cinnamon

½ cup unsweetened almond milk

1 tablespoon flaxseed meal

1 scoop protein powder of your choice (hemp, pea, rice, whey for omnivores)

Water and ice to blend

Put all the liquid and whole food ingredients into a high-speed blender first, followed by the dry ingredients, then blend everything until a fluid consistency is reached. Add more water if needed. Drink immediately.

NUTRITION INFORMATION PER SERVING

Calories	Protein (g)	Carbs (g)	Fat (g)	Sat Fat (g)	Unsat Fat (g)	Fiber (g)
328	28	45	6	0.1	0.4	7

Lunch

KALE AND CARROT SALAD WITH ORANGE CARDAMOM DRESSING

Serves 1

2 handfuls chopped kale, about 2 large leaves

½ cup grated carrots

1 tablespoon chia seeds

FOR THE DRESSING:

2 tablespoons orange juice

1 tablespoon extra-virgin olive oil

½ garlic clove, minced

¼ teaspoon ground cardamom

Dash of sea salt

Dash of ground black pepper

Arrange the kale, carrots, and chia seeds on a serving plate. In a small bowl, whisk together all the ingredients for the dressing, then pour it over the salad.

Warm up yesterday's leftover Wild Salmon with Tangy Apricot Sauce (*omnivore*; or eat the salmon at room temperature if you prefer) or Creamy Carrot Coconut Curry Soup (*vegan*) to serve with the salad.

NUTRITION INFORMATION PER SERVING

	Calories	Protein (g)	Carbs (g)	Fat (g)	Sat Fat (g)	Unsat Fat (g)	Fiber (g)
Omnivore	775	42	44	48	8	40	10
Vegan	750	16	68	51	19	31	18

Snack

ORANGE BELL PEPPER WITH WALNUT PESTO

Makes about 3 cups pesto

7 large garlic cloves

1 cup fresh basil leaves

2 cups walnut halves

½ cup raw pine nuts

2 tablespoons freshly squeezed lemon juice

1 cup extra-virgin olive oil

½ teaspoon sea salt

Dash of ground black pepper

1 orange bell pepper, sliced

Combine the garlic, basil, walnuts, pine nuts, lemon juice, olive oil, salt, and pepper in a high-speed blender or food processor, blending the mixture until it is smooth. Add additional lemon juice, olive oil, salt, or pepper to taste.

Dip the slices of orange bell pepper in some of the pesto for your snack. (Store the remaining pesto in a glass jar in the refrigerator for use in other meals over the next several days.)

NUTRITION INFORMATION PER SERVING

Calories	Protein (g)	Carbs (g)	Fat (g)	Sat Fat (g)	Unsat Fat (g)	Fiber (g)
529	7	16	51	6	43	5

Dinner

ROSEMARY LAMB *(OMNIVORE)* OR LENTILS *(VEGAN)* AND HERBED QUINOA
Serves 2

FOR OMNIVORES:

10 ounces organic, grass-fed ground lamb (makes about 6 meatballs)

FOR VEGANS:

1½ cups barely, or not fully, cooked orange/red lentils

FOR BOTH:

2 teaspoons extra-virgin olive oil

2 tablespoons chopped cashews or other nuts of choice (optional)

1½ teaspoons dried rosemary

1 teaspoon dried thyme

1 teaspoon parsley flakes

1 teaspoon dried sage

½ garlic clove, minced

Pinch of ground black pepper

1½ teaspoons freshly squeezed orange juice

½ cup cooked quinoa, cooked according to package directions (this is enough for just one serving)

Omnivores, in a mixing bowl, combine well the lamb, chopped nuts, rosemary, thyme, parsley, sage, garlic, pepper, and orange juice. Divide the mixture into six equal portions and roll each one in your hand to form 6 medium meatballs. In a skillet, heat the olive oil and brown the meatballs for 15 to 20 minutes, turning as needed.

Vegans, in a skillet set over medium heat, warm the olive oil with the partially cooked lentils. Stir in the chopped nuts, rosemary, thyme, parsley, sage, garlic, pepper, and orange juice, and cook the mixture for about 5 to 7 minutes.

Both omnivores and vegans, spoon the cooked quinoa onto a serving plate.

Omnivores, add to the plate 3 meatballs. (Save the remaining 3 meatballs for tomorrow's lunch.)

Vegans, place half the lentil mixture onto the plate with the quinoa. (Save the remaining lentils for tomorrow's lunch.)

Season to taste and serve warm.

NUTRITION INFORMATION PER SERVING

	Calories	Protein (g)	Carbs (g)	Fat (g)	Sat Fat (g)	Unsat Fat (g)	Fiber (g)
Omnivore	525	33	23	33	11	18	3
Vegan	395	18	51	14	2	9	10

DAY 6: THE FLOW—FATS AND OILS

Thirty years of nutritional advice have left us fatter, sicker, and more poorly nourished. Which is why we find ourselves in the predicament we do: in need of a whole new way to think about eating.

—MICHAEL POLLAN

Meal Plan

	Omnivore	Vegan
Breakfast	Orange Bliss Smoothie	Orange Bliss Smoothie
Lunch	Citrus Fennel Salad Rosemary Lamb	Citrus Fennel Salad Rosemary Lentils
Snack	Avocado and Pumpkin Seeds	Avocado and Pumpkin Seeds
Dinner	Macadamia Nut-Encrusted Halibut with Mango Curry Chutney Seasoned Leeks	Wild Rice and Nut-Stuffed Orange Bell Pepper with Mango Curry Chutney Seasoned Leeks

Whole Detox Emotion Log

At the end of the day, track any emotions that you had on the Whole Detox Emotion Log.

Thought Pattern Activity

The following are some limiting thoughts that relate to the FLOW:

It's difficult to go with the flow of life.
If I eat fat, I'll get fat.
I fear fat.

Pick the limiting thought that seems to ring most true for you. If none of the examples feel true, write down your own limiting thought as it relates to the FLOW.

Next, set your timer for five minutes. Spend that time journaling on that thought, how it has affected your life, and how you feel when you have that thought.

Movement

CHILD'S POSE (BALASANA)

This is one of the most powerful poses to connect you to your breath. It is a relaxing and restorative pose that releases tension in the lower back, massages the internal organs, and gently opens the hips. Go only to the degree that you feel comfortable.

1. Kneel on a mat or blanket.
2. Separate your knees about hip-width apart and sit on your heels, if you can, or put a folded blanket or block under you to come closer down to the floor.
3. Exhale and slowly fold over. Let your forehead rest on the mat or blanket.
4. You can let your arms go back so they are resting by your feet or you can stretch your arms out in front of you, palms down.
5. Maintain this position for three minutes. Take several deep inhalations and exhalations. Feel the flow of air in your abdomen. Observe how you feel.

Affirmation

Spend three minutes saying aloud the following affirmation:

I flow freely and fluidly in every moment.

Feel how your body responds to these words. You can also create your own statement. Feel free to write it on a beautiful notecard or a plain Post-it note and put it in your immediate environment for the day.

Visualization

Set a timer for three minutes. During that time, close your eyes and visualize yourself as moving particles. See where in your body the particles are moving rapidly or too slowly. Allow all of them to come into a synchronous, rhythmic dance. Feel the freedom of this dynamic movement coursing through you.

Meditation

For three minutes, meditate in the presence of running water, such as a stream, river, or even a fountain (small or large). You can also listen to a CD playing sounds of running water. While you are in the moment, listening,

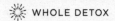

imagine that a generous flow of healthy energy moves through you at a pace that is just right.

DAY 6 RECIPES

Breakfast

ORANGE BLISS SMOOTHIE
Serves 1

½ mango, diced (saved from
yesterday's smoothie)

½ medium carrot, finely diced or grated
to make it easy to blend

½ cup freshly squeezed orange juice

½ cup unsweetened almond milk

½ teaspoon pumpkin spice powder

1 scoop protein powder of your choice
(hemp, pea, rice, whey for omnivores)

Water and ice to blend

Put all the liquid and whole food ingredients into a high-speed blender first, followed by the dry ingredients, then blend everything until a fluid consistency is reached. Add more water if needed. Drink immediately.

NUTRITION INFORMATION PER SERVING

Calories	Protein (g)	Carbs (g)	Fat (g)	Sat Fat (g)	Unsat Fat (g)	Fiber (g)
275	26	35	4	0.1	0.1	3

Lunch

CITRUS FENNEL SALAD WITH ROSEMARY LAMB *(OMNIVORE)* **OR LENTILS** *(VEGAN)*
Serves 1

1 orange, peeled and sectioned

½ fennel bulb, very thinly sliced (save
the other half for tomorrow's lunch;
use the fronds in the dressing)

½ avocado, sliced (leave the pit in the
other ½ and save it for today's snack)

¼ medium shallot, very thinly sliced

2 tablespoons chopped walnut halves

2 tablespoons chopped fresh mint
leaves

FOR THE DRESSING:

1 tablespoon extra-virgin olive oil

1 tablespoon apple cider vinegar

1½ teaspoons honey

1 tablespoon fennel fronds, finely
   chopped

Dash of sea salt

Dash of ground black pepper

In a bowl, gently toss together the orange sections and fennel bulb slices. Add the avocado, shallot, walnuts, and mint, and toss well. Transfer the salad to a serving plate or bowl, and set it aside.

In a small bowl, whisk together the olive oil and apple cider vinegar. Add the honey and fennel fronds, and season the mix with salt and pepper. Pour the dressing over the salad.

Warm up yesterday's leftover Rosemary Lamb (*omnivore*) or Lentils (*vegan*) to serve with the salad.

NUTRITION INFORMATION PER SERVING

	Calories	Protein (g)	Carbs (g)	Fat (g)	Sat Fat (g)	Unsat Fat (g)	Fiber (g)
Omnivore	903	36	53	63	15	45	14
Vegan	773	21	81	44	6	36	21

Snack

AVOCADO AND PUMPKIN SEEDS

Serves 1

½ avocado (saved from lunch)

Sea salt to taste

2 tablespoons roasted pumpkin seeds

Sprinkle the avocado with the salt, then eat it with the pumpkin seeds.

NUTRITION INFORMATION PER SERVING

Calories	Protein (g)	Carbs (g)	Fat (g)	Sat Fat (g)	Unsat Fat (g)	Fiber (g)
287	7	11	25	4	12	7

Dinner

MACADAMIA NUT–ENCRUSTED HALIBUT *(OMNIVORE)*
Serves 2

¼ cup brown rice flour

2 tablespoons flaxseed meal

2 tablespoons melted coconut oil, divided

¼ to ⅓ cup orange juice

¼ cup finely chopped, lightly salted macadamia nuts

2 5-ounce wild-caught halibut fillets

2 tablespoons finely chopped green onion, for garnish

In a small bowl, combine the flour and flaxseed meal, and transfer it to a shallow dish or plate. In a separate shallow dish, combine 1 tablespoon of the melted coconut oil with the orange juice. Put the macadamia nuts in a third shallow dish or on a plate.

Dip a fillet in the flour mixture, coating both sides, then in the coconut oil and orange juice mixture, and finally in the nuts, completely coating the fillet. Repeat the same with the second piece of fish.

In a skillet set over medium heat, warm the remaining tablespoon of coconut oil. Place the fillets in the skillet and cook both sides of each well, about 5 to 7 minutes total, or until done. Remove the fish from the heat.

Transfer 1 fillet to a serving plate, and sprinkle it with the green onion. Optionally, you may top it with the Mango Curry Chutney (recipe follows). (Save the second fillet for tomorrow's lunch.) Serve the halibut alongside the Seasoned Leeks (recipe follows).

NUTRITION INFORMATION PER SERVING

Calories	Protein (g)	Carbs (g)	Fat (g)	Sat Fat (g)	Unsat Fat (g)	Fiber (g)
511	34	23	33	14	26	4

WILD RICE AND NUT–STUFFED ORANGE BELL PEPPER (VEGAN)
Serves 2

1 tablespoon extra-virgin olive oil
½ cup chopped yellow onion
2 garlic cloves, minced
1 cup organic vegetable broth
½ cup uncooked wild rice
½ cup dried sprouted lentils
¼ cup diced celery
¼ cup carrot, sliced in ½-inch-thick rounds

¼ cup raw cashews
2 tablespoons slivered almonds
⅛ teaspoon dried rosemary
⅛ teaspoon ground oregano
Pinch of sea salt
2 large orange bell peppers, stemmed and seeded but left whole

In a large saucepan, heat the olive oil and sauté the onion and garlic until the onion is soft. Add the broth, rice, sprouted lentils, celery, and carrot. Bring the mixture to a boil, then cover the pan, reduce the heat, and let it simmer for 20 to 25 minutes, or until the rice is almost done.

Meanwhile, in a small bowl, combine the cashews, almonds, rosemary, oregano, and salt. When the rice and vegetables are ready, remove them from the heat and stir in the nut and spice mixture, then set it aside.

Fill another saucepan with a few inches of water and set the bell peppers, top side up, in the water. Bring the pot to a boil and cook the peppers for 2 to 3 minutes, or until they are slightly tender. Remove them from the water and place one on a serving plate.

Stuff the pepper with half the rice-nut mixture and spoon any excess of that half-portion around the pepper. Do the same with the second pepper, using the remaining half of the rice-nut mixture. (Save the second stuffed pepper for tomorrow's lunch.)

Serve the stuffed pepper with a dollop of Mango Curry Chutney (recipe follows) and alongside the Seasoned Leeks (recipe follows).

NUTRITION INFORMATION PER SERVING

Calories	Protein (g)	Carbs (g)	Fat (g)	Sat Fat (g)	Unsat Fat (g)	Fiber (g)
587	23	85	20	3	15	14

MANGO CURRY CHUTNEY

Makes about ¾ to 1 cup

½ tablespoon sesame oil

¼ teaspoon ground cayenne pepper

1 tablespoon curry powder

2 tablespoons diced yellow onion

½ tablespoon minced fresh ginger

2 tablespoons golden raisins

1 fresh, ripe mango, cut into strips, or
  ¾ cup frozen mango

¼ cup orange juice

2 tablespoons apple cider vinegar

In a small skillet, heat the oil and add the cayenne pepper, curry powder, and onion. When the onion becomes soft, add the ginger, raisins, and mango, and continue sautéing the mixture for 1 minute.

In a small mixing bowl, combine the orange juice and vinegar. Add this to the skillet, and continue simmering on low heat, stirring frequently, for 15 to 20 minutes, or until the chutney is slightly thickened. Then remove it from the heat.

After the chutney has cooled, store any leftovers in a glass jar in the refrigerator.

NUTRITION INFORMATION PER SERVING

Calories	Protein (g)	Carbs (g)	Fat (g)	Sat Fat (g)	Unsat Fat (g)	Fiber (g)
51	0.4	10	1	0.2	1	1

SEASONED LEEKS

Serves 1

1 tablespoon extra-virgin olive oil

1 cup sliced leeks

Seasoning of your choice (oregano, dill, thyme, etc.)

In a skillet set over medium-high heat, warm the olive oil, then stir-fry the leeks for 3 to 4 minutes, adding whatever herbs or spices you desire. Serve warm.

NUTRITION INFORMATION PER SERVING

Calories	Protein (g)	Carbs (g)	Fat (g)	Sat Fat (g)	Unsat Fat (g)	Fiber (g)
125	1	9	10	1	8	1

DAY 7: THE FIRE—STRESS

Every day we have plenty of opportunities to get angry, stressed, or offended. But what you're doing when you indulge these negative emotions is giving something outside yourself power over your happiness. You can choose to not let little things upset you.

—JOEL OSTEEN

Meal Plan

	Omnivore	Vegan
Breakfast	Spice Shake	Spice Shake
Lunch	Arugula and Fennel Salad Macadamia Nut-Encrusted Halibut with Mango Curry Chutney	Arugula and Fennel Salad Wild Rice and Nut-Stuffed Orange Bell Pepper with Mango Curry Chutney
Snack	Yellow Squash with Walnut Pesto	Yellow Squash with Walnut Pesto
Dinner	Chicken and Cauliflower Curry	Fiery Curry Lentil Soup

Whole Detox Emotion Log

At the end of the day, track any emotions that you had on the Whole Detox Emotion Log.

Thought Pattern Activity

The following are some limiting thoughts that relate to the FIRE:

I can't escape being burnt out.
Life is exhausting.
I can't help eating when I'm stressed.

Pick the limiting thought that seems to ring most true for you. If none of the examples feel true, write down your own limiting thought as it relates to the FIRE.

Next, set your timer for five minutes. Spend that time journaling on that thought, how it has affected your life, and how you feel when you have that thought.

Movement

TAI CHI "PUSH HANDS"

1. Begin by standing comfortably, with your left foot about eight inches in front of your right foot. Let your body weight settle onto your back right foot.
2. Position your hands about six inches in front of your chest, with your palms facing outward. Your hands should be shoulder-width apart. Don't let them move closer together or farther apart when making the movements.
3. Slowly shift your body weight forward onto your left foot. As you move forward, stretch your arms out, making a slow, horizontal circle with your hands.
4. Bring your hands back into your chest, shifting your weight back onto your right foot. Repeat the movement, keeping the same steady motions.

Get your entire body involved, feeling the expansion and contraction. Most important, have fun!

Affirmation

Spend three minutes saying aloud the following affirmation:

I am resilient and powerful from within.

Feel how your body responds to these words. You can also create your own statement. Feel free to write it on a beautiful notecard or a plain Post-it note and put it in your immediate environment for the day.

Visualization

Set a timer for three minutes. During that time, close your eyes and visualize yourself having your inner power center fill with the color yellow. Let the light beam brightly from that inner place, giving you the sensation of warmth, cheerfulness, and empowerment.

Meditation

For three minutes, meditate on your energy and how you can bring it into balance by assessing what needs to be burnt away and what needs additional sparking.

DAY 7 RECIPES

Breakfast

SPICE SHAKE
Serves 1

¼ cup raw almonds, preferably soaked overnight and rinsed well	½ teaspoon ginger powder
	½ teaspoon vanilla extract
2 cups purified water	Pinch of ground nutmeg
1 Medjool date, pitted	Pinch of ground clove
½ teaspoon turmeric powder	1 tablespoon coconut oil
½ teaspoon ground cinnamon	Water and ice to blend

Put all the liquid and whole food ingredients into a high-speed blender first, followed by the dry ingredients, then blend everything until a fluid consistency is reached. Add more water if needed. Drink immediately.

NUTRITION INFORMATION PER SERVING

Calories	Protein (g)	Carbs (g)	Fat (g)	Sat Fat (g)	Unsat Fat (g)	Fiber (g)
346	8	13	32	13	17	5

Lunch

ARUGULA AND FENNEL SALAD WITH MACADAMIA NUT–ENCRUSTED HALIBUT (OMNIVORE) OR NUT-STUFFED ORANGE BELL PEPPER (VEGAN)
Serves 1

1 large handful arugula, about 2 cups
½ fennel bulb, thinly sliced (saved from yesterday)
2 tablespoons raw pine nuts

FOR THE DRESSING:

1 tablespoon freshly squeezed lemon juice	¼ teaspoon dried dill
	Dash of ground black pepper
1 tablespoon extra-virgin olive oil	Dash of sea salt

Arrange the arugula, fennel, and pine nuts on a serving plate.

In a small bowl, whisk together all the ingredients for the dressing, then drizzle it over the salad.

Warm up yesterday's leftover Macadamia Nut–Encrusted Halibut (omnivore) or Wild Rice and Nut–Stuffed Orange Bell Pepper (vegan) to serve with the salad. Topping your leftovers with Mango Curry Chutney is optional.

NUTRITION INFORMATION PER SERVING

	Calories	Protein (g)	Carbs (g)	Fat (g)	Sat Fat (g)	Unsat Fat (g)	Fiber (g)
Omnivore	801	39	37	59	17	47	9
Vegan	877	28	99	46	6	36	19

Snack

YELLOW SQUASH WITH WALNUT PESTO
Serves 1

1 small yellow summer squash, sliced
2 tablespoons Walnut Pesto (saved from Day 5)

Dip the squash slices in the walnut pesto and enjoy!

NUTRITION INFORMATION PER SERVING

Calories	Protein (g)	Carbs (g)	Fat (g)	Sat Fat (g)	Unsat Fat (g)	Fiber (g)
481	5	6	50	6	43	2

Dinner

CHICKEN AND CAULIFLOWER CURRY (OMNIVORE)
Serves 2

1 tablespoon extra-virgin olive oil
½ large yellow onion, diced
2 large garlic cloves, minced
½-inch piece fresh ginger, minced

½ medium yellow bell pepper, cut into 2-inch strips
2 tablespoons unsweetened, full-fat coconut milk

1 teaspoon honey

2 teaspoons curry powder

1 teaspoon turmeric powder

1 teaspoon tapioca flour

¼ teaspoon sea salt

Pinch of ground black pepper

2 cups chopped cauliflower

2 4-ounce organic, free-range, boneless, skinless chicken breasts, cut into 1-inch pieces

1 cup cooked white quinoa

1 tablespoon chopped fresh cilantro

1 tablespoon chopped green onions

In a large skillet set over medium heat, warm the olive oil, then add the onion, garlic, ginger, and bell pepper, and cook the vegetables, stirring occasionally, until they are soft, about 5 to 7 minutes. Stir in the coconut milk, honey, curry powder, turmeric powder, tapioca flour, salt, and pepper. Bring the mixture to a boil, then add the cauliflower and chicken pieces. Reduce the heat to low, cover the skillet, and simmer the mixture for 15 to 20 minutes, or until the chicken is cooked and the cauliflower is soft.

Spoon the prepared quinoa onto a serving plate, and top it with half the hot curry, then garnish the dish with the cilantro and green onions. (Save the remaining half of the curry for tomorrow's lunch.)

NUTRITION INFORMATION PER SERVING

Calories	Protein (g)	Carbs (g)	Fat (g)	Sat Fat (g)	Unsat Fat (g)	Fiber (g)
408	34	39	13	4	7	7

FIERY CURRY LENTIL SOUP (VEGAN)

Serves 2

1 teaspoon extra-virgin olive oil

2 large garlic cloves, minced

½ medium yellow onion, finely diced

½ cup uncooked yellow lentils, rinsed

2 carrots, sliced

1 large yellow potato, cut into 1-inch cubes

4 cups organic vegetable broth

1 teaspoon curry powder

1 teaspoon ground cumin

Dash of sea salt

Dash of ground black pepper

In a large stock pot set over medium heat, warm the olive oil, then add the garlic and onions, sautéing them until they are soft. Add the lentils, carrots, potato, broth, curry powder, cumin, salt, and pepper, and bring the mixture

to a boil. Lower the heat and simmer the soup for 20 to 30 minutes, stirring occasionally, until the lentils are tender.

Serve half the soup warm. (Save the remaining half for tomorrow's lunch.)

NUTRITION INFORMATION PER SERVING

Calories	Protein (g)	Carbs (g)	Fat (g)	Sat Fat (g)	Unsat Fat (g)	Fiber (g)
414	17	79	5	0.4	2	15

DAY 8: THE FIRE—THOUGHTS

It takes but one positive thought when given a chance to survive and thrive to over-power an entire army of negative thoughts.

—ROBERT H. SCHULLER

Meal Plan

	Omnivore	Vegan
Breakfast	Sunshine Smoothie	Sunshine Smoothie
Lunch	Power-Packed Spinach Salad Chicken and Cauliflower Curry	Power-Packed Spinach Salad Fiery Curry Lentil Soup
Snack	Apple with Sunflower Seed Butter	Apple with Sunflower Seed Butter
Dinner	Turkey-Lentil Meatballs Roasted Spaghetti Squash	Seasoned Chickpeas Roasted Spaghetti Squash

Whole Detox Emotion Log

At the end of the day, track any emotions that you had on the Whole Detox Emotion Log.

Thought Pattern Activity

The following are some limiting thoughts that relate to the FIRE:

My thoughts are out of control.
I expect the worst to happen.
It's difficult to escape my negative thoughts.

Pick the limiting thought that seems to ring most true for you. If none of the examples feel true, write down your own limiting thought as it relates to the FIRE.

Next, set your timer for five minutes. Spend that time journaling on that thought, how it has affected your life, and how you feel when you have that thought.

Movement

WARRIOR POSE (VIRABHANDRASANA)

This exercise opens up your solar plexus area and hips. As with all yoga poses, go to your comfortable limit. Nothing should be painful.

1. Stand facing straight ahead with your arms at your sides.
2. Take a deep inhale, and on the exhalation, step your left foot back about three to four feet.
3. Pivot your left foot to a forty-five-degree angle, making sure it is firmly grounded on the mat.
4. Bend your right knee until the knee lines up with your right ankle and your shin is perpendicular to the floor.
5. Raise your arms above your head.
6. Take several deep inhalations and exhalations.
7. Maintain this position for one to two minutes.
8. Repeat the pose on the other side for one to two minutes.

Affirmation

Spend three minutes saying aloud the following affirmation:

Every thought I have frees me into possibilities.

Feel how your body responds to these words. You can also create your own statement. Feel free to write it on a beautiful notecard or a plain Post-it note and put it in your immediate environment for the day.

Visualization

Set a timer for three minutes. During that time, close your eyes and visualize yourself being filled with thoughts. See them as little lights. Find the ones that are burning bright and give you a sense of power and strength. Allow them to become brighter and stronger. As these bright thoughts fill you from within, you feel transformed. Possibilities seem endless; your potential is radiant.

Meditation

Sit with your thoughts for at least three minutes. Be a passive observer of the thoughts that rise and fall. When you are finished, jot down as many of the thoughts as you can remember. See which ones are coming up multiple times. Are they affirming and empowering or defeating and dismal? If the latter, create a new thought to cancel out anything that is draining to your FIRE.

Wait for a couple of hours and try again. See whether your thoughts have shifted.

DAY 8 RECIPES

Breakfast

SUNSHINE SMOOTHIE

Serves 1

1 small banana

1 cup pineapple juice

1 teaspoon freshly squeezed lemon
    juice

1-inch piece fresh ginger, grated

1 scoop protein powder of your choice
    (hemp, pea, rice, whey for omnivores)

Water and ice to blend

Put all the liquid and whole food ingredients into a high-speed blender first, followed by the dry ingredients, then blend everything until a fluid consistency is reached. Add more water if needed. Drink immediately.

NUTRITION INFORMATION PER SERVING

Calories	Protein (g)	Carbs (g)	Fat (g)	Sat Fat (g)	Unsat Fat (g)	Fiber (g)
341	25	57	2	0.1	0.1	3

Lunch

POWER-PACKED SPINACH SALAD WITH CHICKEN AND CAULIFLOWER CURRY (OMNIVORE) OR FIERY CURRY LENTIL SOUP (VEGAN)
Serves 1

1 large handful spinach, about 2 cups	1 tablespoon chia seeds
1½ tablespoons hemp seeds	1 tablespoon minced shallot

FOR THE DRESSING:

1 tablespoon freshly squeezed lemon juice	1½ tablespoons extra-virgin olive oil
½ teaspoon honey	½ teaspoon mustard seeds
	Dash of sea salt

In a serving bowl, combine the spinach leaves with the hemp seeds, chia seeds, and shallot. Set the bowl aside.

In a small bowl, whisk together all the dressing ingredients, then drizzle the dressing over the salad.

Warm up yesterday's leftover Chicken and Cauliflower Curry (omnivore) or Fiery Curry Lentil Soup (vegan) to serve with the salad.

NUTRITION INFORMATION PER SERVING

	Calories	Protein (g)	Carbs (g)	Fat (g)	Sat Fat (g)	Unsat Fat (g)	Fiber (g)
Omnivore	667	38	37	41	8	28	10
Vegan	784	25	97	35	4	23	21

Snack

APPLE WITH SUNFLOWER SEED BUTTER
Serves 1

1 Golden Delicious apple, sliced	2 tablespoons sunflower seed butter

Spread the apple slices with the sunflower seed butter and enjoy!

NUTRITION INFORMATION PER SERVING

Calories	Protein (g)	Carbs (g)	Fat (g)	Sat Fat (g)	Unsat Fat (g)	Fiber (g)
265	6	31	15	2	13	9

Dinner

TURKEY-LENTIL MEATBALLS *(OMNIVORE)*

Serves 2 (makes 6 large meatballs)

1 tablespoon high-oleic sunflower oil or extra-virgin olive oil

½ medium yellow onion, finely chopped

1 garlic clove, minced

¼ cup finely chopped celery

¾ cup finely chopped kale

8 ounces organic, free-range ground turkey

½ cup cooked French green lentils

¼ cup almond meal (other nut meal or nut flour can be substituted, such as hazelnut)

¼ cup finely chopped fresh parsley

1 tablespoon Dijon mustard

1 teaspoon ground ginger

1 tablespoon flaxseed meal

1½ teaspoons sea salt

Freshly ground black pepper to taste

Preheat the oven to 400°F.

In a large skillet, heat the oil, then add the yellow onion and garlic, sautéing them for about a minute. Add the celery and kale, and continue sautéing until the vegetables soften.

In a large bowl, combine by hand the turkey, lentils, almond meal, parsley, mustard, ginger, flaxseed meal, salt, and pepper. Form the mixture into 6 1½-inch round balls, and place the meatballs on a parchment-lined baking sheet.

Bake the meatballs for 25 minutes, until they are lightly browned.

Enjoy 3 meatballs with a serving of the Roasted Spaghetti Squash (recipe follows). (Save the remaining 3 meatballs for tomorrow's lunch.)

NUTRITION INFORMATION PER SERVING

Calories	Protein (g)	Carbs (g)	Fat (g)	Sat Fat (g)	Unsat Fat (g)	Fiber (g)
223	15	12	13	2	6	5

SEASONED CHICKPEAS *(VEGAN)*

Serves 2

1 tablespoon extra-virgin olive oil	2 tablespoons finely chopped fresh parsley
1 tablespoon cumin seeds	
1 shallot, finely chopped	2 tablespoons finely chopped fresh thyme
1 garlic clove, minced	
1½ cups cooked chickpeas	Pinch of sea salt
Zest and juice of ½ lemon	Freshly ground black pepper to taste

In a large sauté pan, gently heat the olive oil, then stir in the cumin seeds, heating them for 1 to 2 minutes. Add the shallot and garlic, and sauté them for 3 to 4 minutes, stirring frequently. Add the chickpeas, stirring until all the ingredients are warmed and blended together.

Remove the pan from the heat, and stir in the lemon zest and juice, parsley, and thyme. Season the mixture with salt and pepper.

Spoon half the chickpeas onto a serving plate, alongside a serving of Roasted Spaghetti Squash (recipe follows). (Save the other half of the chickpeas for tomorrow's lunch.)

NUTRITION INFORMATION PER SERVING

Calories	Protein (g)	Carbs (g)	Fat (g)	Sat Fat (g)	Unsat Fat (g)	Fiber (g)
226	8	29	9	1	6	7

ROASTED SPAGHETTI SQUASH

Serves about 4

1 small spaghetti squash
1 tablespoon extra-virgin olive oil, plus more for drizzling
Sea salt and freshly ground black pepper to taste

Preheat the oven to 400°F.

Cut both ends off the squash, then cut the squash in half lengthwise. Scoop out the seeds and discard them. Drizzle the flesh of each half with the olive oil and sprinkle each with salt and pepper to taste.

Place the squash halves flesh side down in a glass baking dish filled with about ½ inch of water. Roast the squash in the oven for about 20 to 25 minutes, or until it is tender. Insert a knife in the center to check for doneness. Be careful not to overcook them.

When they are ready, remove them from the oven, discard the water, and use a fork to gently scrape out the flesh of both halves of the squash.

Place about a quarter of the "spaghetti" flesh into a large serving bowl. Drizzle it with a little more olive oil, and serve it with 3 Turkey-Lentil Meatballs (omnivore) or half the Seasoned Chickpeas (vegan). (Save the remaining squash flesh for any future snack or meal or for others in your family to enjoy; no more is required in your twenty-one-day program.)

NUTRITION INFORMATION PER SERVING

Calories	Protein (g)	Carbs (g)	Fat (g)	Sat Fat (g)	Unsat Fat (g)	Fiber (g)
93	2	15	4	0.6	3	3

DAY 9: THE FIRE —CARBOHYDRATES AND SUGAR

Everybody's got their poison, and mine is sugar.

—DERRICK ROSE

Meal Plan

	Omnivore	Vegan
Breakfast	Pineapple-Banana Spiced Smoothie	Pineapple-Banana Spiced Smoothie
Lunch	Quinoa, Amaranth, and Pine Nut Salad Turkey-Lentil Meatballs	Quinoa, Amaranth, and Pine Nut Salad Seasoned Chickpeas
Snack	Yellow Bell Pepper with Walnut Pesto	Yellow Bell Pepper with Walnut Pesto
Dinner	Sesame-Tahini Chicken	Black Beans with Tahini

Whole Detox Emotion Log

At the end of the day, track any emotions that you had on the Whole Detox Emotion Log.

Thought Pattern Activity

The following are some limiting thoughts that relate to the FIRE:

The only thing that picks me up is sugar.
I have difficulty finding sweetness in life.
I need quick energy to fuel my quickly moving life.

Pick the limiting thought that seems to ring most true for you. If none of the examples feel true, write down your own limiting thought as it relates to the FIRE.

Next, set your timer for five minutes. Spend that time journaling on that thought, how it has affected your life, and how you feel when you have that thought.

Movement

Stomach crunches: Lie on your back on a mat or blanket and place your hands behind your head. Bend your knees and lift your feet off the floor, pointing your toes toward the ceiling. Contract your stomach muscles and curl your tailbone, lifting your lower back slightly off the floor toward the ceiling. Return to the starting position and repeat for one to three minutes or until you feel a comfortable "burn." Know your limits! Exert yourself, but not to the point where it becomes painful.

Affirmation

Spend three minutes saying aloud the following affirmation:

My life is saturated with sweetness.

Feel how your body responds to these words. You can also create your own statement. Feel free to write it on a beautiful notecard or a plain Post-it note and put it in your immediate environment for the day.

Visualization

Set a timer for three minutes. During that time, close your eyes and visualize yourself inviting a thick, shining liquid of joy to coat your outer being. Then let every cell of your being on the inside feel relaxed and soothed, saturated with the syrupy sweetness of joy.

...inutes, meditate on the word "sweetness." What comes forth? ...editation by making a list of all the ways you can make your life swe... ...ithout indulging in dietary sweeteners.

DAY 9 RECIPES

Breakfast

___

PINEAPPLE-BANANA SPICED SMOOTHIE

Serves 1

- 1 cup unsweetened coconut milk (boxed variety)
- ½ cup pineapple chunks, frozen or fresh
- 1 small banana
- ½ tablespoon coconut oil
- 1 teaspoon turmeric powder
- ½ teaspoon ground cinnamon
- ½ teaspoon ground ginger
- 1 teaspoon chia seeds
- 1 scoop protein powder of your choice (hemp, pea, rice, whey for omnivores)
- Water and ice to blend

Put all the liquid and whole food ingredients into a high-speed blender first, followed by the dry ingredients, then blend everything until a fluid consistency is reached. Add more water if needed. Drink immediately.

NUTRITION INFORMATION PER SERVING

Calories	Protein (g)	Carbs (g)	Fat (g)	Sat Fat (g)	Unsat Fat (g)	Fiber (g)
391	26	38	16	11	2	5

Lunch

___

QUINOA, AMARANTH, AND PINE NUT SALAD WITH TURKEY-LENTIL MEATBALLS
(OMNIVORE) OR SEASONED CHICKPEAS (VEGAN)

Serves 1

- ½ cup cooked quinoa
- ½ cup cooked amaranth
- Pinch of sea salt
- ¼ medium cucumber, diced

½ medium shallot, diced

¼ cup chopped fresh cilantro

¼ cup chopped fresh basil

1½ tablespoons extra-virgin olive oil

1 tablespoon freshly squeezed lemon
juice

2 tablespoons raw pine nuts

Dash of ground black pepper

In a medium bowl, combine the quinoa and amaranth with a pinch of salt. In a separate bowl, toss together the cucumber, shallot, cilantro, basil, olive oil, and lemon juice, then add this to the quinoa-amaranth mixture, combining the salad well. Sprinkle in the pine nuts, and season with pepper to taste.

Serve the salad, warm or cold, with yesterday's leftover Turkey-Lentil Meatballs (*omnivore*) or Seasoned Chickpeas (*vegan*).

NUTRITION INFORMATION PER SERVING

	Calories	Protein (g)	Carbs (g)	Fat (g)	Sat Fat (g)	Unsat Fat (g)	Fiber (g)
Omnivore	794	28	64	49	6	37	12
Vegan	797	21	81	45	5	37	14

Snack

YELLOW BELL PEPPER WITH WALNUT PESTO

Serves 1

1 yellow bell pepper, sliced

2 tablespoons Walnut Pesto (saved from Day 5)

Dip the yellow bell pepper slices in the walnut pesto and savor!

NUTRITION INFORMATION PER SERVING

Calories	Protein (g)	Carbs (g)	Fat (g)	Sat Fat (g)	Unsat Fat (g)	Fiber (g)
529	7	16	51	6	43	5

Dinner

SESAME-TAHINI CHICKEN (OMNIVORE)

Serves 1

¼ cup uncooked organic long-grain
brown rice

½ cup water or organic broth
(vegetable or chicken)

¼ cup cubed yellow squash

1 tablespoon freshly squeezed lemon
juice

2 4-ounce organic, free-range, boneless,
skinless chicken breasts, cubed

Dash of sea salt

Dash of ground black pepper

1 tablespoon sesame oil, divided

½ tablespoon rice vinegar

1 teaspoon minced fresh ginger

1 garlic clove, minced or pressed

2 tablespoons chopped green onions

½ tablespoon unhulled sesame seeds

1 tablespoon tahini

Use a rice cooker to cook the rice with the squash, if one is available. If not, combine the rice with the ½ cup water or broth in a medium saucepan. Toss in the cubed squash, and bring the pot to a boil over medium-high heat. Reduce the heat to low and simmer the mixture, covered, until the rice is tender and the water has been absorbed, 30 to 40 minutes.

While the rice is cooking, in a medium bowl, pour the lemon juice over the chicken breasts and sprinkle them each with salt and pepper.

In a heated skillet, warm ½ tablespoon of the sesame oil, then add the chicken breasts and pan-fry them on medium heat until they are cooked through. Remove them from heat, and set aside half of the chicken. (Save the other half for tomorrow's lunch.)

In a small bowl, whisk the remaining ½ tablespoon sesame oil with the rice vinegar, ginger, and garlic. When the rice and squash have finished cooking and fully cooled, pour the oil and vinegar mixture into the rice and squash, tossing to coat everything. Add the green onion, then the cooked chicken, or keep the chicken on the side if you prefer.

Sprinkle the dish with the sesame seeds and drizzle the chicken with the tahini before serving.

NUTRITION INFORMATION PER SERVING

Calories	Protein (g)	Carbs (g)	Fat (g)	Sat Fat (g)	Unsat Fat (g)	Fiber (g)
526	35	47	22	3	16	4

BLACK BEANS WITH TAHINI *(VEGAN)*
Serves 2

2 teaspoons extra-virgin olive oil	1 large romaine lettuce heart
½ medium red onion, diced	2 teaspoons minced, fresh cilantro
2 garlic cloves, minced	½ avocado, diced or sliced
½ teaspoon ground cumin	2 tablespoons tahini
1½ cups cooked black beans	

In a medium saucepan set over medium heat, warm the olive oil, then add the onion, garlic, and cumin, stirring the mixture for 2 to 3 minutes, or until the onion is soft and translucent. Add the black beans and simmer them until they are warmed through.

On a serving plate, arrange the romaine heart, then spoon half the beans alongside. (Save the remaining half of the beans for tomorrow's lunch.) Garnish the dish with the cilantro and avocado, and drizzle the romaine with tahini.

NUTRITION INFORMATION PER SERVING

Calories	Protein (g)	Carbs (g)	Fat (g)	Sat Fat (g)	Unsat Fat (g)	Fiber (g)
410	16	44	21	3	17	17

DAY 10: THE LOVE—SELF-CARE

Taking good care of you means the people in your life will receive the best of you rather than what's left of you.

—CARL BRYAN

Meal Plan

	Omnivore	Vegan
Breakfast	Emerald Smoothie	Emerald Smoothie
Lunch	Greenie Genie Salad Sesame-Tahini Chicken	Greenie Genie Salad Black Beans with Tahini
Snack	Kiwi and Pistachios	Kiwi and Pistachios
Dinner	Anchovies, White Beans, and Asparagus	White Beans and Asparagus

Whole Detox Emotion Log

At the end of the day, track any emotions that you had on the Whole Detox Emotion Log.

Thought Pattern Activity

The following are some limiting thoughts that relate to the LOVE:

If someone else needs help, I can't say no.
It's selfish to take care of myself or to put myself first.
I think it's wrong to spend time on me.

Pick the limiting thought that seems to ring most true for you. If none of the examples feel true, write down your own limiting thought as it relates to the LOVE.

Next, set your timer for five minutes. Spend that time journaling on that thought, how it has affected your life, and how you feel when you have that thought.

Movement

Focus on your heart and chest area by doing "doorway" stretches: Stand in a doorway within your living or work space and use one arm at a time to push against the doorframe while allowing the chest to expand forward. Alternate arms and repeat the movement for three minutes.

Affirmation

Spend three minutes saying aloud the following affirmation:

Love extends through me and is received by me in equal measure.

Feel how your body responds to these words. You can also create your own statement. Feel free to write it on a beautiful notecard or a plain Post-it note and put it in your immediate environment for the day.

Visualization

Set a timer for three minutes. During that time, close your eyes and visualize your heart as a flower. Reflect on a moment you felt loved and see the flower expanding open. Then connect to a memory in which you gave love to someone and see the flower continue to expand. Visualize your heart "flower" being nourished and opened by this wonderful exchange of giving and receiving love.

Meditation

You will need about ten minutes for this activity. Draw your heart on a piece of paper. Inside the heart, write the names of activities, foods, and people you find to be supportive. Outside the heart, write the names of activities, foods, and people that must remain on the outside of your heart. Meditate for four minutes on your final drawing. Do you find too much on the outside and not enough on the inside? Meditate on four ways you can be more nourishing toward yourself.

DAY 10 RECIPES

Breakfast

EMERALD SMOOTHIE
Serves 1

½ cup unsweetened decaffeinated green tea

½ cup unsweetened coconut milk (boxed variety)

¼ cup apple juice

¼ avocado (leave the pit in the rest and save it for today's and tomorrow's lunches)

¼ cup lightly steamed kale (about 4 large leaves)

½ green apple, sliced (save the rest for today's lunch)

1 scoop protein powder of your choice (hemp, pea, rice, whey for omnivores)

Water and ice to blend

Put all the liquid and whole food ingredients into a high-speed blender first, followed by the dry ingredients, then blend everything until a fluid consistency is reached. Add more water if needed. Drink immediately.

NUTRITION INFORMATION PER SERVING

Calories	Protein (g)	Carbs (g)	Fat (g)	Sat Fat (g)	Unsat Fat (g)	Fiber (g)
310	26	26	12	4	6	7

Lunch

GREENIE GENIE SALAD WITH SESAME-TAHINI CHICKEN (OMNIVORE) OR BLACK BEANS WITH TAHINI (VEGAN)

Serves 1

1 cup chopped broccoli

1 large handful microgreens, about 1 cup

½ green apple (saved from breakfast), sliced

½ avocado (saved from breakfast; save the remaining ¼ for tomorrow's lunch)

4 to 5 walnut halves

FOR THE DRESSING:

1 tablespoon avocado oil

1 tablespoon decaffeinated green tea

1 teaspoon freshly squeezed lime juice

Salt to taste

In a serving bowl, toss together the broccoli, greens, apple, avocado, and walnuts. In a separate small bowl, whisk together all the dressing ingredients and pour the dressing mixture over the salad.

Warm up yesterday's leftover Sesame-Tahini Chicken (omnivore) or Black Beans with Tahini (vegan) to serve with the salad.

NUTRITION INFORMATION PER SERVING

	Calories	Protein (g)	Carbs (g)	Fat (g)	Sat Fat (g)	Unsat Fat (g)	Fiber (g)
Omnivore	535	33	26	36	5	29	12
Vegan	820	23	70	56	7	45	29

Snack

KIWI AND PISTACHIOS

Serves 1

1 kiwi fruit

1 handful unsalted, raw, shelled pistachios, about 3 tablespoons

NUTRITION INFORMATION PER SERVING

Calories	Protein (g)	Carbs (g)	Fat (g)	Sat Fat (g)	Unsat Fat (g)	Fiber (g)
173	5	16	11	1	8	4

Dinner

ANCHOVIES *(OMNIVORE)*, WHITE BEANS, AND ASPARAGUS *(VEGAN)*

Serves 1

FOR OMNIVORES:

4 anchovies (Vital Choice brand preferred)

½ cup cooked Great Northern beans

FOR VEGANS:

¾ cup cooked Great Northern beans

FOR BOTH:

5 asparagus stalks, tough ends removed, cut into bite-size pieces

1 tablespoon avocado oil

1 garlic clove

1 tablespoon minced green onion

2 tablespoons minced fresh parsley

5 green olives, sliced

2 tablespoons raw pine nuts

Omnivores, drain any oil from the anchovies (if applicable), and cut them into bite-size pieces. Set them aside.

Both omnivores and vegans, steam the asparagus for 3 to 4 minutes or until it is bright green.

In a skillet set over medium heat, warm the avocado oil, then add the garlic and green onion, sautéing them for 1 to 2 minutes. Add the asparagus, parsley, beans, and anchovies (omnivore). Sauté for an additional 1 to 2 minutes.

Remove from the heat and transfer the mixture to a serving plate. Sprinkle the dish with the olives and pine nuts.

NUTRITION INFORMATION PER SERVING

	Calories	Protein (g)	Carbs (g)	Fat (g)	Sat Fat (g)	Unsat Fat (g)	Fiber (g)
Omnivore	470	18	32	33	3	27	8
Vegan	498	18	43	31	3	26	11

DAY 11: THE LOVE—MOVEMENT

Every breath we take, every step we make, can be filled with peace, joy, and serenity.

—THICH NHAT HANH

Meal Plan

	Omnivore	Vegan
Breakfast	Green Love Smoothie	Green Love Smoothie
Lunch	The Heart Salad	The Heart Salad
Snack	Seasoned Kale Chips	Seasoned Kale Chips
Dinner	Hearty Turkey Breast Super Spinach	Steamed Nutty Greens with Brown Rice

Whole Detox Emotion Log

At the end of the day, track any emotions that you had on the Whole Detox Emotion Log.

Thought Pattern Activity

The following are some limiting thoughts that relate to the LOVE:

It takes too much energy for me to move.

I have no time to exercise.

I can't do exercises as I'd like, so I don't want to do them at all.

Pick the limiting thought that seems to ring most true for you. If none of the examples feel true, write down your own limiting thought as it relates to the LOVE.

Next, set your timer for five minutes. Spend that time journaling on that thought, how it has affected your life, and how you feel when you have that thought.

Movement

Create a movement that represents you. Find a quiet place and play your favorite music. Sing along if you like! Immerse yourself in the rhythms and melodies. Let your body move organically and breathe deeply. Don't think about it. Don't hesitate for fear you'll look foolish. Express your inner love and merge with the music.

Affirmation

Spend three minutes saying aloud the following affirmation:

Love moves through my heart and blood vessels.

Feel how your body responds to these words. You can also create your own statement. Feel free to write it on a beautiful notecard or a plain Post-it note and put it in your immediate environment for the day.

Visualization

Set a timer for three minutes. During that time, close your eyes and visualize your heart. Place your attention there and see your heart as a green, healthy plant. Imagine that you "feed" your heart love, and each time you do so, it grows leaves, stems, and tendrils that extend throughout your arms and legs. You feel refreshed and healed by the soothing green energy moving through you.

Meditation

For three minutes, engage in a breath-focused meditation: Place both your hands over your heart and, as you inhale, feel your breath expanding your heart chambers and branching blood vessels, relaxing them and making them feel soft and supple. As you exhale, release all the tension held in your circulatory system into your hands while you open your hands up in front of you, palms facing outward. Continue with this pattern of breath until you feel relaxed and heart centered.

DAY 11 RECIPES

Breakfast

GREEN LOVE SMOOTHIE
Serves 1

1 kiwi fruit, peeled and sliced
½ small cucumber, peeled and sliced
1 large handful spinach leaves, about
  1½ cups
1 cup unsweetened coconut water

1 tablespoon raw cacao nibs
1 tablespoon chia seeds
1 scoop protein powder of your choice
  (hemp, pea, rice, whey for omnivores)
Water and ice to blend

Put all the liquid and whole food ingredients into a high-speed blender first, followed by the dry ingredients, then blend everything until a fluid consistency is reached. Add more water if needed. Drink immediately.

NUTRITION INFORMATION PER SERVING

Calories	Protein (g)	Carbs (g)	Fat (g)	Sat Fat (g)	Unsat Fat (g)	Fiber (g)
313	30	31	9	3	2	11

Lunch

THE HEART SALAD
Serves 1

FOR OMNIVORES:
  4 ounces lox

FOR VEGANS:
  ¼ cup cooked cannellini beans
  ¼ cup cooked lima beans

FOR BOTH:
  2 large handfuls spinach leaves, about
    3 cups
  ¼ avocado, diced (saved from
    yesterday)
  ¼ cup broccoli sprouts
  ¼ teaspoon fresh dill

  ¼ cup sliced strawberries, sliced in half
    to resemble heart shapes
  2 tablespoons toasted slivered almonds
  Dash each of sea salt and ground
    black pepper

FOR THE DRESSING:

1 tablespoon flaxseed oil   ½ tablespoon balsamic vinegar
1 tablespoon extra-virgin olive oil

Wash the spinach leaves and put them into a large serving bowl. Add the avocado, broccoli sprouts, and dill, and lightly toss everything. Top the salad with the strawberries and almonds.

Add all the dressing ingredients to a jar with a lid or a shaker cup, and shake to combine them well. Drizzle the salad with the dressing.

Omnivores, eat the salad with the lox; vegans, with the beans.

NUTRITION INFORMATION PER SERVING

	Calories	Protein (g)	Carbs (g)	Fat (g)	Sat Fat (g)	Unsat Fat (g)	Fiber (g)
Omnivore	587	27	19	47	6	39	9
Vegan	562	13	39	42	5	36	15

Snack

SEASONED KALE CHIPS
Serves 2 or more

2 bunches green curly-leaf kale,   Sea salt
  washed and dried   1 teaspoon turmeric powder
2 tablespoons avocado oil

Preheat the oven to 375°F.

Stem the kale by tearing the leafy greens from their tough stems, then tear the greens into smaller pieces, discarding the stems. In a large bowl, toss the leaves with the avocado oil, then add the salt and turmeric, and coat everything well.

Lightly oil two large baking sheets. Spread the leaves evenly on the sheets, and bake them in the oven for 5 minutes. Stir and turn the leaves, and continue baking for another 3 to 5 minutes, or until the leaves are crispy. Watch to be sure the chips do not burn.

(Save half the chips for tomorrow's snack.)

ein (g)	Carbs (g)	Fat (g)	Sat Fat (g)	Unsat Fat (g)	Fiber (g)
3	13	14	2	12	6

Dinner

HEARTY TURKEY BREAST *(OMNIVORE)*

Serves 2

1 tablespoon extra-virgin olive oil
¼ cup chopped green onions
1 garlic clove, minced
½ cup chopped spinach
¼ cup chopped shiitake mushrooms
1 teaspoon dried rosemary
1 teaspoon dried sage

Sea salt and ground black pepper to taste
2 4- to 5-ounce organic, free-range, boneless turkey breasts
Parchment paper
Kitchen twine

Preheat the oven to 375°F.

In a medium skillet, heat the olive oil, then sauté the onions, garlic, spinach, mushrooms, rosemary, and sage until the onions and mushrooms have softened slightly. Season with salt and pepper to taste. Remove the vegetables from the heat and set them aside.

Carefully slice each turkey breast lengthwise and spread open the breasts fully. Cover the meat with parchment paper, then pound it with a wooden or metal mallet (or rolling pin) until each piece is about ¼-inch thick. Trim the breasts until they are roughly a rectangle shape.

Spread a thin layer of the sautéed vegetables on each turkey breast. Tightly roll the breasts lengthwise and secure them using kitchen twine.

In a roasting pan or baking dish, add a thin layer of water, then lay the stuffed breasts in the water. Roast them for about 20 to 25 minutes, or until the turkey is slightly browned. Serve warm with Super Spinach (recipe follows).

(Save one roasted breast for tomorrow's lunch.)

NUTRITION INFORMATION PER SERVING

Calories	Protein (g)	Carbs (g)	Fat (g)	Sat Fat (g)	Unsat Fat (g)	Fiber (g)
192	29	2	8	1	6	0.4

SUPER SPINACH *(OMNIVORE)*
Serves 1

2 large handfuls spinach, about 3 cups   1 teaspoon hemp seeds, or to taste
1 teaspoon sesame oil

In a large skillet, bring about ¼ cup water to a boil. Add the spinach and let it cook until it is wilted, about 2 minutes. Reduce the heat, and add the sesame oil. Sprinkle hemp seeds on top as desired. Serve warm.

NUTRITION INFORMATION PER SERVING

Calories	Protein (g)	Carbs (g)	Fat (g)	Sat Fat (g)	Unsat Fat (g)	Fiber (g)
89	3	8	6	1	4	3

STEAMED NUTTY GREENS WITH BROWN RICE *(VEGAN)*
Serves 2

1 small bunch asparagus, about 12
   stalks, tough ends removed
½ cup sliced Brussels sprouts, about
   6 or 7
¾ cup cooked brown rice
½ avocado, cubed
2 teaspoons apple cider vinegar

2 tablespoons chopped fresh cilantro
½ teaspoon ground oregano
1 tablespoon Walnut Pesto (saved from
   Day 5)
Sea salt and ground black pepper to
   taste
1 tablespoon avocado oil

Steam the asparagus and Brussels sprouts until they are tender.

In a bowl, combine the rice, avocado, vinegar, cilantro, oregano, and pesto. Salt and pepper the mixture to taste.

Arrange half the cooked asparagus and Brussels sprouts around the edge of a serving plate, and drizzle them with the avocado oil. Spoon half the rice mixture into the center of the plate. (Save the other half of the rice and vegetables for tomorrow's lunch.)

NUTRITION INFORMATION PER SERVING

Calories	Protein (g)	Carbs (g)	Fat (g)	Sat Fat (g)	Unsat Fat (g)	Fiber (g)
322	8	32	20	3	17	9

DAY 12: THE LOVE—VEGETABLES

Don't eat vegetables because they are good for you. Eat them for one reason alone.
Because they are gorgeous.

—JILL DUPLEIX

Meal Plan

	Omnivore	Vegan
Breakfast	Mint-Green Smoothie	Mint-Green Smoothie
Lunch	Cucumber Salad Hearty Turkey Breast	Cucumber Salad Steamed Nutty Greens with Brown Rice
Snack	Seasoned Kale Chips	Seasoned Kale Chips
Dinner	Almond Salmon with Swiss Chard	Rosemary-Roasted Cauliflower with Spinach and Tahini

Whole Detox Emotion Log

At the end of the day, track any emotions that you had on the Whole Detox
Emotion Log.

Thought Pattern Activity

The following are some limiting thoughts that relate to the LOVE:

I feel closed off.
It is difficult for me to recover from hurt.
I can't get beyond my grief.

Pick the limiting thought that seems to ring most true for you. If none
of the examples feel true, write down your own limiting thought as it
relates to the LOVE.

Next, set your timer for five minutes. Spend that time journaling on
that thought, how it has affected your life, and how you feel when you have
that thought.

Movement

COBRA POSE (BHUJANGASANA)

This exercise opens up the heart. It is also a good shoulder strengthener. As with all yoga poses, go to your comfortable limit. Nothing should be painful.

1. Lie on your stomach on a mat or blanket with your feet extended out and the tops of your feet and forehead touching the mat.
2. Set your hands under your shoulders and your forearms on the floor, parallel to each other. Inhale and lift your upper torso and head away from the floor into a mild backbend.
3. You may stay in this pose for a minute or so, and then, if you are able, take a deep breath, lift your head and upper body further, almost straightening your arms.
4. Keep pressing the tops of your feet into the mat and let your pubic bone drop down into the mat to stabilize your lower back. Keep your hands pressed firmly against the mat.
5. Breathe out.
6. Continue engaging your legs and pushing your pelvis into the mat. Make sure your arms are not fully straightened, because this may hyper-extend your elbows.
7. Take several deep inhalations and exhalations. Feel your chest opening.
8. Maintain this position for a minute or so. Bend your arms, lower your torso, and rest.
9. Repeat the pose for one to two minutes.

Affirmation

Spend three minutes saying aloud the following affirmation:

I am open to accepting love in my life.

Feel how your body responds to these words. You can also create your own statement. Feel free to write it on a beautiful notecard or a plain Post-it note and put it in your immediate environment for the day.

Visualization

Set a timer for three minutes. During that time, close your eyes and visualize your heart expanding out to meet people in your life who are healing and nourishing, and who love you. Feel your heart field magnify and reach out several feet around you. Bask in the green glow of this magnificent love and healing.

Meditation

For three minutes, shift your consciousness from your head to your heart. Imagine your heart filling with love. To come into this place, you may need to "feel" love from a previous memory or experience, or simply conjure it up.

DAY 12 RECIPES

Breakfast

_____

MINT-GREEN SMOOTHIE

Serves 1

½ cup unsweetened almond milk
1 cup cubed honeydew melon
¼ cup raw almonds
4 to 5 fresh mint leaves

1 scoop protein powder of your choice
(hemp, pea, rice, whey for omnivores)
Water and ice to blend

Put all the liquid and whole food ingredients into a high-speed blender first, followed by the dry ingredients, then blend everything until a fluid consistency is reached. Add more water if needed. Drink immediately.

NUTRITION INFORMATION PER SERVING

Calories	Protein (g)	Carbs (g)	Fat (g)	Sat Fat (g)	Unsat Fat (g)	Fiber (g)
407	33	25	21	1	15	6

Lunch

CUCUMBER SALAD WITH HEARTY TURKEY BREAST *(OMNIVORE)* OR STEAMED NUTTY GREENS WITH BROWN RICE *(VEGAN)*
Serves 1

1 small cucumber, peeled
½ cup shredded green cabbage
½ cup chopped broccoli
2 tablespoons unsalted, raw, shelled pistachios
½ avocado, sliced

1 tablespoon freshly squeezed lime juice
1 tablespoon extra-virgin olive oil
Sea salt and ground black pepper to taste

With a vegetable peeler or spiralizer, slice the cucumber into "noodles."

In a bowl, toss the noodles with the cabbage, broccoli, pistachios, avocado, lime juice, and olive oil. Season with salt and pepper to taste. Serve immediately.

Warm up yesterday's leftover Hearty Turkey Breast (omnivore) or Steamed Nutty Greens with Brown Rice (vegan) to serve with the salad.

NUTRITION INFORMATION PER SERVING

	Calories	Protein (g)	Carbs (g)	Fat (g)	Sat Fat (g)	Unsat Fat (g)	Fiber (g)
Omnivore	747	38	27	57	8	48	13
Vegan	751	17	57	56	8	46	22

Snack

SEASONED KALE CHIPS (LEFTOVER FROM YESTERDAY'S SNACK)
Serves 1

NUTRITION INFORMATION PER SERVING

Calories	Protein (g)	Carbs (g)	Fat (g)	Sat Fat (g)	Unsat Fat (g)	Fiber (g)
174	3	13	14	2	12	6

Dinner

ALMOND SALMON WITH SWISS CHARD *(OMNIVORE)*

Serves 2

2 tablespoons almond meal (make your own by grinding up almonds in a blender)

2 tablespoons extra-virgin olive oil, divided

2 3- to 4-ounce wild-caught salmon fillets

1 garlic clove, minced

1 small bunch (about 5 large leaves) Swiss chard, stemmed and roughly chopped

1 tablespoon balsamic vinegar

Sea salt and ground black pepper to taste

Preheat the oven to 375°F.

In a small bowl, combine well the almond meal and 1 tablespoon of the olive oil. Spread the almond paste over both the salmon fillets, then set the fillets in a glass baking dish and bake them for 15 to 20 minutes, or until they are just cooked through.

Meanwhile, in a sauté pan set over medium heat, warm the remaining tablespoon of olive oil, then add the garlic, and cook it for about 1 minute. Add the chard and cook it until it wilts, about 3 to 4 minutes. Toss the chard with the vinegar, and add salt and pepper to the mixture to taste.

Arrange the Swiss chard on a serving plate, top it with one of the salmon fillets, and eat the dish warm. (Save the second fillet for tomorrow's lunch.)

NUTRITION INFORMATION PER SERVING

Calories	Protein (g)	Carbs (g)	Fat (g)	Sat Fat (g)	Unsat Fat (g)	Fiber (g)
454	36	11	30	4	18	3

ROSEMARY-ROASTED CAULIFLOWER WITH SPINACH AND TAHINI *(VEGAN)*

Serves 2

3 cups chopped cauliflower

2 garlic cloves, minced

1 tablespoon extra-virgin olive oil

2 teaspoons dry rosemary powder

2 tablespoons raw pine nuts

Sea salt and freshly ground black pepper to taste

2 large handfuls spinach, about 3 cups

1 tablespoon tahini

Preheat the oven to 425°F.

In a large mixing bowl, combine the cauliflower with the garlic and olive oil, ensuring all the cauliflower is coated with oil. Sprinkle the mixture with the rosemary and pine nuts, and season it with salt and pepper to taste.

On a baking sheet, spread the cauliflower evenly, then roast the pieces, uncovered, for 20 to 25 minutes, or until the tops and edges are lightly browned.

Serve half the cauliflower immediately on top of either fresh or wilted spinach, and drizzle everything with tahini. (Save the other half of the cauliflower for tomorrow's lunch.)

NUTRITION INFORMATION PER SERVING

Calories	Protein (g)	Carbs (g)	Fat (g)	Sat Fat (g)	Unsat Fat (g)	Fiber (g)
221	6	16	17	2	14	6

DAY 13: THE TRUTH—TRUTHS

If you tell the truth, you don't have to remember anything.

—MARK TWAIN

Meal Plan

	Omnivore	Vegan
Breakfast	Soothing Melon Smoothie	Soothing Melon Smoothie
Lunch	Kale and Mango Salad Almond Salmon	Kale and Mango Salad Rosemary-Roasted Cauliflower
Snack	Toasted Nori	Toasted Nori
Dinner	Thai Coconut Chicken	Thai Coconut Chickpeas

Whole Detox Emotion Log

At the end of the day, track any emotions that you had on the Whole Detox Emotion Log.

Thought Pattern Activity

The following are some limiting thoughts that relate to the TRUTH:

I don't know what is true for me.
It's difficult to tell the truth.
I fear what my life might be like if I spoke my truth.

Pick the limiting thought that seems to ring most true for you. If none of the examples feel true, write down your own limiting thought as it relates to the TRUTH.

Next, set your timer for five minutes. Spend that time journaling on that thought, how it has affected your life, and how you feel when you have that thought.

Movement

Tune in to your authentic voice through chanting, humming, or singing during your activities today.

Affirmation

Spend three minutes saying aloud the following affirmation:

I speak my truth freely.

Feel how your body responds to these words. You can also create your own statement. Feel free to write it on a beautiful notecard or a plain Post-it note and put it in your immediate environment for the day.

Visualization

Set a timer for three minutes. During that time, close your eyes and visualize all the words locked within your throat that you may not have said. See your throat as a cluttered canal. Let the words that most connect to your truth come forward. Imagine that they arrive on the tip of your tongue. Keeping your eyes closed, say them out loud. Repeat this process as many times as you need to, allowing your truth to come forward and be expressed.

Meditation

For at least three minutes, meditate using sound by chanting each vowel sound: "ah," "ee," "eye," "ooh," "eww." To do this, breathe in deeply, and on the exhale, release "ah," then repeat the rhythm of breaths with the other vowel sounds.

DAY 13 RECIPES

Breakfast

SOOTHING MELON SMOOTHIE
Serves 1

1 small banana	Pinch of ground cardamom
½ cup cubed cantaloupe	1 scoop protein powder of your choice
½ cup cubed honeydew melon	(hemp, pea, rice, whey for omnivores)
1 tablespoon flaxseed meal	Water and ice to blend
½ cup unsweetened coconut water	

Put all the liquid and whole food ingredients into a high-speed blender first, followed by the dry ingredients, then blend everything until a fluid consistency is reached. Add more water if needed. Drink immediately.

NUTRITION INFORMATION PER SERVING

Calories	Protein (g)	Carbs (g)	Fat (g)	Sat Fat (g)	Unsat Fat (g)	Fiber (g)
320	29	45	5	0.4	0.2	7

Lunch

KALE AND MANGO SALAD WITH ALMOND SALMON *(OMNIVORE)* OR ROSEMARY-ROASTED CAULIFLOWER *(VEGAN)*
Serves 1

2 handfuls baby kale, about 3 cups	1 cup cubed fresh mango
½ green apple, sliced	

FOR THE DRESSING:

4 tablespoons orange juice	½ tablespoon extra-virgin olive oil
1 tablespoon freshly squeezed lemon	Dash of sea salt
juice	Dash of ground black pepper

In a serving bowl, toss together the kale, apple, and mango. Set the mixture aside. In a small bowl, whisk together all the dressing ingredients, and pour it over the fruits and greens. Warm up yesterday's leftover Almond Salmon (*omnivore*) or Rosemary-Roasted Cauliflower (*vegan*) to serve with the salad.

NUTRITION INFORMATION PER SERVING

	Calories	Protein (g)	Carbs (g)	Fat (g)	Sat Fat (g)	Unsat Fat (g)	Fiber (g)
Omnivore	769	43	74	39	5	25	13
Vegan	576	15	87	26	3	21	17

Snack

TOASTED NORI

Serves 1

3 sheets pressed nori

1 tablespoon sesame oil

Sea salt

Dash of turmeric powder

Preheat the oven to 250°F.

Cut each nori sheet into wide strips using clean scissors. Place the nori strips on a baking sheet. Lightly brush them front and back with sesame oil, then sprinkle them with sea salt and turmeric.

Bake the nori for 10 to 15 minutes, watching to be sure they do not burn. Let them cool before serving.

NUTRITION INFORMATION PER SERVING

Calories	Protein (g)	Carbs (g)	Fat (g)	Sat Fat (g)	Unsat Fat (g)	Fiber (g)
149	3	4	14	2	12	0

Dinner

THAI COCONUT CHICKEN *(OMNIVORE)* OR CHICKPEAS *(VEGAN)*

Serves 2

FOR OMNIVORES:

8 ounces organic, free-range, boneless chicken breasts, cut into 1-inch-thick strips

FOR VEGANS:

1½ cups cooked chickpeas

FOR BOTH:

1 tablespoon coconut oil	1 teaspoon sea salt
2 garlic cloves, minced	1 cup unsweetened, full-fat coconut
1-inch piece fresh ginger, minced	milk
¼ cup diced yellow onion	1 small zucchini, cubed
2 tablespoons curry powder	2 small red potatoes, cubed
⅛ teaspoon ground black pepper	

In a large skillet set over medium-high heat, warm the coconut oil, then add the garlic, ginger, and onion, sautéing until the onion becomes soft and translucent. Stir in the curry powder, pepper, and salt. Cook the mixture for about 1 minute. Add the coconut milk, zucchini, and potatoes, coating everything well, then add the chicken (omnivore) or the chickpeas (vegan). Stir the ingredients consistently until everything is cooked through.

Serve half the mixture warm. (Save the other half for tomorrow's lunch.)

NUTRITION INFORMATION PER SERVING

	Calories	Protein (g)	Carbs (g)	Fat (g)	Sat Fat (g)	Unsat Fat (g)	Fiber (g)
Omnivore	439	32	34	21	17	2	4
Vegan	390	9	47	21	17	2	7

DAY 14: THE TRUTH—AFFIRMATIONS

Words mean more than what is set down on paper. It takes the human voice to infuse them with deeper meaning.

—MAYA ANGELOU

Meal Plan

	Omnivore	Vegan
Breakfast	Mango-Mint Smoothie	Mango-Mint Smoothie
Lunch	Bitters-Sweet Salad Thai Coconut Chicken	Bitters-Sweet Salad Thai Coconut Chickpeas
Snack	Rainbow Fruit and Nut Salad	Rainbow Fruit and Nut Salad
Dinner	Halibut Stew	Mung Bean Stew

Whole Detox Emotion Log

At the end of the day, track any emotions that you had on the Whole Detox Emotion Log.

Thought Pattern Activity

The following are some limiting thoughts that relate to the TRUTH:

I've been taught that it's impolite to disagree.
I am at a loss for words.
I am afraid to say what I really want to say.

Pick the limiting thought that seems to ring most true for you. If none of the examples feel true, write down your own limiting thought as it relates to the TRUTH.

Next, set your timer for five minutes. Spend that time journaling on that thought, how it has affected your life, and how you feel when you have that thought.

Movement

Do five rounds of gentle neck rolls in both counterclockwise and clockwise directions. Feel where there is tenderness and gently massage that area. Also, take five minutes to lightly massage your jaw, mouth, and throat area.

Affirmation

Spend three minutes saying aloud the following affirmation:

My words are crafted with honesty, integrity, and truth.

Feel how your body responds to these words. You can also create your own statement. Feel free to write it on a beautiful notecard or a plain Post-it note and put it in your immediate environment for the day.

Visualization

Set a timer for three minutes. During that time, close your eyes and visualize your mouth as a spinning wheel of words. See your mouth as a moving wheel that can generate words of your choice. Allow certain words to come forward that speak to your inner truth, perhaps something you would like to say but haven't said. Let them spin on the wheel until they have been shaped with honesty and integrity. Say them out loud at the end of the visualization.

Meditation

Sit still for five minutes and observe any and all sounds in your environment. Notice each of them without engagement.

DAY 14 RECIPES

Breakfast

MANGO-MINT SMOOTHIE
Serves 1

1 cup cubed fresh mango
1½ cups unsweetened coconut water
2 tablespoons freshly chopped mint
 leaves (about 4–6 whole mint leaves)

1 scoop protein powder of your choice
 (hemp, pea, rice, whey for omnivores)
Water and ice to blend

Put all the liquid and whole food ingredients into a high-speed blender first, followed by the dry protein powder, then blend everything until a fluid consistency is reached. Add more water if needed. Drink immediately.

NUTRITION INFORMATION PER SERVING

Calories	Protein (g)	Carbs (g)	Fat (g)	Sat Fat (g)	Unsat Fat (g)	Fiber (g)
308	28	46	3	0.6	0	8

Lunch

BITTERS-SWEET SALAD WITH THAI COCONUT CHICKEN *(OMNIVORE)* OR CHICKPEAS *(VEGAN)*
Serves 1

1 cup arugula
1 cup dandelion greens

¼ cup shredded carrots
2 radishes, sliced

FOR THE DRESSING:

1 tablespoon honey   ½ teaspoon mustard seeds

1 tablespoon sesame oil

In a serving bowl, toss together the arugula, dandelion greens, carrots, and radishes. In a small mixing bowl, whisk together all the dressing ingredients, then pour the dressing over the salad.

Warm up yesterday's leftover Thai Coconut Chicken (*omnivore*) or Chickpeas (*vegan*) to serve with the salad.

NUTRITION INFORMATION PER SERVING

	Calories	Protein (g)	Carbs (g)	Fat (g)	Sat Fat (g)	Unsat Fat (g)	Fiber (g)
Omnivore	674	35	61	36	19	15	8
Vegan	625	12	79	36	19	15	11

Snack

RAINBOW FRUIT AND NUT SALAD

Serves 1

1 kiwi fruit, peeled and sliced

1 cup cubed honeydew melon

2 strawberries, sliced

5–6 blueberries

½ small banana, sliced

3 to 4 fresh mint leaves, chopped

3 tablespoons pecan pieces

1 tablespoon unsweetened, shredded coconut

1 teaspoon honey

1 tablespoon freshly squeezed lime juice

In a small bowl, combine all the ingredients and serve immediately.

NUTRITION INFORMATION PER SERVING

Calories	Protein (g)	Carbs (g)	Fat (g)	Sat Fat (g)	Unsat Fat (g)	Fiber (g)
353	4	50	18	4	12	8

Dinner

HALIBUT *(OMNIVORE)* OR MUNG BEAN *(VEGAN)* STEW
Serves 2

FOR OMNIVORES:

8 ounces wild-caught halibut, skin removed, cut into 1-inch pieces

FOR VEGANS:

1½ cups cooked mung beans

FOR BOTH:

⅔ cup unsweetened, full-fat coconut milk

3 cups organic vegetable broth

1 tablespoon freshly squeezed lime juice

2 teaspoons grated or minced fresh ginger

2 carrots, sliced into bite-size strips

3-inch piece fresh lemongrass

2 cups chopped cauliflower

½ teaspoon Thai green curry paste

4 fresh basil leaves, chopped

Sea salt and freshly ground black pepper to taste

In a large saucepan set over medium-high heat, combine the halibut (omnivore) or mung beans (vegan) with the coconut milk, broth, lime juice, ginger, carrots, lemongrass, cauliflower, and curry paste. Bring the mixture to a quick boil, then reduce the heat, gently simmering for about 10 to 15 minutes, or until the fish or beans are cooked through.

Top the soup with the chopped basil, and season it with salt and pepper to taste.

NUTRITION INFORMATION PER SERVING

	Calories	Protein (g)	Carbs (g)	Fat (g)	Sat Fat (g)	Unsat Fat (g)	Fiber (g)
Omnivore	370	29	21	20	15	3	6
Vegan	405	16	50	18	14	1	17

DAY 15: THE TRUTH—LIQUID FOODS

A first-rate soup is more creative than a second-rate painting.

—ABRAHAM MASLOW

Meal Plan

	Omnivore	Vegan
Breakfast	Pomegranate-Apple Smoothie	Pomegranate-Apple Smoothie
Lunch	Rainbow Salad Halibut Stew	Rainbow Salad Mung Bean Stew
Snack	Dates and Almonds	Dates and Almonds
Dinner	Shiitake-Sea Plant Soup	Shiitake-Sea Plant Soup

Whole Detox Emotion Log

At the end of the day, track any emotions that you had on the Whole Detox Emotion Log.

Thought Pattern Activity

The following are some limiting thoughts that relate to the TRUTH:

I feel closed off.
I am not free to be me.
My true self feels shut down.

Pick the limiting thought that seems to ring most true for you. If none of the examples feel true, write down your own limiting thought as it relates to the TRUTH.

Next, set your timer for five minutes. Spend that time journaling on that thought, how it has affected your life, and how you feel when you have that thought.

Movement

PLOW POSE (HALASANA)

This exercise lengthens the back of your neck and can aid in balancing the throat. As with all yoga poses, go to your comfortable limit. If this pose seems too daunting for you, modify it accordingly, or simply spend the time doing gentle neck rolls. Nothing should be painful.

1. Fold two blankets into firm rectangles about one to two feet across and stack them together on the floor.
2. Lie down on your back with your shoulders and torso on the blankets, with your head extending beyond the folded edges.
3. Bend your knees, keeping your feet flat on the floor. Your arms should be parallel at your sides.
4. On an exhale, push your feet off the floor, lifting your bent legs, and bring your hands to your mid-back, just above your waist, to support your body.
5. Straighten your legs and allow them to extend back over your head. Your toes will touch the floor behind you. You may let your hands go and extend the arms to lie along the floor.
6. Keep your neck long.
7. Remain in the pose for one to three minutes, then roll back down on an exhale.

Affirmation

Spend three minutes saying aloud the following affirmation:

My throat is open and moist to release my authentic voice.

Feel how your body responds to these words. You can also create your own statement. Feel free to write it on a beautiful notecard or a plain Post-it note and put it in your immediate environment for the day.

Visualization

Set a timer for three minutes. During that time, close your eyes and visualize your throat as an open canal. Fill it with healing aquamarine light. Let this light cast out any stuck words, dryness, or scratchy patches. Imagine your throat as smooth, soft, and open to your deepest truths.

Meditation

Meditate using a conscious "sipping" exercise, using either water, tea, or broth, in which you take a sip and envision that the liquid carries healing for your throat, thyroid, and authentic voice. Meditate for as long as it takes to empty a glass of water, or a cup of tea or broth. It may take as long as five minutes.

DAY 15 RECIPES

Breakfast

POMEGRANATE-APPLE SMOOTHIE
Serves 1

1 cup pomegranate juice
½ green apple, sliced
1 handful spinach, about 1½ cups

1 scoop protein powder of your choice
  (hemp, pea, rice, whey for omnivores)
Water and ice to blend

Put all the liquid and whole food ingredients into a high-speed blender first, followed by the dry protein powder, then blend everything until a fluid consistency is reached. Add more water if needed. Drink immediately.

NUTRITION INFORMATION PER SERVING

Calories	Protein (g)	Carbs (g)	Fat (g)	Sat Fat (g)	Unsat Fat (g)	Fiber (g)
315	26	51	2	0	0	4

Lunch

RAINBOW SALAD WITH HALIBUT *(OMNIVORE)* OR MUNG BEAN *(VEGAN)* STEW
Serves 1

½ red bell pepper, diced
1 carrot, sliced in rounds
½ small yellow squash, sliced
1 cup baby kale

¼ cup finely sliced red cabbage
5 walnut halves, chopped
1 teaspoon unhulled sesame seeds
Freshly ground black pepper to taste

FOR THE DRESSING:

2 tablespoons freshly squeezed lemon
   juice
1½ tablespoons extra-virgin olive oil
¼ teaspoon minced fresh ginger

¾ teaspoon honey
Pinch of ground cayenne pepper
Pinch of sea salt

In a serving bowl, toss together the bell pepper, carrot, squash, kale, cabbage, walnuts, and sesame seeds, and season with black pepper to taste. In a small bowl, whisk together all the dressing ingredients, then pour the dressing over the salad.

Warm up yesterday's leftover Halibut (Omnivore) or Mung Bean (Vegan) Stew to serve with the salad.

NUTRITION INFORMATION PER SERVING

	Calories	Protein (g)	Carbs (g)	Fat (g)	Sat Fat (g)	Unsat Fat (g)	Fiber (g)
Omnivore	750	35	47	50	19	27	12
Vegan	785	22	76	48	18	25	23

Snack

DATES AND ALMONDS
Serves 1

2 Medjool dates
1 handful raw almonds, about 12

Calories	Protein (g)	Carbs (g)	Fat (g)	Sat Fat (g)	Unsat Fat (g)	Fiber (g)
123	3	14	7	0.5	6	3

Dinner

SHIITAKE–SEA PLANT SOUP
Serves 2

FOR OMNIVORES:

6 ounces organic, free-range, boneless
   chicken breasts, cubed

FOR VEGANS:

1 cup cooked adzuki beans

FOR BOTH:

4 cups organic vegetable broth	1 cup dulse flakes
1½ cups shredded bok choy	1 tablespoon coconut aminos
5 large shiitake mushrooms, sliced	1 teaspoon sea salt
1 green onion, finely chopped	½ cup cooked brown rice

In a large saucepan set over medium-low heat, combine the chicken (*omnivore*) or beans (*vegan*) with the broth, bok choy, mushrooms, onion, dulse, coconut aminos, and salt, and allow the mixture to simmer for about 15 to 20 minutes. Stir in the rice, and serve half the soup warm. (Save the other half for tomorrow's lunch.)

NUTRITION INFORMATION PER SERVING

	Calories	Protein (g)	Carbs (g)	Fat (g)	Sat Fat (g)	Unsat Fat (g)	Fiber (g)
Omnivore	243	26	27	3	0.4	1	5
Vegan	297	15	56	2	0.2	0.4	13

DAY 16: THE INSIGHT—MOODS AND COGNITION

Be curious always! For knowledge will not acquire you; you must acquire it.

—BERTRAND RUSSELL

Meal Plan

	Omnivore	Vegan
Breakfast	Pomegranate-Berry Smoothie	Pomegranate-Berry Smoothie
Lunch	Purple Kale and Cabbage Salad Shiitake-Seaplant Soup (with chicken)	Purple Kale and Cabbage Salad Shiitake-Seaplant Soup (with beans)
Snack	Berry and Nut Cobbler	Berry and Nut Cobbler
Dinner	Wild Salmon with Blackberry-Basil Sauce Super Spinach	Purple Rice and Vegetables with Blackberry-Cashew Cream

Whole Detox Emotion Log

At the end of the day, track any emotions that you had on the Whole Detox Emotion Log.

Thought Pattern Activity

The following are some limiting thoughts that relate to the INSIGHT:

I'm not good at learning new things.
I am not intuitive.
I can't focus my attention.

Pick the limiting thought that seems to ring most true for you. If none of the examples feel true, write down your own limiting thought as it relates to the INSIGHT.

Next, set your timer for five minutes. Spend that time journaling on that thought, how it has affected your life, and how you feel when you have that thought.

Movement

Allow yourself to do some gentle neck rolls to loosen up your neck and head area. Lift your chin and let your eyes gaze up toward your forehead for a couple of seconds, then return to facing straight ahead. After a couple of seconds, tilt your chin down and let your gaze fall on your chest, then return to facing straight ahead. Repeat a few times, to the level of comfort.

Affirmation

Spend three minutes saying aloud the following affirmation:

My moods are balanced and my thinking is clear and precise.

Feel how your body responds to these words. You can also create your own statement. Feel free to write it on a beautiful notecard or a plain Post-it note and put it in your immediate environment for the day.

Visualization

Set a timer for three minutes. During that time, close your eyes and visualize your mind as being clear and bright. The light transforms any blocks or barriers to clear your thinking. Your neurons communicate rapidly back and forth, transmitting information seamlessly. Your mood is brightened by the light, and you feel balanced.

Meditation

For six minutes, envision your mind as a suitcase, tightly packed with excessive thoughts, stress, and unrealized ideas and dreams. Now see your mind let go of all the excesses, one by one, emptying itself out. After the meditation, make a conscious effort to scrutinize everything you put into the suitcase of your mind.

DAY 16 RECIPES

Breakfast

POMEGRANATE-BERRY SMOOTHIE
Serves 1

1 cup pomegranate juice
½ cup fresh blackberries
½ cup hibiscus tea, cooled
½ small banana, sliced
⅛ teaspoon ground cardamom
1 scoop protein powder of your choice
  (hemp, pea, rice, whey for omnivores)
Water and ice to blend

Put all the liquid and whole food ingredients into a high-speed blender first, followed by the dry protein powder, then blend everything until a fluid consistency is reached. Add more water if needed. Drink immediately.

NUTRITION INFORMATION PER SERVING

Calories	Protein (g)	Carbs (g)	Fat (g)	Sat Fat (g)	Unsat Fat (g)	Fiber (g)
336	27	54	3	0	0.3	5

Lunch

PURPLE KALE AND CABBAGE SALAD WITH SHIITAKE–SEA PLANT SOUP
Serves 1

1 cup chopped purple kale

½ cup chopped red cabbage

⅓ cup thinly sliced red apple

2 tablespoons chopped walnuts

FOR THE DRESSING:

1 tablespoon freshly squeezed lemon juice

½ tablespoon Dijon mustard

1 teaspoon honey

1 tablespoon extra-virgin olive oil

Sea salt and ground black pepper to taste

In a serving bowl, combine the kale, cabbage, apple, and walnuts. In a small bowl, whisk together all the dressing ingredients, then pour the dressing over the salad.

Warm up yesterday's leftover Shiitake–Sea Plant Soup to serve with the salad.

NUTRITION INFORMATION PER SERVING

	Calories	Protein (g)	Carbs (g)	Fat (g)	Sat Fat (g)	Unsat Fat (g)	Fiber (g)
Omnivore	563	31	53	27	3	25	9
Vegan	617	20	82	26	3	21	17

Snack

BERRY AND NUT COBBLER
Serves 4

1 teaspoon plus 2 tablespoons coconut oil

1 cup blueberries, frozen or fresh

1 cup blackberries

1 cup raspberries

½ cup chopped pecans

½ cup chopped walnuts

1 cup gluten-free oats

1 tablespoon flaxseed meal

1 tablespoon honey

Preheat the oven to 375°F.

Grease a 9 × 9 glass baking dish with 1 teaspoon of the coconut oil.

In a medium bowl, combine the blueberries, blackberries, and raspberries. In another bowl, combine the pecans, walnuts, oats, flaxseed meal, and honey with the remaining 2 tablespoons of coconut oil.

Spread the berry mixture evenly in the greased baking dish. Sprinkle the nut and oat mixture on top. Bake the cobbler for 20 to 25 minutes, or until the berries are gently bubbling. Remove it from the oven and allow it to cool.

Spoon a quarter of the cobbler onto a dish and eat it mindfully. (Save the remaining cobbler for tomorrow's snack plus future additional snacks.)

NUTRITION INFORMATION PER SERVING

Calories	Protein (g)	Carbs (g)	Fat (g)	Sat Fat (g)	Unsat Fat (g)	Fiber (g)
206	4	18	15	4	9	4

Dinner

WILD SALMON WITH BLACKBERRY-BASIL SAUCE *(OMNIVORE)*

Serves 2

¼ cup freshly squeezed lime juice	1 tablespoon coconut oil
1 tablespoon extra-virgin olive oil	2 cups fresh blackberries
Dash of sea salt	5 fresh basil leaves (purple basil
1 garlic clove, minced	preferred)
2 4-ounce wild-caught salmon fillets	1 cup purified water

In a large bowl, combine the lime juice, olive oil, sea salt, and garlic. Dip each salmon fillet into the bowl, coating both well.

In a skillet set over low heat, melt the coconut oil, and add the coated salmon fillets. Cover the skillet and let the salmon cook for 7 to 10 minutes, turning them halfway through to cook on their other sides.

In a saucepan set over medium heat, combine the blackberries, basil, and water. Allow the berries to reach a boil, then reduce the heat to gently simmer them until they take on the consistency of a thick sauce, about 8 to 10 minutes. Add more water if needed.

On a serving plate, place 1 salmon fillet. Season it with black pepper to taste, and spoon half the sauce over the top. Serve it with Super Spinach (recipe on page 301). (Save the other salmon fillet for tomorrow's lunch.)

NUTRITION INFORMATION PER SERVING

Calories	Protein (g)	Carbs (g)	Fat (g)	Sat Fat (g)	Unsat Fat (g)	Fiber (g)
398	25	17	27	11	16	7

PURPLE RICE AND VEGETABLES WITH BLACKBERRY-CASHEW CREAM *(VEGAN)*
Serves 2

¼ cup uncooked purple/black rice

2 cups stemmed, chopped purple kale

2 cups shredded red cabbage

2 cups chopped cauliflower

FOR THE CREAM:

¾ cup raw cashews

¾ cup fresh blackberries

1 tablespoon freshly squeezed lemon juice

1 tablespoon walnut oil

¼ cup water, or as needed for blending

Sea salt to taste

Cook the purple rice in a rice cooker if available. If not, cook it on the stove-top according to the package instructions.

Meanwhile, in a vegetable steamer, heat about 1 cup of water. Steam the kale, cabbage, and cauliflower, allowing the vegetables to cook lightly yet not lose color.

In a high-speed blender or food processor, blend together all the ingredients for the cream.

On a serving plate, arrange a bed of half the cooked rice topped with half the vegetables, then drizzle everything with half the blackberry-cashew cream. (Save the remaining half-portions for tomorrow's lunch.)

NUTRITION INFORMATION PER SERVING

Calories	Protein (g)	Carbs (g)	Fat (g)	Sat Fat (g)	Unsat Fat (g)	Fiber (g)
547	16	58	32	5	24	10

DAY 17: THE INSIGHT—VISUALIZATIONS

Your vision will become clear only when you can look into your own heart.
Who looks outside, dreams; who looks inside, awakens.

—CARL JUNG

Meal Plan

	Omnivore	Vegan
Breakfast	Berryananda Smoothie	Berryananda Smoothie
Lunch	Cool Blue Salad Wild Salmon with Blackberry-Basil Sauce	Cool Blue Salad Purple Rice and Vegetables with Blackberry-Cashew Cream
Snack	Berry and Nut Cobbler	Berry and Nut Cobbler
Dinner	Coconut Cod Fillet with Plum-Lavender Sauce Steamed Broccoli	Purple Buddha Bowl

Whole Detox Emotion Log

At the end of the day, track any emotions that you had on the Whole Detox Emotion Log.

Thought Pattern Activity

The following are some limiting thoughts that relate to the INSIGHT:

I have difficulty seeing the big picture.
I lack vision about where my life is going.
It's difficult for me to zoom out of my everyday view and have perspective on the larger whole of my life.

Pick the limiting thought that seems to ring most true for you. If none of the examples feel true, write down your own limiting thought as it relates to the INSIGHT.

Next, set your timer for five minutes. Spend that time journaling on that thought, how it has affected your life, and how you feel when you have that thought.

Movement

Strengthen your eyes by doing a simple three-minute eye-stretching activity in which you look up with both eyes, then to the right, down, and to the left. Repeat the pattern three times. Do the series again but in the opposite direction.

Affirmation

Spend three minutes saying aloud the following affirmation:

My inner vision is aligned with my outer sight.

Feel how your body responds to these words. You can also create your own statement. Feel free to write it on a beautiful notecard or a plain Post-it note and put it in your immediate environment for the day.

Visualization

Set a timer for three minutes. During that time, close your eyes and visualize not your outer eyes but an inner eye at your forehead. Allow this inner, wise eye to look into your future. Visualize your next couple of years. Imagine the best vision possible for yourself. Bring that vision back with you after the three minutes end, and jot a couple of notes about what you discovered.

Meditation

Close your eyes and fix your gaze toward your forehead, especially at the end of the day before bedtime. After three minutes, with your fingertips, gently tap the area around the eyes.

DAY 17 RECIPES

Breakfast

BERRYANANDA SMOOTHIE

Serves 1

- 1 small banana
- 1 cup frozen blueberries
- 1 cup unsweetened almond milk
- ¼ teaspoon ground cardamom
- ¼ teaspoon ground cinnamon
- 1 teaspoon bee pollen granules (optional)
- 1 scoop protein powder of your choice (hemp, pea, rice, whey for omnivores)
- Water and ice to blend

Put all the liquid and whole food ingredients into a high-speed blender first, followed by the dry protein powder, then blend everything until a fluid consistency is reached. Add more water if needed. Drink immediately.

NUTRITION INFORMATION PER SERVING

Calories	Protein (g)	Carbs (g)	Fat (g)	Sat Fat (g)	Unsat Fat (g)	Fiber (g)
334	27	48	6	0.1	0.4	7

Lunch

COOL BLUE SALAD WITH WILD SALMON *(OMNIVORE)* OR PURPLE RICE AND VEGETABLES *(VEGAN)*

Serves 1

- 2 cups baby kale
- ½ cup fresh blueberries
- ¼ cup cubed cucumber

FOR THE DRESSING:

- 1 tablespoon hempseed oil
- 1 tablespoon freshly squeezed lemon juice
- ¼ teaspoon lemon zest
- 2 fresh purple basil leaves, chopped finely
- Sea salt and ground black pepper to taste

In a serving bowl, combine the kale, blueberries, and cucumber. In a separate bowl, whisk together all the dressing ingredients, and drizzle the dressing over the salad.

Warm up yesterday's leftover Wild Salmon (*omnivore*) or Purple Rice and Vegetables (*vegan*) to serve with the salad.

NUTRITION INFORMATION PER SERVING

	Calories	Protein (g)	Carbs (g)	Fat (g)	Sat Fat (g)	Unsat Fat (g)	Fiber (g)
Omnivore	635	30	43	41	12	28	12
Vegan	784	21	85	47	7	37	15

Snack

BERRY AND NUT COBBLER (LEFTOVER FROM YESTERDAY'S SNACK)

NUTRITION INFORMATION PER SERVING

Calories	Protein (g)	Carbs (g)	Fat (g)	Sat Fat (g)	Unsat Fat (g)	Fiber (g)
206	4	18	15	4	9	4

Dinner

COCONUT COD FILLET WITH PLUM-LAVENDER SAUCE *(OMNIVORE)*
Serves 2

- 2 tablespoons coconut oil, melted
- 2 tablespoons unsweetened shredded coconut
- 1/8 teaspoon ground cardamom
- Pinch of sea salt
- 1/8 teaspoon freshly ground black pepper
- 2 4-ounce wild-caught cod fillets

FOR THE PLUM-LAVENDER SAUCE:

- 2 plums, pitted and sliced
- 2 tablespoons extra-virgin olive oil
- 1 1/4 tablespoons freshly squeezed lemon juice
- 2 teaspoons lavender buds, ground in a mortar and pestle
- 1/2 teaspoon sea salt

In a large bowl, whisk together the coconut oil, shredded coconut, cardamom, salt, and pepper. Set the mixture aside.

Set a large skillet over low heat. Dip each cod fillet into the oil and spice mixture, then lay both fillets in the heated skillet. Cover the skillet and let the cod cook, flipping the fillets to cook their other sides after about 5 minutes for a total cooking time of 10 minutes.

Meanwhile, make the sauce. In a small saucepan, warm the plums in about ¼ cup water. When they have softened, after about 1 minute, add the olive oil, lemon juice, lavender, and salt. Heat the mixture for about 2 minutes, stirring constantly.

Place 1 cooked cod fillet on a serving plate and drizzle it with half the sauce. Serve the cod with Steamed Broccoli (recipe follows). (Save the remaining fillet for tomorrow's lunch.)

NUTRITION INFORMATION PER SERVING

Calories	Protein (g)	Carbs (g)	Fat (g)	Sat Fat (g)	Unsat Fat (g)	Fiber (g)
349	21	12	25	11	14	2

STEAMED BROCCOLI *(OMNIVORE)*
Serves 1

1½ cups chopped broccoli   1 teaspoon chia seeds
1 teaspoon extra-virgin olive oil

In a saucepan or pot fitted with a steamer basket, bring about ¼ cup water to a boil. Add the broccoli to the steamer basket, cover the pot, and let the broccoli steam for about 1 minute, or until the pieces turn bright green.

Transfer the broccoli to a serving dish. Drizzle the broccoli with the olive oil, and sprinkle the chia seeds on top as desired. Serve warm.

NUTRITION INFORMATION PER SERVING

Calories	Protein (g)	Carbs (g)	Fat (g)	Sat Fat (g)	Unsat Fat (g)	Fiber (g)
87	4	7	6	1	5	4

PURPLE BUDDHA BOWL *(VEGAN)*

Serves 2

¼ cup uncooked purple/black rice

1 tablespoon coconut oil

½ cup diced red onion

1 garlic clove, minced

2½ cups chopped broccoli

1 cup cooked adzuki beans (you may want to cook them with the rice)

2 purple carrots, diced

2 tablespoons hemp seeds

½ red bell pepper, sliced

½ avocado, cubed

1 tablespoon flaxseed oil

Sea salt and ground black pepper to taste

Dash of ground cayenne pepper

Cook the rice in a rice cooker if available. If not, cook it in a saucepan on the stovetop according to the package instructions.

In a large skillet set over medium heat, melt the coconut oil, then sauté the onion and garlic in the oil for about 2 minutes, or until the onion becomes soft. Add the broccoli, cooked beans, carrots, hemp seeds, and bell pepper. (If you opt to cook the beans with the rice, omit them in this step.) Stir and heat the mixture until the colors of the broccoli and carrots are bright, about 1 to 2 minutes.

Into a large, wide serving bowl, spoon half the cooked rice (or half the rice and beans), then half the cooked vegetables, then half the avocado cubes. Drizzle everything with half the flaxseed oil, and season it with salt, black pepper, and cayenne. (Save the other half-portions of everything for tomorrow's lunch.)

NUTRITION INFORMATION PER SERVING

Calories	Protein (g)	Carbs (g)	Fat (g)	Sat Fat (g)	Unsat Fat (g)	Fiber (g)
568	19	70	26	8	13	18

DAY 18: THE INSIGHT—SPICES

Variety is the spice of life.

—WILLIAM COWPER

Meal Plan

	Omnivore	Vegan
Breakfast	Cacao-Coconut Smoothie	Cacao-Coconut Smoothie
Lunch	Zesty Purple Spiral Salad Coconut Cod Fillet	Zesty Purple Spiral Salad Purple Buddha Bowl
Snack	Blueberries and Pecans	Blueberries and Pecans
Dinner	Ginger Chicken with Blackberry Sauce Purple Potatoes	Spiced Eggplant Purple Potatoes

Whole Detox Emotion Log

At the end of the day, track any emotions that you had on the Whole Detox Emotion Log.

Thought Pattern Activity

The following are some limiting thoughts that relate to the INSIGHT:

To feel alive, I need to feel like I'm living on the edge.
I am too spicy for most people.
My life lacks spice and intensity.

Pick the limiting thought that seems to ring most true for you. If none of the examples feel true, write down your own limiting thought as it relates to the INSIGHT.

Next, set your timer for five minutes. Spend that time journaling on that thought, how it has affected your life, and how you feel when you have that thought.

Movement

DOWNWARD FACING DOG (ADHO MUKHA SVANASANA)

This pose increases blood flow to your head while calming and energizing the entire body. As with all yoga poses, go to your comfortable limit. Nothing should be painful.

1. Kneel on all fours on the floor, a mat, or a blanket with your back flat.
2. Walk your hands farther forward, keeping your palms flat on the floor.
3. Spread your fingers and establish solid contact with the floor, mat, or blanket.
4. Exhale as you lift your tailbone and straighten your legs.
5. Keep your feet flat on the floor, and lengthen your spine. Keep lifting your tailbone toward the ceiling while keeping your heels as close to the floor as you can. Do not lock your knees but keep them activated.
6. Maintain straight arms, keeping contact with the floor with your hands. Your palms should press firmly into the mat.
7. After holding this pose for up to three minutes, lower your tailbone, bend your knees, walk your hands back, and return to your original position to rest. You may repeat the activity a few more times, stretching each time just a little bit deeper than the previous time, to the level of comfort.

Affirmation

Spend three minutes saying aloud the following affirmation:

My life is filled with healthy intensity and flavorful moments.

Feel how your body responds to these words. You can also create your own statement. Feel free to write it on a beautiful notecard or a plain Post-it note and put it in your immediate environment for the day.

Visualization

Set a timer for three minutes. During that time, close your eyes and visualize yourself as a kaleidoscope of colors on the inside. See yourself as a brightly colored mosaic. Feel the intensity of your inner artwork. Let it invigorate every cell of your being.

Meditation

Watch your thoughts intently in a six-minute meditation. Adjust their speed, allowing them to move in slow motion and then speeding them up as fast as you'd like them to go. See how you feel when you look attentively and carefully at your thoughts versus letting them whiz by you in a whirlwind. While you do this activity, remain detached and free from their influence.

DAY 18 RECIPES

Breakfast

CACAO-COCONUT SMOOTHIE

Serves 1

1 cup unsweetened coconut milk
  (boxed variety)

1 teaspoon honey

1 tablespoon raw cacao nibs

1 tablespoon unsweetened cocoa
  powder

1 teaspoon flaxseed meal

1 scoop protein powder of your choice
  (hemp, pea, rice, whey for omnivores)

Water and ice to blend

Put all the liquid and whole food ingredients into a high-speed blender first, followed by the dry ingredients, then blend everything until a fluid consistency is reached. Add more water if needed. Drink immediately.

NUTRITION INFORMATION PER SERVING

Calories	Protein (g)	Carbs (g)	Fat (g)	Sat Fat (g)	Unsat Fat (g)	Fiber (g)
259	27	13	12	8	0.3	3

Lunch

ZESTY PURPLE SPIRAL SALAD WITH COCONUT COD FILLET *(OMNIVORE)* OR PURPLE BUDDHA BOWL *(VEGAN)*

Serves 1

2 large red cabbage leaves

¼ red cabbage, sliced lengthwise

1 large shallot, sliced into ringlets

1 tablespoon grated carrot

2 tablespoons raw pine nuts

1 tablespoon flaxseed oil

1 tablespoon freshly squeezed lemon juice

½ teaspoon lemon zest

1 teaspoon honey

Sea salt and ground black pepper to taste

Lay the 2 cabbage leaves inside a serving bowl, overlapping to cover the bottom surface.

In a small mixing bowl, combine the sliced cabbage, shallot, carrot, and pine nuts. Add the flaxseed oil, lemon juice, lemon zest, and honey. Combine the mixture well, seasoning with salt and pepper to taste. Then spoon it into the middle of the cabbage leaves in the serving bowl.

Either eat the salad taco style (rolled up in the cabbage leaves) or dig into the salad with a fork.

Warm up yesterday's leftover Coconut Cod Fillet (omnivore) or Purple Buddha Bowl (vegan) to serve with the salad.

NUTRITION INFORMATION PER SERVING

	Calories	Protein (g)	Carbs (g)	Fat (g)	Sat Fat (g)	Unsat Fat (g)	Fiber (g)
Omnivore	655	27	44	45	13	30	10
Vegan	873	25	102	46	10	29	26

Snack

BLUEBERRIES AND PECANS
Serves 1

1 cup fresh blueberries   1 handful pecans, about 8 halves

NUTRITION INFORMATION PER SERVING

Calories	Protein (g)	Carbs (g)	Fat (g)	Sat Fat (g)	Unsat Fat (g)	Fiber (g)
167	2	23	9	1	8	5

Dinner

GINGER CHICKEN WITH BLACKBERRY SAUCE *(OMNIVORE)*
Serves 1

1 tablespoon extra-virgin olive oil

2 tablespoons coconut aminos

1-inch piece fresh ginger, thinly sliced

1 teaspoon sea salt

1 4-ounce organic, free-range, boneless chicken breast, cut into strips

FOR THE SAUCE:

¼ cup fresh blackberries

1 tablespoon apple cider vinegar

1 teaspoon grated fresh ginger

½ teaspoon sea salt

1 teaspoon minced fresh mint leaves

In a skillet set over medium heat, warm the olive oil, then add the coconut aminos, ginger, salt, and chicken strips, stir-frying until the chicken is cooked through, about 7 to 10 minutes.

In a small saucepan set over medium heat, combine all the sauce ingredients, mashing the berries with a fork to release their juices. Let the mixture simmer, stirring it constantly, until it thickens slightly, approximately 2 minutes.

Arrange the chicken on a serving plate and drizzle it with the sauce. Serve immediately with Purple Potatoes (recipe follows).

NUTRITION INFORMATION PER SERVING

Calories	Protein (g)	Carbs (g)	Fat (g)	Sat Fat (g)	Unsat Fat (g)	Fiber (g)
301	27	11	16	2	13	2

SPICED EGGPLANT *(VEGAN)*

Serves 1

1 tablespoon extra-virgin olive oil
1 small red onion, finely chopped
1 garlic clove, minced
⅛ teaspoon ground cinnamon
⅛ teaspoon ground cardamom
1 teaspoon sea salt
1 small eggplant, peeled and cubed

½ medium tomato, chopped
3 shiitake mushrooms, diced
2 tablespoons raw pine nuts
1 teaspoon freshly squeezed lemon juice
Ground black pepper to taste

In a skillet set over medium heat, warm the olive oil, then add the onion, garlic, cinnamon, cardamom, and salt, sautéing the mixture until the onions are translucent, about 2 minutes. Add the eggplant and cook it until it's soft, about 5 to 7 minutes. Lower the heat, then stir in the tomato, mushrooms, and pine nuts and let warm for about 30 seconds. Drizzle the ingredients with lemon juice and add black pepper to taste.

Serve the eggplant with Purple Potatoes (recipe follows).

NUTRITION INFORMATION PER SERVING

Calories	Protein (g)	Carbs (g)	Fat (g)	Sat Fat (g)	Unsat Fat (g)	Fiber (g)
388	9	36	27	3	21	15

PURPLE POTATOES

Serves 1

2 small purple potatoes, cubed
½ tablespoon coconut oil
½ teaspoon dried rosemary

½ teaspoon turmeric powder
½ teaspoon sea salt

In a large skillet, boil the potatoes in just enough water to cover them. Cook them for about 7 to 10 minutes, until they are soft yet still firm in texture. Rinse the potatoes in a colander.

Drain any excess water from the skillet, and set it over medium heat. Melt the coconut oil in the skillet, then add the rosemary, turmeric, and salt, and transfer the potatoes into the spiced oil. Stir to coat the potatoes well. After about 1 minute, remove the skillet from the heat.

Serve the potatoes warm, with either the Ginger Chicken (*omnivore*) or the Spiced Eggplant (*vegan*).

NUTRITION INFORMATION PER SERVING

Calories	Protein (g)	Carbs (g)	Fat (g)	Sat Fat (g)	Unsat Fat (g)	Fiber (g)
298	6	54	7	6	1	6

DAY 19: THE SPIRIT—CONNECTION

The true way to be humble is not to stoop until you are smaller than yourself but to stand at your real height against some higher nature that will show you what the real smallness of your greatness is.

—PHILLIPS BROOKS

Meal Plan

	Omnivore	Vegan
Breakfast	Pear-Coconut Smoothie	Pear-Coconut Smoothie
Lunch	Arugula with Seed Medley	Arugula with Seed Medley
Snack	Divine Cleansing Broth	Divine Cleansing Broth
Dinner	Lemony Sole (Soul) with Turnips and Carrots	Enlightenment (Raw) Soup

Whole Detox Emotion Log

At the end of the day, track any emotions that you had on the Whole Detox Emotion Log.

Thought Pattern Activity

The following are some limiting thoughts that relate to the SPIRIT:

It is difficult for me to feel connected to a greater whole.

I don't feel inspired by my life.

I feel alone and disconnected from my everyday life.

Pick the limiting thought that seems to ring most true for you. If none of the examples feel true, write down your own limiting thought as it relates to the SPIRIT.

Next, set your timer for five minutes. Spend that time journaling on that thought, how it has affected your life, and how you feel when you have that thought.

Movement

Let your nervous system experience the contracting strength and relaxation of doing a whole-body progressive relaxation activity. Lie flat on your back, and insert a cushion under your knees if you need some lower-back support. Start the exercise by closing your eyes and tensing up all your muscles, starting with your feet and moving into your legs, torso, hands and arms, and face. Once your body is fully contracted, imagine what you want to let go of . . . and with a deep exhale, slowly let go of each part of your body, starting with where you tensed up first, your feet, and at the same time, release what you no longer need in your mind (maybe "stress" or "difficulty with my job"). Let the relaxation wash through your being, and feel your nervous system relax and calm down. Repeat this process three times and feel your body being connected throughout.

Affirmation

Spend three minutes saying aloud the following affirmation:

I am united with all of life.

Feel how your body responds to these words. You can also create your own statement. Feel free to write it on a beautiful notecard or a plain Post-it note and put it in your immediate environment for the day.

Visualization

Set a timer for three minutes. During that time, close your eyes and visualize a white, glitter-like coating over your entire being. Imagine that this coating represents your highest potential and purpose in life. Spend time basking in this glow of your illuminated self, feeling connection with all life within you and in your environment.

Meditation

For three minutes, meditate on the color white as you sit quietly on a cushion or chair.

DAY 19 RECIPES

Breakfast

PEAR-COCONUT SMOOTHIE

Serves 1

1 pear, sliced
1 cup unsweetened coconut water

1 scoop protein powder of your choice
(hemp, pea, rice, whey for omnivores)
Water and ice to blend

Put all the liquid and whole food ingredients into a high-speed blender first, followed by the dry protein powder, then blend everything until a fluid consistency is reached. Add more water if needed. Drink immediately.

NUTRITION INFORMATION PER SERVING

Calories	Protein (g)	Carbs (g)	Fat (g)	Sat Fat (g)	Unsat Fat (g)	Fiber (g)
269	26	37	3	0.4	0.1	8

Lunch

ARUGULA WITH SEED MEDLEY

Serves 1

2 cups arugula
½ cup diced cucumber

1 tablespoon chia seeds
1 tablespoon hemp seeds

FOR THE DRESSING:

1 tablespoon freshly squeezed lemon
juice
1 tablespoon tahini

⅛ teaspoon turmeric powder
⅛ teaspoon ground black pepper
Pinch of sea salt

In a serving bowl, combine the arugula, cucumber, chia seeds, and hemp seeds. In a separate small bowl, whisk together all the dressing ingredients and drizzle the dressing over the salad.

NUTRITION INFORMATION PER SERVING

Calories	Protein (g)	Carbs (g)	Fat (g)	Sat Fat (g)	Unsat Fat (g)	Fiber (g)
205	8	12	15	2	9	5

Snack

DIVINE CLEANSING BROTH
Serves 3

- 7 cups purified water
- 2 carrots, sliced
- 3 celery stalks, diced
- ¼ cup chopped fresh parsley
- ¼ cup finely sliced green onions
- ¼ cup chopped leeks
- 5-inch piece burdock root, finely diced
- 7 shiitake mushrooms, sliced
- 1½ teaspoons freshly squeezed lemon juice
- 1 teaspoon sea salt
- Ground black pepper to taste

In a large saucepan or soup pot, bring all the ingredients to a boil, then lower the heat and gently simmer the soup for 30 minutes. Serve the soup warm, spooning up one-third of it for today's snack. (Save the remaining two-thirds for the next two days' snacks.)

NUTRITION INFORMATION PER SERVING

Calories	Protein (g)	Carbs (g)	Fat (g)	Sat Fat (g)	Unsat Fat (g)	Fiber (g)
60	2	13	0.2	0	0.1	3

Dinner

LEMONY SOLE (SOUL) WITH TURNIPS AND CARROTS *(OMNIVORE)*
Serves 1

- 1 tablespoon freshly squeezed lemon juice
- 1 cup unsweetened coconut milk (boxed variety)

1 teaspoon dried thyme

1 teaspoon ground oregano

Pinch of sea salt

Freshly ground pepper to taste

1 5-ounce wild-caught sole fillet

2 medium turnips, cut into bite-size pieces

1 large carrot, cut into bite-size pieces

In a large skillet set over medium heat, combine the lemon juice, coconut milk, thyme, oregano, and salt, and season with pepper to taste. Gently add the sole fillet and let each side cook for 3 to 5 minutes, or until thoroughly cooked.

In a saucepan fitted with a steamer basket, boil ¼ to ½ cup water. Add the turnips and carrots to the steamer basket, and steam them until they are soft yet still colorful and firm, about 7 to 10 minutes.

Serve the sole alongside the steamed vegetables while they're still warm.

NUTRITION INFORMATION PER SERVING

Calories	Protein (g)	Carbs (g)	Fat (g)	Sat Fat (g)	Unsat Fat (g)	Fiber (g)
291	30	25	7	5	1	6

ENLIGHTENMENT (RAW) SOUP *(VEGAN)*

Serves 1

3 celery stalks

1 red bell pepper

2 cups spinach

½ avocado

1 green onion, diced

1 garlic clove

¼ cup raw cashews

2 tablespoons unhulled sesame seeds

1 teaspoon dulse flakes

3 fresh basil leaves

½ teaspoon dried dill

¼ teaspoon turmeric powder

Dash of ground cayenne pepper

1 teaspoon sea salt

Blend all the ingredients together in a high-speed blender or food processor. Thin the soup with purified water as desired. Serve it in a soup bowl, unheated.

NUTRITION INFORMATION PER SERVING

Calories	Protein (g)	Carbs (g)	Fat (g)	Sat Fat (g)	Unsat Fat (g)	Fiber (g)
544	14	42	39	5	24	18

DAY 20: THE SPIRIT—MEDITATION

Meditation is to dive all the way within, beyond thought, to the source of thought and pure consciousness. It enlarges the container, every time you transcend. When you come out, you come out refreshed, filled with energy and enthusiasm for life.

—DAVID LYNCH

Meal Plan

	Omnivore	Vegan
Breakfast	Mango-Coconut Smoothie	Mango-Coconut Smoothie
Lunch	Sweet-Sour Slaw	Sweet-Sour Slaw
Snack	Divine Cleansing Broth	Divine Cleansing Broth
Dinner	Creamy Spiced Cauliflower Soup with Lamb	Creamy Spiced Cauliflower Soup

Whole Detox Emotion Log

At the end of the day, track any emotions that you had on the Whole Detox Emotion Log.

Thought Pattern Activity

The following are some limiting thoughts that relate to the SPIRIT:

I can't meditate.

Sitting still is a waste of time.

I need to be always going somewhere or doing something.

Pick the limiting thought that seems to ring most true for you. If none of the examples feel true, write down your own limiting thought as it relates to the SPIRIT.

Next, set your timer for five minutes. Spend that time journaling on that thought, how it has affected your life, and how you feel when you have that thought.

Movement

HALF LOTUS (ARDHA PADMASANA)

As with all yoga poses, go to your comfortable limit. Nothing should be painful. Be careful with this pose if you have knee issues. Go with a modified pose if you are unable to complete the pose in its description below.

1. Sit on a mat or cushion.
2. Place one foot on the opposite thigh and the other foot on the floor beneath the opposite thigh.
3. Ideally both knees are on the floor; however, do not be discouraged if you cannot achieve this. Honor where your body is.

Alternatively, you can modify the pose by sitting with both feet on the floor, one in front of the other.

Once you have established your comfort in this pose, spend a couple of minutes here breathing deeply and fully.

Now, alternate your legs and repeat the same pose.

Affirmation

Spend three minutes saying aloud the following affirmation:

I move into the mystery of life with grace and ease.

Feel how your body responds to these words. You can also create your own statement. Feel free to write it on a beautiful notecard or a plain Post-it note and put it in your immediate environment for the day.

Visualization

Set a timer for three minutes. During that time, close your eyes and visualize rays of sunlight beaming down into every cell of your body, cleansing and purifying you of all toxins. Take your time to let the sunbeams radiate fully and completely from the outside to the inside.

Meditation

Meditate for seven minutes while basking in sunlight or while imagining that you are engulfed by a glow of purifying sunlight.

DAY 20 RECIPES

Breakfast

MANGO-COCONUT SMOOTHIE
Serves 1

1 cup diced mango

1 cup unsweetened coconut milk
(boxed variety)

¼ cup unsweetened coconut water

1 scoop protein powder of your choice
(hemp, pea, rice, whey for omnivores)

Water and ice to blend

Put all the liquid and whole food ingredients into a high-speed blender first, followed by the dry protein powder, then blend everything until a fluid consistency is reached. Add more water if needed. Drink immediately.

NUTRITION INFORMATION PER SERVING

Calories	Protein (g)	Carbs (g)	Fat (g)	Sat Fat (g)	Unsat Fat (g)	Fiber (g)
325	25	39	8	5	0.3	4

Lunch

SWEET-SOUR SLAW
Serves 1

1 cup diced green cabbage

½ cup diced red cabbage

1 pear, sliced

1 tablespoon diced white onion

2 tablespoons chopped walnuts

2 tablespoons golden raisins

FOR THE DRESSING:

1 tablespoon Dijon mustard

1 teaspoon honey

1 tablespoon apple cider vinegar

1 tablespoon flaxseed oil

½ teaspoon fennel seeds

Pinch of ground cayenne pepper

Pinch of sea salt

я a serving bowl, combine the cabbages, pear, onion, walnuts, and raisins. In a separate small bowl, whisk together all the dressing ingredients and drizzle the dressing over the salad.

NUTRITION INFORMATION PER SERVING

Calories	Protein (g)	Carbs (g)	Fat (g)	Sat Fat (g)	Unsat Fat (g)	Fiber (g)
468	5	65	24	2	20	11

Snack

DIVINE CLEANSING BROTH

Enjoy one serving—half—of yesterday's leftovers

NUTRITION INFORMATION PER SERVING

Calories	Protein (g)	Carbs (g)	Fat (g)	Sat Fat (g)	Unsat Fat (g)	Fiber (g)
60	2	13	0.2	0	0.1	3

Dinner

CREAMY SPICED CAULIFLOWER SOUP *(VEGAN)* WITH LAMB *(OMNIVORE)*
Serves 2

FOR OMNIVORES:

½ pound organic, grass-fed, boneless lamb, cubed

FOR BOTH:

2 teaspoons coconut oil

½ medium yellow onion, diced

2 garlic cloves, minced

Pinch of crushed red pepper flakes

1 teaspoon ground cumin

1 teaspoon turmeric powder

Pinch of ground coriander

Pinch of ground cardamom

Pinch of sea salt

Dash of ground black pepper

½ large head cauliflower, roughly chopped

1 cup unsweetened, full-fat coconut milk

2 cups organic vegetable broth

1 bay leaf

1 tablespoon cashew nut butter

In a large soup pot set over medium heat, warm the coconut oil.

Omnivores, add the lamb and sauté it for several minutes before adding the onion and garlic.

Both omnivores and vegans, sauté the onion and garlic, stirring occasionally, until the onions become translucent, about 3 minutes. Add the red pepper flakes, cumin, turmeric, coriander, cardamom, salt, and black pepper, and stir the mixture well for about 1 minute. Then add the cauliflower, coconut milk, broth, bay leaf, and cashew nut butter. Bring the soup to a boil, then reduce the heat and let it simmer gently for about 15 minutes, until the cauliflower is tender and, for omnivores, the lamb is cooked.

Ladle half the soup into a serving bowl and serve it warm. (Save the remaining half for tomorrow's lunch.)

NUTRITION INFORMATION PER SERVING

	Calories	Protein (g)	Carbs (g)	Fat (g)	Sat Fat (g)	Unsat Fat (g)	Fiber (g)
Omnivore	550	32	23	40	29	5	6
Vegan	390	9	23	33	26	2	6

DAY 21: THE SPIRIT—FASTING

I continue to be drawn to clarity and simplicity. "Less is more" remains my mantra.

—STÉPHANE ROLLAND

Meal Plan

	Omnivore	Vegan
Breakfast	Pear-Ginger Smoothie	Pear-Ginger Smoothie
Lunch	Pure and Simple Detox Salad Creamy Spiced Cauliflower Soup with Lamb	Pure and Simple Detox Salad Creamy Spiced Cauliflower Soup
Snack	Divine Cleansing Broth	Divine Cleansing Broth
Dinner	Coconut-Flaked Halibut with White Onion	Divine Rainbow Noodles with Heavenly Basil-Cauliflower Pesto

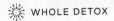

Whole Detox Emotion Log

At the end of the day, track any emotions that you had on the Whole Detox Emotion Log.

Thought Pattern Activity

The following are some limiting thoughts that relate to the SPIRIT:

I never have enough.
I need to eat to feel secure and fulfilled.
I feel scared when I "go without."

Pick the limiting thought that seems to ring most true for you. If none of the examples feel true, write down your own limiting thought as it relates to the SPIRIT.

Next, set your timer for five minutes. Spend that time journaling on that thought, how it has affected your life, and how you feel when you have that thought.

Movement

Gentle bouncing is excellent stimulation for the lymphatic system. You can jump on a trampoline, jump rope, or just jump in place. The up-and-down rhythmic gravitational force causes the lymph system's one-way valves to open and close. This motion increases the flow of lymphatic fluid and oxygen uptake, and promotes detoxification through the lungs, skin, and lymph.

Affirmation

Spend three minutes saying aloud the following affirmation:

I am filled with the abundance of life.

Feel how your body responds to these words. You can also create your own statement. Feel free to write it on a beautiful notecard or a plain Post-it note and put it in your immediate environment for the day.

Visualization

Set a timer for three minutes. During that time, close your eyes and visualize yourself as a vast universe. See your inner self filled with planets, stars, and galaxies. Imagine that your being is the expanse of all that lives and exists. Feel nourished and abundant by seeing this interconnection within you.

Meditation

What is your favorite food to eat? Meditate for seven minutes on that food; see it as a symbol or a metaphor for what you are really experiencing by eating that food on the level of your soul. In the meditation, what comes forth from your thought patterns, childhood, and the sensation of eating that food?

DAY 21 RECIPES

Breakfast

PEAR-GINGER SMOOTHIE
Serves 1

1 small ripe pear, cored
1-inch piece fresh ginger, minced
¼ teaspoon ground ginger
½ cup water

1 scoop protein powder of your choice
    (hemp, pea, rice, whey for omnivores)
Water and ice to blend

Put all the liquid and whole food ingredients into a high-speed blender first, followed by the dry protein powder, then blend everything until a fluid consistency is reached. Add more water if needed. Drink immediately.

NUTRITION INFORMATION PER SERVING

Calories	Protein (g)	Carbs (g)	Fat (g)	Sat Fat (g)	Unsat Fat (g)	Fiber (g)
223	25	29	2	0	0.1	6

Lunch

PURE AND SIMPLE DETOX SALAD WITH CREAMY SPICED CAULIFLOWER SOUP (*VEGAN*) WITH LAMB (*OMNIVORE*)

Serves 1

1 cup chopped romaine lettuce

½ cup chopped cucumber

1 tablespoon chia seeds

1 tablespoon freshly squeezed lemon juice

1 tablespoon hempseed oil

Simply combine everything in a serving bowl, coating all the ingredients with lemon juice and hempseed oil.

Warm up yesterday's Creamy Spiced Cauliflower Soup (*vegan*) with Lamb (*omnivore*) to serve with the salad.

NUTRITION INFORMATION PER SERVING

	Calories	Protein (g)	Carbs (g)	Fat (g)	Sat Fat (g)	Unsat Fat (g)	Fiber (g)
Omnivore	733	34	31	56	30	19	11
Vegan	573	11	31	49	27	16	11

Snack

DIVINE CLEANSING BROTH

Enjoy the remaining serving of leftovers from Day 19

NUTRITION INFORMATION PER SERVING

Calories	Protein (g)	Carbs (g)	Fat (g)	Sat Fat (g)	Unsat Fat (g)	Fiber (g)
60	2	13	0.2	0	0.1	3

Dinner

COCONUT-FLAKED HALIBUT WITH WHITE ONION *(OMNIVORE)*
Serves 1

1 teaspoon coconut oil

1 small white onion, sliced thinly

2 tablespoons coconut flour

2 tablespoons unsweetened coconut flakes

2 tablespoons flaxseed meal

2 tablespoons coconut oil, melted, divided

¼ cup unsweetened, full-fat coconut milk

1 5-ounce halibut fillet

1 tablespoon finely chopped green onion, for garnish

In a small skillet set over low heat, warm the 1 teaspoon coconut oil, then add the onion, sautéing it until it is lightly browned.

While the onion is cooking, prepare the fish. In a shallow bowl or plate, combine the coconut flour, coconut flakes, and flaxseed meal. In a separate shallow bowl, combine 1 tablespoon of the melted coconut oil with the coconut milk. Dip both sides of the halibut fillet first into the oil and milk mixture, then into the flour and meal mixture, completely coating the fillet.

In a skillet set over medium heat, add the remaining 1 tablespoon of melted coconut oil, then gently place the fillet into the pan, and cook it about 5 minutes on each side, depending on its thickness.

Serve the fillet topped with a sprinkle of chopped green onion and alongside the sautéed onions.

NUTRITION INFORMATION PER SERVING

Calories	Protein (g)	Carbs (g)	Fat (g)	Sat Fat (g)	Unsat Fat (g)	Fiber (g)
559	34	13	42	33	6	7

DIVINE RAINBOW NOODLES WITH HEAVENLY BASIL-CAULIFLOWER PESTO *(VEGAN)*
Serves 1

1 red bell pepper, sliced thinly

1 carrot, sliced into "noodles" with a
vegetable peeler

1 small zucchini, sliced into "noodles"
with a vegetable peeler or spiralizer

1 small yellow squash, sliced into

"noodles" with a vegetable peeler or
spiralizer

2 tablespoons Heavenly Basil-
Cauliflower Pesto (recipe follows)

Sliced green onions, for garnish

On a serving plate, gently combine the bell pepper, carrot, zucchini, and
yellow squash with the pesto, and garnish the dish with the green onions.

NUTRITION INFORMATION PER SERVING

Calories	Protein (g)	Carbs (g)	Fat (g)	Sat Fat (g)	Unsat Fat (g)	Fiber (g)
96	4	20	1	0.1	0.3	6

HEAVENLY BASIL-CAULIFLOWER PESTO *(VEGAN)*
Makes about ½ cup, or about four servings

1 cup tightly packed fresh basil leaves
(purple basil preferred)

1 cup chopped cauliflower

2 garlic cloves

1 teaspoon sea salt

½ cup raw pine nuts

½ cup extra-virgin olive oil

Place all the ingredients in a high-speed blender or food processor, and
blend the mixture until it's smooth. Add more oil if needed for a better flow.
Save any leftover pesto in a glass jar for future use.

NUTRITION INFORMATION PER SERVING

Calories	Protein (g)	Carbs (g)	Fat (g)	Sat Fat (g)	Unsat Fat (g)	Fiber (g)
131	2	3	13	1	11	1

CHAPTER 12

WHOLE DETOX FOR LIFE

Congratulations! You've completed your twenty-one-day Whole Detox and brought a whole new rainbow of possibilities into your life. You've taken some exciting steps toward clearing up symptoms, losing weight, boosting your vitality, and tapping into new reserves of purpose and meaning. You've learned something about which foods sap your energy and discovered some new foods that have brought more color, flavor, and sparkle into your life. You've found out more about the toxic barriers that are holding you back, and you've found some new ways to break through them and move on to a new level of inspiration.

I'm excited for the new possibilities you have unlocked, and I want to help you make the most of them. So let's talk about what comes next.

WHOLE DETOX: WHAT COMES NEXT?

Right after the program: Reintroduce foods you have eliminated while enjoying a daily rainbow of good food.

One month later: Complete the Whole Detox Spectrum Quiz again and identify which system of full-spectrum health is most out of balance now. Focus on bringing that system back into balance through food, lifestyle, color, or any combination of the three.

Six months later: Complete another entire Whole Detox. After the twenty-one days, you can try reintroducing foods that didn't work for you the last time. Then continue to do your monthly check-in with your systems of health through the Whole Detox Spectrum Quiz.

Going forward: Every six months, complete another Whole Detox. If you like, you can try reintroducing foods that you haven't yet been able to tolerate. Use the Whole Detox Food Reintroduction Symptoms Tracker to track your progress.

RIGHT AFTER THE PROGRAM:
REINTRODUCE FOODS AND CONSUME THE RAINBOW

You've just spent twenty-one days finding out what it's like when your body isn't burdened by problem foods. You've also found out how great it feels to eat from the full spectrum of the rainbow. Now it's time to figure out which foods you can bring back into your daily diet while also continuing to eat a rainbow-colored diet.

What is Reintroduction?

As we saw in chapter 1, Whole Detox begins at the ROOT, pulling out any food that might trigger inflammation. Inflammation is a response from your immune system that can be healing when it is acute and specific but becomes highly problematic when it is chronic.

The following foods frequently trigger inflammation, which is why we pulled them from our twenty-one-day detox:

- Alcohol
- Caffeine (chocolate, coffee, soft drinks, tea)
- Dairy products (cheese, milk, yogurt)
- Eggs
- Gluten (barley, spelt, wheat, and, in some cases, oats)
- Peanuts
- Processed carbohydrates
- Processed meats
- Shellfish
- Sugar and sweeteners (includes artificial ones)
- Soy

However, after a twenty-one-day Whole Detox, your immune system has become healthier without the daily interference of foods you had before you started the program. Using the following protocol, you can find whether you can now eat foods that formerly gave you trouble.

The Reintroduction Protocol

Make a list of the foods and beverages you have omitted and would like to add back into your diet.

For example:

- Caffeine (coffee, soda, tea)
- Chocolate
- Corn (chips, fresh corn, tortillas)
- Dairy products (cheese, milk, yogurt)
- Eggs
- Shellfish (lobster, shrimp)
- Soy (miso, soy sauce, tofu)

1. *Find a simple version of the first food you want to test.* Ensure that the food you test is simple enough in composition and not a complex food with multiple ingredients. For example, if you are testing corn, you will want to test a pure corn product in multiple forms that you typically eat, like organic corn on the cob or a straightforward corn chip or a simple-ingredient corn tortilla, not a corn chip with gluten-containing spices or a high-fructose corn syrup sweetener. If you try the food in a complex version with multiple ingredients and you have a problematic reaction, you won't know whether you're reacting to the problem food or to one of the other ingredients.

2. *While maintaining your baseline diet, add in two daily servings of the test food.* For example, if you are reintroducing cheese, you might have one slice of cheese with your daily smoothie and another with your salad at lunch.

3. *Allow four to six hours after you consume a new food before eating any more of it.* If you notice symptoms at any point, stop eating the food and pull it from your diet for at least six months. If you're okay, continue on to the next serving.

4. *Observe your symptoms the day after the food challenge.* If you notice symptoms, stop eating it immediately. If you manage two successful symptom-free days (one of those days is the day you challenged the food), you can now add the food back into your diet. Don't overdo it, though; you might provoke another bad reaction. Stick to two to five times a week for any formerly problematic food. Rotating foods is always a good idea.

5. *Reintroduce the next food.* If you have successfully introduced the first food, you can reintroduce the next food. If you had problematic symptoms from the first food, wait for those symptoms to fully subside. Then, after two symptom-free days, introduce the next food.

You can use the Food Reintroduction Symptoms Tracker (see page 384) to keep a record of the process.

If a food gives you problems, don't despair. You can try to reintroduce it again in another six to twelve months, after your immune system has become stronger. You may be able to enjoy it in small amounts or at times when you're not too stressed. Listen to your intuition and let your body tell you what you are able to handle. You might also consult a functional medicine practitioner to work with you more closely to figure out which foods are right for you through laboratory testing.

COMMON REACTIONS FROM PROBLEM FOODS

- Digestion difficulties, such as gas or bloating
- Changes in bowel movements, such as diarrhea or constipation
- Skin rashes, itching, acne, rosacea, and/or hives
- Extreme fatigue
- Chills or temperature shifts, such as flushing and atypical body heat
- Pain in the joints or throughout the body

Consuming the Rainbow

As you have seen, Whole Detox isn't just about taking foods out. It's also about making sure you get the right foods to fortify your system. The more you support your system with healthy, colorful, whole foods, the more you will be able to tolerate life's stresses and perhaps also some of the foods that gave you problems before.

Remember is to get the full rainbow every day. Make sure you eat at least one food from each of the seven colors on a daily basis. You can use the Rainbow Tracker (see page 385) to help ensure you're covering the entire rainbow. I suggest using the tracker for twenty-one days, which is typically how long it takes to create a new habit.

BECOMING AWARE OF COLOR

One of the most transformative results of Whole Detox is how much your awareness of color grows. You will find yourself noticing how different colored foods affect you, and also how color affects you in other domains: the clothes you wear, the colors you choose for your home, the objects you bring in to brighten up your work space. I encourage you to remain open to the healing, energizing, and inspiring properties of color!

ONE MONTH LATER: START YOUR MONTHLY CHECK-IN

Once you've finished the process of reintroducing problem foods, give yourself a month to process the results of your Whole Detox. Then check in by retaking the entire Whole Detox Spectrum Quiz (see pages 35–41). Use your score to determine which of your seven systems is most out of balance. Then focus on that system for the next month. You can restore balance with food, lifestyle, color, or any combination of the three.

SIX MONTHS LATER: COMPLETE ANOTHER WHOLE DETOX

The exciting thing about this approach is that each time you conduct a Whole Detox, your experience will be profoundly different. Barriers that existed before may now have disappeared; new challenges, perhaps in different systems, will have emerged. As long as we are alive, we will face some barriers to health and fulfillment. Learning how to remove each new barrier as it appears offers us a continual process of discovery and growth—and an ongoing opportunity to deepen our relationship with ourselves.

GOING FORWARD

- Continue your monthly check-in
- Repeat Whole Detox every six months

As I tell my patients, we can learn more about ourselves, breaking through barriers and accessing new potential. Accordingly, each time you complete a Whole Detox, your experience will teach you something you didn't expect. You might find yourself working on different systems of health or returning again and again to the same one or two systems, but each time the issues that arise will seem slightly different and the possibilities you unlock will take you to new places.

Throughout your journey, however, you can count on the Whole Detox Spectrum Quiz to guide you, helping you identify where your strengths lie and your toxic barriers appear. Clarifying and healing one set of issues makes room for some new issues to come to the surface, in an ongoing process of detoxification and renewal.

This is why I'd like you also to use the Whole Detox Food Reintroduction Systems Tracker (see page 384) to track your progress from one week to the next. As "happy," "energized," and "symptom-free" become your new normal, you might forget how far you've come. And even if some of the same issues recur—as they do for most of us—your Systems Tracker will help you realize that they are returning in new forms. Often we are making progress even when it doesn't feel like it, and the Systems Tracker can help you see that.

THE POWER OF SYSTEMS

One of the extraordinary things about Whole Detox is how work on one system of health profoundly affects all the other systems. Even tiny, incremental adjustments—starting to eat a colorful food, adding in a few minutes of daily exercise, taking five minutes to meditate or do a yoga stretch—can, over time, be transformative, because one small change leads to another, and then another, and then another. Likewise, a modification in the ROOT can quickly produce changes in one of the other systems, which can lead to a change in yet another system, and then another, and then another.

Although Whole Detox moves through the systems of health in a linear fashion, the systems are less a straight line than a web, a dynamic interconnected network. Some people feel overwhelmed by the idea that we are truly a web and that anything we do is going to have an impact: from teeny tiny actions to great big huge actions. Don't get stuck or stagnated on trying to figure out how to be perfect; just move through your colors, go where you feel drawn, and you will be on the path of healing. Let yourself be guided by the inspiration of color and the information you now have about food and lifestyle as you continue to live a full-spectrum life!

UNIVERSAL CONVERSION CHART

OVEN TEMPERATURE EQUIVALENTS

250°F = 120°C   400°F = 200°C
275°F = 135°C   425°F = 220°C
300°F = 150°C   450°F = 230°C
325°F = 160°C   475°F = 240°C
350°F = 180°C   500°F = 260°C
375°F = 190°C

MEASUREMENT EQUIVALENTS

Measurements should always be level unless directed otherwise.

⅛ teaspoon = 0.5 mL
¼ teaspoon = 1 mL
½ teaspoon = 2 mL
1 teaspoon = 5 mL
1 tablespoon = 3 teaspoons = ½ fluid ounce = 15 mL
2 tablespoons = ⅓ cup = 1 fluid ounce = 30 mL
4 tablespoons = ½ cup = 2 fluid ounces = 60 mL
5⅓ tablespoons = ⅓ cup = 3 fluid ounces = 80 mL
8 tablespoons = ½ cup = 4 fluid ounces = 120 mL
10⅔ tablespoons = ⅔ cup = 5 fluid ounces = 160 mL
12 tablespoons = ½ cup = 6 fluid ounces = 180 mL
16 tablespoons = 1 cup = 8 fluid ounces = 240 mL

SHOPPING LISTS

OMNIVORE SHOPPING LISTS
THE ROOT

PRODUCE

Apples, red	2 (1 small, 1 medium)
Avocado	1 medium
Beets with their greens	2 medium
Bell pepper, red	2 small
Broccoli	1 cup, chopped
Carrots	3 (1 small, 2 medium)
Cauliflower	1 cup, chopped
Grapefruit	1
Grapes, red	7
Kale	4 medium to large leaves
Lettuce, red- or green-leaf	2 cups roughly chopped
Mushroom, portobello	1
Mushrooms, shiitake	6
Onion, red	2 medium
Radishes	4
Raspberries	About 1½ cups
Strawberries	About 1 cup
Swiss chard	2 medium to large leaves
Tomatoes	2 medium
Turnip	1 medium

GROCERY

Almond butter	2 tablespoons
Bee pollen granules (optional)	1 tablespoon
Hummus	½ cup
Quinoa (red variety preferred)	¼ cup uncooked (½ cup cooked)
Sesame seeds, unhulled	1 tablespoon
Sunflower seeds, raw	1 tablespoon
Tomato juice, low-sodium, bottled	2 cups
Walnut halves (red variety preferred)	8

MEAT AND FISH

Chicken breasts, organic, free-range, boneless, skinless	2 breasts, 4 ounces each
Flank steak, organic, grass-fed	4 to 6 ounces
Ground beef, organic, grass-fed	⅓ pound
Ground turkey, organic, free-range, lean	½ pound

THE FLOW

PRODUCE

Apricots	3
Arugula or other leafy greens	2 cups
Avocado	1 medium
Banana	1 small
Bell pepper, orange	1 large
Cabbage, red	1 small head (need ½ cup shredded)
Carrots	3 medium
Fennel bulb with fronds	1
Green onions	3
Kale	2 large leaves
Leek	1 medium
Mangoes	2
Mixed greens	1 cup

Nectarine (or orange, if you prefer)	1
Onion, yellow	1 small (need 2 tablespoons diced)
Oranges (save the zest)	2
Peach	2 small
Shallot	1 medium

FRESH HERBS

| Basil | 1 cup leaves |
| Mint | 2 tablespoons chopped |

GROCERY

Brown rice flour	¼ cup
Cashews, raw (or other nuts of choice; optional)	2 tablespoons
Coconut flakes, unsweetened	1 tablespoon
Dates, Medjool	2
Macadamia nuts, lightly salted	10 whole nuts plus ¼ cup finely chopped
Orange juice	2¼ cups
Pine nuts, raw	½ cup
Pumpkin seeds, roasted	2 tablespoons
Quinoa	¼ cup uncooked (½ cup cooked)
Raisins, golden	2 tablespoons
Sunflower oil, high oleic, or extra-virgin olive oil	1 tablespoon
Vegetable broth, organic	1¼ cups
Walnut halves	2 cups plus 2 tablespoons

MEAT AND FISH

Cod, wild-caught	3 ounces
Ground lamb, organic, grass-fed	10 ounces
Halibut, wild-caught	2 fillets, 5 ounces each
Salmon, wild-caught	1 8- to 10-ounce fillet (with its skin)

THE FIRE

PRODUCE

Apple, Golden Delicious	1
Arugula	2 cups
Bananas	2 small
Bell peppers, yellow	1½
Cauliflower	2 cups chopped
Celery	1 to 2 stalks (need ¼ cup finely chopped)
Cucumber	¼ medium
Green onions	1 to 2 (need 3 tablespoons chopped)
Kale	1 to 2 leaves (need ¾ cup finely chopped)
Onion, yellow	1 large
Pineapple chunks, frozen or fresh	½ cup
Shallots	2 medium to large
Spaghetti squash	1 small
Spinach	2 cups
Summer squash, yellow	1 small plus ¼ cup cubed

FRESH HERBS

Basil	¼ cup chopped
Cilantro	5 tablespoons chopped
Parsley	¼ cup finely chopped

GROCERY

Almonds, raw	¼ cup
Amaranth	3 tablespoons uncooked (½ cup cooked)
Date, Medjool	1
Lentils, French green	¼ cup uncooked (½ cup cooked)
Mustard, Dijon	1 tablespoon
Pineapple juice	1 cup
Pine nuts, raw	2 tablespoons
Quinoa	¾ cup uncooked (1½ cups cooked)
Rice, brown, long grain	¼ cup uncooked

Rice vinegar	½ tablespoon
Sesame seeds, unhulled	½ tablespoon
Sunflower oil, high-oleic, or extra-virgin olive oil	1 tablespoon
Sunflower seed butter	2 tablespoons
Tahini	1 tablespoon
Tapioca flour	1 teaspoon
Vegetable broth, organic (optional)	½ cup

MEAT AND FISH

Chicken breasts, organic, free-range, boneless, skinless	4 breasts, 4 ounces each
Ground turkey, organic, free-range	8 ounces

THE LOVE

PRODUCE

Apple, green	1
Asparagus stalks	5
Avocado	1 large
Broccoli	1½ cups chopped
Broccoli sprouts	¼ cup
Cabbage, green	½ head or 1 small (need ½ cup shredded)
Cucumber	1½ small
Green onions	1 bunch
Honeydew melon	1 cup cubed
Kale, green curly-leaf	2½ to 3 bunches
Kiwi fruits	2
Microgreens	About 1 cup
Mushrooms, shiitake	¼ cup chopped
Spinach	8½ to 9 cups
Strawberries	About 2 (need ¼ cup sliced)
Swiss chard	1 bunch (about 5 large leaves)

FRESH HERBS

Dill	¼ teaspoon
Mint	4 to 5 leaves
Parsley	2 tablespoons minced

GROCERY

Almond meal	2 tablespoons
Almonds, raw	¼ cup
Almonds, toasted, slivered	2 tablespoons
Apple juice	¼ cup
Avocado oil	4 tablespoons
Cacao nibs, raw	1 tablespoon
Green tea, decaffeinated	⅔ cup
Olives, green	5
Pine nuts, raw	2 tablespoons
Pistachios, unsalted, raw, shelled	5 tablespoons
Walnut halves	4 to 5
White beans (Great Northern)	3 tablespoons uncooked (½ cup cooked)
Other	Parchment paper, kitchen string

MEAT AND FISH

Anchovies (Vital Choice brand preferred)	4
Lox	4 ounces
Salmon, wild-caught	2 fillets, 3 to 4 ounces each
Turkey breasts, organic, free-range, boneless	2 breasts, 4 to 5 ounces each

THE TRUTH

PRODUCE

Apple, green	1
Arugula	1 cup
Banana	1 medium
Bell pepper, red	½

Bok choy	1 to 2 heads (need 1½ cups chopped)
Cabbage, red	Less than ¼ head (need ¼ cup finely sliced)
Cantaloupe	½ cup cubed
Carrots	4
Cauliflower	2 cups chopped
Dandelion greens	1 cup
Green onion	1
Honeydew melon	1½ cups cubed
Kale, baby	4 cups
Kiwi fruit	1
Mango	2 cups cubed
Mushrooms, shiitake	5 large
Onion, yellow	¼ cup diced
Potatoes, red	2 small
Radishes	2
Spinach	1½ cups
Squash, yellow	½ small
Strawberries	2
Zucchini	1 small

FRESH HERBS

Basil	4 leaves
Lemongrass	3-inch piece
Mint	7 or 8 leaves

GROCERY

Almonds, raw	12
Coconut, unsweetened, shredded	1 tablespoon
Dates, Medjool	2
Dulse flakes	1 cup
Nori, pressed	3 sheets
Orange juice	4 tablespoons
Pecan pieces	½ cup
Pomegranate juice	1 cup

Rice, brown	½ cup cooked
Sesame seeds, unhulled	1 teaspoon
Thai green curry paste	½ teaspoon
Vegetable broth, organic	7 cups
Walnut halves	5

MEAT AND FISH

| Chicken breasts, organic, free-range, boneless | 14 ounces total |
| Halibut, wild-caught | 8 ounces |

THE INSIGHT

PRODUCE

Apple, red	⅓ cup sliced
Banana	1 medium
Blackberries	3¾ cups
Blueberries, frozen or fresh	3½ cups
Broccoli	1½ cups chopped
Cabbage, red	1 large
Carrot	1 tablespoon shredded
Cucumber	¼ cup cubed
Kale, baby	2 cups
Kale, purple	3 cups chopped
Plums	2
Potatoes, purple	2 small
Raspberries	1 cup
Shallot	1 large
Spinach	3 cups

FRESH HERBS

| Basil, purple | 7 leaves |
| Mint | 1 teaspoon minced |

GROCERY

Bee pollen granules (optional)	1 teaspoon
Cacao nibs, raw	1 tablespoon
Cocoa powder, unsweetened	1 tablespoon
Coconut, unsweetened, shredded	2 tablespoons
Hempseed oil	1 tablespoon
Hibiscus tea	½ cup
Mustard, Dijon	½ tablespoon
Oats, gluten-free	1 cup
Pecan halves	8
Pecans	½ cup chopped
Pine nuts, raw	2 tablespoons
Pomegranate juice	1 cup
Walnuts	¾ cup chopped

MEAT AND FISH

Chicken breast, organic, free-range, boneless	1 breast, 4 ounces
Cod, wild-caught	2 fillets, 4 ounces each
Salmon, wild-caught	2 fillets, 4 ounces each

THE SPIRIT

PRODUCE

Arugula	2 cups
Burdock root	5-inch piece
Cabbage, green	¼ to ½ head (need 1 cup diced)
Cabbage, red	¼ head (need ½ cup diced)
Carrots	3
Cauliflower	½ large head
Celery	3 stalks
Cucumber	1 cup diced
Green onions	1 small bunch

Leeks	¼ cup chopped
Mango, frozen or fresh	1 cup diced
Mushrooms, shiitake	7
Onion, white	1 medium or 2 small
Onion, yellow	½ medium
Pears	3
Romaine lettuce	1 cup chopped
Turnips	2 medium

FRESH HERBS

Parsley	¼ cup chopped

GROCERY

Cashew nut butter	1 tablespoon
Coconut flakes, unsweetened	2 tablespoons
Coconut flour	2 tablespoons
Hempseed oil	1 tablespoon
Mustard, Dijon	1 tablespoon
Raisins, golden	2 tablespoons
Tahini	1 tablespoon
Vegetable broth, organic	2 cups
Walnuts	2 tablespoons chopped

MEAT AND FISH

Halibut, wild-caught	1 fillet, 5 ounces
Lamb, organic, grass-fed, boneless	8 ounces
Sole, wild-caught	1 fillet, 5 ounces

VEGAN SHOPPING LISTS
THE ROOT

PRODUCE

Apples, red	2 (1 small, 1 medium)
Avocado	1 medium
Beets with their greens	2 medium
Bell pepper, red	2 small
Broccoli	1 cup chopped
Carrots	3 (1 small, 2 medium)
Cauliflower	1 cup, chopped
Grapefruit	1
Grapes, red	7
Kale	4 large leaves
Lettuce, red- or green-leaf	2 cups roughly chopped
Mushroom, portobello	1
Mushrooms, shiitake	6
Onion, red	2 medium
Radishes	4
Raspberries	About 1½ cups
Strawberries	About 1 cup
Swiss chard	2 medium to large leaves
Tomatoes	2 medium
Turnip	1 medium

GROCERY

Adzuki beans	½ cup uncooked (1½ cups cooked)
Almond butter	2 tablespoons
Bee pollen granules (optional)	1 tablespoon
Black beans	¼ cup uncooked (¾ cup cooked)
Chickpeas	½ cup uncooked (1½ cups cooked)
Hummus	½ cup
Kidney beans	¼ cup uncooked (¾ cup cooked)

Quinoa (red variety preferred)	¼ cup uncooked (½ cup cooked) plus 2 tablespoons uncooked
Sesame seeds, unhulled	1 tablespoon
Sunflower seeds, raw	1 tablespoon
Tomato juice, low-sodium, bottled	2 cups
Walnut halves (red variety preferred)	8

THE FLOW

PRODUCE

Avocado	1 medium
Banana	1 small
Bell peppers, orange	3 large
Cabbage, red	1 small head (need ½ cup shredded)
Carrots	12 medium to large
Celery	1 to 2 stalks (need ¼ cup diced)
Fennel bulb with fronds	1
Kale	2 large leaves
Leek	1 small to medium
Mangoes	2
Mixed greens	1 cup
Nectarine (or orange, if you prefer)	1
Onion, yellow	1 small to medium
Oranges (save the zest)	2
Peach	2 small
Shallot	1 medium

FRESH HERBS

Basil	1 cup leaves
Mint	2 tablespoons chopped

GROCERY

Almond butter	3 tablespoons
Almonds, slivered	2 tablespoons
Cashews, raw	6 tablespoons
Coconut flakes, unsweetened	1 tablespoon
Dates, Medjool	2
Lentils, dried, sprouted	½ cup uncooked
Lentils, orange/red	¾ cup uncooked (1½ cups cooked)
Macadamia nuts, lightly salted	10
Orange juice	¾ cup
Pine nuts, raw	¾ cup
Pumpkin seeds, roasted	2 tablespoons
Quinoa	¼ cup uncooked (½ cup cooked)
Raisins, golden	2 tablespoons
Sunflower oil, high oleic	1 tablespoon
Sunflower seeds, raw	¼ cup
Tahini	2 tablespoons
Vegetable broth, organic	3 cups
Walnut halves	2 cups plus 2 tablespoons
Wild rice	½ cup uncooked

THE FIRE

PRODUCE

Apple, Golden Delicious	1
Arugula	2 cups
Avocado	1 small
Bananas	2 small
Bell pepper, yellow	1
Carrots	2
Cucumber	½ small
Onion, red	1 small
Onion, yellow	1 small
Pineapple chunks, frozen or fresh	½ cup

Potato, yellow	1 large
Romaine lettuce heart	1 large
Shallots	3 medium to large
Spinach	2 cups
Summer squash, yellow	1 small

FRESH HERBS

Basil	¼ cup chopped
Cilantro	5 tablespoons chopped
Parsley	2 tablespoons chopped
Thyme	2 tablespoons chopped

GROCERY

Almonds, raw	¼ cup
Amaranth	3 tablespoons uncooked (½ cup cooked)
Black beans	½ cup uncooked (1½ cups cooked)
Chickpeas	½ cup uncooked (1½ cups cooked)
Date, Medjool	1
Lentils, yellow	½ cup uncooked
Pineapple juice	1 cup
Pine nuts, raw	2 tablespoons
Quinoa	¼ cup uncooked (½ cup cooked)
Sunflower seed butter	2 tablespoons
Tahini	2 tablespoons
Vegetable broth, organic	4 cups

THE LOVE

PRODUCE

Apple, green	1
Asparagus stalks	1 large bunch
Avocados	2 large
Broccoli	1½ cups chopped

Broccoli sprouts	¼ cup
Brussels sprouts	6 or 7
Cabbage, green	½ head or 1 small (need ½ cup shredded)
Cauliflower	3 cups chopped
Cucumber	I medium
Green onions	2
Honeydew melon	1 cup cubed
Kale, green curly-leaf	2½ to 3 bunches
Kiwi fruits	2
Microgreens	About 1 cup
Spinach	7½ cups
Strawberries	About 2 (need ¼ cup sliced)

FRESH HERBS

Cilantro	2 tablespoons chopped
Dill	¼ teaspoon
Mint	4 to 5 leaves
Parsley	2 tablespoons minced

GROCERY

Almonds, raw	¼ cup
Almonds, toasted, slivered	2 tablespoons
Apple juice	¼ cup
Avocado oil	5 tablespoons
Cacao nibs, raw	1 tablespoon
Cannellini beans	2 tablespoons uncooked (¼ cup cooked)
Green tea, decaffeinated	⅔ cup
Lima beans	2 tablespoons uncooked (¼ cup cooked)
Olives, green	5
Pine nuts, raw	4 tablespoons
Pistachios, unsalted, raw, shelled	5 tablespoons
Rice, brown	¼ cup uncooked (¾ cup cooked)
Tahini	1 tablespoon
Walnut halves	4 to 5
White beans, Great Northern	¼ cup uncooked (¾ cup cooked)

THE TRUTH

PRODUCE

Apple, green	1
Arugula	1 cup
Banana	1 medium
Bell pepper, red	½
Bok choy	1 to 2 heads (need 1½ cups chopped)
Cabbage, red	Less than ¼ head (need ¼ cup finely sliced)
Cantaloupe	½ cup cubed
Carrots	4
Cauliflower	2 cups chopped
Dandelion greens	1 cup
Green onion	1
Honeydew melon	1½ cups cubed
Kale, baby	4 cups
Kiwi fruit	1
Mango	2 cups cubed
Mushrooms, shiitake	5 large
Onion, yellow	¼ cup diced
Potatoes, red	2 small
Radishes	2
Spinach	1½ cups
Squash, yellow	½ small
Strawberries	2
Zucchini	1 small

FRESH HERBS

Basil	4 leaves
Lemongrass	3-inch piece
Mint	7 or 8 leaves

GROCERY

Adzuki beans	1/3 cup uncooked (1 cup cooked)
Almonds, raw	12
Chickpeas	1/2 cup uncooked (1 1/2 cups cooked)
Coconut, unsweetened, shredded	1 tablespoon
Dates, Medjool	2
Dulse flakes	1 cup
Mung beans	1/2 cup uncooked (1 1/2 cups cooked)
Nori, pressed	3 sheets
Orange juice	4 tablespoons
Pecan pieces	1/2 cup
Pomegranate juice	1 cup
Rice, brown	1/2 cup cooked
Sesame seeds, unhulled	1 teaspoon
Thai green curry paste	1/2 teaspoon
Vegetable broth, organic	7 cups
Walnut halves	5

THE INSIGHT

PRODUCE

Apple, red	1/3 cup sliced
Avocado	1/2
Bananas	1 1/2 small
Bell pepper, red	1/2
Blackberries	2 1/4 cups
Blueberries, frozen or fresh	3 1/2 cups
Broccoli	2 1/2 cups chopped
Cabbage, red	1 large
Carrots	1 tablespoon shredded
Carrots, purple	2
Cauliflower	2 cups chopped
Cucumber	1/4 cup cubed
Eggplant	1 small

Kale, baby	2 cups
Kale, purple	1 cup chopped
Mushrooms, shiitake	3
Onions, red	2 small
Potatoes, purple	2 small
Raspberries	1 cup
Shallot	1 large
Tomato	½ medium

FRESH HERBS

| Basil (purple preferred) | 2 leaves |

GROCERY

Adzuki beans	⅓ cup uncooked (1 cup cooked)
Bee pollen granules (optional)	1 teaspoon
Cacao nibs, raw	1 tablespoon
Cashews, raw	¾ cup
Cocoa powder, unsweetened	1 tablespoon
Hempseed oil	1 tablespoon
Hibiscus tea	½ cup
Mustard, Dijon	½ tablespoon
Oats, gluten-free	1 cup
Pecan halves	8
Pecans	½ cup chopped
Pine nuts, raw	4 tablespoons
Pomegranate juice	1 cup
Rice, purple/black	½ cup uncooked
Walnut oil	1 tablespoon
Walnuts	¾ cup chopped

THE SPIRIT

PRODUCE

Arugula	2 cups
Avocado	1 small
Bell peppers, red	2
Burdock root	5-inch piece
Cabbage, green	¼ to ½ head (need 1 cup diced)
Cabbage, red	¼ head (need ½ cup diced)
Carrots	3
Cauliflower	1 large head
Celery	3 stalks
Cucumber	1 cup diced
Green onions	1 bunch
Leeks	¼ cup chopped
Mango, frozen or fresh	1 cup diced
Onion, white	1 medium or 2 small
Onion, yellow	1 small
Mushrooms, shiitake	7
Pears	3
Romaine lettuce	1 cup chopped
Spinach	2 cups
Squash, yellow	1 small
Zucchini	1 small

FRESH HERBS

Basil (purple variety preferred for most of it)	2 cups leaves
Parsley	¼ cup chopped

GROCERY

Cashew nut butter	1 tablespoon
Cashews, raw	¼ cup
Dulse flakes	1 teaspoon
Hempseed oil	1 tablespoon

Mustard, Dijon	1 tablespoon
Pine nuts, raw	½ cup
Raisins, golden	2 tablespoons
Sesame seeds, unhulled	2 tablespoons
Tahini	1 tablespoon
Vegetable broth, organic	2 cups
Walnuts	2 tablespoons chopped

WHOLE DETOX TRACKING CHARTS

WHOLE DETOX EMOTION LOG

The Whole Detox Emotion Log is designed to help you track and see patterns in your emotions over time. At the end of each day, simply go through each of the emotions listed and put an X in boxes that correspond to the emotions you felt that day. After you've completed one week of this activity, look at any patterns that may be obvious, such as a predominance of one emotion (e.g., fear) or a pattern of emotions that feel uplifting or nonserving. You can match this information to your food intake to see how your daily emotions might be driving your food choices. Additionally, you may want to use the results of your Whole Detox Emotion Log to fuel your journaling process or your engagement in other therapies with a qualified practitioner.

	ROOT			FLOW			FIRE		
	1	2	3	4	5	6	7	8	9
Able to express self									
Angry									
Appreciative									
Authentic									
Aware									
Balanced									
Compassionate									
Courageous									
Creative									
Daring									
Energetic									
Fearful									
Forgiving									
Frustrated									
Grateful									
Grieving									
Happy									
Helpful									
Honest									
Interested									
Joyful									
Loving									
Optimistic									
Peaceful									
Playful									
Relaxed									
Sad									
Self-accepting									
Solutions-oriented									
Upset									
Worried									
Other (please list):									

LOVE			TRUTH			INSIGHT			SPIRIT		
10	11	12	13	14	15	16	17	18	19	20	21

WHOLE DETOX FOOD REINTRODUCTION
SYMPTOMS TRACKER

The Food Reintroduction Symptoms Tracker is a tool you use to help you gauge your reactions to the foods that you eliminated as part of the twenty-one-day Whole Detox. See the instructions for reintroducing foods on pages 354–56.

WHOLE DETOX FOOD REINTRODUCTION SYMPTOMS TRACKER

Date	Time	Food	Symptoms (e.g., rash, bloating, loss of energy, joint pain)
	____:____ A.M. / P.M.		
	____:____ A.M. / P.M.		
	____:____ A.M. / P.M.		
	____:____ A.M. / P.M.		
	____:____ A.M. / P.M.		
	____:____ A.M. / P.M.		
	____:____ A.M. / P.M.		
	____:____ A.M. / P.M.		
	____:____ A.M. / P.M.		
	____:____ A.M. / P.M.		

RAINBOW TRACKER

Use the Rainbow Tracker after you have completed your twenty-one-day Whole Detox. It is intended to help you continue to focus on getting the rainbow variety of colors on a daily basis, so your seven systems feel nourished and complete. Each time you have natural, whole foods (not anything artificially dyed or colored) that correspond to the colors listed, just put an X in the box of that color. By the end of the day, check to see if you have the full spectrum of your rainbow!

RAINBOW TRACKER

Date	Red: ROOT	Orange: FLOW	Yellow: FIRE	Green: LOVE	Aqua-marine: TRUTH	Indigo: INSIGHT	White: SPIRIT

WHOLE DETOX SYSTEMS TRACKER

The Whole Detox Systems Tracker will help you track the progress of your seven systems of health over time, after you have completed your twenty-one-day Whole Detox, so you can see the subtle changes and improvements. Use this form to log your *no* responses from the Whole Detox Spectrum Quiz (see pages 35–41) and plot your scores in the corresponding system sections. What you are looking for is to have lower *no* scores over time. You can compare your *no* scores among all the systems at a specific time point. You can also look at your scores within a particular system over time to see if the numbers go down, indicating an improvement.

WHOLE DETOX SYSTEMS TRACKER

Date	The ROOT	The FLOW	The FIRE	The LOVE	The TRUTH	The INSIGHT	The SPIRIT

RESOURCES

WHOLE DETOX PROGRAMS

To find out about further participation in online Whole Detox programs, visit my websites:

Dr. Deanna Minich: www.drdeannaminich.com

Whole Detox: www.whole-detox.com

The online Whole Detox program is also twenty-one days in duration and is available throughout the year. You would follow the program as outlined in the book but with a larger community through social media. Additional benefits are live webinars with Dr. Deanna Minich.

HEALTH PROFESSIONALS

If you want to work with a Certified Food & Spirit Practitioner, who has been trained in the Seven Systems of Full-Spectrum Health, see the website: www.foodandspiritprofessional.com.

To learn more about becoming a Certified Food & Spirit Practitioner, visit the program website for information: www.foodandspiritprofessional.com.

To learn more about functional medicine and finding a Certified Functional Medicine Practitioner, visit the Institute for Functional Medicine website: www.functionalmedicine.org.

If you have dental amalgams, consider getting them removed and replaced with a functional or biological dentist who takes the necessary precautions. Check out the International Academy of Biological Dentistry and Medicine to find a practitioner: https://iabdm.org.

THE DETOX SUMMIT

If you are interested in listening to more cutting-edge information about detox, everything from nutrition to emotions to spiritual health, you will want to listen to The Detox Summit, a virtual online summit of thirty leaders in Whole Detox organized and led by Dr. Deanna Minich: http://thedetoxsummit.com.

SOCIAL MEDIA

Whole Detox Fan Page: www.facebook.com/wholedetox

Whole Detox Community Page: www.facebook.com/groups/FullSpectrum DetoxCommunity

Deanna Minich, Ph.D.: www.facebook.com/deanna.minich

Certified Food & Spirit Practitioner Program: www.facebook.com/Certified -Food-Spirit-Practitioner-Program-703507403030620

Twitter: www.twitter.com/drdeannaminich

Pinterest: www.pinterest.com/foodandspirit

YouTube: www.youtube.com/foodandspirit

OTHER BOOKS AND MATERIALS BY DR. DEANNA MINICH TO SUPPORT YOU THROUGH THE WHOLE DETOX PROGRAM

All of these are available at www.amazon.com:

An A–Z Guide to Food Additives: Never Eat What You Can't Pronounce (Conari Press, 2009)—A pocketbook listing the important food additives in foods. What's good and what's not? This book will rate ingredients and foods using a simple scoring system of A through F. It is concise and targeted for the busy consumer. Make sure you have this in your purse, backpack, or pocket while shopping!

The Complete Handbook of Quantum Healing: An A–Z Self-Healing Guide for Over 100 Common Ailments (Red Wheel / Weiser, 2010)—A reference book full of Whole Detox nutrition and lifestyle suggestions for specific ailments. You may want to review it for specific ailments you have so you can fine-tune your detox modalities to fit you specifically.

Nourish Your Whole Self Cards—A creative, inspirational deck of 56 cards, each with an affirmation and visual to add greater nourishment to your eating experience throughout Whole Detox. Pick a card before, during, or after a meal, or even at the start of the day to see what eating message is waiting for you. Read more about the card you chose in the accompanying booklet.

WHERE TO GET FOODS, EQUIPMENT, AND PRODUCTS FOR THE WHOLE DETOX PROGRAM

Seafood
Get quality seafood at Vital Choice: www.vitalchoice.com.

Seaweeds
Make sure your edible seaweeds are organically certified and carefully harvested. Maine Coast Sea Vegetables specializes in sustainably harvested seaweeds from the North Atlantic: www.seaveg.com/shop.

Spices
For single spices or simple blends, a great choice is Frontier Natural Products Co-op brands, including Simply Organic: www.simplyorganic.com.

Teeny Tiny Spice Company has a wide variety of mixed spices (tandoori masala, vindaloo, etc.): www.teenytinyspice.com. (Use coupon code "FOOD+SPIRIT" to receive 10% off.)

Teas
Pukka Herbs: www.pukkaherbs.com

Rishi Tea: www.rishi-tea.com

Teeccino gluten-free herbal teas: www.teeccino.com (Use coupon code "FOOD&SPIRIT" to receive 15% off.)

Yogi teas: www.yogiproducts.com

Green Food Powders
Whole-food, green food powder—pHresh Greens: www.phreshproducts .com/food-spirit (Use coupon code "foodspirit" to receive 10% off.)

Professional-Grade Dietary Supplements
Allergy Research Group: www.allergyresearchgroup.com

Biotics Research: www.bioticsresearch.com

Designs for Health: www.designsforhealth.com

Douglas Laboratories: www.douglaslabs.com

Innate Response: www.innateresponse.com

Metagenics: www.metagenics.com; Food & Spirit: www.foodandspirit.com /shop/metagenics-food-spirit-store (Receive 20% off your first order and 10% off every subsequent order.)

MicroNourish: www.micronutrients.com

Nature's Sunshine Products: www.naturessunshine.com/us/shop

Nordic Naturals: www.nordicnaturals.com/consumers.php

Nutrilite: www.nutrilite.com

ProThera/Klaire Labs: www.protherainc.com

Pure Encapsulations: www.pureencapsulations.com

Thorne Research: www.thorne.com

Vital Nutrients: www.vitalnutrients.net

Xymogen: www.xymogen.com

Blenders

Buy yourself a high-speed blender—any of the different brands available on the market, including Blendtec, Ninja, NutriBullet, or Vitamix. They all work well for making morning smoothies.

Water Filters

Here is the best, most thorough guide to finding a good water filter: www .ewg.org/tap-water/getawaterfilter.php.

Personal Care Products

General

Dr. Bronner's soap and toothpaste products: www.drbronner.com

Desert Essence personal care items: www.desertessence.com

Seventh Generation toilet paper, tampons, and other household goods: www.seventhgeneration.com

Hair

Morrocco Method, especially Sapphire Volumizer Mist, which is a combination of ionized water with essential oils: http://tinyurl.com/fsmorrocco method

Skin

Aubrey Organics: www.aubrey-organics.com

MyChelle: www.mychelle.com

Simply Divine Botanicals, especially the Black Velvet Fabulous Foaming Facial Cleanser and Skincredible Revitalizing Sandalwood Elixir: www .simplydivinebotanicals.com

INFORMATIONAL WEBSITES

These websites provide information on lifestyle medicine, nutrition, and personal growth that may be useful to you:

American College of Nutrition, for research into nutrition science and the prevention and treatment of disease: www.americancollegeofnutrition.org

Environmental Working Group (EWG), for the "Dirty Dozen Plus" list of the most pesticide-laden fruits and vegetables, updates on mercury levels in fish, and many other resources on the quality of foods, household products, and our environment: www.ewg.org

Green Med Info, for the latest research into the use of natural substances in disease prevention and treatment: www.greenmedinfo.com

The Grief Recovery Institute, for assistance with grief counseling: www .griefrecoverymethod.com

HeartMath Institute, for biofeedback and heart rate variability devices: www .heartmath.com and www.heartmath.org

MindBodyGreen, for blogs, videos, and information on mind and body: www.mindbodygreen.com

Natural Resources Defense Council (NRDC), for mercury levels in fish: www.nrdc.org/health/effects/mercury/guide.asp

Dr. Jeffrey Bland's Personalized Lifestyle Medicine Institute: www.plm institute.org

The World's Healthiest Foods, a website with practical nutrition information: http://whfoods.com

Yoga Alliance, to find a yoga teacher: www.yogaalliance.org

ACKNOWLEDGMENTS

At times our own light goes out and is rekindled by a spark from another person.
Each of us has cause to think with deep gratitude of those who have lighted the
flame within us.

—ALBERT SCHWEITZER

Just as a human being comprises a spectrum of systems, so too does a book. A book is an artful synthesis of thoughts, experience, and people, which is what makes it so satisfying to write. One of my favorite parts of creating the tapestry is giving gratitude to all the people whose beautiful threads I had the opportunity to weave together.

The ROOT: There is nothing more grounding than a solid, supportive family who help you to feel safe and protected in all you do. I thank my generous, loving parents, John and Sharon, who have been incredible and wonderful at every step of my life journey, all while teaching me through their examples. I am deeply grateful for the gift of having them both in my life in the present day and for showing me the power of choice on the spectrum of health and disease. A huge thanks to my sister, Brenda, who has always been my advocate.

The FLOW: I am flowing with boundless thanks to all the creative people in my life and to those who have inspired me to create and to go with the organic flow of my emotions through art, including my aunt Kim and my brother Ian. I thank Wendy Alfaro for providing me with the creative inspiration for colorful, whole-foods-based recipes and for helping me to think more expansively about food combinations. I am indebted to Barb Schiltz's creative culinary eye as she put the finishing touches on the recipes in this book.

The FIRE: So many people have allowed me to ignite the Food & Spirit message to the world by supporting the business, including team members Kimberlee, Marchel, and Laura. Kimberlee, a special hug to you for your fiery loyalty and dedication in working with me for several years. You have all been amazing to work with—thank you for keeping your flame burning bright for this work. Sean Bonsell, thanks for stepping in with your creative flair to get ideas into motion. Thanks to all the Certified Food & Spirit Practitioners who have committed to the Food & Spirit full-spectrum approach of whole-self healing. I am still burning bright with the experience of doing the Detox Summit in August 2014, and I thank everyone for being part of that event, including the experts and the team behind the scenes making it all happen. I appreciate all the people who have taken part in the many detox programs I've offered over the years. A huge thanks to Dhrumil Purohit for his laser-like leadership and business coaching. Thanks to all the wonderful colleagues who have helped me grow within the business realm, giving me guidance to make my dream a reality, including Aviva Romm, Pilar Gerasimo, Amy Myers, Howard Hoffman, and Alejandro Junger.

The LOVE: I bow to my life partner and love, Mark, for being my teacher, friend, and supporter. You encourage my passion, dreams, and heartfelt wishes to come forth in the highest and most meaningful way. I thank my dear friends and healers, including Scott Whittaker, Char Sundust, Patrice Connelly, Alan Pritz, Barbara Maddoux, Barb Schiltz, Mark Houston, Lyra Heller, Kristi Hughes, Caroline Myss, Mink Fire, Gay McCray, Lorraine Leas, Janet Ridgeway, Joel Kahn, Michael Stone, John Principe, Sayer Ji, Annie Basu, Andy Maxwell, Hong and Mike Curley, Anthony William, and Anna Kong.

The TRUTH: I can still remember the initial phone call with my soon-to-be literary agent, Stephanie Tade. I am so grateful for her initial enthusiasm and eventual guidance through the publishing "birth canal" and for assisting me with pivotal decisions. If it weren't for her, I might not have met the utterly brilliant and lovely soul Rachel Kranz, who helped me shift into my authentic truth through choosing the right words and expressions. Rachel, thank you for being a master of words and for bridging the spectrum between the grounding of facts and the flowing art of people's lives. Gideon Weil, my amazing editor at HarperCollins, you have been outstanding in seeing the vision of this work very early on and providing gentle coaching and steering when needed. So many people sing your praises, and you can now count me as one of the choir! Finally, I want to thank my mom a second time, for teaching me the importance of being in my truth and the necessity of honesty in one's life. I now realize how precious it was to learn from her that it's perfectly fine to be different and to revel in the uniqueness of who I am. Thanks, Mom, for being my truth-shining star.

The INSIGHT: Several people have illuminated my neurons with an understanding of systems thinking and through inspiring the depth of scientific intellect needed to write this book, including all my teachers in nutritional and functional medicine. My biggest thanks goes to Dr. Jeffrey Bland, who has a multitude of titles. His best known is probably the Father of Functional Medicine, but now I add to the list Father of Nutritional Detoxification. It was Dr. Bland who forged the early path in detoxification, doing studies, publishing papers, and paving the way for "detox" to become what it is today. I also want to thank my many other teachers in biochemistry, nutrition, and functional medicine, including Drs. Phyllis Bowen, Maria Sapuntzakis, Clare Hasler, Henkjan Verkade, Folkert Kuipers, and Roel Vonk; everyone at the Institute for Functional Medicine, especially Laurie Hofmann; Drs. Patrick Hanaway, Mark Hyman, Kristi Hughes, and Dan Lukaczer; the Detox Module Team, including Bob Rountree, Rick Mayfield, Mary Ellen Chalmers, and T. R. Morris; all my wise physician teachers at the Functional Medicine Research Center, Jack Kornberg, Joe Lamb, and Bob Lerman.

The SPIRIT: For the soul and spirit of all I do, I give humble, immense thanks to God; in all the divine forms I feel the oneness and grace of life.

BIBLIOGRAPHY

NOTE: Entries are listed in order of their reference in the text.

INTRODUCTION: WHY WHOLE DETOX?

Chan, S. Y., and J. Loscalzo. "The Emerging Paradigm of Network Medicine in the Study of Human Disease." *Circulation Research* 111, no. 3 (2012): 359–74. doi:10.1161/CIRCRES AHA.111.258541.

Westerhoff, H. V., and B. O. Palsson. "The Evolution of Molecular Biology into Systems Biology." *Nature Biotechnology* 22, no. 10 (2004): 1249–52.

Edmondson, D., J. D. Newman, W. Whang, and K. W. Davidson. "Emotional Triggers in Myocardial Infarction: Do They Matter?" *European Heart Journal* 34, no. 4 (2013): 300–6. doi:10.1093/eurheartj/ehs398.

Strike, P. C., and A. Steptoe. "Behavioral and Emotional Triggers of Acute Coronary Syndromes: A Systematic Review and Critique." *Psychosomatic Medicine* 67, no. 2 (2005): 179–86.

Buckley, T., D. Sunari, A. Marshall, R. Bartrop, S. McKinley, and G. Tofler. "Physiological Correlates of Bereavement and the Impact of Bereavement Interventions." *Dialogues in Clinical Neuroscience* 14, no. 2 (2012): 129–39.

Steptoe, A., A. Shankar, P. Demakakos, and J. Wardle. "Social Isolation, Loneliness, and All-Cause Mortality in Older Men and Women." *PNAS* 110, no. 15 (2013): 5797–801. doi:10.1073/pnas.1219686110.

Luo, Y., L. C. Hawkley, L. J. Waite, and J. T. Cacioppo. "Loneliness, Health, and Mortality in Old Age: A National Longitudinal Study." *Social Science and Medicine* 74, no. 6 (2012): 907–14. doi:10.1016/j.socscimed.2011.11.028.

CHAPTER 1: WHOLE DETOX FOR YOUR WHOLE SELF

Dickerson, S. S. and M. E. Kemeny. "Acute Stressors and Cortisol Responses: A Theoretical Integration and Synthesis of Laboratory Research." *Psychological Bulletin* 130, no. 3 (2004): 355–91.

Khalfa, S., S. D. Bella, M. Roy, I. Peretz, and S. J. Lupien. "Effects of Relaxing Music on Salivary Cortisol Level After Psychological Stress." *Annals of the New York Academy of Sciences* no. 999 (2003): 374–76.

Maslow, A. H. "A Theory of Human Motivation." *Psychological Review* 50, no. 4 (1943): 370–96. psychclassics.yorku.ca.

Csikszentmihalyi, Mihaly. *Flow: The Psychology of Optimal Experience.* New York: Harper and Row, 1990.

Cantin, M., and J. Genest. "The Heart as an Endocrine Gland." *Pharmacological Research Communications* 20, suppl. 3 (1988): 1–22.

CHAPTER 3: THE ROOT

Segerstrom, S. C., and G. E. Miller. "Psychological Stress and the Human Immune System: A Meta-Analytic Study of 30 Years of Inquiry." *Psychological Bulletin* 130, no. 4 (2004): 601–30.

Avitsur, R., S. Levy, N. Goren, and R. Grinshpahet. "Early Adversity, Immunity and Infectious Disease." *Stress* 18, no. 3 (2015): 289–96.

Carlsson, E., A. Frostell, J. Ludvigsson, and M. Faresjö. "Psychological Stress in Children May Alter the Immune Response." *Journal of Immunology* 192, no. 5 (2014): 2071–81. doi:10.4049/jimmunol.1301713.

Dube, S. R., D. Fairweather, W. S. Pearson, V. J. Felitti, R. F. Anda, and J. B. Croft. "Cumulative Childhood Stress and Autoimmune Diseases in Adults." *Psychosomatic Medicine* 71, no. 2 (2009): 243–50. doi:10.1097/PSY.0b013e3181907888.

Tian, R., G. Hou, D. Li, and T.-F. Yuan. "A Possible Change Process of Inflammatory Cytokines in the Prolonged Chronic Stress and Its Ultimate Implications for Health." *Scientific World Journal* 2014 (2014): 780616. doi:10.1155/2014/780616.

Rutledge, T., S. E. Reis, M. Olson, J. Owens, S. F. Kelsey, C. J. Pepine, S. Mankad, et al. "Social Networks Are Associated with Lower Mortality Rates Among Women with Suspected Coronary Disease: The National Heart, Lung, and Blood Institute–Sponsored Women's Ischemia Syndrome Evaluation Study." *Psychosomatic Medicine* 66, no. 6 (2004): 882–88.

Cohen, S., W. J. Doyle, R. Turner, C. M. Alper, and D. P. Skoner. "Sociability and Susceptibility to the Common Cold." *Psychological Science* 14, no. 5 (2003): 389–95.

Pinquart, M., and P. R. Duberstein. "Associations of Social Networks with Cancer Mortality: A Meta-Analysis." *Critical Reviews in Oncology/Hematology* 75, no. 2 (2010): 122–37. doi:10.1016/j.critrevonc.2009.06.003.

Pressman, S. D., S. Cohen, G. E. Miller, A. Barkin, B. S. Rabin, and J. J. Treanor. "Loneliness, Social Network Size, and Immune Response to Influenza Vaccination in College Freshmen." *Health Psychology* 24, no. 3 (2005): 297–306.

Sroykham, W., J. Wongsathikun, and Y. Wongsawat. "The Effects of Perceiving Color in Living Environment on QEEG, Oxygen Saturation, Pulse Rate, and Emotion Regulation in Humans." *Conference Proceedings: IEEE Engineering in Medicine and Biology Society* 2014 (2014): 6226–29. doi:10.1109/EMBC.2014.6945051.

Bertrams, A., R. F. Baumeister, C. Englert, and P. Furley. "Ego Depletion in Color Priming Research: Self-Control Strength Moderates the Detrimental Effect of Red on Cognitive Test Performance." *Personal and Social Psychology Bulletin* 41, no. 3 (2015): 311–22. doi:10.1177/0146167214564968.

Buechner, V. L., M. A. Maier, S. Lichtenfeld, and S. Schwarz. "Red—Take a Closer Look." *PLoS ONE* 9, no. 9 (2014): e108111. doi:10.1371/journal.pone.0108111.

Young, S. G., A. J. Elliot, R. Feltman, and N. Ambady. "Red Enhances the Processing of Facial Expressions of Anger." *Emotion* 13, no. 3 (2013): 380–84. doi:10.1037/a0032471.

Genschow, O., L. Reutner, and M. Wänke. "The Color Red Reduces Snack Food and Soft Drink Intake." *Appetite* 58, no. 2 (2012): 699–702. doi:10.1016/j.appet.2011.12.023.

Ley, S. H., Q. Sun, W. C. Willett, A. H. Eliassen, K. Wu, A. Pan, F. Grodstein, and F. B. Hu. "Associations Between Red Meat Intake and Biomarkers of Inflammation and Glucose Metabolism in Women." *American Journal of Clinical Nutrition* 99, no. 2 (2014): 352–60. doi:10.3945 /ajcn.113.075663.

Montonen, J., H. Boeing, A. Fritsche, E. Schleicher, H. G. Joost, M. B. Schulze, A. Steffen, and T. Pischon. "Consumption of Red Meat and Whole-Grain Bread in Relation to Biomarkers of Obesity, Inflammation, Glucose Metabolism and Oxidative Stress." *European Journal of Nutrition* 52, no. 1 (2013): 337–45. doi:10.1007/s00394-012-0340-6.

Sinha, R., M. Kulldorff, W. H. Chow, J. Denobile, and N. Rothman. "Dietary Intake of Heterocyclic Amines, Meat-Derived Mutagenic Activity, and Risk of Colorectal Adenomas." *Cancer Epidemiology, Biomarkers and Prevention* 10, no. 5 (2001): 559–62.

Li, Z., A. Wong, S. M. Henning, Y. Zhang, A. Jones, A. Zerlin, G. Thames, S. Bowerman, C. H. Tseng, and D. Heber. "Hass Avocado Modulates Postprandial Vascular Reactivity and Postprandial Inflammatory Responses to a Hamburger Meal in Healthy Volunteers." *Food and Function* 4, no. 3 (2013): 384–91. doi:10.1039/c2fo30226h.

Shaughnessy, D. T., L. M. Gangarosa, B. Schliebe, D. M. Umbach, Z. Xu, B. MacIntosh, M. G. Knize, et al. "Inhibition of Fried Meat–Induced Colorectal DNA Damage and Altered Systemic Genotoxicity in Humans by Crucifera, Chlorophyllin, and Yogurt." *PLoS ONE* 6, no. 4 (2011): e18707. doi:10.1371/journal.pone.0018707.

Dashwood, R. "Chlorophylls as Anticarcinogens (Review)." *International Journal of Oncology* 10, no. 4 (1997): 721–27.

United States Department of Agriculture, Agricultural Research Service. "National Nutrient Database for Standard Reference Release 28." http://ndb.nal.usda.gov/ndb/foods.

Houston, M. C. "The Role of Mercury and Cadmium Heavy Metals in Vascular Disease, Hypertension, Coronary Heart Disease, and Myocardial Infarction." *Alternative Therapies in Health and Medicine* 13, no. 2 (2007): S128–33.

Driscoll, C. T., R. P. Mason, H. M. Chan, D. J. Jacob, and N. Pirrone. "Mercury as a Global Pollutant: Sources, Pathways, and Effects." *Environmental Science and Technology* 47, no. 10 (2013): 4967–83. doi:10.1021/es305071v.

Zwicker, J. D., D. J. Dutton, and J. C. H. Emery. "Longitudinal Analysis of the Association Between Removal of Dental Amalgam, Urine Mercury and 14 Self-Reported Health Symptoms." *Environmental Health* 13 (2014): 95. doi:10.1186/1476-069X-13-95.

Cech, I., M. H. Smolensky, M. Afshar, G. Broyles, M. Barczyk, K. Burau, and R. Emery. "Lead and Copper in Drinking Water Fountains—Information for Physicians." *Southern Medical Journal* 99, no. 2 (2006): 137–42.

James, S. C. "Metals in Municipal Landfill Leachate and Their Health Effects." *American Journal of Public Health* 65, no. 5 (1977): 429–32.

Olmedo, P., A. Pla, A. F. Hernández, F. Barbier, L. Ayouni, and F. Gil. "Determination of Toxic Elements (Mercury, Cadmium, Lead, Tin and Arsenic) in Fish and Shellfish Samples. Risk Assessment for the Consumers." *Environment International* 59 (2013): 63–72. doi:10.1016/j .envint.2013.05.005.

Consumer Reports. "How Much Arsenic Is in Your Rice? Consumer Reports' New Data and Guidelines Are Important for Everyone but Especially for Gluten Avoiders." November 2014. Accessed September 7, 2015. http://www.consumerreports.org/cro/magazine /2015/01/how-much-arsenic-is-in-your-rice/index.htm.

Yoshinaga, J., K. Yamasaki, A. Yonemura, Y. Ishibashi, T. Kaido, K. Mizuno, M. Takagi, and A. Tanaka. "Lead and Other Elements in House Dust of Japanese Residences—Source of Lead and Health Risks Due to Metal Exposure." *Environmental Pollution* 189 (2014): 223–28. doi:10.1016/j.envpol.2014.03.003.

Butte, W., and B. Heinzow. "Pollutants in House Dust as Indicators of Indoor Contamination." *Reviews of Environmental Contamination and Toxicology* 175 (2002): 1–46.

Fergusson, J. E., and N. D. Kim. "Trace Elements in Street and House Dusts: Sources and Speciation." *Science of the Total Environment* 100 (1991): 125–50. doi:10.1016/0048-9697 (91)90376-P.

Zakaria, A., and Y. B. Ho. "Heavy Metals Contamination in Lipsticks and Their Associated Health Risks to Lipstick Consumers." *Regulatory Toxicology and Pharmacology* 73, no. 1 (2015): 191–95. doi:10.1016/j.yrtph.2015.07.005.

Hepp, N. M. "Determination of Total Lead in 400 Lipsticks on the U.S. Market Using a Validated Microwave-Assisted Digestion, Inductively Coupled Plasma-Mass Spectrometric Method." *Journal of Cosmetic Science* 63, no. 3 (2012): 159–76.

Associated Press. "FDA to Examine Claim That Lipstick Lead Levels Unsafe." *Seattle Times*. October 13, 2007. Accessed September 7, 2015. http://www.seattletimes.com/nation-world /fda-to-examine-claim-that-lipstick-lead-levels-unsafe/.

Yokoi, K., and A. Konomi. "Toxicity of So-Called Edible Hijiki Seaweed (*Sargassum fusiforme*) Containing Inorganic Arsenic." *Regulatory Toxicology and Pharmacology* 63, no. 2 (2012): 291–97. doi:10.1016/j.yrtph.2012.04.006.

Hong, Y. S., K. H. Song, and J. Y. Chung. "Health Effects of Chronic Arsenic Exposure." *Journal of Preventative Medicine and Public Health* 47, no. 5 (2014): 245–52. doi:10.3961/jpmph .14.035.

Nash, R. A. "Metals in Medicine." *Alternative Therapies in Health and Medicine* 11, no. 4 (2005): 18–25.

Adal, A. "Heavy Metal Toxicity." *Medscape*. Last modified March 24, 2015. Accessed September 7, 2015. http://emedicine.medscape.com/article/814960-overview.

Peters, J. L., M. P. Fabian, and J. I. Levy. "Combined Impact of Lead, Cadmium, Polychlorinated Biphenyls and Non-Chemical Risk Factors on Blood Pressure in NHANES." *Environmental Research* 132 (2014): 93–99. doi:10.1016/j.envres.2014.03.038.

Hara, A., L. Thijs, K. Asayama, Y. M. Gu, L. Jacobs, Z. Y. Zhang, Y. P. Liu, T. S. Nawrot, and J. A. Staessen. "Blood Pressure in Relation to Environmental Lead Exposure in the National Health and Nutrition Examination Survey 2003 to 2010." *Hypertension* 65, no. 1 (2015): 62–69. doi:10.1161/HYPERTENSIONAHA.114.04023.

Zalewska, M., J. Trefon, and H. Milnerowicz. "The Role of Metallothionein Interactions with Other Proteins." *Proteomics* 14, no. 11 (2014): 1343–56. doi:10.1002/pmic.201300496.

Rotruck, J. T., A. L. Pope, H. E. Ganther, A. B. Swanson, D. G. Hafeman, and W. G. Hoekstra. "Selenium: Biochemical Role as a Component of Glutathione Peroxidase." *Science* 179, no. 4073 (1973): 588–90.

The World's Healthiest Foods. "Selenium." Accessed September 7, 2015. http://www .whfoods.com/genpage.php?tname=nutrient&dbid=95.

The World's Healthiest Foods. "Zinc." Accessed September 7, 2015. http://www.whfoods .com/genpage.php?tname=nutrient&dbid=115.

Kodama, M., T. Kodama, M. Murakami, and M. Kodama. "Vitamin C Infusion Treatment Enhances Cortisol Production of the Adrenal via the Pituitary ACTH Route." *In Vivo* (Athens, Greece) 8, no. 6 (1994): 1079–85.

Peters, E. M., R. Anderson, D. C. Nieman, H. Fickl, and V. Jogessar. "Vitamin C Supplementation Attenuates the Increases in Circulating Cortisol, Adrenaline and Anti-Inflammatory Polypeptides Following Ultramarathon Running." *International Journal of Sports Medicine* 22, no. 7 (2001): 537–43.

Peters, E. M., R. Anderson, and A. J. Theron. "Attenuation of Increase in Circulating Cortisol and Enhancement of the Acute Phase Protein Response in Vitamin C–Supplemented Ultra-marathoners." *International Journal of Sports Medicine* 22, no. 2 (2001): 120–26.

Sorice, A., E. Guerriero, F. Capone, G. Colonna, G. Castello, and S. Costantini. "Ascorbic Acid: Its Role in Immune System and Chronic Inflammation Diseases." *Mini Reviews in Medicinal Chemistry* 14, no. 5 (2014): 444–52.

Mann, D. "Red Foods: The New Health Powerhouses?" WebMD. Last modified April 1, 2008. Accessed September 7, 2015. http://www.webmd.com/food-recipes/red-foods-the -new-health-powerhouses.

Nutrition Data. "Foods Highest in Vitamin C." Accessed September 7, 2015. http://nutrition data.self.com/foods-011101000000000000000-w.html?mbid=enews_nd0823.

Boyer, J., and R. H. Liu. "Apple Phytochemicals and Their Health Benefits." *Nutrition Journal* 3 (2004): 5.

Min, Y. D., C. H. Choi, H. Bark, H. Y. Son, H. H. Park, S. Lee, J. W. Park, et al. "Quercetin Inhibits Expression of Inflammatory Cytokines Through Attenuation of NF-kappaB and p38 MAPK in HMC-1 Human Mast Cell Line." *Inflammation Research* 56, no. 5 (2007): 210–15.

Park, H. J., C. M. Lee, I. D. Jung, J. S. Lee, Y. I. Jeong, J. H. Chang, S. H. Chun, et al. "Quercetin Regulates Th1/Th2 Balance in a Murine Model of Asthma." *International Immunopharmacology* 9, no. 3 (2009): 261–67. doi:10.1016/j.intimp.2008.10.021.

Chung, S., H. Yao, S. Caito, J. W. Hwang, G. Arunachalam, and I. Rahman. "Regulation of SIRT1 in Cellular Functions: Role of Polyphenols." *Archives of Biochemistry and Biophysics* 501, no. 1 (2010): 79–90. doi:10.1016/j.abb.2010.05.003.

Environmental Working Group. "Apples Top Dirty Dozen List for Fifth Year in a Row." News release. February 25, 2015. Accessed September 7, 2015. http://www.ewg.org/release /apples-top-dirty-dozen-list-fifth-year-row.

Hodges, R. E., and D. M. Minich. "Modulation of Metabolic Detoxification Pathways Using Foods and Food-Derived Components: A Scientific Review with Clinical Application." *Journal of Nutrition and Metabolism* 2015 (2015): 760689. doi:10.1155/2015/760689.

Gajowik, A., and M. M. Dobrzyńska. "Lycopene—Antioxidant with Radioprotective and Anti-cancer Properties. A Review." *Roczniki Państwowego Zakładu Higieny* 65, no. 4 (2014): 263–71.

Rao, A. V., M. R. Ray, and L. G. Rao. "Lycopene." *Advances in Food and Nutrition Research* 51 (2006): 99–164.

Agarwal, A., H. Shen, S. Agarwal, and A. V. Rao. "Lycopene Content of Tomato Products: Its Stability, Bioavailability and In Vivo Antioxidant Properties." *Journal of Medicinal Food* 4, no. 1 (Spring 2001): 9–15.

Unlu, N. Z., T. Bohn, D. M. Francis, H. N. Nagaraja, S. K. Clinton, and S. J. Schwartz. "Lyco-pene from Heat-Induced Cis-Isomer-Rich Tomato Sauce Is More Bioavailable than from All-Trans-Rich Tomato Sauce in Human Subjects." *British Journal of Nutrition* 98, no. 1 (2007): 140–46.

Vallverdú-Queralt, A., J. Regueiro, J. F. Rinaldi de Alvarenga, X. Torrado, and R. M. Lamuela-Raventos. "Carotenoid Profile of Tomato Sauces: Effect of Cooking Time and Content of Extra Virgin Olive Oil." *International Journal of Molecular Sciences* 16, no. 5 (2015): 9588–99. doi:10.3390/ijms16059588.

Bugianesi, R., M. Salucci, C. Leonardi, R. Ferracane, G. Catasta, E. Azzini, and G. Maiani. "Effect of Domestic Cooking on Human Bioavailability of Naringenin, Chlorogenic Acid, Lyco-pene and Beta-Carotene in Cherry Tomatoes." *European Journal of Nutrition* 43, no. 6 (2004): 360–66.

Casas-Grajales, S., and P. Muriel. "Antioxidants in Liver Health." *World Journal of Gastrointestinal Pharmacology and Therapeutics* 6, no. 3 (2015): 59–72. doi:10.4292/wjgpt.v6.i3.59.

Meng, S., J. Cao, Q. Feng, J. Peng, and Y. Hu. "Roles of Chlorogenic Acid on Regulating Glucose and Lipids Metabolism: A Review." *Evidence-Based Complementary and Alternative Medicine* 2013 (2013): 801457. doi:10.1155/2013/801457.

Oschman, J. L., G. Chevalier, and R. Brown. "The Effects of Grounding (Earthing) on Inflammation, the Immune Response, Wound Healing, and Prevention and Treatment of Chronic Inflammatory and Autoimmune Diseases." *Journal of Inflammation Research* 8 (2015): 83–96. doi:10.2147/JIR.S69656.

Chevalier, G. "The Effect of Grounding the Human Body on Mood." *Psychological Reports* 116, no. 2 (2015): 534–43. doi:10.2466/06.PR0.116k21w5.

Chevalier, G., S. T. Sinatra, J. L. Oschman, and R. M. Delany. "Earthing (Grounding) the Human Body Reduces Blood Viscosity—A Major Factor in Cardiovascular Disease." *Journal of Alternative and Complementary Medicine* 19, no. 2 (2013): 102–10. doi:10.1089/acm .2011.0820.

Sokal, K., and P. Sokal. "Earthing the Human Organism Influences Bioelectrical Processes." *Journal of Alternative and Complementary Medicine* 18, no. 3 (2012): 229–34. doi:10.1089/acm .2010.0683.

Chevalier, G., S.T. Sinatra, J. L. Oschman, K. Sokal, and P. Sokal. "Earthing: Health Implications of Reconnecting the Human Body to the Earth's Surface Electrons." *Journal of Environmental and Public Health* 2012 (2012): 291541. doi:10.1155/2012/291541.

CHAPTER 4: THE FLOW

Denton, D. A., M. J. McKinley, and R. S. Weisinger. "Hypothalamic Integration of Body Fluid Regulation." *PNAS* 93, no. 14 (1996): 7397–404.

Schug, T. T., A. Janesick, B. Blumberg, and J. J. Heindel. "Endocrine Disrupting Chemicals and Disease Susceptibility." *Journal of Steroid Biochemistry and Molecular Biology* 127, nos. 3–5 (2011): 204–15. doi:10.1016/j.jsbmb.2011.08.007.

Győrffy, Z., D. Dweik, and E. Girasek. "Reproductive Health and Burn-Out Among Female Physicians: Nationwide, Representative Study from Hungary." *BMC Women's Health* 14 (2014): 121. doi:10.1186/1472-6874-14-121.

Liu, F., W. N. Liu, Q. X. Zhao, and M. M. Han. "Study on Environmental and Psychological Risk Factors for Female Infertility." [Article in Chinese; abstract in English.] *Zhonghua Lao Dong Wei Sheng Zhi Ye Bing Za Zhi* 31, no. 12 (2013): 922–23.

Fido, A. "Emotional Distress in Infertile Women in Kuwait." *International Journal of Fertility and Women's Medicine* 49, no. 1 (2004): 24–28.

Peterson, B. D, C. S. Sejbaek, M. Pirritano, and L. Schmidt. "Are Severe Depressive Symptoms Associated with Infertility-Related Distress in Individuals and Their Partners?" *Human Reproduction* 29, no. 1 (2014): 76–82. doi:10.1093/humrep/det412.

Lynch, C. D., R. Sundaram, J. M. Maisog, A. M. Sweeney, and G. M. Buck Louis. "Preconception Stress Increases the Risk of Infertility: Results from a Couple-Based Prospective Cohort Study—The Life Study." *Human Reproduction* 29, no. 5 (2014): 1067–75. doi:10.1093 /humrep/deu032.

Pauli, S. A., and S. L. Berga. "Athletic Amenorrhea: Energy Deficit or Psychogenic Challenge?" *Annals of the New York Academy of Sciences* 1205 (2010): 33–38. doi:10.1111/j.1749 -6632.2010.05663.x.

Podfigurna-Stopa, A., S. Luisi, C. Regini, K. Katulski, G. Centini, B. Meczekalski, and F. Petraglia. "Mood Disorders and Quality of Life in Polycystic Ovary Syndrome." *Gynecological Endocrinology* 31, no. 6 (2015): 431–34. doi:10.3109/09513590.2015.1009437.

Sköld, H. N., T. Amundsen, P. A. Svensson, I. Mayer, J. Bjelvenmark, and E. Forsgren. "Hormonal Regulation of Female Nuptial Coloration in a Fish." *Hormones and Behavior* 54, no. 4 (2008): 549–56. doi:10.1016/j.yhbeh.2008.05.018.

De Serrano, A. R., C. J. Weadick, A. C. Price, and F. H. Rodd. "Seeing Orange: Prawns Tap Into a Pre-Existing Sensory Bias of the Trinidadian Guppy." *Proceedings of the Royal Society B: Biological Sciences* 279, no. 1741 (2012): 3321–28. doi:10.1098/rspb.2012.0633.

Locatello, L., M. B. Rasotto, J. P. Evans, and A. Pilastro. "Colourful Male Guppies Produce Faster and More Viable Sperm." *Journal of Evolutionary Biology* 19, no. 5 (2006): 1595–602.

Helfenstein, F., S. Losdat, A. P. Møller, J. D. Blount, and H. Richner. "Sperm of Colourful Males Are Better Protected Against Oxidative Stress." *Ecology Letters* 13, no. 2 (2010): 213–22. doi:10.1111/j.1461-0248.2009.01419.x.

O'Fallon, J. V., and B. P. Chew. "The Subcellular Distribution of Beta-Carotene in Bovine Corpus Luteum." *Proceedings of the Society for Experimental Biology and Medicine* 177, no. 3 (1984): 406–11.

Arellano-Rodriguez, G., C. A. Meza-Herrera, R. Rodriguez-Martinez, R. Dionisio-Tapia, D. M. Hallford, M. Mellado, and A. Gonzalez-Bulnes. "Short-Term Intake of Beta-Carotene-Supplemented Diets Enhances Ovarian Function and Progesterone Synthesis in Goats." *Journal of Animal Physiology and Animal Nutrition* (Berlin) 93, no. 6 (2009): 710–15. doi:10.1111/j.1439-0396.2008.00859.x.

Meza-Herrera, C. A., F. Vargas-Beltran, H. P. Vergara-Hernandez, U. Macias-Cruz, L. Avendaño-Reyes, R. Rodriguez-Martinez, G. Arellano-Rodriguez, and F. G. Veliz-Deras. "Betacarotene Supplementation Increases Ovulation Rate Without an Increment in LH Secretion in Cyclic Goats." *Reproductive Biology* 13, no. 1 (2013): 51–57. doi:10.1016/j.repbio.2013.01.171.

Czeczuga-Semeniuk, E., and S. Wołczyński. "Dietary Carotenoids in Normal and Pathological Tissues of Corpus Uteri." *Folia Histochemica et Cytobiologica* 46, no. 3 (2008): 283–90. doi:10.2478/v10042-008-0040-5.

Ruder, E. H., T. J. Hartman, R. H. Reindollar, and M. B. Goldman. "Female Dietary Antioxidant Intake and Time to Pregnancy Among Couples Treated for Unexplained Infertility." *Fertility and Sterility* 101, no. 3 (2014): 759–66. doi:10.1016/j.fertnstert.2013.11.008.

Miles, E. A., P. S. Noakes, L. S. Kremmyda, M. Vlachava, N. D. Diaper, G. Rosenlund, H. Urwin, et al. "The Salmon in Pregnancy Study: Study Design, Subject Characteristics, Maternal Fish and Marine n–3 Fatty Acid Intake, and Marine n–3 Fatty Acid Status in Maternal and Umbilical Cord Blood." *American Journal of Clinical Nutrition* 94, no. 6 suppl. (2011): 1986S–1992S. doi:10.3945/ajcn.110.001636.

Imhoff-Kunsch, B., V. Briggs, T. Goldenberg, and U. Ramakrishnan. "Effect of n–3 Long-Chain Polyunsaturated Fatty Acid Intake During Pregnancy on Maternal, Infant, and Child Health Outcomes: A Systematic Review." *Paediatric and Perinatal Epidemiology* 26, no. 1, suppl. 1 (2012): 91–107. doi:10.1111/j.1365-3016.2012.01292.x.

Klebanoff, M. A., M. Harper, Y. Lai, J. Thorp Jr., Y. Sorokin, M. W. Varner, R. J. Wapner, et al. "Fish Consumption, Erythrocyte Fatty Acids, and Preterm Birth." *Obstetrics and Gynecology* 117, no. 5 (2011): 1071–77. doi:10.1097/AOG.0b013e31821645dc.

Furuhjelm, C., K. Warstedt, J. Larsson, M. Fredriksson, M. F. Böttcher, K. Fälth-Magnusson, and K. Duchén. "Fish Oil Supplementation in Pregnancy and Lactation May Decrease the Risk of Infant Allergy." *Acta Paediatrica* 98, no. 9 (2009): 1461–67. doi:10.1111/j.1651-2227.2009.01355.x.

Feng, Y., Y. Ding, J. Liu, Y. Tian, Y. Yang, S. Guan, and C. Zhang. "Effects of Dietary Omega-3/Omega-6 Fatty Acid Ratios on Reproduction in the Young Breeder Rooster." *BMC Veterinary Research* 11 (2015): 73. doi:10.1186/s12917-015-0394-9.

Wathes, D. C., D. R. Abayasekara, and R. J. Aitken. "Polyunsaturated Fatty Acids in Male and Female Reproduction." *Biology of Reproduction* 77, no. 2 (2007): 190–201.

Rahman, M. M., C. Gasparini, G. M. Turchini, and J. P. Evans. "Experimental Reduction in Dietary Omega-3 Polyunsaturated Fatty Acids Depresses Sperm Competitiveness." *Biology Letters* 10, no. 9 (2014): 20140623. doi:10.1098/rsbl.2014.0623.

Wabner, C. L., and C. Y. Pak. "Effect of Orange Juice Consumption on Urinary Stone Risk Factors." *Journal of Urology* 149, no. 6 (1993): 1405–8.

Ishii, H., M. Nagashima, M. Tanno, A. Nakajima, and S. Yoshino. "Does Being Easily Moved to Tears as a Response to Psychological Stress Reflect Response to Treatment and the General Prognosis in Patients with Rheumatoid Arthritis?" *Clinical and Experimental Rheumatology* 21, no. 5 (2003): 611–16.

Benito, M. J., M. J. González-García, M. Tesón, N. García, I. Fernández, M. Calonge, and A. Enríquez-de-Salamanca. "Intra- and Inter-Day Variation of Cytokines and Chemokines in Tears of Healthy Subjects." *Experimental Eye Research* 120 (2014): 43–49. doi:10.1016/j.exer.2013.12.017.

Sawada, T., K. Matsuo, and I. Hashimoto. "Psychological Effects of Emotional Crying in Adults: Events That Elicit Crying and Social Reactions to Crying." [Article in Japanese; abstract in English.] *Shinrigaku Kenkyu* 82, no. 6 (2012): 514–22.

Pinazo-Durán, M. D., C. Galbis-Estrada, S. Pons-Vázquez, J. Cantú-Dibildox, C. Marco-Ramírez, and J. Benítez-del-Castillo. "Effects of a Nutraceutical Formulation Based on the Combination of Antioxidants and ω-3 Essential Fatty Acids in the Expression of Inflammation and Immune Response Mediators in Tears from Patients with Dry Eye Disorders." *Clinical Interventions in Aging* 8 (2013): 139–48. doi:10.2147/CIA.S40640.

Liu, A., and J. Ji. "Omega-3 Essential Fatty Acids Therapy for Dry Eye Syndrome: A Meta-Analysis of Randomized Controlled Studies." *Medical Science Monitor* 20 (2014): 1583–89. doi:10.12659/MSM.891364.

Genuis, S. J., S. Beesoon, and D. Birkholz. "Biomonitoring and Elimination of Perfluorinated Compounds and Polychlorinated Biphenyls Through Perspiration: Blood, Urine, and Sweat Study." *ISRN Toxicology* 2013 (2013): 483832. doi:10.1155/2013/483832.

Genuis, S. J., S. Beesoon, R. A. Lobo, and D. Birkholz. "Human Elimination of Phthalate Compounds: Blood, Urine, and Sweat (BUS) Study." *Scientific World Journal* 2012 (2012): 615068. doi:10.1100/2012/615068.

Genuis, S. J., S. Beesoon, D. Birkholz, and R. A. Lobo. "Human Excretion of Bisphenol A: Blood, Urine, and Sweat (BUS) Study." *Journal of Environmental and Public Health* 2012 (2012): 185731. doi:10.1155/2012/185731.

James, J. W., and R. Friedman. *The Grief Recovery Handbook, 20th Anniversary Expanded Edition: The Action Program for Moving Beyond Death, Divorce, and Other Losses Including Health, Career, and Faith.* New York: William Morrow, 2009.

Minich, D. M. "Essential Fatty Acid Absorption and Metabolism." Ph.D. thesis, Rijksuniversiteit Groningen, 1999. Accessed September 7, 2015. http://www.direct-ms.org/pdf/NutritionFats/EFA%20metabolism.pdf.

Lavialle, M., I. Denis, P. Guesnet, and S. Vancassel. "Involvement of Omega-3 Fatty Acids in Emotional Responses and Hyperactive Symptoms." *Journal of Nutritional Biochemistry* 21, no. 10 (2010): 899–905. doi:10.1016/j.jnutbio.2009.12.005.

Grosso, G., A. Pajak, S. Marventano, S. Castellano, F. Galvano, C. Bucolo, F. Drago, and F. Caraci. "Role of Omega-3 Fatty Acids in the Treatment of Depressive Disorders: A Comprehensive Meta-Analysis of Randomized Clinical Trials." *PLoS ONE* 9, no. 5 (2014): e96905. doi:10.1371/journal.pone.0096905.

Spector, A. A., and H. Y. Kim. "Discovery of Essential Fatty Acids." *Journal of Lipid Research* 56, no. 1 (2015): 11–21. doi:10.1194/jlr.R055095.

Perica, M. M., and I. Delas. "Essential Fatty Acids and Psychiatric Disorders." *Nutrition in Clinical Practice* 26, no. 4 (2011): 409–25. doi:10.1177/0884533611411306.

Haag, M. "Essential Fatty Acids and the Brain." *Canadian Journal of Psychiatry* 48, no. 3 (2003): 195–203.

Gehrig, K. A., and J. G. Dinulos. "Acrodermatitis Due to Nutritional Deficiency." *Current Opinion in Pediatrics* 22, no. 1 (2010): 107–12. doi:10.1097/MOP.0b013e328335107f.

Finner, A. M. "Nutrition and Hair: Deficiencies and Supplements." *Dermatologic Clinics* 31, no. 1 (2013): 167–72. doi:10.1016/j.det.2012.08.015.

Das, U. N. "Essential Fatty Acids and Their Metabolites as Modulators of Stem Cell Biology with Reference to Inflammation, Cancer, and Metastasis." *Cancer Metastasis Reviews* 30, nos. 3–4 (2011): 311–24. doi:10.1007/s10555-011-9316-x.

The World's Healthiest Foods. "Omega-3 Fatty Acids." Accessed September 7, 2015. http://www.whfoods.com/genpage.php?tname=nutrient&dbid=84.

United States Department of Agriculture, Agricultural Research Service. "National Nutrient Database for Standard Reference Release 28." http://ndb.nal.usda.gov/ndb/foods.

Daley, C. A., A. Abbott, P. S. Doyle, G. A. Nader, and S. Larson. "A Review of Fatty Acid Profiles and Antioxidant Content in Grass-Fed and Grain-Fed Beef." *Nutrition Journal* 9 (2010): 10. doi:10.1186/1475-2891-9-10.

Bourre, J. M. "Where to Find Omega-3 Fatty Acids and How Feeding Animals with Diet Enriched in Omega-3 Fatty Acids to Increase Nutritional Value of Derived Products for Human: What Is Actually Useful?" *Journal of Nutrition, Health, and Aging* 9, no. 4 (2005): 232–42.

Simopoulos, A. P. "Evolutionary Aspects of Diet, the Omega-6/Omega-3 Ratio and Genetic Variation: Nutritional Implications for Chronic Diseases." *Biomedicine and Pharmacotherapy* 60, no. 9 (2006): 502–7.

Jandacek, R. J., and P. Tso. "Factors Affecting the Storage and Excretion of Toxic Lipophilic Xenobiotics." *Lipids* 36, no. 12 (2001): 1289–305.

Moreira, A. P., T. F. Texeira, A. B. Ferreira, C. Peluzio Mdo, and C. Alfenas Rde. "Influence of a High-Fat Diet on Gut Microbiota, Intestinal Permeability and Metabolic Endotoxaemia." *British Journal of Nutrition* 108, no. 5 (2012): 801–9. doi:10.1017/S0007114512001213.

Fukui, H. "Gut-Liver Axis in Liver Cirrhosis: How to Manage Leaky Gut and Endotoxemia." *World Journal of Hepatology* 7, no. 3 (2015): 425–42. doi:10.4254/wjh.v7.i3.425.

Pendyala, S., J. M. Walker, and P. R. Holt. "A High-Fat Diet Is Associated with Endotoxemia That Originates from the Gut." *Gastroenterology* 142, no. 5 (2012): 1100–101.e2. doi:10.1053/j.gastro.2012.01.034.

United States Department of Agriculture, Agricultural Research Service. "National Nutrient Database for Standard Reference Release 28." http://ndb.nal.usda.gov/ndb/foods.

Sirato-Yasumoto, S., M. Katsuta, Y. Okuyama, Y. Takahashi, and T. Ide. "Effect of Sesame Seeds Rich in Sesamin and Sesamolin on Fatty Acid Oxidation in Rat Liver." *Journal of Agricultural and Food Chemistry* 49, no. 5 (2001): 2647–51.

Ide, T., Y. Nakashima, H. Iida, S. Yasumoto, and M. Katsuta. "Lipid Metabolism and Nutrigenomics—Impact of Sesame Lignans on Gene Expression Profiles and Fatty Acid Oxidation in Rat Liver." *Forum of Nutrition* 61 (2009): 10–24. doi:10.1159/000212735.

Callaway, J. C. "Hempseed as a Nutritional Resource: An Overview." *Euphytica* 140 (2004): 65–72. doi:10.1007/s10681-004-4811-6.

Goyal, A., V. Sharma, N. Upadhyay, S. Gill, and M. Sihag. "Flax and Flaxseed Oil: An Ancient

Medicine and Modern Functional Food." *Journal of Food Science and Technology* 51, no. 9 (2014): 1633–53. doi:10.1007/s13197-013-1247-9.

Tur, J. A., M. M. Bibiloni, A. Sureda, and A. Pons. "Dietary Sources of Omega-3 Fatty Acids: Public Health Risks and Benefits." *British Journal of Nutrition* 107, suppl. 2 (2012): S23–52. doi:10.1017/S0007114512001456.

DebMandal, M., and S. Mandal. "Coconut (*Cocos nucifera* L.: *Arecaceae*): In Health Promotion and Disease Prevention." *Asian Pacific Journal of Tropical Medicine* 4, no. 3 (2011): 241–47. doi:10.1016/S1995-7645(11)60078-3.

Cicerale, S., L. J. Lucas, and R. S. Keast. "Antimicrobial, Antioxidant and Anti-Inflammatory Phenolic Activities in Extra-Virgin Olive Oil." *Current Opinion in Biotechnology* 23, no. 2 (2012): 129–35. doi:10.1016/j.copbio.2011.09.006.

Ortiz-Avila, O., M. Esquivel-Martínez, B. E. Olmos-Orizaba, A. Saavedra-Molina, A. R. Rodriguez-Orozco, and C. Cortés-Rojo. "Avocado Oil Improves Mitochondrial Function and Decreases Oxidative Stress in Brain of Diabetic Rats." *Journal of Diabetes Research* 2015 (2015): 485759. doi:10.1155/2015/485759.

Ortiz-Avila, O., M. A. Gallegos-Corona, L. A. Sánchez-Briones, E. Calderón-Cortés, R. Montoya-Pérez, A. R. Rodriguez-Orozco, J. Campos-García, et al. "Protective Effects of Dietary Avocado Oil on Impaired Electron Transport Chain Function and Exacerbated Oxidative Stress in Liver Mitochondria from Diabetic Rats." *Journal of Bioenergetics and Biomembranes* 47, no. 4 (2015): 337–53.

Alasalvar, C., and B. W. Bolling. "Review of Nut Phytochemicals, Fat-Soluble Bioactives, Antioxidant Components and Health Effects." *British Journal of Nutrition* 113, suppl. 2 (2015): S68–78. doi:10.1017/S0007114514003729.

Fardet, A. "A Shift Toward a New Holistic Paradigm Will Help to Preserve and Better Process Grain Products' Food Structure for Improving Their Health Effects." *Food and Function* 6, no. 2 (2015): 363–82. doi:10.1039/c4fo00477a.

Kaulmann, A., and T. Bohn. "Carotenoids, Inflammation, and Oxidative Stress—Implications of Cellular Signaling Pathways and Relation to Chronic Disease Prevention." *Nutrition Research* 34, no. 11 (2014): 907–29. doi:10.1016/j.nutres.2014.07.010.

Talavera, F., and B. P. Chew. "Comparative Role of Retinol, Retinoic Acid and Beta-Carotene on Progesterone Secretion by Pig Corpus Luteum In Vitro." *Journal of Reproduction and Fertility* 82, no. 2 (1988): 611–15.

Graves-Hoagland, R. L., T. A. Hoagland, and C. O. Woody. "Effect of Beta-Carotene and Vitamin A on Progesterone Production by Bovine Luteal Cells." *Journal of Dairy Science* 71, no. 4 (1988): 1058–62.

Ribaya-Mercado, J. D. "Influence of Dietary Fat on Beta-Carotene Absorption and Bioconversion into Vitamin A." *Nutrition Reviews* 60, no. 4 (2002): 104–10.

Lemmens, L., I. J. Colle, S. van Buggenhout, A. M. van Loey, and M. E. Hendrickx. "Quantifying the Influence of Thermal Process Parameters on In Vitro β-Carotene Bioaccessibility: A Case Study on Carrots." *Journal of Agriculture and Food Chemistry* 59, no. 7 (2011): 3162–67. doi:10.1021/jf104888y.

Rizza, S., R. Muniyappa, M. Iantorno, J. A. Kim, H. Chen, P. Pullikotil, N. Senese, et al. "Citrus Polyphenol Hesperidin Stimulates Production of Nitric Oxide in Endothelial Cells While Improving Endothelial Function and Reducing Inflammatory Markers in Patients with Metabolic Syndrome." *Journal of Clinical Endocrinology and Metabolism* 96, no. 5 (2011): E782–92. doi:10.1210/jc.2010-2879.

Gupta, C., and D. Prakash. "Phytonutrients as Therapeutic Agents." *Journal of Complementary and Integrative Medicine* 11, no. 3 (2014): 151–69.

CHAPTER 5: THE FIRE

Nater, U. M., R. La Marca, L. Florin, A. Moses, W. Langhans, M. M. Koller, and U. Ehlert. "Stress-Induced Changes in Human Salivary Alpha-Amylase Activity—Associations with Adrenergic Activity." Psychoneuroendocrinology 31, no. 1 (2006): 49–58.

Morse, D. R., G. R. Schacterle, L. Furst, M. Zaydenberg, and R. L. Pollack. "Oral Digestion of a Complex-Carbohydrate Cereal: Effects of Stress and Relaxation on Physiological and Salivary Measures." American Journal of Clinical Nutrition 49, no. 1 (1989): 97–105.

Moloney, R. D., L. Desbonnet, G. Clarke, T. G. Dinan, and J. F. Cryan. "The Microbiome: Stress, Health and Disease." Mammalian Genome 25, nos. 1–2 (2014): 49–74. doi:10.1007/s00335 -013-9488-5.

Kellman, R. The Microbiome Diet: The Scientifically Proven Way to Restore Your Gut Health and Achieve Permanent Weight Loss. Boston: Da Capo Lifelong, 2015.

Ishizaki, M., H. Nakagawa, Y. Morikawa, R. Honda, Y. Yamada, N. Kawakami; and Japan Work Stress and Health Cohort Study Group. "Influence of Job Strain on Changes in Body Mass Index and Waist Circumference: 6-Year Longitudinal Study." Scandinavian Journal of Work, Environment and Health 34, no. 4 (2008): 288–96.

Brunner, E. J., T. Chandola, and M. G. Marmot. "Prospective Effect of Job Strain on General and Central Obesity in the Whitehall II Study." American Journal of Epidemiology 165, no. 7 (2007): 828–37.

Steptoe, A., M. Cropley, J. Griffith, and K. Joekes. "The Influence of Abdominal Obesity and Chronic Work Stress on Ambulatory Blood Pressure in Men and Women." International Journal of Obesity and Related Metabolic Disorders 23, no. 11 (1999): 1184–91.

Nyberg, S. T., E. I. Fransson, K. Heikkilä, K. Ahola, L. Alfredsson, J. B. Bjorner, M. Borritz, et al. "Job Strain as a Risk factor for Type 2 Diabetes: A Pooled Analysis of 124,808 Men and Women." Diabetes Care 37, no. 8 (2014): 2268–75. doi:10.2337/dc13-2936.

Huth, C., B. Thorand, J. Baumert, J. Kruse, R. T. Emeny, A. Schneider, C. Meisinger, and K. H. Ladwig. "Job Strain as a Risk Factor for the Onset of Type 2 Diabetes Mellitus: Findings from the MONICA/KORA Augsburg Cohort Study." Psychosomatic Medicine 76, no. 7 (2014): 562–68. doi:10.1097/PSY.0000000000000084.

Koponen, A., J. Vahtera, J. Pitkäniemi, M. Virtanen, J. Pentti, N. Simonsen-Rehn, M. Kivimäki, and S. Suominen. "Job Strain and Supervisor Support in Primary Care Health Centres and Glycaemic Control Among Patients with Type 2 Diabetes: A Cross-Sectional Study." BMJ Open 3, no. 5 (2013): e002297. doi:10.1136/bmjopen-2012-002297.

Eriksson, A. K., M. van den Donk, A. Hilding, and C. G. Östenson. "Work Stress, Sense of Coherence, and Risk of Type 2 Diabetes in a Prospective Study of Middle-Aged Swedish Men and Women." Diabetes Care 36, no. 9 (2013): 2683–89. doi:10.2337/dc12-1738.

Lett, A. M., P. S. Thondre, and A. J. Rosenthal. "Yellow Mustard Bran Attenuates Glycaemic Response of a Semi-Solid Food in Young Healthy Men." International Journal of Food Sciences and Nutrition 64, no. 2 (2013): 140–46. doi:10.3109/09637486.2012.728201.

Marinangeli, C. P., and P. J. Jones. "Whole and Fractionated Yellow Pea Flours Reduce Fasting Insulin and Insulin Resistance in Hypercholesterolaemic and Overweight Human Subjects." British Journal of Nutrition 105, no. 1 (2011): 110–17. doi:10.1017/S0007114510003156.

Kim, Y., H. Y. Yang, A. J. Kim, and Y. Lim. "Academic Stress Levels Were Positively Associated with Sweet Food Consumption Among Korean High-School Students." Nutrition 29, no. 1 (2013): 213–18. doi:10.1016/j.nut.2012.08.005.

Baumeister, R. F. "Self-Regulation, Ego Depletion, and Inhibition." Neuropsychologia 65 (2014): 313–19. doi:10.1016/j.neuropsychologia.2014.08.012.

Gröpel, P., R. F. Baumeister, and J. Beckmann. "Action Versus State Orientation and Self-Control Performance After Depletion." *Personal and Social Psychology Bulletin* 40, no. 4 (2014): 476–87. doi:10.1177/0146167213516636.

DeWall, C. N., R. F. Baumeister, N. L. Mead, and K. D. Vohs. "How Leaders Self-Regulate Their Task Performance: Evidence That Power Promotes Diligence, Depletion, and Disdain." *Journal of Personal and Social Psychology* 100, no. 1 (2011): 47–65. doi:10.1037/a0020932.

Palimeri, S., E. Palioura, and E. Diamanti-Kandarakis. "Current Perspectives on the Health Risks Associated with the Consumption of Advanced Glycation End Products: Recommendations for Dietary Management." *Diabetes, Metabolic Syndrome and Obesity* 8 (2015): 415–26. doi:10.2147/DMSO.S63089.

Bartłomiej, S., R. K. Justyna, and N. Ewa. "Bioactive Compounds in Cereal Grains—Occurrence, Structure, Technological Significance and Nutritional Benefits—A Review." *Food Sciences Technology International* 18, no. 6 (2012): 559–68. doi:10.1177/1082013211433079.

Fernie, A. R., F. Carrari, and L. J. Sweetlove. "Respiratory Metabolism: Glycolysis, the TCA Cycle and Mitochondrial Electron Transport." *Current Opinion in Plant Biology* 7, no. 3 (2004): 254–61.

Stough, C., A. Scholey, J. Lloyd, J. Spong, S. Myers, and L. A. Downey. "The Effect of 90 Day Administration of a High Dose Vitamin B-Complex on Work Stress." *Human Psychopharmacology* 26, no. 7 (2011): 470–76. doi:10.1002/hup.1229.

Kennedy, D. O., R. Veasey, A. Watson, F. Dodd, E. Jones, S. Maggini, and C. F. Haskell. "Effects of High-Dose B Vitamin Complex with Vitamin C and Minerals on Subjective Mood and Performance in Healthy Males." *Psychopharmacology* (Berlin) 211, no. 1 (2010): 55–68. doi:10.1007/s00213-010-1870-3.

Southgate, D. A. "Digestion and Metabolism of Sugars." *American Journal of Clinical Nutrition* 62, suppl. 1 (1995): 203S–10S.

Swithers, S. "Artificial Sweeteners Produce the Counterintuitive Effect of Inducing Metabolic Derangements." *Trends in Endocrinology and Metabolism* 24, no. 9 (2013): 431–41.

Suez, J., T. Korem, D. Zeevi, G. Zilberman-Schapira, C. Thaiss, O. Maza, D. Israeli, et al. "Artificial Sweeteners Induce Glucose Intolerance by Altering the Gut Microbiota." *Nature* 514, no. 7521 (2014): 181–86.

Yang, Q. "Gain Weight by 'Going Diet'? Artificial Sweeteners and the Neurobiology of Sugar Cravings: Neuroscience 2010." *Yale Journal of Biology and Medicine* 83, no. 2 (2010): 101–8.

Vazquez-Roque, M., and A. S. Oxentenko. "Nonceliac Gluten Sensitivity." *Mayo Clinic Proceedings* 90, no. 9 (2015): 1272–77. doi:10.1016/j.mayocp.2015.07.009.

Mansueto, P., A. Seidita, A. D'Alcamo, and A. Carroccio. "Non-Celiac Gluten Sensitivity: Literature Review." *Journal of the American College of Nutrition* 33, no. 1 (2014): 39–54. doi:10.1080/07315724.2014.869996.

Flood, J. E., L. S. Roe, and B. J. Rolls. "The Effect of Increased Beverage Portion Size on Energy Intake at a Meal." *Journal of the American Dietetic Association* 106, no. 12 (2006): 1984–90; discussion 1990–91.

Davy, B. M., E. A. Dennis, A. L. Dengo, K. L. Wilson, and K. P. Davy. "Water Consumption Reduces Energy Intake at a Breakfast Meal in Obese Older Adults." *Journal of the American Dietetic Association* 108, no. 7 (2008): 1236–39. doi:10.1016/j.jada.2008.04.013.

Dennis, E. A., A. L. Dengo, D. L. Comber, K. D. Flack, J. Savla, K. P. Davy, and B. M. Davy. "Water Consumption Increases Weight Loss During a Hypocaloric Diet Intervention in Middle-Aged and Older Adults." *Obesity* (Silver Spring) 18, no. 2 (2010): 300–7. doi:10.1038/oby.2009.235.

Taylor, A. G., L. E. Goehler, D. I. Galper, K. E. Innes, and C. Bourguignon. "Top-Down and Bottom-Up Mechanisms in Mind–Body Medicine: Development of an Integrative Framework for Psychophysiological Research." *Explore* (New York) 6, no. 1 (2010): 29–41. doi:10.1016/j.explore.2009.10.004.

CHAPTER 6: THE LOVE

Ogawa, T., and A. J. de Bold. "The Heart as an Endocrine Organ." *Endocrine Connections* 3, no. 2 (2014): R31–44. doi:10.1530/EC-14-0012.

McGrath, M. F., M. L. de Bold, and A. J. de Bold. "The Endocrine Function of the Heart." *Trends in Endocrinology and Metabolism* 16, no. 10 (2005): 469–77.

De Bold, A. J., K. K. Ma, Y. Zhang, M. L. de Bold, M. Bensimon, and A. Khoshbaten. "The Physiological and Pathophysiological Modulation of the Endocrine Function of the Heart." *Canadian Journal of Physiology and Pharmacology* 79, no. 8 (2001): 705–14.

Miller, S. B., L. Dolgoy, M. Friese, and A. Sita. "Dimensions of Hostility and Cardiovascular Response to Interpersonal Stress." *Journal of Psychosomatic Research* 41, no. 1 (1996): 81–95.

Suarez, E. C., E. Harlan, M. C. Peoples, and R. B. Williams Jr. "Cardiovascular and Emotional Responses in Women: The Role of Hostility and Harassment." *Health Psychology* 12, no. 6 (1993): 459–68.

Vitaliano, P. P., J. Russo, S. L. Bailey, H. M. Young, and B. S. McCann. "Psychosocial Factors Associated with Cardiovascular Reactivity in Older Adults." *Psychosomatic Medicine* 55, no. 2 (1993): 164–77.

Buckley, T., S. McKinley, G. Tofler, and R. Bartrop. "Cardiovascular Risk in Early Bereavement: A Literature Review and Proposed Mechanisms." *International Journal of Nursing Studies* 47, no. 2 (2010): 229–38. doi:10.1016/j.ijnurstu.2009.06.010.

Carey, I. M., S. M. Shah, S. DeWilde, T. Harris, C. R. Victor, and D. G. Cook. "Increased Risk of Acute Cardiovascular Events After Partner Bereavement: A Matched Cohort Study." *JAMA Internal Medicine* 174, no. 4 (2014): 598–605. doi:10.1001/jamainternmed.2013 .14558.

Levin, A. "In Young Women, Depression Can Mean Literal Heartbreak." *EurekAlert!*. June 28, 2004. Accessed November 9, 2015. http://www.eurekalert.org/pub_releases/2004-06 /cfta-iyw062804.php.

News Staff. "Literal Heartbreak: The Cardiovascular Impact of Rejection." *Science 2.0* (blog). September 28, 2010. Accessed September 27, 2015. http://www.science20.com/news _articles/literal_heartbreak_cardiovascular_impact_rejection.

Crawford, C. "Why a Broken Heart Literally Hurts." Health Guidance for Better Health, Accessed November 9, 2015. http://www.healthguidance.org/entry/15607/1/Why-a -Broken-Heart-Literally-Hurts.html.

Jurkiewicz, R., and B. W. Romano. "Coronary Artery Disease and Experiences of Losses." [Article in English, Portuguese, Spanish.] *Arquivos Brasileiros de Cardiologia* 93, no. 4 (2009): 345–59.

Kaprio, J., M. Koskenvuo, and H. Rita. "Mortality After Bereavement: A Prospective Study of 95,647 Widowed Persons." *American Journal of Public Health* 77, no. 3 (1987): 283–87.

Luecken, L. J. "Childhood Attachment and Loss Experiences Affect Adult Cardiovascular and Cortisol Function." *Psychosomatic Medicine* 60, no. 6 (1998): 765–72.

Arch, J. J., K. W. Brown, D. J. Dean, L. N. Landy, K. D. Brown, and M. L. Laudenslager. "Self-Compassion Training Modulates Alpha-Amylase, Heart Rate Variability, and Subjective

Responses to Social Evaluative Threat in Women." *Psychoneuroendocrinology* 42 (2014): 49–58. doi:10.1016/j.psyneuen.2013.12.018.

Kemper, K. J., D. Powell, C. C. Helms, and D. B. Kim-Shapiro. "Loving-Kindness Meditation's Effects on Nitric Oxide and Perceived Well-Being: A Pilot Study in Experienced and Inexperienced Meditators." *Explore* (New York) 11, no. 1 (2015): 32–39. doi:10.1016/j .explore.2014.10.002.

Schäfer, A., and K. W. Kratky. "The Effect of Colored Illumination on Heart Rate Variability." *Forschende Komplementärmedizin* 13, no. 3 (2006): 167–73.

Peck, M. Scott. *The Road Less Traveled.* New York: Simon & Schuster, 1978.

Park, B. J., Y. Tsunetsugu, T. Kasetani, T. Kagawa, and Y. Miyazaki. "The Physiological Effects of Shinrin-Yoku (Taking in the Forest Atmosphere or Forest Bathing): Evidence from Field Experiments in 24 Forests Across Japan." *Environmental Health and Preventive Medicine* 15, no. 1 (2010): 18–26. doi:10.1007/s12199-009-0086-9.

Ochiai, H., H. Ikei, C. Song, M. Kobayashi, A. Takamatsu, T. Miura, T. Kagawa, et al. "Physiological and Psychological Effects of Forest Therapy on Middle-Aged Males with High-Normal Blood Pressure." *International Journal of Environmental Research and Public Health* 12, no. 3 (2015): 2532–42. doi:10.3390/ijerph120302532.

Mao, G. X., Y. B. Cao, X. G. Lan, Z. H. He, Z. M. Chen, Y. Z. Wang, X. L. Hu, et al. "Therapeutic Effect of Forest Bathing on Human Hypertension in the Elderly." *Journal of Cardiology* 60, no. 6 (2012): 495–502. doi:10.1016/j.jjcc.2012.08.003.

Lee, J., B. J. Park, Y. Tsunetsugu, T. Ohira, T. Kagawa, and Y. Miyazaki. "Effect of Forest Bathing on Physiological and Psychological Responses in Young Japanese Male Subjects." *Public Health* 125, no. 2 (2011): 93–100. doi:10.1016/j.puhe.2010.09.005.

Shaughnessy, D. T., L. M. Gangarosa, B. Schliebe, D. M. Umbach, Z. Xu, B. MacIntosh, M. G. Knize, et al. "Inhibition of Fried Meat-Induced Colorectal DNA Damage and Altered Systemic Genotoxicity in Humans by Crucifera, Chlorophyllin, and Yogurt." *PLoS ONE* 6, no. 4 (2011): e18707. doi:10.1371/journal.pone.0018707.

Dashwood, R., S. Yamane, and R. Larsen. "Study of the Forces of Stabilizing Complexes Between Chlorophylls and Heterocyclic Amine Mutagens." *Environmental and Molecular Mutagenesis* 27, no. 3 (1996): 211–18.

Walsh, M. C., L. Brennan, E. Pujos-Guillot, J. L. Sébédio, A. Scalbert, A. Fagan, D. G. Higgins, and M. J. Gibney. "Influence of Acute Phytochemical Intake on Human Urinary Metabolomic Profiles." *American Journal of Clinical Nutrition* 86, no. 6 (2007): 1687–93.

Dhonukshe-Rutten, R. A., J. H. de Vries, A. de Bree, N. van der Put, W. A. van Staveren, and L. C. de Groot. "Dietary Intake and Status of Folate and Vitamin B12 and Their Association with Homocysteine and Cardiovascular Disease in European Populations." *European Journal of Clinical Nutrition* 63, no. 1 (2009): 18–30.

Waśkiewicz, A., E. Sygnowska, and G. Broda. "Dietary Intake of Vitamins B6, B12 and Folate in Relation to Homocysteine Serum Concentration in the Adult Polish Population—WOBASZ Project." *Kardiologia Polska* 68, no. 3 (2010): 275–82.

Jones, P. J., and S. S. Abumweis. "Phytosterols as Functional Food Ingredients: Linkages to Cardiovascular Disease and Cancer." *Current Opinion in Clinical Nutrition and Metabolic Care* 12, no. 2 (2009): 147–51.

Sirotkin, A. V., and A. H. Harrath. "Phytoestrogens and Their Effects." *European Journal of Pharmacology* 741 (2014): 230–36. doi:10.1016/j.ejphar.2014.07.057.

Jenkins, D. J., C. W. Kendall, A. Marchie, D. Faulkner, E. Vidgen, K. G. Lapsley, E. A. Trautwein, et al. "The Effect of Combining Plant Sterols, Soy Protein, Viscous Fibers, and Almonds in Treating Hypercholesterolemia." *Metabolism* 52, no. 11 (2003): 1478–83.

Jenkins, D. J., C. W. Kendall, A. Marchie, A. L. Jenkins, L. S. Augustin, D. S. Ludwig, N. D. Barnard, and J. W. Anderson. "Type 2 Diabetes and the Vegetarian Diet." *American Journal of Clinical Nutrition* 78, no. 3 suppl. (2003): 610S–16S.

USDA Agricultural Research Service. National Nutrient Database "Phytosterol." Last modified December 7, 2011. Accessed September 27, 2015. http://ndb.nal.usda.gov/.

Thompson, H. J., J. Heimendinger, A. Diker, C. O'Neill, A. Haegele, B. Meinecke, P. Wolfe, et al. "Dietary Botanical Diversity Affects the Reduction of Oxidative Biomarkers in Women Due to High Vegetable and Fruit Intake." *Journal of Nutrition* 136, no. 8 (2006): 2207–12.

Liu, R. H. "Health Benefits of Fruit and Vegetables Are from Additive and Synergistic Combinations of Phytochemicals." *American Journal of Clinical Nutrition* 78, no. 3 suppl. (2003): 517S–20S.

Rylott, E. L., V. Gunning, K. Tzafestas, H. Sparrow, E. J. Johnston, A. S. Brentnall, J. R. Potts, and N. C. Bruce. "Phytodetoxification of the Environmental Pollutant and Explosive 2,4,6-Trinitrotoluene." *Plant Signaling and Behavior* 10, no. 1 (2015): e977714. doi:10.4161 /15592324.2014.977714.

Hannink, N., S. J. Rosser, C. E. French, A. Basran, J. A. Murray, S. Nicklin, and N. C. Bruce. "Phytodetoxification of TNT by Transgenic Plants Expressing a Bacterial Nitroreductase." *Nature Biotechnology* 19, no. 12 (2001): 1168–72.

Khalesi, S., C. Irwin, and M. Schubert. "Flaxseed Consumption May Reduce Blood Pressure: A Systematic Review and Meta-Analysis of Controlled Trials." *Journal of Nutrition* 145, no. 4 (2015): 758–65. doi:10.3945/jn.114.205302.

Goyal, A., V. Sharma, N. Upadhyay, S. Gill, and M. Sihag. "Flax and Flaxseed Oil: An Ancient Medicine and Modern Functional Food." *Journal of Food Science and Technology* 51, no. 9 (2014): 1633–53. doi:10.1007/s13197-013-1247-9.

Peterson, J., J. Dwyer, H. Adlercreutz, A. Scalbert, P. Jacques, and M. L. McCullough. "Dietary Lignans: Physiology and Potential for Cardiovascular Disease Risk Reduction." *Nutrition Reviews* 68, no. 10 (2010): 571–603. doi:10.1111/j.1753-4887.2010.00319.x.

Adolphe, J. L., S. J. Whiting, B. H. Juurlink, L. U. Thorpe, and J. Alcorn. "Health Effects with Consumption of the Flax Lignan Secoisolariciresinol Diglucoside." *British Journal of Nutrition* 103, no. 7 (2010): 929–38. doi:10.1017/S0007114509992753.

Thompson, L. U., B. A. Boucher, Z. Lui, M. Cotterchio, and N. Kreiger. "Phytoestrogen Content of Foods Consumed in Canada, Including Isoflavones, Lignans and Coumestan." *Nutrition and Cancer* 54, no. 2 (2006): 184–201.

Feldman, E. B. "Fruits and Vegetables and the Risk of Stroke." *Nutrition Reviews* 59, no. 1, pt. 1 (2001): 24–27.

Mizrahi, A., P. Knekt, J. Montonen, M. A. Laaksonen, M. Heliövaara, and R. Järvinen. "Plant Foods and the Risk of Cerebrovascular Diseases: A Potential Protection of Fruit Consumption." *British Journal of Nutrition* 102, no. 7 (2009): 1075–83. doi:10.1017 /S0007114509359097.

Virtanen, J. K., T. H. Rissanen, S. Voutilainen, and T. P. Tuomainen. "Mercury as a Risk Factor for Cardiovascular Diseases." *Journal of Nutritional Biochemistry* 18, no. 2 (2007): 75–85.

Caciari, T., A. Sancini, M. Fioravanti, A. Capozzella, T. Casale, L. Montuori, M. Fiaschetti, et al. "Cadmium and Hypertension in Exposed Workers: A Meta-Analysis." *International Journal of Occupational Medicine and Environmental Health* 26, no. 3 (2013): 440–56. doi:10.2478/s13382 -013-0111-5.

Rosin, A. "The Long-Term Consequences of Exposure to Lead." *Israel Medical Association Journal* 11, no. 11 (2009): 689–94.

Uchikawa, T., I. Maruyama, S. Kumamoto, Y. Ando, and A. Yasutake. "Chlorella Suppresses Methylmercury Transfer to the Fetus in Pregnant Mice." *Journal of Toxicological Sciences* 36, no. 5 (2011): 675–80.

Rai, L. C., J. P. Gaur, and H. D. Kumar. "Protective Effects of Certain Environmental Factors on the Toxicity of Zinc, Mercury, and Methylmercury to Chlorella Vulgaris." *Environmental Research* 25, no. 2 (1981): 250–59.

Omura, Y., and S. L. Beckman. "Role of Mercury (Hg) in Resistant Infections and Effective Treatment of Chlamydia Trachomatis and Herpes Family Viral Infections (and Potential Treatment for Cancer) by Removing Localized Hg Deposits with Chinese Parsley and Delivering Effective Antibiotics Using Various Drug Uptake Enhancement Methods." *Acupuncture and Electro-Therapeutics Research* 20, nos. 3–4 (1995): 195–229.

Alcocer-Varela, J., A. Iglesias, L. Llorente, and D. Alarcón-Segovia. "Effects of L-Canavanine on T Cells May Explain the Induction of Systemic Lupus Erythematosus by Alfalfa." *Arthritis and Rheumatism* 28, no. 1 (1985): 52–57.

Malinow, M. R., E. J. Bardana Jr., B. Pirofsky, S. Craig, and P. McLaughlin. "Systemic Lupus Erythematosus-Like Syndrome in Monkeys Fed Alfalfa Sprouts: Role of a Nonprotein Amino Acid." *Science* 216, no. 4544 (1982): 415–17.

Xiao, Z., G. E. Lester, Y. Luo, and Q. Wang. "Assessment of Vitamin and Carotenoid Concentrations of Emerging Food Products: Edible Microgreens." *Journal of Agricultural and Food Chemistry* 60, no. 31 (2012): 7644–51. doi:10.1021/jf300459b.

Scholz, S., and G. Williamson. "Interactions Affecting the Bioavailability of Dietary Polyphenols In Vivo." *International Journal for Vitamin and Nutrition Research* 77, no. 3 (2007): 224–35.

Naito, Y., and T. Yoshikawa. "Green Tea and Heart Health." *Journal of Cardiovascular Pharmacology* 54, no. 5 (2009): 385–90. doi:10.1097/FJC.0b013e3181b6e7a1.

CHAPTER 7: THE TRUTH

M. L. Pelchat and S. Schaefer. "Dietary monotony and food cravings in young and elderly adults." *Physiological and Behavior* 68, no. 3 (January 2000): 353-9.

C. Noel and R. Dando. "The effect of emotional state on taste perception." *Appetite* 95 (1 December 2015): 89-95. doi: 10.1016/j.appet.2015.06.003. Epub 2015 Jun 27.

Devillier, P., E. Naline, and S. Grassin-Delyle. "The Pharmacology of Bitter Taste Receptors and Their Role in Human Airways." *Pharmacology and Therapeutics* 155 (2015): 11–12. doi:10.1016/j.pharmthera.2015.08.001.

Clark, A. A., C. D. Dotson, A. E. Elson, A. Voigt, U. Boehm, W. Meyerhof, N. I. Steinle, and S. D. Munger. "TAS2R Bitter Taste Receptors Regulate Thyroid Function." *FASEB Journal* 29, no. 1 (2015): 164–72. doi:10.1096/fj.14-262246.

Maehashi, K., and L. Huang. "Bitter Peptides and Bitter Taste Receptors." *Cellular and Molecular Life Sciences* 66, no. 10 (2009): 1661–71. doi:10.1007/s00018-009-8755-9.

Rozengurt, E. "Taste Receptors in the Gastrointestinal Tract. I. Bitter Taste Receptors and Alpha-Gustducin in the Mammalian Gut." *American Journal of Physiology: Gastrointestinal and Liver Physiology* 291, no. 2 (2006): G171–77.

Denke, C., M. Rotte, H. J. Heinze, and M. Schaefer. "Lying and the Subsequent Desire for Toothpaste: Activity in the Somatosensory Cortex Predicts Embodiment of the Moral-Purity Metaphor." *Cerebral Cortex* (September 11, 2014): bhu170.

Kreutz, G., S. Bongard, S. Rohrmann, V. Hodapp, and D. Grebe. "Effects of Choir Singing or Listening on Secretory Immunoglobulin A, Cortisol, and Emotional State." *Journal of Behavioral Medicine* 27, no. 6 (2004): 623–35.

Grape, C., M. Sandgren, L. O. Hansson, M. Ericson, and T. Theorell. "Does Singing Promote Well-Being?: An Empirical Study of Professional and Amateur Singers During a Singing Lesson." *Integrative Physiological and Behavioral Science* 38, no. 1 (2003): 65–74.

Lee, Y. Y., M. F. Chan, and E. Mok. "Effectiveness of Music Intervention on the Quality of Life of Older People." *Journal of Advanced Nursing* 66, no. 12 (2010): 2677–87. doi:10.1111/j.1365-2648.2010.05445.x.

Coulton, S., S. Clift, A. Skingley, and J. Rodriguez. "Effectiveness and Cost-Effectiveness of Community Singing on Mental Health-Related Quality of Life of Older People: Randomised Controlled Trial." *British Journal of Psychiatry* 207, no. 3 (2015): 250–55. doi:10.1192/bjp.bp.113.129908.

MacArtain, P., C. I. Gill, M. Brooks, R. Campbell, and I. R. Rowland. "Nutritional Value of Edible Seaweeds." *Nutrition Reviews* 65, no. 12, pt. 1 (2007): 535–43.

Rajapakse, N., and S. K. Kim. "Nutritional and Digestive Health Benefits of Seaweed." *Advances in Food and Nutrition Research* 64 (2011): 17–28. doi:10.1016/B978-0-12-387669-0.00002-8.

Fitton, J. H., D. N. Stringer, and S. S. Karpiniec. "Therapies from Fucoidan: An Update." *Marine Drugs* 13, no. 9 (2015): 5920–46. doi:10.3390/md13095920.

Abuajah, C. I., A. C. Ogbonna, and C. M. Osuji. "Functional Components and Medicinal Properties of Food: A Review." *Journal of Food Science and Technology* 52, no. 5 (2015): 2522–29. doi:10.1007/s13197-014-1396-5.

Rose, M., J. Lewis, N. Langford, M. Baxter, S. Origgi, M. Barber, H. MacBain, and K. Thomas. "Arsenic in Seaweed—Forms, Concentration and Dietary Exposure." *Food and Chemical Toxicology* 45, no. 7 (2007): 1263–67.

Yokoi, K., and A. Konomi. "Toxicity of So-Called Edible Hijiki Seaweed (*Sargassum fusiforme*) Containing Inorganic Arsenic." *Regulatory Toxicology and Pharmacology* 63, no. 2 (2012): 291–97. doi:10.1016/j.yrtph.2012.04.006.

Skibola, C. F. "The Effect of *Fucus Vesiculosus*, an Edible Brown Seaweed, upon Menstrual Cycle Length and Hormonal Status in Three Pre-Menopausal Women: A Case Report." *BMC Complementary and Alternative Medicine* 4 (2004): 10.

Ramaekers, M. G., P. A. Luning, R. M. Ruijschop, C. M. Lakemond, J. H. Bult, G. Gort, and M. A. van Boekel. "Aroma Exposure Time and Aroma Concentration in Relation to Satiation." *British Journal of Nutrition* 111, no. 3 (2014): 554–62. doi:10.1017/S0007114513002729.

Carwile, J. L., X. Ye, X. Zhou, A. M. Calafat, and K. B. Michels. "Canned Soup Consumption and Urinary Bisphenol A: A Randomized Crossover Trial." *Journal of the American Medical Association* 306, no. 20 (2011): 2218–20. doi:10.1001/jama.2011.1721.

Flood, J. E., and B. J. Rolls. "Soup Preloads in a Variety of Forms Reduce Meal Energy Intake." *Appetite* 49, no. 3 (2007): 626–34.

Hord, N. G. "Dietary Nitrates, Nitrites, and Cardiovascular Disease." *Current Atherosclerosis Reports* 13, no. 6 (2011): 484–92. doi:10.1007/s11883-011-0209-9.

Hodges, R. E., and D. M. Minich. "Modulation of Metabolic Detoxification Pathways Using Foods and Food-Derived Components: A Scientific Review with Clinical Application." *Journal of Nutrition and Metabolism* 2015 (2015): 760689. doi:10.1155/2015/760689.

Llewellyn, C. H., C. H. van Jaarsveld, D. Boniface, S. Carnell, and J. Wardle. "Eating Rate Is a Heritable Phenotype Related to Weight in Children." *American Journal of Clinical Nutrition* 88, no. 6 (2008): 1560–66. doi:10.3945/ajcn.2008.26175.

Dalen, J., B. W. Smith, B. M. Shelley, A. L. Sloan, L. Leahigh, and D. Begay. "Pilot Study: Mindful Eating and Living (MEAL): Weight, Eating Behavior, and Psychological Outcomes Associated with a Mindfulness-Based Intervention for People with Obesity." *Complementary Therapies in Medicine* 18, no. 6 (2010): 260–64. doi:10.1016/j.ctim.2010.09.008.

Katterman, S. N., B. M. Kleinman, M. M. Hood, L. M. Nackers, and J. A. Corsica. "Mindfulness Meditation as an Intervention for Binge Eating, Emotional Eating, and Weight Loss: A Systematic Review." *Eating Behaviors* 15, no. 2 (2014): 197–204. doi:10.1016/j.eatbeh.2014.01.005.

Rolls, B. J., L. S. Roe, and J. S. Meengs. "Larger Portion Sizes Lead to a Sustained Increase in Energy Intake over 2 Days." *Journal of the American Dietetic Association* 106, no. 4 (2006): 543–49.

Appleton, K. M., and L. McGowan. "The Relationship Between Restrained Eating and Poor Psychological Health Is Moderated by Pleasure Normally Associated with Eating." *Eating Behaviors* 7, no. 4 (2006): 342–47.

CHAPTER 8: THE INSIGHT

Craft, S., B. Cholerton, and L. D. Baker. "Insulin and Alzheimer's Disease: Untangling the Web." *Journal of Alzheimer's Disease* 33, suppl. 1 (2013): S263–75.

Cholerton, B., L. D. Baker, and S. Craft. "Insulin, Cognition, and Dementia." *European Journal of Pharmacology* 719, nos. 1–3 (2013): 170–79. doi:10.1016/j.ejphar.2013.08.008.

Cholerton, B., L. D. Baker, and S. Craft. "Insulin Resistance and Pathological Brain Ageing." *Diabetic Medicine* 28, no. 12 (2011): 1463–75. doi:10.1111/j.1464-5491.2011.03464.x.

De la Monte, S. M. "Type 3 Diabetes Is Sporadic Alzheimer's Disease: Mini-Review." *European Neuropsychopharmacology* 24, no. 12 (2014): 1954–60. doi:10.1016/j.euroneuro.2014.06.008.

Berg, J. M., J. L. Tymoczko, and L. Stryer. "Each Organ Has a Unique Metabolic Profile." Section 30.2 in *Biochemistry*, 5th ed. New York: W. H. Freeman, 2002.

McCraty, R., M. Atkinson, and R. T. Bradley. "Electrophysiological Evidence of Intuition: Part 2. A System-Wide Process?" *Journal of Alternative and Complementary Medicine* 10, no. 2 (2004): 325–36.

Petter, M., C. T. Chambers, and J. MacLaren Chorney. "The Effects of Mindfulness-Based Attention on Cold Pressor Pain in Children." *Pain Research and Management* 18, no. 1 (2013): 39–45.

Mizrahi, M. C., R. Reicher-Atir, S. Levy, S. Haramati, D. Wengrower, E. Israeli, and E. Goldin. "Effects of Guided Imagery with Relaxation Training on Anxiety and Quality of Life Among Patients with Inflammatory Bowel Disease." *Psychology and Health* 27, no. 12 (2012): 1463–79. doi:10.1080/08870446.2012.691169.

Gedde-Dahl, M., and E. A. Fors. "Impact of Self-Administered Relaxation and Guided Imagery Techniques During Final Trimester and Birth." *Complementary Therapies in Clinical Practice* 18, no. 1 (2012): 60–65. doi:10.1016/j.ctcp.2011.08.008.

Abdoli, S., K. Rahzani, M. Safaie, and A. Sattari. "A Randomized Control Trial: The Effect of Guided Imagery with Tape and Perceived Happy Memory on Chronic Tension Type Headache." *Scandinavian Journal of Caring Sciences* 26, no. 2 (2012): 254–61. doi:10.1111/j.1471-6712.2011.00926.x.

Mannix, L. K., R. S. Chandurkar, L. A. Rybicki, D. L. Tusek, and G. D. Solomon. "Effect of Guided Imagery on Quality of Life for Patients with Chronic Tension-Type Headache." *Headache* 39, no. 5 (1999): 326–34.

Mehta, R., and R. J. Zhu. "Blue or Red? Exploring the Effect of Color on Cognitive Task Performances." *Science* 323, no. 5918 (2009): 1226–29. doi:10.1126/science.1169144.

Viola, A. U., L. M. James, L. J. Schlangen, and D. J. Dijk. "Blue-Enriched White Light in the Workplace Improves Self-Reported Alertness, Performance and Sleep Quality." *Scandinavian Journal of Work, Environment and Health* 34, no. 4 (2008): 297–306.

Phipps-Nelson, J., J. R. Redman, L. J. Schlangen, and S. M. Rajaratnam. "Blue Light Exposure Reduces Objective Measures of Sleepiness During Prolonged Nighttime Performance Testing." *Chronobiology International* 26, no. 5 (2009): 891–912. doi:10.1080/07420520903044364.

Gabel, V., M. Maire, C. F. Reichert, S. L. Chellappa, C. Schmidt, V. Hommes, A. U. Viola, and C. Cajochen. "Effects of Artificial Dawn and Morning Blue Light on Daytime Cognitive Performance, Well-Being, Cortisol and Melatonin Levels." *Chronobiology International* 30, no. 8 (2013): 988–97. doi:10.3109/07420528.2013.793196.

Taillard, J., A. Capelli, P. Sagaspe, A. Anund, T. Akerstedt, and P. Philip. "In-Car Nocturnal Blue Light Exposure Improves Motorway Driving: A Randomized Controlled Trial." *PLoS ONE* 7, no. 10 (2012): e46750. doi:10.1371/journal.pone.0046750.

The Doc. "7 Great Examples of Scientific Discoveries Made in Dreams." *Famous Scientists* (blog). Accessed September 28, 2015. http://www.famousscientists.org/7-great-examples-of-scientific-discoveries-made-in-dreams/.

Whyte, A. R., and C. M. Williams. "Effects of a Single Dose of a Flavonoid-Rich Blueberry Drink on Memory in 8 to 10 Year Old Children." *Nutrition* 31, no. 3 (2015): 531–34. doi:10.1016/j.nut.2014.09.013.

Campbell, E. L., M. Chebib, and G. A. Johnston. "The Dietary Flavonoids Apigenin and (-)-Epigallocatechin Gallate Enhance the Positive Modulation by Diazepam of the Activation by GABA of Recombinant GABA(A) Receptors." *Biochemical Pharmacology* 68, no. 8 (2004): 1631–38.

Cho, S., J. H. Park, A. N. Pae, D. Han, D. Kim, N. C. Cho, K. T. No, et al. "Hypnotic Effects and GABAergic Mechanism of Licorice (*Glycyrrhiza glabra*) Ethanol Extract and Its Major Flavonoid Constituent Glabrol." *Bioorganic and Medicinal Chemistry* 20, no. 11 (2012): 3493–501. doi:10.1016/j.bmc.2012.04.011.

Jäger, A. K., and L. Saaby. "Flavonoids and the CNS." *Molecules* 16, no. 2 (2011): 1471–85. doi:10.3390/molecules16021471.

Kavvadias, D., V. Monschein, P. Sand, P. Riederer, and P. Schreier. "Constituents of Sage (*Salvia Officinalis*) with In Vitro Affinity to Human Brain Benzodiazepine Receptor." *Planta Medica* 69, no. 2 (2003): 113–17.

Nielsen, M., S. Frøkjaer, and C. Braestrup. "High Affinity of the Naturally-Occurring Biflavonoid, Amentoflavon, to Brain Benzodiazepine Receptors In Vitro." *Biochemical Pharmacology* 37, no. 17 (1988): 3285–87.

Medina, J. H., A. C. Paladini, C. Wolfman, M. Levi de Stein, D. Calvo, L. E. Diaz, and C. Peña. "Chrysin (5,7-di-OH-flavone), a Naturally-Occurring Ligand for Benzodiazepine Receptors, with Anticonvulsant Properties." *Biochemical Pharmacology* 40, no. 10 (1990): 2227–31.

Salgueiro, J. B., P. Ardenghi, M. Dias, M. B. Ferreira, I. Izquierdo, and J. H. Medina. "Anxiolytic Natural and Synthetic Flavonoid Ligands of the Central Benzodiazepine Receptor Have No Effect on Memory Tasks in Rats." *Pharmacology, Biochemistry, and Behavior* 58, no. 4 (1997): 887–91.

Viola, H., C. Wasowski, M. Levi de Stein, C. Wolfman, R. Silveira, F. Dajas, J. H. Medina, and A. C. Paladini. "Apigenin, a Component of Matricaria Recutita Flowers, Is a Central Benzodiazepine Receptors-Ligand with Anxiolytic Effects." *Planta Medica* 61, no. 3 (1995): 213–16.

Wolfman, C., H. Viola, A. Paladini, F. Dajas, and J. H. Medina. "Possible Anxiolytic Effects of Chrysin, a Central Benzodiazepine Receptor Ligand Isolated from Passiflora Coerulea." *Pharmacology, Biochemistry, and Behavior* 47, no. 1 (1994): 1–4.

Papanikolaou, Y., H. Palmer, M. A. Binns, D. J. Jenkins, and C. E. Greenwood. "Better Cognitive Performance Following a Low-Glycaemic-Index Compared with a High-Glycaemic-

Index Carbohydrate Meal in Adults with Type 2 Diabetes." *Diabetologia* 49, no. 5 (2006): 855–62.

Greenwood, C. E., R. J. Kaplan, S. Hebblethwaite, and D. J. Jenkins. "Carbohydrate-Induced Memory Impairment in Adults with Type 2 Diabetes." *Diabetes Care* 26, no. 7 (2003): 1961–66.

Mahoney, C. R., H. A. Taylor, R. B. Kanarek, and P. Samuel. "Effect of Breakfast Composition on Cognitive Processes in Elementary School Children." *Physiology and Behavior* 85, no. 5 (2005): 635–45.

Ciok, J., and A. Dolna. "Carbohydrates and Mental Performance—The Role of Glycemic Index of Food Products." [In Polish.] *Polski Merkuriusz Lekarski* 20, no. 117 (2006): 367–70.

Lakhan, S. E., and A. Kirchgessner. "The Emerging Role of Dietary Fructose in Obesity and Cognitive Decline." *Nutrition Journal* 12, no. 1 (2013): 114.

Abdel-Salam, O. M., N. A. Salem, M. E. El-Shamarka, J. S. Hussein, N. A. Ahmed, and M. E. El-Nagar. "Studies on the Effects of Aspartame on Memory and Oxidative Stress in Brain of Mice." *European Review for Medical and Pharmacological Sciences* 16, no. 15 (2012): 2092–101.

Collison, K. S., N. J. Makhoul, M. Z. Zaidi, S. M. Saleh, B. Andres, A. Inglis, R. Al-Rabiah, and F. A. Al-Mohanna. "Gender Dimorphism in Aspartame-Induced Impairment of Spatial Cognition and Insulin Sensitivity." *PLoS ONE* 7, no. 4 (2012): e31570. doi:10.1371/journal .pone.0031570.

Cai, W., J. Uribarri, L. Zhu, X. Chen, S. Swamy, Z. Zhao, F. Grosjean, et al. "Oral Glycotoxins Are a Modifiable Cause of Dementia and the Metabolic Syndrome in Mice and Humans." *PNAS* 111, no. 13 (2014): 4940–45. doi:10.1073/pnas.1316013111.

Győréné, K. G., A. Varga, and A. Lugasi. "A Comparison of Chemical Composition and Nutritional Value of Organically and Conventionally Grown Plant Derived Foods." [In Hungarian.] *Orvosi Hetilap* 147, no. 43 (2006): 2081–90.

Nafar, F., and K. M. Mearow. "Coconut Oil Attenuates the Effects of Amyloid-β on Cortical Neurons In Vitro." *Journal of Alzheimer's Disease* 39, no. 2 (2014): 233–37. doi:10.3233/JAD -131436.

Ford, P. A., K. Jaceldo-Siegl, J. W. Lee, W. Youngberg, and S. Tonstad. "Intake of Mediterranean Foods Associated with Positive Affect and Low Negative Affect." *Journal of Psychosomatic Research* 74, no. 2 (2013): 142–48. doi:10.1016/j.jpsychores.2012.11.002.

Conner, T. S., K. L. Brookie, A. C. Richardson, and M. A. Polak. "On Carrots and Curiosity: Eating Fruit and Vegetables Is Associated with Greater Flourishing in Daily Life." *British Journal of Health Psychology* 20, no. 2 (2015): 413–27. doi:10.1111/bjhp.12113.

Ritchie, K., I. Carrière, A. de Mendonca, F. Portet, J. F. Dartigues, O. Rouaud, P. Barberger-Gateau, and M. L. Ancelin. "The Neuroprotective Effects of Caffeine: A Prospective Population Study (the Three City Study)." *Neurology* 69, no. 6 (2007): 536–45.

Santos, C., J. Costa, J. Santos, A. Vaz-Carneiro, and N. Lunet. "Caffeine Intake and Dementia: Systematic Review and Meta-Analysis." *Journal of Alzheimer's Disease* 20, suppl. 1 (2010): S187–204. doi:10.3233/JAD-2010-091387.

Júdice, P. B., J. P. Magalhães, D. A. Santos, C. N. Matias, A. I. Carita, P. A. Armada-Da-Silva, L. B. Sardinha, and A. M. Silva. "A Moderate Dose of Caffeine Ingestion Does Not Change Energy Expenditure but Decreases Sleep Time in Physically Active Males: A Double-Blind Randomized Controlled Trial." *Applied Physiology, Nutrition, and Metabolism* 38, no. 1 (2013): 49–56. doi:10.1139/apnm-2012-0145.

Martin, F. P., N. Antille, S. Rezzi, and S. Kochhar. "Everyday Eating Experiences of Chocolate and Non-Chocolate Snacks Impact Postprandial Anxiety, Energy and Emotional States." *Nutrients* 4, no. 6 (2012): 554–67. doi:10.3390/nu4060554.

Smit, H. J., E. A. Gaffan, and P. J. Rogers. "Methylxanthines Are the Psycho-Pharmacologically Active Constituents of Chocolate." *Psychopharmacology* (Berlin) 176, nos. 3–4 (2004): 412–19.

Sudarma, V., S. Sukmaniah, and P. Siregar. "Effect of Dark Chocolate on Nitric Oxide Serum Levels and Blood Pressure in Prehypertension Subjects." *Acta Medic Indonesiana* 43, no. 4 (2011): 224–28.

Field, D. T., C. M. Williams, and L. T. Butler. "Consumption of Cocoa Flavanols Results in an Acute Improvement in Visual and Cognitive Functions." *Physiology and Behavior* 103, nos. 3–4 (2011): 255–60. doi:10.1016/j.physbeh.2011.02.013.

Radin, D., G. Hayssen, and J. Walsh. "Effects of Intentionally Enhanced Chocolate on Mood." *Explore* (New York) 3, no. 5 (2007): 485–92.

Grassi, D., G. Desideri, S. Necozíone, F. Ruggieri, J. B. Blumberg, M. Stornello, and C. Ferri. "Protective Effects of Flavanol-Rich Dark Chocolate on Endothelial Function and Wave Reflection During Acute Hyperglycemia." *Hypertension* 60, no. 3 (2012): 827–32. doi:10.1161/HYPERTENSIONAHA.112.193995.

Shiah, Y. J., and D. Radin. "Metaphysics of the Tea Ceremony: A Randomized Trial Investigating the Roles of Intention and Belief on Mood While Drinking Tea." *Explore* (New York) 9, no. 6 (2013): 355–60. doi:10.1016/j.explore.2013.08.005.

Rankin, C. W., J. O. Nriagu, J. K. Aggarwal, T. A. Arowolo, K. Adebayo, and A. R. Flegal. "Lead Contamination in Cocoa and Cocoa Products: Isotopic Evidence of Global Contamination." *Environmental Health Perspectives* 113, no. 10 (2005): 1344–48. doi:10.1289/ehp.8009.

Krecisz, B., D. Chomiczewska, M. Kiec-Swierczynska, and A. Kaszuba. "Systemic Contact Dermatitis to Nickel Present in Cocoa in 14-Year-Old Boy." *Pediatric Dermatology* 28, no. 3 (2011): 335–36. doi:10.1111/j.1525-1470.2011.01235.x.

Radenahmad, N., F. Saleh, I. Sayoh, K. Sawangjaroen, P. Subhadhirasakul, P. Boonyoung, W. Rundorn, and W. Mitranun. "Young Coconut Juice Can Accelerate the Healing Process of Cutaneous Wounds." *BMC Complementary and Alternative Medicine* 12 (2012): 252. doi:10.1186/1472-6882-12-252.

Radenahmad, N., F. Saleh, K. Sawangjaroen, U. Vongvatcharanon, P. Subhadhirasakul, W. Rundorn, B. Withyachumnarnkul, and J. R. Connor. "Young Coconut Juice, a Potential Therapeutic Agent That Could Significantly Reduce Some Pathologies Associated with Alzheimer's Disease: Novel Findings." *British Journal of Nutrition* 105, no. 5 (2011): 738–46. doi:10.1017/S0007114510004241.

Yong, J. W. H., L. Ge, Y. F. Ng, and S. N. Tan. "The Chemical Composition and Biological Properties of Coconut (*Cocos Nucifera* L.) Water." *Molecules* 14, no. 12 (2009): 5144–64. doi:10.3390/molecules14125144.

Gómez-Pinilla, F. "Brain Foods: The Effects of Nutrients on Brain Function." *Nature Reviews Neuroscience* 9, no. 7 (2008): 568–78. doi:10.1038/nrn2421.

Reger, M. A., S. T. Henderson, C. Hale, B. Cholerton, L. D. Baker, G. S. Watson, K. Hyde, D. Chapman, and S. Craft. "Effects of Beta-Hydroxybutyrate on Cognition in Memory-Impaired Adults." *Neurobiology of Aging* 25, no. 3 (2004): 311–14.

Appleton, K. M., P. J. Rogers, and A. R. Ness. "Updated Systematic Review and Meta-Analysis of the Effects of n–3 Long-Chain Polyunsaturated Fatty Acids on Depressed Mood." *American Journal of Clinical Nutrition* 91, no. 3 (2010): 757–70. doi:10.3945/ajcn.2009.28313.

Kraguljac, N. V., V. M. Montori, M. Pavuluri, H. S. Chai, B. S. Wilson, and S. S. Unal. "Efficacy of Omega-3 Fatty Acids in Mood Disorders—A Systematic Review and Meta-Analysis." *Psychopharmacology Bulletin* 42, no. 3 (2009): 39–54.

Ng, T. P., P. C. Chiam, T. Lee, H. C. Chua, L. Lim, and E. H. Kua. "Curry Consumption and Cognitive Function in the Elderly." *American Journal of Epidemiology* 164, no. 9 (2006): 898–906.

Kirkham, S., R. Akilen, S. Sharma, and A. Tsiami. "The Potential of Cinnamon to Reduce Blood Glucose Levels in Patients with Type 2 Diabetes and Insulin Resistance." *Diabetes, Obesity and Metabolism* 11, no. 12 (2009): 1100–13. doi:10.1111/j.1463-1326.2009.01094.x.

Shukitt-Hale, B., D. F. Bielinski, F. C. Lau, L. M. Willis, A. N. Carey, and J. A. Joseph. "The Beneficial Effects of Berries on Cognition, Motor Behaviour and Neuronal Function in Ageing." *British Journal of Nutrition* 114, no. 10 (2015): 1542–49.

Malin, D. H., D. R. Lee, P. Goyarzu, Y. H. Chang, L. J. Ennis, E. Beckett, B. Shukitt-Hale, and J. A. Joseph. "Short-Term Blueberry-Enriched Diet Prevents and Reverses Object Recognition Memory Loss in Aging Rats." *Nutrition* 27, no. 3 (2011): 338–42. doi:10.1016/j.nut.2010.05.001.

Krikorian, R., M. D. Shidler, T. A. Nash, W. Kalt, M. R. Vinqvist-Tymchuk, B. Shukitt-Hale, and J. A. Joseph. "Blueberry Supplementation Improves Memory in Older Adults." *Journal of Agricultural and Food Chemistry* 58, no. 7 (2010): 3996–4000. doi:10.1021/jf9029332.

Rendeiro, C., D. Vauzour, M. Rattray, P. Waffo-Téguo, J. M. Mérillon, L. T. Butler, C. M. Williams, and J. P. Spencer. "Dietary Levels of Pure Flavonoids Improve Spatial Memory Performance and Increase Hippocampal Brain-Derived Neurotrophic Factor." *PLoS ONE* 8, no. 5 (2013): e63535. doi:10.1371/journal.pone.0063535.

Joseph, J. A., B. Shukitt-Hale, and L. M. Willis. "Grape Juice, Berries, and Walnuts Affect Brain Aging and Behavior." *Journal of Nutrition* 139, no. 9 (2009): 1813S–1817S. doi:10.3945/jn.109.108266.

Galli, R. L., B. Shukitt-Hale, K. A. Youdim, and J. A. Joseph. "Fruit Polyphenolics and Brain Aging: Nutritional Interventions Targeting Age-Related Neuronal and Behavioral Deficits." *Annals of the New York Academy of Sciences* 959 (2002): 128–32.

Tan, L., H. P. Yang, W. Pang, H. Lu, Y. D. Hu, J. Li, S. J. Lu, W. Q. Zhang, and Y. G. Jiang. "Cyanidin-3-O-Galactoside and Blueberry Extracts Supplementation Improves Spatial Memory and Regulates Hippocampal ERK Expression in Senescence-Accelerated Mice." *Biomedical and Environmental Sciences* 27, no. 3 (2014): 186–96. doi:10.3967/bes2014.007.

Krikorian, R., E. L. Boespflug, D. E. Fleck, A. L. Stein, J. D. Wightman, M. D. Shidler, and S. Sadat-Hossieny. "Concord Grape Juice Supplementation and Neurocognitive Function in Human Aging." *Journal of Agricultural and Food Chemistry* 60, no. 23 (2012): 5736–42. doi:10.1021/jf300277g.

Krikorian, R., T. A. Nash, M. D. Shidler, B. Shukitt-Hale, and J. A. Joseph. "Concord Grape Juice Supplementation Improves Memory Function in Older Adults with Mild Cognitive Impairment." *British Journal of Nutrition* 103, no. 5 (2010): 730–34. doi:10.1017/S0007114509992364.

CHAPTER 9: THE SPIRIT

Van Wijk, R., and E. P. van Wijk. "An Introduction to Human Biophoton Emission." *Forschende Komplementärmedizin und Klassische Naturheilkunde* 12, no. 2 (2005): 77–83.

Van Wijk, E. P., J. Ackerman, and R. van Wijk. "Effect of Meditation on Ultraweak Photon Emission from Hands and Forehead." *Forschende Komplementärmedizin und Klassische Naturheilkunde* 12, no. 2 (2005): 107–12.

Van Wijk, E. P., R. Lüdtke, and R. van Wijk. "Differential Effects of Relaxation Techniques on Ultraweak Photon Emission." *Journal of Alternative and Complementary Medicine* 14, no. 3 (2008): 241–50. doi:10.1089/acm.2007.7185.

Kamal, A. H., and S. Komatsu. "Involvement of Reactive Oxygen Species and Mitochondrial Proteins in Biophoton Emission in Roots of Soybean Plants Under Flooding Stress." *Journal of Proteome Research* 14, no. 5 (2015): 2219–36. doi:10.1021/acs.jproteome.5b00007.

Winkler, R., H. Guttenberger, and H. Klima. "Ultraweak and Induced Photon Emission After Wounding of Plants." *Photochemistry and Photobiology* 85, no. 4 (2009): 962–65. doi:10.1111 /j.1751-1097.2009.00537.x.

Kim, M. "Blue Light from Electronics Disturbs Sleep, Especially for Teenagers." *Washington Post*. September 1, 2014. Accessed September 28, 2015. http://www.washingtonpost .com/national/health-science/blue-light-from-electronics-disturbs-sleep-especially-for -teenagers/2014/08/29/3edd2726-27a7-11e4-958c-268a320a60ce_story.html.

Claustrat, B., and J. Leston. "Melatonin: Physiological Effects in Humans." *Neurochirurgie* 61, nos. 2–3 (2015): 77–84. doi:10.1016/j.neuchi.2015.03.002.

Carpenter, D. O. "Human Disease Resulting from Exposure to Electromagnetic Fields." *Reviews on Environmental Health* 28, no. 4 (2013): 159–72. doi:10.1515/reveh-2013-0016.

EMFs.info: Electric and Magnetic Fields and Health. "Sources." Accessed September 28, 2015. http://www.emfs.info/sources/.

Feychting, M., A. Ahlbom, and L. Kheifets. "EMF and Health." *Annual Review of Public Health* 26 (2005): 165–89.

Miller, A. B., and L. M. Green. "Electric and Magnetic Fields at Power Frequencies." *Chronic Diseases in Canada* 29, suppl. 1 (2010): 69–83.

Kheifets, L., J. Monroe, X. Vergara, G. Mezei, and A. A. Afifi. "Occupational Electromagnetic Fields and Leukemia and Brain Cancer: An Update to Two Meta-Analyses." *Journal of Occupational and Environmental Medicine* 50, no. 6 (2008): 677–88. doi:10.1097/JOM .0b013e3181757a27.

Ferreri, F., G. Curcio, P. Pasqualetti, L. De Gennaro, R. Fini, and P. M. Rossini. "Mobile Phone Emissions and Human Brain Excitability." *Annals of Neurology* 60, no. 2 (2006): 188–96.

Berk, M., S. Dodd, and M. Henry. "Do Ambient Electromagnetic Fields Affect Behaviour? A Demonstration of the Relationship Between Geomagnetic Storm Activity and Suicide." *Bioelectromagnetics* 27, no. 2 (2006): 151–55.

Rohan, M. L., R. T. Yamamoto, C. T. Ravichandran, K. R. Cayetano, O. G. Morales, D. P. Olson, G. Vitaliano, S. M. Paul, and B. M. Cohen. "Rapid Mood-Elevating Effects of Low Field Magnetic Stimulation in Depression." *Biological Psychiatry* 76, no. 3 (2014): 186–93. doi:10.1016/j .biopsych.2013.10.024.

Galace de Freitas, D., F. B. Marcondes, R. L. Monteiro, S. G. Rosa, P. Maria de Moraes Barros Fucs, and T. Y. Fukuda. "Pulsed Electromagnetic Field and Exercises in Patients with Shoulder Impingement Syndrome: A Randomized, Double-Blind, Placebo-Controlled Clinical Trial." *Archives of Physical Medicine and Rehabilitation* 95, no. 2 (2014): 345–52. doi:10.1016/j .apmr.2013.09.022.

Valentini, E., M. Ferrara, F. Presaghi, L. De Gennaro, and G. Curcio. "Systematic Review and Meta-Analysis of Psychomotor Effects of Mobile Phone Electromagnetic Fields." *Occupational and Environmental Medicine* 67, no. 10 (2010): 708–16. doi:10.1136/oem.2009 .047027.

Rikk, J., K. J. Finn, I. Liziczai, Z. Radák, Z. Bori, and F. Ihász. "Influence of Pulsing Electromagnetic Field Therapy on Resting Blood Pressure in Aging Adults." *Electromagnetic Biology and Medicine* 32, no. 2 (2013): 165–72. doi:10.3109/15368378.2013.776420.

Sutbeyaz, S. T., N. Sezer, F. Koseoglu, and S. Kibar. "Low-Frequency Pulsed Electromagnetic Field Therapy in Fibromyalgia: A Randomized, Double-Blind, Sham-Controlled

Clinical Study." *Clinical Journal of Pain* 25, no. 8 (2009): 722–28. doi:10.1097/AJP .0b013e3181a68a6c.

Piatkowski, J., S. Kern, and T. Ziemssen. "Effect of BEMER Magnetic Field Therapy on the Level of Fatigue in Patients with Multiple Sclerosis: A Randomized, Double-Blind Controlled Trial." *Journal of Alternative and Complementary Medicine* 15, no. 5 (2009): 507–11. doi:10.1089 /acm.2008.0501.

Ganesan, K., A. C. Gengadharan, C. Balachandran, B. M. Manohar, and R. Puvanakrishnan. "Low Frequency Pulsed Electromagnetic Field—A Viable Alternative Therapy for Arthritis." *Indian Journal of Experimental Biology* 47, no. 12 (2009): 939–48.

Meesters, Y., V. Dekker, L. J. Schlangen, E. H. Bos, and M. J. Ruiter. "Low-Intensity Blue-Enriched White Light (750 Lux) and Standard Bright Light (10,000 Lux) Are Equally Effective in Treating SAD. A Randomized Controlled Study." *BMC Psychiatry* 11 (2011): 17. doi:10.1186/1471-244X-11-17.

Pail, G., W. Huf, E. Pjrek, D. Winkler, M. Willeit, N. Praschak-Rieder, and S. Kasper. "Bright-Light Therapy in the Treatment of Mood Disorders." *Neuropsychobiology* 64, no. 3 (2011): 152–62. doi:10.1159/000328950.

Magnusson, A., and D. Boivin. "Seasonal Affective Disorder: An Overview." *Chronobiology International* 20, no. 2 (2003): 189–207.

Blask, D. E., G. C. Brainard, R. T. Dauchy, J. P. Hanifin, L. K. Davidson, J. A. Krause, L. A. Sauer, et al. "Melatonin-Depleted Blood from Premenopausal Women Exposed to Light at Night Stimulates Growth of Human Breast Cancer Xenografts in Nude Rats." *Cancer Research* 65, no. 23 (2005): 11174–84.

Jim, H. S., J. E. Pustejovsky, C. L. Park, S. C. Danhauer, A. C. Sherman, G. Fitchett, T. V. Merluzzi, et al. "Religion, Spirituality, and Physical Health in Cancer Patients: A Meta-Analysis." *Cancer* 121, no. 21 (2015): 3760–68. doi:10.1002/cncr.29353.

Williams, A. L. "Perspectives on Spirituality at the End of Life: A Meta-Summary." *Palliative and Supportive Care* 4, no. 4 (2006): 407–17.

Grant, E., S. A. Murray, M. Kendall, K. Boyd, S. Tilley, and D. Ryan. "Spiritual Issues and Needs: Perspectives from Patients with Advanced Cancer and Nonmalignant Disease. A Qualitative Study." *Palliative and Supportive Care* 2, no. 4 (2004): 371–78.

Martínez, B. B., and R. P. Custódio. "Relationship Between Mental Health and Spiritual Well-Being Among Hemodialysis Patients: A Correlation Study." *São Paulo Medical Journal* 132, no. 1 (2014): 23–27. doi:10.1590/1516-3180.2014.1321606.

Wirz-Justice, A., A. Bader, U. Frisch, R. D. Stieglitz, J. Alder, J. Bitzer, I. Hösli, et al. "A Randomized, Double-Blind, Placebo-Controlled Study of Light Therapy for Antepartum Depression." *Journal of Clinical Psychiatry* 72, no. 7 (2011): 986–93. doi:10.4088 /JCP.10m06188blu.

Klerman, E. B., J. F. Duffy, D. J. Dijk, and C. A. Czeisler. "Circadian Phase Resetting in Older People by Ocular Bright Light Exposure." *Journal of Investigative Medicine* 49, no. 1 (2001): 30–40.

Martiny, K. "Adjunctive Bright Light in Non-Seasonal Major Depression." *Acta Psychiatrica Scandinavica: Supplementum* 425 (2004): 7–28.

Loving, R. T., D. F. Kripke, and S. R. Shuchter. "Bright Light Augments Antidepressant Effects of Medication and Wake Therapy." *Depression and Anxiety* 16, no. 1 (2002): 1–3.

Lam, R. W., E. M. Goldner, L. Solyom, and R. A. Remick. "A Controlled Study of Light Therapy for Bulimia Nervosa." *American Journal of Psychiatry* 151, no. 5 (1994): 744–50.

Christakis, N., and J. Fowler. "Connected." ConnectedtheBook.com. Accessed September 28, 2015. http://connectedthebook.com/.

Cheng, C. W., G. B. Adams, L. Perin, M. Wei, X. Zhou, B. S. Lam, S. Da Sacco, et al. "Prolonged Fasting Reduces IGF-1/PKA to Promote Hematopoietic-Stem-Cell-Based Regeneration and Reverse Immunosuppression." *Cell Stem Cell* 14, no. 6 (2014): 810–23. doi:10.1016/j .stem.2014.04.014.

Mendelsohn, A. R., and J. W. Larrick. "Prolonged Fasting/Refeeding Promotes Hematopoietic Stem Cell Regeneration and Rejuvenation." *Rejuvenation Research* 17, no. 4 (2014): 385–89. doi:10.1089/rej.2014.1595.

Hussin, N. M., S. Shahar, N. I. Teng, W. Z. Ngah, and S. K. Das. "Efficacy of Fasting and Calorie Restriction (FCR) on Mood and Depression Among Ageing Men." *Journal of Nutrition, Health and Aging* 17, no. 8 (2013): 674–80. doi:10.1007/s12603-013-0344-9.

Teng, N. I., S. Shahar, Z. A. Manaf, S. K. Das, C. S. Taha, and W. Z. Ngah. "Efficacy of Fasting Calorie Restriction on Quality of Life Among Aging Men." *Physiology and Behavior* 104, no. 5 (2011): 1059–64. doi:10.1016/j.physbeh.2011.07.007.

Liu, J. D., D. Goodspeed, Z. Sheng, B. Li, Y. Yang, D. J. Kliebenstein, and J. Braam. "Keeping the Rhythm: Light/Dark Cycles During Postharvest Storage Preserve the Tissue Integrity and Nutritional Content of Leafy Plants." *BMC Plant Biology* 15 (2015): 92. doi:10.1186 /s12870-015-0474-9.

Sutherland, E. G., C. Ritenbaugh, S. J. Kiley, N. Vuckovic, and C. Elder. "An HMO-Based Prospective Pilot Study of Energy Medicine for Chronic Headaches: Whole-Person Outcomes Point to the Need for New Instrumentation." *Journal of Alternative and Complementary Medicine* 15, no. 8 (2009): 819–26.

Lu, D. F., L. K. Hart, S. K. Lutgendorf, and Y. Perkhounkova. "The Effect of Healing Touch on the Pain and Mobility of Persons with Osteoarthritis: A Feasibility Study." *Geriatric Nursing* 34, no. 4 (2013): 314–22. doi:10.1016/j.gerinurse.2013.05.003.

Hart, L. K., M. I. Freel, P. J. Haylock, and S. K. Lutgendorf. "The Use of Healing Touch in Integrative Oncology." *Clinical Journal of Oncology Nursing* 15, no. 5 (2011): 519–25. doi:10.1188/11.CJON.519-525.

Richeson, N. E., J. A. Spross, K. Lutz, and C. Peng. "Effects of Reiki on Anxiety, Depression, Pain, and Physiological Factors in Community-Dwelling Older Adults." *Research in Gerontological Nursing* 3, no. 3 (2010): 187–99. doi:10.3928/19404921-20100601-01.

Bourque, A. L., M. E. Sullivan, and M. R. Winter. "Reiki as a Pain Management Adjunct in Screening Colonoscopy." *Gastroenterology Nursing* 35, no. 5 (2012): 308–12.

Bowden, D., L. Goddard, and J. Gruzelier. "A Randomised Controlled Single-Blind Trial of the Effects of Reiki and Positive Imagery on Well-Being and Salivary Cortisol." *Brain Research Bulletin* 81, no. 1 (2010): 66–72. doi:10.1016/j.brainresbull.2009.10.002.

Díaz-Rodríguez, L., M. Arroyo-Morales, C. Fernández-de-las-Peñas, F. García-Lafuente, C. García-Royo, and I. Tomás-Rojas. "Immediate Effects of Reiki on Heart Rate Variability, Cortisol Levels, and Body Temperature in Health Care Professionals with Burnout." *Biological Research for Nursing* 13, no. 4 (2011): 376–82. doi:10.1177/1099800410389166.

Vickers, A. J., A. M. Cronin, A. C. Maschino, G. Lewith, H. MacPherson, N. E. Foster, K. J. Sherman, et al. "Acupuncture for Chronic Pain: Individual Patient Data Meta-Analysis." *JAMA Internal Medicine* 172, no. 19 (2012): 1444–53. doi:10.1001/archinternmed.2012 .3654.

Mackay, N., S. Hansen, and O. McFarlane. "Autonomic Nervous System Changes During Reiki Treatment: A Preliminary Study." *Journal of Alternative and Complementary Medicine* 10, no. 6 (2004): 1077–81.

Buettner, D. *The Blue Zones: 9 Lessons for Living Longer from the People Who've Lived the Longest.* Reprint Edition. Washington, DC: National Geographic, 2010.

CHAPTER 10: HOW TO GET THE MOST FROM YOUR WHOLE DETOX

Kinnier, R. T., C. Hofsess, R. Pongratz, and C. Lambert. "Attributions and Affirmations for Overcoming Anxiety and Depression." *Psychology and Psychotherapy* 82, pt. 2 (2009): 153–69. doi:10.1348/147608308X389418.

Epton, T., P. R. Harris, R. Kane, G. M. van Koningsbruggen, and P. Sheeran. "The Impact of Self-Affirmation on Health-Behavior Change: A Meta-Analysis." *Health Psychology* 34, no. 3 (2015): 187–96. doi:10.1037/hea0000116.

Gelernter, R., G. Lavi, L. Yanai, R. Brooks, Y. Bar, Z. Bistrizer, and M. Rachmiel. "Effect of Auditory Guided Imagery on Glucose Levels and on Glycemic Control in Children with Type 1 Diabetes Mellitus." *Journal of Pediatric Endocrinology and Metabolism* (August 14, 2015). doi: 10.1515/jpem-2015-0150.

Giacobbi Jr., P. R., M. E. Stabler, J. Stewart, A. M. Jaeschke, J. L. Siebert, and G. A. Kelley. "Guided Imagery for Arthritis and Other Rheumatic Diseases: A Systematic Review of Randomized Controlled Trials." *Pain Management Nursing* 16, no. 5 (2015): 792–803. doi:10.1016/j .pmn.2015.01.003.

Kwekkeboom, K. L., and L. C. Bratzke. "A Systematic Review of Relaxation, Meditation, and Guided Imagery Strategies for Symptom Management in Heart Failure." *Journal of Cardiovascular Nursing* (June 10, 2015).

Marchand, W. R. "Mindfulness-Based Stress Reduction, Mindfulness-Based Cognitive Therapy, and Zen Meditation for Depression, Anxiety, Pain, and Psychological Distress." *Journal of Psychiatric Practice* 18, no. 4 (2012): 233–52. doi:10.1097/01.pra.0000416014.53215.86.

Tang, Y.-Y., B. K. Hölzel, and M. I. Posner. "The Neuroscience of Mindfulness Meditation." *Nature Reviews Neuroscience* 16, no. 4 (2015): 213–25. doi:10.1038/nrn3916.

Bhasin, M. K., J. A. Dusek, B. H. Chang, M. G. Joseph, J. W. Denninger, G. L. Fricchione, H. Benson, and T. A. Libermann. "Relaxation Response Induces Temporal Transcriptome Changes in Energy Metabolism, Insulin Secretion and Inflammatory Pathways." *PLoS ONE* 8, no. 5 (2013): e62817. doi:10.1371/journal.pone.0062817.

Dusek, J. A., H. H. Otu, A. L. Wohlhueter, M. Bhasin, L. F. Zerbini, M. G. Joseph, H. Benson, and T. A. Libermann. "Genomic Counter-Stress Changes Induced by the Relaxation Response." *PLoS ONE* 3, no. 7 (2008): e2576. doi:10.1371/journal.pone.0002576.

INDEX